D1565308

COLLECTED WORKS OF

OSCAR WILDE

COLLECTED WORKS OF

OSCAR WILDE

INCLUDING

The Poems, Novels, Plays, Essays and Fairy Tales

GREYSTONE PRESS

New York

BY GEORGE MC KIBBIN & SON; BROOKLYN, NEW YORK
PRINTED IN THE UNITED STATES OF AMERICA

CONTENTS

POEMS

POEMS

POEMS

THE BALLAD OF READING GAOL

I

He did not wear his scarlet coat,
For blood and wine are red,
And blood and wine were on his hands
When they found him with the dead,
The poor dead woman whom he loved,
And murdered in her bed.

He walked amongst the Trial Men
In a suit of shabby gray;
A cricket cap was on his head,
And his step seemed light and gay;
But I never saw a man who looked
So wistfully at the day.

I never saw a man who looked
With such a wistful eye
Upon that little tent of blue
Which prisoners call the sky,
And at every drifting cloud that went
With sails of silver by.

I walked, with other souls in pain,
Within another ring,
And was wondering if the man had done
A great or little thing,
When a voice behind me whispered low,
"*That fellow's got to swing.*"

Dear Christ! the very prison walls
Suddenly seemed to reel,
And the sky above my head became
Like a casque of scorching steel;
And, though I was a soul in pain,
My pain I could not feel.

I only knew what haunted thought
Quickened his step, and why
He looked upon the garish day
With such a wistful eye;
The man had killed the thing he loved,
And so he had to die.

Yet each man kills the thing he loves,
By each let this be heard,
Some do it with a bitter look,
Some with a flattering word,
The coward does it with a kiss,
The brave man with a sword!

Some kill their love when they are young,
And some when they are old;
Some strangle with the hands of Lust,
Some with the hands of Gold:
The kindest use a knife, because
The dead so soon grow cold.

Some love too little, some too long,
Some sell, and others buy;
Some do the deed with many tears,
And some without a sigh:
For each man kills the thing he loves,
Yet each man does not die.

He does not die a death of shame
On a day of dark disgrace,
Nor have a noose about his neck,
Nor a cloth upon his face,
Nor drop feet foremost through the floor
Into an empty space.

He does not sit with silent men
Who watch him night and day;

Who watch him when he tries to weep,
And when he tries to pray;
Who watch him lest himself should rob
The prison of its prey.

He does not wake at dawn to see
Dread figures throng his room,
The shivering Chaplain robed in white,
The Sheriff stern with gloom,
And the Governor all in shiny black,
With the yellow face of Doom.

He does not rise in piteous haste
To put on convict-clothes,
While some coarse-mouthed Doctor gloats, and notes
Each new and nerve-twitched pose,
Fingering a watch whose little ticks
Are like horrible hammer-blows.

He does not feel that sickening thirst
That sands one's throat, before
The hangman with his gardener's gloves
Comes through the padded door,
And binds one with three leathern thongs,
That the throat may thirst no more.

He does not bend his head to hear
The Burial Office read,
Nor, while the anguish of his soul
Tells him he is not dead,
Cross his own coffin, as he moves
Into the hideous shed.

He does not stare upon the air
Through a little roof of glass:
He does not pray with lips of clay
For his agony to pass;
Nor feel upon his shuddering cheek
The kiss of Caiaphas.

II

Six weeks the guardsman walked the yard,
In the suit of shabby gray:
His cricket cap was on his head,
And his step was light and gay,
But I never saw a man who looked
So wistfully at the day.

I never saw a man who looked
With such a wistful eye
Upon that little tent of blue
Which prisoners call the sky,
And at every wandering cloud that trailed
Its ravelled fleeces by.

He did not wring his hands, as do
Those witless men who dare
To try to rear the changeling Hope
In the cave of black Despair:
He only looked upon the sun,
And drank the morning air.

He did not wring his hands nor weep,
Nor did he peek or pine,
But he drank the air as though it held
Some healthful anodyne;
With open mouth he drank the sun
As though it had been wine!

And I and all the souls in pain,
Who tramped the other ring,
Forgot if we ourselves had done
A great or little thing,
And watched with gaze of dull amaze
The man who had to swing.

For strange it was to see him pass
With a step so light and gay,
And strange it was to see him look
So wistfully at the day,
And strange it was to think that he
Had such a debt to pay.

The oak and elm have pleasant leaves
That in the spring-time shoot:
But grim to see is the gallows-tree,
With its alder-bitten root,
And, green or dry, a man must die
Before it bears its fruit!

The loftiest place is the seat of grace
For which all worldlings try:
But who would stand in hempen band
Upon a scaffold high,
And through a murderer's collar take
His last look at the sky?

It is sweet to dance to violins
When Love and Life are fair:
To dance to flutes, to dance to lutes
Is delicate and rare:
But it is not sweet with nimble feet
To dance upon the air!

So with curious eyes and sick surmise
We watched him day by day,
And wondered if each one of us
Would end the self-same way,
For none can tell to what red Hell
His sightless soul may stray.

At last the dead man walked no more
Amongst the Trial Men,
And I knew that he was standing up
In the black dock's dreadful pen,
And that never would I see his face
For weal or woe again.

Like two doomed ships that pass in storm
We had crossed each other's way:
But we made no sign, we said no word,
We had no word to say;
For we did not meet in the holy night,
But in the shameful day.

A prison wall was round us both,
Two outcast men we were:
The world had thrust us from its heart,
And God from out His care:
And the iron gin that waits for Sin
Had caught us in its snare.

III

In Debtors' Yard the stones are hard,
And the dripping wall is high,
So it was there he took the air
Beneath the leaden sky,
And by each side a warder walked,
For fear the man might die.

Or else he sat with those who watched
His anguish night and day;
Who watched him when he rose to weep,
And when he crouched to pray;
Who watched him lest himself should rob
Their scaffold of its prey.

The Governor was strong upon
The Regulations Act:
The Doctor said that Death was but
A scientific fact:
And twice a day the Chaplain called,
And left a little tract.

And twice a day he smoked his pipe,
And drank his quart of beer:
His soul was resolute, and held
No hiding-place for fear;
He often said that he was glad
The hangman's day was near.

But why he said so strange a thing
No warder dared to ask:
For he to whom a watcher's doom
Is given as his task,
Must set a lock upon his lips,
And make his face a mask.

Or else he might be moved, and try
To comfort or console:
And what should Human Pity do
Pent up in Murderers' Hole?
What word of grace in such a place
Could help a brother's soul?

With slouch and swing around the ring
We trod the Fools' Parade!
We did not care: we knew we were
The Devils' Own Brigade:
And shaven head and feet of lead
Make a merry masquerade.

We tore the tarry rope to shreds
With blunt and bleeding nails;
We rubbed the doors, and scrubbed the floors,
And cleaned the shining rails:
And, rank by rank, we soaped the plank,
And clattered with the pails.

We sewed the sacks, we broke the stones,
We turned the dusty drill:
We banged the tins, and bawled the hymns,
And sweated on the mill:
But in the heart of every man
Terror was lying still.

So still it lay that every day
Crawled like a weed-clogged wave:
And we forgot the bitter lot
That waits for fool and knave,
Till once, as we tramped in from work,
We passed an open grave.

With yawning mouth the horrid hole
Gaped for a living thing;
The very mud cried out for blood
To the thirsty asphalte ring:
And we knew that ere one dawn grew fair
The fellow had to swing.

Right in we went, with soul intent
On Death and Dread and Doom:
The hangman, with his little bag,
Went shuffling through the gloom:
And I trembled as I groped my way
Into my numbered tomb.

That night the empty corridors
Were full of forms of Fear,
And up and down the iron town
Stole feet we could not hear,
And through the bars that hide the stars
White faces seemed to peer.

He lay as one who lies and dreams
In a pleasant meadow-land,
The watchers watched him as he slept,
And could not understand
How one could sleep so sweet a sleep
With a hangman close at hand.

But there is no sleep when men must weep
Who never yet have wept:
So we—the fool, the fraud, the knave—
That endless vigil kept,
And through each brain on hands of pain
Another's terror crept.

Alas! it is a fearful thing
To feel another's guilt!
For, right within, the sword of Sin
Pierced to its poisoned hilt,
And as molten lead were the tears we shed
For the blood we had not spilt.

The warders with their shoes of felt
Crept by each padlocked door,
And peeped and saw, with eyes of awe,
Gray figures on the floor,
And wondered why men knelt to pray
Who never prayed before.

All through the night we knelt and prayed,
Mad mourners of a corse!
The troubled plumes of midnight shook
Like the plumes upon a hearse:
And as bitter wine upon a sponge
Was the savour of Remorse.

The gray cock crew, the red cock crew,
But never came the day:
And crooked shapes of Terror crouched,
In the corners where we lay:
And each evil sprite that walks by night
Before us seemed to play.

They glided past, they glided fast,
Like travellers through a mist:
They mocked the moon in a rigadoon
Of delicate turn and twist,
And with formal pace and loathsome grace
The phantoms kept their tryst.

With mop and mow, we saw them go,
Slim shadows hand in hand:
About, about, in ghostly rout
They trod a saraband:
And the damned grotesques made arabesques,
Like the wind upon the sand!

With the pirouettes of marionettes,
They tripped on pointed tread:
But with flutes of Fear they filled the ear,
As their grisly masque they led,
And loud they sang, and long they sang,
For they sang to wake the dead.

"*Oho!*" they cried, "*the world is wide,*
But fettered limbs go lame!
And once, or twice, to throw the dice
Is a gentlemanly game,
But he does not win who plays with Sin
In the secret House of Shame."

No things of air these antics were,
That frolicked with such glee:
To men whose lives were held in gyves,
And whose feet might not go free,
Ah! wounds of Christ! they were living things,
Most terrible to see.

Around, around, they waltzed and wound;
Some wheeled in smirking pairs;
With the mincing step of a demirep
Some sidled up the stairs:
And with subtle sneer, and fawning leer,
Each helped us at our prayers.

The morning wind began to moan,
But still the night went on:
Through its giant loom the web of gloom
Crept till each thread was spun:
And, as we prayed, we grew afraid
Of the Justice of the Sun.

The moaning wind went wandering round
The weeping prison wall:
Till like a wheel of turning steel
We felt the minutes crawl:
O moaning wind! what had we done
To have such a seneschal?

At last I saw the shadowed bars,
Like a lattice wrought in lead,
Move right across the whitewashed wall
That faced my three-plank bed,
And I knew that somewhere in the world
God's dreadful dawn was red.

At six o'clock we cleaned our cells,
  At seven all was still,
But the sough and swing of a mighty
      wing
  The prison seemed to fill,
For the Lord of Death with icy
      breath
  Had entered in to kill.

He did not pass in purple pomp,
  Nor ride a moon-white steed.
Three yards of cord and a sliding
      board
  Are all the gallows' need:
So with rope of shame the Herald
      came
  To do the secret deed.

We were as men who through a fen
  Of filthy darkness grope:
We did not dare to breathe a prayer,
  Or to give our anguish scope:
Something was dead in each of us,
  And what was dead was Hope.

For Man's grim Justice goes its way
  And will not swerve aside:
It slays the weak, it slays the strong,
  It has a deadly stride:
With iron heel it slays the strong
  The monstrous parricide!

We waited for the stroke of eight:
  Each tongue was thick with thirst:
For the stroke of eight is the stroke
      of Fate
  That makes a man accursed,
And Fate will use a running noose
  For the best man and the worst.

We had no other thing to do,
  Save to wait for the sign to come:
So, like things of stone in a valley
      lone,
  Quiet we sat and dumb:
But each man's heart beat thick and
      quick,
  Like a madman on a drum!

With sudden shock the prison-clock
  Smote on the shivering air,
And from all the gaol rose up a wail
  Of impotent despair,
Like the sound the frightened marshes
      hear
  From some leper in his lair.

And as one sees most fearful things
  In the crystal of a dream,
We saw the greasy hempen rope
  Hooked to the blackened beam,
And heard the prayer the hangman's
      snare
  Strangled into a scream.

And all the woe that moved him so
  That he gave that bitter cry,
And the wild regrets, and the bloody
      sweats,
  None knew so well as I:
For he who lives more lives than one
  More deaths that one must die.

IV

There is no chapel on the day
  On which they hang a man:
The Chaplain's heart is far too sick,
  Or his face is far too wan,
Or there is that written in his eyes
  Which none should look upon.

So they kept us close till nigh on
      noon,
  And then they rang the bell,
And the warders with their jingling
      keys
  Opened each listening cell,
And down the iron stair we tramped,
  Each from his separate Hell.

Out into God's sweet air we went,
  But not in wonted way,
For this man's face was white with fear,
  And that man's face was gray,
And I never saw sad men who looked
  So wistfully at the day.

I never saw sad men who looked
  With such a wistful eye
Upon that little tent of blue
  We prisoners called the sky,
And at every happy cloud that passed
  In such strange freedom by.

But there were those amongst us all
  Who walked with downcast head,
And knew that, had each got his due,
  They should have died instead:
He had but killed a thing that lived,
  Whilst they had killed the dead.

For he who sins a second time
  Wakes a dead soul to pain,
And draws it from its spotted shroud
  And makes it bleed again,
And makes it bleed great gouts of blood,
  And makes it bleed in vain!

Like ape or clown, in monstrous garb
  With crooked arrows starred,
Silently we went round and round
  The slippery asphalte yard;
Silently we went round and round,
  And no man spoke a word.

Silently we went round and round,
  And through each hollow mind
The Memory of dreadful things
  Rushed like a dreadful wind,
And Horror stalked before each man,
  And Terror crept behind.

The warders strutted up and down,
  And watched their herd of brutes,
Their uniforms were spick and span,
  And they wore their Sunday suits,
But we knew the work they had been at,
  By the quicklime on their boots.

For where a grave had opened wide
  There was no grave at all:
Only a stretch of mud and sand
  By the hideous prison-wall,
And a little heap of burning lime,
  That the man should have his pall.

For he has a pall, this wretched man,
  Such as few men can claim:
Deep down below a prison-yard,
  Naked, for greater shame,
He lies, with fetters on each foot,
  Wrapt in a sheet of flame!

And all the while the burning lime
  Eats flesh and bone away,
It eats the brittle bones by night,
  And the soft flesh by day,
It eats the flesh and bone by turns,
  But it eats the heart alway.

For three long years they will not sow
  Or root or seedling there:
For three long years the unblessed spot
  Will sterile be and bare,
And look upon the wondering sky
  With unreproachful stare.

They think a murderer's heart would taint
  Each simple seed they sow.
It is not true! God's kindly earth
  Is kindlier than men know,
And the red rose would but glow more red,
  The white rose whiter blow.

Out of his mouth a red, red rose!
  Out of his heart a white!

For who can say by what strange way,
Christ brings His will to light,
Since the barren staff the pilgrim bore
Bloomed in the great Pope's sight?

But neither milk-white rose nor red
May bloom in prison air;
The shard, the pebble, and the flint,
Are what they give us there:
For flowers have been known to heal
A common man's despair.

So never will wine-red rose or white,
Petal by petal, fall
On that stretch of mud and sand that lies
By the hideous prison-wall,
To tell the men who tramp the yard
That God's Son died for all.

Yet though the hideous prison-wall
Still hems him round and round,
And a spirit may not walk by night
That is with fetters bound,
And a spirit may but weep that lies
In such unholy ground,

He is at peace—this wretched man—
At peace, or will be soon:
There is no thing to make him mad,
Nor does Terror walk at noon,
For the lampless Earth in which he lies
Has neither Sun nor Moon.

They hanged him as a beast is hanged:
They did not even toll
A requiem that might have brought
Rest to his startled soul,
But hurriedly they took him out,
And hid him in a hole.

The warders stripped him of his clothes,
And gave him to the flies:
They mocked the swollen purple throat,
And the stark and staring eyes:
And with laughter loud they heaped the shroud
In which the convict lies.

The Chaplain would not kneel to pray
By his dishonoured grave:
Nor mark it with that blessed Cross
That Christ for sinners gave,
Because the man was one of those
Whom Christ came down to save.

Yet all is well; he has but passed
To Life's appointed bourne:
And alien tears will fill for him
Pity's long-broken urn,
For his mourners will be outcast men,
And outcasts always mourn.

V

I know not whether Laws be right,
Or whether Laws be wrong;
All that we know who lie in gaol
Is that the wall is strong;
And that each day is like a year,
A year whose days are long.

But this I know, that every Law
That men have made for Man,
Since first Man took his brother's life,
And the sad world began,
But straws the wheat and saves the chaff
With a most evil fan.

This too I know—and wise it were
If each could know the same—
That every prison that men build
Is built with bricks of shame,
And bound with bars lest Christ should see
How men their brothers maim.

With bars they blur the gracious moon,
And blind the goodly sun:
And they do well to hide their Hell,
For in it things are done
That Son of God nor son of Man
Ever should look upon!

The vilest deeds like poison weeds
Bloom well in prison-air:
It is only what is good in Man
That wastes and withers there:
Pale Anguish keeps the heavy gate,
And the warder is Despair.

For they starve the little frightened child
Till it weeps both night and day:
And they scourge the weak, and flog the fool,
And gibe the old and gray,
And some grow mad, and all grow bad,
And none a word may say.

Each narrow cell in which we dwell
Is a foul and dark latrine,
And the fetid breath of living Death
Chokes up each grated screen,
And all, but Lust, is turned to dust
In Humanity's machine.

The brackish water that we drink
Creeps with a loathsome slime,
And the bitter bread they weigh in scales
Is full of chalk and lime,
And Sleep will not lie down, but walks
Wild-eyed, and cries to Time.

But though lean Hunger and green Thirst
Like asp with adder fight,
We have little care of prison fare,
For what chills and kills outright
Is that every stone one lifts by day
Becomes one's heart by night.

With midnight always in one's heart,
And twilight in one's cell,
We turn the crank, or tear the rope,
Each in his separate Hell,
And the silence is more awful far
Than the sound of a brazen bell.

And never a human voice comes near
To speak a gentle word:
And the eye that watches through the door
Is pitiless and hard:
And by all forgot, we rot and rot,
With soul and body marred.

And thus we rust Life's iron chain
Degraded and alone:
And some men curse, and some men weep,
And some men make no moan:
But God's eternal Laws are kind
And break the heart of stone.

And every human heart that breaks,
In prison-cell or yard,
Is as that broken box that gave
Its treasure to the Lord,
And filled the unclean leper's house
With the scent of costliest nard.

Ah! happy they whose hearts can break
And peace of pardon win!
How else may man make straight his plan
And cleanse his soul from Sin?
How else but through a broken heart
May Lord Christ enter in?

And he of the swollen purple throat,
And the stark and staring eyes,
Waits for the holy hands that took
The Thief to Paradise;
And a broken and a contrite heart
The Lord will not despise.

The man in red who reads the Law
  Gave him three weeks of life,
Three little weeks in which to heal
  His soul of his soul's strife,
And cleanse from every blot of blood
  The hand that held the knife.

And with tears of blood he cleansed the hand,
  The hand that held the steel:
For only blood can wipe out blood,
  And only tears can heal:
And the crimson stain that was of Cain
  Became Christ's snow-white seal.

VI

In Reading gaol by Reading town
  There is a pit of shame,
And in it lies a wretched man
  Eaten by teeth of flame,
In a burning winding-sheet he lies,
  And his grave has got no name.

And there, till Christ call forth the dead,
  In silence let him lie:
No need to waste the foolish tear,
  Or heave the windy sigh:
The man had killed the thing he loved,
  And so he had to die.

And all men kill the thing they love,
  By all let this be heard,
Some do it with a bitter look,
  Some with a flattering word,
The coward does it with a kiss,
  The brave man with a sword!

C. 3. 3.

CHARMIDES

I

He was a Grecian lad, who coming home
  With pulpy figs and wine from Sicily
Stood at his galley's prow, and let the foam
  Blow through his crisp brown curls unconsciously,
And holding wind and wave in boy's despite
Peered from his dripping seat across the wet and stormy night.

Till with the dawn he saw a burnished spear
  Like a thin thread of gold against the sky,
And hoisted sail, and strained the creeking gear,
  And bade the pilot head her lustily
Against the nor-west gale, and all day long
Held on his way, and marked the rowers' time with measured song.

And when the faint Corinthian hills were red
  Dropped anchor in a little sandy bay,
And with fresh boughs of olive crowned his head,
  And brushed from cheek and throat the hoary spray,
And washed his limbs with oil, and from the hold
Brought out his linen tunic and his sandals brazen-soled.

And a rich robe stained with the fishes' juice
Which of some swarthy trader he had bought
Upon the sunny quay at Syracuse,
And was with Tyrian broideries inwrought,
And by the questioning merchants made his way
Up through the soft and silver woods, and when the laboring day

Had spun its tangled web of crimson cloud,
Clomb the high hill, and with swift silent feet
Crept to the fane unnoticed by the crowd
Of busy priests, and from some dark retreat
Watched the young swains his frolic playmates bring
The firstling of their little flock, and the shy shepherd fling

The crackling salt upon the flame, or hang
His studded crook against the temple wall
To Her who keeps away the ravenous fang
Of the base wolf from homestead and from stall;
And then the clear-voiced maidens 'gan to sing,
And to the altar each man brought some goodly offering,

A beechen cup brimming with milky foam,
A fair cloth wrought with cunning imagery
Of hounds in chase, a waxen honey-comb
Dripping with oozy gold which scarce the bee
Had ceased from building, a black skin of oil
Meet for the wrestlers, a great boar the fierce and white-tusked spoil

Stolen from Artemis that jealous maid
To please Athena, and the dappled hide
Of a tall stag who in some mountain glade
Had met the shaft; and then the herald cried,
And from the pillared precinct one by one
Went the glad Greeks well pleased that they their simple vows had done.

And the old priest put out the waning fires
Save that one lamp whose restless ruby glowed
For ever in the cell, and the shrill lyres
Came fainter on the wind, as down the road
In joyous dance these country folk did pass,
And with stout hands the warder closed the gates of polished brass.

Long time he lay and hardly dared to breathe,
And heard the cadenced drip of spilt-out wine,
And the rose-petals falling from the wreath
As the night breezes wandered through the shrine,
And seemed to be in some entrancèd swoon
Till through the open roof above the full and brimming moon

Flooded with sheeny waves the marble floor,
When from his nook upleapt the venturous lad,
And flinging wide the cedar-carven door
Beheld an awful image saffron-clad
And armed for battle! the gaunt Griffin glared
From the huge helm, and the long lance of wreck and ruin flared

Like a red rod of flame, stony and steeled
The Gorgon's head its leaden eyeballs rolled,
And writhed its snaky horrors through the shield,
And gaped aghast with bloodless lips and cold
In passion impotent, while with blind gaze
The blinking owl between the feet hooted in shrill amaze.

The lonely fisher as he trimmed his lamp
Far out at sea off Sunium, or cast
The net for tunnies, heard a brazen tramp
Of horses smite the waves, and a wild blast
Divide the folded curtains of the night,
And knelt upon the little poop, and prayed in holy fright.

And guilty lovers in their venery
Forgat a little while their stolen sweets,
Deeming they heard dread Dian's bitter cry;
And the grim watchmen on their lofty seats
Ran to their shields in haste precipitate,
Or strained black-bearded throats across the dusky parapet.

For round the temple rolled the clang of arms,
And the twelve Gods leapt up in marble fear,
And the air quaked with dissonant alarums
Till huge Poseidon shook his mighty spear,
And on the frieze the prancing horses neighed,
And the low tread of hurrying feet rang from the cavalcade.

Ready for death with parted lips he stood,
And well content at such a price to see
That calm wide brow, that terrible maidenhood.
The marvel of that pitiless chastity,
Ah! well content indeed, for never wight
Since Troy's young shepherd prince had seen so wonderful a sight.

Ready for death he stood, but lo! the air
Grew silent, and the horses ceased to neigh,
And off his brow he tossed the clustering hair,
And from his limbs he threw the cloak away,
For whom would not such love make desperate,
And nigher came, and touched her throat, and with hands violate

Undid the cuirass, and the crocus gown,
And bared the breasts of polished ivory,

Till from the waist the peplos falling down
Left visible the secret mystery
Which no lover will Athena show,
The grand cool flanks, the crescent thighs, the bossy hills of snow.

Those who have never known a lover's sin
Let them not read my ditty, it will be
To their dull ears so musicless and thin
That they will have no joy of it, but ye
To whose wan cheeks now creeps the lingering smile,
Ye who have learned who Eros is,—O listen yet a-while.

A little space he let his greedy eyes
Rest on the burnished image, till mere sight
Half swooned for surfeit of such luxuries,
And then his lips in hungering delight
Fed on her lips, and round the towered neck
He flung his arms, nor cared at all his passion's will to check.

Never I ween did lover hold such tryst,
For all night long he murmured honeyed word,
And saw her sweet unravished limbs, and kissed
Her pale and argent body undisturbed,
And paddled with the polished throat, and pressed
His hot and beating heart upon her chill and icy breast.

It was as if Numidian javelins
Pierced through and through his wild and whirling brain,
And his nerves thrilled like throbbing violins
In exquisite pulsation, and the pain
Was such sweet anguish that he never drew
His lips from hers till overhead the lark of warning flew.

They who have never seen the daylight peer
Into a darkened room, and drawn the curtain,
And with dull eyes and wearied from some dear
And worshipped body risen, they for certain
Will never know of what I try to sing,
How long the last kiss was, how fond and late his lingering.

The moon was girdled with a crystal rim,
The sign which shipmen say is ominous
Of wrath in heaven, the wan stars were dim,
And the low lightening east was tremulous
With the faint fluttering wings of flying dawn,
Ere from the silent sombre shrine this lover had withdrawn.

Down the steep rock with hurried feet and fast
Clomb the brave lad, and reached the cave of Pan,
And heard the goat-foot snoring as he passed,
And leapt upon a grassy knoll and ran

Like a young fawn unto an olive wood
Which in a shady valley by the well-built city stood.

And sought a little stream, which well he knew,
For oftentimes with boyish careless shout
The green and crested grebe he would pursue,
Or snare in woven net the silver trout,
And down amid the startled reeds he lay
Panting in breathless sweet affright, and waited for the day.

On the green bank he lay, and let one hand
Dip in the cool dark eddies listlessly,
And soon the breath of morning came and fanned
His hot flushed cheeks, or lifted wantonly
The tangled curls from off his forehead, while
He on the running water gazed with strange and secret smile.

And soon the shepherd in rough woollen cloak
With his long crook undid the wattled cotes,
And from the stack a thin blue wreath of smoke
Curled through the air across the ripening oats,
And on the hill the yellow house-dog bayed
As through the crisp and rustling fern the heavy cattle strayed.

And when the light-foot mower went a-field
Across the meadows laced with threaded dew,
And the sheep bleated on the misty weald,
And from its nest the wakening corn-crake flew,
Some woodmen saw him lying by the stream
And marvelled much that any lad so beautiful could seem,

Nor deemed him born of mortals, and one said,
"It is young Hylas, that false runaway
Who with a Naïad now would make his bed
Forgetting Herakles," but others, "Nay,
It is Narcissus, his own paramour,
Those are the fond and crimson lips no woman can allure."

And when they nearer came a third one cried,
"It is young Dionysos who has hid
His spear and fawnskin by the river side
Weary of hunting with the Bassarid,
And wise indeed were we away to fly,
They live not long who on the gods immortal come to spy."

So turned they back, and feared to look behind,
And told the timid swain how they had seen
Amid the reeds some woodland God reclined,
And no man dared to cross the open green,
And on that day no olive-tree was slain,
Nor rushes cut, but all deserted was the fair domain.

Save when the neat-herd's lad, his empty pail
 Well slung upon his back, with leap and bound
Raced on the other side, and stopped to hail
 Hoping that he some comrade new had found,
And gat no answer, and then half afraid
Passed on his simple way, or down the still and silent glade.

A little girl ran laughing from the farm
 Not thinking of love's secret mysteries,
And when she saw the white and gleaming arm
 And all his manlihood, with longing eyes
Whose passion mocked her sweet virginity
Watched him a-while, and then stole back sadly and wearily.

Far off he heard the city's hum and noise,
 And now and then the shriller laughter where
The passionate purity of brown-limbed boys
 Wrestled or raced in the clear healthful air,
And now and then a little tinkling bell
As the shorn wether led the sheep down to the mossy well.

Through the gray willows danced the fretful gnat,
 The grasshopper chirped idly from the tree,
In sleek and oily coat the water-rat
 Breasting the little ripples manfully
Made for the wild-duck's nest, from bough to bough
Hopped the shy finch, and the huge tortoise crept across the slough.

On the faint wind floated the silky seeds,
 As the bright scythe swept through the waving grass,
The ousel-cock splashed circles in the reeds
 And flecked with silver whorls the forest's glass,
Which scarce had caught again its imagery
Ere from its bed the dusky tench leapt at the dragon-fly.

But little care had he for anything
 Though up and down the beech the squirrel played,
And from the copse the linnet 'gan to sing
 To her brown mate her sweetest serenade,
Ah! little care indeed, for he had seen
The breasts of Pallas and the naked wonder of the Queen.

But when the herdsman called his straggling goats
 With whistling pipe across the rocky road,
And the shard-beetle with its trumpet-notes
 Boomed through the darkening woods, and seemed to bode
Of coming storm, and the belated crane
Passed homeward like a shadow, and the dull big drops of rain

Fell on the pattering fig-leaves, up he rose,
 And from the gloomy forest went his way

Past sombre homestead and wet orchard-close,
And came at last unto a little quay,
And called his mates a-board, and took his seat
On the high poop, and pushed from land, and loosed the dripping sheet,

And steered across the bay, and when nine suns
Passed down the long and laddered way of gold,
And nine pale moons had breathed their orisons
To the chaste stars their confessors, or told
Their dearest secret to the downy moth
That will not fly at noonday, through the foam and surging froth

Came a great owl with yellow sulphurous eyes
And lit upon the ship, whose timbers creaked
As though the lading of three argosies
Were in the hold, and flopped its wings, and shrieked,
And darkness straightway stole across the deep,
Sheathed was Orion's sword, dread Mars himself fled down the steep,

And the moon hid behind a tawny mask
Of drifting cloud, and from the ocean's marge
Rose the red plume, the huge and hornèd casque,
The seven cubit spear, the brazen targe!
And clad in bright and burnished panoply
Athena strode across the stretch of sick and shivering sea!

To the dull sailors' sight her loosened locks
Seemed like the jagged storm-rack, and her feet
Only the spume that floats on hidden rocks,
And marking how the rising waters beat
Against the rolling ship, the pilot cried
To the young helmsman at the stern to luff to windward side.

But he, the over-bold adulterer,
A dear profaner of great mysteries,
An ardent amorous idolater,
When he beheld those grand relentless eyes
Laughed loud for joy, and crying out "I come"
Leapt from the lofty poop into the chill and churning foam.

Then fell from the high heaven one bright star,
One dancer left the circling galaxy,
And back to Athens on her clattering car
In all the pride of venged divinity
Pale Pallas swept with shrill and steely clank,
And a few gurgling bubbles rose where her boy lover sank.

And the mast shuddered as the gaunt owl flew,
With mocking hoots after the wrathful Queen,
And the old pilot bade the trembling crew
Hoist the big sail, and told how he had seen
Close to the stern a dim and giant form,
And like a dripping swallow the stout ship dashed through the storm.

And no man dared to speak of Charmides
Deeming that he some evil thing had wrought,
And when they reached the strait Symplegades
They beached their galley on the shore, and sought
The toll-gate of the city hastily,
And in the market showed their brown and pictured pottery.

II

But some good Triton-god had ruth, and bare
The boy's drowned body back to Grecian land,
And mermaids combed his dank and dripping hair
And smoothed his brow, and loosed his clinching hand,
Some brought sweet spices from far Araby,
And others made the halcyon sing her softest lullaby.

And when he neared his old Athenian home,
A mighty billow rose up suddenly
Upon whose oily back the clotted foam
Lay diapered in some strange fantasy,
And clasping him unto its glassy breast,
Swept landward, like a white-maned Steed upon a venturous quest!

Now where Colonos leans unto the sea
There lies a long and level stretch of lawn,
The rabbit knows it, and the mountain bee
For it deserts Hymettus, and the Faun
Is not afraid, for never through the day
Comes a cry ruder than the shout of shepherd lads at play.

But often from the thorny labyrinth
And tangled branches of the circling wood
The stealthy hunter sees young Hyacinth
Hurling the polished disk, and draws his hood
Over his guilty gaze, and creeps away,
Nor dares to wind his horn, or—else at the first break of day

The Dryads come and throw the leathern ball
Along the reedy shore, and circumvent
Some goat-eared Pan to be their seneschal
For fear of bold Poseidon's ravishment,
And loose their girdles, with shy timorous eyes,
Lest from the surf his azure arms and purple beard should rise.

On this side and on that a rocky cave,
Hung with yellow-bell'd laburnum, stands,
Smooth is the beach, save where some ebbing wave
Leaves its faint outline etched upon the sands,
As though it feared to be too soon forgot
By the green rush, its playfellow,—and yet, it is a spot

So small, that the inconstant butterfly
Could steal the hoarded honey from each flower

Ere it was noon, and still not satisfy
Its over-greedy love,—within an hour
A sailor boy, were he but rude enow
To land and pluck a garland for his galley's painted prow,

Would almost leave the little meadow bare,
For it knows nothing of great pageantry,
Only a few narcissi here and there
Stand separate in sweet austerity,
Dotting the unmown grass with silver stars,
And here and there a daffodil waves tiny scimetars.

Hither the billow brought him, and was glad
Of such dear servitude, and where the land
Was virgin of all waters laid the lad
Upon the golden margent of the strand,
And like a lingering lover oft returned
To kiss those pallid limbs which once with intense fire burned,

Ere the wet seas had quenched that holocaust,
That self-fed flame, that passionate lustihead,
Ere grisly death with chill and nipping frost
Had withered up those lilies white and red
Which, while the boy would through the forest range,
Answered each other in a sweet antiphonal counter-change.

And when at dawn the wood-nymphs, hand-in-hand,
Threaded the bosky dell, their satyr spied
The boy's pale body stretched upon the sand,
And feared Poseidon's treachery, and cried,
And like bright sunbeams flitting through a glade,
Each startled Dryad sought some safe and leafy ambuscade.

Save one white girl, who deemed it would not be
So dread a thing to feel a sea-god's arms
Crushing her breasts in amorous tyranny,
And longed to listen to those subtle charms
Insidious lovers weave when they would win
Some fencèd fortress, and stole back again, nor thought it sin

To yield her treasure unto one so fair.
And lay beside him, thirsty with love's drouth,
Called him soft names, played with his tangled hair,
And with hot lips made havoc of his mouth
Afraid he might not wake, and then afraid
Lest he might wake too soon, fled back, and then, fond renegade,

Returned to fresh assault, and all day long
Sat at his side, and laughed at her new toy,
And held his hand, and sang her sweetest song,
Then frowned to see how froward was the boy
Who would not with her maidenhood entwine,
Nor knew that three days since his eyes had looked on Proserpine,

Nor knew what sacrilege his lips had done,
But said, "He will awake, I know him well,
He will awake at evening when the sun
Hangs his red shield on Corinth's citadel,
This sleep is but a cruel treachery
To make me love him more, and in some cavern of the sea

"Deeper than ever falls the fisher's line
Already a huge Triton blows his horn,
And weaves a garland from the crystalline
And drifting ocean-tendrils to adorn
The emerald pillars of our bridal bed,
For sphered in foaming silver, and with coral-crownèd head.

"We two will sit upon a throne of pearl,
And a blue wave will be our canopy,
And at our feet the water-snakes will curl
In all their amethystine panoply
Of diamonded mail, and we will mark
The mullets swimming by the mast of some storm-foundered bark,

"Vermilion-finned with eyes of bossy gold
Like flakes of crimson light, and the great deep
His glassy-portaled chamber will unfold,
And we will see the painted dolphins sleep
Cradled by murmuring halcyons on the rocks
Where Proteus in quaint suit of green pastures his monstrous flocks.

"And tremulous opal hued anemones
Will wave their purple fringes where we tread
Upon the mirrored floor, and argosies
Of fishes flecked with tawny scales will thread
The drifting cordage of the shattered wreck,
And honey-colored amber beads our twining limbs will deck."

But when that baffled Lord of War the Sun
With gaudy pennon flying passed away
Into his brazen House, and one by one
The little yellow stars began to stray
Across the field of heaven, ah! then indeed
She feared his lips upon her lips would never care to feed,

And cried, "Awake, already the pale moon
Washes the trees with silver, and the wave
Creeps gray and chilly up this sandy dune,
The croaking frogs are out, and from the cave
The night-jar shrieks, the fluttering bats repass,
And the brown stoat with hollow flanks creeps through the dusky grass.

"Nay, though thou art a God, be not so coy,
For in yon stream there is a little reed

That often whispers how a lovely boy
Lay with her once upon a grassy mead,
Who when his cruel pleasure he had done
Spread wings of rustling gold and soared aloft into the sun.

"Be not so coy, the laurel trembles still
With great Apollo's kisses, and the fir
Whose clustering sisters fringe the sea-ward hill
Hath many a tale of that bold ravisher
Whom men call Boreas, and I have seen
The mocking eyes of Hermes through the poplar's silvery sheen.

"Even the jealous Naiads call me fair,
And every morn a young and ruddy swain
Wooes me with apples and with locks of hair,
And seeks to soothe my virginal disdain
By all the gifts the gentle wood-nymphs love;
But yesterday he brought to me an iris-plumaged dove

"With little crimson feet, which with its store
Of seven spotted eggs the cruel lad
Had stolen from the lofty sycamore
At daybreak when her amorous comrade had
Flown off in search of berried juniper
Which most they love; the fretful wasp, that earliest vintager

"Of the blue grapes, hath not persistency
So constant as this simple shepherd-boy
For my poor lips, his joyous purity
And laughing sunny eyes might well decoy
A Dryad from her oath to Artemis;
For very beautiful is he, his mouth was made to kiss.

"His argent forehead, like a rising moon
Over the dusky hills of meeting brows,
Is crescent shaped, the hot and Tyrian noon
Leads from the myrtle-grove no goodlier spouse
For Cytheraea, the first silky down
Fringes his blushing cheeks, and his young limbs are strong and brown:

"And he is rich, and fat and fleecy herds
Of bleating sheep upon his meadows lie,
And many an earthen bowl of yellow curds
Is in his homestead for the thievish fly
To swim and drown in, the pink clover mead
Keeps its sweet store for him, and he can pipe on oaten reed.

"And yet I love him not, it was for thee
I kept my love, I knew that thou would'st come
To rid me of this pallid chastity;
Thou fairest flower of the flowerless foam
Of all the wide Aegean, brightest star
Of ocean's azure heavens where the mirrored planets are!

"I knew that thou would'st come, for when at first
The dry wood burgeoned, and the sap of Spring
Swelled in my green and tender bark or burst
To myriad multitudinous blossoming
Which mocked the midnight with its mimic moons
That did not dread the dawn, and first the thrushes' rapturous tunes

"Startled the squirrel from its granary,
And cuckoo flowers fringed the narrow lane,
Through my young leaves a sensuous ecstasy
Crept like new wine, and every mossy vein
Throbbed with the fitful pulse of amorous blood,
And the wild winds of passion shook my slim stem's maidenhood.

"The trooping fawns at evening came and laid
Their cool black noses on my lowest boughs
And on my topmost branch the blackbird made
A little nest of grasses for his spouse,
And now and then a twittering wren would light
On a thin twig which hardly bare the weight of such delight.

"I was the Attic shepherd's trysting place,
Beneath my shadow Amaryllis lay,
And round my trunk would laughing Daphnis chase
The timorous girl, till tired out with play
She felt his hot breath stir her tangled hair,
And turned, and looked, and fled no more from such delightful snare.

"Then come away unto my ambuscade
Where clustering woodbine weaves a canopy
For amorous pleasaunce, and the rustling shade
Of Paphian myrtles seems to sanctify
The dearest rites of love, there in the cool
And green recesses of its furthest depth there is a pool,

"The ouzel's haunt, the wild bee's pasturage;
For round its rim great creamy lilies float
Through their flat leaves in verdant anchorage,
Each cup a white-sailed golden-laden boat
Steered by a dragon-fly,—be not afraid
To leave this wan and wave-kissed shore, surely the place were made

"For lovers such as we, the Cyprian Queen,
One arm around her boyish paramour,
Strays often there at eve, and I have seen
The moon strip off her misty vestiture
For young Endymion's eyes, be not afraid,
The panther feet of Dian never tread that secret glade.

"Nay, if thou wil'st, back to the beating brine,
Back to the boisterous billow let us go,
And walk all day beneath the hyaline
Huge vault of Neptune's watery portico,
And watch the purple monsters of the deep
Sport in ungainly play, and from his lair keen Xiphias leap.

"For if my mistress find me lying here
She will not ruth or gentle pity show,
But lay her boar-spear down, and with austere
Relentless fingers string the cornel bow,
And draw the feathered notch against her breast,
And loose the archèd cord, ay, even now upon the quest

"I hear her hurrying feet,—awake, awake,
Thou laggard in love's battle! once at least
Let me drink deep of passion's wine, and slake
My parchèd being with the nectarous feast
Which even Gods affect! O come Love come,
Still we have time to reach the cavern of thine azure home."

Scarce had she spoken when the shuddering trees
Shook, and the leaves divided, and the air
Grew conscious of a God, and the gray seas
Crawled backward, and a long and dismal blare
Blew from some tasseled horn, a sleuth-hound bayed
And like a flame a barbèd reed flew whizzing down the glade.

And where the little flowers of her breast
Just brake in to their milky blossoming,
This murderous paramour, this unbidden guest,
Pierced and struck deep in horrid chambering,
And plowed a bloody furrow with its dart,
And dug a long red road, and cleft with wingèd death her heart.

Sobbing her life out with a bitter cry
On the boy's body fell the Dryad maid,
Sobbing for incomplete virginity,
And raptures unenjoyed, and pleasures dead,
And all the pain of things unsatisfied,
And the bright drops of crimson youth crept down her throbbing side.

Ah! pitiful it was to hear her moan,
And very pitiful to see her die
Ere she had yielded up her sweets, or known
The joy of passion, that dread mystery
Which not to know is not to live at all,
And yet to know is to be held in death's most deadly thrall.

But as it hapt the Queen of Cytheré,
Who with Adonis all night long had lain
Within some shepherd's hut in Arcady,

On team of silver doves and gilded wane
Was journeying Paphos-ward, high up afar
From mortal ken between the mountains and the morning star,

And when low down she spied the hapless pair,
And heard the Oread's faint despairing cry,
Whose cadence seemed to play upon the air
As though it were a viol, hastily
She bade her pigeons fold each straining plume,
And dropt to earth, and reached the strand, and saw their dolorous doom.

For as a gardener turning back his head
To catch the last notes of the linnet, mows
With careless scythe too near some flower bed,
And cuts the thorny pillar of the rose,
And with the flower's loosened loveliness
Strews the brown mold, or as some shepherd lad in wantonness

Driving his little flock along the mead
Treads down two daffodils which side by side
Have lured the lady-bird with yellow brede
And made the gaudy moth forget its pride,
Treads down their brimming golden chalices
Under light feet which were not made for such rude ravages,

Or as a schoolboy tired of his book
Flings himself down upon the reedy grass
And plucks two water-lilies from the brook,
And for a time forgets the hour glass,
Then wearies of their sweets, and goes his way,
And lets the hot sun kill them, even so these lovers lay.

And Venus cried, "It is dread Artemis
Whose bitter hand hath wrought this cruelty,
Or else that mightier mayde whose care it is
To guard her strong and stainless majesty
Upon the hill Athenian,—alas!
That they who loved so well unloved into Death's house should pass."

So with soft hands she laid the boy and girl
In the great golden waggon tenderly,
Her white throat whiter than a moony pearl
Just threaded with a blue vein's tapestry
Had not yet ceased to throb, and still her breast
Swayed like a wind-stirred lily in ambiguous unrest.

And then each pigeon spread its milky van,
The bright car soared into the dawning sky,
And like a cloud the aerial caravan
Passed over the Aegean silently,

Till the faint air was troubled with the song
From the wan mouths that call on bleeding Thammuz all night long.

But when the doves had reached their wonted goal
Where the wide stair of orbèd marble dips
Its snows into the sea, her fluttering soul
Just shook the trembling petals of her lips
And passed into the void, and Venus knew
That one fair maid the less would walk amid her retinue,

And bade her servants carve a cedar chest
With all the wonder of this history,
Within whose scented womb their limbs should rest
Where olive-trees make tender the blue sky
On the low hills of Paphos, and the fawn
Pipes in the noonday, and the nightingale sings on till dawn.

Nor failed they to obey her hest, and ere
The morning bee had stung the daffodil
With tiny fretful spear, or from its lair
The waking stag had leapt across the rill
And roused the ousel, or the lizard crept
Athwart the sunny rock, beneath the grass their bodies slept.

And when day brake, within that silver shrine
Fed by the flames of cressets tremulous,
Queen Venus knelt and prayed to Proserpine
That she whose beauty made Death amorous
Should beg a guerdon from her pallid Lord,
And let desire pass across dread Charon's icy ford.

III

In melancholy moonless Acheron,
Far from the goodly earth and joyous day,
Where no spring ever buds, nor ripening sun
Weighs down the apple trees, nor flowery May
Checkers with chestnut blooms the grassy floor,
Where thrushes never sing, and piping linnets mate no more,

There by a dim and dark Lethaean well,
Young Charmides was lying, wearily
He plucked the blossoms from the asphodel,
And with its little rifled treasury
Strewed the dull waters of the dusky stream,
And watched the white stars founder, and the land was like a dream.

When as he gazed into the watery glass
And through his brown hair's curly tangles scanned
His own wan face, a shadow seemed to pass

Across the mirror, and a little hand
Stole into his, and warm lips timidly
Brushed his pale cheeks, and breathed their secret forth into a sigh.

Then turned he around his weary eyes and saw,
And ever nigher still their faces came,
And nigher ever did their young mouths draw
Until they seemed one perfect rose of flame,
And longing arms around her neck he cast,
And felt her throbbing bosom, and his breath came hot and fast,

And all his hoarded sweets were hers to kiss,
And all her maidenhood was his to slay,
And limb to limb in long and rapturous bliss
Their passion waxed and waned,— O why essay
To pipe again of love too venturous reed!
Enough, enough that Eros laughed upon that flowerless mead,

Too venturous poesy O why essay
To pipe again of passion! fold thy wings
O'er daring Icarus and bid thy lay
Sleep hidden in the lyre's silent strings,
Till thou hast found the old Castilian rill,
Or from the Lesbian waters plucked drowned Sappho's golden quill!

Enough, enough that he whose life had been
A fiery pulse of sin, a splendid shame,
Could in the loveless land of Hades glean
One scorching harvest from those fields of flame
Where passion walks with naked unshod feet
And is not wounded,—ah! enough that once their lips could meet

In that wild throb when all existences
Seem narrowed to one single ecstasy
Which dies through its own sweetness and the stress
Of too much pleasure, ere Persephone
Had made them serve her by the ebon throne
Of the pale God who in the fields of Enna loosed her zone.

PANTHEA

Nay, let us walk from fire unto fire,
From passionate pain to deadlier delight,—
I am too young to live without desire,
Too young art thou to waste this summer night
Asking those idle questions which of old
Man sought of seer and oracle, and no reply was told.

For sweet, to feel is better than to know,
And wisdom is a childless heritage,
One pulse of passion—youth's first fiery glow,—

Are worth the hoarded proverbs of the sage:
Vex not thy soul with dead philosophy,
Have we not lips to kiss with, hearts to love, and eyes to see!

Dost thou not hear the murmuring nightingale
Like water bubbling from a silver jar,
So soft she sings the envious moon is pale,
That high in heaven she hung so far
She cannot hear that love-enraptured tune,–
Mark how she wreathes each horn with mist, yon late and laboring moon.

White lilies, in whose cups the gold bees dream,
The fallen snow of petals where the breeze
Scatters the chestnut blossom, or the gleam
Of all our endless sins, our vain endeavour
Enough for thee, dost thou desire more?
Alas! the Gods will give naught else from their eternal store.

For our high Gods have sick and wearied grown
Of boyish limbs in water,–are not these
For wasted days of youth to make atone
By pain or prayer or priest, and never, never,
Hearken they now to either good or ill,
But send their rain upon the just and the unjust at will.

They sit at ease, our Gods they sit at ease,
Strewing with leaves of rose their scented wine,
They sleep, they sleep, beneath the rocking trees
Where asphodel and yellow lotus twine,
Mourning the old glad days before they knew
What evil things the heart of man could dream, and dreaming do.

And far beneath the brazen floor, they see
Like swarming flies the crowd of little men,
The bustle of small lives, then wearily
Back to their lotus-haunts they turn again
Kissing each other's mouths, and mix more deep
The poppy-seeded draught which brings soft purple-lidded sleep.

There all day long the golden-vestured sun,
Their torch-bearer, stands with his torch a-blaze,
And when the gaudy web of noon is spun
By its twelve maidens through the crimson haze
Fresh from Endymion's arms comes forth the moon,
And the immortal Gods in toils of mortal passions swoon.

There walks Queen Juno through some dewy mead,
Her grand white feet flecked with the saffron dust
Of wind-stirred lilies, while young Ganymede

Leaps in the hot and amber-foaming must,
His curls all tossed, as when the eagle bare
The frightened boy from Ida through the blue Ionian air.

There in the green heart of some garden close
Queen Venus with the shepherd at her side,
Her warm soft body like the brier rose
Which would be white yet blushes at its pride,
Laughs low for love, till jealous Salmacis
Peers through the myrtle-leaves and sighs for pain of lonely bliss.

There never does that dreary north-wind blow
Which leaves our English forests bleak and bare,
Nor ever falls the swift white-feathered snow,
Nor doth the red-toothed lightning ever dare
To wake them in the silver-fretted night
When we lie weeping for some sweet sad sin, some dead delight.

Alas! they know the far Lethæan spring,
The violet-hidden waters well they know,
Where one whose feet with tired wandering
Are faint and broken may take heart and go,
And from those dark depths cool and crystalline
Drink, and draw balm, and sleep for sleepless souls, and anodyne.

But we oppress our natures, God or Fate
Is our enemy, we starve and feed
On vain repentance–O we are born too late!
What balm for us in bruisèd poppy seed
Who crowd into one finite pulse of time
The joy of infinite love and the fierce pain of infinite crime.

O we are wearied of this sense of guilt,
Wearied of pleasures paramour despair,
Wearied of every temple we have built,
Wearied of every right, unanswered prayer,
For man is weak; God sleeps: and heaven is high:
One fiery-colored moment: one great love: and lo! we die.

Ah! but no ferry-man with laboring pole
Nears his black shallop to the flowerless strand,
No little coin of bronze can bring the soul
Over Death's river to the sunless land,
Victim and wine and vow are all in vain,
The tomb is sealed; the soldiers watch; the dead rise not again.

We are resolved into the supreme air,
We are made one with what we touch and see,
With our heart's blood each crimson sun is fair,
With our young lives each spring-impassioned tree

Flames into green, the wildest beasts that range
The moor our kinsmen are, all life is one, and all is change.

With beat of systole and of diastole
One grand great light throbs through earth's giant heart,
And mighty waves of single Being roll
From nerve-less germ to man, for we are part
Of every rock and bird and beast and hill,
One with the things that prey on us, and one with what we kill.

From lower cells of waking life we pass
To full perfection; thus the world grows old:
We who are godlike now were once a mass
Of quivering purple flecked with bars of gold,
Unsentient or of joy or misery,
And tossed in terrible tangles of some wild and wind-swept sea.

This hot hard flame with which our bodies burn
Will make some meadow blaze with daffodil,
Ay! and those argent breasts of thine will turn
To water-lilies; the brown fields men till
Will be more fruitful for our love to-night,
Nothing is lost in nature, all things live in Death's despite.

The boy's first kiss, the hyacinth's first bell,
The man's last passion, and the last red spear
That from the lily leaps, the asphodel
Which will not let its blossoms blow for fear
Of too much beauty, and the timid shame
Of the young bridegroom at his lover's eyes,—these with the same

One sacrament are consecrate, the earth
Not we alone hath passions hymeneal,
The yellow buttercups that shake for mirth
At daybreak know a pleasure not less real
Than we do, when in some fresh-blossoming wood
We draw the spring into our hearts, and feel that life is good.

So when men bury us beneath the yew
Thy crimson-stainèd mouth a rose will be,
And thy soft eyes lush bluebells dimmed with dew,
And when the white narcissus wantonly
Kisses the wind its playment, some faint joy
Will thrill our dust, and we will be again fond maid and boy.

And thus without life's conscious torturing pain
In some sweet flower we will feel the sun,
And from the linnet's throat will sing again,
And as two gorgeous-mailèd snakes will run

Over our graves, or as two tigers creep
Through the hot jungle where the yellow-eyed huge lions sleep

And give them battle! How my heart leaps up
To think of that grand living after death
In beast and bird and flower, when this cup,
Being filled too full of spirit, bursts for breath,
And with the pale leaves of some autumn day
The soul earth's earliest conqueror becomes earth's last great prey.

O think of it! We shall inform ourselves
Into all sensuous life, the goat-foot Faun,
The Centaur, or the merry bright-eyed Elves
That leave their dancing rings to spite the dawn
Upon the meadows, shall not be more near
Than you and I to nature's mysteries, for we shall hear

The thrush's heart beat, and the daisies grow,
And the wan snowdrop sighing for the sun
On sunless days in winter, we shall know
By whom the silver gossamer is spun,
Who paints the diapered fritillaries,
On what wide wings from shivering pine to pine the eagle flies.

Ay! had we never loved at all, who knows
If yonder daffodil had lured the bee
Into its gilded womb, or any rose
Had hung with crimson lamps its little tree!
Methinks no leaf would ever bud in spring,
But for the lovers' lips that kiss, the poet's lips that sing.

Is the light vanished from our golden sun,
Or is this dædal-fashioned earth less fair,
That we are nature's heritors, and one
With every pulse of life that beats the air?
Rather new suns across the sky shall pass,
New splendour come unto the flower, new glory to the grass.

And we two lovers shall not sit afar,
Critics of nature, but the joyous sea
Shall be our raiment, and the bearded star
Shoot arrows at our pleasure! We shall be
Part of the mighty universal whole,
And through all æons mix and mingle with the Kosmic Soul!

We shall be notes in that great Symphony
Whose cadence circles through the rhythmic spheres,
And all the live World's throbbing heart shall be
One with our heart, the stealthy creeping years
Have lost their terrors now, we shall not die,
The Universe itself shall be our Immortality!

RAVENNA

A YEAR ago I breathed the Italian air,—
And yet, methinks this northern Spring is fair,—
These fields made golden with the flower of March,
The throstle singing on the fathered larch,
The cawing rooks, the wood-doves fluttering by,
The little clouds that race across the sky;
And fair the violet's gentle drooping head,
The primrose, pale for love uncomforted,
The rose that burgeons on the climbing briar,
The crocus-bed, (that seems a moon of fire
Round-girdled with a purple marriage-ring);
And all the flowers of our English Spring,
Fond snow-drops, and the bright-starred daffodil.
Up starts the lark beside the murmuring mill,
And breaks the gossamer-threads of early dew;
And down the river, like a flame of blue,
Keene as an arrow flies the water-king,
While the brown linnets in the greenwood sing.
A year ago!—it seems a little time
Since last I saw that lordly southern clime,
Where flower and fruit to purple radiance blow,
And like bright lamps the fabled apples grow.
Full Spring it was—and by rich flowing vines,
Dark olive-groves and noble forest-pines,
I rode at will; the moist glad air was sweet,
The white road rang beneath my horse's feet,
And musing on Ravenna's ancient name,
I watched the day till, marked with wounds of flame,
The turquoise sky to burnished gold was turned.

O how my heart with boyish passion burned,
When far away across the sedge and mere
I saw that Holy City rising clear,
Crowned with her crown of towers!—On and on
I galloped, racing with the setting sun,
And ere the crimson after-glow was passed,
I stood within Ravenna's walls at last!

II

How strangely still! no sound of life or joy
Startles the air! no laughing shepherd-boy
Pipes on his reed, nor ever through the day
Comes the glad sound of children at their play:

O sad, and sweet, and silent! surely here
A man might dwell apart from troublous fear,
Watching the tide of seasons as they flow
From amorous Spring to Winter's rain and snow,
And have no thought of sorrow;—here, indeed,
Are Lethe's waters, and that fatal weed
Which makes a man forget his fatherland.

Ay! amid lotus-meadows dost thou stand,
Like Proserpine, with poppy-laden head,
Guarding the holy ashes of the dead.
For though thy brood of warrior sons hath ceased,
Thy noble dead are with thee!—they at least
Are faithful to thine honour:—guard them well,
O childless city! for a mighty spell,
To wake men's hearts to dream of things sublime,
Are the lone tombs where rest the Great of Time.

III

Yon lonely pillar, rising on the plain,
Marks where the bravest knight of France was slain,—
The Prince of chivalry, the Lord of war,
Gaston de Foix: for some untimely star
Led him against thy city, and he fell,
As falls some forest-lion fighting well.
Taken from life while life and love were new,
He lies beneath God's seamless veil of blue;
Tall lance-like reeds wave sadly o'er his head,
And oleanders bloom to deeper red,
Where his bright youth flowed crimson on the ground.

Look farther north unto that broken mound,—
There, prisoned now within a lordly tomb
Raised by a daughter's hand, in lonely gloom,
Huge-limbed Theodoric, the Gothic king,
Sleeps after all his weary conquering.
Time hath not spared his ruin,—wind and rain
Have broken down his stronghold; and again
We see that Death is mighty lord of all,
And king and clown to ashen dust must fall.

Mighty indeed *their* glory! yet to me
Barbaric king, or knight of chivalry,
Or the great queen herself, were poor and vain
Beside the grave where Dante rests from pain.
His gilded shrine lies open to the air;
And cunning sculptor's hands have carven there
The calm white brow, as calm as earliest morn,
The eyes that flashed with passionate love and scorn,
The lips that sang of Heaven and of Hell,
The almond-face which Giotto drew so well,

The weary face of Dante;–to this day,
Here in his place of resting, far away
From Arno's yellow waters, rushing down
Through the wide bridges of that fairy town,
Where the tall tower of Giotto seems to rise
A marble lily under sapphire skies!
Alas! my Dante! thou hast known the pain
Of meaner lives,–the exile's galling chain,
How steep the stairs within king's houses are,
And all the petty miseries which mar
Man's nobler nature with the sense of wrong.
Yet this dull world is grateful for thy song;
Our nations do thee homage,–even she,
That cruel queen of vine-clad Tuscany,
Who bound with crown of thorns thy living brow,
Hath decked thine empty tomb with laurels now,
And begs in vain the ashes of her son.

O mightiest exile! all thy grief is done:
Thy soul walks now beside thy Beatrice;
Ravenna guards thine ashes: sleep in peace.

IV

How lone this palace is; how grey the walls!
No minstrel now wakes echoes in these halls.
The broken chain lies rusting on the door,
And noisome weeds have split the marble floor:
Here lurks the snake, and here the lizards run
By the stone lions blinking in the sun.
Byron dwelt here in love and revelry
For two long years–a second Anthony,
Who of the world another Actium made!–
Yet suffered not his royal soul to fade,
Or lyre to break, or lance to grow less keen,
'Neath any wiles of an Egyptian queen.
For from the East there came a mighty cry,
And Greece stood up to fight for Liberty,
And called him from Ravenna: never knight
Rode forth more nobly to wild scenes of fight!
None fell more bravely on ensanguined field,
Borne like a Spartan back upon his shield!
O Hellas! Hellas! in thine hour of pride,
Thy day of might, remember him who died
To wrest from off thy limbs the trammelling chain:
O Salamis! O lone Platæan plain!
O tossing waves of wild Eubœan sea!
O wind-swept heights of lone Thermopylæ!
He loved you well–ay, not alone in word,
Who freely gave to thee his lyre and sword,
Like Æschylus at well-fought Marathon:

And England, too, shall glory in her son,
Her warrior-poet, first in song and fight.
No longer now shall Slander's venomed spite
Crawl like a snake across his perfect name,
Or mar the lordly scutcheon of his fame.

For as the olive-garland of the race
Which lights with joy each eager runner's face,
As the red cross which saveth men in war,
As a flame-bearded beacon seen from far
By mariners upon a storm-tossed sea,—
Such was his love for Greece and Liberty!

Byron, thy crowns are ever fresh and green:
Red leaves of rose from Sapphic Mitylene
Shall bind thy brows; the myrtle blooms for thee,
In hidden glades by lonely Castaly;
The laurels wait thy coming: all are thine,
And round thy head one perfect wreath will twine.

V

The pine-tops rocked before the evening breeze
With the hoarse murmur of the wintry seas,
And the tall stems were streaked with amber bright;—
I wandered through the wood in wild delight,
Some startled bird, with fluttering wings and fleet,
Made snow of all the blossoms: at my feet,
Like silver crowns, the pale narcissi lay,
And small birds sang on every twining spray.
O waving trees, O forest liberty!
Within your haunts at least a man is free,
And half forgets the weary world of strife:
The blood flows hotter, and a sense of life
Wakes i' the quickening veins, while once again
The woods are filled with gods we fancied slain.
Long time I watched, and surely hoped to see
Some goat-foot Pan make merry minstrelsy
Amid the reeds! some startled Dryad-maid
In girlish flight! or lurking in the glade,
The soft brown limbs, the wanton treacherous face
Of woodland god! Queen Dian in the chase,
White-limbed and terrible, with look of pride,
And leash of boar-hounds leaping at her side!
Or Hylas mirrored in the perfect stream.

O idle heart! O fond Hellenic dream!
Ere long, with melancholy rise and swell,
The evening chimes, the convent's vesper-bell
Struck on mine ears amid the amorous flowers.
Alas! alas! these sweet and honied hours

Had 'whelmed my heart like some encroaching sea,
And drowned all thoughts of black Gethsemane.

VI

O lone Ravenna! many a tale is told
Of thy great glories in the days of old:
Two thousand years have passed since thou didst see
Cæsar ride forth in royal victory.
Mighty thy name when Rome's lean eagles flew
From Britain's isles to far Euphrates blue;
And of the peoples thou wast noble queen,
Till in thy streets the Goth and Hun were seen.
Discrowned by man, deserted by the sea,
Thou sleepest, rocked in lonely misery!
No longer now upon thy swelling tide,
Pine-forest like, thy myriad galleys ride!
For where the brass-beaked ships were wont to float,
The weary shepherd pipes his mournful note;
And the white sheep are free to come and go
Where Adria's purple waters used to flow.

O fair! O sad! O Queen uncomforted!
In ruined loveliness thou liest dead,
Alone of all thy sisters; for at last
Italia's royal warrior hath passed
Rome's lordliest entrance, and hath worn his crown
In the high temples of the Eternal Town!
The Palatine hath welcomed back her king,
And with his name the seven mountains ring!

And Naples hath outlived her dream of pain,
And mocks her tyrant! Venice lives again,
New risen from the waters! and the cry
Of Light and Truth, of Love and Liberty,
Is heard in lordly Genoa, and where
The marble spires of Milan wound the air,
Rings from the Alps to the Sicilian shore,
And Dante's dream is now a dream no more.

But thou, Ravenna, better loved than all,
Thy ruined palaces are but a pall
That hides thy fallen greatness! and thy name
Burns like a grey and flickering candle-flame,
Beneath the noon-day splendour of the sun
Of new Italia! for the night is done,
The night of dark oppression, and the day
Hath dawned in passionate splendour: far away
The Austrian hounds are hunted from the land,
Beyond those ice-crowned citadels which stand
Girdling the plain of royal Lombardy,
From the far West unto the Eastern sea.

I know, indeed, that sons of thine have died
In Lissa's waters, by the mountain-side
Of Aspromonte, on Novara's plain,—
Nor have thy children died for thee in vain:
And yet, methinks, thou hast not drunk this wine
From grapes new-crushed of Liberty divine,
Thou hast not followed that immortal Star
Which leads the people forth to deeds of war.
Weary of life, thou liest in silent sleep,
As one who marks the lengthening shadows creep,
Careless of all the hurrying hours that run,
Mourning some day of glory, for the sun
Of freedom hath not shown to thee his face,
And thou hast caught no flambeau in the race.

Yet wake not from thy slumbers,—rest thee well,
Amidst thy fields of amber asphodel,
Thy lily-sprinkled meadows,—rest thee there,
To mock all human greatness: who would dare
To vent the paltry sorrows of his life
Before thy ruins, or to praise the strife
Of kings' ambition, and the barren pride
Of warrior nations! wert not thou the Bride
Of the wild Lord of Adria's stormy sea!
The Queen of double Empires! and to thee
Were not the nations given as thy prey!
And now—thy gates lie open night and day,
The grass grows green on every tower and hall,
The ghastly fig hath cleft thy bastioned wall;
And where thy mailèd warriors stood at rest
The midnight owl hath made her secret nest.
O fallen! fallen! from thy high estate,
O city trammelled in the toils of Fate,
Doth nought remain of all thy glorious days,
But a dull shield, a crown of withered bays!

Yet who beneath this night of wars and fears,
From tranquil tower can watch the coming years;
Who can fortell what joys the day shall bring,
Or why before the dawn the linnets sing?
Thou, even thou, mayst wake, as wakes the rose
To crimson splendour from its grave of snows;
As the rich corn-fields rise to red and gold
From these brown lands, now stiff with Winter's cold
As from the storm-rack comes a perfect star!

O much-loved city! I have wandered far
From the wave-circled islands of my home,

Have seen the gloomy mystery of the Dome
Rise slowly from the drear Campagna's way,
Clothed in the royal purple of the day:
I from the city of the violet crown
Have watched the sun by Corinth's hill go down,
And marked the "myriad laughter" of the sea
From starlit hills of flower-starred Arkady;
Yet back to thee returns my perfect love,
As to its forest-nest the evening dove.

O poet's city! one who scarce has seen
Some twenty summers cast their doublets green,
For Autumn's livery, would seek in vain
To wake his lyre to sing a louder strain,
Or tell thy days of glory;—poor indeed
Is the low murmur of the shepherd's reed,
Where the loud clarion's blast should shake the sky,
And flame across the heavens! and to try
Such lofty themes were folly: yet I know
That never felt my heart a nobler glow
Than when I woke the silence of thy street
With clamorous trampling of my horse's feet,
And saw the city which now I try to sing,
After long days of weary travelling.

VII

Adieu, Ravenna! but a year ago,
I stood and watched the crimson sunset glow
From the lone chapel on thy marshy plain:
The sky was as a shield that caught the stain
Of blood and battle from the dying sun,
And in the west the circling clouds had spun
A royal robe, which some great God might wear,
While into ocean-seas of purple air
Sank the gold galley of the Lord of Light.

Yet here the gentle stillness of the night
Brings back the swelling tide of memory,
And wakes again my passionate love for thee:
Now is the Spring of Love, yet soon will come
On meadow and tree the Summer's lordly bloom:
And soon the grass with brighter flowers will blow,
And send up lilies for some boy to mow.
Then before long the Summer's conqueror,
Rich Autumn-time, the season's usurer,
Will lend his hoarded gold to all the trees,
And see it scattered by the spendthrift breeze;
And after that the Winter cold and drear.
So runs the perfect cycle of the year.
And so from youth to manhood do we go,

And fall to weary days and locks of snow.
Love only knows no winter; never dies:
Nor cares for frowning storms or leaden skies.
And mine for thee shall never pass away,
Though my weak lips may falter in my lay.

Adieu! Adieu! yon silent evening star,
The night's ambassador, doth gleam afar,
And bid the shepherd bring his flocks to fold.
Perchance before our inland seas of gold
Are garnered by the reapers into sheaves,
Perchance before I see the Autumn leaves,
I may behold thy city; and lay down
Low at thy feet the poet's laurel crown.

Adieu! Adieu! yon silver lamp, the moon,
Which turns our midnight into perfect noon,
Doth surely light thy towers, guarding well
Where Dante sleeps, where Byron loved to dwell.

THE GARDEN OF EROS

It is full summer now, the heart of June,
Not yet the sun-burnt reapers are a-stir
Upon the upland meadow where too soon
Rich autumn time, the season's usurer,
Will lend his hoarded gold to all the trees,
And see his treasure scattered by the wild and spendthrift breeze.

Too soon indeed! yet here the daffodil,
That love-child of the Spring, has lingered on
To vex the rose with jealousy, and still
The harebell spreads her azure pavilion,
And like a strayed and wandering reveller
Abandoned of its brothers, whom long since June's messenger

The missel-thrush has frighted from the glade,
One pale narcissus loiters fearfully
Close to a shadowy nook, where half afraid
Of their own loveliness some violets lie
That will not look the gold sun in the face
For fear of too much splendour,—ah! methinks it is a place

Which should be trodden by Persephone
When wearied of the flowerless fields of Dis!
Or danced on by the lads of Arcady!
The hidden secret of eternal bliss
Known to the Grecian here a man might find,

Ah! you and *I* may find it now if Love and Sleep be kind.

There are the flowers which mourning Herakles
Strewed on the tomb of Hylas, columbine,
Its white doves all a-flutter where the breeze
Kissed them too harshly, the small celandine,
That yellow-kirtled chorister of eve,
And lilac lady's-smock,–but let them bloom alone and leave

Yon spired holly-hock red-crocketed
To sway its silent chimes, else must the bee,
Its little bell-ringer, go seek instead
Some other pleasaunce; the anemone
That weeps at daybreak, like a silly girl
Before her love, and hardly lets the butterflies unfurl

Their painted wings beside it,–bid it pine
In pale virginity; the winter snow
Will suit it better than those lips of thine
Whose fires would but scorch it, rather go
And pluck that amorous flower which blooms alone,
Fed by the pander wind with dust of kisses not its own.

The trumpet-mouths of red convolvulus
So dear to maidens, creamery meadow-sweet
Whiter than Juno's throat and odorous
As all Arabia, hyacinths the feet
Of Huntress Dian would be loath to mar
For any dappled fawn,–pluck these, and those fond flowers which are

Fairer than what Queen Venus trod upon
Beneath the pines of Ida, eucharis,
That morning star which does not dread the sun,
And budding marjoram which but to kiss
Would sweeten Cytheræa's lips and make
Adonis jealous,–these for thy head,–and for thy girdle take

Yon curving spray of purple clematis
Whose gorgeous dye outflames the Tyrian King,
And fox-gloves with their nodding chalices,
But that one narciss which the startled Spring
Let from her kirtle fall when first she heard
In her own woods the wild tempestuous song of summer's bird,

Ah! leave it for a subtle memory
Of those sweet tremulous days of rain and sun,
When April laughed between her tears to see
The early primrose with shy footsteps run
From the gnarled oak-tree roots till all the wold,
Spite of its brown and trampled leaves, grew bright with shimmering gold.

Nay, pluck it too, it is not half so sweet
As thou thyself, my soul's idolatry!

And when thou art a-wearied at thy feet
Shall oxlips weave their brightest tapestry,
For thee the woodbine shall forget its pride
And veil its tangled whorls, and thou shalt walk on daisies pied.

And I will cut a reed by yonder spring
And make the wood-gods jealous, and old Pan
Wonder what young intruder dares to sing
In these still haunts, where never foot of man
Should tread at evening, lest he chance to spy
The marble limbs of Artemis and all her company.

And I will tell you why the jacinth wears
Such dread embroidery of dolorous moan,
And why the hapless nightingale forbears
To sing her song at noon, but weeps alone
When the fleet swallow sleeps, and rich men feast,
And why the laurel trembles when she sees the lightening east.

And I will sing how sad Proserpina
Unto a grave and gloomy Lord was wed,
And lure the silver-breasted Helena
Back from the lotus meadows of the dead,
So shalt thou see that awful loveliness
For which two mighty Hosts met fearfully in war's abyss!

And then I'll pipe to thee that Grecian tale
How Cynthia loves the lad Endymion,
And hidden in a gray and misty veil
Hies to the cliffs of Latmos, once the Sun
Leaps from his ocean bed, in fruitless chase
Of those pale flying feet which fade away in his embrace.

And if my flute can breathe sweet melody,
We may behold Her face who long ago
Dwelt among men by the Ægean sea,
And whose sad house with pillaged portico
And friezeless wall and columns toppled down
Looms o'er the ruins of that fair and violet-cinctured town.

Spirit of Beauty! tarry still a-while,
They are not dead, thine ancient votaries,
Some few there are to whom thy radiant smile
Is better than a thousand victories,
Though all the nobly slain of Waterloo
Rise up in wrath against them! tarry still, there are a few,

Who for thy sake would give their manlihood
And consecrate their being, I at least
Have done so, made thy lips my daily food,
And in thy temples found a goodlier feast
Than this starved age can give me, spite of all
Its new-found creeds so skeptical and so dogmatical.

Here not Cephissos, not Ilissos flows,
The woods of white Colonos are not here,
On our bleak hills the olive never blows,
No simple priest conducts his lowing steer
Up the steep marble way, nor through the town
Do laughing maidens bear to thee the crocus-flowered gown.

Yet tarry! for the boy who loved thee best,
Whose very name should be a memory
To make thee linger, sleeps in silent rest
Beneath the Roman walls, and melody
Still mourns her sweetest lyre, none can play
The lute of Adonais, with his lips Song passed away.

Nay, when Keats died the Muses still had left
One silver voice to sing his threnody,
But ah! too soon of it we were bereft
When on that riven night and stormy sea
Panthea claimed her singer as her own,
And slew the mouth that praised her; since which time we walk alone,

Save for that fiery heart, that morning star
Of re-arisen England, whose clear eye
Saw from our tottering throne and waste of war
The grand Greek limbs of young Democracy
Rise mightily like Hesperus and bring
The great Republic! him at least thy love hath taught to sing,

And he hath been with thee at Thessaly,
And seen white Atalanta fleet of foot
In passionless and fierce virginity
Hunting the tuskèd boar, his honeyed lute
Hath pierced the cavern of the hollow hill,
And Venus laughs to know one knee will bow before her still.

And he hath kissed the lips of Proserpine,
And sung the Galilæan's requiem,
That wounded forehead dashed with blood and wine
He hath discrowned, the Ancient Gods in him
Have found their last, most ardent worshipper,
And the new Sign grows gray and dim before its conqueror

Spirit of Beauty! tarry with us still,
It is not quenched the torch of poesy,
The star that shook above the Eastern hill
Holds unassailed its argent armory
From all the gathering gloom and fretful fight—
O tarry with us still! for through the long and common night,

Morris, our sweet and simple Chaucer's child,
Dear heritor of Spenser's tuneful reed,
With soft and sylvan pipe has oft beguiled

The weary soul of man in troublous need,
And from the far and flowerless fields of ice
Has brought fair flowers meet to make an earthly paradise.

We know them all, Gudrun the strong man's bride,
Aslaug and Olafson we know them all,
How giant Grettir fought and Sigurd died,
And what enchantment held the king in thrall
When lonely Brynhild wrestled with the powers
That war against all passion, ah! how oft through summer hours,

Long listless summer hours when the noon
Being enamored of a damask rose
Forgets to journey westward, till the moon
The pale usurper of its tribute grows
From a thin sickle to a silver shield
And chides its loitering car—how oft, in some cool grassy field

Far from the cricket-ground and noisy eight
At Bagley, where the rustling blue-bells come
Almost before the blackbird finds a mate
And overstay the swallow, and the hum
Of many murmuring bees flits through the leaves,
Have I lain poring on the dreamy tales his fancy weaves,

And through their unreal woes and mimic pain
Wept for myself, and so was purified,
And in their simple mirth grew glad again;
For as I sailed upon that pictured tide
The strength and splendour of the storm was mine
Without the storm's red ruin, for the singer is divine.

The little laugh of water falling down
Is not so musical, the clammy gold
Close hoarded in the tiny waxen town
Has less of sweetness in it, and the old
Half-withered reeds that waved in Arcady
Touched by his lips break forth again to fresher harmony.

Spirit of Beauty tarry yet a-while!
Although the cheating merchants of the mart
With iron roads profane our lovely isle,
And break on whirring wheels the limbs of Art,
Ay! though the crowded factories beget
The blind-worm Ignorance that slays the soul, O tarry yet!

For One at least there is,—He bears his name
From Dante and the seraph Gabriel,—
Whose double laurels burn with deathless flame
To light thine altar; He too loves thee well
Who saw old Merlin lured in Vivien's snare,
And the white feet of angels coming down the golden stair,

Loves thee so well, that all the world for him
A gorgeous-colored vestiture must wear,
And Sorrow take a purple diadem,
Or else be no more Sorrow, and Despair
Gild its own thorns, and Pain, like Adon, be
Even in anguish beautiful;—such is the empery

Which painters hold, and such the heritage
This gentle, solemn Spirit doth possess,
Being a better mirror of his age
In all his pity, love, and weariness,
Than those who can but copy common things,
And leave the soul unpainted with its mighty questionings.

But they are few, and all romance has flown,
And men can prophesy about the sun,
And lecture on his arrows—how, alone,
Through a waste void the soulless atoms run,
How from each tree its weeping nymph has fled,
And that no more 'mid English reeds a Naïad shows her head.

Methinks these new actæons boast too soon
That they have spied on beauty; what if we
Have analysed the rainbow, robbed the moon
Of her most ancient, chastest mystery,
Shall I, the last Endymion, lose all hope
Because rude eyes peer at my mistress through a telescope!

What profit if this scientific age
Burst through our gates with all its retinue
Of modern miracles! Can it assuage
One lover's breaking heart? what can it do
To make one life more beautiful, one day
More god-like in its period? but now the Age of Clay

Returns in horrid cycle, and the earth
Hath borne again a noisy progeny
Of ignorant Titans, whose ungodly birth
Hurls them against the august hierarchy
Which sat upon Olympus, to the Dust
They have appealed, and to that barren arbiter they must

Repair for judgment, let them, if they can,
From Natural Warfare and insensate Chance,
Create the new ideal rule for man!
Methinks that was not my inheritance;
For I was nurtured otherwise, my soul
Passes from higher heights of life to a more supreme goal.

Lo! while we spake the earth did turn away
Her visage from the God, and Hecate's boat
Rose silver-laden, till the jealous day
Blew all its torches out: I did not note
The waning hours, to young Endymions
Time's palsied fingers count in vain his rosary of suns!—

Mark how the yellow iris wearily
Leans back its throat, as though it would be kissed
By its false chamberer, the dragon-fly,
Who, like a blue vein on a girl's white wrist,
Sleeps on that snowy primrose of the night,
Which 'gins to flush with crimson shame, and die beneath the light.

Come let us go, against the pallid shield
Of the wan sky the almond blossoms gleam,
The corn-crake nested in the unmown field
Answers its mate, across the misty stream
On fitful wing the startled curlews fly,
And in his sedgy bed the lark, for joy that Day is nigh,

Scatters the pearlèd dew from off the grass,
In tremulous ecstasy to greet the sun,
Who soon in gilded panoply will pass
Forth from yon orange-curtained pavilion
Hung in the burning east, see, the red rim
O'ertops the expectant hills! it is the God! for love of him

Already the shrill lark is out of sight,
Flooding with waves of song this silent dell,—
Ah! there is something more in that bird's flight
Than could be tested in a crucible!—
But the air freshens, let us go,—why soon
The woodmen will be here; how we have lived this night of June!

THE BURDEN OF ITYS

This English Thames is holier far than Rome,
Those harebells like a sudden flush of sea
Breaking across the woodland, with the foam
Of meadow-sweet and white anemone
To fleck their blue waves,—God is likelier there,
Than hidden in that crystal-hearted star the pale monks bear!

Those violet-gleaming butterflies that take
Yon creamy lily for their pavilion
Are monsignores, and where the rushes shake
A lazy pike lies basking in the sun
His eyes half-shut,—He is some mitred old
Bishop *in partibus!* look at those gaudy scales all green and gold!

The wind the restless prisoner of the trees
Does well for Palæstrina, one would say
The mighty master's hands were on the keys
Of the Maria organ, which they play

When early on some sapphire Easter morn
In a high litter red as blood or sin the Pope is borne

From his dark house out to the balcony
Above the bronze gates and the crowded square,
Whose very fountains seem for ecstasy
To toss their silver lances in the air,
And stretching out weak hands to East and West
In vain sends peace to peaceless lands, to restless nations rest.

Is not yon lingering orange afterglow
That stays to vex the moon more fair than all
Rome's lordliest pageants! strange, a year ago
I knelt before some crimson Cardinal
Who bare the Host across the Esquiline,
And now—those common poppies in the wheat seem twice as fine.

The blue-green beanfields yonder, tremulous
With the last shower, sweeter perfume bring
Through this cool evening than the odorous
Flame-jewelled censers the young deacons swing,
When the gray priest unlocks the curtained shrine,
And makes God's body from the common fruit of corn and vine.

Poor Fra Giovanni bawling at the mass
Were out of tune now, for a small brown bird
Sings overhead, and through the long cool grass
I see that throbbing throat which once I heard
On starlit hills of flower-starred Arcady,
Once where the white and crescent sand of Salamis meets the sea.

Sweet is the swallow twittering on the eaves
At daybreak, when the mower whets his scythe,
And stock-doves murmur, and the milkmaid leaves
Her little lonely bed, and carols blithe
To see the heavy-lowing cattle wait
Stretching their huge and dripping mouths across the farmyard gate.

And sweet the hops upon the Kentish leas,
And sweet the wind that lifts the new-mown hay,
And sweet the fretful swarms of grumbling bees
That round and round the linden blossoms play;
And sweet the heifer breathing in the stall,
And the green bursting figs that hang upon the red-brick wall.

And sweet to hear the cuckoo mock the spring
While the last violet loiters by the well,
And sweet to hear the shepherd Daphnis sing
The song of Linus through a sunny dell
Of warm Arcadia where the corn is gold
And the slight lithe-limbed reapers dance about the wattled fold.

And sweet with young Lycoris to recline
In some Illyrian valley far away,
Where canopied on herbs amaracine
We too might waste the summer-trancèd day
Matching our reeds in sportive rivalry,
While far beneath us frets the troubled purple of the sea.

But sweeter far if silver-sandalled foot
Of some long-hidden God should ever tread
The Nuneham meadows, if with reeded flute
Pressed to his lips some Faun might raise his head
By the green water-flags, ah! sweet indeed
To see the heavenly herdsman call his white-fleeced flock to feed.

Then sing to me thou tuneful chorister,
Though what thou sing'st be thine own requiem!
Tell me thy tale thou hapless chronicler
Of thine own tragedies! do not contemn
These unfamiliar haunts, this English field,
For many a lovely coronal our northern isle can yield,

Which Grecian meadows know not, many a rose,
Which all day long in vales Æolian
A lad might seek in vain for, overgrows
Our hedges like a wanton courtesan
Unthrifty of her beauty, lilies too
Ilissus never mirrored star our streams, and cockles blue

Dot the green wheat which, though they are the signs
For swallows going south, would never spread
Their azure tints between the Attic vines;
Even that little weed of ragged red,
Which bids the robin pipe, in Arcady
Would be a trespasser, and many an unsung elegy

Sleeps in the reeds that fringe our winding Thames
Which to awake were sweeter ravishment
Than ever Syrinx wept for, diadems
Of brown be-studded orchids which were meant
For Cytheræa's brows are hidden here
Unknown to Cytheræa, and by yonder pasturing steer

There is a tiny yellow daffodil,
The butterfly can see it from afar,
Although one summer evening's dew could fill
Its little cup twice over ere the star
Had called the lazy shepherd to his fold
And be no prodigal, each leaf is flecked with spotted gold

As if Jove's gorgeous leman Danaë
Hot from his gilded arms had stooped to kiss
The trembling petals, or young Mercury
Low-flying to the dusky ford of Dis
Had with one feather of his pinions
Just brushed them!—the slight stem which bears the burdens of its suns

Is hardly thicker than the gossamer,
Or poor Arachne's silver tapestry,—
Men say it bloomed upon the sepulchre
Of One I sometime worshipped, but to me
It seems to bring diviner memories
Of faun-loved Heliconian glades and blue nymph-haunted seas,

Of an untrodden vale at Tempe where
On the clear river's marge Narcissus lies,
The tangle of the forest in his hair,
The silence of the woodland in his eyes,
Wooing that drifting imagery which is
No sooner kissed than broken, memories of Salmacis.

Who is not boy or girl and yet is both,
Fed by two fires and unsatisfied
Through their excess, each passion being loath
For love's own sake to leave the other's side,
Yet killing love by staying, memories
Of Oreads peeping through the leaves of silent moonlit trees.

Of lonely Ariadne on the wharf
At Naxos, when she saw the treacherous crew
Far out at sea, and waved her crimson scarf
And called the false Theseus back again nor knew
That Dionysos on an amber pard
Was close behind her: memories of what Maeonia's bard

With sightless eyes beheld, the wall of Troy,
Queen Helen lying in the carven room,
And at her side an amorous red-lipped boy
Trimming with dainty hand his helmet's plume,
And far away the moil, the shout, the groan,
As Hector shielded off the spear and Ajax hurled the stone;

Of wingèd Perseus with his flawless sword
Cleaving the snaky tresses of the witch,
And all those tales imperishably stored
In little Grecian urns, freightage more rich
Than any gaudy galleon of Spain
Bare from the Indies ever! these at least bring back again,

For well I know they are not dead at all,
The ancient Gods of Grecian poesy,
They are asleep, and when they hear thee call
Will wake and think 'tis very Thessaly,
This Thames the Daulian waters, this cool glade
The yellow-irised mead where once young Itys laughed and played.

If it was thou dear jasmine-cradled bird
Who from the leafy stillness of thy throne
Sang to the wondrous boy, until he heard
The horn of Atalanta faintly blown
Across the Cumnor hills, and wandering
Through Bagley wood at evening found the Attic poet's spring,—

Ah! tiny sober-suited advocate
  That pleadest for the moon against the day!
If thou didst make the shepherd seek his mate
  On that sweet questing, when Proserpina
Forgot it was not Sicily and leant
Across the mossy Sandford stile in ravished wonderment,—

Light-winged and bright-eyed miracle of the wood!
  If ever thou didst soothe with melody
One of that little clan, that brotherhood
  Which loved the morning-star of Tuscany
More than the perfect sun of Raphael,
And is immortal, sing to me! for I too love thee well,

Sing on! sing on! let the dull world grow young,
  Let elemental things take form again,
And the old shapes of Beauty walk among
  The simple garths and open crofts, as when
The son of Leto bare the willow rod,
And the soft sheep and shaggy goats followed the boyish God.

Sing on! sing on! and Bacchus will be here
  Astride upon his gorgeous Indian throne,
And over whimpering tigers shake the spear
  With yellow ivy crowned and gummy cone,
While at his side the wanton Bassarid
Will throw the lion by the mane and catch the mountain kid!

Sing on! and I will wear the leopard skin,
  And steal the moonèd wings of Ashtaroth,
Upon whose icy chariot we could win
  Cithæron in an hour e'er the froth
Has overbrimmed the wine-vat or the Faun
Ceased from the treading! ay, before the flickering lamp of dawn

Has scared the hooting owlet to its nest,
  And warned the bat to close its filmy vans,
Some Mænad girl with vine-leaves on her breast
  Will filch their beechnuts from the sleeping Pans
So softly that the little nested thrush
Will never wake, and then with shrilly laugh and leap will rush

Down the green valley where the fallen dew
  Lies thick beneath the elm and count her store,
Till the brown Satyrs in a jolly crew
  Trample the loosestrife down along the shore,
And where their hornéd master sits in state
Bring strawberries and bloomy plums upon a wicker crate!

Sing on! and soon with passion-wearied face
  Through the cool leaves Apollo's lad will come,
The Tyrian prince his bristled boar will chase
  Adown the chestnut copses all a-bloom,
And ivory-limbed, gray-eyed, with look of pride,
After yon velvet-coated deer the virgin maid will ride.

Sing on! and I the dying boy will see
Stain with his purple blood the waxen bell
That overweighs the jacinth, and to me
The wretched Cyprian her woe will tell,
And I will kiss her mouth and streaming eyes,
And lead her to the myrtle-hidden grove where Adon lies!

Cry out aloud on Itys! memory
That foster-brother of remorse and pain
Drops poison in mine ear–O to be free,
To burn one's old ships! and to launch again
Into the white-plumed battle of the waves
And fight old Proteus for the spoil of coral-flowered caves?

O for Medea with her poppied spell!
O for the secret of the Colchian shrine!
O for one leaf of that pale asphodel
Which binds the tired brows of Proserpine,
And sheds such wondrous dews at eve that she
Dreams of the fields of Enna, by the far Sicilian sea,

Where oft the golden-girdled bee she chased
From lily to lily on the level mead,
Ere yet her sombre Lord had bid her taste
The deadly fruit of that pomegranate seed,
Ere the black steeds had harried her away
Down to the faint and flowerless land, the sick and sunless day.

O for one midnight and as paramour
The Venus of the little Melian farm!
O that some antique statue for one hour
Might wake to passion, and that I could charm
The Dawn at Florence from its dumb despair,
Mix with those mighty limbs and make that giant breast my lair!

Sing on! sing on! I would be drunk with life,
Drunk with the trampled vintage of my youth,
I would forget the wearying wasted strife,
The riven vale, the Gorgon eyes of Truth,
The prayerless vigil and the cry for prayer,
The barren gifts, the lifted arms, the dull insensate air!

Sing on! sing on! O feathered Niobe,
Thou canst make sorrow beautiful, and steal
From joy its sweetest music, not as we
Who by dead voiceless silence strive to heal
Our too untented wounds, and do but keep
Pain barricaded in our hearts, and murder pillowed sleep.

Sing louder yet, why must I still behold
The wan white face of that deserted Christ,
Whose bleeding hands my hands did once infold.
Whose smitten lips my lips so oft have kissed,

And now in mute and marble misery
Sits in His lone dishonored House
and weeps, perchance for me.

O memory cast down thy wreathèd
shell!
Break thy hoarse lute O sad Mel-
pomené!
O sorrow, sorrow keep thy cloistered
cell
Nor dim with tears this limpid
Castaly!
Cease, cease, sad bird, thou dost the
forest wrong
To vex its sylvan quiet with such
wild impassioned song!

Cease, cease, or if 'tis anguish to be
dumb
Take from the pastoral thrush her
simpler air,
Whose jocund carelessness doth more
become
This English woodland than thy
keen despair,
Ah! cease and let the north wind
bear thy lay
Back to the rocky hills of Thrace, the
stormy Daulian bay.

A moment more, the startled leaves
had stirred,
Endymion would have passed across
the mead
Moonstruck with love, and this still
Thames had heard
Pan plash and paddle groping for
some reed
To lure from her blue cave that
Naiad maid
Who for such piping listens half in
joy and half afraid.

A moment more, the waking dove
had cooed,
The silver daughter of the silver
sea
With the fond gyves of clinging
hands had wooed
Her wanton from the chase, the
Dryope
Had thrust aside the branches of her
oak
To see the lusty gold-haired lad rein
in his snorting yoke.

A moment more, the trees had
stooped to kiss
Pale Daphne just awakening from
the swoon
Of tremulous laurels, lonely Salmacis
Had bared his barren beauty to the
moon,
And through the vale with sad volup-
tuous smile
Antinous had wandered, the red lotus
of the Nile.

Down leaning from his black and
clustering hair
To shade those slumberous eyelids'
caverned bliss,
Or else on yonder grassy slope with
bare
High-tuniced limbs unravished
Artemis
Had bade her hounds give tongue,
and roused the deer
From his green ambuscade with shrill
hallo and pricking spear.

Lie still, lie still, O passionate heart,
lie still!
O Melancholy, fold thy raven
wing!
O sobbing Dryad, from thy hollow
hill
Come not with such desponded
answering!
No more thou wingèd Marsyas complain,
Apollo loveth not to hear such
troubled songs of pain!

It was a dream, the glade is tenantless,
No soft Ionian laughter moves the air,
The Thames creeps on in sluggish leadenness,
And from the copse left desolate and bare
Fled is young Bacchus with his revelry,
Yet still from Nuneham wood there comes that thrilling melody

So sad, that one might think a human heart
Brake in each separate note, a quality
Which music sometimes has, being the Art
Which is most nigh to tears and memory,
Poor mourning Philomel, what dost thou fear?
Thy sister doth not haunt these fields, Pandion is not here,

Here is no cruel Lord with murderous blade,
No woven web of bloody heraldries,
But mossy dells for roving comrades made,
Warm valleys where the tired student lies
With half-shut book, and many a winding walk
Where rustic lovers stray at eve in happy simple talk.

The harmless rabbit gambols with its young
Across the trampled towing-path, where late
A troop of laughing boys in jostling throng
Cheered with their noisy cries the racing eight;
The gossamer, with ravelled silver threads,
Works at its little loom, and from the dusky red-caved sheds

Of the lone Farm a flickering light shines out
Where the swinked shepherd drives his bleating flock,
Back to their wattled sheep-cotes, a faint shout
Comes from some Oxford boat at Sandford lock,
And starts the moor-hen from the sedgy rill,
And the dim lengthening shadows flit like swallows up the hill.

The heron passes homeward to the mere,
The blue mist creeps among the shivering trees,
Gold world by world the silent stars appear,
And like a blossom blown before the breeze,
A white moon drifts across the shimmering sky,
Mute arbitress of all thy sad, thy rapturous threnody.

She does not heed thee, wherefore should she heed,
She knows Endymion is not far away,
'Tis I, 'tis I, whose soul is as the reed
Which has no message of its own to play,
So pipes another's bidding, it is I,
Drifting with every wind on the wide sea of misery.

Ah! the brown bird has ceased: one exquisite trill
About the sombre woodland seems to cling,
Dying in music, else the air is still,
So still that one might hear the bat's small wing
Wander and wheel above the pines, or tell
Each tiny dewdrop dripping from the bluebell's brimming cell.
And far across the lengthening wold,
Across the willowy flats and thickets brown,
Magdalen's tall tower tipped with tremulous gold
Marks the long High Street of the little town,
And warns me to return; I must not wait,
Hark! 'tis the curfew booming from the bell of Christ Church Gate.

HUMANITAD

It is full winter now: the trees are bare,
Save where the cattle huddle from the cold
Beneath the pine, for it doth never wear
The Autumn's gaudy livery whose gold
Her jealous brother pilfers, but is true
To the green doublet; bitter is the wind, as though it blew

From Saturn's cave; a few thin wisps of hay
Lie on the sharp black hedges, where the wain
Dragged the sweet pillage of a summer's day
From the low meadows up the narrow lane;
Upon the half-thawed snow the bleating sheep
Press close against the hurdles, and the shivering housedogs creep

From the shut stable to the frozen stream
And back again disconsolate, and miss
The bawling shepherds and the noisy team;
And overhead in circling listlessness
The cawing rooks whirl round the frosted stack,
Or crowd the dripping boughs; and in the fen the ice-pools crack

Where the gaunt bittern stalks among the reeds
And flaps his wings, and stretches back his neck,
And hoots to see the moon; across the meads
Limps the poor frightened hare, a little speck;
And a stray seamew with its fretful cry
Flits like a sudden drift of snow against the dull gray sky.

Full winter: and a lusty goodman brings
His load of faggots from the chilly byre,
And stamps his feet upon the hearth, and flings
The sappy billets on the waning fire,

And laughs to see the sudden lightning scare
His children at their play; and yet,—the Spring is in the air,

Already the slim crocus stirs the snow,
And soon yon blanchèd fields will bloom again
With nodding cowslips for some lad to mow,
For with the first warm kisses of the rain
The winter's icy sorrow breaks to tears,
And the brown thrushes mate, and with bright eyes the rabbit peers

From the dark warren where the fir-cones lie,
And treads one snowdrop under foot and runs
Over the mossy knoll, and blackbirds fly
Across our path at evening, and the suns
Stay longer with us; ah! how good to see
Grass-girdled Spring in all her joy of laughing greenery

Dance through the hedges till the early rose,
(That sweet repentance of the thorny briar!)
Burst from its sheathèd emerald and disclose
The little quivering disk of golden fire
Which the bees know so well, for with it come
Pale boy's love, sops-in-wine, and daffodillies all in bloom.

Then up and down the field the sower goes,
While close behind the laughing younker scares,
With shrilly whoop the black and thievish crows.
And then the chestnut-tree its glory wears,
And on the grass the creamy blossom falls
In odorous excess, and faint half-whispered madrigals

Steal from the bluebells' nodding carillons
Each breezy morn, and then white jessamine,
That star of its own heaven, snap-dragons
With lolling crimson tongues, and eglantine
In dusty velvets clad usurp the bed
And woodland empery, and when the lingering rose hath shed

Red leaf by leaf its folded panoply,
And pansies closed their purple-lidded eyes,
Chrysanthemums from gilded argosy
Unload their gaudy scentless merchandise
And violets getting overbold withdraw
From their shy nooks, and scarlet berries dot the leafless haw.

O happy field! and O thrice happy tree!
Soon will your queen in daisy-flowered smock,
And crown of flower-de-luce trip down the lea,
Soon will the lazy shepherds drive their flock

Back to the pasture by the pool, and soon
Through the green leaves will float the hum of murmuring bees at noon.

Soon will the glade be bright with bellamour,
The flower which wantons love, and those sweet nuns
Vale-lilies in their snowy vestiture
Will tell their bearded pearls, and carnations
With mitred dusky leaves will scent the wind,
And straggling traveller's joy each hedge with yellow stars will bind.

Dear Bride of Nature and most bounteous Spring!
That can'st give increase to the sweet-breath'd kine,
And to the kid its little horns, and bring
The soft and silky blossoms to the vine,
Where is that old nepenthe which of yore
Man got from poppy root and glossy-berried mandragore!

There was a time when any common bird
Could make me sing in unison, a time
When all the strings of boyish life were stirred
To quick response or more melo dious rhyme
By every forest idyll;—do I change?
Or rather doth some evil thing through thy fair pleasaunce range?

Nay, nay, thou art the same: 'tis I who seek
To vex with sighs thy simple solitude,
And because fruitless tears bedew my cheek
Would have thee weep with me in brotherhood;
Fool! shall each wronged and restless spirit dare
To taint such wine with the salt poison of his own despair!

Thou art the same: 'tis I whose wretched soul
Takes discontent to be its paramour,
And gives its kingdom to the rude control
Of what should be its servitor,—for sure
Wisdom is somewhere, though the stormy sea
Contain it not, and the huge deep answer " 'Tis not in me."

To burn with one clear flame, to stand erect
In natural honor, not to bend the knee
In profitless prostrations whose effect
Is by itself condemned, what alchemy
Can teach me this? what herb Medea brewed
Will bring the unexultant peace of essence not subdued?

The minor chord which ends the harmony,
And for its answering brother waits in vain,
Sobbing for incompleted melody
Dies a swan's death; but I the heir of pain

A silent Memnon with blank lidless eyes
Wait for the light and music of those suns which never rise.

The quanched-out torch, the lonely cypress-gloom,
The little dust stored in the narrow urn,
The gentle XAIPE of the Attic tomb,—
Were not these better far than to return
To my old fitful restless malady,
Or spend my days within the voiceless cave of misery?

Nay! for perchance that poppy-crownèd God
Is like the watcher by a sick man's bed
Who talks of sleep but gives it not; his rod
Hath lost its virtue, and, when all is said,
Death is too rude, too obvious a key
To solve one single secret in a life's philosophy.

And love! that noble madness, whose august
And inextinguishable might can slay
The soul with honeyed drugs,—alas! I must
From such sweet ruin play the runaway,
Although too constant memory never can
Forget the archèd splendor of those brows Olympian

Which for a little season made my youth
So soft a swoon of exquisite indolence
That all the chiding of more prudent Truth
Seemed the thin voice of jealousy,—O Hence
Thou huntress deadlier than Artemis!
Go seek some other quarry! for of thy too perilous bliss

My lips have drunk enough,—no more, no more,—
Though Love himself should turn his gilded prow
Back to the troubled waters of this shore
Where I am wrecked and stranded, even now
The chariot wheels of passion sweep too near,
Hence! Hence! I pass unto a life more barren, more austere.

More barren—ay, those arms will never lean
Down through the trellised vines and draw my soul
In sweet reluctance through the tangled green;
Some other head must wear that aureole,
For I am Hers who loves not any man
Whose white and stainless bosom bears the sign Gorgonian.

Let Venus go and chuck her dainty page,
And kiss his mouth, and toss his curly hair,
With net and spear and hunting equipage
Let young Adonis to his tryst repair,
But me her fond and subtle-fashioned spell
Delights no more, though I could win her dearest citadel.

Ay, though I were that laughing shepherd boy
Who from Mount Ida saw the little cloud
Pass over Tenedos and lofty Troy
And knew the coming of the Queen, and bowed
In wonder at her feet, not for the sake
Of a new Helen would I bid her hand the apple take.

Then rise supreme Athena argent-limbed!
And, if my lips be musicless, inspire
At least my life: was not thy glory hymned
By one who gave to thee his sword and lyre
Like Æschylus at well-fought Marathon,
And died to show that Milton's England still could bear a son!

And yet I cannot tread the portico
And live without desire, fear and pain,
Or nurture that wise calm which long ago
The grave Athenian master taught to men,
Self-poised, self-centered, and self-comforted,
To watch the world's vain phantasies go by with unbowed head.

Alas! that serene brow, those eloquent lips,
Those eyes that mirrored all eternity,
Rest in their own Colonos, an eclipse
Hath come on Wisdom, and Mnemosyne
Is childless; in the night which she had made
For lofty secure flight Athena's owl itself hath strayed.

Nor much with Science do I care to climb,
Although by strange and subtle witchery
She draw the moon from heaven: the Muse of Time
Unrolls her gorgeous-colored tapestry
To no less eager eyes; often indeed
In the great epic of Polymnia's scroll I love to read

How Asia sent her myriad hosts to war
Against a little town, and panoplied
In gilded mail with jewelled scimetar,
White-shielded, purple-crested, rode the Mede
Between the waving poplars and the sea
Which men call Artemisium, till he saw Thermopylae

Its steep ravine spanned by a narrow wall,
And on the nearer side a little brood
Of careless lions holding festival!
And stood amazèd at such hardihood,
And pitched his tent upon the reedy shore,
And stayed two days to wonder, and then crept at midnight o'er

Some unfrequented height, and coming down
The autumn forests treacherously slew
What Sparta held most dear and was the crown
Of far Eurotas, and passed on, nor knew

How God had staked an evil net for him
In the small bay of Salamis,—and yet, the page grows dim.

Its cadenced Greek delights me not, I feel
With such a goodly time too out of tune
To love it much: for like the Dial's wheel
That from its blinded darkness strikes the noon
Yet never sees the sun, so do my eyes
Restlessly follow that which from my cheated vision flies.

O for one grand unselfish simple life
To teach us what is Wisdom! speak ye hills
Of lone Helvellyn, for this note of strife
Shunned your untroubled crags and crystal rills,
Where is that Spirit which living blamelessly
Yet dared to kiss the smitten mouth of his own century!

Speak ye Ridalian laurels! where is He
Whose gentle head ye sheltered, that pure soul
Whose gracious days of uncrowned majesty
Through lowliest conduct touched the lofty goal
Where Love and Duty mingle! Him at least
The most high Laws were glad of, he had sat at Wisdom's feast,

But we are Learning's changelings, known by rote
The clarion watchword of each Grecian school
And follow none, the flawless sword which smote
The pagan Hydra is an effete tool
Which we ourselves have blunted, what man now
Shall scale the august ancient heights and to old Reverence bow?

One such indeed I saw, but, Ichabod!
Gone is that last dear son of Italy,
Who being man died for the sake of God,
And whose unrisen bones sleep peacefully.
O guard him, guard him well, my Giotto's tower,
Thou marble lily of the lily town! let not the lower

Of the rude tempest vex his slumber, or
The Arno with its tawny troubled gold
O'erleap its marge, no mightier conqueror
Clomb the high Capitol in the days of old
When Rome was indeed Rome, for Liberty
Walked like a Bride beside him, at which sight pale Mystery

Fled shrieking to her furthest somberest cell
With an old man who grabbled rusty keys,
Fled shuddering for that immemorial knell
With which oblivion buries dynasties
Swept like a wounded eagle on the blast,
As to the holy heart of Rome the great triumvir passed.

He knew the holiest heart and heights of Rome,
He drave the base wolf from the lion's lair,
And now lies dead by that empyreal dome
Which overtops Valdarno hung in air
By Brunelleschi—O Melpomene
Breathe through thy melancholy pipe thy sweetest threnody!

Breathe through the tragic stops such melodies
That Joy's self may grow jealous, and the Nine
Forget a-while their discreet emperies,
Mourning for him who on Rome's lordliest shrine
Lit for men's lives the light of Marathon,
And bare to sun-forgotten fields the fire of the sun!

O guard him, guard him well, my Giotto's tower,
Let some young Florentine each eventide
Bring coronals of that enchanted flower
Which the dim woods of Vallombrosa hide,
And deck the marble tomb wherein he lies
Whose soul is as some mighty orb unseen of mortal eyes.

Some mighty orb whose cycled wanderings,
Being tempest-driven to the furthest rim
Where Chaos meets Creation and the wings
Of the eternal chanting Cherubim
Are pavilioned on Nothing, passed away
Into a moonless void—and yet, though he is dust and clay,

He is not dead, the immemorial Fates
Forbid it, and the closing shears refrain,
Lift up your heads ye everlasting gates!
Ye argent clarions sound a loftier strain!
For the vile thing he hated lurks within
Its sombre house, alone with God and memories of sin.

Still what avails it that she sought her cave
That murderous mother of red harlotries?
At Munich on the marble architrave
The Grecian boys die smiling, but the seas
Which wash Ægina fret in loneliness
Not mirroring their beauty, so our lives grow colourless

For lack of our ideals, if one star
Flame torch-like in the heavens the unjust
Swift daylight kills it, and no trump of war
Can wake to passionate voice the silent dust
Which was Mazzini once! rich Niobe
For all her stony sorrows hath her sons, but Italy!

What Easter Day shall make her children rise,
Who were not Gods yet suffered? what sure feet
Shall find their graveclothes folded? what clear eyes

Shall see them bodily? O it were meet
To roll the stone from off the sepulchre
And kiss the bleeding roses of their wounds, in love of Her

Our Italy! our mother visible!
Most blessed among nations and most sad,
For whose dear sake the young Calabrian fell
That day at Aspromonte and was glad
That in an age when God was bought and sold
One man could die for Liberty! but we, burnt out and cold,

See Honour smitten on the cheek and gyves
Bind the sweet feet of Mercy: Poverty
Creeps through our sunless lanes and with sharp knives
Cuts the warm throats of children stealthily,
And no word said:–O we are wretched men
Unworthy of our great inheritance! where is the pen

Of austere Milton? where the mighty sword
Which slew its master righteously? the years
Have lost their ancient leader, and no word
Breaks from the voiceless tripod on our ears;
While as a ruined mother in some spasm
Bears a base child and loathes it, so our best enthusiasm

Genders unlawful children, Anarchy
Freedom's own Judas, the vile prodigal
License who steals the gold of Liberty
And yet has nothing, Ignorance the real
One Fratricide since Cain, Envy the asp
That stings itself to anguish, Avarice whose palsied grasp

Is in its extent stiffened, moneyed Greed
For whose dull appetite men waste away
Amid the whirr of wheels and are the seed
Of things which slay their sower, these each day
Sees rife in England, and the gentle feet
Of Beauty tread no more the stones of each unlovely street.

What even Cromwell spared is desecrated
By weed and worm, left to the stormy play
Of wind and beating snow, or renovated
By more destructful hands: Time's worst decay
Will wreathe its ruins with some loveliness,
But these new Vandals can but make a rainproof barrenness.

Where is that Art which bade the Angels sing
Through Lincoln's lofty choir, till the air
Seems from such marble harmonies to ring
With sweeter song than common lips can dare

To draw from actual reed? ah! where is now
The cunning hand which made the flowering hawthorn branches bow

For Southwell's arch, and carved the House of One
Who loved the lilies of the field with all
Our dearest English flowers? the same sun
Rises for us: the season's natural
Weave the same tapestry of green and gray:
The unchanged hills are with us: but that Spirit hath passed away.

And yet perchance it may be better so,
For Tyranny is an incestuous Queen,
Murder her brother is her bedfellow,
And the Plague chambers with her: in obscene
And bloody paths her treacherous feet are set;
Better the empty desert and a soul inviolate!

For gentle brotherhood, the harmony
Of living in the healthful air, the swift
Clean beauty of strong limbs when men are free
And women chaste, these are the things which lift
Our souls up more than even Agnolo's
Gaunt blinded Sibyl poring o'er the scroll of human woes,

Or Titian's little maiden on the stair
White as her own sweet lily and as tall,
Or Mona Lisa smiling through her hair,—
Ah! somehow life is bigger after all
Than any painted angel could we see
The God that is within us! The old Greek serenity

Which curbs the passion of that level line
Of marble youths, who with untroubled eyes
And chastened limbs ride round Athena's shrine
And mirror her divine economies,
And balanced symmetry of what in man
Would else wage ceaseless warfare,—this at least within the span

Between our mother's kisses and the grave
Might so inform our lives, that we could win
Such mighty empires that from her cave
Temptation would grow hoarse, and pallid Sin
Would walk ashamed of his adulteries,
And Passion creep from out the House of Lust with startled eyes.

To make the Body and the Spirit one
With all right things, till no thing live in vain
From morn to noon, but in sweet unison
With every pulse of flesh and throb of pain
The Soul in flawless essence high enthroned,
Against all outer vain attack invincibly bastioned,

Mark with serene impartiality
The strife of things, and yet be comforted,

Knowing that by the chain causality
All separate existences are wed
Into one supreme whole, whose utterance
Is joy, or holier praise! ah! surely this were governance

Of life in most august omnipresence,
Through which the rational intellect would find
In passion its expression, and mere sense
Ignoble else, lend fire to the mind,
And being joined with it in harmony
More mystical than that which binds the stars planetary

Strike from their several tones one octave chord
Whose cadence being measureless would fly
Through all the circling spheres, then to its Lord
Return refreshed with its new empery
And more exultant power,—this indeed
Could we but reach it were to find the last, the perfect creed.

Ah! it was easy when the world was young
To keep one's life free and inviolate,
From our sad lips another song is rung,
By our own hands our heads are desecrate,
Wanderers in drear exile and dispossessed
Of what should be our own, we can but feed on wild unrest.

Somehow the grace, the bloom of things has flown,
And of all men we are most wretched who
Must live each other's lives and not our own
For very pity's sake and then undo
All that we live for—it was otherwise
When soul and body seemed to blend in mystic symphonies.

But we have left those gentle haunts to pass
With weary feet to the new Calvary,
Where we behold, as one who in a glass
Sees his own face, self-slain Humanity,
And in the dumb reproach of that sad gaze
Learn what an awful phantom the red hand of man can raise.

O smitten mouth! O forehead crowned with thorn!
O chalice of all common miseries!
Thou for our sakes that loved thee not hast borne
An agony of endless centuries,
And we were vain and ignorant nor knew
That when we stabbed thy heart it was our own real hearts we slew.

Being ourselves the sowers and the seeds,
The night that covers and the lights that fade,
The spear that pierces and the side that bleeds,
The lips betraying and the life betrayed;
The deep hath calm: the moon hath rest: but we
Lords of the natural world are yet our own dread enemy.

Is this the end of all that primal force
Which, in its changes being still the same,
From eyeless Chaos cleft its upward course,
Through ravenous seas and whirling rocks and flame,
Till the suns met in heaven and began
Their cycles, and the morning stars sang, and the Word was Man!

Nay, nay, we are but crucified, and though
The bloody sweat falls from our brows like rain,
Loosen the nails–we shall come down I know,
Stanch the red wounds–we shall be whole again,
No need have we of hyssop-laden rod,
That which is purely human, that is Godlike that is God.

THE SPHINX

In a dim corner of my room,
For longer than my fancy thinks,
A beautiful and silent Sphinx
Has watched me through the shifting gloom.

Inviolate and immobile
She does not rise, she does not stir
For silver moons are nought to her,
And nought to her the suns that reel.

Red follows grey across the air
The waves of moonlight ebb and flow
But with the dawn she does not go
And in the night-time she is there.

Dawn follows Dawn, and Nights grow old
And all the while this curious cat
Lies crouching on the Chinese mat
With eyes of satin rimmed with gold.

Upon the mat she lies and leers,
And on the tawny throat of her
Flutters the soft and silky fur
Or ripples to her pointed ears.

Come forth my lovely seneschal,
So somnolent, so statuesque,
Come forth you exquisite grotesque,
Half woman and half animal,

Come forth my lovely languorous Sphinx,
And put your head upon my knee
And let me stroke your throat and see
Your body spotted like the Lynx,

And let me touch those curving claws
Of yellow ivory, and grasp
The tail that like a monstrous Asp
Coils round your heavy velvet paws.

A thousand weary centuries
Are thine, while I have hardly seen
Some twenty summers cast their green
For Autumn's gaudy liveries,

But you can read the Hieroglyphs
On the great sandstone obelisks,
And you have talked with Basilisks
And you have looked on Hippogriffs

O tell me, were you standing by
When Isis to Osiris knelt,
And did you watch the Egyptian melt
Her union for Anthony,

And drink the jewel-drunken wine,
And bend her head in mimic awe
To see the huge pro-consul draw
The salted tunny from the brine?

And did you mark the Cyprian kiss
With Adon on his catafalque,
And did you follow Amanalk
The god of Heliopolis?

And did you talk with Thoth, and did
You hear the moon-horned Io weep,
And know the painted kings who sleep
Beneath the wedge-shaped Pyramid?

Lift up your large black satin eyes
Which are like cushions where one sinks,
Fawn at my feet, fantastic Sphinx,
And sing me all your memories.

Sing to me of the Jewish maid
Who wandered with the Holy Child,
And how you led them through the wild,
And how they slept beneath your shade.

Sing to me of that odorous
Green eve when crouching by the marge
You heard from Adrian's gilded barge
The laughter of Antinous,

And lapped the stream, and fed your drouth,
And watched with hot and hungry stare
The ivory body of that rare
Young slave with his pomegranate mouth.

Sing to me of the Labyrinth
In which the two-formed bull was stalled,
Sing to me of the night you crawled
Across the temple's granite plinth

When through the purple corridors
The screaming scarlet Ibis flew
In terror, and a horrid dew
Dripped from the moaning Mandragores,

And the great torpid crocodile
Within the tank shed slimy tears,
And tore the jewels from his ears
And staggered back into the Nile,

And the Priests cursed you with shrill psalms
As in your claws you seized their snake
And crept away with it to slake
Your passion by the shuddering palms.

Who were your lovers, who were they
Who wrestled for you in the dust?
Which was the vessel of your Lust,
What Leman had you every day?

Did giant lizards come and crouch
Before you on the reedy banks?
Did Gryphons with great metal flanks
Leap on you in your trampled couch,

Did monstrous hippopotami
Come sidling to you in the mist
Did gilt-scaled dragons write and twist
With passion as you passed them by?

And from that brick-built Lycian tomb
What horrible Chimaera came
With fearful heads and fearful flame
To breed new wonders from your womb?

Or had you shameful secret guests
And did you harry to your home
Some Nereid coiled in amber foam
With curious rock-crystal breasts;

Or did you, treading through the froth,
Call to the brown Sidonian
For tidings of Leviathan,
Leviathan of Behemoth?

Or did you when the sun was set,
Climb up the cactus-covered slope
To meet your swarthy Ethiop
Whose body was of polished jet?

Or did you while the earthen skiffs
Dropt down the gray Nilotic flats
At twilight, and the flickering bats
Flew round the temple's triple glyphs

Steal to the border of the bar
And swim across the silent lake
And slink into the vault and make
The Pyramid your lupanar,

Till from each black sarcophagus
Rose up the painted, swathèd dead,
Or did you lure unto your bed
The ivory-horned Trageophos?

Or did you love the God of flies
Who plagued the Hebrews and was splashed
With wine unto the waist, or Pasht
Who had green beryls for her eyes?

Or that young God, the Tyrian,
Who was more amorous than the dove
Of Ashtaroth, or did you love
The God of the Assyrian,

Whose wings that like transparent talc
Rose high above his hawk-faced head
Painted with silver and with red
And ribbed with rods of Oreichalch?

Or did huge Apis from his car
Leap down and lay before your feet
Big blossoms of the honey-sweet,
And honey-coloured nenuphar?

How subtle secret is your smile;
Did you love none then? Nay I know
Great Ammon was your bedfellow,
He lay with you beside the Nile.

The river-horses in the slime
Trumpeted when they saw him come
Odorous with Syrian galbanum
And smeared with spikenard and with thyme.

He came along the river bank
Like some tall galley argent-sailed
He strode across the waters, mailed
In beauty and the waters sank.

He strode across the desert sand,
He reached the valley where you lay,
He waited till the dawn of day,
Then touched your black breasts with his hand.

You kissed his mouth with mouth of flame,
You made the hornèd-god your own,
You stood behind him on his throne;
You called him by his secret name,

You whispered monstrous oracles
 Into the caverns of his ears,
 With blood of goats and blood of steers
You taught him monstrous miracles,

While Ammon was your bedfellow
 Your chamber was the steaming Nile
 And with your curved Archaic smile
You watched his passion come and go.

With Syrian oils his brows were bright
 And wide-spread as a tent at noon
 His marble limbs made pale the moon
And lent the day a larger light,

His long hair was nine cubits span
 And coloured like that yellow gem
 Which hidden in their garments' hem,
The merchants bring from Kurdistan.

His face was as the must that lies
 Upon a vat of new-made wine,
 The seas could not insapphirine
The perfect azure of his eyes.

His thick, soft throat was white as milk
 And threaded with thin veins of blue
 And curious pearls like frozen dew
Were broidered on his flowing silk.

On pearl and porphyry pedestalled
 He was too bright to look upon
 For on his ivory breast there shone
The wondrous ocean-emerald,–

That mystic, moonlight jewel which
 Some diver of the Colchian caves
 Had found beneath the blackening waves
And carried to the Colchian witch.

Before his gilded galiot
 Ran naked vine-wreathed corybants
 And lines of swaying elephants
Knelt down to draw his chariot,

And lines of swarthy Nubians
 Bore up his litter as he rode
 Down the great granite-paven road,
Between the nodding peacock fans.

The merchants brought him steatite
 From Sidon in their painted ships;
 The meanest cup that touched his lips
Was fashioned from a chrysolite.

The merchants brought him cedar chests
 Of rich apparel, bound with cords;
 His train was borne by Memphian lords;
Young kings were glad to be his guests.

Ten hundred shaven priests did bow
 To Ammon's altar day and night,
 Ten hundred lamps did wave their light
Through Ammon's carven house,– and now

Foul snake and speckled adder with
 Their young ones crawl from stone to stone
 For ruined is the house, and prone
The great rose-marble monolith;

Wild ass or strolling jackal comes
 And crouches in the mouldering gates,
 Wild satyrs call unto their mates
Across the fallen fluted drums.

And on the summit of the pile,
 The blue-faced ape of Horus sits
 And gibbers while the fig-tree splits
The pillars of the peristyle.

The God is scattered here and there;
  Deep hidden in the windy sand
  I saw his giant granite hand
Still clenched in impotent despair.

And many a wandering caravan
  Of stately negroes, silken-shawled,
  Crossing the desert, halts appalled
Before the neck that none can span.

And many a bearded Bedouin
  Draws back his yellow-striped burnous
  To gaze upon the Titan thews
Of him who was thy paladin.

Go seek his fragments on the moor,
  And wash them in the evening dew,
  And from their pieces make anew
Thy mutilated paramour.

Go seek them where they lie alone
  And from their broken pieces make
  Thy bruisèd bedfellow! And wake
Mad passions in the senseless stone!

Charm his dull ear with Syrian hymns;
  He loved your body; oh be kind!
  Pour spikenard on his hair and wind
Soft rolls of linen round his limbs;

Wind round his head the figured coins,
  Stain with red fruits the pallid lips;
  Weave purple for his shrunken hips,
And purple for his barren loins!

Away to Egypt! Have no fear;
  Only one God has ever died,
  Only one God has let His side
Be wounded by a soldier's spear.

But these, thy lovers, are not dead;
  Still by the hundred-cubit gate
  Dog-faced Anubis sits in state
With lotus lilies for thy head.

Still from his chair of porphyry
  Giant Memnon strains his lidless eyes
  Across the empty land and cries
Each yellow morning unto thee.

And Nilus with his broken horn
  Lies in his black and oozy bed
  And till thy coming will not spread
His waters on the withering corn.

Your lovers are not dead, I know,
  And will rise up and hear thy voice
  And clash their symbols and rejoice
And run to kiss your mouth,—and so

Set wings upon your argosies!
  Set horses to your ebon car!
  Back to your Nile! Or if you are
Grown sick of dead divinities;

Follow some roving lion's spoor
  Across the copper-coloured plain,
  Reach out and hale him by the mane
And bid him be your paramour!

Crouch by his side upon the grass
  And set your white teeth in his throat,
  And when you hear his dying note,
Lash your long flanks of polished brass

And take a tiger for your mate,
  Whose amber sides are flecked with black,
  And ride upon his gilded back
In triumph through the Theban gate,

And toy with him in amorous jests,
  And when he turns and snarls and gnaws,
  Oh smite him with your jasper claws
And bruise him with your agate breasts!

Why are you tarrying? Get hence!
I weary of your sullen ways.
I weary of your steadfast gaze,
Your somnolent magnificence.

Your horrible and heavy breath
Makes the light flicker in the lamp,
And on my brow I feel the damp
And dreadful dews of night and death,

Your eyes are like fantastic moons
That shiver in some stagnant lake,
Your tongue is like a scarlet snake
That dances to fantastic tunes.

Your pulse makes poisonous melodies,
And your black throat is like the hole
Left by some torch or burning coal
On Saracenic tapestries.

Away! the sulphur-coloured stars
Are hurrying through the Western gate!
Away! Or it may be too late
To climb their silent silver cars!

See, the dawn shivers round the gray,
Gilt-dialled towers, and the rain
Streams down each diamonded pane
And blurs with tears the wannish day.

What snake-tressed fury, fresh from Hell,
With uncouth gestures and unclean,
Stole from the poppy-drowsy queen
And led you to a student's cell?

What songless, tongueless ghost of sin
Crept through the curtains of the night
And saw my taper burning bright,
And knocked and bade you enter in?

Are there not others more accursed,
Whiter with leprosies than I?
Are Abana and Pharphar dry,
That you come here to slake your thirst?

False Sphinx! False Sphinx! By reedy Styx,
Old Charon, leaning on his oar,
Waits for my coin. Go thou before
And leave me to my crucifix,

Whose pallid burden, sick with pain,
Watches the world with wearied eyes.
And weeps for every soul that dies,
And weep for every soul in vain!!.

ELEUTHERIA

SONNET TO LIBERTY

Not that I love thy children, whose dull eyes
See nothing save their own unlovely woe,
Whose minds know nothing, nothing care to know,—
But that the roar of thy Democracies,
Thy reigns of Terror, thy great Anarchies,
Mirror my wildest passions like the sea,
And give my rage a brother——! Liberty!
For his sake only do thy dissonant cries
Delight my discreet soul, else might all kings

By bloody knout or treacherous cannonades
Rob nations of their rights inviolate
And I remain unmoved—and yet, and yet,
These Christs that die upon the barricades,
God knows it I am with them, in some things.

AVE IMPERATRIX

Set in this stormy Northern sea,
Queen of these restless fields of tide,
England! what shall men say of thee,
Before whose feet the worlds divide?

The earth, a brittle globe of glass,
Lies in the hollow of thy hand,
And through its heart of crystal pass,
Like shadows through a twilight land,

The spears of crimson-suited war,
The long white-crested waves of fight,
And all the deadly fires which are
The torches of the lords of Night.

The yellow leopards, strained and lean,
The treacherous Russian knows so well,
With gaping blackened jaws are seen
Leap through the hail of screaming shell.

The strong sea-lion of England's wars
Hath left his sapphire cave of sea,
To battle with the storm that mars
The star of England's chivalry.

The brazen-throated clarion blows
Across the Pathan's reedy fen,
And the high steeps of Indian snows
Shake to the tread of armèd men.

And many an Afghan chief, who lies
Beneath his cool pomegranate-trees,
Clutches his sword in fierce surmise
When on the mountain-side he sees

The fleet-foot Marri scout, who comes
To tell how he hath heard afar
The measured roll of English drums
Beat at the gates of Kandahar.

For southern wind and east wind meet
Where, girt and crowned by sword and fire,
England with bare and bloody feet
Climbs the steep road of wide empire.

O lonely Himalayan height,
Gray pillar of the Indian sky,
Where saw'st thou last in clanging fight,
Our winged dogs of Victory?

The almond groves of Samarcand,
Bokhara, where red lilies blow,
And Oxus, by whose yellow sand
The grave white-turbaned merchants go:

And on from thence to Ispahan,
The gilded garden of the sun,
Whence the long dusty caravan
Brings cedar and vermilion;

And that dread city of Cabool
Set at the mountain's scarpèd feet,
Whose marble tanks are ever full
With water for the noon-day heat:

Where through the narrow straight Bazaar
A little maid Circassian
Is led, a present from the Czar
Unto some old and bearded khan,—

Here have our wild war-eagles flown,
And flapped wide wings in fiery fight;
But the sad dove, that sits alone
In England—she hath no delight.

In vain the laughing girl will lean
To greet her love with love-lit eyes:
Down in some treacherous black ravine,
Clutching his flag, the dead boy lies.

And many a moon and sun will see
The lingering wistful children wait
To climb upon their father's knee;
And in each house made desolate

Pale women who have lost their lord
Will kiss the relics of the slain—
Some tarnished epaulet—some sword—
Poor toys to soothe such anguished pain.

For not in quiet English fields
Are these, our brothers, laid to rest.
Where we might deck their broken shields
With all the flowers the dead love best.

For some are by the Delhi walls,
And many in the Afghan land,
And many where the Ganges falls
Through seven mouths of shifting sand.

And some in Russian waters lie,
And others in the seas which are
The portals to the East, or by
The wind-swept heights of Trafalgar.

O wandering graves! O restless sleep!
O silence of the sunless day!
O still ravine! O stormy deep!
Give up your prey! Give up your prey!

And thou whose wounds are never healed,
Whose weary race is never won,
O Cromwell's England! must thou yield
For every inch of ground a son?

Go! crown with thorns thy gold-crowned head,
Change thy glad song to song of pain;
Wind and wild wave have got thy dead,
And will not yield them back again.

Wave and wild wind and foreign shore
Possess the flower of English land—
Lips that thy lips shall kiss no more,
Hands that shall never clasp thy hand.

What profit now that we have bound
The whole round world with net of gold,
If hidden in our heart is found
The care that groweth never old?

What profit that our galleys ride,
Pine-forest-like, on every main?
Ruin and wreck are at our side,
Grim warders of the House of pain.

Where are the brave, the strong, the fleet?
Where is our English chivalry?
Wild grasses are their burial-sheet,
And sobbing waves their threnody.

O loved ones lying far away,
What word of love can dead lips send!
O wasted dust! O senseless clay!
Is this the end! is this the end!

Peace, peace! we wrong the noble dead
To vex their solemn slumber so:
Though childless, and with thorn-crowned head,
Up the steep road must England go,

Yet when this fiery web is spun,
Her watchmen shall decry from far
The young Republic like a sun
Rise from these crimson seas of war.

TO MILTON

Milton! I think thy spirit hath passed away
From these white cliffs, and high embattled-towers;
This gorgeous fiery-colored world of ours
Seems fallen into ashes dull and gray,
And the age changed unto a mimic play
Wherein we waste our else too-crowded hours:
For all our pomp and pageantry and powers
We are but fit to delve the common clay,
Seeing this little isle on which we stand,
This England, this sea-lion of the sea,
By ignorant demagogues is held in fee,
Who love her not: Dear God! is this the land
Which bare a triple empire in her hand
When Cromwell spake the word Democracy!

LOUIS NAPOLEON

Eagle of Austerlitz! where were thy wings
When far away upon a barbarous strand,
In fight unequal, by an obscure hand,
Fell the last scion of thy brood of Kings!

Poor boy! thou wilt not flaunt thy cloak of red,
Nor ride in state through Paris in the van
Of thy returning legions, but instead
Thy mother France, free and republican,

Shall on thy dead and crownless forehead place
The better laurels of a soldier's crown,
That not dishonored should thy soul go down
To tell the mighty Sire of thy race

That France hath kissed the mouth of Liberty,
And found it sweeter than his honeyed bees,
And that the giant wave Democracy
Breaks on the shores where Kings lay couched at ease.

SONNET

On the Massacre of the Christians in Bulgaria.

Christ, dost Thou live indeed? or are Thy bones
Still straightened in their rock-hewn sepulchre?
And was Thy Rising only dreamed by her
Whose love of Thee for all her sin atones?
For here the air is horrid with men's groans,
The priests who call upon Thy name are slain,
Dost Thou not hear the bitter wail of pain
From those whose children lie upon the stones?
Come down, O Son of God! incestuous gloom
Curtains the land, and through the starless night
Over Thy Cross the Crescent moon I see!
If Thou in very truth didst burst the tomb
Come down, O Son of Man! and show Thy might
Lest Mahomet be crowned instead of Thee!

QUANTUM MUTATA

There was a time in Europe long ago,
When no man died for freedom anywhere,
But England's lion leaping from its lair
Laid hands on the oppressor! it was so
While England could a great Republic show.
Witness the men of Piedmont, chiefest care
Of Cromwell, when with impotent despair
The Pontiff in his painted portico
Trembled before our stern embassadors.
How comes it then that from such high estate
We have thus fallen, save that Luxury
With barren merchandise piles up the gate
Where nobler thoughts and deeds should enter by:
Else might we still be Milton's heritors.

LIBERTATIS SACRA FAMES

Albeit nurtured in democracy,
And liking best that state republican
Where every man is Kinglike and no man
Is crowned above his fellows, yet I see
Spite of this modern fret for Liberty,
Better the rule of One, whom all obey,
Than to let clamorous demagogues betray
Our freedom with the kiss of anarchy.
Wherefore I love them not whose hands profane
Plant the red flag upon the piled-up street
For no right cause, beneath whose ignorant reign
Arts, Culture, Reverence, Honor, all things fade,
Save Treason and the dagger of her trade,
And Murder with his silent bloody feet.

THEORETIKOS

This mighty empire hath but feet of clay;
Of all its ancient chivalry and might
Our little island is forsaken quite:
Some enemy hath stolen its crown of bay,
And from its hills that voice hath passed away
Which spake of Freedom: O come out of it,
Come out of it, my Soul, thou art not fit
For this vile traffic-house, where day by day
Wisdom and reverence are sold at mart,
And the rude people rage with ignorant cries
Against an heritage of centuries.
It mars my calm: wherefore in dreams of Art
And loftiest culture I would stand apart,
Neither for God, nor for His enemies.

ROSA MYSTICA

HELAS

To drift with every passion till my soul
Is a stringed lute on which all winds can play,
Is it for this that I have given away
Mine ancient wisdom, and austere control?—
Methinks my life is a twice-written scroll
Scrawled over on some boyish holiday
With idle songs for pipe and virelay
Which do but mar the secret of the whole.
Surely that was a time I might have trod
The sunlit heights, and from life's dissonance
Struck one clear chord to reach the ears of God;
Is that time dead? lo! with a little rod
I did but touch the honey of romance—
And must I lose a soul's inheritance?

REQUIESCAT

Tread lightly, she is near
Under the snow,
Speak gently, she can hear
The daisies grow.

All her bright golden hair
Tarnished with rust,
She that was young and fair
Fallen to dust.

Lily-like, white as snow,
She hardly knew
She was a woman, so
Sweetly she grew.

Coffin-board, heavy stone,
Lie on her breast,
I vex my heart alone
She is at rest.

Peace, Peace, she cannot hear
Lyre or sonnet,
All my life's buried here,
Heap earth upon it.

Avignon.

SALVE SATURNIA TELLUS

I REACHED the Alps: the soul within me burned
Italia, my Italia, at thy name:
And when from out the mountain's heart I came
And saw the land for which my life had yearned,
I laughed as one who some great prize had earned:
And musing on the story of thy fame
I watched the day, till marked with wounds of flame
The turquoise sky to burnished gold was turned,
The pine-trees waved as waves a woman's hair,
And in the orchards every twining spray
Was breaking into flakes of blossoming foam:
But when I knew that far away at Rome
In evil bonds a second Peter lay,
I wept to see the land so very fair.

TURIN.

SAN MINIATO

SEE, I have climbed the mountain side
Up to this holy house of God,
Where once that Angel-Painter trod
Who saw the heavens opened wide,

And throned upon the crescent moon
The Virginal white Queen of Grace,—
Mary! could I but see thy face
Death could not come at all too soon.

O crowned by God with thorns and pain!
Mother of Christ! O mystic wife!
My heart is weary of this life
And over-sad to sing again.

O crowned by God with love and flame!
O crowned by Christ the Holy One!
O listen ere the searching sun
Show to the world my sin and shame.

AVE MARIA PLENA GRATIA

WAS this his coming! I had hoped to see
A scene of wondrous glory, as was told
Of some great God who in a rain of gold
Broke open bars and fell on Danae:
Or a dread vision as when Semele
Sickening for love and unappeased desire
Prayed to see God's clear body, and the fire
Caught her white limbs and slew her utterly:
With such glad dreams I sought this holy place,
And now with wondering eyes and heart I stand
Before this supreme mystery of Love:
A kneeling girl with passionless pale face,
An angel with a lily in his hand,
And over both with outstretched wings the Dove.

FLORENCE.

ITALIA

ITALIA! thou art fallen, though with sheen
Of battle-spears thy clamorous armies stride
From the North Alps to the Sicilian tide!
Ay! fallen, though the nations hail thee Queen

Because rich gold in every town is seen,
And on thy sapphire lake, in tossing pride
Of wind-filled vans thy myriad galleys ride
Beneath one flag of red and white and green.
O Fair and Strong! O Strong and Fair in vain!
Look southward where Rome's desecrated town
Lies mourning for her God-anointed King?
Look heavenward! shall God allow this thing?
Nay! but some flame-girt Raphael shall come down,
And smite the Spoiler with the sword of pain.

VENICE.

SONNET

I WANDERED in Scoglietto's green retreat,
The oranges on each o'erhanging spray
Burned as bright lamps of gold to shame the day;
Some startled bird with fluttering wings and fleet
Made snow of all the blossoms, at my feet
Like silver moons the pale narcissi lay:
And the curved waves that streaked the sapphire bay
Laughed i' the sun, and life seemed very sweet.
Outside the young boy-priest passed singing clear,
"Jesus the Son of Mary has been slain,
O come and fill his sepulchre with flowers."
Ah, God! Ah, God! those dear Hellenic hours
Had drowned all memory of thy bitter pain,
The Cross, the Crown, the Soldiers, and the Spear.

GENOA, *Holy Week.*

ROME UNVISITED

I

THE corn has turned from gray to red,
Since first my spirit wandered forth
From the drear cities of the north,
And to Italia's mountains fled.

And here I set my face toward home,
For all my pilgrimage is done,
Although, methinks, yon blood-red sun
Marshals the way to Holy Rome.

O Blessèd Lady, who dost hold
Upon the seven hills thy reign!
O Mother without blot or stain,
Crowned with bright crowns of triple gold!

O Roma, Roma, at thy feet
I lay this barren gift of song!
For, ah! the way is steep and long
That leads unto thy sacred street.

II

And yet what joy it were for me
To turn my feet unto the south,
And journeying toward the Tiber mouth
To kneel again at Fiesole!

And wandering through the tangled pines
That break the gold of Arno's stream,
To see the purple mist and gleam
Of morning on the Apennines.

By many a vineyard-hidden home,
Orchard, and olive-garden gray,
Till from the drear Campagna's way
The seven hills bear up the dome!

III

A pilgrim from the northern seas—
What joy for me to seek alone
The wondrous Temple, and the throne
Of Him who holds the awful keys!

When, bright with purple and with gold,
Come priest and holy Cardinal,
And borne above the heads of all
The gentle Shepherd of the Fold.

O joy to see before I die
The only God-anointed King,
And hear the silver trumpets ring
A triumph as He passes by.

Or at the altar of the shrine
Holds high the mystic sacrifice,
And shows a God to human eyes
Beneath the veil of bread and wine.

IV

For lo, what changes time can bring!
The cycles of revolving years
May free my heart from all its fears,—
And teach my lips a song to sing.

Before yon field of trembling gold
Is garnered into dusty sheaves,
Or ere the autumn's scarlet leaves
Flutter as birds adown the wold,

I may have run the glorious race,
And caught the torch while yet aflame,
And called upon the holy name
Of Him who now doth hide His face.

ARONA.

URBS SACRA ÆTERNA

ROME! what a scroll of History thine has been!
In the first days thy sword republican
Ruled the whole world for many an age's span:
Then of thy peoples thou wert crownèd Queen,
Till in thy streets the bearded Goth was seen;
And now upon thy walls the breezes fan
(Ah, city crowned by God, discrowned by man!)
The hated flag of red and white and green.
When was thy glory! when in search for power
Thine eagles flew to greet the double sun,
And all the nations trembled at thy rod?
Nay, but thy glory tarried for this hour,
When pilgrims kneel before the Holy One,
The prisoned shepherd of the Church of God.

SONNET

On Hearing the Dies Irae Sung in the Sistine Chapel.

NAY, Lord, not thus! white lilies in the spring,
Sad olive-groves, or silver-breasted dove,
Teach me more clearly of Thy life and love
Than terrors of red flame and thundering.
The empurpled vines dear memories of Thee bring:
A bird at evening flying to its nest,

Tells me of One who had no place of rest:
I think it is of Thee the sparrows sing.
Come rather on some autumn afternoon,
When red and brown are burnished on the leaves,
And the fields echo to the gleaner's song,
Come when the splendid fulness of the moon
Looks down upon the rows of golden sheaves,
And reap Thy harvest: we have waited long.

EASTER DAY

The silver trumpets rang across the Dome:
The people knelt upon the ground with awe:
And borne upon the necks of men I saw,
Like some great God, the Holy Lord of Rome.
Priest-like, he wore a robe more white than foam,
And, king-like, swathed himself in royal red,
Three crowns of gold rose high upon his head:
In splendor and in light the Pope passed home.
My heart stole back across wide wastes of years
To One who wandered by a lonely sea,
And sought in vain for any place of rest:
"Foxes have holes, and every bird its nest,
I, only I, must wander wearily,
And bruise My feet, and drink wine salt with tears."

E TENEBRIS

Come down, O Christ, and help me! reach thy hand,
For I am drowning in a stormier sea
Than Simon on Thy lake of Galilee:
The wine of life is spilt upon the sand,
My heart is as some famine-murdered land,
Whence all good things have perished utterly,
And well I know my soul in Hell must lie
If I this night before God's throne should stand.
"He sleeps perchance, or rideth to the chase,
Like Baal, when his prophets howled that name
From morn to noon on Carmel's smitten height."
Nay, peace, I shall behold before the night,
The feet of brass, the robe more white than flame,
The wounded hands, the weary human face.

VITA NUOVA

I stood by the unvintageable sea
Till the wet waves drenched face and hair with spray,
The long red fires of the dying day
Burned in the west; the wind piped drearily;
And to the land the clamorous gulls did flee:
"Alas!" I cried, "my life is full of pain,
And who can garner fruit or golden grain,

From these waste fields which travail ceaselessly!"
My nets gaped wide with many a break and flaw
 Nathless I threw them as my final cast
 Into the sea, and waited for the end.
When lo! a sudden glory! and I saw
 The argent splendor of white limbs ascend,
 And in that joy forgot my tortured past.

MADONNA MIA

A LILY girl, not made for this world's pain,
 With brown, soft hair close braided by her ears,
 And longing eyes half veiled by slumb'rous tears
Like bluest water seen through mists of rain;
Pale cheeks whereon no love hath left its stain,
 Red underlip drawn in for fear of love,
 And white throat, whiter than the silvered dove,
Through whose wan marble creeps one purple vein.
Yet, though my lips shall praise her without cease,
 Even to kiss her feet I am not bold,
 Being o'ershadowed by the wings of awe.
Like Dante, when he stood with Beatrice
 Beneath the flaming Lion's breast and saw
 The seventh Crystal, and the Stair of Gold.

THE NEW HELEN

Where hast thou been since round the walls of Troy
 The sons of God fought in that great emprise?
  Why dost thou walk our common earth again?
Hast thou forgotten that impassioned boy,
  His purple galley, and his Tyrian men,
 And treacherous Aphrodite's mocking eyes?
For surely it was thou, who, like a star
 Hung in the silver silence of the night,
 Didst lure the Old World chivalry and might
Into the clamorous crimson waves of war!

Or didst thou rule the fire-laden moon?
 In amorous Sidon was thy temple built
  Over the light and laughter of the sea?
 Where, behind lattice scarlet-wrought and gilt,
  Some brown-limbed girl did weave thee tapestry,
 All through the waste and wearied hours of noon;
Till her wan cheek with flame of passion burned,
 And she rose up the sea-washed lips to kiss
Of some glad Cyprian sailor, safe returned
 From Calpé and the cliffs of Herakles!

No! thou art Helen, and none other one!

It was for thee that young Sarpedôn died,
And Memnôn's manhood was untimely spent;
It was for thee gold-crested Hector tried
With Thetis' child that evil race to run,
In the last year of thy beleaguerment;
Ay! even now the glory of thy fame
Burns in those fields of trampled asphodel,
Where the high lords whom Ilion knew so well
Clash ghostly shields, and call upon thy name.

Where hast thou been? in that enchanted land
Whose slumbering vales forlorn Calypso knew,
Where never mower rose to greet the day
But all unswathed the trammeling grasses grew,
And the sad shepherd saw the tall corn stand
Till summer's red had changed to withered gray?
Didst thou lie there by some Lethæan stream
Deep brooding on thine ancient memory,
The crash of broken spears, the fiery gleam
From shivered helm, the Grecian battle-cry?

Nay, thou were hidden in that hollow hill
With one who is forgotten utterly,
That discrowned Queen men call the Erycine;
Hidden away that never might'st thou see
The face of her, before whose mouldering shrine
To-day at Rome the silent nations kneel;
Who gat from joy no joyous gladdening,
But only Love's intolerable pain,
Only a sword to pierce her heart in twain,
Only the bitterness of child-bearing.

The lotos-leaves which heal the wounds of Death
Lie in thy hand; O, be thou kind to me,
While yet I know the summer of my days;
For hardly can my tremulous lips draw breath
To fill the silver trumpet with thy praise,
So bowed am I before thy mystery;
So bowed and broken on Love's terrible wheel,
That I have lost all hope and heart to sing,
Yet care I not what ruin time may bring
If in thy temple thou wilt let me kneel.

Alas, alas, thou wilt not tarry here,
But, like that bird, the servant of the sun,
Who flies before the north wind and the home.
So wilt thou fly our evil land and drear,
Back to the tower of thine old delight,
And the red lips of young Euphorion;
Nor shall I ever see thy face again,
But in this poisonous garden must I stay,

Crowning my brows with the thorn-crown of pain,
Till all my loveless life shall pass away.

O Helen! Helen! Helen! Yet awhile,
Yet for a little while, O tarry here,
Till the dawn cometh and the shadows flee!
For in the gladsome sunlight of thy smile
Of heaven or hell I have no thought or fear,
Seeing I know no other god but thee:
No other god save him, before whose feet
In nets of gold the tired planets move,
The incarnate spirit of spiritual love
Who in thy body holds his joyous seat.

Thou wert not born as common women are!
But, girt with silver splendor of the foam,
Didst from the depths of sapphire seas arise!
And at thy coming some immortal star,
Bearded with flame, blazed in the Eastern skies;
And waked the shepherds on thine island home.
Thou shalt not die! no asps of Egypt creep
Close at thy heels to taint the delicate air;
No sullen-blooming poppies stain thy hair,
Those scarlet heralds of eternal sleep.

Lily of love, pure and inviolate!
Tower of ivory! red rose of fire!
Thou hast come down our darkness to illume:
For we, close-caught in the wide nets of Fate,
Wearied with waiting for the World's Desire,
Aimlessly wandered in the house of gloom.
Aimlessly sought some slumberous anodyne
For wasted lives, for lingering wretchedness,
Till we beheld thy re-arisen shrine,
And the white glory of thy loveliness.

WIND FLOWERS

IMPRESSION DU MATIN

The Thames nocturne of blue and gold
Changed to a Harmony in gray:
A barge with ochre-colored hay
Dropt from the wharf: and chill and cold

The yellow fog came creeping down
The bridges, till the houses' walls
Seemed changed to shadows, and St. Paul's
Loomed like a bubble o'er the town.

Then suddenly arose the clang
Of waking life; the streets were stirred
With country waggons: and a bird
Flew to the glistening roofs and sang.

But one pale woman all alone,
The daylight kissing her wan hair,
Loitered beneath the gas lamp's flare,
With lips of flame and heart of stone.

MAGDALEN WALKS

The little white clouds are racing over the sky,
And the fields are strewn with the gold of the flower of March
The daffodil breaks underfoot, and the tasselled larch
Sways and swings as the thrush goes hurrying by.

A delicate odor is borne on the wings of the morning breeze,
The odor of leaves, and of grass, and of newly upturned earth,
The birds are singing for joy of the Spring's glad birth,
Hopping from branch to branch on the rocking trees,

And all the woods are alive with the murmur and sound of Spring,
And the rosebud breaks into pink on the climbing brier,
And the crocus-bed is a quivering moon of fire
Girdled round with the belt of an amethyst ring.

And the plane to the pine-tree is whispering some tale of love
Till it rustles with laughter and tosses its mantle of green
And the gloom of the wych-elm's hollow is lit with the iris sheen
Of the burnished rainbow throat and the silver breast of a dove.

See! the lark starts up from his bed in the meadow there,
Breaking the gossamer threads and the nets of dew,
And flashing a-down the river, a flame of blue!
The kingfisher flies like an arrow, and wounds the air.

ATHANASIA

To that gaunt House of Art which lacks for naught
Of all the great things men have saved from Time,
The withered body of a girl was brought
Dead ere the world's glad youth had touched its prime,
And seen by lonely Arabs lying hid
In the dim wound of some black pyramid.

But when they had unloosed the linen band
Which swathed the Egyptian's body,—lo! was found
Closed in the wasted hollow of her hand
A little seed, which sown in English ground
Did wondrous snow of starry blossoms bear,
And spread rich odors through our springtide air.

With such strange arts this flower did allure
That all forgotten was the asphodel,
And the brown bee, the lily's paramour,
Forsook the cup where he was wont to dwell,

For not a thing of earth it seemed to be,
But stolen from some heavenly Arcady.

In vain the sad narcissus, wan and white
At its own beauty, hung across the stream,
The purple dragon-fly had no delight
With its gold-dust to make his wings a-gleam,
Ah! no delight the jasmine-bloom to kiss,
Or brush the rain-pearls from the eucharis.

For love of it the passionate nightingale
Forgot the hills of Thrace, the cruel king,
And the pale dove no longer cared to sail
Through the wet woods at time of blossoming,
But round this flower of Egypt sought to float,
With silvered wing and amethystine throat.

While the hot sun blazed in his tower of blue
A cooling wind crept from the land of snows,
And the warm south with tender tears of dew
Drenched its white leaves when Hesperos uprose
Amid those sea-green meadows of the sky
On which the scarlet bars of sunset lie.

But when o'er wastes of lily-haunted field
The tired birds had stayed their amorous tune,
And broad and glittering like an argent shield
High in the sapphire heavens hung the moon,
Did no strange dream or evil memory make
Each tremulous petal of its blossoms shake?

Ah no! to this bright flower a thousand years
Seemed but the lingering of a summer's day,
It never knew the tide of cankering fears
Which turn a boy's gold hair to withered gray,
The dread desire of death it never knew,
Or how all folk that they were born must rue.

For we to death with pipe and dancing go,
Nor would we pass the ivory gate again,
As some sad river wearied of its flow
Through the dull plains, the haunts of common men,
Leaps lover-like into the terrible sea!
And counts it gain to die so gloriously.

We mar our lordly strength in barren strife
With the world's legions led by clamorous care,
It never feels decay but gathers life
From the pure sunlight and the supreme air,
We live beneath Time's wasting sovereignty,
It is the child of all eternity.

SERENADE

For Music

THE western wind is blowng fair
  Across the dark Ægean sea,
And at the secret marble stair
  My Tyrian galley waits for thee.
Come down! the purple sail is spread,
  The watchman sleeps within the town.
O leave thy lily-flowered bed,
  O lady mine come down, come down!

She will not come, I know her well,
  Of lover's vows she hath no care,
And little good a man can tell
  Of one so cruel and so fair.
True love is but a woman's toy,
  They never know the lover's pain,
And I who loved as loves a boy
  Must love in vain, must love in vain.

O noble pilot tell me true
  Is that the sheen of golden hair?
Or is it but the tangled dew
  That binds the passion-flowers there?
Good sailor come and tell me now
  Is that my lady's lily hand?
Or is it but the gleaming prow,
  Or is it but the silver sand?

No! no! 'tis not the tangled dew,
  'Tis not the silver-fretted sand,
It is my own dear Lady true
  With golden hair and lily hand!
O noble pilot steer for Troy,
  Good sailor ply the laboring oar,
This is the Queen of life and joy
  Whom we must bear from Grecian shore!

The waning sky grows faint and blue,
  It wants an hour still of day,
Aboard! aboard! my gallant crew,
  O Lady mine away! away!
O noble pilot steer for Troy,
  Good sailor ply the laboring oar,
O loved as only loves a boy!
  O loved for ever evermore!

ENDYMION

For Music

THE apple trees are hung with gold,
  And birds are loud in Arcady,
The sheep lie bleating in the fold,
The wild goat runs across the wold,
But yesterday his love he told,
  I know he will come back to me.
O rising moon! O Lady moon!
  Be you my lover's sentinel,
  You cannot choose but know him well,
For he is shod with purple shoon,
You cannot choose but know my love,
  For he a shepherd's crook doth bear,
And he is soft as any dove,
  And brown and curly is his hair.

The turtle now has ceased to call
  Upon her crimson-footed groom,
The gray wolf prowls about the stall,
The lily's singing seneschal
Sleeps in the lily-bell, and all
  The violet hills are lost in gloom.
O risen moon! O holy moon!
  Stand on the top of Helice,
  And if my own true love you see,
Ah! if you see the purple shoon,
The hazel crook, the lad's brown hair,
  The goat-skin wrapped about his arm,
Tell him that I am waiting where
  The rushlight glimmers in the Farm.

The falling dew is cold and chill,
  And no bird sings in Arcady,
The little fauns have left the hill,
Even the tired daffodil
Has closed its gilded doors, and still
  My lover comes not back to me.
False moon! False moon! O waning moon!
  Where is my own true lover gone,
  Where are the lips vermilion,
The shepherd's crook, the purple shoon?
Why spread that silver pavilion,
  Why wear that veil of drifting mist?
Ah! thou hast young Endymion,
  Thou hast the lips that should be kissed!

LA BELLA DONNA DELLA MIA MENTE

My limbs are wasted with a flame,
  My feet are sore with travelling,
For calling on my Lady's name
  My lips have now forgot to sing.

O Linnet in the wild-rose brake
  Strain for my Love thy melody,
O Lark sing louder for love's sake
  My gentle Lady passeth by.

She is too fair for any man
  To see or hold his heart's delight,
Fairer than Queen or courtezan
  Or moon-lit water in the night.

Her hair is bound with myrtle leaves,
  (Green leaves upon her golden hair!)
Green grasses through the yellow sheaves
Of autumn corn are not more fair.

Her little lips, more made to kiss
  Than to cry bitterly for pain,
Are tremulous as brook-water is,
  Or roses after evening rain.

Her neck is like white melilote
  Flushing for pleasure of the sun,
The throbbing of the linnet's throat
  Is not so sweet to look upon.

As a pomegranate, cut in twain,
  White-seeded, is her crimson mouth,
Her cheeks are as the fading stain
  Where the peach reddens to the south.

O twining hands! O delicate
  White body made for love and pain!
O House of Love! O desolate
  Pale flower beaten by the rain!

CHANSON

A ring of gold and a milk-white dove
  Are goodly gifts for thee,
And a hempen rope for your own love
  To hang upon a tree.

For you a House of Ivory
  (Roses are white in the rose-bower)!
A narrow bed for me to lie
  (White, O white is the hemlock flower)!

Myrtle and jessamine for you
  (O the red rose is fair to see)!
For me the cypress and the rue
  (Fairest of all is rosemary)!

For you three lovers of your hand
  (Green grass where a man lies dead)!
For me three paces on the sand
  (Plant lilies at my head)!

FLOWERS OF GOLD

IMPRESSIONS

I

Les Silhouettes

The sea is flecked with bars of gray,
The dull dead wind is out of tune,
And like a withered leaf the moon
Is blown across the stormy bay.

Etched clear upon the pallid sand
The black boat lies: a sailor boy
Clambers aboard in careless joy
With laughing face and gleaming hand.

And overhead the curlews cry,
Where through the dusky upland grass
The young brown-throated reapers pass,
Like silhouettes against the sky.

II

La Fuite de la Lune

To outer senses there is peace,
A dreamy peace on either hand,
Deep silence in the shadowy land,
Deep silence where the shadows cease.

Save for a cry that echoes shrill
From some lone bird disconsolate;
A corncrake calling to its mate;
The answer from the misty hill.

And suddenly the moon withdraws
Her sickle from the lightening skies,
And to her sombre cavern flies,
Wrapped in a veil of yellow gauze.

THE GRAVE OF KEATS

Rid of the world's injustice, and his pain,
He rests at last beneath God's veil of blue:
Taken from life when life and love were new
The youngest of the martyrs here is lain,
Fair as Sebastian, and as early slain.
No cypress shades his grave, no funeral yew,
But gentle violets weeping with the dew
Weave on his bones an ever-blossoming chain.
O proudest heart that broke for misery!
O sweetest lips since those of Mitylene!
O poet-painter of our English land!
Thy name was writ in water—it shall stand:
And tears like mine will keep thy memory green,
As Isabella did her Basil tree.

Rome.

THEOCRITUS

A Villanelle

O singer of Persephone!
In the dim meadows desolate
Dost thou remember Sicily?

Still through the ivy flits the bee
Where Amaryllis lies in state;
O Singer of Persephone!

Simaetha calls on Hecate
  And hears the wild dogs at the gate:
Dost thou remember Sicily?

Still by the light and laughing sea
  Poor Polypheme bemoans his fate:
O Singer of Persephone!

And still in boyish rivalry
  Young Daphnis challenges his mate:
Dost thou remember Sicily?

Slim Lacon keeps a goat for thee,
  For thee the jocund shepherds wait,
O Singer of Persephone!
Dost thou remember Sicily?

IN THE GOLD ROOM

A Harmony

Her ivory hands on the ivory keys
  Strayed in a fitful fantasy,
Like the silver gleam when the poplar trees
  Rustle their pale leaves listlessly,
  Or the drifting foam of a restless sea
When the waves show their teeth in the flying breeze.

Her gold hair fell on the wall of gold
  Like the delicate gossamer tangles spun
On the burnished disk of the marigold,
  Or the sun-flower turning to meet the sun
  When the gloom of the jealous night is done,
And the spear of the lily is aureoled.

And her sweet red lips on these lips of mine
  Burned like the ruby fire set
In the swinging lamp of a crimson shrine,
  Or the bleeding wounds of the pomegranate,
  Or the heart of the lotus drenched and wet
With the spilt-out blood of the rose-red wine.

BALLADE DE MARGUERITE

Normande

I am weary of lying within the chase
When the knights are meeting in market-place.

Nay, go not thou to the red-roofed town
Lest the hooves of the war-horse tread thee down.

But I would not go where the Squires ride,
I would only walk by my Lady's side.

Alack! and alack! thou art over bold,
A Forester's son may not eat off gold.

Will she love me the less that my Father is seen
Each Martinmas day in a doublet green?

Perchance she is sewing at tapestrie,
Spindle and loom are not meet for thee.

Ah, if she is working the arras bright
I might ravel the threads by the fire-light.

Perchance she is hunting of the deer,
How could you follow o'er hill and mere?

Ah, if she is riding with the court,
I might run beside her and wind the morte.

Perchance she is kneeling in S. Denys,
(On her soul may our Lady have gramercy!)

Ah, if she is praying in lone chapelle,
I might swing the censer and ring the bell.

Come in my son, for you look sae pale,
Thy father shall fill thee a stoup of ale.

But who are these knights in bright array?
Is it a pageant the rich folks play?

'Tis the King of England from over sea,
Who has come unto visit our fair countrie.

But why does the curfew tool sae low
And why do the mourners walk a-row?

O 'tis Hugh of Amiens my sister's son
Who is lying stark, for his day is done.

Nay, nay, for I see white lilies clear,
It is no strong man who lies on the bier.

O 'tis old Dame Jeannette that kept the hall,
I knew she would die at the autumn fall.

Dame Jeannette had not that gold-brown hair,
Old Jeannette was not a maiden fair.

O 'tis none of our kith and none of our kin,
(Her soul may our Lady assoil from sin!)

But I hear the boy's voice chanting sweet,
"Elle est morte, la Marguerite."

Come in my son and lie on the bed,
And let the dead folk bury their dead.

O mother, you know I loved her true:
O mother, hath one grave room for two?

THE DOLE OF THE KING'S DAUGHTER

Breton

Seven stars in the still water,
And seven in the sky;
Seven sins on the King's daughter,
Deep in her soul to lie.

Red roses are at her feet,
(Roses are red in her red-gold hair,)
And O where her bosom and girdle meet
Red roses are hidden there.

Fair is the knight who lieth slain
Amid the rush and reed,
See the lean fishes that are fain
Upon dead men to feed.

Sweet is the page that lieth there,
(Cloth of gold is goodly prey,)
See the black ravens in the air,
Black, O black as the night are they.

What do they there so stark and dead?
(There is blood upon her hand)
Why are the lilies flecked with red?
(There is blood on the river sand.)

There are two that ride from the south and east,
And two from the north and west,
For the black raven a goodly feast,
For the King's daughter rest.

There is one man who loves her true
(Red, O red, is the stain of gore!)
He hath duggen a grave by the darksome yew,
(One grave will do for four.)

No moon in the still heaven,
In the black water none,
The sins on her soul are seven,
The sin upon his is one.

AMOR INTELLECTUALIS

Oft have we trod the vales of Castaly
And heard sweet notes of sylvan music blown
From antique reeds to common folk unknown
And often launched our bark upon that sea
Which the nine muses hold in empery,
And plowed free furrows through the wave and foam,
Nor spread reluctant sail for more safe home
Till we had freighted well our argosy.
Of which despoilèd treasures these remain,
Sordello's passion, and the honeyed line
Of young Endymion, lordly Tamburlaine
Driving him pampered jades, and more than these,
The seven-fold vision of the Florentine,
And grave-browed Milton's solemn harmonies.

SANTA DECCA

The Gods are dead: no longer do we bring
To gray-eyed Pallas crowns of olive-leaves!
Demeter's child no more hath tithe of sheaves,
And in the noon the careless shepherds sing,
For Pan is dead, and all the wantoning
By secret glade and devious haunt is o'er:
Young Hylas seeks the water-springs no more;
Great Pan is dead, and Mary's Son is King.

And yet—perchance in this sea-trancèd isle,
Chewing the bitter fruit of memory,
Some God lies hidden in the asphodel.
Ah Love! if such there be then it were well
For us to fly his anger: nay, but see
The leaves are stirring: let us watch a-while.

Corfu.

A VISION

Two crownèd Kings and One that stood alone
With no green weight of laurels round his head,
But with sad eyes as one uncomforted,
And wearied with man's never-ceasing moan
For sins no bleating victim can atone,
And sweet long lips with tears and kisses fed.
Girt was he in a garment black and red,
And at his feet I marked a broken stone
Which sent up lilies, dove-like, to his knees,
Now at their sight, my heart being lit with flame
I cried to Beatricé, "Who are these?"
"Æschylos first, the second Sophokles,
And last (wide stream of tears!) Euripides."

IMPRESSION DE VOYAGE

The sea was sapphire colored, and the sky
Burned like a heated opal through the air,
We hoisted sail; the wind was blowing fair
For the blue lands that to the eastward lie.
From the steep prow I marked with quickening eye
Zakynthos, every olive grove and creek,
Ithaca's cliff, Lycaon's snowy peak,
And all the flower-strewn hills of Arcady.
The flapping of the sail against the mast,
The ripple of the water on the side,
The ripple of girls' laughter at the stern,
The only sounds:—when 'gan the West to burn,
And a red sun upon the seas to ride,
I stood upon the soil of Greece at last!

Katakolo.

THE GRAVE OF SHELLEY

Like burnt-out torches by a sick man's bed
Gaunt cypress-trees stand round the sun-bleached stone;
Here doth the little night-owl make her throne,
And the slight lizard show his jewelled head.
And, where the chaliced poppies flame to red,
In the still chamber of yon pyramid
Surely some Old-World Sphinx lurks darkly hid,
Grim warder of this pleasaunce of the dead.

Ah! sweet indeed to rest within the womb
Of Earth, great mother of eternal sleep,
But sweeter far for thee a restless tomb
In the blue cavern of an echoing deep,
Or where the tall ships founder in the gloom
Against the rocks of some wave-shattered steep.

Rome.

BY THE ARNO

The oleander on the wall
Grows crimson in the dawning light,
Though the gray shadows of the night
Lie yet on Florence like a pall.

The dew is bright upon the hill,
And bright the blossoms overhead,
But ah! the grasshoppers have fled,
The little Attic song is still.

Only the leaves are gently stirred
By the soft breathing of the gale,
And in the almond-scented vale
The lonely nightingale is heard

The day will make thee silent soon,
O nightingale sing on for love!
While yet upon the shadowy grove
Splinter the arrows of the moon.

Before across the silent lawn
In sea-green mist the morning steals,
And to love's frightened eyes reveals
The long white fingers of the dawn.

Fast climbing up the eastern sky
To grasp and slay the shuddering night,
All careless of my heart's delight,
Or if the nightingale should die.

IMPRESSIONS DE THEATRE

FABIEN DEI FRANCHI

To My Friend Henry Irving

The silent room, the heavy creeping shade,
The dead that travel fast, the opening door,
The murdered brother rising through the floor,
The ghost's white fingers on thy shoulders laid,
And then the lonely duel in the glade,
The broken swords, the stifled scream, the gore,
Thy grand revengeful eyes when all is o'er,—
These things are well enough,—but thou wert made
For more august creation! frenzied Lear
Should at thy bidding wander on the heath
With the shrill fool to mock him, Romeo
For thee should lure his love, and desperate fear
Pluck Richard's recreant dagger from its sheath—
Thou trumpet set for Shakespeare's lips to blow!

PHEDRE

To Sarah Bernhardt

How vain and dull this common world must seem
To such a One as thou, who should'st have talked
At Florence with Mirandola, or walked
Through the cool olives of the Academe:

Thou should'st have gathered reeds from a green stream
For goat-foot Pan's shrill piping, and have played
With the white girls in that Phaeacian glade
Where grave Odysseus wakened from his dream.

Ah! surely once some urn of Attic clay
Held thy wan dust, and thou hast come again
Back to this common world so dull and vain,
For thou wert weary of the sunless day,
The heavy fields of scentless asphodel,
The loveless lips with which men kiss in Hell.

I
PORTIA
To Ellen Terry

I MARVEL not Bassanio was so bold
To peril all he had upon the lead,
Or that proud Aragon bent low his head,
Or that Morocco's fiery heart grew cold:
For in that gorgeous dress of beaten gold
Which is more golden than the golden sun,
No woman Veronesé looked upon
Was half so fair as thou whom I behold.
Yet fairer when with wisdom as your shield
The sober-suited lawyer's gown you donned
And would not let the laws of Venice yield
Antonio's heart to that accursèd Jew—
O Portia! take my heart; it is thy due:
I think I will not quarrel with the bond.

WRITTEN AT THE LYCEUM THEATRE

II
QUEEN HENRIETTA MARIA
To Ellen Terry

IN THE lone tent, waiting for victory,
She stands with eyes marred by the mists of pain,
Like some wan lily overdrenched with rain;
The clamorous clang of arms, the ensanguined sky,
War's ruin, and the wreck of chivalry,
To her proud soul no common fear can bring:
Bravely she tarrieth for her Lord the King,
Her soul a-flame with passionate ecstasy.
O Hair of Gold! O crimson lips! O Face
Made for the luring and the love of man!
With thee I do forget the toil and stress,
The loveless road that knows no resting place,
Time's straitened pulse, the soul's dread weariness,
My freedom and my life republican!

WRITTEN AT THE LYCEUM THEATRE

III

CAMMA

To Ellen Terry

As ONE who poring on a Grecian urn
 Scans the fair shapes some Attic hand hath made,
 God with slim goddess, goodly man with maid,
And for their beauty's sake is loath to turn
And face the obvious day, must I not yearn
 For many a secret moon of indolent bliss,
 When is the midmost shrine of Artemis
I see thee standing, antique-limbed, and stern?

And yet—methinks I'd rather see thee play
 That serpent of old Nile, whose witchery
Made Emperors drunken,—come, great Egypt, shake
Our stage with all thy mimic pageants! Nay,
 I am growing sick of unreal passions, make
 The world thine Actium, me thine Anthony!

WRITTEN AT THE LYCEUM THEATRE

THE FOURTH MOVEMENT

IMPRESSION

Le Réveillon

THE SKY is laced with fitful red,
 The circling mists and shadows flee,
 The dawn is rising from the sea,
Like a white lady from her bed.

And jagged brazen arrows fall
 Athwart the feathers of the night,
 And a long wave of yellow light
Breaks silently on tower and hall,

And spreading wide across the wold
 Wakes into flight some fluttering bird,
 And all the chestnut tops are stirred,
And all the branches streaked with gold.

AT VERONA

How STEEP the stairs within Kings' houses are
 For exile-wearied feet as mine to tread,
 And O how salt and bitter is the bread
Which falls from this Hound's table,—better far
That I had died in the red ways of war,
 Or that the gate of Florence bare my head,
 Than to live thus, by all things comraded
Which seek the essence of my soul to mar.

"Curse God and die: what better hope than this?
 He hath forgotten thee in all the bliss

Of his gold city, and eternal day"—
Nay peace: behind my prison's blinded bars
I do possess what none can take away,
My love, and all the glory of the stars.

APOLOGIA

Is IT thy will that I should wax and wane,
Barter my cloth of gold for hodden gray,
And at thy pleasure weave that web of pain
Whose brightest threads are each a wasted day?

Is it thy will—Love that I love so well—
That my Soul's House should be a tortured spot
Wherein, like evil paramours, must dwell
The quenchless flame, the worm that dieth not?

Nay, if it be thy will I shall endure,
And sell ambition at the common mart,
And let dull failure be my vestiture,
And sorrow dig its grave within my heart.

Perchance it may be better so—at least
I have not made my heart a heart of stone,
Nor starved my boyhood of its goodly feast,
Nor walked where Beauty is a thing unknown.

Many a man hath done so; sought to fence
In straitened bonds the soul that should be free,
Trodden the dusty road of common sense,
While all the forest sang of liberty,

Not marking how the spotted hawk in flight
Passed on wide pinion through the lofty air,
To where the steep untrodden mountain height
Caught the last tresses of the Sun God's hair.

Or how the little flower he trod upon,
The daisy, that white-feathered shield of gold,
Followed with wistful eyes the wandering sun
Content if once its leaves were aureoled.

But surely it is something to have been
The best belovèd for a little while,
To have walked hand in hand with Love, and seen
His purple wings flit once across thy smile.

Ay! though the gorgèd asp of passion feed
On my boy's heart, yet have I burst the bars,
Stood face to face with Beauty, known indeed
The Love which moves the Sun and all the stars!

QUIA MULTUM AMAVI

Dear heart I think the young impassioned priest
When first he takes from out the hidden shrine
His God imprisoned in the Eucharist,
And eats the Bread, and drinks the Dreadful Wine,

Feels not such awful wonder as I felt
When first my smitten eyes beat full on thee,
And all night long before thy feet I knelt
Till thou wert wearied of Idolatry.

Ah! had'st thou liked me less and loved me more,
Through all those summer days of joy and rain,
I had not now been sorrow's heritor,
Or stood a lackey in the House of Pain.

Yet, though remorse, youth's white-faced seneschal
Tread on my heels with all his retinue,
I am most glad I loved thee—think of all
The sums that go to make one speedwell blue!

SILENTIUM AMORIS

As oftentimes the too resplendent sun
Hurries the pallid and reluctant moon
Back to her sombre cave, ere she hath won
A single ballad from the nightingale,
So doth thy Beauty make my lips to fail,
And all my sweetest singing out of tune.

And as at dawn across the level mead
On wings impetuous some wind will come,
And with its too harsh kisses break the reed
Which was its only instrument of song,
So my too stormy passions work me wrong,
And for excess of Love my Love is dumb.

But surely unto thee mine eyes did show
Why I am silent, and my lute unstrung;
Else it were better we should part, and go,
Thou to some lips of sweeter melody,
And I to nurse the barren memory
Of unkissed kisses, and songs never sung.

HER VOICE

The wild bee reels from bough to bough
With his furry coat and his gauzy wing.
Now in a lily-cup, and now
Setting a jacinth bell a-swing,
In his wandering;
Sit closer love: it was here I trow
I made that vow,

Swore that two lives should be like one
As long as the sea-gull loved the sea,

As long as the sunflower sought the
sun—
It shall be, I said, for eternity
'Twixt you and me!
Dear friend, those times are over and
done,
Love's web is spun.

Look upward where the poplar trees
Sway and sway in the summer air,
Here in the valley never a breeze
Scatters the thistledown, but there
Great winds blow fair
From the mighty murmuring mys-
tical seas,
And the wave-lashed leas.

Look upward where the white gull
screams
What does it see that we do not
see?
Is that a star? or the lamp that
gleams
On some outward voyaging
argosy,—
Ah! can it be
We have lived our lives in land of
dreams!
How sad it seems.

Sweet, there is nothing left to say
But this, that love is never lost.
Keen winter stabs the breasts of May
Whose crimson roses burst his
frost,
Ships tempest-tossed
Will find a harbour in some bay,
And so we may.

And there is nothing left to do
But to kiss once again, and part,
Nay, there is nothing we should rue,
I have my beauty,—you your Art.
Nay, do not start,
One world was not enough for two
Like me and you.

MY VOICE

Within this restless, hurried, modern
world
We took our heart's full pleasure—
You and I,
And now the white sails of our ship
are furled,
And spent the lading of our argosy.

Wherefore my cheeks before their
time are wan,
For very weeping is my gladness
fled,
Sorrow hath paled my lip's vermilion,
And Ruin draws the curtains of my
bed.

But all this crowded life has been to
thee
No more than lyre, or lute, or
subtle spell
Of viols, or the music of the sea
That sleeps, a mimic echo, in the
shell.

TAEDIUM VITAE

To stab my youth with desperate
knife, to wear
This paltry age's gaudy livery,
To let each base hand filch my
treasury,
To mesh my soul within a woman's
hair,
And be mere Fortune's lackeyed
groom,—I swear,
I love it not! these things are less
to me
Than the thin foam that frets upon
the sea,
Less than the thistle-down of summer
air
Which hath no seed: better to
stand aloof
Far from these slanderous fools who
mock my life

Knowing me not, better the lowliest roof
Fit for the meanest hind to sojourn in,
Than to go back to that hoarse cave of strife
Where my white soul first kissed the mouth of sin.

FLOWER OF LOVE

Sweet, I blame you not, for mine the fault was,
Had I not been made of common clay
I had climbed the higher heights unclimbed yet,
Seen the fuller air, the larger day.

From the wildness of my wasted passion I had
Struck a better, clearer song,
Lit some lighter light of freer freedom, battled
With some Hydra-headed wrong.

Had my lips been smitten into music by the
Kisses that but made them bleed,
You had walked with Bice and the angels on
That verdant and enamelled mead.

I had trod the road which Dante treading saw
The suns of seven circles shine,
Ay! perchance had seen the heavens opening, as
They opened to the Florentine.

And the mighty nations would have crowned me,
Who am crownless now and without name,
And some orient dawn had found me kneeling
On the threshold of the House of Fame

I had sat within that marble circle where the
Oldest bard is as the young,
And the pipe is ever dropping honey, and the
Lyre's strings are ever strung.

Keats had lifted up his hymeneal curls from out
The poppy-seeded wine,
With ambrosial mouth had kissed my forehead,
Clasped the hand of noble love in mine.

And at springtime, when the apple-blossoms
Brush the burnished bosom of the dove,
Two young lovers lying in an orchard would
Have read the story of our love.

Would have read the legend of my passion,
Known the bitter secret of my heart,
Kissed as we have kissed, but never parted as
We two are fated now to part.

For the crimson flower of our life is eaten by
The canker-worm of truth,
And no hand can gather up the fallen withered
Petals of the rose of youth.

Yet I am not sorry that I loved you—ah! what
Else had I a boy to do,—
For the hungry teeth of time devour, and the
Silent-footed years pursue.

Rudderless, we drift athwart a tempest, and
When once the storm of youth is past,
Without lyre, without lute or chorus, Death a
Silent pilot comes at last.

And within the grave there is no pleasure, for
The blind-worm battens on the root,
And Desire shudders into ashes, and the tree of
Passion bears no fruit.

Ah! what else had I to do but love you, God's
Own mother was less dear to me,
And less dear the Cytheraean rising like an
Argent lily from the sea.

I have made my choice, have lived my poems,
And, though youth is gone in wasted days,
I have found the lover's crown of myrtle
Better than the poet's crown of bays.

MISCELLANEOUS POEMS

THE TRUE KNOWLEDGE

Thou knowest all—I seek in vain
What lands to till or sow with seed—
The land is black with briar and weed,
Nor cares for falling tears or rain.

Thou knowest all—I sit and wait
With blinded eyes and hands that fail,
Till the last lifting of the veil,
And the first opening of the gate.

Thou knowest all—I cannot see.
I trust I shall not live in vain,
I know that we shall meet again,
In some divine eternity.

A LAMENT

O well for him who lives at ease
With garnered gold in wide domain,
Nor heeds the plashing of the rain,
The crashing down of forest trees.

O well for him who ne'er hath known
The travail of the hungry years,
A father grey with grief and tears,
A mother weeping all alone.

But well for him whose feet hath trod
The weary road of toil and strife,
Yet from the sorrows of his life
Builds ladders to be nearer God.

WASTED DAYS

A fair slim boy not made for this world's pain.
With hair of gold thick clustering round his ears,
And longing eyes half veiled by foolish tears
Like bluest water seen through mists of rain:

Pale cheeks whereon no kiss hath left its stain,
Red under lip drawn for fear of Love,
And white throat whiter than the breast of dove.
Alas! alas! if all should be in vain.

Behind, wide fields, and reapers all a-row
In heat and labour toiling wearily,
To no sweet sound of laughter or of lute.
The sun is shooting wide its crimson glow,
Still the boy dreams: nor knows that night is nigh,
And in the night-time no man gathers fruit.

LOTUS LEAVES

I

THERE is no peace beneath the moon,—
Ah! in those meadows is there peace
Where, girdled with a silver fleece,
As a bright shepherd, strays the moon?

Queen of the gardens of the sky,
Where stars like lilies, white and fair,
Shine through the mists of frosty air,
Oh, tarry, for the dawn is nigh!

Oh, tarry, for the envious day
Stretches long hands to catch thy feet.
Alas! but thou art overfleet,
Alas! I know thou wilt not stay.

II

Eastward the dawn has broken red,
The circling mists and shadows flee;
Aurora rises from the sea,
And leaves the crocus-flowered bed.

Eastward the silver arrows fall,
Splintering the veil of holy night:
And a long wave of yellow light
Breaks silently on tower and hall.

And speeding wide across the wold
Wakes into flight some fluttering bird;
And all the chestnut tops are stirred,
And all the branches streaked with gold.

III

To outer senses there is peace,
A dream-like peace on either hand,
Deep silence in the shadowy land,
Deep silence where the shadows cease,

Save for a cry that echoes shrill
From some lone bird disconsolate;
A curlew calling to its mate;
The answer from the distant hill.

And, herald of my love to Him
Who, waiting for the dawn, doth lie,
The orbèd maiden leaves the sky,
And the white firs grow more dim.

IV

Up sprang the sun to run his race,
The breeze blew fair on meadow and lea,
But in the west I seemed to see
The likeness of a human face.

A linnet on the hawthorn spray
  Sang of the glories of the spring,
  And made the flow'ring copses ring
With gladness for the new-born day.

A lark from out the grass I trod
  Flew wildly, and was lost to view
  In the great seamless veil of blue
That hangs before the face of God.

The willow whispered overhead
  That death is but a newer life
  And that with idle words of strife
We bring dishonour on the dead.

I took a branch from off the tree,
  And hawthorn branches drenched with dew,
  I bound them with a sprig of yew,
And made a garland fair to see.

I laid the flowers where He lies
  (Warm leaves and flowers on the stones):
  What joy I had to sit alone
Till evening broke on tired eyes:

Till all the shifting clouds had spun
  A robe of gold for God to wear
  And into seas of purple air
Sank the bright galley of the sun.

V

Shall I be gladdened for the day,
  And let my inner heart be stirred
  By murmuring tree or song of bird,
And sorrow at the wild winds' play?

Not so, such idle dreams belong
  To souls of lesser depth than mine;
  I feel that I am half divine;
I know that I am great and strong.

I know that every forest tree
  By labour rises from the root
  I know that none shall gather fruit
By sailing on the barren sea.

IMPRESSIONS

I

Le Jardin

The lily's withered chalice falls
  Around its rod of dusty gold,
  And from the beech trees on the wold
The last wood-pigeon coos and calls.

The gaudy leonine sunflower
  Hangs black and barren on its stalk,
  And down the windy garden walk
The dead leaves scatter,–hour by hour.

Pale privet-petals white as milk
  Are blown into a snowy mass;
  The roses lie upon the grass,
Like little shreds of crimson silk.

II

La Mer

A white mist drifts across the shrouds,
  A wild moon in this wintry sky
  Gleams like an angry lion's eye
Out of a mane of tawny clouds.

The muffled steersman at the wheel
  Is but a shadow in the gloom;–
  And in the throbbing engine room
Leap the long rods of polished steel.

The shattered storm has left its trace
  Upon this huge and heaving dome,
  For the thin threads of yellow foam
Float on the waves like ravelled lace.

UNDER THE BALCONY

O BEAUTIFUL STAR with the crimson mouth!
O moon with the brows of gold!
Rise up, rise up, from the odorous south!
And light for my love her way,
Lest her feet should stray
On the windy hill and the wold!
O beautiful star with the crimson mouth!
O moon with the brows of gold!

O ship that shakes on the desolate sea!
O ship with the wet, white sail!
Put in, put in, to the port to me!
For my love and I would go
To the land where the daffodils blow
In the heart of a violet dale!
O ship that shakes on the desolate sea!
O ship with the wet, white sail!

O rapturous bird with the low, sweet note!
O bird that sits on the spray!
Sing on, sing on, from your soft brown throat!
And my love in her little bed
Will listen, and lift her head
From the pillow, and come my way!
O rapturous bird with the low, sweet note!
O bird that sits on the spray!

O blossom that hangs in the tremulous air!
O blossom with lips of snow!
Come down, Come down, for my love to wear!
You will die in her head in a crown,
You will die in a fold of her gown,
To her little light heart you will go!
O blossom that hangs in the tremulous air!
O blossom with lips of snow!

A FRAGMENT

BEAUTIFUL star with the crimson lips
And flagrant daffodil hair,
Come back, come back, in the shaking ships
O'er the much-overrated sea,
To the hearts that are sick for thee
With a woe worse than mal de mer—
O beautiful stars with the crimson lips
And the flagrant daffodil hair.

O ship that shakes on the desolate sea,
Neath the flag of the wan White Star,
Thou bringest a brighter star with thee
From the land of the Philistine,
Where Niagara's reckoned fine
And Tupper is popular—
O ship that shakes on the desolate sea,
Neath the flag of the wan White Star.

LE JARDIN DES TUILERIES

THIS winter air is keen and cold,
And keen and cold this winter sun,
But round my chair the children run
Like little things of dancing gold.

Sometimes about the painted kiosk
The mimic soldiers strut and stride,
Sometimes the blue-eyed brigands hide
In the bleak tangles of the bosk.

And sometimes, while the old nurse cons
Her book, they steal across the square,
And launch their paper navies where
Huge Triton writhes in greenish bronze.

And now in mimic flight they flee,
And now they rush, a boisterous band—
And, tiny hand on tiny hand,
Climb up the black and leafless tree.

Ah! cruel tree! if I were you,
And children climbed me, for their sake
Though it be winter I would break
Into spring blossoms white and blue!

SONNET

On the Sale by Auction of Keats' Love Letters

These are the letters which Endymion wrote
To one he loved in secret and apart,
And now the brawlers of the auction-mart
Bargain and bid for each tear-blotted note,
Aye! for each separate pulse of passion quote
The merchant's price! I think they love not art
Who break the crystal of a poet's heart,
That small and sickly eyes may glare or gloat.

Is it not said, that many years ago,
In a far Eastern town some soldiers ran
With torches through the midnight, and began
To wrangle for mean raiment, and to throw
Dice for the garments of a wretched Man,
Not knowing the God's wonder, or His woe?

THE NEW REMORSE

The sin was mine; I did not understand.
So now is music prisoned in her cave,
Save where some ebbing desultory wave
Frets with its restless whirls this meagre strand.
And in the withered hollow of this land
Hath Summer dug herself so deep a grave,
That hardly can the leaden willow crave
One silver blossom from keen Winter's hand.
But who is this that cometh by the shore?
(Nay, love, look up and wonder!) Who is this
Who cometh in dyed garments from the South?
It is thy new-found Lord, and he shall kiss
The yet unravished roses of thy mouth,
And I shall weep and worship, as before.

AN INSCRIPTION

Go, little book,
To him who, on a lute with horns of pearl,
Sang of the white feet of the Golden Girl:
And bid him look
Into thy pages: it may hap that he
May find that golden maidens dance through thee.

THE HARLOT'S HOUSE

We caught the tread of dancing feet,
We loitered down the moonlit street,
And stopped beneath the Harlot's House.
Inside, above the din and fray,
We heard the loud musicians play
The "Treues Liebes," of Strauss.

Like strange mechanical grotesques,
Making fantastic arabesques,
The shadows raced across the blind.
We watched the ghostly dancers spin,
To sound of horn and violin,
Like black leaves wheeling in the wind.

Like wire-pulled Automatons,
Slim silhouetted skeletons
Went sidling through the slow quadrille,
Then took each other by the hand,
And danced a stately saraband;
Their laughter echoed thin and shrill.

Sometimes a clock-work puppet pressed
A phantom lover to her breast,
Sometimes they seemed to try and sing.
Sometimes a horrible Marionette
Came out, and smoked its cigarette
Upon the steps like a live thing.

Then turning to my love I said,
"The dead are dancing with the dead,
The dust is whirling with the dust."
But she, she heard the violin,
And left my side and entered in:
Love passed into the House of Lust.

Then suddenly the tune went false,
The dancers wearied of the waltz,
The shadows ceased to wheel and whirl,
And down the long and silent street,
The dawn with silver-sandalled feet,
Crept like a frightened girl.

THE PICTURE OF DORIAN GRAY

CHAPTER I

The studio was filled with the rich odour of roses, and when the light summer wind stirred amidst the trees of the garden there came through the open door the heavy scent of the lilac, or the more delicate perfume of the pink-flowering thorn.

From the corner of the divan of Persian saddle-bags on which he was lying, smoking, as was his custom, innumerable cigarettes, Lord Henry Wotton could just catch the gleam of the honey-sweet and honey-coloured blossoms of a laburnum, whose tremulous branches seemed hardly able to bear the burden of a beauty so flamelike as theirs; and now and then the fantastic shadows of birds in flight flitted across the long tussore-silk curtains that were stretched in front of the huge window, producing a kind of momentary Japanese effect, and making him think of those pallid jade-faced painters of Tokio who, through the medium of an art that is necessarily immobile, seek to convey the sense of swiftness and motion. The sullen murmur of the bees shouldering their way through the long unmown grass, or circling with monotonous insistence round the dusty gilt horns of the straggling woodbine, seemed to make the stillness more oppressive. The dim roar of London was like the burdon note of a distant organ.

In the centre of the room, clamped to an upright easel, stood the full-length portrait of a young man of extraordinary personal beauty, and in front of it, some little distance away, was sitting the artist himself, Basil Hallward, whose sudden disappearance some years ago caused, at the time, such public excitement, and gave rise to so many strange conjectures.

As the painter looked at the gracious and comely form he had so skilfully mirrored in his art, a smile of pleasure passed across his face, and seemed about to linger there. But he suddenly started up, and, closing his eyes, placed his fingers upon the lids, as though he sought to imprison within his brain some curious dream from which he feared he might awake.

"It is your best work, Basil, the best thing you have ever done," said Lord Henry, languidly. "You must certainly send it next year to the Grosvenor. The Academy is too large and too vulgar. Whenever I have gone there, there have either been so many people that I have not been able to see the pictures, which was dreadful, or so many pictures that I have not been able to see the people, which was worse. The Grosvenor is really the only place."

"I don't think I shall send it anywhere," he answered, tossing his head back in that odd way that used to make his friends laugh at him at Oxford. "No; I won't send it anywhere."

Lord Henry elevated his eyebrows, and looked at him in amazement through the thin blue wreaths of smoke that curled up in such fanciful whorls from his heavy opium-tainted cigarette.

"Not send it anywhere? My dear fellow, why? Have you any reason? What odd chaps you painters are! You do anything in the world to gain a reputation. As soon as you have one, you seem to want to throw it away. It is silly of you, for there is only one thing in the world worse than being talked about, and that is not being talked about. A portrait like this would set you far above all the young men in England, and make the old men quite jealous, if old men are ever capable of any emotion."

"I know you will laugh at me," he replied, "but I really can't exhibit it. I have put too much of myself into it."

Lord Henry stretched himself out on the divan and laughed.

"Yes, I knew you would; but it is quite true, all the same."

"Too much of yourself in it! Upon my word, Basil, I didn't know you were so vain; and I really can't see any resemblance between you, with your rugged strong face and your coal-black hair, and this young Adonis, who looks as if he was made out of ivory and rose-leaves. Why, my dear Basil, he is a Narcissus, and you—well, of course you have an intellectual expression, and all that. But beauty, real beauty, ends where an intellectual expression begins. Intellect is in itself a mode of exaggeration, and destroys the harmony of any face. The moment one sits down to think, one becomes all nose, or all forehead, or something horrid. Look at the successful men in any of the learned professions. How perfectly hideous they are! Except, of course, in the church. But then in the church they don't think. A bishop keeps on saying at the age of eighty what he was told to say when he was a boy of eighteen, and as a natural consequence he always looks absolutely delightful. Your mysterious young friend, whose name you have never told me, but whose picture really fascinates me, never thinks. I feel quite sure of that. He is some brainless, beautiful creature, who should always be here in winter when we have no flowers to look at, and always here in summer when we want something to chill our intelligence. Don't flatter yourself, Basil, you are not in the least like him."

"You don't understand me, Harry," answered the artist. "Of course I am not like him. I know that perfectly well. Indeed, I should be sorry to look like him. You shrug your shoulders? I am telling you the truth. There is a fatality about all physical and intellectual distinction, the sort of fatality that seems to dog through history the faltering steps of kings. It is better not to be different from one's fellows. The ugly and the stupid have the best of it in this world. They can sit at their ease and gape at the play. If they know nothing of victory, they are at least spared the knowledge of defeat. They live as we all should live, undisturbed, indifferent, and without disquiet. They neither bring ruin upon others, nor ever receive it, from alien hands. Your rank and wealth, Harry; my brains, such as they are—my art, whatever it may be worth; Dorian Gray's good looks—we shall all suffer for what the gods have given us, suffer terribly."

"Dorian Gray? Is that his name?" asked Lord Henry, walking across the studio towards Basil Hallward.

"Yes, that is his name. I didn't intend to tell it to you."

"But why not?"

"Oh, I can't explain. When I like people immensely I never tell their names to any one. It is like surrendering a part of them. I have grown to love secrecy. It seems to be the one thing that can make modern life mysterious or marvellous to us. The commonest thing is delightful if one only hides it. When I leave town now I never tell my people where I am going. If I did, I would lose all my pleasure. It is a silly habit, I dare say, but somehow it seems to bring a great deal of romance into one's life. I suppose you think me awfully foolish about it?"

"Not at all," answered Lord Henry, "not at all, my dear Basil. You seem to forget that I am married, and the one charm of marriage is that it makes a life of deception absolutely necessary for both parties. I never know where my wife is, and my wife never knows what I am doing. When we meet—we do meet occasionally, when we dine out together, or go down to the Duke's—we tell each other the most absurd stories with the most serious faces. My wife is very good at it—much better, in fact, than I am. She never gets confused over her dates, and I always do. But when she does find me out, she makes no row at all. I sometimes wish she would; but she merely laughs at me."

"I hate the way you talk about your married life, Harry," said Basil Hallward, strolling towards the door that led into the garden. "I believe that you are really a very good husband, but that you are thoroughly ashamed of your own virtues. You are an extraordinary fellow. You never say a moral thing, and you never do a wrong thing. Your cynicism is simply a pose."

"Being natural is simply a pose, and the most irritating pose I know," cried Lord Henry, laughing; and the two young men went out into the garden together, and ensconced themselves on a long bamboo seat that stood in the shade of a tall laurel bush. The sunlight slipped over the polished leaves. In the grass, white daisies were tremulous.

After a pause, Lord Henry pulled out his watch. "I am afraid I must be going, Basil," he murmured, "and before I go, I insist on your answering a question I put to you some time ago."

"What is that?" said the painter, keeping his eyes fixed on the ground.

"You know quite well."

"I do not, Harry."

"Well, I will tell you what it is. I want you to explain to me why you won't exhibit Dorian Gray's picture. I want the real reason."

"I told you the real reason."

"No, you did not. You said it was because there was too much of yourself in it. Now, that is childish."

"Harry," said Basil Hallward, looking him straight in the face, "every portrait that is painted with feeling is a portrait of the artist, not of the sitter. The sitter is merely the accident, the occasion. It is not he who is revealed by the painter; it is rather the painter who, on the coloured canvas, reveals himself. The reason I will not exhibit this picture is that I am afraid that I have shown in it the secret of my own soul."

Lord Henry laughed. "And what is that?" he asked.

"I will tell you," said Hallward; but an expression of perplexity came over his face.

"I am all expectation, Basil," continued his companion, glancing at him.

"Oh, there is really very little to tell, Harry," answered the painter; "and I am afraid you will hardly understand it. Perhaps you will hardly believe it."

Lord Henry smiled, and, leaning down, plucked a pink-petalled daisy from the grass, and examined it. "I am quite sure I shall understand it," he replied, gazing intently at the little golden white-feathered disk, "and as for believing things, I can believe anything, provided that it is quite incredible."

The wind shook some blossoms from the trees, and the heavy lilac-blooms, with their clustering stars, moved to and fro in the languid air. A grasshopper began to chirrup by the wall, and like a blue thread a long thin dragon-fly floated past on its brown gauze wings. Lord Henry felt as if he could hear Basil Hallward's heart beating, and wondered what was coming.

"The story is simply this," said the painter after some time. "Two months ago I went to a crush at Lady Brandon's. You know we poor artists have to show ourselves in society from time to time, just to remind the public that we are not savages. With an evening coat and a white tie, as you told me once, anybody, even a stock-broker, can gain a reputation for being civilized. Well, after I had been in the room about ten minutes, talking to huge overdressed dowagers and tedious Academicians, I suddenly became conscious that some one was looking at me. I turned halfway round, and saw Dorian Gray for the first time. When our eyes met, I felt that I was growing pale. A curious sensation of terror came over me. I knew that I had come face to face with some one whose mere personality was so fascinating that, if I allowed it to do so, it would absorb my whole nature, my whole soul, my very art itself. I did not want any external influence in my life. You know yourself, Harry, how independent I am by nature. I have always been my own master; had at least always been so, till I met Dorian Gray. Then—but I don't know how to explain it to you. Something seemed to tell me that I was on the verge of a terrible crisis in my life. I had a strange feeling that Fate had in store for me exquisite joys and exquisite sorrows. I grew afraid, and turned to quit the room. It was not conscience that made me do it: it was a sort of cowardice. I take no credit to myself for trying to escape."

"Conscience and cowardice are really the same things, Basil. Conscience is the trade-name of the firm. That is all."

"I don't believe that, Harry, and I don't believe you do either. However, whatever was my motive—and it may have been pride, for I used to be very proud—I certainly struggled to the door. There, of course, I stumbled against Lady Brandon. 'You are not going to run away so soon, Mr. Hallward?' she screamed out. You know her curiously shrill voice?"

"Yes; she is a peacock in everything but beauty," said Lord Henry, pulling the daisy to bits with his long, nervous fingers.

"I could not get rid of her. She brought me up to Royalties, and people with Stars and Garters, and elderly ladies with gigantic tiaras and parrot noses.

She spoke of me as her dearest friend. I had only met her once before, but she took it into her head to lionize me. I believe some picture of mine had made a great success at the time, at least had been chattered about in the penny newspapers, which is the nineteenth-century standard of immortality. Suddenly I found myself face to face with the young man whose personality had so strangely stirred me. We were quite close, almost touching. Our eyes met again. It was reckless of me, but I asked Lady Brandon to introduce me to him. Perhaps it was not so reckless, after all. It was simply inevitable. We would have spoken to each other without any introduction. I am sure of that. Dorian told me so afterwards. He, too, felt that we were destined to know each other."

"And how did Lady Brandon describe this wonderful young man?" asked his companion. "I know she goes in for giving a rapid *précis* of all her guests. I remember her bringing me up to a truculent and red-faced old gentleman covered all over with orders and ribbons, and hissing into my ear, in a tragic whisper which must have been perfectly audible to everybody in the room, the most astounding details. I simply fled. I like to find out people for myself. But Lady Brandon treats her guests exactly as an auctioneer treats his goods. She either explains them entirely away, or tells one everything about them except what one wants to know."

"Poor Lady Brandon! You are hard on her, Harry!" said Hallward, listlessly.

"My dear fellow, she tried to found a *salon*, and only succeeded in opening a restaurant. How could I admire her? But tell me, what did she say about Mr. Dorian Gray?"

"Oh, something like 'Charming boy—poor dear mother and I absolutely inseparable. Quite forget what he does—afraid he—doesn't do anything—oh, yes, plays the piano—or is it the violin, dear Mr. Gray?' Neither of us could help laughing, and we became friends at once."

"Laughter is not at all a bad beginning for a friendship, and it is far the best ending for one," said the young lord, plucking another daisy.

Hallward shook his head. "You don't understand what friendship is, Harry," he murmured—"or what enmity is, for that matter. You like every one; that is to say, you are indifferent to every one."

"How horribly unjust of you!" cried Lord Henry, tilting his hat back, and looking up at the little clouds that, like ravelled skeins of glossy white silk, were drifting across the hollowed turquoise of the summer sky. "Yes, horribly unjust of you. I make a great difference between people. I choose my friends for their good looks, my acquaintances for their good characters, and my enemies for their good intellects. A man cannot be too careful in the choice of his enemies. I have not got one who is a fool, they are all men of some intellectual power, and consequently they all appreciate me. Is that very vain of me? I think it is rather vain."

"I should think it was, Harry. But according to your category I must be merely an acquaintance."

"My dear old Basil, you are much more than an acquaintance."

"And much less than a friend. A sort of brother, I suppose?"

"Oh, brothers! I don't care for brothers. My elder brother won't die, and my younger brothers seem never to do anything else."

"Harry!" exclaimed Hallward, frowning.

"My dear fellow, I am not quite serious. But I can't help detesting my relations. I suppose it comes from the fact that none of us can stand other people having the same faults as ourselves. I quite sympathize with the rage of the English democracy against what they call the vices of the upper orders. The masses feel that drunkenness, stupidity, and immorality should be their own special property, and that if any one of us makes an ass of himself he is poaching on their preserves. When poor Southwark got into the Divorce Court, their indignation was quite magnificent. And yet I don't suppose that ten per cent. of the proletariat live correctly."

"I don't agree with a single word that you have said, and, what is more, Harry, I feel sure that you don't either."

Lord Henry stroked his pointed brown beard, and tapped the toe of his patent-leather boot with a tasselled ebony cane. "How English you are, Basil! That is the second time you have made that observation. If one puts forward an idea to a true Englishman—always a rash thing to do—he never dreams of considering whether the idea is right or wrong. The only thing he considers of any importance is whether one believes it oneself. Now, the value of an idea has nothing whatsoever to do with the sincerity of the man who expresses it. Indeed, the probabilities are that the more insincere the man is, the more purely intellectual will the idea be, as in that case it will not be coloured by either his wants, his desires, or his prejudices. However, I don't propose to discuss politics, sociology, or metaphysics with you. I like persons better than principles, and I like persons with no principles better than anything else in the world. Tell me more about Mr. Dorian Gray. How often do you see him?"

"Every day. I couldn't be happy if I didn't see him every day. He is absolutely necessary to me."

"How extraordinary! I thought you would never care for anything but your art."

"He is all my art to me now," said the painter, gravely. "I sometimes think, Harry, that there are only two eras of any importance in the world's history. The first is the appearance of a new medium for art, and the second is the appearance of a new personality for art also. What the invention of oil-painting was to the Venetians, the face of Antinous was to late Greek sculpture, and the face of Dorian Gray will some day be to me. It is not merely that I paint from him, draw from him, sketch from him. Of course I have done all that. But he is much more to me than a model or a sitter. I won't tell you that I am dissatisfied with what I have done of him, or that his beauty is such that Art cannot express it. There is nothing that Art cannot express, and I know that the work I have done, since I met Dorian Gray, is good work, is the best work of my life. But in some curious way—I wonder will you understand me?—his personality has suggested to me an entirely new manner in art, an entirely new mode of style. I see things differently, I think of them differently. I can now re-create life in a way that was hidden from me before. 'A dream of form in days of thought:'—who is it who says that? I forget; but it is what Dorian Gray has been to me. The merely visible presence of this lad—for he seems to me little more than a lad, though he is really over twenty —his merely visible presence—ah! I wonder can you realize all that that means? Unconsciously he defines for me the lines of a fresh school, a school that is to have in it all the passion of the romantic spirit, all the perfection of the spirit that is Greek. The harmony of soul and body—how much that is! We in our madness have separated the two, and have invented a realism that is vulgar, an ideality that is void. Harry! if you only knew what Dorian Gray is to me! You remember that landscape of mine, for which Agnew offered me such a huge price, but which I would not part with? It is one of the best things I have ever done. And why is it so? Because, while I was painting it, Dorian Gray sat beside me. Some subtle influence passed from him to me, and for the first time in my life I saw in the plain woodland the wonder I had always looked for, and always missed."

"Basil, this is extraordinary! I must see Dorian Gray."

Hallward got up from his seat, and walked up and down the garden. After some time he came back. "Harry," he said, "Dorian Gray is to me simply a motive in art. You might see nothing in him. I see everything in him. He is never more present in my work than when no image of him is there. He is a suggestion, as I have said, of a new manner. I find him in the curves of certain lines, in the loveliness and subtleties of certain colours. That is all."

"Then why won't you exhibit his portrait?" asked Lord Henry.

"Because, without intending it, I have put into it some expression of all this curious artistic idolatry, of which, of course, I have never cared to speak to him. He knows nothing about it. He shall never know anything about it. But the world might guess it; and I will not bare my soul to their shallow, prying eyes. My heart shall never be put under their microscope. There is too much of myself in the thing, Harry—too much of myself!"

"Poets are not so scrupulous as you are. They know how useful passion is for publication. Nowadays a broken heart will run to many editions."

"I hate them for it," cried Hallward. "An artist should create beautiful things, but should put nothing of his own life into them. We live in an age when men treat art as if it were meant to be a form of autobiography. We have lost the abstract sense of beauty. Some day I will show the world what it is; and for that reason the world shall never see my portrait of Dorian Gray."

"I think you are wrong, Basil, but I won't argue with you. It is only the intellectually lost who ever argue. Tell me, is Dorian Gray very fond of you?"

The painter considered for a few moments. "He likes me," he answered after a pause; "I know he likes me. Of course I flatter him dreadfully. I find a strange pleasure in saying things to him that I know I shall be sorry for having said. As a rule, he is charming to me, and we sit in the studio and talk of a thousand things. Now and then, however, he is horribly thoughtless, and seems to take a real delight in giving me pain. Then I feel, Harry, that I have given away my whole soul to some one who treats it as if it were a flower to put in his coat, a bit of decoration to charm his vanity, an ornament for a summer's day."

"Days in summer, Basil, are apt to linger," murmured Lord Henry. "Perhaps you will tire sooner than he will. It is a sad thing to think of, but there is no doubt that Genius lasts longer than Beauty. That accounts for the fact that we all take such pains to over-educate ourselves. In the wild struggle for existence, we want to have something that endures, and so we fill our minds with rubbish and facts, in the silly hope of keeping our place. The thoroughly well-informed man—that is the modern idea. And the mind of the thoroughly well-informed man is a dreadful thing. It is like a bric-à-brac shop, all monsters and dust, with everything priced above its proper value. I think you will tire first, all the same. Some day you will look at your friend and he will seem to you to be a little out of drawing, or you won't like his tone of colour, or something. You will bitterly reproach him in your own heart, and seriously think that he has behaved very badly to you. The next time he calls, you will be perfectly cold and indifferent. It will be a great pity, for it will alter you. What you have told me is quite a romance, a romance of art one might call it, and the worst of having a romance of any kind is that it leaves one so unromantic."

"Harry, don't talk like that. As long as I live, the personality of Dorian Gray will dominate me. You can't feel what I feel. You change too often."

"Ah, my dear Basil, that is exactly why I can feel it. Those who are faithful know only the trivial side of love: it is the faithless who know love's tragedies." And Lord Henry struck a light on a dainty silver case, and began to smoke a cigarette with a self-conscious and satisfied air, as if he had summed up the world in a phrase. There was a rustle of chirruping sparrows in the green lacquer leaves of the ivy, and the blue cloud-shadows chased themselves across the grass like swallows. How pleasant it was in the garden! And how delightful other people's emotions were!—much more delightful than their ideas, it seemed to him. One's own soul, and the passions of one's friends—those were the fascinating things in life. He pictured to himself with silent amusement the tedious luncheon that he had missed by staying so long with Basil Hallward. Had he gone to his aunt's, he would have been sure to have met Lord Goodbody there, and the whole conversation would have been about the feeding of the poor, and the necessity for model lodging-houses. Each class would have preached the importance of those virtues, for whose exercise there was no necessity in their own lives. The rich would have spoken on the value of thrift, and the idle grown eloquent over the dignity of labour. It was charming to have escaped all that! As he thought of his aunt, an idea seemed to strike him. He turned to Hallward, and said, "My dear fellow, I have just remembered."

"Remembered what, Harry?"

"Where I heard the name of Dorian Gray."

"Where was it?" asked Hallward, with a slight frown.

"Don't look so angry, Basil. It was at my aunt, Lady Agatha's. She told me she had discovered a wonderful young man, who was going to help her in the

East End, and that his name was Dorian Gray. I am bound to state that she never told me he was good-looking. Women have no appreciation of good looks; at least, good women have not. She said that he was very earnest, and had a beautiful nature. I at once pictured to myself a creature with spectacles and lank hair, horribly freckled, and tramping about on huge feet. I wish I had known it was your friend."

"I am very glad you didn't, Harry."

"Why?"

"I don't want you to meet him."

"You don't want me to meet him?"

"No."

"Mr. Dorian Gray is in the studio, sir," said the butler, coming into the garden.

"You must introduce me now," cried Lord Henry, laughing.

The painter turned to his servant, who stood blinking in the sunlight. "Ask Mr. Gray to wait, Parker: I shall be in in a few moments." The man bowed, and went up the walk.

Then he looked at Lord Henry. "Dorian Gray is my dearest friend," he said. "He has a simple and beautiful nature. Your aunt was quite right in what she said of him. Don't spoil him. Don't try to influence him. Your influence would be bad. The world is wide, and has many marvellous people in it. Don't take away from me the one person who gives to my art whatever charm it possesses; my life as an artist depends on him. Mind, Harry, I trust you." He spoke very slowly, and the words seemed wrung out of him almost against his will.

"What nonsense you talk!" said Lord Henry, smiling, and, taking Hallward by the arm, he almost led him into the house.

CHAPTER II

As THEY entered they saw Dorian Gray. He was seated at the piano, with his back to them, turning over the pages of a volume of Schumann's "Forest Scenes." "You must lend me these, Basil," he cried. "I want to learn them. They are perfectly charming."

"That depends entirely on how you sit to-day, Dorian."

"Oh, I am tired of sitting, and I don't want a life-sized portrait of myself," answered the lad, swinging round on the music-stool, in a wilful, petulant manner. When he caught sight of Lord Henry, a faint blush coloured his cheeks for a moment, and he started up. "I beg your pardon, Basil, but I didn't know you had any one with you."

"This is Lord Henry Wotton, Dorian, an old Oxford friend of mine. I have just been telling him what a capital sitter you were, and now you have spoiled everything."

"You have not spoiled my pleasure in meeting you, Mr. Gray," said Lord Henry, stepping forward and extending his hand. My aunt has often spoken to me about you. You are one of her favourites, and, I am afraid, one of her victims, also."

"I am in Lady Agatha's black books at present," answered Dorian, with a funny look of penitence. "I promised to go to a club in Whitechapel with her last Tuesday, and I really forgot all about it. We were to have played a duet together—three duets, I believe. I don't know what she will say to me. I am far too frightened to call."

"Oh, I will make your peace with my aunt. She is quite devoted to you. And I don't think it really matters about your not being there. The audience probably thought it was a duet. When Aunt Agatha sits down to the piano she makes quite enough noise for two people."

"That is very horrid to her, and not very nice to me," answered Dorian, laughing.

Lord Henry looked at him. Yes, he was certainly wonderfully handsome, with his finely-curved scarlet lips, his frank blue eyes, his crisp gold hair. There was something in his face that made one trust him at once. All the candour of youth was there, as well as all youth's passionate purity. One felt that he had kept himself unspotted from the world. No wonder Basil Hallward worshipped him.

"You are too charming to go in for philanthropy, Mr. Gray—far too charming." And Lord Henry flung himself down on the divan, and opened his cigarette-case.

The painter had been busy mixing his colours and getting his brushes ready. He was looking worried, and when he heard Lord Henry's last remark he glanced at him, hesitated for a moment, and then said, "Harry, I want to finish this picture to-day. Would you think it awfully rude of me if I asked you to go away?"

Lord Henry smiled, and looked at Dorian Gray. "Am I to go, Mr. Gray?" he asked.

"Oh, please don't, Lord Henry. I see that Basil is in one of his sulky moods; and I can't bear him when he sulks. Besides, I want you to tell me why I should not go in for philanthropy."

"I don't know that I shall tell you that, Mr. Gray. It is so tedious a subject that one would have to talk seriously about it. But I certainly shall not run away, now that you have asked me to stop. You don't really mind, Basil, do you? You have often told me that you liked your sitters to have some one to chat to."

Hallward bit his lip. "If Dorian wishes it, of course you must stay. Dorian's whims are laws to everybody, except himself."

Lord Henry took up his hat and gloves. "You are very pressing, Basil, but I am afraid I must go. I have promised to meet a man at the Orleans. Good-bye, Mr. Gray. Come and see me some afternoon in Curzon Street. I am nearly always at home at five o'clock. Write to me when you are coming. I should be sorry to miss you."

"Basil," cried Dorian Gray, "if Lord Henry Wotton goes I shall go too. You never open your lips while you are painting, and it is horribly dull standing on a platform and trying to look pleasant. Ask him to stay. I insist upon it."

"Stay, Harry, to oblige Dorian, and to oblige me," said Hallward, gazing intently at his picture. "It is quite true, I never talk when I am working, and never listen either, and it must be dreadfully tedious for my unfortunate sitters. I beg you to stay."

"But what about my man at the Orleans?"

The painter laughed. "I don't think there will be any difficulty about that. Sit down again, Harry. And now, Dorian, get up on the platform, and don't move about too much, or pay any attention to what Lord Henry says. He has a very bad influence over all his friends, with the single exception of myself."

Dorian Gray stepped up on the dais, with the air of a young Greek martyr, and made a little *moue* of discontent to Lord Henry, to whom he had rather taken a fancy. He was so unlike Basil. They made a delightful contrast. And he had such a beautiful voice. After a few moments he said to him, "Have you really a very bad influence, Lord Henry? As bad as Basil says?"

"There is no such thing as a good influence, Mr. Gray. All influence is immoral—immoral from the scientific point of view."

"Why?"

"Because to influence a person is to give him one's own soul. He does not think his natural thoughts, or burn with his natural passions. His virtues are not real to him. His sins, if there are such things as sins, are borrowed. He becomes an echo of some one else's music, an actor of a part that has not been written for him. The aim of life is self-development. To realize one's nature perfectly—that is what each of us is here for. People are afraid of themselves, nowadays. They have forgotten the highest of all duties, the duty that one owes to one's self. Of course they are charitable. They feed the hungry, and clothe the beggar. But their own souls starve, and are naked. Courage has gone out of our race. Perhaps we never really had it. The terror of society, which is the basis of morals, the terror of God, which is the secret of religion—these are the two things that govern us. And yet——"

"Just turn your head a little more to the right, Dorian, like a good boy," said the painter, deep in his work, and conscious only that a look had come into the lad's face that he had never seen there before.

"And yet," continued Lord Henry, in his low, musical voice, and with that graceful wave of the hand that was always so characteristic of him, and that he had even in his Eton days, "I believe that if one man were to live out his life fully and completely, were to give form to every feeling, expression to every thought, reality to every dream—I believe that the world would gain such a fresh impulse of joy that we would forget all the maladies of mediaevalism, and return to the Hellenic ideal—to something finer, richer, than the Hellenic ideal, it may be. But the bravest man amongst us is afraid of himself. The mutilation of the savage has its tragic survival in the self-denial that mars our lives. We are punished for our refusals. Every impulse that we strive to strangle broods in the mind, and poisons us. The body sins once, and has done with its sin, for action is a mode of purification. Nothing remains then but the recollection of a pleasure, or the luxury of a regret. The only way to get rid of a temptation is to yield to it. Resist it, and your soul grows sick with longing for the things it has forbidden to itself, with desire for what its monstrous laws have made monstrous and unlawful. It has been said that the great events of the world take place in the brain. It is in the brain, and the brain only, that the great sins of the world take place also. You, Mr. Gray, you yourself, with your rose-red youth and your rose-white boyhood, you have had passions that have made you afraid, thoughts that have filled you with terror, day-dreams and sleeping dreams whose mere memory might stain your cheek with shame—"

"Stop!" faltered Dorian Gray, "stop! you bewilder me. I don't know what to say. There is some answer to you, but I cannot find it. Don't speak. Let me think. Or, rather, let me try not to think."

For nearly ten minutes he stood there, motionless, with parted lips, and eyes strangely bright. He was dimly conscious that entirely fresh influences were at work within him. Yet they seemed to him to have come really from himself. The few words that Basil's friend had said to him—words spoken by chance, no doubt, and with wilful paradox in them—had touched some secret chord that had never been touched before, but that he felt was now vibrating and throbbing to curious pulses.

Music had stirred him like that. Music had troubled him many times. But music was not articulate. It was not a new world, but rather another chaos, that it created in us. Words! Mere words! How terrible they were! How clear, and vivid, and cruel. One could not escape from them. And yet what a subtle magic there was in them. They seemed to be able to give a plastic form to formless things, and to have a music of their own as sweet as that of viol or of lute. Mere words! Was there anything so real as words?

Yes, there had been things in his boyhood that he had not understood. He understood them now. Life suddenly had become fiery-coloured to him. It seemed to him that he had been walking in fire. Why had he not known it?

With his subtle smile, Lord Henry watched him. He knew the precise psychological moment when to say nothing. He felt intensely interested. He was amazed at the sudden impression that his words had produced, and, remembering a book that he had read when he was sixteen, a book which had revealed to him much that he had not known before, he wondered whether Dorian Gray was passing through a similar experience. He had merely shot an arrow into the air. Had it hit the mark? How fascinating the lad was!

Hallward painted away with that marvellous bold touch of his, that had the true refinement and perfect delicacy that in art, at any rate, comes only from strength. He was unconscious of the silence.

"Basil, I am tired of standing," cried Dorian Gray, suddenly. "I must go out and sit in the garden. The air is stifling here."

"My dear fellow, I am so sorry. When I am painting, I can't think of anything else. But you never sat better. You were perfectly still. And I have caught the effect I wanted—the half-parted lips and the bright look in the eyes. I don't know what Harry has been saying to you, but he has certainly made you have the most wonderful expression. I suppose he has been paying you compliments. You mustn't believe a word that he says."

"He has certainly not been paying me compliments. Perhaps that is the reason that I don't believe anything he has told me."

"You know you believe it all," said Lord Henry, looking at him with his dreamy, languorous eyes. "I will go out to the garden with you. It is horribly hot in the studio. Basil, let us have something iced to drink, something with strawberries in it."

"Certainly, Harry. Just touch the bell, and when Parker comes I will tell him what you want. I have got to work up this background, so I will join you later on. Don't keep Dorian too long. I have never been in better form for painting than I am to-day. This is going to be my masterpiece. It is my masterpiece as it stands."

Lord Henry went out to the garden, and found Dorian Gray burying his face in the great cool lilac-blossoms, feverishly drinking in their perfume as if it had been wine. He came close to him, and put his hand upon his shoulder. "You are quite right to do that," he murmured. "Nothing can cure the soul but the senses, just as nothing can cure the senses but the soul."

The lad started and drew back. He was bare-headed, and the leaves had tossed his rebellious curls and tangled all their gilded threads. There was a look of fear in his eyes, such as people have when they are suddenly awakened. His finely-chiselled nostrils quivered, and some hidden nerve shook the scarlet of his lips and left them trembling.

"Yes," continued Lord Henry, "that is one of the great secrets of life—to cure the soul by means of the senses, and the senses by means of the soul. You are a wonderful creation. You know more than you think you know, just as you know less than you want to know."

Dorian Gray frowned and turned his head away. He could not help liking the tall, graceful young man who was standing by him. His romantic olive-coloured face and worn expression interested him. There was something in his low, languid voice that was absolutely fascinating. His cool, white, flower-like hands, even, had a curious charm. They moved, as he spoke, like music, and seemed to have a language of their own. But he felt afraid of him, and ashamed of being afraid. Why had it been left for a stranger to reveal him to himself? He had known Basil Hallward for months, but the friendship between them had never altered him. Suddenly there had come some one across his life who seemed to have disclosed to him life's mystery. And, yet, what was there to be afraid of? He was not a schoolboy or a girl. It was absurd to be frightened.

"Let us go and sit in the shade," said Lord Henry. "Parker has brought out the drinks, and if you stay any longer in this glare you will be quite spoiled, and Basil will never paint you again. You really must not allow yourself to become sunburnt. It would be unbecoming."

"What can it matter?" cried Dorian Gray, laughing, as he sat down on the seat at the end of the garden.

"It should matter everything to you, Mr. Gray."

"Why?"

"Because you have the most marvellous youth, and youth is the one thing worth having."

"I don't feel that, Lord Henry."

"No, you don't feel it now. Some day, when you are old and wrinkled and ugly, when thought has seared your forehead with its lines, and passion branded your lips with its hideous fires, you will feel it, you will feel it terribly. Now, wherever you go, you charm the world. Will it always be so? . . . You have a wonderfully beautiful face, Mr. Gray. Don't frown. You have. And Beauty is a form of Genius—is higher, indeed, than Genius, as it needs no explanation. It is of the great facts of the world, like sunlight, or spring-time, or the reflection in dark waters of that silver shell we call the moon. It cannot be questioned. It has its divine right of sovereignty. It makes princes of those who have it. You smile? Ah! when you have lost it you won't smile. . . . People say sometimes that Beauty is only superficial. That may be so. But at least it is not so superficial as Thought is. To me, Beauty is the wonder of wonders. It is only shallow people who do not judge by appearances. The true mystery of the world is the visible, not the invisible. . . . Yes, Mr. Gray, the gods have been good to you. But what the gods give they quickly take away. You have only a few years in which to live really, perfectly, and fully. When your youth goes, your beauty will go with it, and then you will suddenly discover that there are no triumphs left for you, or have to content yourself with those mean triumphs that the memory of your past will make more bitter than defeats. Every month as it wanes brings you nearer to something dreadful. Time is jealous of you, and wars against your lilies and your roses. You will become sallow, and hollow-cheeked, and dull-eyed. You will suffer horribly. . . . Ah! realize your youth while you have it. Don't squander the gold of your days, listening to the tedious, trying to improve the hopeless failure, or giving away your life to the ignorant, the common, and the vulgar. These are the sickly aims, the false ideals, of our age. Live! Live the wonderful life that is in you! Let nothing be lost upon you. Be always searching for new sensations. Be afraid of nothing. . . . A new Hedonism—that is what our century wants. You might be its visible symbol. With your personality there is nothing you could not do. The world belongs to you for a season. . . . The moment I met you I saw that you were quite unconscious of what you really are, of what you really might be. There was so much in you that charmed me that I felt I must tell you something about yourself. I thought how tragic it would be if you were wasted. For there is such a little time that your youth will last—such a little time. The common hill-flowers wither, but they blossom again. The laburnum will be as yellow next June as it is now. In a month there will be purple stars on the clematis, and year after year the green night of its leaves will hold its purple stars. But we never get back our youth. The pulse of joy that beats in us at twenty, becomes sluggish. Our limbs fail, our senses rot. We degenerate into hideous puppets, haunted by the memory of the passions of which we were too much afraid, and the exquisite temptations that we had not the courage to yield to. Youth! Youth! There is absolutely nothing in the world but youth!"

Dorian Gray listened, open-eyed and wondering. The spray of lilac fell from his hand upon the gravel. A furry bee came and buzzed round it for a moment. Then it began to scramble all over the oval stellated globe of its tiny blossoms. He watched it with that strange interest in trivial things that we try to develop when things of high import make us afraid, or when we are stirred by some new emotion for which we cannot find expression, or when some thought that terrifies us lays sudden siege to the brain and calls on us to yield. After a time the bee flew away. He saw it creeping into the stained trumpet of a Tyrian convolvulus. The flower seemed to quiver, and then swayed gently to and fro.

Suddenly the painter appeared at the door of the studio, and made staccato signs for them to come in. They turned to each other, and smiled.

"I am waiting," he cried. "Do come in. The light is quite perfect, and you can bring your drinks."

They rose up, and sauntered down the walk together. Two green-and-white butterflies fluttered past them, and in the pear-tree at the corner of the garden a thrush began to sing.

"You are glad you have met me, Mr. Gray," said Lord Henry, looking at him.

"Yes, I am glad now. I wonder shall I always be glad?"

"Always! That is a dreadful word. It makes me shudder when I hear it. Women are so fond of using it. They spoil every romance by trying to make it last forever. It is a meaningless word, too. The only difference between a caprice and a life-long passion is that the caprice lasts a little longer."

As they entered the studio, Dorian Gray put his hand upon Lord Henry's arm. "In that case, let our friendship be a caprice," he murmured, flushing at his own boldness, then stepped up on the platform and resumed his pose.

Lord Henry flung himself into a large wicker arm-chair and watched him. The sweep and dash of the brush on the canvas made the only sound that broke the stillness, except when, now and then, Hallward stepped back to look at his work from a distance. In the slanting beams that streamed through the open doorway the dust danced and was golden. The heavy scent of the roses seemed to brood over everything.

After about a quarter of an hour Hallward stopped painting, looked for a long time at Dorian Gray, and then for a long time at the picture, biting the end of one of his huge brushes, and frowning. "It is quite finished," he cried at last, and stooping down he wrote his name in long vermilion letters on the left-hand corner of the canvas.

Lord Henry came over and examined the picture. It was certainly a wonderful work of art, and a wonderful likeness as well.

"My dear fellow, I congratulate you most warmly," he said. "It is the finest portrait of modern times. Mr. Gray, come over and look at yourself."

The lad started, as if awakened from some dream. "Is it really finished?" he murmured, stepping down from the platform.

"Quite finished," said the painter. "And you have sat splendidly to-day. I am awfully obliged to you."

"That is entirely due to me," broke in Lord Henry. "Isn't it, Mr. Gray?"

Dorian made no answer, but passed listlessly in front of his picture and turned towards it. When he saw it he drew back, and his cheeks flushed for a moment with pleasure. A look of joy came into his eyes, as if he had recognized himself for the first time. He stood there motionless and in wonder, dimly conscious that Hallward was speaking to him, but not catching the meaning of his words. The sense of his own beauty came on him like a revelation. He had never felt it before. Basil Hallward's compliments had seemed to him to be merely the charming exaggerations of friendship. He had listened to them, laughed at them, forgotten them. They had not influenced his nature. Then had come Lord Henry Wotton with his strange panegyric on youth, his terrible warning of its brevity. That had stirred him at the time, and now, as he stood gazing at the shadow of his own loveliness, the full reality of the description flashed across him. Yes, there would be a day when his face would be wrinkled and wizened, his eyes dim and colourless, the grace of his figure broken and deformed. The scarlet would pass away from his lips, and the gold steal from his hair. The life that was to make his soul would mar his body. He would become dreadful, hideous, and uncouth.

As he thought of it, a sharp pang of pain struck through him like a knife, and made each delicate fibre of his nature quiver. His eyes deepened into amethyst, and across them came a mist of tears. He felt as if a hand of ice had been laid upon his heart.

"Don't you like it?" cried Hallward at last, stung a little by the lad's silence, not understanding what it meant.

"Of course he likes it," said Lord Henry. "Who wouldn't like it? It is one of the greatest things in modern art. I will give you anything you like to ask for it. I must have it."

"It is not my property, Harry."

"Whose property is it?"

"Dorian's, of course," answered the painter.

"He is a very lucky fellow."

"How sad it is!" murmured Dorian Gray, with his eyes still fixed upon his own portrait. "How sad it is! I shall grow old, and horrible, and dreadful. But this picture will remain always young. It will never be older than this particular day of June. . . . If it were only the other way! If it were I who was to be always young, and the picture that was to grow old! For that—for that—I would give everything! Yes, there is nothing in the whole world I would not give! I would give my soul for that!"

"You would hardly care for such an arrangement, Basil," cried Lord Henry, laughing. "It would be rather hard lines on your work."

"I should object very strongly, Harry," said Hallward.

Dorian Gray turned and looked at him. "I believe you would, Basil. You like your art better than your friends. I am no more to you than a green bronze figure. Hardly as much, I dare say."

The painter stared in amazement. It was so unlike Dorian to speak like that. What had happened? He seemed quite angry. His face was flushed and his cheeks burning.

"Yes," he continued, "I am less to you than your ivory Hermes or your silver Faun. You will like them always. How long will you like me? Till I have my first wrinkle, I suppose. I know, now, that when one loses one's good looks, whatever they may be, one loses everything. Your picture has taught me that. Lord Henry Wotton is perfectly right. Youth is the only thing worth having. When I find that I am growing old, I shall kill myself."

Hallward turned pale, and caught his hand. "Dorian! Dorian!" he cried, "don't talk like that. I have never had such a friend as you, and I shall never have such another. You are not jealous of material things, are you?—you who are finer than any of them!"

"I am jealous of everything whose beauty does not die. I am jealous of the portrait you have painted of me. Why should it keep what I must lose? Every moment that passes takes something from me, and gives something to it. Oh, if it were only the other way! If the picture could change, and I could be always what I am now! Why did you paint it? It will mock me some day—mock me horribly!" The hot tears welled into his eyes; he tore his hand away, and, flinging himself on the divan, he buried his face in the cushions, as though he was praying.

"This is your doing, Harry," said the painter, bitterly.

Lord Henry shrugged his shoulders. "It is the real Dorian Gray—that is all."

"It is not."

"If it is not, what have I to do with it?"

"You should have gone away when I asked you," he muttered.

"I stayed when you asked me," was Lord Henry's answer.

"Harry, I can't quarrel with my two best friends at once, but between you both you have made me hate the finest piece of work I have ever done, and I will destroy it. What is it but canvas and colour? I will not let it come across our three lives and mar them."

Dorian Gray lifted his golden head from the pillow, and with pallid face and tear-stained eyes looked at him, as he walked over to the deal painting-table that was set beneath the high curtained window. What was he doing there? His fingers were straying about among the litter of tin tubes and dry brushes, seeking for something. Yes, it was for the long palette-knife, with its thin blade of lithe steel. He had found it at last. He was going to rip up the canvas.

With a stifled sob the lad leaped from the couch, and, rushing over to Hallward, tore the knife out of his hand, and flung it to the end of the studio. "Don't, Basil, don't!" he cried. "It would be murder!"

"I am glad you appreciate my work at last, Dorian," said the painter, coldly, when he had recovered from his surprise. "I never thought you would."

"Appreciate it? I am in love with it, Basil. It is part of myself. I feel that."

"Well, as soon as you are dry, you shall be varnished, and framed, and sent home. Then you can do what you like with yourself." And he walked across the room and rang the bell for tea. "You will have tea, of course, Dorian? And so will you, Harry? Or do you object to such simple pleasures?"

"I adore simple pleasures," said Lord Henry. "They are the last refuge of the complex. But I don't like scenes, except on the stage. What absurd fellows you are, both of you! I wonder who it was defined man as a rational animal. It was the most premature definition ever given. Man is many things, but he is not rational. I am glad he is not, after all: though I wish you chaps would not squabble over the picture. You had much better let me have it, Basil. This silly boy doesn't really want it, and I really do."

"If you let any one have it but me, Basil, I shall never forgive you!" cried Dorian Gray; "and I don't allow people to call me a silly boy."

"You know the picture is yours, Dorian. I gave it to you before it existed."

"And you know you have been a little silly, Mr. Gray, and that you don't really object to being reminded that you are extremely young."

"I should have objected very strongly this morning, Lord Henry."

"Ah! this morning! You have lived since then."

There came a knock at the door, and the butler entered with a laden tea-tray and set it down upon a small Japanese table. There was a rattle of cups and saucers and the hissing of a fluted Georgian urn. Two globe-shaped china dishes were brought in by a page. Dorian Gray went over and poured out the tea. The two men sauntered languidly to the table, and examined what was under the covers.

"Let us go to the theatre to-night," said Lord Henry. "There is sure to be something on, somewhere. I have promised to dine at White's, but it is only with an old friend, so I can send him a wire to say that I am ill, or that I am prevented from coming in consequence of a subsequent engagement. I think that would be a rather nice excuse: it would have all the surprise of candour."

"It is such a bore putting on one's dress-clothes," muttered Hallward. "And, when one has them on, they are so horrid."

"Yes," answered Lord Henry, dreamily, "the costume of the nineteenth century is detestable. It is so sombre, so depressing. Sin is the only real colour-element left in modern life."

"You really must not say things like that before Dorian, Harry."

"Before which Dorian? The one who is pouring out tea for us, or the one in the picture?"

"Before either."

"I should like to come to the theatre with you, Lord Henry," said the lad.

"Then you shall come; and you will come too, Basil, won't you?"

"I can't really. I would sooner not. I have a lot of work to do."

"Well, then, you and I will go, Mr. Gray."

"I should like that awfully."

The painter bit his lip and walked over, cup in hand, to the picture. "I shall stay with the real Dorian," he said, sadly.

"Is it the real Dorian?" cried the original of the portrait, strolling across to him. "Am I really like that?"

"Yes; you are just like that."

"How wonderful, Basil!"

"At least you are like it in appearance. But it will never alter," sighed Hallward. "That is something."

"What a fuss people make about fidelity!" exclaimed Lord Henry. "Why, even in love it is purely a question of physiology. It has nothing to do with our own will. Young men want to be faithful, and are not; old men want to be faithless, and cannot: that is all one can say."

"Don't go to the theatre to-night, Dorian," said Hallward. "Stop and dine with me."

"I can't, Basil."

"Why?"

"Because I have promised Lord Henry Wotton to go with him."

"He won't like you any better for keeping your promises. He always breaks his own. I beg you not to go."

Dorian Gray laughed and shook his head.

"I entreat you."

The lad hesitated, and looked over at Lord Henry, who was watching them from the tea-table with an amused smile.

"I must go, Basil," he answered.

"Very well," said Hallward; and he went over and laid down his cup on the tray. "It is rather late, and, as you have to dress, you had better lose no time. Good-bye, Harry. Good-bye, Dorian. Come and see me soon. Come to-morrow."

"Certainly."

"You won't forget?"

"No, of course not," cried Dorian.

"And . . . Harry!"

"Yes, Basil?"

"Remember what I asked you, when we were in the garden this morning?"

"I have forgotten it."

"I trust you."

"I wish I could trust myself," said Lord Henry, laughing. "Come, Mr. Gray, my hansom is outside, and I can drop you at your own place. Good-bye, Basil. It has been a most interesting afternoon."

As the door closed behind them, the painter flung himself down on a sofa, and a look of pain came into his face.

CHAPTER III

At half-past twelve next day Lord Henry Wotton strolled from Curzon Street over to the Albany to call on his uncle, Lord Fermor, a genial if somewhat rough-mannered old bachelor, whom the outside world called selfish because it derived no particular benefit from him, but who was considered generous by Society as he fed the people who amused him. His father had been our ambassador at Madrid when Isabella was young, and Prim unthought of, but had retired from the Diplomatic Service in a capricious moment of annoyance on not being offered the Embassy at Paris, a post to which he considered that he was fully entitled by reason of his birth, his indolence, the good English of his despatches, and his inordinate passion for pleasure. The son, who had been his father's secretary, had resigned along with his chief, somewhat foolishly as was thought at the time, and on succeeding some months later to the title, had set himself to the serious study of the great aristocratic art of doing absolutely nothing. He had two large town houses, but preferred to live in chambers as it was less trouble, and took most of his meals at his club. He paid some attention to the management of his collieries in the Midland counties, excusing himself for this taint of industry on the ground that the one advantage of having coal was that it enabled a gentleman to afford the decency of burning wood on his own hearth. In politics he was a Tory, except when the Tories were in office, during which period he roundly abused them for being a pack of Radicals. He was a hero to his valet, who bullied him, and a terror to most of his relations, whom he bullied in turn. Only England could have produced him, and he always said that the country was going to the dogs. His principles were out of date, but there was a good deal to be said for his prejudices.

When Lord Henry entered the room, he found his uncle sitting in a rough shooting coat, smoking a cheroot and grumbling over *The Times*. "Well, Harry," said the old gentleman, "what brings you out so early? I thought you dandies never got up until two, and were not visible until five."

"Pure family affection, I assure you, Uncle George. I want to get something out of you."

"Money, I suppose," said Lord Fermor, making a wry face. "Well, sit down and tell me all about it. Young people, nowadays, imagine that money is everything."

"Yes," murmured Lord Henry, settling his buttonhole in his coat; "and when they grow older they know it. But I don't want money. It is only people who pay their bills who want that, Uncle George, and I never pay mine. Credit is the capital of a younger son, and one lives charmingly upon it. Besides, I always deal with Dartmoor's tradesmen, and consequently they never bother me. What I want is information; not useful information, of course; useless information."

"Well, I can tell you anything that is in an English Blue-book, Harry, although those fellows nowadays write a lot of nonsense. When I was in the Diplomatic, things were much better. But I hear they let them in now by examination. What can you expect? Examinations, sir, are pure humbug from beginning to end. If a man is a gentleman, he knows quite enough, and if he is not a gentleman, whatever he knows is bad for him."

"Mr. Dorian Gray does not belong to Blue-books, Uncle George," said Lord Henry, languidly.

"Mr. Dorian Gray? Who is he?" asked Lord Fermor, knitting his bushy white eyebrows.

"That is what I have come to learn, Uncle George. Or rather, I know who he is. He is the last Lord Kelso's grandson. His mother was a Devereux, Lady Margaret Devereux. I want you to tell me about his mother. What was she like? Whom did she marry? You have known nearly everybody in your time, so you might have known her. I am very much interested in Mr. Gray at present. I have only just met him."

"Kelso's grandson!" echoed the old gentleman. "Kelso's grandson! . . . Of course. . . . I knew his mother intimately. I believe I was at her christening. She was an extraordinarily beautiful girl, Margaret Devereux, and made all the men frantic by running away with a penniless young fellow, a mere nobody, sir, a subaltern in a foot regiment, or something of that kind. Certainly. I remember the whole thing as if it happened yesterday. The poor chap was killed in a duel at Spa a few months after the marriage. There was an ugly story about it. They said Kelso got some rascally adventurer, some Belgian brute, to insult his son-in-law in public, paid him, sir, to do it, paid him, and that the fellow spitted his man as if he had been a pigeon. The thing was hushed up, but, egad, Kelso ate his chop alone at the club for some time afterwards. He brought his daughter back with him, I was told, and she never spoke to him again. Oh, yes; it was a bad business. The girl died too, died within a year. So she left a son, did she? I had forgotten that. What sort of a boy is he? If he is like his mother he must be a good-looking chap."

"He is very good-looking," assented Lord Henry.

"I hope he will fall into proper hands," continued the old man. "He should have a pot of money waiting for him if Kelso did the right thing by him. His mother had money too. All the Selby property came to her, through her grandfather. Her grandfather hated Kelso, thought him a mean dog. He was, too. Came to Madrid once when I was there. Egad, I was ashamed of him. The Queen used to ask me about the English noble who was always quarrelling with the cabmen about their fares. They made quite a story of it. I didn't dare show my face at Court for a month. I hope he treated his grandson better than he did the jarvies."

"I don't know," answered Lord Henry. "I fancy that the boy will be well off. He is not of age yet. He has Selby, I know. He told me so. And . . . his mother was very beautiful?"

"Margaret Devereux was one of the loveliest creatures I ever saw, Harry. What on earth induced her to behave as she did, I never could understand. She could have married anybody she chose. Carlington was mad after her. She was romantic though. All the women of that family were. The men were a poor lot, but, egad! the women were wonderful. Carlington went on his knees to her. Told me so himself. She laughed at him, and there wasn't a girl in London at the time who wasn't after him. And by the way, Harry, talking about silly marriages, what is this humbug your father tells me about Dartmoor wanting to marry an American? Ain't English girls good enough for him?"

"It is rather fashionable to marry Americans just now, Uncle George."

"I'll back English women against the world, Harry," said Lord Fermor, striking the table with his fist.

"The betting is on the Americans."

"They don't last, I am told," muttered his uncle.

"A long engagement exhausts them, but they are capital at a steeplechase. They take things flying. I don't think Dartmoor has a chance."

"Who are her people?" grumbled the old gentleman. "Has she got any?"

Lord Henry shook his head. "American girls are as clever at concealing their parents, as English women are at concealing their past," he said, rising to go.

"They are pork-packers, I suppose?"

"I hope so, Uncle George, for Dartmoor's sake. I am told that pork-packing is the most lucrative profession in America, after politics."

"Is she pretty?"

"She behaves as if she was beautiful. Most American women do. It is the secret of their charm."

"Why can't these American women stay in their own country? They are always telling us that it is the Paradise for women."

"It is. That is the reason why, like Eve, they are so excessively anxious to get out of it," said Lord Henry. "Good-bye, Uncle George. I shall be late for lunch, if I stop any longer. Thanks for giving me the information I wanted. I always like to know everything about my new friends, and nothing about my old ones."

"Where are you lunching, Harry?"

"At Aunt Agatha's. I have asked myself and Mr. Gray. He is her latest *protege*."

"Humph! Tell your Aunt Agatha, Harry, not to bother me with any more of her charity appeals. I am sick of them. Why, the good woman thinks that I have nothing to do but write cheques for her silly fads."

"All right, Uncle George, I'll tell her, but it won't have any effect. Philanthropic people lose all sense of humanity. It is their distinguishing characteristic."

The old gentleman growled approvingly, and rang the bell for his servant. Lord Henry passed up the low arcade into Burlington Street, and turned his steps in the direction of Berkeley Square.

So that was the story of Dorian Gray's parentage. Crudely as it had been told to him, it had yet stirred him by its suggestion of a strange, almost modern romance. A beautiful woman risking everything for a mad passion. A few wild weeks of happiness cut short by a hideous, treacherous crime. Months of voiceless agony, and then a child born in pain. The mother snatched away by death, the boy left to solitude and the tyranny of an old and loveless man. Yes; it was an interesting background. It posed the lad, made him more perfect as it were. Behind every exquisite thing that existed, there was something tragic. Worlds had to be in travail, that the meanest flower might blow. . . . And how charming he had been at dinner the night before, as with startled eyes and lips parted in frightened pleasure he had sat opposite to him at the club, the red candleshades staining to a richer rose the wakening wonder of his face. Talking to him was like playing upon an exquisite violin. He answered to every touch and thrill of the bow. . . . There was something terribly enthralling in the exercise of influence. No other activity was like it. To project one's soul into some gracious form, and let it tarry there for a moment; to hear one's own intellectual views echoed back to one with all the added music of passion and youth; to convey one's temperament into another as though it were a subtle fluid or a strange perfume: there was a real joy in that—perhaps the most satisfying joy left to us in an age so limited and vulgar as our own, an age grossly carnal in its pleasures, and grossly common in its aims. . . . He was a marvellous type, too, this lad, whom by so curious a chance he had met in Basil's studio, or could be fashioned into a marvellous type, at any rate. Grace was his, and the white purity of boyhood, and beauty such as old Greek marbles have kept for us. There was nothing that one could not do with him. He could be made a Titan or a toy. What a pity it was that such beauty was destined to fade! . . . And Basil? From a psychological point of view, how interesting he was! The new manner in art, the fresh mode of looking at life, suggested so strangely by the merely visible presence of one who was unconscious of it all; the silent spirit that dwelt in dim woodland, and walked unseen in open field, suddenly showing herself, Dryad-like and not afraid, because in his soul who sought for her there had been awakened that wonderful vision to which alone are wonderful things revealed; the mere shapes and patterns of things becoming, as it were, refined, and gaining a kind of symbolical value, as though they were themselves patterns of some other and more perfect form whose shadow they made real: how strange it all was! He remembered something like it in history. Was it not Plato, that artist in thought, who had first analyzed it? Was it not Buonarotti who had carved it in the coloured marbles of a sonnet-sequence? But in our own country it was strange. . . . Yes; he would try to be to Dorian Gray what, without knowing it, the lad was to the painter who had fashioned the wonderful portrait. He would seek to dominate him—had already, indeed, half done so. He would make that wonderful spirit his own. There was something fascinating in this son of Love and Death.

Suddenly he stopped, and glanced up at the houses. He found that he had passed his aunt's some distance, and smiling to himself, turned back. When he entered the somewhat sombre hall the butler told him that they had gone in to lunch. He gave one of the footmen his hat and stick and passed into the dining-room.

"Late as usual, Harry," cried his aunt, shaking her head at him.

He invented a facile excuse, and having taken the vacant seat next to her, looked round to see who was there. Dorian bowed to him shyly from the end of the table, a flush of pleasure stealing into his cheek. Opposite was the Duchess of Harley, a lady of admirable good-nature and good temper, much liked by every one who knew her, and of those ample architectural proportions that in women who are not Duchesses are described by contemporary historians as stoutness. Next to her sat, on her right, Sir Thomas Burdon, a Radical member of Parliament, who followed his leader in public life and in private life followed the best cooks, dining with the Tories, and thinking with the Liberals, in accordance with a wise and well-known rule. The post on her left was occupied by Mr. Erskine of Treadley, an old gentleman of considerable charm and culture, who had fallen, however, into bad habits of silence, having, as he explained once to Lady Agatha, said everything that he had to say before he was thirty. His own neighbour was Mrs. Vandeleur, one of his aunt's oldest friends, a perfect saint amongst women, but so dreadfully dowdy that she reminded one of a badly bound hymn book. Fortunately for him she had on the other side Lord Faudel, a most intelligent middle-aged mediocrity, as bad as a Ministerial statement in the House of Commons, with whom she was conversing in that intensely earnest manner which is the one unpardonable error, as he remarked once himself, that all really good people fall into, and from which none of them ever quite escape.

"We are talking about poor Dartmoor, Lord Henry," cried the Duchess, nodding pleasantly to him across the table. "Do you think he will really marry this fascinating young person?"

"I believe she has made up her mind to propose to him, Duchess."

"How dreadful!" exclaimed Lady Agatha. "Really, some one should interfere."

"I am told, on excellent authority, that her father keeps an American dry-goods store," said Sir Thomas Burdon, looking supercilious.

"My uncle has already suggested pork-packing, Sir Thomas."

"Dry-goods! What are American dry-goods?" asked the Duchess, raising her large hands in wonder, and accentuating the verb.

"American novels," answered Lord Henry, helping himself to some quail.

The Duchess looked puzzled.

"Don't mind him, my dear," whispered Lady Agatha. "He never means anything that he says."

"When America was discovered," said the Radical member, and he began to give some wearisome facts. Like all people who try to exhaust a subject, he exhausted his listeners. The Duchess sighed, and exercised her privilege of interruption. "I wish to goodness it never had been discovered at all!" she exclaimed. "Really, our girls have no chance nowadays. It is most unfair."

"Perhaps, after all, America never has been discovered," said Mr. Erskine; "I myself would say that it had merely been detected."

"Oh! but I have seen specimens of the inhabitants," answered the Duchess, vaguely. "I must confess that most of them are extremely pretty. And they dress well, too. They get all their dresses in Paris. I wish I could afford to do the same."

"They say that when good Americans die they go to Paris," chuckled Sir Thomas, who had a large wardrobe of Humour's cast-off clothes.

"Really! And where do bad Americans go when they die?" inquired the Duchess.

"They go to America," murmured Lord Henry.

Sir Thomas frowned. "I am afraid that your nephew is prejudiced against that great country," he said to Lady Agatha. "I have travelled all over it, in cars provided by the directors, who, in such matters, are extremely civil. I assure you that it is an education to visit it."

"But must we really see Chicago in order to be educated?" asked Mr. Erskine, plaintively. "I don't feel up to the journey."

Sir Thomas waved his hand. "Mr. Erskine of Treadley has the world on his shelves. We practical men like to see things, not to read about them. The Americans are an extremely interesting people. They are absolutely reasonable. I think that is their distinguishing characteristic. Yes, Mr. Erskine, an absolutely reasonable people. I assure you there is no nonsense about the Americans."

"How dreadful!" cried Lord Henry. "I can stand brute force, but brute reason is quite unbearable. There is something unfair about its use. It is hitting below the intellect."

"I do not understand you," said Sir Thomas, growing rather red.

"I do, Lord Henry," murmured Mr. Erskine, with a smile.

"Paradoxes are all very well in their way . . ." rejoined the Baronet.

"Was that a paradox?" asked Mr. Erskine. "I did not think so. Perhaps it was. Well, the way of paradoxes is the way of truth. To test Reality we must see it on the tight-rope. When the Verities become acrobats we can judge them."

"Dear me!" said Lady Agatha, "how you men argue! I am sure I never can make out what you are talking about. Oh! Harry, I am quite vexed with you. Why do you try to persuade our nice Mr. Dorian Gray to give up the East End? I assure you he would be quite invaluable. They would love his playing."

"I want him to play to me," cried Lord Henry, smiling, and he looked down the table and caught a bright answering glance.

"But they are so unhappy in Whitechapel," continued Lady Agatha.

"I can sympathize with everything, except suffering," said Lord Henry, shrugging his shoulders. "I cannot sympathize with that. It is too ugly, too horrible, too distressing. There is something terribly morbid in the modern sympathy with pain. One should sympathize with the colour, the beauty, the joy of life. The less said about life's sores the better."

"Still, the East End is a very important problem," remarked Sir Thomas, with a grave shake of the head.

"Quite so," answered the young lord. "It is the problem of slavery, and we try to solve it by amusing the slaves."

The politician looked at him keenly. "What change do you propose, then?" he asked.

Lord Henry laughed. "I don't desire to change anything in England except the weather," he answered. "I am quite content with philosophic contemplation. But, as the nineteenth century has gone bankrupt through an over-expenditure of sympathy, I would suggest that we should appeal to Science to put us straight. The advantage of the emotions is that they lead us astray, and the advantage of Science is that it is not emotional."

"But we have such grave responsibilties," ventured Mrs. Vandeleur, timidly.

"Terribly grave," echoed Lady Agatha.

Lord Henry looked over at Mr. Erskine. "Humanity takes itself too seriously. It is the world's original sin. If the caveman had known how to laugh, History would have been different."

"You are really very comforting," warbled the Duchess. "I have always felt rather guilty when I came to see your dear aunt, for I take no interest at all in the East End. For the future I shall be able to look her in the face without a blush."

"A blush is very becoming, Duchess," remarked Lord Henry.

"Only when one is young," she answered. "When an old woman like myself blushes, it is a very bad sign. Ah! Lord Henry, I wish you would tell me how to become young again."

He thought for a moment. "Can you remember any great error that you committed in your early days, Duchess?" he asked, looking at her across the table.

"A great many, I fear,'" she cried.

"Then commit them over again," he said, gravely. "To get back one's youth, one has merely to repeat one's follies."

"A delightful theory!" she exclaimed. "I must put it into practice."

"A dangerous theory," came from Sir Thomas's tight lips. Lady Agatha shook her head, but could not help being amused. Mr. Erskine listened.

"Yes," he continued, "that is one of the great secrets of life. Nowadays most people die of a sort of creeping common sense, and discover when it is too late that the only things one never regrets are one's mistakes."

A laugh ran round the room.

He played with the idea, and grew wilful; tossed it into the air and transformed it; let it escape and recaptured it; made it iridescent with fancy, and winged it with paradox. The praise of folly, as he went on, soared into a philosophy, and Philosophy herself became young, and catching the mad music of Pleasure, wearing, one might fancy, her wine-stained robe and wreath of ivy, danced like a Bacchante over the hills of life, and mocked the slow Silenus for being sober. Facts fled before her like frightened forest things. Her white feet trod the huge press at which wise Omar sits, till the seething grape-juice rose round her bare limbs in waves of purple bubbles, or crawled in red foam over the vat's black, dripping, sloping sides. It was an extraordinary improvisation. He felt that the eyes of Dorian Gray were fixed on him, and the consciousness that amongst his audience there was one whose temperament he wished to fascinate, seemed to give his wit keenness, and to lend colour to his imagination. He was brilliant, fantastic, irresponsible. He charmed his listeners out of themselves, and they followed his pipe laughing. Dorian Gray never took his gaze off him, but sat like one under a spell, smiles chasing each other over his lips, and wonder growing grave in his darkening eyes.

At last, liveried in the costume of the age, Reality entered the room in the shape of a servant to tell the Duchess that her carriage was waiting. She wrung her hands in mock despair. "How annoying!" she cried. "I must go. I have to call for my husband at the club, to take him to some absurd meeting at Willis's Rooms, where he is going to be in the chair. If I am late he is sure to be furious, and I couldn't have a scene in this bonnet. It is far too fragile. A harsh word would ruin it. No, I must go, dear Agatha. Good-bye, Lord

Henry, you are quite delightful, and dreadfully demoralizing. I am sure I don't know what to say about your views. You must come and dine with us some night. Tuesday? Are you disengaged Tuesday?"

"For you I would throw over anybody, Duchess," said Lord Henry, with a bow.

"Ah! that is very nice, and very wrong of you," she cried; "so mind you come;" and she swept out of the room, followed by Lady Agatha and the other ladies.

When Lord Henry had sat down again, Mr. Erskine moved round, and taking a chair close to him, placed his hand upon his arm.

"You talk books away," he said; "why don't you write one?"

"I am too fond of reading books to care to write them, Mr. Erskine. I should like to write a novel certainly, a novel that would be as lovely as a Persian carpet and as unreal. But there is no literary public in England for anything except newspapers, primers, and encyclopædies. Of all people in the world the English have the least sense of the beauty of literature."

"I fear you are right," answered Mr. Erskine. "I myself used to have literary ambitions, but I gave them up long ago. And now, my dear young friend, if you will allow me to call you so, may I ask if you really meant all that you said to us at lunch?"

"I quite forget what I said," smiled Lord Henry. "Was it all very bad?"

"Very bad indeed. In fact I consider you extremely dangerous, and if anything happens to our good Duchess we shall all look on you as being primarily responsible. But I should like to talk to you about life. The generation into which I was born was tedious. Some day, when you are tired of London, come down to Treadley, and expound to me your philosophy of pleasure over some admirable Burgundy I am fortunate enough to possess."

"I shall be charmed. A visit to Treadley would be a great privilege. It has a perfect host, and a perfect library."

"You will complete it," answered the old gentleman, with a courteous bow. "And now I must bid good-bye to your excellent aunt. I am due at the Athenæum. It is the hour when we sleep there."

"All of you, Mr. Erskine?"

"Forty of us, in forty arm-chairs. We are practising for an English Academy of Letters."

Lord Henry laughed, and rose. "I am going to the Park," he cried.

As he was passing out of the door Dorian Gray touched him on the arm. "Let me come with you," he murmured.

"But I thought you had promised Basil Hallward to go and see him," answered Lord Henry.

"I would sooner come with you; yes, I feel I must come with you. Do let me. And you will promise to talk to me all the time? No one talks so wonderfully as you do."

"Ah! I have talked quite enough for to-day," said Lord Henry, smiling. "All I want now is to look at life. You may come and look at it with me, if you care to."

CHAPTER IV

One afternoon, a month later, Dorian Gray was reclining in a luxurious arm-chair, in the little library of Lord Henry's house in Mayfair. It was, in its way, a very charming room, with its high panelled wainscoting of olive-stained oak, its cream-coloured frieze and ceiling of raised plaster-work, and its brick-dust felt carpet strewn with silk long-fringed Persian rugs. On a tiny satinwood table stood a statuette by Clodion, and beside it lay a copy of "Les Cent Nouvelles," bound for Margaret of Valois by Clovis Eve, and powdered with the gilt daisies that Queen had selected for her device. Some large blue china jars and parrot-tulips were ranged on the mantelshelf, and through the small leaded panes of the window streamed the apricot-coloured light of a summer day in London.

Lord Henry had not yet come in. He was always late on principle, his principle being that punctuality is the thief of time. So the lad was looking rather sulky, as with listless fingers he turned over the pages of an elaborately-illustrated edition of "Manon Lescaut" that he had found in one of the book-cases. The formal monotonous ticking of the Louis Quatorze clock annoyed him. Once or twice he thought of going away.

At last he heard a step outside, and the door opened. "How late you are, Harry!" he murmured.

"I am afraid it is not Harry, Mr. Gray," answered a shrill voice.

He glanced quickly round, and rose to his feet. "I beg your pardon. I thought——"

"You thought it was my husband. It is only his wife. You must let me introduce myself. I know you quite well by your photographs. I think my husband has got seventeen of them."

"Not seventeen, Lady Henry?"

"Well, eighteen, then. And I saw you with him the other night at the Opera." She laughed nervously as she spoke, and watched him with her vague forget-me-not eyes. She was a curious woman, whose dresses always looked as if they had been designed in a rage and put on in a tempest. She was usually in love with somebody, and, as her passion was never returned, she had kept all her illusions. She tried to look picturesque, but only succeeded in being untidy. Her name was Victoria, and she had a perfect mania for going to church.

"That was at 'Lohengrin,' Lady Henry, I think?"

"Yes; it was at dear 'Lohengrin.' I like Wagner's music better than anybody's. It is so loud that one can talk the whole time without other people hearing what one says. That is a great advantage: don't you think so, Mr. Gray?"

The same nervous staccato laugh broke from her thin lips, and her fingers began to play with a long tortoise-shell paper-knife.

Dorian smiled, and shook his head: "I am afraid I don't think so, Lady

Henry. I never talk during music—at least, during good music. If one hears bad music, it is one's duty to drown it in conversation."

"Ah! that is one of Harry's views, isn't it, Mr. Gray? I always hear Harry's views from his friends. It is the only way I get to know of them. But you must not think I don't like good music. I adore it, but I am afraid of it. It makes me too romantic. I have simply worshipped pianists—two at a time, sometimes, Harry tells me. I don't know what it is about them. Perhaps it is that they are foreigners. They all are, ain't they? Even those that are born in England become foreigners after a time, don't they? It is so clever of them, and such a compliment to art. Makes it quite cosmopolitan, doesn't it? You have never been to any of my parties, have you, Mr. Gray? You must come. I can't afford orchids, but I spare no expense in foreigners. They make one's rooms look so picturesque. But here is Harry!—Harry, I came in to look for you, to ask you something—I forget what it was—and I found Mr. Gray here. We have had such a pleasant chat about music. We have quite the same ideas. No; I think our ideas are quite different. But he has been most pleasant. I am so glad I've seen him."

"I am charmed, my love, quite charmed," said Lord Henry, elevating his dark crescent-shaped eyebrows and looking at them both with an amused smile. "So sorry I am late, Dorian. I went to look after a piece of old brocade in Wardour Street, and had to bargain for hours for it. Nowadays people know the price of everything, and the value of nothing."

"I am afraid I must be going," exclaimed Lady Henry, breaking an awkward silence with her silly sudden laugh. "I have promised to drive with the Duchess. Good-bye, Mr. Gray. Good-bye, Harry. You are dining out, I suppose? So am I. Perhaps I shall see you at Lady Thornbury's."

"I dare say, my dear," said Lord Henry, shutting the door behind her, as, looking like a bird of paradise that had been out all night in the rain, she flitted out of the room, leaving a faint odour of frangi-pani. Then he lit a cigarette, and flung himself down on the sofa.

"Never marry a woman with straw-coloured hair, Dorian," he said, after a few puffs.

"Why, Harry?"

"Because they are so sentimental."

"But I like sentimental people."

"Never marry at all, Dorian. Men marry because they are tired; women because they are curious: both are disappointed."

"I don't think I am likely to marry, Harry. I am too much in love. That is one of your aphorisms. I am putting it into practice, as I do everything that you say."

"Who are you in love with?" asked Lord Henry, after a pause.

"With an actress," said Dorian Gray, blushing.

Lord Henry shrugged his shoulders. "That is a rather commonplace *debut.*"

"You would not say so of you saw her, Harry."

"Who is she?"

"Her name is Sibyl Vane."

"Never heard of her."

"No one has. People will some day, however. She is a genius."

"My dear boy, no woman is a genius. Women are a decorative sex. They never have anything to say, but they say it charmingly. Women represent the triumph of matter over mind, just as men represent the triumph of mind over morals."

"Harry, how can you?"

"My dear Dorian, it is quite true. I am analyzing women at present, so I ought to know. The subject is not so abstruse as I thought it was. I find that, ultimately, there are only two kinds of women, the plain and the coloured. The plain women are very useful. If you want to gain a reputation for respectability, you have merely to take them down to supper. The other women are very charming. They commit one mistake, however. They paint in order to try and look young. Our grandmothers painted in order to try and talk brilliantly. *Rouge* and *esprit* used to go together. That is all over now. As long as a woman can look ten years younger than her own daughter, she is perfectly satisfied. As for conversation, there are only five women in London worth talking to and two of these can't be admitted into decent society. However, tell me about your genius. How long have you known her?"

"Ah! Harry, your views terrify me."

"Never mind that. How long have you known her?"

"About three weeks."

"And where did you come across her?"

"I will tell you, Harry; but you mustn't be unsympathetic about it. After all, it never would have happened if I had not met you. You filled me with a wild desire to know everything about life. For days after I met you, something seemed to throb in my veins. As I lounged in the Park, or strolled down Piccadilly, I used to look at every one who passed me, and wonder, with a mad curiosity, what sort of lives they led. Some of them fascinated me. Others filled me with terror. There was an exquisite poison in the air. I had a passion for sensations. . . . Well, one evening about seven o'clock, I determined to go out in search of some adventure. I felt that this grey, monstrous London of ours, with its myriads of people, its sordid sinners, and its splendid sins, as you once phrased it, must have something in store for me. I fancied a thousand things. The mere danger gave me a sense of delight. I remembered what you had said to me on that wonderful evening when we first dined together, about the search for beauty being the real secret of life. I don't know what I expected, but I went out and wandered eastward, soon losing my way in a labyrinth of grimy streets and black, grassless squares. About half-past eight I passed by an absurd little theatre, with great flaring gas-jets and gaudy playbills. A hideous Jew, in the most amazing waistcoat I ever beheld in my life, was standing at the entrance, smoking a vile cigar. He had greasy ringlets, and an enormous diamond blazed in the centre of a soiled shirt. 'Have a box, My Lord?' he said, when he saw me, and he took off his hat with an air of gorgeous servilitv. There was something about him, Harry, that amused me.

He was such a monster. You will laugh at me, I know, but I really went in and paid a whole guinea for the stage-box. To the present day I can't make out why I did so; and yet if I hadn't—my dear Harry, if I hadn't, I should have missed the greatest romance of my life. I see you are laughing. It is horrid of you!"

"I am not laughing, Dorian; at least I am not laughing at you. But you should not say the greatest romance of your life. You should say the first romance of your life. You will always be loved, and you will always be in love with love. A *grande passion* is the privilege of people who have nothing to do. That is the one use of the idle classes of a country. Don't be afraid. There are exquisite things in store for you. This is merely the beginning."

"Do you think my nature so shallow?" cried Dorian Gray, angrily.

"No; I think your nature so deep."

"How do you mean?"

"My dear boy, the people who love only once in their lives are really the shallow people. What they call their loyalty, and their fidelity, I call either the lethargy of custom or their lack of imagination. Faithfulness is to the emotional life what consistency is to the life of the intellect—simply a confession of failure. Faithfulness! I must analyze it some day. The passion for property is in it. There are many things that we would throw away if we were not afraid that others might pick them up. But I don't want to interrupt you. Go on with your story."

"Well, I found myself seated in a horrid little private box, with a vulgar drop-scene staring me in the face. I looked out from behind the curtain, and surveyed the house. It was a tawdry affair, all Cupids and cornucopias, like a third-rate wedding-cake. The gallery and pit were fairly full, but the two rows of dingy stalls were quite empty, and there was hardly a person in what I suppose they called the dress-circle. Women went about with oranges and ginger-beer, and there was a terrible consumption of nuts going on."

"It must have been just like the palmy days of the British Drama."

"Just like, I should fancy, and very depressing. I began to wonder what on earth I should do, when I caught sight of the play-bill. What do you think the play was, Harry?"

"I should think 'The Idiot Boy, or Dumb but Innocent.' Our fathers used to like that sort of piece, I believe. The longer I live, Dorian, the more keenly I feel that whatever was good enough for our fathers is not good enough for us. In art, as in politics, *les grandpères ont toujours tort.*"

"This play was good enough for us, Harry. It was 'Romeo and Juliet.' I must admit I was rather annoyed at the idea of seeing Shakespeare done in such a wretched hole of a place. Still, I felt interested, in a sort of way. At any rate, I determined to wait for the first act. There was a dreadful orchestra, presided over by a young Hebrew who sat at a cracked piano, that nearly drove me away, but at last the drop-scene was drawn up, and the play began. Romeo was a stout elderly gentleman, with corked eyebrows, a husky tragedy voice, and a figure like a beer-barrel. Mercutio was almost as bad. He was played by the low-comedian, who had introduced gags of his own and was on most friendly terms with the pit. They were both as grotesque as the scenery, and that looked as if it had come out of a country-booth. But Juliet! Harry, imagine a girl, hardly seventeen years of age, with a little flower-like face, a small Greek head with plaited coils of dark-brown hair, eyes that were violet wells of passion, lips that were like the petals of a rose. She was the loveliest thing I had ever seen in my life. You said to me once that pathos left you unmoved, but that beauty, mere beauty, could fill your eyes with tears. I tell you, Harry, I could hardly see this girl for the mist of tears that came across me. And her voice—I never heard such a voice. It was very low at first, with deep mellow notes, that seemed to fall singly upon one's ear. Then it became a little louder, and sounded like a flute or a distant haut-bois. In the garden-scene it had all the tremulous ecstasy that one hears just before dawn when nightingales are singing. There was moments, later on, when it had the wild passion of violins. You know how a voice can stir one. Your voice and the voice of Sibyl Vane are two things that I shall never forget. When I close my eyes, I hear them, and each of them says something different. I don't know which to follow. Why should I not love her? Harry, I do love her. She is everything to me in life. Night after night I go to see her play. One evening she is Rosalind, and the next evening she is Imogen. I have seen her die in the gloom of an Italian tomb, sucking the poison from her lover's lips. I have watched her wandering through the forest of Arden, disguised as a pretty boy in hose and doublet and dainty cap. She has been mad, and has come into the presence of a guilty king, and given him rue to wear, and bitter herbs to taste of. She has been innocent, and the black hands of jealousy have crushed her reed-like throat. I have seen her in every age and in every costume. Ordinary women never appeal to one's imagination. They are limited to their century. No glamour ever transfigures them. One knows their minds as easily as one knows their bonnets. One can always find them. There is no mystery in any of them: they ride in the Park in the morning, and chatter at tea-parties in the afternoon. They have their stereotyped smile, and their fashionable manner. They are quite obvious. But an actress! How different an actress is! Harry! why didn't you tell me that the only thing worth loving is an actress?"

"Because I have loved so many of them, Dorian."

"Oh, yes, horrid people with dyed hair and painted faces."

"Don't run down dyed hair and painted faces. There is an extraordinary charm in them, sometimes," said Lord Henry.

"I wish now I had not told you about Sibyl Vane."

"You could not have helped telling me, Dorian. All through your life you will tell me everything you do."

"Yes, Harry, I believe that is true, I cannot help telling you things. You have a curious influence over me. If I ever did a crime, I would come and confess it to you. You would understand me."

"People like you—the wilful sunbeams of life—don't commit crimes, Dorian. But I am much obliged for the compliment, all the same. And now tell me—reach me the matches, like a good boy: thanks:—what are your actual relations with Sibyl Vane?"

Dorian Gray leaped to his feet, with flushed cheeks and burning eyes. "Harry! Sibyl Vane is sacred!"

"It is only the sacred things that are worth touching, Dorian," said Lord Henry, with a strange touch of pathos in his voice. "But why should you be annoyed? I suppose she will belong to you some day. When one is in love, one always begins by deceiving one's self, and one always ends by deceiving others. That is what the world calls a romance. You know her, at any rate, I suppose?"

"Of course I know her. On the first night I was at the theatre, the horrid old Jew came round to the box after the performance was over, and offered to take me behind the scenes and introduce me to her. I was furious with him, and told him that Juliet had been dead for hundreds of years, and that her body was lying in a marble tomb in Verona. I think, from his blank look of amazement, that he was under the impression that I had taken too much champagne, or something."

"I am not surprised."

"Then he asked me if I wrote for any of the newspapers. I told him I never even read them. He seemed terribly disappointed at that, and confided to me that all the dramatic critics were in a conspiracy against him, and that they were every one of them to be bought."

"I should not wonder if he was quite right there. But, on the other hand, judging from their appearance, most of them cannot be at all expensive."

"Well, he seemed to think they were beyond his means," laughed Dorian. "By this time, however, the lights were being put out in the theatre, and I had to go. He wanted me to try some cigars that he strongly recommended. I declined. The next night, of course, I arrived at the place again. When he saw me he made a low bow, and assured me that I was a munificent patron of art. He was a most offensive brute, though he had an extraordinary passion for Shakespeare. He told me once, with an air of pride, that his five bankruptcies were entirely due to 'The Bard,' as he insisted on calling him. He seemed to think it a distinction."

"It was a distinction, my dear Dorian—a great distinction. Most people become bankrupt through having invested too heavily in the prose of life. To have ruined one's self over poetry is an honour. But when did you first speak to Miss Sibyl Vane?"

"The third night. She had been playing Rosalind. I could not help going round. I had thrown her some flowers, and she had looked at me; at least I fancied that she had. The old Jew was persistent. He seemed determined to take me behind, so I consented. It was curious my not wanting to know her, wasn't it?"

"No; I don't think so."

"My dear Harry, why?"

"I will tell you some other time. Now I want to know about the girl."

"Sibyl? Oh, she was so shy, and so gentle. There is something of a child about her. Her eyes opened wide in exquisite wonder when I told her what I thought of her performance, and she seemed quite unconscious of her power.

I think we were both rather nervous. The old Jew stood grinning at the doorway of the dusty greenroom, making elaborate speeches about us both, while we stood looking at each other like children. He would insist on calling me 'My Lord,' so I had to assure Sibyl that I was not anything of the kind. She said quite simply to me, 'You look more like a prince. I must call you Prince Charming.' "

"Upon my word, Dorian, Miss Sibyl knows how to pay compliments."

"You don't understand her, Harry. She regarded me merely as a person in a play. She knows nothing of life. She lives with her mother, a faded tired woman who played Lady Capulet in a sort of magenta dressing-wrapper on the first night, and looks as if she had seen better days."

"I know that look. It depresses me," murmured Lord Henry, examining his rings.

"The Jew wanted to tell me her history, but I said it did not interest me."

"You were quite right. There is always something infinitely mean about other people's tragedies."

"Sibyl is the only thing I care about. What is it to me where she came from? From her little head to her little feet, she is absolutely and entirely divine. Every night of my life I go to see her act, and every night she is more marvellous."

"That is the reason, I suppose, that you never dine with me now. I thought you must have some curious romance on hand. You have; but it is not quite what I expected."

"My dear Harry, we either lunch or sup together every day, and I have been to the Opera with you several times," said Dorian, opening his blue eyes in wonder.

"You always come dreadfully late."

"Well, I can't help going to see Sibyl play," he cried, "even if it is only for a single act. I get hungry for her presence; and when I think of the wonderful soul that is hidden away in that little ivory body, I am filled with awe."

"You can dine with me to-night, Dorian, can't you?"

He shook his head. "To-night she is Imogen," he answered, "and to-morrow night she will be Juliet."

"When is she Sibyl Vane?"

"Never."

"I congratulate you."

"How horrid you are! She is all the great heroines of the world in one. She is more than an individual. You laugh, but I tell you she has genius. I love her, and I must make her love me. You, who know all the secrets of life, tell me how to charm Sibyl Vane to love me! I want to make Romeo jealous. I want the dead lovers of the world to hear our laughter, and grow sad. I want a breath of our passion to stir their dust into consciousness, to wake their ashes into pain. My God, Harry, how I worship her!" He was walking up and down the room as he spoke. Hectic spots of red burned on his cheeks. He was terribly excited.

Lord Henry watched him with a subtle sense of pleasure. How different he was now from the shy, frightened boy he had met in Basil Hallward's studio! His nature had developed like a flower, had borne blossoms of scarlet flame. Out of its secret hiding-place had crept his Soul, and Desire had come to meet it on the way.

"And what do you propose to do?" said Lord Henry, at last.

"I want you and Basil to come with me some night and see her act. I have not the slightest fear of the result. You are certain to acknowledge her genius. Then we must get her out of the Jew's hands. She is bound to him for three years—at least for two years and eight months—from the present time. I shall have to pay him something, of course. When all that is settled, I shall take a West End theatre and bring her out properly. She will make the world as mad as she has made me."

"That would be impossible, my dear boy."

"Yes, she will. She has not merely art, consummate art-instinct, in her but she has personality also; and you have often told me that it is personalities, not principles, that move the age."

"Well, what night shall we go?"

"Let me see. To-day is Tuesday. Let us fix to-morrow. She plays Juliet to-morrow."

"All right. The Bristol at eight o'clock; and I will get Basil."

"Not eight, Harry, please. Half-past six. We must be there before the curtain rises. You must see her in the first act, where she meets Romeo."

"Half-past six! What an hour! It will be like having a meat-tea, or reading an English novel. It must be seven. No gentleman dines before seven. Shall you see Basil between this and then? Or shall I write to him?"

"Dear Basil! I have not laid eyes on him for a week. It is rather horrid of me, as he has sent me my portrait in the most wonderful frame, specially designed by himself, and, though I am a little jealous of the picture for being a whole month younger than I am, I must admit that I delight in it. Perhaps you had better write to him. I don't want to see him alone. He says things that annoy me. He gives me good advice."

Lord Henry smiled. "People are very fond of giving away what they need most themselves. It is what I call the depth of generosity."

"Oh, Basil is the best of fellows, but he seems to me to be just a bit of a Philistine. Since I have known you, Harry, I have discovered that."

"Basil, my dear boy, puts everything that is charming in him into his work. The consequence is that he has nothing left for life but his prejudices, his principles, and his common sense. The only artists I have ever known, who are personally delightful, are bad artists. Good artists exist simply in what they make, and consequently are perfectly uninteresting in what they are. A great poet, a really great poet, is the most unpoetical of all creatures. But inferior poets are absolutely fascinating. The worse their rhymes are, the more picturesque they look. The mere fact of having published a book of second-rate sonnets makes a man quite irresistible. He lives the poetry that he cannot write. The others write the poetry that they dare not realize."

"I wonder is that really so, Harry?" said Dorian Gray, putting some perfume on his handkerchief out of a large gold-topped bottle that stood on the table. "It must be, if you say it. And now I'm off. Imogen is waiting for me. Don't forget about to-morrow. Good-bye."

As he left the room Lord Henry's heavy eyelids drooped, and he began to think. Certainly few people had ever interested him so much as Dorian Gray, and yet the lad's mad adoration of some one else caused him not the slightest pang of annoyance or jealousy. He was pleased by it. It made him a more interesting study. He had always been enthralled by the methods of natural science, but the ordinary subject matter of that science had seemed to him trivial and of no import. And so he had begun by vivisecting himself, as he had ended by vivisecting others. Human life—that appeared to him the one thing worth investigating. Compared to it there was nothing else of any value. It was true that as one watched life in its curious crucible of pain and pleasure, one could not wear over one's face a mask of glass, nor keep the sulphurous fumes from troubling the brain and making the imagination turbid with monstrous fancies and misshapen dreams. There were poisons so subtle that to know their properties one had to sicken of them. There were maladies so strange that one had to pass through them if one sought to understand their nature. And, yet, what a great reward one received! How wonderful the whole world became to one! To note the curious hard logic of passion, and the emotional coloured life of the intellect—to observe where they met, and where they separated, at what point they were in unison, and at what point they were at discord—there was a delight in that. What matter what the cost was? One could never pay too high a price for any sensation.

He was conscious—and the thought brought a gleam of pleasure into his brown agate eyes—that it was through certain words of his, musical words said with musical utterance, that Dorian Gray's soul had turned to this white girl and bowed in worship before her. To a large extent the lad was his own creation. He had made him premature. That was something. Ordinary people waited till life disclosed to them its secrets, but to the few, to the elect, the mysteries of life were revealed before the veil was drawn away. Sometimes this was the effect of art, and chiefly of the art of literature, which dealt immediately with the passions and the intellect. But now and then a complex personality took the place and assumed the office of art, was indeed, in its way, a real work of art, Life having its elaborate masterpieces, just as poetry has, or sculpture, or painting.

Yes, the lad was premature. He was gathering his narvest while it was yet spring. The pulse and passion of youth were in him, but he was becoming self-conscious. It was delightful to watch him. With his beautiful face, and his beautiful soul, he was a thing to wonder at. It was no matter how it all ended, or was destined to end. He was like one of those gracious figures in a pageant or a play, whose joys seem to be remote from one, but whose sorrows stir one's sense of beauty, and whose wounds are like red roses.

Soul and body, body and soul—how mysterious they were! There was animalism in the soul, and the body had its moments of spirituality. The senses could refine, and the intellect could degrade. Who could say where the fleshly impulse ceased, or the psychical impulse began? How shallow were the arbitrary definitions of ordinary psychologists! And yet how difficult to decide between the claims of the various schools! Was the soul a shadow seated in the house of sin? Or was the body really in the soul, as Giordano Bruno thought? The separation of spirit from matter was a mystery, and the union of spirit with matter was a mystery also.

He began to wonder whether we could ever make psychology so absolute a science that each little spring of life would be revealed to us. As it was, we always misunderstood ourselves, and rarely understood others. Experience was of no ethical value. It was merely the name men gave to their mistakes. Moralists had, as a rule, regarded it as a mode of warning, had claimed for it a certain ethical efficacy in the formation of character, had praised it as something that taught us what to follow and showed us what to avoid. But there was no motive power in experience. It was as little of an active cause as conscience itself. All that it really demonstrated was that our future would be the same as our past, and that the sin we had done once, and with loathing, we would do many times, and with joy.

It was clear to him that the experimental method was the only method by which one could arrive at any scientific analysis of the passions; and certainly Dorian Gray was a subject made to his hand, and seemed to promise rich and fruitful results. His sudden mad love for Sibyl Vane was a psychological phenomenon of no small interest. There was no doubt that curiosity had much to do with it, curiosity and the desire for new experiences; yet it was not a simple but rather a very complex passion. What there was in it of the purely sensuous instinct of boyhood had been transformed by the workings of the imagination, changed into something that seemed to the lad himself to be remote from sense, and was for that very reason all the more dangerous. It was the passions about whose origin we deceived ourselves that tyrannized most strongly over us. Our weakest motives were those of whose nature we were conscious. It often happened that when we thought we were experimenting on others we were really experimenting on ourselves.

While Lord Henry sat dreaming on these things, a knock came to the door, and his valet entered, and reminded him it was time to dress for dinner. He got up and looked out into the street. The sunset had smitten into scarlet gold the upper windows of the houses opposite. The panes glowed like plates of heated metal. The sky above was like a faded rose. He thought of his friend's young fiery-coloured life, and wondered how it was all going to end.

When he arrived home, about half-past twelve o'clock, he saw a telegram lying on the hall table. He opened it, and found it was from Dorian Gray. It was to tell him that he was engaged to be married to Sibyl Vane.

CHAPTER V

"MOTHER, mother, I am so happy!" whispered the girl, burying her face in the lap of the faded, tired-looking woman who, with back turned to the shrill intrusive light, was sitting in the one arm-chair that their dingy sitting-room contained. "I am so happy!" she repeated, "and you must be happy too!"

Mrs. Vane winced, and put her thin bismuth-whitened hands on her daughter's head. "Happy!" she echoed, "I am only happy, Sibyl, when I see you act. You must not think of anything but your acting. Mr. Isaacs has been very good to us, and we owe him money."

The girl looked up and pouted. "Money, mother?" she cried. "What does money matter? Love is more than money."

"Mr. Isaacs has advanced us fifty pounds to pay off our debts, and to get a proper outfit for James. You must not forget that, Sibyl. Fifty pounds is a very large sum. Mr. Isaacs has been most considerate."

"He is not a gentleman, mother, and I hate the way he talks to me," said the girl, rising to her feet, and going over to the window.

"I don't know how we could manage without him," answered the elder woman, querulously.

Sibyl Vane tossed her head and laughed. "We don't want him any more, mother. Prince Charming rules life for us now." Then she paused. A rose shook in her blood, and shadowed her cheeks. Quick breaths parted the petals of her lips. They trembled. Some southern wind of passion swept over her, and stirred the dainty folds of her dress. "I love him," she said, simply.

"Foolish child! foolish child!" was the parrot-phrase flung in answer. The waving of crooked, false-jewelled fingers gave grotesqueness to the words.

The girl laughed again. The joy of a caged bird was in her voice. Her eyes caught the melody and echoed it in radiance: then closed for a moment, as though to hide their secret. When they opened, the mist of a dream had passed across them.

Thin-lipped wisdom spoke at her from the worn chair, hinted at prudence, quoted from that book of cowardice whose author apes the name of common sense. She did not listen. She was free in her prison of passion. Her prince, Prince Charming, was with her. She had called on Memory to remake him. She had sent her soul to search for him, and it had brought him back. His kiss burned again upon her mouth. Her eyelids were warm with his breath.

Then Wisdom altered its method and spoke of espial and discovery. This young man might be rich. If so, marriage should be thought of. Against the shell of her ear broke the waves of worldly cunning. The arrows of craft shot by her. She saw the thin lips moving, and smiled.

Suddenly she felt the need to speak. The wordy silence troubled her. "Mother, mother," she cried, "why does he love me so much? I know why I love him. I love him because he is like what Love himself should be. But what does he see in me? I am not worthy of him. And yet–why, I cannot tell–though I feel so much beneath him, I don't feel humble. I feel proud, terribly proud. Mother, did you love my father as I love Prince Charming?"

The elder woman grew pale beneath the coarse powder that daubed her cheeks, and her dry lips twitched with a spasm of pain. Sibyl rushed to her, flung her arms round her neck, and kissed her. "Forgive me, mother. I know it pains you to talk about our father. But it only pains you because you loved him so much. Don't look so sad. I am as happy to-day as you were twenty years ago. Ah! let me be happy forever!"

"My child, you are far too young to think of falling in love. Besides, what do you know of this young man. You don't even know his name. The whole thing is most inconvenient, and really, when James is going away to Australia, and I have so much to think of, I must say that you should have shown more consideration. However, as I said before, if he is rich . . ."

"Ah! mother, mother, let me be happy!"

Mrs. Vane glanced at her, and with one of those false theatrical gestures that so often become a mode of second nature to a stage-player, clasped her in her arms. At this moment the door opened, and a young lad with rough brown hair came into the room. He was thick-set of figure, and his hands and feet were large, and somewhat clumsy in movement. He was not so finely bred as his sister. One would hardly have guessed the close relationship that existed between them. Mrs. Vane fixed her eyes on him, and intensified her smile. She mentally elevated her son to the dignity of an audience. She felt sure that the *tableau* was interesting.

"You might keep some of your kisses for me, Sibyl, I think," said the lad, with a good-natured grumble.

"Ah! but you don't like being kissed, Jim," she cried. "You are a dreadful old bear." And she ran across the room and hugged him.

James Vane looked into his sister's face with tenderness. "I want you to come out with me for a walk, Sibyl. I don't suppose I shall ever see this horrid London again. I am sure I don't want to."

"My son, don't say such dreadful things," murmured Mrs. Vane, taking up a tawdry theatrical dress, with a sigh, and beginning to patch it. She felt a little disappointed that he had not joined the group. It would have increased the theatrical picturesqueness of the situation.

"Why not, mother? I mean it."

"You pain me, my son. I trust you will return from Australia in a position of affluence. I believe there is no society of any kind in the Colonies, nothing that I would call society; so when you have made your fortune you must come back and assert yourself in London."

"Society!" muttered the lad. "I don't want to know anything about that. I should like to make some money to take you and Sibyl off the stage. I hate it."

"Oh, Jim!" said Sibyl, laughing, "how unkind of you! But are you really going for a walk with me? That will be nice! I was afraid you were going to say good-bye to some of your friends—to Tom Hardy, who gave you that hideous pipe, or Ned Langton, who makes fun of you for smoking it. It is very sweet of you to let me have your last afternoon. Where shall we go? Let us go to the Park."

"I am too shabby," he answered, frowning. "Only swell people go to the Park."

"Nonsense, Jim," she whispered, stroking the sleeve of his coat.

He hesitated for a moment. "Very well," he said at last, "but don't be too long dressing." She danced out of the door. One could hear her singing as she ran upstairs. Her little feet pattered overhead.

He walked up and down the room two or three times. Then he turned to the still figure in the chair. "Mother, are my things ready?" he asked.

"Quite ready, James," she answered, keeping her eyes on her work. For some months past she had felt ill at ease when she was alone with this rough, stern son of hers. Her shallow secret nature was troubled when their eyes met. She used to wonder if he suspected anything. The silence, for he made no other observation, became intolerable to her. She began to complain. Women defend themselves by attacking, just as they attack by sudden and strange surrenders. "I hope you will be contented, James, with your sea-faring life," she said. "You must remember that it is your own choice. You might have entered a solicitor's office. Solicitors are a very respectable class, and in the country often dine with the best families."

"I hate offices, and I hate clerks," he replied. "But you are quite right. I have chosen my own life. All I say is, watch over Sibyl. Don't let her come to any harm. Mother, you must watch over her."

"James, you really talk very strangely. Of course I watch over Sibyl."

"I hear a gentleman comes every night to the theatre, and goes behind to talk to her. Is that right? What about that?"

"You are speaking about things you don't understand, James. In the profession we are accustomed to receive a great deal of most gratifying attention. I myself used to receive many bouquets at one time. That was when acting was really understood. As for Sibyl, I do not know at present whether her attachment is serious or not. But there is no dobut that the young man in question is a perfect gentleman. He is always most polite to me. Besides, he has the appearance of being rich, and the flowers he sends are lovely."

"You don't know his name, though," said the lad, harshly.

"No," answered his mother, with a placid expression in her face. "He has not yet revealed his real name. I think it is quite romantic of him. He is probably a member of the aristocracy."

James Vane bit his lip. "Watch over Sibyl, mother," he cried, "watch over her."

"My son, you distress me very much. Sibyl is always under my special care. Of course, if this gentleman is wealthy, there is no reason why she could not contract an alliance with him. I trust he is one of the aristocracy. He has all the appearance of it, I must say. It might be a most brilliant marriage for Sibyl. They would make a charming couple. His good looks are really quite remarkable; everybody notices them."

The lad muttered something to himself, and drummed on the windowpane with his coarse fingers. He had just turned round to say something, when the door opened, and Sibyl ran in.

"How serious you both are!" she cried. "What is the matter?"

"Nothing," he answered. "I suppose one must be serious sometimes. Goodbye, mother. I will have my dinner at five o'clock. Everything is packed, except my shirts, so you need not trouble."

"Good-bye, my son," she answered, with a bow of strained stateliness. She was extremely annoyed at the tone he had adopted with her, and there was something in his look that had made her feel afraid.

"Kiss me, mother," said the girl. Her flower-like lips touched the withered cheek, and warmed its frost.

"My child! my child!" cried Mrs. Vane, looking up to the ceiling in search of an imaginary gallery.

"Come, Sibyl," said her brother, impatiently. He hated his mother's affectations.

They went out into the flickering wind-blown sunlight, and strolled down the dreary Euston Road. The passers-by glanced in wonder at the sullen, heavy youth, who, in coarse, ill-fitting clothes, was in the company of such a graceful, refined-looking girl. He was like a common gardener walking with a rose.

Jim frowned from time to time when he caught the inquisitive glance of some stranger. He had that dislike of being stared at which comes on geniuses late in life, and never leaves the commonplace. Sibyl, however, was quite unconscious of the effect she was producing. Her love was trembling in laughter on her lips. She was thinking of Prince Charming, and, that she might think of him all the more, she did not talk of him, but prattled on about the ship in which Jim was going to sail, about the gold he was certain to find, about the wonderful heiress whose life he was to save from the wicked, red-shirted bushrangers. For he was not to remain a sailor, or a super-cargo, or whatever he was going to be. Oh, no! A sailor's existence was dreadful. Fancy being cooped up in a horrid ship, with the hoarse, hump-backed waves trying to get in, and a black wind blowing the masts down, and tearing the sails into long screaming ribands! He was to leave the vessel at Melbourne, bid a polite good-bye to the captain, and go off at once to the gold-fields. Before a week was over he was to come across a large nugget of pure gold, the largest nugget that had ever been discovered, and bring it down to the coast in a waggon guarded by six mounted policemen. The bushrangers were to attack them three times, and be defeated with immense slaughter. Or, no. He was not to go to the gold-fields at all. They were horrid places, where men got intoxicated, and shot each other in bar-rooms, and used bad language. He was to be a nice sheep-farmer, and one evening, as he was riding home, he was to see the beautiful heiress being carried off by a robber on a black horse, and give chase, and rescue her. Of course she would fall in love with him, and he with her, and they would get married, and come home, and live in an immense house in London. Yes, there were delightful things in store for him. But he must be very good, and not lose his temper, or spend his money foolishly. She was only a year older than he was, but she knew so much more of life. He must be sure, also, to write to her by every mail, and to say his prayers each night before he went to sleep. God was very good, and would watch over him. She would pray for him too, and in a few years he would come back quite rich and happy.

The lad listened sulkily to her, and made no answer. He was heart-sick at leaving home.

Yet it was not this alone that made him gloomy and morose. Inexperienced though he was, he had still a strong sense of the danger of Sibyl's position. This young dandy who was making love to her could mean her no good. He was a gentleman, and he hated him for that, hated him through some curious race-instinct for which he could not account, and which for that reason was all the more dominant within him. He was conscious also of the shallowness and vanity of his mother's nature, and in that saw infinite peril for Sibyl and Sibyl's happiness. Children begin by loving their parents; as they grow older they judge them; sometimes they forgive them.

His mother! He had something on his mind to ask her, something that he had brooded on for many months of silence. A chance phrase that he had heard at the theatre, a whispered sneer that had reached his ears one night as he waited at the stage-door, had set loose a train of horrible thoughts. He remembered it as if it had been the lash of a hunting-crop across his face. His brows knit together into a wedge-like furrow, and with a twitch of pain he bit his under-lip.

"You are not listening to a word I am saying, Jim," cried Sibyl, "and I am making the most delightful plans for your future. Do say something."

"What do you want me to say?"

"Oh! that you will be a good boy, and not forget us," she answered, smiling at him.

He shrugged his shoulders. "You are more likely to forget me, than I am to forget you, Sibyl."

She flushed. "What do you mean, Jim?" she asked.

"You have a new friend, I hear. Who is he? Why have you not told me about him? He means you no good."

"Stop, Jim!" she exclaimed. "You must not say anything against him. I love him."

"Why, you don't even know his name," answered the lad. "Who is he? I have a right to know."

"He is called Prince Charming. Don't you like the name? Oh! you silly boy! you should never forget it. If you only saw him, you would think him the most wonderful person in the world. Some day you will meet him: when you come back from Australia. You will like him so much. Everybody likes him, and I . . . love him. I wish you could come to the theatre to-night. He is going to be there, and I am to play Juliet. Oh! how I shall play it! Fancy, Jim, to be in love and play Juliet! To have him sitting there! To play for his delight! I am afraid I may frighten the company, frighten or enthrall them. To be in love is to surpass one's self. Poor dreadful Mr. Isaacs will be shouting 'genius' to his loafers at the bar. He has preached me as a dogma; to-night he will announce me as a revelation. I feel it. And it is all his, his only, Prince Charming, my wonderful lover, my god of graces. But I am poor beside him. Poor? What does that matter? When poverty creeps in at the door, love flies in through the window. Our proverbs want re-writing. They were made in winter, and it is summer now; spring-time for me, I think, a very dance of blossoms in blue skies."

"He is a gentleman," said the lad, sullenly.

"A Prince!" she cried, musically. "What more do you want?"

"He wants to enslave you."

"I shudder at the thought of being free."

"I want you to beware of him."

"To see him is to worship him, to know him is to trust him."

"Sibyl, you are mad about him."

She laughed, and took his arm. "You dear old Jim, you talk as if you were a hundred. Some day you will be in love yourself. Then you will know what it is. Don't look so sulky. Surely you should be glad to think that, though you are going away, you leave me happier than I have ever been before. Life has been hard for us both, terribly hard and difficult. But it will be different now. You are going to a new world, and I have found one. Here are two chairs; let us sit down and see the smart people go by."

They took their seats amidst a crowd of watchers. The tulip-beds across the road flamed like throbbing rings of fire. A white dust, tremulous cloud of orris-root it seemed, hung in the panting air. The brightly-coloured parasols danced and dipped like monstrous butterflies.

She made her brother talk of himself, his hopes, his prospects. He spoke slowly and with effort. They passed words to each other as players at a game pass counters. Sibyl felt oppressed. She could not communicate her joy. A faint smile curving that sullen mouth was all the echo she could win. After some time she became silent. Suddenly she caught a glimpse of golden hair and laughing lips, and in an open carriage with two ladies Dorian Gray drove past.

She started to her feet. "There he is!" she cried.

"Who?" said Jim Vane.

"Prince Charming," she answered, looking after the victoria.

He jumped up, and seized her roughly by the arm. "Show him to me. Which is he? Point him out. I must see him!" he exclaimed; but at that moment the Duke of Berwick's four-in-hand came between, and when it had left the space clear, the carriage had swept out of the Park.

"He is gone," murmured Sibyl, sadly. "I wish you had seen him."

"I wish I had, for as sure as there is a God in heaven, if he ever does you any wrong, I shall kill him."

She looked at him in horror. He repeated his words. They cut the air like a dagger. The people round began to gape. A lady standing close to her tittered.

"Come away, Jim; come away," she whispered. He followed her doggedly as she passed through the crowd. He felt glad at what he had said.

When they reached the Achilles Statue she turned round. There was pity in her eyes that became laughter on her lips. She shook her head at him. "You are foolish, Jim, utterly foolish; a bad-tempered boy, that is all. How can you say such horrible things? You don't know what you are talking about. You are simply jealous and unkind. Ah! I wish you would fall in love. Love makes people good, and what you said was wicked."

"I am sixteen," he answered, "and I know what I am about. Mother is no help to you. She doesn't understand how to look after you. I wish now that I was not going to Australia at all. I have a great mind to chuck the whole thing up. I would, if my articles hadn't been signed."

"Oh, don't be so serious, Jim. You are like one of the heroes of those silly melodramas mother used to be so fond of acting in. I am not going to quarrel with you. I have seen him, and oh! to see him is perfect happiness. We won't quarrel. I know you would never harm any one I love, would you?"

"Not as long as you love him, I suppose," was the sullen answer.

"I shall love him for ever!" she cried.

"And he?"

"For ever, too!"

"He had better."

She shrank from him. Then she laughed and put her hand on his arm. He was merely a boy.

At the Marble Arch they hailed an omnibus, which left them close to their shabby home in the Euston Road. It was after five o'clock, and Sibyl had to lie down for a couple of hours before acting. Jim insisted that she should do so. He said that he would sooner part with her when their mother was not present. She would be sure to make a scene, and he detested scenes of every kind.

In Sibyl's own room they parted. There was jealousy in the lad's heart, and a fierce, murderous hatred of the stranger who, as it seemed to him, had come between them. Yet, when her arms were flung around his neck, and her fingers strayed through his hair, he softened, and kissed her with real affection. There were tears in his eyes as he went downstairs.

His mother was waiting for him below. She grumbled at his unpunctuality, as he entered. He made no answer, but sat down to his meagre meal. The flies buzzed round the table, and crawled over the stained cloth. Through the rumble of omnibuses, and the clatter of street-cabs, he could hear the droning voice devouring each minute that was left to him.

After some time, he thrust away his plate, and put his head in his hands. He felt that he had a right to know. It should have been told to him before, if it was as he suspected. Leaden with fear, his mother watched him. Words dropped mechanically from her lips. A tattered lace handkerchief twitched in her fingers. When the clock struck six, he got up, and went to the door. Then he turned back, and looked at her. Their eyes met. In hers he saw a wild appeal for mercy. It enraged him.

"Mother, I have something to ask you," he said. Her eyes wandered vaguely about the room. She made no answer. "Tell me the truth. I have a right to know. Were you married to my father?"

She heaved a deep sigh. It was a sigh of relief. The terrible moment, the moment that night and day, for weeks and months, she had dreaded, had come at last, and yet she felt no terror. Indeed in some measure it was a disappointment to her. The vulgar directness of the question called for a direct answer. The situation had not been gradually led up to. It was crude. It reminded her of a bad rehearsal.

"No," she answered, wondering at the harsh simplicity of life.

"My father was a scoundrel then!" cried the lad, clenching his fists.

She shook her head. "I knew he was not free. We loved each other very much. If he had lived, he would have made provision for us. Don't speak against him, my son. He was your father, and a gentleman. Indeed he was highly connected."

An oath broke from his lips. "I don't care for myself," he exclaimed, "but don't let Sibyl . . . It is a gentleman, isn't it, who is in love with her, or says he is? Highly connected, too, I suppose."

For a moment a hideous sense of humiliation came over the woman. Her head drooped. She wiped her eyes with shaking hands. "Sibyl has a mother," she murmured; "I had none."

The lad was touched. He went towards her, and stooping down he kissed her. "I am sorry if I have pained you by asking about my father," he said, "but I could not help it. I must go now. Good-bye. Don't forget that you will have only one child now to look after, and believe me that if this man wrongs my sister, I will find out who he is, track him down, and kill him like a dog. I swear it."

The exaggerated folly of the threat, the passionate gesture that accompanied it, the mad melodramatic words, made life seem more vivid to her. She was familiar with the atmosphere. She breathed more freely, and for the first time in many months she really admired her son. She would have liked to have continued the scene on the same emotional scale, but he cut her short. Trunks had to be carried down, and mufflers looked for. The lodging-house drudge bustled in and out. There was the bargaining with the cab-man. The moment was lost in vulgar details. It was with a renewed feeling of disappointment that she waved the tattered lace handkerchief from the window, as her son drove away. She was conscious that a great opportunity had been wasted. She consoled herself by telling Sibyl how desolate she felt her life would be, now that she had only one child to look after. She remembered the phrase. It had pleased her. Of the threat she said nothing. It was vividly and dramatically expressed. She felt that they would all laugh at it some day.

CHAPTER VI

"I SUPPOSE you have heard the news, Basil?" said Lord Henry that evening, as Hallward was shown into a little private room at the Bristol where dinner had been laid for three.

"No, Harry," answered the artist, giving his hat and coat to the bowing waiter. "What is it? Nothing about politics, I hope? They don't interest me. There is hardly a single person in the House of Commons worth painting; though many of them would be the better for a little whitewashing."

"Dorian Gray is engaged to be married," said Lord Henry, watching him as he spoke.

Hallward started, and then frowned. "Dorian engaged to be married!" he cried. "Impossible!"

"It is perfectly true."

"To whom?"

"To some little actress or other."

"I can't believe it. Dorian is far too sensible."

"Dorian is far too wise not to do foolish things now and then, my dear Basil."

"Marriage is hardly a thing that one can do now and then, Harry."

"Except in America," rejoined Lord Henry, languidly. "But I didn't say he was married. I said he was engaged to be married. There is a great difference. I have a distinct remembrance of being married, but I have no recollection at all of being engaged. I am inclined to think that I never was engaged."

"But think of Dorian's birth, and position, and wealth. It would be absurd for him to marry so much beneath him."

"If you want to make him marry this girl tell him that, Basil. He is sure to do it, then. Whenever a man does a thoroughly stupid thing, it is always from the noblest motives."

"I hope the girl is good, Harry. I don't want to see Dorian tied to some vile creature, who might degrade his nature and ruin his intellect."

"Oh, she is better than good—she is beautiful," murmured Lord Henry, sipping a glass of vermouth and orange-bitters. "Dorian says she is beautiful; and he is not often wrong about things of that kind. Your portrait of him has quickened his appreciation of the personal appearance of other people. It has had that excellent effect, amongst others. We are to see her to-night, if that boy doesn't forget his appointment."

"Are you serious?"

"Quite serious, Basil. I should be miserable if I thought I should ever be more serious than I am at the present moment."

"But do you approve of it, Harry?" asked the painter, walking up and down the room, and biting his lip. "You can't approve of it, possibly. It is some silly infatuation."

"I never approve, or disapprove, of anything now. It is an absurd attitude to take towards life. We are not sent into the world to air our moral prejudices. I never take any notice of what common people say, and I never interfere with what charming people do. If a personality fascinates me, whatever mode of expression that personality selects is absolutely delightful to me. Dorian Gray falls in love with a beautiful girl who acts Juliet, and proposes to marry her. Why not? If he wedded Messalina he would be none the less interesting. You know I am not a champion of marriage. The real drawback to marriage is that it makes one unselfish. And unselfish people are colourless. They lack individuality. Still, there are certain temperaments that marriage makes more complex. They retain their egotism, and add to it many other egos. They are forced to have more than one life. They become highly organized, and to be highly organized is, I should fancy, the object of man's existence. Besides, every experience is of value, and, whatever one may say against marriage, it is certainly an experience. I hope that Dorian Gray will make this girl his wife, passionately adore her for six months, and then suddenly become fascinated by some one else. He would be a wonderful study."

"You don't mean a single word of all that, Harry; you know you don't. If Dorian Gray's life were spoiled, no one would be sorrier than yourself. You are much better than you pretend to be."

Lord Henry laughed. "The reason we all like to think so well of others is that we are all afraid for ourselves. The basis of optimism is sheer terror. We think that we are generous because we credit our neighbour with the possession of those virtues that are likely to be a benefit to us. We praise the banker that we may overdraw our account, and find good qualities in the highwayman in the hope that he may spare our pockets. I mean everything that I have said. I have the greatest contempt for optimism. As for a spoiled life, no life is spoiled but one whose growth is arrested. If you want to mar a nature, you have merely to reform it. As for marriage, of course that would be silly, but there are other and more interesting bonds between men and women. I will certainly encourage them. They have the charm of being fashionable. But here is Dorian himself. He will tell you more than I can."

"My dear Harry, my dear Basil, you must both congratulate me!" said the lad, throwing off his evening cape with its satin-lined wings, and shaking each of his friends by the hand in turn. "I have never been so happy. Of course it is sudden: all really delightful things are. And yet it seems to me to be the one thing I have been looking for all my life." He was flushed with excitement and pleasure, and looked extraordinarily handsome.

"I hope you will always be very happy, Dorian," said Hallward, "but I don't quite forgive you for not having let me know of your engagement. You let Harry know."

"And I don't forgive you for being late for dinner," broke in Lord Henry, putting his hand on the lad's shoulder, and smiling as he spoke. "Come, let us sit down and try what the new *chef* here is like, and then you will tell us how it all came about."

"There is really not much to tell," cried Dorian, as they took their seats at the small round table. "What happened was simply this. After I left you yesterday evening, Harry, I dressed, had some dinner at that little Italian restaurant in Rupert Street, you introduced me to, and went down at eight o'clock to the theatre. Sibyl was playing Rosalind. Of course the scenery was dreadful, and the Orlando absurd. But Sibyl! You should have seen her! When she came on in her boy's clothes she was perfectly wonderful. She wore a moss-coloured velvet jerkin with cinnamon sleeves, slim brown cross-gartered hose, a dainty little green cap with a hawk's feather caught in a jewel, and a hooded cloak lined with dull red. She had never seemed to me more exquisite. She had all the delicate grace of that Tanagra figurine that you have in your studio, Basil. Her hair clustered round her face like dark leaves round a pale rose. As for her acting—well, you shall see her to-night. She is simply a born artist. I sat in the dingy box absolutely enthralled. I forgot that I was in London and in the nineteenth century. I was away with my love in a forest that no man had ever seen. After the performance was over I went behind, and spoke to her. As we were sitting together, suddenly there came into her eyes a look that I had never seen there before. My lips moved toward hers. We kissed each other. I can't describe to you what I felt at that moment. It seemed to me that all my life had been narrowed to one perfect point of rose-coloured joy. She trembled all over, and shook like a white narcissus. Then she flung herself on her knees and kissed my hands. I feel that I should not tell you all this, but I can't help it. Of course our engagement is a dead secret. She has not even told her own mother. I don't know what my guardian will say. Lord Radley is sure to be furious. I don't care. I shall be of age in less than a year, and then I can do what I like. I have been right, Basil, haven't I, to take my love out of poetry, and to find my wife in Shakespeare's plays? Lips that Shakespeare taught to speak have whispered their secret in my ear. I have had the arms of Rosalind around me, and kissed Juliet on the mouth."

"Yes, Dorian, I suppose you were right," said Hallward, slowly.

"Have you seen her to-day?" asked Lord Henry.

Dorian Gray shook his head. "I left her in the forest of Arden, I shall find her in an orchard in Verona."

Lord Henry sipped his champagne in a meditative manner. "At what particular point did you mention the word marriage, Dorian? And what did she say in answer? Perhaps you forgot all about it."

"My dear Harry, I did not treat it as a business transaction, and I did not make any formal proposal. I told her that I loved her, and she said she was not worthy to be my wife. Not worthy! Why the whole world is nothing to me compared with her."

"Women are wonderfully practical," murmured Lord Henry, "much more practical than we are. In situations of that kind we often forget to say anything about marriage, and they always remind us."

Hallward laid his hand upon his arm. "Don't, Harry. You have annoyed Dorian. He is not like other men. He would never bring misery upon any one. His nature is too fine for that."

Lord Henry looked across the table. "Dorian is never annoyed with me," he answered. "I asked the question for the best reason possible, for the only reason, indeed, that excuses one for asking any question—simply curiosity. I have a theory that it is always the women who propose to us, and not we who propose to the women. Except, of course, in the middle-class life. But then the middle classes are not modern."

Dorian Gray laughed, and tossed his head. "You are quite incorrigible, Harry; but I don't mind. It is impossible to be angry with you. When you see Sibyl Vane you will feel that the man who could wrong her would be a beast, a beast without a heart. I cannot understand how any one can wish to shame the thing he loves. I love Sibyl Vane. I want to place her on a pedestal of gold, and to see the world worship the woman who is mine. What is marriage? An irrevocable vow. You mock at it for that. Ah! don't mock. It is an irrevocable vow that I want to take. Her trust makes me faithful, her belief makes me good. When I am with her, I regret all that you have taught me. I become different from what you have known me to be. I am changed, and the mere touch of Sibyl Vane's hand makes me forget you and all your wrong, fascinating, poisonous, delightful theories."

"And those are . . . ?" asked Lord Henry, helping himself to some salad.

"Oh, your theories about life, your theories about love, your theories about pleasure. All your theories, in fact, Harry."

"Pleasure is the only thing worth having a theory about," he answered, in his slow, melodious voice. "But I am afraid I cannot claim my theory as my own. It belongs to Nature, not to me. Pleasure is Nature's test, her sign of approval. When we are happy we are always good, but when we are good we are not always happy."

"Ah! but what do you mean by good?" cried Basil Hallward.

"Yes," echoed Dorian, leaning back in his chair, and looking at Lord Henry over the heavy clusters of purple-lipped irises that stood in the centre of the table, "what do you mean by good, Harry?"

"To be good is to be in harmony with one's self," he replied, touching the thin stem of his glass with his pale, fine-pointed fingers. "Discord is to be forced to be in harmony with others. One's own life—that is the important thing. As for the lives of one's neighbors, if one wishes to be a prig or a Puritan, one can flaunt one's moral views about them, but they are not one's concern. Besides, Individualism has really the higher aim. Modern morality consists in accepting the standard of one's age. I consider that for any man of culture to accept the standard of his age is a form of the grossest immorality."

"But, surely, if one lives merely for one's self, Harry, one pays a terrible price for doing so?" suggested the painter.

"Yes, we are overcharged for everything nowadays. I should fancy that the real tragedy of the poor is that they can afford nothing but self-denial. Beautiful sins, like beautiful things, are the privilege of the rich."

"One has to pay in other ways but money."

"What sort of ways, Basil?"

"Oh! I should fancy in remorse, in suffering, in . . . well, in the consciousness of degradation."

Lord Henry shrugged his shoulders. "My dear fellow, mediaeval art is charming, but mediaeval emotions are out of date. One can use them in fiction, of course. But then the only things that one can use in fiction are the things that one has ceased to use in fact. Believe me, no civilized man ever regrets a pleasure, and no uncivilized man ever knows what a pleasure is."

"I know what pleasure is," cried Dorian Gray. "It is to adore some one."

"That is certainly better than being adored," he answered, toying with some fruits. "Being adored is a nuisance. Women treat us just as Humanity treats its gods. They worship us, and are always bothering us to do something for them."

"I should have said that whatever they ask for they had first given to us," murmured the lad, gravely. "They create Love in our natures. They have a right to demand it back."

"That is quite true, Dorian," cried Hallward.

"Nothing is ever quite true," said Lord Henry.

"This is," interrupted Dorian. "You must admit, Harry, that women give to men the very gold of their lives."

"Possibly," he sighed, "but they invariably want it back in such very small change. That is the worry. Women, as some witty Frenchman once put it, inspire us with the desire to do masterpieces, and always prevent us from carrying them out."

"Harry, you are dreadful! I don't know why I like you so much."

"You will always like me, Dorian," he replied. "Will you have some coffee, you fellows? Waiter, bring coffee, and *fine-champagne*, and some cigarettes. No; don't mind the cigarettes; I have some. Basil, I can't allow you to smoke cigars. You must have a cigarette. A cigarette is the perfect type of a perfect pleasure. It is exquisite, and it leaves one unsatisfied. What more can one want? Yes, Dorian, you will always be fond of me. I represent to you all the sins you have never had the courage to commit."

"What nonsense you talk, Harry!" cried the lad, taking a light from a fire-breathing silver dragon that the waiter had placed on the table. "Let us go down to the theatre. When Sibyl comes on the stage you will have a new ideal of life. She will represent something to you that you have never known."

"I have known everything," said Lord Henry, with a tired look in his eyes, "but I am always ready for a new emotion. I am afraid, however, that, for me at any rate, there is no such thing. Still, your wonderful girl may thrill me. I love acting. It is so much more real than life. Let us go. Dorian, you will come with me. I am so sorry, Basil, but there is only room for two in the brougham. You must follow us in a hansom."

They got up and put on their coats, sipping their coffee standing. The painter was silent and preoccupied. There was a gloom over him. He could not bear this marriage, and yet it seemed to him to be better than many other things that might have happened. After a few minutes, they all passed downstairs. He drove off by himself, as had been arranged, and watched the flashing lights of the little brougham in front of him. A strange sense of loss came over him. He felt that Dorian Gray would never again be to him all that he had been in the past. Life had come between them. . . . His eyes darkened, and the crowded, flaring streets became blurred to his eyes. When the cab drew up at the theatre, it seemed to him that he had grown years older.

CHAPTER VII

For some reason or other, the house was crowded that night, and the fat Jew manager who met them at the door was beaming from ear to ear with an oily, tremulous smile. He escorted them to their box with a sort of pompous humility, waving his fat jewelled hands, and talking at the top of his voice. Dorian Gray loathed him more than ever. He felt as if he had come to look for Miranda and had been met by Caliban. Lord Henry, upon the other hand, rather liked him. At least he declared he did, and insisted on shaking him by the hand, and assuring him that he was proud to meet a man who had discovered a real genius and gone bankrupt over a poet. Hallward amused himself with watching the faces in the pit. The heat was terribly oppressive, and the huge sunlight flamed like a monstrous dahlia with petals of yellow fire. The youths in the gallery had taken off their coats and waistcoats and hung them over the side. They talked to each other across the theatre, and shared their oranges with the tawdry girls who sat beside them. Some women were laughing in the pit. Their voices were horribly shrill and discordant. The sound of the popping of corks came from the bar.

"What a place to find one's divinity in!" said Lord Henry.

"Yes!" answered Dorian Gray. "It was here I found her, and she is divine beyond all living things. When she acts you will forget everything. These common, rough people, with their coarse faces and brutal gestures, become quite different when she is on the stage. They sit silently and watch her. They weep and laugh as she wills them to do. She makes them as responsive as a violin. She spiritualizes them, and one feels that they are of the same flesh and blood as one's self."

"The same flesh and blood as one's self! Oh, I hope not!" exclaimed Lord Henry, who was scanning the occupants of the gallery through his opera-glass.

"Don't pay any attention to him, Dorian," said the painter. "I understand what you mean, and I believe in this girl. Any one you love must be marvellous, and any girl that has the effect you describe must be fine and noble. To spiritualize one's age—that is something worth doing. If this girl can give a soul to those who have lived without one, if she can create the sense of beauty in people whose lives have been sordid and ugly, if she can strip them of their selfishness and lend them tears for sorrows that are not their own, she is worthy of all your adoration, worthy of the adoration of the world. This marriage is quite right. I did not think so at first, but I admit it now. The gods made Sibyl Vane for you. Without her you would have been incomplete."

"Thanks, Basil," answered Dorian Gray, pressing his hand. "I knew that you would understand me. Harry is so cynical, he terrifies me. But here is the orchestra. It is quite dreadful, but it only lasts for about five minutes. Then the curtain rises, and you will see the girl to whom I am going to give all my life, to whom I have given everything that is good in me."

A quarter of an hour afterwards, amidst an extraordinary turmoil of applause, Sibyl Vane stepped on the stage. Yes, she was certainly lovely to look at—one of the loveliest creatures, Lord Henry thought, that he had ever seen. There was something of the fawn in her shy grace and startled eyes. A faint blush, like the shadow of a rose in a mirror of silver, came to her cheeks as she glanced at the crowded, enthusiastic house. She stepped back a few paces, and her lips seemed to tremble. Basil Hallward leaped to his feet and began to applaud. Motionless, and as one in a dream, sat Dorian Gray, gazing at her. Lord Henry peered through his glasses, murmuring, "Charming! charming!"

The scene was the hall of Capulet's house, and Romeo in his pilgrim's dress had entered with Mercutio and his other friends. The band, such as it was, struck up a few bars of music, and the dance began. Through the crowd of ungainly, shabbily-dressed actors, Sibyl Vane moved like a creature from a finer world. Her body swayed, while she danced, as a plant sways in the water. The curves of her throat were the curves of the white lily. Her hands seemed to be made of cool ivory.

Yet she was curiously listless. She showed no sign of joy when her eyes rested on Romeo. The few words she had to speak—

Good pilgrim, you do wrong your hand too much,
Which mannerly devotion shows in this;
For saints have hands that pilgrims' hands do touch,
And palm to palm is holy palmers' kiss—

with the brief dialogue that follows, were spoken in a thoroughly artificial manner. The voice was exquisite, but from the point of view of tone it was absolutely false. It was wrong in colour. It took away all life from the verse. It made the passion unreal.

Dorian Gray grew pale as he watched her. He was puzzled and anxious. Neither of his friends dared to say anything to him. She seemed to them to be absolutely incompetent. They were horribly disappointed.

Yet they felt that the true test of any Juliet is the balcony scene of the second act. They waited for that. If she failed there, there was nothing in her.

She looked charming as she came out in the moonlight. That could not be denied. But the staginess of her acting was unbearable, and grew worse as she went on. Her gestures became absurdly artificial. She overemphasized everything that she had to say. The beautiful passage—

Thou knowest the mask of night is on my face,
Else would a maiden blush bepaint my cheek
For that which thou hast heard me speak tonight—

was declaimed with the painful precision of a school-girl who has been taught to recite by some second-rate professor of elocution. When she leaned over the balcony and came to those wonderful lines—

Although I joy in thee,
I have no joy of this contract tonight;
It is too rash, too unadvised, too sudden;
Too like the lightning, which doth cease to be
Ere one can say, "It lightens." Sweet, good-night!
This bud of love by summer's ripening breath
May prove a beauteous flower when next we meet—

she spoke the words as though they conveyed no meaning to her. It was not nervousness. Indeed, so far from being nervous, she was absolutely self-contained. It was simply bad art. She was a complete failure.

Even the common, uneducated audience of the pit and gallery lost their interest in the play. They got restless, and began to talk loudly and to whistle. The Jew manager, who was standing at the back of the dress-circle, stamped and swore with rage. The only person unmoved was the girl herself.

When the second act was over there came a storm of hisses, and Lord Henry got up from his chair and put on his coat. "She is quite beautiful, Dorian," he said, "but she can't act. Let us go."

"I am going to see the play through," answered the lad, in a hard, bitter voice. "I am awfully sorry that I have made you waste an evening, Harry. I apologize to you both."

"My dear Dorian, I should think Miss Vane was ill," interrupted Hallward. "We will come some other night."

"I wish she were ill," he rejoined. "But she seems to me to be simply callous and cold. She has entirely altered. Last night she was a great artist. This evening she is merely a common-place, mediocre actress."

"Don't talk like that about any one you love, Dorian. Love is a more wonderful thing than Art."

"They are both simply forms of imitation," remarked Lord Henry. "But do let us go. Dorian, you must not stay here any longer. It is not good for one's morals to see bad acting. Besides, I don't suppose you will want your wife to act. So what does it matter if she plays Juliet like a wooden doll? She is very lovely, and if she knows as little about life as she does about acting, she will be a delightful experience. There are only two kinds of people who are really fascinating—people who know absolutely everything, and people who know absolutely nothing. Good heavens, my dear boy, don't look so tragic! The secret of remaining young is never to have an emotion that is unbecoming. Come to the club with Basil and myself. We will smoke cigarettes and drink to the beauty of Sibyl Vane. She is beautiful. What more can you want?"

"Go away, Harry," cried the lad. "I want to be alone. Basil, you must go. Ah! can't you see that my heart is breaking?" The hot tears came to his eyes. His lips trembled, and rushing to the back of the box, he leaned up against the wall, hiding his face in his hands.

"Let us go, Basil," said Lord Henry, with a strange tenderness in his voice; and the two young men passed out together.

A few moments afterwards the footlights flared up, and the curtain rose on the third act. Dorian Gray went back to his seat. He looked pale, and proud, and indifferent. The play dragged on, and seemed interminable. Half of the audience went out, tramping in heavy boots, and laughing. The whole thing was a *fiasco.* The last act was played to almost empty benches. The curtain went down on a titter, and some groans.

As soon as it was over, Dorian Gray rushed behind the scenes into the greenroom. The girl was standing there alone, with a look of triumph on her face. Her eyes lit with an exquisite fire. There was a radiance about her. Her parted lips were smiling over some secret of their own.

When he entered, she looked at him and an expression of infinite joy came over her. "How badly I acted to-night, Dorian!" she cried.

"Horribly!" he answered, gazing at her in amazement, "horribly! It was dreadful. Are you ill? You have no idea what it was. You have no idea what I suffered."

The girl smiled. "Dorian," she answered, lingering over his name with long-drawn music in her voice, as though it were sweeter than honey to the red petals of her mouth—"Dorian, you should have understood. But you understand now, don't you?"

"Understand what?" he asked angrily.

"Why I was so bad to-night. Why I shall always be bad. Why I shall never act well again."

He shrugged his shoulders. "You are ill, I suppose. When you are ill you shouldn't act. You make yourself ridiculous. My friends were bored. I was bored."

She seemed not to listen to him. She was transfigured with joy. An ecstasy of happiness dominated her.

"Dorian, Dorian," she cried, "before I knew you, acting was the one reality of my life. It was only in the theatre that I lived. I thought that it was all true. I was Rosalind one night, and Portia the other. The joy of Beatrice was my joy, and the sorrows of Cordelia were mine also. I believed in everything. The common people who acted with me seemed to me to be godlike. The painted scenes were my world. I knew nothing but shadows, and I thought them real. You came—oh, my beautiful love!—and you freed my soul from prison. You taught me what reality really is. To-night, for the first time in my life, I saw through the hollowness, the sham, the silliness of the empty pageant in which I had always played. To-night, for the first time, I became conscious that the Romeo was hideous, and old, and painted, and that the moonlight in the orchard was false, that the scenery was vulgar, and that the words I had to speak were unreal, were not my words, were not what I wanted to say. You had brought me something higher, something of which all art is but a reflection. You had made me understand what love really is. My love! my love! Prince Charming! Prince of life! I have grown sick of shadows. You are more to me than all art can ever be. What have I to do with the puppets of a play? When I came on to-night, I could not understand how it was that everything had gone from me. I thought that I was going to be wonderful. I found that I could do nothing. Suddenly it dawned on my soul what it all meant. The knowledge was exquisite to me. I heard them hissing, and I smiled. What could they know of love such as ours? Take me away, Dorian—take me away with you, where we can be quite alone. I hate the stage. I might mimic a passion that I do not feel, but I cannot mimic one that burns me like fire. Oh, Dorian, Dorian, you understand now what it signifies? Even if I could do it, it would be profanation for me to play at being in love. You have made me see that."

He flung himself down on the sofa, and turned away his face. "You have killed my love," he muttered.

She looked at him in wonder, and laughed. He made no answer. She came across to him, and with her little fingers stroked his hair. She knelt down and pressed his hands to her lips. He drew them away, and a shudder ran through him.

Then he leaped up, and went to the door. "Yes," he cried, "you have killed my love. You used to stir my imagination. Now you don't even stir my curiosity. You simply produce no effect. I loved you because you were marvellous, because you had genius and intellect, because you realized the dreams of great poets and gave shape and substance to the shadows of art. You have thrown it all away. You are shallow and stupid. My God! how mad I was to love you! What a fool I have been! You are nothing to me now. I will never see you again. I will never think of you. I will never mention your name. You don't know what you were to me, once. Why, once . . . Oh, I can't bear to think of it! I wish I had never laid eyes upon you! You have spoiled the romance of my life. How little you can know of love, if you say it mars your art! Without your art you are nothing. I would have made you famous, splendid, magnificent. The world would have worshipped you, and you would have borne my name. What are you now? A third-rate actress with a pretty face."

The girl grew white, and trembled. She clenched her hands together, and her voice seemed to catch in her throat. "You are not serious, Dorian?" she murmured. "You are acting."

"Acting! I leave that to you. You do it so well," he answered, bitterly.

She rose from her knees, and, with a piteous expression of pain in her face, came across the room to him. She put her hand upon his arm, and looked into his eyes. He thrust her back. "Don't touch me!" he cried.

A low moan broke from her, and she flung herself at his feet, and lay there like a trampled flower. "Dorian, Dorian, don't leave me!" she whispered. "I am so sorry I didn't act well. I was thinking of you all the time. But I will try—indeed, I will try. It came so suddenly across me, my love for you. I think I should never have known it if you had not kissed me—if we had not kissed each other. Kiss me again, my love. Don't go away from me. I couldn't bear it. Oh! don't go away from me. My brother . . . No; never mind. He didn't mean it. He was in jest. . . . But you, oh! can't you forgive me for to-night? I will work so hard, and try to improve. Don't be cruel to me because I love you better than anything in the world. After all, it is only once that I have not pleased you. But you are quite right, Dorian. I should have shown myself more of an artist. It was foolish of me; and yet I couldn't help it. Oh, don't leave me, don't leave me." A fit of passionate sobbing choked her. She crouched on the floor like a wounded thing, and Dorian Gray, with his beautiful eyes, looked down at her, and his chiselled lips curled in exquisite disdain. There is always something ridiculous about the emotions of people whom one has ceased to love. Sibyl Vane seemed to him to be absurdly melodramatic. Her tears and sobs annoyed him.

"I am going," he said at last, in his calm, clear voice. "I don't wish to be unkind, but I can't see you again. You have disappointed me."

She wept silently, and made no answer, but crept nearer. Her little hands stretched blindly out, and appeared to be seeking for him. He turned on his heel, and left the room. In a few moments he was out of the theatre.

Where he went to he hardly knew. He remembered wandering through dimly-lit streets, past gaunt black-shadowed archways and evil-looking houses. Women with hoarse voices and harsh laughter had called after him. Drunkards had reeled by cursing, and chattering to themselves like monstrous apes. He had seen grotesque children huddled upon doorsteps, and heard shrieks and oaths from gloomy courts.

As the dawn was just breaking he found himself close to Covent Garden. The darkness lifted, and, flushed with faint fires, the sky hollowed itself into a perfect pearl. Huge carts filled with nodding lilies rumbled slowly down the polished empty street. The air was heavy with the perfume of the flowers, and their beauty seemed to bring him an anodyne for his pain. He followed into the market, and watched the men unloading their waggons. A white-smocked carter offered him some cherries. He thanked him, wondered why he refused to accept any money for them, and began to eat them listlessly. They had been plucked at midnight, and the coldness of the moon had entered into them. A long line of boys carrying crates of striped tulips, and of yellow and red roses, defiled in front of him, threading their way through the huge jade-green piles of vegetables. Under the portico, with its grey sun-bleached pillars, loitered a troop of draggled bareheaded girls, waiting for the auction to be over. Others crowded round the swinging doors of the coffee-house in the piazza. The heavy cart-horses slipped and stamped upon the rough stones, shaking their bells and trappings. Some of the drivers were lying asleep on a pile of sacks. Iris-necked, and pink-footed, the pigeons ran about picking up seeds.

After a little while, he hailed a hansom, and drove home. For a few moments he loitered upon the doorstep, looking round at the silent Square with its blank close-shuttered windows, and its staring blinds. The sky was pure opal now, and the roofs of the houses glistened like silver against it. From some chimney opposite a thin wreath of smoke was rising. It curled, a violet riband, through the nacre-coloured air.

In the huge gilt Venetian lantern, spoil of some Doge's barge, that hung from the ceiling of the great oak-panelled hall of entrance, lights were still burning from three flickering jets: thin blue petals of flame they seemed, trimmed with white fire. He turned them out, and, having thrown his hat and cape on the table, passed through the library towards the door of his bedroom, a large octagonal chamber on the ground floor that, in his new-born feeling for luxury, he had just had decorated for himself, and hung with some curious Renaissance tapestries that had been discovered stored in a disused attic at Selby Royal. As he was turning the handle of the door, his eye fell upon the portrait Basil Hallward had painted of him. He started back as if in surprise. Then he went on into his own room, looking somewhat puzzled. After he had taken the buttonhole out of his coat, he seemed to hesitate. Finally he came back, went over to the picture, and examined it. In the dim arrested light that struggled through the cream-coloured silk blinds, the face appeared to him to be a little changed. The expression looked different. One would have said that there was a touch of cruelty in the mouth. It was certainly strange.

He turned round, and, walking to the window, drew up the blind. The bright dawn flooded the room, and swept the fantastic shadows into dusky corners, where they lay shuddering. But the strange expression that he had noticed in the face of the portrait seemed to linger there, to be more intensified even. The quivering, ardent sunlight showed him the lines of cruelty round the mouth as clearly as if he had been looking into a mirror after he had done some dreadful thing.

He winced, and, taking up from the table an oval glass framed in ivory Cupids, one of Lord Henry's many presents to him, glanced hurriedly into its polished depths. No line like that warped his red lips. What did it mean?

He rubbed his eyes, and came close to the picture, and examined it again. There were no signs of any change when he looked into the actual painting, and yet there was no doubt that the whole expression had altered. It was not a mere fancy of his own. The thing was horribly apparent.

He threw himself into a chair, and began to think. Suddenly there flashed across his mind what he had said in Basil Hallward's studio the day the picture had been finished. Yes, he remembered it perfectly. He had uttered a mad wish that he himself might remain young, and the portrait grow old; that his own beauty might be untarnished, and the face on the canvas bear the burden of his passions and his sins; that the painted image might be seared with the lines of suffering and thought, and that he might keep all the delicate bloom and loveliness of his then just conscious boyhood. Surely his wish had not been fulfilled? Such things were impossible. It seemed monstrous even to think of them. And, yet, there was the picture before him, with the touch of cruelty in the mouth.

Cruelty! Had he been cruel? It was the girl's fault, not his. He had dreamed of her as a great artist, had given his love to her because he had thought her great. Then she had disappointed him. She had been shallow and unworthy. And, yet, a feeling of infinite regret came over him, as he thought of her lying at his feet sobbing like a little child. He remembered with what callousness he had watched her. Why had he been made like that? Why had such a soul been given to him? But he had suffered also. During the three terrible hours that the play had lasted, he had lived centuries of pain, æon upon æon of torture. His life was well worth hers. She had marred him for a moment, if he had wounded her for an age. Besides, women were better suited to bear sorrow than men. They lived on their emotions. They only thought of their emotions. When they took lovers, it was merely to have some one with whom they could have scenes. Lord Henry had told him that, and Lord Henry knew what women were. Why should he trouble about Sibyl Vane? She was nothing to him now.

But the picture? What was he to say of that? It held the secret of his life, and told his story. It had taught him to love his own beauty. Would it teach him to loathe his own soul? Would he ever look at it again?

No; it was merely an illusion wrought on the troubled senses. The horrible night that he had passed had left phantoms behind it. Suddenly there had fallen upon his brain that tiny scarlet speck that makes men mad. The picture had not changed. It was folly to think so.

Yet it was watching him, with its beautiful marred face and its cruel smile. Its bright hair gleamed in the early sunlight. Its blue eyes met his own. A sense of infinite pity, not for himself, but for the painted image of himself, came over him. It had altered already, and would alter more. Its gold would wither into grey. Its red and white roses would die. For every sin that he committed, a stain would fleck and wreck its fairness. But he would not sin. The picture, changed or unchanged, would be to him the visible emblem of conscience. He would resist temptation. He would not see Lord Henry any more—would not, at any rate, listen to those subtle poisonous theories that in Basil Hallward's garden had first stirred within him the passion for impossible things. He would go back to Sibyl Vane, make her amends, marry her, try to love her again. Yes, it was his duty to do so. She must have suffered more than he had. Poor child! He had been selfish and cruel to her. The fascination that she had exercised over him would return. They would be happy together. His life with her would be beautiful and pure.

He got up from his chair, and drew a large screen right in front of the portrait, shuddering as he glanced at it. "How horrible!" he murmured to himself, and he walked across to the window and opened it. When he stepped out on to the grass, he drew a deep breath. The fresh morning air seemed to drive away all his sombre passions. He thought only of Sibyl. A faint echo of his love came back to him. He repeated her name over and over again. The birds that were singing in the dew-drenched garden seemed to be telling the flowers about her.

CHAPTER VIII

It was long past noon when he awoke. His valet had crept several times on tiptoe into the room to see if he was stirring, and had wondered what made his young master sleep so late. Finally his bell sounded, and Victor came in softly with a cup of tea, and a pile of letters, on a small tray of old Sèvres china, and drew back the olive-satin curtains, with their shimmering blue lining, that hung in front of the three tall windows.

"Monsieur has slept well this morning," he said, smiling.

"What o'clock is it, Victor?" asked Dorian Gray, drowsily.

"One hour and a quarter, Monsieur."

How late it was! He sat up, and, having sipped some tea, turned over his letters. One of them was from Lord Henry, and had been brought by hand that morning. He hesitated for a moment, and then put it aside. The others he opened listlessly. They contained the usual collection of cards, invitations to dinner, tickets for private views, programmes of charity concerts, and the like, that are showered on fashionable young men every morning during the season. There was a rather heavy bill, for a chased silver Louis-Quinze toilet-set, that he had not yet had the courage to send on to his guardians, who were extremely old-fashioned people and did not realize that we live in an age when unnecessary things are our only necessities; and there were several very courteouslv worded communications from Jermyn Street money-lenders offering to advance any sum of money at a moment's notice and at the most reasonable rates of interest.

After about ten minutes he got up, and, throwing on an elaborate dressing-gown of silk-embroidered cashmere wool, passed into the onyx-paved bathroom. The cool water refreshed him after his long sleep. He seemed to have forgotten all that he had gone through. A dim sense of having taken part in some strange tragedy came to him once or twice, but there was the unreality of a dream about it.

As soon as he was dressed, he went into the library and sat down to a light French breakfast, that had been laid out for him on a small round table close to the open window. It was an exquisite day. The warm air seemed laden with spices. A bee flew in, and buzzed round the blue-dragon bowl that, filled with sulphur-yellow roses, stood before him. He felt perfectly happy.

Suddenly his eye fell on the screen that he had placed in front of the portrait, and he started.

"Too cold for Monsieur?" asked his valet, putting an omelette on the table. "I shut the window?"

Dorian shook his head. "I am not cold," he murmured.

Was it all true? Had the portrait really changed? Or had it been simply his own imagination that had made him see a look of evil where there had been a look of joy? Surely a painted canvas could not alter? The thing was absurd. It would serve as a tale to tell Basil some day. It would make him smile.

And, yet, how vivid was his recollection of the whole thing! First in the dim twilight, and then in the bright dawn, he had seen the touch of cruelty round the warped lips. He almost dreaded his valet leaving the room. He knew that when he was alone he would have to examine the portrait. He was afraid of certainty. When the coffee and cigarettes had been brought and the man turned to go, he felt a wild desire to tell him to remain. As the door was closing behind him he called him back. The man stood waiting for his orders. Dorian looked at him for a moment. "I am not at home to any one, Victor," he said, with a sigh. The man bowed and retired.

Then he rose from the table, lit a cigarette and flung himself down on a luxuriously-cushioned couch that stood facing the screen. The screen was an old one, of gilt Spanish leather, stamped and wrought with a rather florid Louis-Quatorze pattern. He scanned it curiously, wondering if ever before it had concealed the secret of a man's life.

Should he move it aside, after all? Why not let it stay there? What was the use of knowing? If the thing was true, it was terrible. If it was not true, why trouble about it? But what if, by some fate or deadlier chance, eyes other than his spied behind, and saw the horrible change? What should he do if Basil Hallward came and asked to look at his own picture? Basil would be sure to do that. No; the thing had to be examined, and at once. Anything would be better than this dreadful state of doubt.

He got up, and locked both doors. At least he would be alone when he looked upon the mask of his shame. Then he drew the screen aside, and saw himself face to face. It was perfectly true. The portrait had altered.

As he often remembered afterwards, and always with no small wonder, he found himself at first gazing at the portrait with a feeling of almost scientific interest. That such a change should have taken place was incredible to him. And yet it was a fact. Was there some subtle affinity between the chemical atoms, that shaped themselves into form and colour on the canvas, and the soul that was within him? Could it be that what that soul thought, they realized?—that what it dreamed, they made true? Or was there some other, more terrible reason? He shuddered, and felt afraid, and, going back to the couch, lay there, gazing at the picture in sickened horror.

One thing, however, he felt that it had done for him. It had made him conscious how unjust, how cruel, he had been to Sibyl Vane. It was not too late to make reparation for that. She could still be his wife. His unreal and selfish love would yield to some higher influence, would be transformed into some nobler passion, and the portrait that Basil Hallward had painted of him would be a guide to him through life, would be to him what holiness is to some, and conscience to others, and the fear of God to us all. There were opiates for remorse, drugs that could lull the moral sense to sleep. But here was a visible symbol of the degradation of sin. Here was an ever-present sign of the ruin men brought upon their souls.

Three o'clock struck, and four, and the half-hour rang its double chime, but Dorian Gray did not stir. He was trying to gather up the scarlet threads of life, and to weave them into a pattern; to find his way through the sanguine labyrinth of passion through which he was wandering. He did not know what to do, or what to think. Finally, he went over to the table and wrote a passionate letter to the girl he had loved, imploring her forgiveness, and accusing himself of madness. He covered page after page with wild words of sorrow, and wilder words of pain. There is a luxury in self-reproach. When we blame ourselves we feel that no one else has a right to blame us. It is the confession, not the priest, that gives us absolution. When Dorian had finished the letter, he felt that he had been forgiven.

Suddenly there came a knock to the door, and he heard Lord Henry's voice outside. "My dear boy, I must see you. Let me in at once. I can't bear your shutting yourself up like this."

He made no answer at first, but remained quite still. The knocking still continued, and grew louder. Yes, it was better to let Lord Henry in, and to explain to him the new life he was going to lead, to quarrel with him if it became necessary to quarrel, to part if parting was inevitable. He jumped up, drew the screen hastily across the picture, and unlocked the door.

"I am so sorry for it all, Dorian," said Lord Henry, as he entered. "But you must not think too much about it."

"Do you mean about Sibyl Vane?" asked the lad.

"Yes, of course," answered Lord Henry, sinking into a chair, and slowly pulling off his yellow gloves. "It is dreadful, from one point of view, but it was not your fault. Tell me, did you go behind and see her, after the play was over?"

"Yes."

"I felt sure you had. Did you make a scene with her?"

"I was brutal, Harry, perfectly brutal. But it is all right now. I am not sorry for anything that has happened. It has taught me to know myself better."

"Ah, Dorian, I am so glad you take it in that way! I was afraid I would find you plunged in remorse, and tearing that nice curly hair of yours."

"I have got through all that," said Dorian, shaking his head, and smiling. "I am perfectly happy now. I know what conscience is, to begin with. It is not what you told me it was. It is the divinest thing in us. Don't sneer at it, Harry, any more—at least not before me. I want to be good. I can't bear the idea of my soul being hideous."

"A very charming artistic basis for ethics, Dorian! I congratulate you on it. But how are you going to begin?"

"By marrying Sibyl Vane."

"Marrying Sibyl Vane!" cried Lord Henry, standing up, and looking at him in perplexed amazement. "But, my dear Dorian——"

"Yes, Harry, I know what you are going to say. Something dreadful about marriage. Don't say it. Don't ever say things of that kind to me again. Two days ago I asked Sibyl to marry me. I am not going to break my word to her. She is to be my wife."

"Your wife! Dorian! . . . Didn't you get my letter? I wrote to you this morning, and sent the note down, by my own man."

"Your letter? Oh, yes, I remember. I have not read it yet, Harry. I was afraid there might be something in it that I wouldn't like. You cut life to pieces with your epigrams."

"You know nothing, then?"

"What do you mean?"

Lord Henry walked across the room, and, sitting down by Dorian Gray, took both his hands in his own, and held them tightly. "Dorian," he said, "my letter—don't be frightened—was to tell you that Sibyl Vane is dead."

A cry of pain broke from the lad's lips, and he leaped to his feet, tearing his hands away from Lord Henry's grasp. "Dead! Sibyl dead! It is not true! It is a horrible lie! How dare you say it?"

"It is quite true, Dorian," said Lord Henry, gravely. "It is in all the morning papers. I wrote down to you to ask you not to see any one till I came. There will have to be an inquest, of course, and you must not be mixed up in it. Things like that make a man fashionable in Paris. But in London people are so prejudiced. Here, one should never make one's *debut* with a scandal. One should reserve that to give an interest to one's old age. I suppose they don't know your name at the theatre? If they don't, it is all right. Did any one see you going round to her room? That is an important point."

Dorian did not answer for a few moments. He was dazed with horror. Finally he stammered, in a stifled voice, "Harry, did you say an inquest? What did you mean by that? Did Sibyl——? Oh, Harry, I can't bear it! But be quick. Tell me everything at once."

"I have no doubt it was not an accident, Dorian, though it must be put in that way to the public. It seems that as she was leaving the theatre with her mother, about half-past twelve or so, she said she had forgotten something upstairs. They waited some time for her, but she did not come down again. They ultimately found her lying dead on the floor of her dressing room. She had swallowed something by mistake, some dreadful thing they use at theatres. I don't know what it was, but it had either prussic acid or white lead in it. I should fancy it was prussic acid, as she seems to have died instantaneously."

"Harry, Harry, it is terrible!" cried the lad.

"Yes; it is very tragic, of course, but you must not get yourself mixed up in it. I see by *The Standard* that she was seventeen. I should have thought she was almost younger than that. She looked such a child, and seemed to know so little about acting. Dorian, you mustn't let this thing get on your nerves. You must come and dine with me, and afterwards we will look in at the Opera. It is a Patti night, and everybody will be there. You can come to my sister's box. She has got some smart women with her."

"So I have murdered Sibyl Vane," said Dorian Gray, half to himself, "murdered her as surely as if I had cut her little throat with a knife. Yet the roses are not less lovely for all that. The birds sing just as happily in my garden. And to-night I am to dine with you, and then go on to the Opera, and sup somewhere, I suppose, afterwards. How extraordinarily dramatic life is! If I had read all this in a book, Harry, I think I would have wept over it. Somehow, now that it has happened actually, and to me, it seems far too wonderful for tears. Here is the first passionate love-letter I have ever written in my life. Strange, that my first passionate love-letter should have been addressed to a dead girl. Can they feel, I wonder, those white silent people we call the dead? Sibyl! Can she feel, or know, or listen? Oh, Harry, how I loved her once! It seems years ago to me now. She was everything to me. Then came that dreadful night—was it really only last night?—when she played so badly, and my heart almost broke. She explained it all to me. It was terribly pathetic. But I was not moved a bit. I thought her shallow. Suddenly something happened that made me afraid. I can't tell you what it was, but it was terrible. I said I would go back to her. I felt I had done wrong. And now she is dead. My God! my God! Harry, what shall I do? You don't know the danger I am in, and there is nothing to keep me straight. She would have done that for me. She had no right to kill herself. It was selfish of her."

"My dear Dorian," answered Lord Henry, taking a cigarette from his case, and producing a gold-latten matchbox, "the only way a woman can ever reform a man is by boring him so completely that he loses all possible interest in life. If you had married this girl you would have been wretched. Of course you would have treated her kindly. One can always be kind to people about whom one cares nothing. But she would have soon found out that you were absolutely indifferent to her. And when a woman finds that out about her husband, she either becomes dreadfully dowdy, or wears very smart bonnets that some other woman's husband has to pay for. I say nothing about the social mistake, which would have been abject, which, of course, I would not have allowed, but I assure you that in any case the whole thing would have been an absolute failure."

"I suppose it would," muttered the lad, walking up and down the room, and looking horribly pale. "But I thought it was my duty. It is not my fault that this terrible tragedy has prevented my doing what was right. I remember your saying once that there is a fatality about good resolutions—that they are always made too late. Mine certainly were."

"Good resolutions are useless attempts to interfere with scientific laws. Their origin is pure vanity. Their result is absolutely *nil*. They give us, now and then, some of those luxurious sterile emotions that have a certain charm for the weak. That is all that can be said for them. They are simply cheques that men draw on a bank where they have no account."

"Harry," cried Dorian Gray, coming over and sitting down beside him, "why is it that I cannot feel this tragedy as much as I want to? I don't think I am heartless. Do you?"

"You have done too many foolish things during the last fortnight to be entitled to give yourself that name, Dorian," answered Lord Henry, with his sweet, melancholy smile.

The lad frowned. "I don't like that explanation, Harry," he rejoined, "but I am glad you don't think I'm heartless. I am nothing of the kind. I know I am not. And yet I must admit that this thing that has happened does not affect me as it should. It seems to me to be simply like a wonderful ending to a wonderful play. It has all the terrible beauty of a Greek tragedy, a tragedy in which I took a great part, but by which I have not been wounded."

"It is an interesting question," said Lord Henry, who found an exquisite pleasure in playing on the lad's unconscious egotism—"an extremely interesting question. I fancy that the true explanation is this. It often happens that the real tragedies of life occur in such an inartistic manner that they hurt us by their crude violence, their absolute incoherence, their absurd want of meaning, their entire lack of style. They affect us just as vulgarity affects us. They give us an impression of sheer brute force, and we revolt against that. Sometimes, however, a tragedy that possesses artistic elements of beauty crosses our lives. If these elements of beauty are real, the whole thing simply appeals to our sense of dramatic effect. Suddenly we find that we are no longer the actors, but the spectators of the play. Or rather we are both. We watch ourselves, and the mere wonder of the spectacle enthralls us. In the present case, what is it that has really happened? Some one has killed herself for love of you. I wish that I had ever had such an experience. It would have made me in love with love for the rest of my life. The people who have adored me—there have not been very many, but there have been some—have always insisted on living on, long after I had ceased to care for them, or they to care for me. They have become stout and tedious, and when I meet them they go in at once for reminiscences. That awful memory of woman! What a fearful thing it is! And what an utter intellectual stagnation it reveals! One should absorb the colour of life, but one should never remember its details. Details are always vulgar."

"I must sow poppies in my garden," sighed Dorian.

"There is no necessity," rejoined his companion. "Life has always poppies in her hands. Of course, now and then things linger. I once wore nothing but violets all through one season, as a form of artistic mourning for a romance that would not die. Ultimately, however, it did die. I forget what killed it. I think it was her proposing to sacrifice the whole world for me. That is always a dreadful moment. It fills one with the terror of eternity. Well—would you believe it?—a week ago, at Lady Hampshire's, I found myself seated at dinner next the lady in question, and she insisted on going over the whole thing again, and digging up the past, and raking up the future. I had buried my romance in a bed of asphodel. She dragged it out again, and assured me that I had spoiled her life. I am bound to state that she ate an enormous dinner, so I did not feel any anxiety. But what a lack of taste she showed! The one charm of the past is that it is the past. But women never know when the curtain has fallen. They always want a sixth act, and as soon as the interest of the play is entirely over they propose to continue it. If they were allowed their own way, every comedy would have a tragic ending, and every tragedy would culminate in a farce. They are charmingly artificial, but they have no sense of art. You are more fortunate than I am. I assure you, Dorian, that not one of the women I have known would have done for me what Sibyl Vane did for you. Ordinary women always console themselves. Some of them do it by going in for sentimental colours. Never trust a woman who wears mauve, whatever her age may be, or a woman over thirty-five who is fond of pink ribbons. It always means that they have a history. Others find a great consolation in suddenly discovering the good qualities of their husbands. They flaunt their conjugal felicity in one's face, as if it were the most fascinating of sins. Religion consoles some. Its mysteries have all the charm of a flirtation, a woman once told me, and I can quite understand it. Besides, nothing makes one so vain as being told that one is a sinner. Conscience makes egotists of us all. Yes; there is really no end to the consolations that women find in modern life. Indeed, I have not mentioned the most important one."

"What is that, Harry?" said the lad, listlessly.

"Oh, the obvious consolation. Taking some one else's admirer when one loses one's own. In good society that always whitewashes a woman. But really, Dorian, how different Sibyl Vane must have been from all the women one meets! There is something to me quite beautiful about her death. I am glad I am living in a century when such wonders happen. They make one believe in the reality of the things we all play with, such as romance, passion, and love."

"I was terribly cruel to her. You forget that."

"I am afraid that women appreciate cruelty, downright cruelty, more than anything else. They have wonderfully primitive instincts. We have emancipated them, but they remain slaves looking for their masters, all the same. They love being dominated. I am sure you were splendid. I have never seen you really and absolutely angry, but I can fancy how delightful you looked. And, after all, you said something to me the day before yesterday that seemed to me at the time to be merely fanciful, but that I see now was absolutely true, and it holds the key to everything."

"What was that, Harry?"

"You said to me that Sibyl Vane represented to you all the heroines of romance—that she was Desdemona one night, and Ophelia the other; that if she died as Juliet, she came to life as Imogen."

"She will never come to life again now," muttered the lad, burying his face in his hands.

"No, she will never come to life. She has played her last part. But you must think of that lonely death in the tawdry dressing-room simply as a strange lurid fragment from some Jacobean tragedy, as a wonderful scene from Webster, or Ford, or Cyril Tourneur. The girl never really lived, and so she has never really died. To you at least she was always a dream, a phantom that flitted through Shakespeare's plays and left them lovelier for its presence, a reed through which Shakespeare's music sounded richer and more full of joy. The moment she touched actual life, she marred it, and it marred her, and so she passed away. Mourn for Ophelia, if you like. Put ashes on your head because Cordelia was strangled. Cry out against Heaven because the daughter of Brabantio died. But don't waste your tears over Sibyl Vane. She was less real than they are."

There was a silence. The evening darkened in the room. Noiselessly, and with silver feet, the shadows crept in from the garden. The colours faded wearily out of things.

After some time Dorian Gray looked up. "You have explained me to myself, Harry," he murmured, with something of a sigh of relief. "I felt all that you have said, but somehow I was afraid of it, and I could not express it to myself. How well you know me! But we will not talk again of what has happened. It has been a marvellous experience. That is all. I wonder if life has still in store for me anything as marvellous."

"Life has everything in store for you, Dorian. There is nothing that you, with your extraordinary good looks, will not be able to do."

"But suppose, Harry, I became haggard, and old, and wrinkled? What then?"

"Ah, then," said Lord Henry, rising to go, "then, my dear Dorian, you would have to fight for your victories. As it is, they are brought to you. No, you must keep your good looks. We live in an age that reads too much to be wise, and that thinks too much to be beautiful. We cannot spare you. And now you had better dress, and drive down to the club. We are rather late, as it is."

"I think I shall join you at the Opera, Harry. I feel too tired to eat anything. What is the number of your sister's box?"

"Twenty-seven, I believe. It is on the grand tier. You will see her name on the door. But I am sorry you won't come and dine."

"I don't feel up to it," said Dorian, listlessly. "But I am awfully obliged to you for all that you have said to me. You are certainly my best friend. No one has ever understood me as you have."

"We are only at the beginning of our friendship, Dorian," answered Lord Henry, shaking him by the hand. "Good-bye. I shall see you before nine-thirty, I hope. Remember, Patti is singing."

As he closed the door behind him, Dorian Gray touched the bell, and in a few minutes Victor appeared with the lamps and drew the blinds down. He waited impatiently for him to go. The man seemed to take an interminable time over everything.

As soon as he had left, he rushed to the screen, and drew it back. No; there was no further change in the picture. It had received the news of Sibyl Vane's death before he had known of it himself. It was conscious of the events of life as they occurred. The vicious cruelty that marred the fine lines of the mouth had, no doubt, appeared at the very moment that the girl had drunk the poison, whatever it was. Or was it indifferent to results? Did it merely take cognizance of what passed within the soul? He wondered, and hoped that some day he would see the change taking place before his very eyes, shuddering as he hoped it.

Poor Sibyl! what a romance it had all been! She had often mimicked death on the stage. Then Death himself had touched her, and taken her with him. How had she played that dreadful last scene? Had she cursed him, as she died? No; she had died for love of him, and love would always be a sacrament to him now. She had atoned for everything, by the sacrifice she had made of her life. He would not think any more of what she had made him go through, on that horrible night at the theatre. When he thought of her, it would be as a wonderful tragic figure sent on to the world's stage to show the supreme reality of Love. A wonderful tragic figure? Tears came to his eyes as he remembered her childlike look and winsome fanciful ways and shy tremulous grace. He brushed them away hastily, and looked again at the picture.

He felt that the time had really come for making his choice. Or had his choice already been made? Yes, life had decided that for him—life, and his own infinite curiosity about life. Eternal youth, infinite passion, pleasure subtle and secret, wild joys and wilder sins—he was to have all these things. The portrait was to bear the burden of his shame: that was all.

A feeling of pain crept over him as he thought of the desecration that was in store for the fair face on the canvas. Once, in boyish mockery of Narcissus, he had kissed, or feigned to kiss, those painted lips that now smiled so cruelly at him. Morning after morning he had sat before the portrait wondering at its beauty, almost enamoured of it, as it seemed to him at times. Was it to alter now with every mood to which he yielded? Was it to become a monstrous and loathsome thing, to be hidden away in a locked room, to be shut out from the sunlight that had so often touched to brighter gold the waving wonder of its hair? The pity of it! the pity of it!

For a moment he thought of praying that the horrible sympathy that existed between him and the picture might cease. It had changed in answer to a prayer; perhaps in answer to a prayer it might remain unchanged. And, yet, who, that knew anything about Life, would surrender the chance of remaining always young, however fantastic that chance might be, or with what fateful consequences it might be fraught? Besides, was it really under his control? Had it indeed been prayer that had produced the substitution? Might there not be some curious scientific reason for it all? If thought could exercise its influence upon a living organism, might not thought exercise an influence upon dead and inorganic things? Nay, without thought or conscious desire, might not things external to ourselves vibrate in unison with our moods and passions, atom calling to atom in secret love or strange affinity? But the reason was of no importance. He would never again tempt by a prayer any terrible power. If the picture was to alter, it was to alter. That was all. Why inquire too closely into it?

For there would be a real pleasure in watching it. He would be able to follow his mind into its secret places. This portrait would be to him the most magical of mirrors. As it had revealed to him his own body, so it would reveal to him his own soul. And when winter came upon it, he would still be standing where spring trembles on the verge of summer. When the blood crept from its face, and left behind a pallid mask of chalk with leaden eyes, he would keep the glamour of boyhood. Not one blossom of his loveliness would ever fade. Not one pulse of his life would ever weaken. Like the gods of the Greeks, he would be strong, and fleet, and joyous. What did it matter what happened to the coloured image on the canvas? He would be safe. That was everything.

He drew the screen back into its former place in front of the picture, smiling as he did so, and passed into his bedroom, where his valet was already waiting for him. An hour later he was at the Opera, and Lord Henry was leaning over his chair.

CHAPTER IX

As HE was sitting at breakfast next morning, Basil Hallward was shown into the room.

"I am glad I have found you, Dorian," he said gravely. "I called last night, and they told me you were at the Opera. Of course I knew that was impossible. But I wish you had left word where you had really gone to. I passed a dreadful evening, half afraid that one tragedy might be followed by another. I think you might have telegraphed for me when you heard of it first. I read of it quite by chance in a late edition of *The Globe*, that I picked up at the club. I came here at once, and was miserable at not finding you. I can't tell you how heartbroken I am about the whole thing. I know what you must suffer. But where were you? Did you go down and see the girl's mother? For a moment I thought of following you there. They gave the address in the paper. Somewhere in the Euston Road, isn't it? But I was afraid of intruding upon a sorrow that I could not lighten. Poor woman! What a state she must be in! And her only child, too! What did she say about it all?"

"My dear Basil, how do I know?" murmured Dorian Gray, sipping some pale-yellow wine from a delicate gold-beaded bubble of Venetian glass, and looking dreadfully bored. "I was at the Opera. You should have come on there. I met Lady Gwendolyn, Harry's sister, for the first time. We were in her box. She is perfectly charming; and Patti sang divinely. Don't talk about horrid subjects. If one doesn't talk about a thing, it has never happened. It is simply expression, as Harry says, that gives reality to things. I may mention that she was not the woman's only child. There is a son, a charming fellow, I believe. But he is not on the stage. He is a sailor, or something. And now, tell me about yourself and what you are painting."

"You went to the Opera?" said Hallward, speaking very slowly, and with a strained touch of pain in his voice. "You went to the Opera while Sibyl Vane was lying dead in some sordid lodging? You can talk to me of other women being charming, and of Patti singing divinely, before the girl you loved has even the quiet of a grave to sleep in? Why, man, there are horrors in store for that little white body of hers!"

"Stop, Basil! I won't hear it!" cried Dorian, leaping to his feet. "You must not tell me about things. What is done is done. What is past is past."

"You call yesterday the past?"

"What has the actual lapse of time got to do with it? It is only shallow people who require years to get rid of an emotion. A man who is master of himself can end a sorrow as easily as he can invent a pleasure. I don't want to be at the mercy of my emotions. I want to use them, to enjoy them, and to dominate them."

"Dorian, this is horrible! Something has changed you completely. You look exactly like the same wonderful boy who, day after day, used to come down to my studio to sit for his picture. But you were simple, natural, and affectionate then. You were the most unspoiled creature in the whole world. Now, I don't know what has come over you. You talk as if you had no heart, no pity in you. It is all Harry's influence. I see that."

The lad flushed up, and, going to the window, looked out for a few moments on the green, flickering, sun-lashed garden. "I owe a great deal to Harry, Basil," he said, at last, "more than I owe to you. You only taught me to be vain."

"Well, I am punished for that, Dorian—or shall be some day."

"I don't know what you mean, Basil," he exclaimed, turning round. "I don't know what you want. What do you want?"

"I want the Dorian Gray I used to paint," said the artist, sadly.

"Basil," said the lad, going over to him, and putting his hand on his shoulder, "you have come too late. Yesterday when I heard that Sibyl Vane had killed herself——"

"Killed herself! Good heavens! is there no doubt about that?" cried Hallward, looking up at him with an expression of horror.

"My dear Basil! Surely you don't think it was a vulgar accident? Of course she killed herself."

The elder man buried his face in his hands. "How fearful," he muttered, and a shudder ran through him.

"No," said Dorian Gray, "there is nothing fearful about it. It is one of the great romantic tragedies of the age. As a rule, people who act lead the most commonplace lives. They are good husbands, or faithful wives, or something tedious. You know what I mean—middle-class virtue, and all that kind of thing. How different Sibyl was! She lived her finest tragedy. She was always a heroine. The last night she played—the night you saw her—she acted badly because she had known the reality of love. When she knew its unreality, she died, as Juliet might have died. She passed again into the sphere of art. There is something of the martyr about her. Her death has all the pathetic uselessness of martyrdom, all its wasted beauty. But as I was saying, you must not think I have not suffered. If you had come in yesterday at a particular moment—about half-past five, perhaps, or a quarter to six—you would have found me in tears. Even Harry, who was here, who brought me the news, in fact, had no idea what I was going through. I suffered immensely. Then it passed away. I cannot repeat an emotion. No one can, except sentimentalists. And you are awfully unjust, Basil. You come down here to console me. That is charming of you. You find me consoled, and you are furious. How like a sympathetic person! You remind me of a story Harry told me about a certain philanthropist who spent twenty years of his life in trying to get some grievance redressed, or some unjust law altered—I forget exactly what it was. Finally he succeeded, and nothing could exceed his disappointment. He had absolutely nothing to do, almost died of *ennui*, and became a confirmed misanthrope. And besides, my dear old Basil, if you really want to console me, teach me rather to forget what has happened, or to see it from a proper artistic point of view. Was it not Gautier who used to write about *la consolation des arts?* I remember picking up a little vellum-covered book in your studio one day and chancing on that delightful phrase. Well, I am not like that young man you told me of when we were down at Marlow together, the young man who used to say that yellow satin could console one for all the miseries of life. I love beautiful things that one can touch and handle. Old brocades, green bronzes, lacquerwork, carved ivories, exquisite surroundings, luxury, pomp, there is much to be got from all these. But the artistic temperament that they create, or at any rate reveal, is still more to me. To become the spectator of one's own life, as Harry says, is to escape the suffering of life. I know you are surprised at my talking to you like this. You have not realized how I have developed. I was a schoolboy when you knew me. I am a man now. I have new passions, new thoughts, new ideas. I am different, but you must not like me less. I am changed, but you must always be my friend. Of course I am very fond of Harry. But I know that you are better than he is. You are not stronger—you are too much afraid of life—but you are better. And how happy we used to be together! Don't leave me, Basil, and don't quarrel with me. I am what I am. There is nothing more to be said."

The painter felt strangely moved. The lad was infinitely dear to him, and his personality had been the great turning-point in his art. He could not bear the idea of reproaching him any more. After all, his indifference was probably merely a mood that would pass away. There was so much in him that was good, so much in him that was noble.

"Well, Dorian," he said, at length, with a sad smile, "I won't speak to you again about this horrible thing, after to-day. I only trust your name won't be mentioned in connection with it. The inquest is to take place this afternoon. Have they summoned you?"

Dorian shook his head, and a look of annoyance passed over his face at the mention of the word "inquest." There was something so crude and vulgar about everything of the kind. "They don't know my name," he answered.

"But surely she did?"

"Only my Christian name, and that I am quite sure she never mentioned to any one. She told me once that they were all rather curious to learn who I was, and that she invariably told them my name was Prince Charming. It was pretty of her. You must do me a drawing of Sibyl, Basil. I should like to have something more of her than the memory of a few kisses and some broken pathetic words."

"I will try and do something, Dorian, if it would please you. But you must come and sit to me yourself again. I can't get on without you."

"I can never sit to you again, Basil. It is impossible!" he exclaimed, starting back.

The painter stared at him. "My dear boy, what nonsense!" he cried. "Do you mean to say you don't like what I did for you? Where is it? Why have you pulled the screen in front of it? Let me look at it? It is the best thing I have ever done. Do take the screen away, Dorian. It is simply disgraceful of your servant hiding my work like that. I felt the room looked different as I came in."

"My servant has nothing to do with it, Basil. You don't imagine I let him arrange my room for me? He settles my flowers for me sometimes—that is all. No; I did it myself. The light was too strong on the portrait."

"Too strong! Surely not, my dear fellow? It is an admirable place for it. Let me see it." And Hallward walked towards the corner of the room.

A cry of terror broke from Dorian Gray's lips, and he rushed between the painter and the screen. "Basil," he said, looking very pale, "you must not look at it. I don't wish you to."

"Not look at my own work! you are not serious. Why shouldn't I look at it?" exclaimed Hallward, laughing.

"If you try to look at it, Basil, on my word of honour I will never speak to you again as long as I live. I am quite serious. I don't offer any explanation, and you are not to ask for any. But, remember, if you touch this screen, everything is over between us."

Hallward was thunderstruck. He looked at Dorian Gray in absolute amazement. He had never seen him like this before. The lad was actually pallid with rage. His hands were clenched, and the pupils of his eyes were like disks of blue fire. He was trembling all over.

"Dorian!"

"Don't speak!"

"But what is the matter? Of course I won't look at it if you don't want me to," he said, rather coldly, turning on his heel, and going over towards the window. "But, really, it seems rather absurd that I shouldn't see my own work, especially as I am going to exhibit it in Paris in the autumn. I shall probably have to give it another coat of varnish before that, so I must see it some day, and why not to-day?"

"To exhibit it! You want to exhibit it?" exclaimed Dorian Gray, a strange sense of terror creeping over him. Was the world going to be shown his secret? Were people to gape at the mystery of his life? That was impossible. Something—he did not know what—had to be done at once.

"Yes; I don't suppose you will object to that. Georges Petit is going to collect all my best pictures for a special exhibition in the Rue de Sèze, which will open the first week in October. The portrait will only be away a month. I should think you could easily spare it for that time. In fact, you are sure to be out of town. And if you keep it always behind a screen, you can't care much about it."

Dorian Gray passed his hand over his forehead. There were beads of perspiration there. He felt that he was on the brink of a horrible danger. "You told me a month ago that you would never exhibit it," he cried. "Why have you changed your mind? You people who go in for being consistent have just as many moods as others have. The only difference is that your moods are rather meaningless. You can't have forgotten that you assured me most solemnly that nothing in the world would induce you to send it to any exhibition. You told Harry exactly the same thing." He stopped suddenly, and a gleam of light came into his eyes. He remembered that Lord Henry had said to him once, half seriously, and half in jest, "If you want to have a strange quarter of an hour, get Basil to tell you why he won't exhibit your picture. He told me why he wouldn't, and it was a revelation to me." Yes, perhaps, Basil, too, had his secret. He would ask him and try.

"Basil," he said, coming over quite close, and looking him straight in the face, "we have each of us a secret. Let me know yours, and I shall tell you mine. What was your reason for refusing to exhibit my picture?"

The painter shuddered in spite of himself. "Dorian, if I told you, you might like me less than you do, and you would certainly laugh at me. I could not bear your doing either of those two things. If you wish me never to look at your picture again, I am content. I have always you to look at. If you wish the best work I have ever done to be hidden from the world, I am satisfied. Your friendship is dearer to me than any fame or reputation."

"No, Basil, you must tell me," insisted Dorian Gray. "I think I have a right to know." His feeling of terror had passed away, and curiosity had taken its place. He was determined to find out Basil Hallward's mystery.

"Let us sit down, Dorian," said the painter, looking troubled. "Let us sit down. And just answer me one question. Have you noticed in the picture something curious?—something that probably at first did not strike you, but that revealed itself to you suddenly?"

"Basil!" cried the lad, clutching the arms of his chair with trembling hands, and gazing at him with wild, startled eyes.

"I see you did. Don't speak. Wait till you hear what I have to say. Dorian, from the moment I met you, your personality had the most extraordinary influence over me. I was dominated, soul, brain, and power by you. You became to me the visible incarnation of that unseen ideal whose memory haunts us artists like an exquisite dream. I worshipped you. I grew jealous of every one to whom you spoke. I wanted to have you all to myself. I was only happy when I was with you. When you were away from me you were still present in my art. . . . Of course I never let you know anything about this. It would have been impossible. You would not have understood it. I hardly understood it myself. I only knew that I had seen perfection face to face, and that the world had become wonderful to my eyes—too wonderful, perhaps, for in such mad worships there is peril, the peril of losing them, no less than the peril of keeping them. . . . Weeks and weeks went on, and I grew more and more absorbed in you. Then came a new development. I had drawn you as Paris in dainty armour, and as Adonis with huntsman's cloak and polished boar-spear. Crowned with heavy lotus-blossoms you had sat on the prow of Adrian's barge, gazing across the green turbid Nile. You had leaned over the still pool of some Greek woodland, and seen in the water's silent silver the marvel of your own face. And it had all been what art should be, unconscious, ideal, and remote. One day, a fatal day I sometimes think, I determined to paint a wonderful portrait of you as you actually are, not in the costume of dead ages, but in your own dress and in your own time. Whether it was the Realism of the method or the mere wonder of your own personality, thus directly presented to me without mist or veil, I cannot tell. But I know that as I worked at it, every flake and film of colour seemed to me to reveal my secret. I grew afraid that others would know of my idolatry. I felt, Dorian, that I had told too much, that I had put too much of myself into it. Then it was that I resolved never to allow the picture to be exhibited. You were a little annoyed; but then you did not realize all that it meant to me. Harry, to whom I talked about it, laughed at me. But I did not mind that. When the picture was finished, and I sat alone with it, I felt that I was right. . . . Well, after a few days the thing left my studio, and as soon as I had got rid of the intolerable fascination of its presence it seemed to me that I had been foolish in imagining that I had seen anything in it, more than that you were extremely good-looking and that I could paint. Even now I cannot help feeling that it is a mistake to think that the passion one feels in creation is ever really shown in the work one creates. Art is always more abstract than we fancy. Form and colour tell us of form and colour—that is all. It often seems to me that art conceals the artist far more completely than it ever reveals him. And so when I got this offer from Paris I determined to make your portrait the principal thing in my exhibition. It never occurred to me that you would refuse. I see now that you were right. The picture cannot be shown. You must not be angry with me, Dorian, for what I have told you. As I said to Harry, once, you are made to be worshipped."

Dorian Gray drew a long breath. The colour came back to his cheeks, and a smile played about his lips. The peril was over. He was safe for the time. Yet he could not help feeling infinite pity for the painter who had just made this strange confession to him, and wondered if he himself would ever be so dominated by the personality of a friend. Lord Henry had the charm of being very dangerous. But that was all. He was too clever and too cynical to be really fond of. Would there ever be some one who would fill him with a strange idolatry? Was that one of the things that life had in store?

"It is extraordinary to me, Dorian," said Hallward, "that you should have seen this in the portrait. Did you really see it?"

"I saw something in it," he answered, "something that seemed to me very curious."

"Well, you don't mind my looking at the thing now?"

Dorian shook his head. "You must not ask me that, Basil. I could not possibly let you stand in front of that picture."

"You will some day, surely?"

"Never."

"Well, perhaps you are right. And now good-bye, Dorian. You have been the one person in my life who has really influenced my art. Whatever I have done that is good, I owe to you. Ah! you don't know what it cost me to tell you all that I have told you."

"My dear Basil," said Dorian, "what have you told me? Simply that you felt that you admired me too much. That is not even a compliment."

"It was not intended as a compliment. It was a confession. Now that I have made it, something seems to have gone out of me. Perhaps one should never put one's worship into words."

"It was a disappointing confession."

"Why, what did you expect, Dorian? You didn't see anything else in the picture, did you? There was nothing else to see?"

"No; there was nothing else to see. Why do you ask? But you mustn't talk about worship. It is foolish. You and I are friends, Basil, and we must always remain so."

"You have got Harry," said the painter, sadly.

"Oh, Harry?" cried the lad, with a ripple of laughter. "Harry spends his days in saying what is incredible, and his evenings in doing what is improbable. Just the sort of life I would like to lead. But still I don't think I would go to Harry if I were in trouble. I would sooner go to you, Basil."

"You will sit to me again?"

"Impossible!"

"You spoil my life as an artist by refusing, Dorian. No man came across two ideal things. Few come across one."

"I can't explain it to you, Basil, but I must never sit to you again. There is something fatal about a portrait. It has a life of its own. I will come and have tea with you. That will be just as pleasant."

"Pleasanter for you, I am afraid," murmured Hallward, regretfully. "And now good-bye. I am sorry you won't let me look at the picture once again. But that can't be helped. I quite understand what you feel about it."

As he left the room, Dorian Gray smiled to himself. Poor Basil! how little he knew of the true reason! And how strange it was that, instead of having been forced to reveal his own secret, he had succeeded, almost by chance, in wresting a secret from his friend! How much that strange confession explained to him! The painter's absurd fits of jealousy, his wild devotion, his extravagant panegyrics, his curious reticences—he understood them all now, and he felt sorry. There seemed to him to be something tragic in a friendship so coloured by romance.

He sighed and touched a bell. The portrait must be hidden away at all costs. He could not run such a risk of discovery again. It had been mad of him to have allowed the thing to remain, even for an hour, in a room to which any of his friends had access.

CHAPTER X

WHEN his servant entered, he looked at him steadfastly, and wondered if he had thought of peering behind the screen. The man was quite impassive, and waited for his orders. Dorian lit a cigarette, and walked over to the glass and glanced into it. He could see the reflection of Victor's face perfectly. It was like a placid mask of servility. There was nothing to be afraid of, there. Yet he thought it best to be on his guard.

Speaking very slowly, he told him to tell the housekeeper that he wanted to see her, and then to go to the frame-maker and ask him to send two of his men round at once. It seemed to him that as the man left the room his eyes wandered in the direction of the screen. Or was that merely his own fancy?

After a few moments, in her black silk dress with old-fashioned thread mittens on her wrinkled hands, Mrs. Leaf bustled into the library. He asked for the key of the schoolroom.

"The old schoolroom, Mr. Dorian?" she exclaimed. "Why, it is full of dust. I must get it arranged, and put it straight before you go into it. It is not fit for you to see, sir. It is not, indeed."

"I don't want it put straight, Leaf. I only want the key."

"Well, sir, you'll be covered with cobwebs if you go into it. Why, it hasn't been opened for nearly five years, not since his lordship died."

He winced at the mention of his grandfather. He had hateful memories of him. "That does not matter," he answered. "I simply want to see the place —that is all. Give me the key."

"And here is the key, sir," said the old lady, going over the contents of her bunch with tremulously uncertain hands. "Here is the key. I'll have it off the bunch in a moment. But you don't think of living up there, sir, and you so comfortable here?"

"No, no," he cried, petulantly. "Thank you, Leaf. That will do."

She lingered for a few moments, and was garrulous over some detail of the household. He sighed, and told her to manage things as she thought best. She left the room, wreathed in smiles.

As the door closed, Dorian put the key in his pocket, and looked round the room. His eye fell on a large purple satin coverlet heavily embroidered with gold, a splendid piece of late seventeenth-century Venetian work that his grandfather had found in a convent near Bologna. Yes, that would serve to wrap the dreadful thing in. It had perhaps served often as a pall for the dead. Now it was to hide something that had a corruption of its own, worse than the corruption of death itself—something that would breed horrors and yet would never die. What the worm was to the corpse, his sins would be to the painted image on the canvas. They would mar its beauty, and eat away its grace. They would defile it, and make it shameful. And yet the thing would still live on. It would be always alive.

He shuddered, and for a moment he regretted that he had not told Basil the true reason why he had wished to hide the picture away. Basil would have helped him to resist Lord Henry's influence, and the still more poisonous influences that came from his own temperament. The love that he bore him—for it was really love—had nothing in it that was not noble and intellectual. It was not that mere physical admiration of beauty that is born of the senses, and that dies when the senses tire. It was such love as Michael Angelo had known, and Montaigne, and Winckelmann, and Shakespeare himself. Yes, Basil could have saved him. But it was too late now. The past could always be annihilated. Regret, denial, or forgetfulness could do that. But the future was inevitable. There were passions in him that would find their terrible outlet, dreams that would make the shadow of their evil real.

He took up from the couch the great purple-and-gold texture that covered it, and, holding it in his hands, passed behind the screen. Was the face on the canvas viler than before? It seemed to him that it was unchanged; and yet his loathing of it was intensified. Gold hair, blue eyes, and rose-red lips—they all were there. It was simply the expression that had altered. That was horrible in its cruelty. Compared to what he saw in it of censure or rebuke, how shallow Basil's reproaches about Sibyl Vane had been!—how shallow, and of what little account! His own soul was looking out at him from the canvas and calling him to judgment. A look of pain came across him, and he flung the rich pall over the picture. As he did so, a knock came to the door. He passed out as his servant entered.

"The persons are here, Monsieur."

He felt that the man must be got rid of at once. He must not be allowed to know where the picture was being taken to. There was something sly about him, and he had thoughtful, treacherous eyes. Sitting down at the writing-table, he scribbled a note to Lord Henry, asking him to send him round something to read, and reminding him that they were to meet at eight-fifteen that evening.

"Wait for an answer," he said, handing it to him, "and show the men in here."

In two or three minutes there was another knock, and Mr. Hubbard himself, the celebrated frame-maker of South Audley Street, came in with a somewhat rough-looking young assistant. Mr. Hubbard was a florid, red-whiskered little man, whose admiration for art was considerably tempered by the inveterate impecuniosity of most of the artists who dealt with him. As a rule, he never left his shop. He waited for people to come to him. But he always made an exception in favor of Dorian Gray. There was something about Dorian that charmed everybody. It was a pleasure even to see him.

"What can I do for you, Mr. Gray?" he said, rubbing his fat freckled hands. "I thought I would do myself the honour of coming round in person. I have just got a beauty of a frame, sir. Picked it up at a sale. Came from Fonthill, I believe. Admirably suited for a religious subject, Mr. Gray."

"I am so sorry you have given yourself the trouble of coming round, Mr. Hubbard. I shall certainly drop in and look at the frame–though I don't go in much at present for religious art–but to-day I only want a picture carried to the top of the house for me. It is rather heavy, so I thought I would ask you to lend me a couple of your men."

"No trouble at all, Mr. Gray. I am delighted to be of any service to you. Which is the work of art, sir?"

"This," replied Dorian, moving the screen back. "Can you move it, covering and all, just as it is? I don't want it to get scratched going upstairs."

"There will be no difficulty, sir," said the genial frame-maker, beginning, with the aid of his assistant, to unhook the picture from the long brass chains by which it was suspended. "And, now, where shall we carry it to, Mr. Gray?"

"I will show you the way, Mr. Hubbard, if you will kindly follow me. Or perhaps you had better go in front. I am afraid it is right at the top of the house. We will go up by the front staircase, as it is wider."

He held the door open for them, and they passed out into the hall and began the ascent. The elaborate character of the frame had made the picture extremely bulky, and now and then, in spite of the obsequious protests of Mr. Hubbard, who had the true tradesman's spirited dislike of seeing a gentleman doing anything useful, Dorian put his hand to it so as to help them.

"Something of a load to carry, sir," gasped the little man, when they reached the top landing. And he wiped his shiny forehead.

"I am afraid it is rather heavy," murmured Dorian, as he unlocked the door that opened into the room that was to keep for him the curious secret of his life and hide his soul from the eyes of men.

He had not entered the place for more than four years–not, indeed, since he had used it first as a playroom when he was a child, and then as a study when he grew somewhat older. It was a large, well-proportioned room, which had been specially built by the last Lord Kelso for the use of the little grandson whom, for his strange likeness to his mother, and also for other reasons, he had always hated and desired to keep at a distance. It appeared to Dorian to have but little changed. There was the huge Italian *cassone*, with its fantastically-painted panels and its tarnished gilt mouldings, in which he had so often hidden himself as a boy. There the satinwood bookcase filled with his dog-eared schoolbooks. On the wall behind it was hanging the same ragged Flemish tapestry where a faded king and queen were playing chess in a garden, while a company of hawkers rode by, carrying hooded birds on their gauntleted wrists. How well he remembered it all! Every moment of his lonely childhood came back to him as he looked round. He recalled the stainless purity of his boyish life, and it seemed horrible to him that it was here the fatal portrait was to be hidden away. How little he had thought, in those dead days, of all that was in store for him!

But there was no other place in the house so secure from prying eyes as this. He had the key, and no one else could enter it. Beneath its purple pall, the face painted on the canvas could grow bestial, sodden, and unclean. What did it matter? No one could see it. He himself would not see it. Why should he watch the hideous corruption of his soul? He kept his youth—that was enough. And, besides, might not his nature grow finer, after all? There was no reason that the future should be so full of shame. Some love might come across his life, and purify him, and shield him from those sins that seemed to be already stirring in spirit and in flesh—those curious unpictured sins whose very mystery lent them their subtlety and their charm. Perhaps, some day, the cruel look would have passed away from the scarlet sensitive mouth, and he might show to the world Basil Hallward's masterpiece.

No; that was impossible. Hour by hour, and week by week, the thing upon the canvas was growing old. It might escape the hideousness of sin, but the hideousness of age was in store for it. The cheeks would become hollow or flaccid. Yellow crow's-feet would creep round the fading eyes and make them horrible. The hair would lose its brightness, the mouth would gape or droop, would be foolish or gross, as the mouths of old men are. There would be the wrinkled throat, the cold, blue-veined hands, the twisted body, that he remembered in the grandfather who had been so stern to him in his boyhood. The picture had to be concealed. There was no help for it.

"Bring it in, Mr. Hubbard, please," he said, wearily, turning round. "I am sorry I kept you waiting so long. I was thinking of something else."

"Always glad to have a rest, Mr. Gray," answered the frame-maker, who was still gasping for breath. "Where shall we put it, sir?"

"Oh, anywhere. Here: this will do. I don't want to have it hung up. Just lean it against the wall. Thanks."

"Might one look at the work of art, sir?"

Dorian started. "It would not interest you, Mr. Hubbard," he said, keeping his eye on the man. He felt ready to leap upon him and fling him to the ground if he dared to lift the gorgeous hanging that concealed the secret of his life. "I shan't trouble you any more now. I am much obliged for your kindness in coming round."

"Not at all, not at all, Mr. Gray. Ever ready to do anything for you, sir." And Mr. Hubbard tramped downstairs, followed by the assistant, who glanced back at Dorian with a look of shy wonder in his rough, uncomely face. He had never seen any one so marvellous.

When the sound of their footsteps had died away, Dorian locked the door, and put the key in his pocket. He felt safe now. No one would ever look upon the horrible thing. No eye but his would ever see his shame.

On reaching the library he found that it was just after five o'clock, and that the tea had been already brought up. On a little table of dark perfumed wood thickly encrusted with nacre, a present from Lady Radley, his guardian's wife, a pretty professional invalid, who had spent the preceding winter in Cairo, was lying a note from Lord Henry, and beside it was a book bound in yellow paper, the cover slightly torn and the edges soiled. A copy of the third edition of *The St. James Gazette* had been placed on the tea-tray. It was evident that Victor had returned. He wondered if he had met the men in the hall as they were leaving the house, and had wormed out of them what they had been doing. He would be sure to miss the picture—had no doubt missed it already, while he had been laying the tea-things. The screen had not been set back, and a blank space was visible on the wall. Perhaps some night he might find him creeping upstairs and trying to force the door of the room. It was a horrible thing to have a spy in one's house. He had heard of rich men who had been blackmailed all their lives by some servant who had read a letter, or overheard a conversation, or picked up a card with an address, or found beneath a pillow a withered flower or a shred of crumpled lace.

He sighed, and, having poured himself out some tea, opened Lord Henry's note. It was simply to say that he sent him round the evening paper, and a book that might interest him, and that he would be at the club at eight-fifteen. He opened *The St. James* languidly, and looked through it. A red pencil-mark on the fifth page caught his eye. It drew attention to the following paragraph:—

"Inquest on an Actress.—An inquest was held this morning at the Bell Tavern, Hoxton Road, by Mr. Danby, the District Coroner, on the body of Sibyl Vane, a young actress recently engaged at the Royal Theatre, Holborn. A verdict of death by misadventure was returned. Considerable sympathy was expressed for the mother of the deceased, who was greatly affected during the giving of her own evidence and that of Dr. Birrell, who had made the post-mortem examination of the deceased."

He frowned, and, tearing the paper in two went across the room and flung the pieces away. How ugly it all was! And how horribly real ugliness made things! He felt a little annoyed with Lord Henry for having sent him the report. And it was certainly stupid of him to have marked it with red pencil. Victor might have read it. The man knew more than enough English for that.

Perhaps he had read it, and had begun to suspect something. And, yet, what did it matter? What had Dorian Gray to do with Sibyl Vane's death? There was nothing to fear. Dorian Gray had not killed her.

His eye fell on the yellow book that Lord Henry had sent him. What was it, he wondered. He went towards the little pearl-coloured octagonal stand, that had always looked to him like the work of some strange Egyptian bees that wrought in silver, and taking up the volume, flung himself into an arm-chair, and began to turn over the leaves. After a few minutes he became absorbed. It was the strangest book that he had ever read. It seemed to him that in exquisite raiment, and to the delicate sound of flutes, the sins of the world were passing in dumb show before him. Things that he had dimly dreamed of were suddenly made real to him. Things of which he had never dreamed were gradually revealed.

It was a novel without a plot, and with only one character, being indeed, simply a psychological study of a certain young Parisian, who spent his life trying to realize in the nineteenth century all the passions and modes of thought that belonged to every century except his own, and to sum up, as it were, in himself the various moods through which the world-spirit had ever passed, loving for their mere artificiality those renunciations that men have unwisely called virtue, as much as those natural rebellions that wise men still call sin. The style in which it was written was that curious jewelled style, vivid and obscure at once, full of *argot* and of archaisms, of technical expressions and of elaborate paraphrases, that characterizes the work of some of the finest artists of the French school of *Symbolistes*. There were in it metaphors as monstrous as orchids, and as subtle in colour. The life of the senses was described in the terms of mystical philosophy. One hardly knew at times whether one was reading the spiritual ecstasies of some mediaeval saint or the morbid confessions of a modern sinner. It was a poisonous book. The heavy odor of incense seemed to cling about its pages and to trouble the brain. The mere cadence of the sentences, the subtle monotony of their music, so full as it was of complex refrains and movements elaborately repeated, produced in the mind of the lad, as he passed from chapter to chapter, a form of reverie, a malady of dreaming, that made him unconscious of the falling day and creeping shadows.

Cloudless, and pierced by one solitary star, a copper-green sky gleamed through the windows. He read on by its wan light till he could read no more. Then, after his valet had reminded him several times of the lateness of the hour, he got up, and, going into the next room, placed the book on the little Florentine table that always stood at his bedside, and began to dress for dinner.

It was almost nine o'clock before he reached the club, where he found Lord Henry sitting alone, in the morning-room, looking very much bored.

"I am so sorry, Harry," he cried, "but really it is entirely your fault. That book you sent me so fascinated me that I forgot how the time was going."

"Yes: I thought you would like it," replied his host, rising from his chair.

"I didn't say I liked it, Harry. I said it fascinated me. There is a great difference."

"Ah, you have discovered that?" murmured Lord Henry. And they passed into the dining-room.

CHAPTER XI

For years, Dorian Gray could not free himself from the influence of this book. Or perhaps it would be more accurate to say that he never sought to free himself from it. He procured from Paris no less than nine large-paper copies of the first edition, and had them bound in different colours, so that they might suit his various moods and the changing fancies of a nature over which he seemed, at times, to have almost entirely lost control. The hero, the wonderful young Parisian, in whom the romantic and the scientific temperaments were so strangely blended, became to him a kind of prefiguring type of himself. And, indeed, the whole book seemed to him to contain the story of his own life, written before he had lived it.

In one point he was more fortunate than the novel's fantastic hero. He never knew—never, indeed, had any cause to know—that somewhat grotesque dread of mirrors, and polished metal surfaces, and still waters, which came upon the young Parisian so early in his life, and was occasioned by the sudden decay of a beauty that had once, apparently, been so remarkable. It was with an almost cruel joy—and perhaps in nearly every joy, as certainly in every pleasure, cruelty has its place—that he used to read the latter part of the book, with its really tragic, if somewhat over-emphasized, account of the sorrow and despair of one who had himself lost what in others, and in the world, he had most dearly valued.

For the wonderful beauty that had so fascinated Basil Hallward, and many others besides him, seemed never to leave him. Even those who had heard the most evil things against him, and from time to time strange rumours about his mode of life crept through London and became the chatter of the clubs, could not believe anything to his dishonour when they saw him. He had always the look of one who had kept himself unspotted from the world. Men who talked grossly became silent when Dorian Gray entered the room. There was something in the purity of his face that rebuked them. His mere presence seemed to recall to them the memory of the innocence that they had tarnished. They wondered how one so charming and graceful as he was could have escaped the stain of an age that was at once sordid and sensual.

Often, on returning home from one of those mysterious and prolonged absences that gave rise to such strange conjecture among those who were his friends, or thought that they were so, he himself would creep upstairs to the locked room, open the door with the key that never left him now, and stand, with a mirror, in front of the portrait that Basil Hallward had painted of him, looking now at the evil and aging face on the canvas, and now at the fair young face that laughed back at him from the polished glass. The very sharpness of the contrast used to quicken his sense of pleasure. He grew more and more enamoured of his own beauty, more and more interested in the corruption of his own soul. He would examine with minute care, and sometimes with monstrous and terrible delight, the hideous lines that seared the wrinkling forehead or crawled around the heavy sensual mouth, wondering sometimes which were the more horrible, the signs of sin or the signs of age. He would place his white hands beside the coarse bloated hands of the picture, and smile. He mocked the misshapen body and the failing limbs.

There were moments, indeed, at night, when, lying sleepless in his own delicately-scented chamber, or in the sordid room of the little ill-famed tavern near the Docks, which, under an assumed name, and in disguise, it was his habit to frequent, he would think of the ruin he had brought upon his soul, with a pity that was all the more poignant because it was purely selfish. But moments such as these were rare. That curiosity about life which Lord Henry had first stirred in him, as they sat together in the garden of their friend, seemed to increase with gratification. The more he knew, the more he desired to know. He had mad hungers that grew more ravenous as he fed them.

Yet he was not really reckless, at any rate in his relations to society. Once or twice every month during the winter, and on each Wednesday evening while the season lasted, he would throw open to the world his beautiful house and have the most celebrated musicians of the day to charm his guests with the wonders of their art. His little dinners, in the settling of which Lord Henry always assisted him, were noted as much for the careful selection and placing of those invited, as for the exquisite taste shown in the decoration of the table, with its subtle symphonic arrangements of exotic flowers, and embroidered cloths, and antique plate of gold and silver. Indeed, there were many, especially among the very young men, who saw, or fancied that they saw, in Dorian Gray the true realization of a type of which they had often dreamed in Eton or Oxford days, a type that was to combine something of the real culture of the scholar with all the grace and distinction and perfect manner of a citizen of the world. To them he seemed to be of the company of those whom Dante describes as having sought to "make themselves perfect by the worship of beauty." Like Gautier, he was one for whom "the visible world existed."

And certainly, to him Life itself was the first, the greatest, of the arts, and for it all the other arts seemed to be but a preparation. Fashion, by which what is really fantastic becomes for a moment universal, and Dandyism, which, in its own way, is an attempt to assert the absolute modernity of beauty, had, of course, their fascination for him. His mode of dressing, and the particular styles that from time to time he affected, had their marked influence on the young exquisites of the Mayfair balls and Pall Mall Club windows, who copied him in everything that he did, and tried to reproduce the accidental charm of his graceful, though to him only half-serious fopperies.

For, while he was but too ready to accept the position that was almost immediately offered to him on his coming of age, and found, indeed, a subtle pleasure in the thought that he might really become to the London of his own day what to imperial Neronian Rome the author of the "Satyricon" once had been, yet in his inmost heart he desired to be something more than a mere *arbiter elegantiarum*, to be consulted on the wearing of a jewel, or the knotting of a necktie, or the conduct of a cane. He sought to elaborate some new scheme of life that would have its reasoned philosophy and its ordered principles, and find in the spiritualizing of the senses its highest realization.

The worship of the senses has often, and with much justice, been decried, men feeling a natural instinct of terror about passions and sensations that seem stronger than themselves, and that they are conscious of sharing with the less highly organized forms of existence. But it appeared to Dorian Gray that the true nature of the senses had never been understood, and that they had remained savage and animal merely because the world had sought to starve them into submission or to kill them by pain, instead of aiming at making them elements of a new spirituality, of which a fine instinct for beauty was to be the dominant characteristic. As he looked back upon man moving through History, he was haunted by a feeling of loss. So much had been surrendered! and to such little purpose! There had been mad wilful rejections, monstrous forms of self-torture and self-denial, whose origin was fear, and whose result was a degradation infinitely more terrible than that fancied degradation from which, in their ignorance, they had sought to escape, Nature, in her wonderful irony, driving out the anchorite to feed with the wild animals of the desert and giving to the hermit the beasts of the field as his companions.

Yes: there was to be, as Lord Henry had prophesied, a new Hedonism that was to re-create life, and to save it from that harsh, uncomely Puritanism that is having, in our own day, its curious revival. It was to have its service of the intellect, certainly; yet, it was never to accept any theory or system that would involve the sacrifice of any mode of passionate experience. Its aim, indeed, was to be experience itself, and not the fruits of experience, sweet or bitter as they might be. Of the asceticism that deadens the senses, as of the vulgar profligacy that dulls them, it was to know nothing. But it was to teach man to concentrate himself upon the moments of a life that is itself but a moment.

There are few of us who have not sometimes wakened before dawn, either after one of those dreamless nights that make us almost enamoured of death, or one of those nights of horror and misshapen joy, when through the chambers of the brain sweep phantoms more terrible than reality itself, and instinct with that vivid life that lurks in all grotesques, and that lends to Gothic art its enduring vitality, this art being, one might fancy, especially the art of those whose minds have been troubled with the malady of reverie. Gradually white fingers creep through the curtains, and they appear to tremble. In black fantastic shapes, dumb shadows crawl into the corners of the room, and crouch there. Outside, there is the stirring of birds among the leaves, or the sound of men going forth to their work, or the sigh and sob of the wind coming down from the hills, and wandering round the silent house, as though it feared to wake the sleepers, and yet must needs call forth sleep from her purple cave. Veil after veil of thin dusky gauze is lifted, and by degrees the forms and colours of things are restored to them, and we watch the dawn remaking the world in its antique pattern. The wan mirrors get back their mimic life. The flameless tapers stand where we had left them, and beside them lies the half-cut book that we had been studying, or the wired flower that we had worn at the ball, or the letter that we had been afraid to read, or that we had read too often. Nothing seems to us changed. Out of the unreal shadows of the night comes back the real life that we had known. We have to resume it where we had left off, and there steals over us a terrible sense of the necessity for the continuance of energy in the same wearisome round of stereotyped habits, or a wild longing, it may be, that our eyelids might open some morning upon a world that had been refashioned anew in the darkness for our pleasure, a world in which things would have fresh shapes and colours, and be changed, or have other secrets, a world in which the past would have little or no place, or survive, at any rate, in no conscious form of obligation or regret, the remembrance even of joy having its bitterness, and the memories of pleasure their pain.

It was the creation of such worlds as these that seemed to Dorian Gray to be the true object, or amongst the true objects, of life; and in his search for sensations that would be at once new and delightful, and possess that element of strangeness that is so essential to romance, he would often adopt certain modes of thought that he knew to be really alien to his nature, abandon himself to their subtle influences, and then, having, as it were, caught their colour and satisfied his intellectual curiosity, leave them with that curious indifference that is not incompatible with a real ardour of temperament, and that indeed, according to certain modern psychologists, is often a condition of it.

It was rumoured of him once that he was about to join the Roman Catholic communion; and certainly the Roman ritual had always a great attraction for him. The daily sacrifice, more awful really than all the sacrifices of the antique world, stirred him as much by its superb rejection of the evidence of the senses as by the primitive simplicity of its elements and the eternal pathos of the human tragedy that it sought to symbolize. He loved to kneel down on the cold marble pavement, and watch the priest, in his stiff flowered dalmatic, slowly and with white hands moving aside the veil of the tabernacle, or raising aloft the jewelled lantern-shaped monstrance with that pallid wafer that at times, one would fain think, is indeed the "*panis caelestis*," the bread of angels, or, robed in the garments of the Passion of Christ, breaking the Host into the chalice, and smiting his breast for his sins. The fuming censers, that the grave boys, in their lace and scarlet, tossed into the air like great gilt flowers, had their subtle fascination for him. As he passed out, he used to look with wonder at the black confessionals, and long to sit in the dim shadow of one of them and listen to men and women whispering through the worn grating the true story of their lives.

But he never fell into the error of arresting his intellectual development by any formal acceptance of creed or system, or of mistaking, for a house in which to live, an inn that is but suitable for the sojourn of a night or for a few hours of a night in which there are no stars and the moon is in travail. Mysticism, with its marvellous power of making common things strange to us, and the subtle antinomianism that always seems to accompany it, moved him for a season; and for a season he inclined to the materialistic doctrines of the *Darwinismus* movement in Germany, and found a curious pleasure in tracing the thoughts and passions of men to some pearly cell in the brain, or some white nerve in the body, delighting in the conception of the absolute dependence of the spirit on certain physical conditions, morbid or healthy, normal or diseased. Yet, as has been said of him before, no theory of life seemed to him to be of any importance compared with life itself. He felt keenly conscious of how barren all intellectual speculation is when separated from action and experiment. He knew that the senses, no less than the soul, have their spiritual mysteries to reveal.

And so he would now study perfumes, and the secrets of their manufacture, distilling heavily-scented oils, and burning odorous gums from the East. He saw that there was no mood of the mind that had not its counterpart in the sensuous life, and set himself to discover their true relations, wondering what there was in frankincense that made one mystical, and in ambergris that stirred one's passions, and in violets that woke the memory of dead romances, and in musk that troubled the brain, and in Champak that stained the imagination; and seeking often to elaborate a real psychology of perfumes, and to estimate the several influences of sweet-smelling roots, and scented pollen-laden flowers, of aromatic balms, and of dark and fragrant woods, of spikenard that sickens, of hovenia that makes men mad, and of aloes that are said to be able to expel melancholy from the soul.

At another time he devoted himself entirely to music, and in a long latticed room, with a vermilion-and-gold ceiling and walls of olive-green lacquer, he used to give curious concerts in which mad gypsies tore wild music from little zithers, or grave yellow-shawled Tunisians plucked at the strained strings of monstrous lutes, while grinning Negroes beat monotonously upon copper drums, and, crouching upon scarlet mats, slim turbaned Indians blew through long pipes of reed or brass, and charmed, or feigned to charm, great hooded snakes and horrible horned adders. The harsh intervals and shrill discords of barbaric music stirred him at times when Schubert's grace, and Chopin's beautiful sorrows, and the mighty harmonies of Beethoven himself, fell unheeded on his ear. He collected together from all parts of the world the strangest instruments that could be found, either in the tombs of dead nations or among the few savage tribes that have survived contact with Western civilizations, and loved to touch and try them. He had the mysterious *juruparis* of the Rio Negro Indians, that women are not allowed to look at, and that even youths may not see till they have been subjected to fasting and scourging, and the earthen jars of the Peruvians that have the shrill cries of birds, and flutes of human bones such as Alfonso de Ovalle heard in Chile, and the sonorous green jaspers that are found near Cuzco and give forth a note of singular sweetness. He had painted gourds filled with pebbles that rattled when they were shaken; the long *clarin* of the Mexicans, into which the performer does not blow, but through which he inhales the air; the harsh *ture* of the Amazon tribes, that is sounded by the sentinels who sit all day long in high trees, and can be heard, it is said, at a distance of three leagues; the *teponaztli*, that has two vibrating tongues of wood, has her monsters, things of bestial shape and with an elastic gum obtained from the milky juice of plants; the *Yotl-bells* of the Aztecs, that are hung in clusters like grapes; and a huge cylindrical drum, covered with the skins of great serpents, like the one that Bernal Diaz saw when he went with Cortes into the Mexican temple, and of whose doleful sound he has left us so vivid a description. The fantastic character of these instruments fascinated him, and he felt a curious delight in the thought that Art, like Nature, has her monsters, things of bestial shape and with hideous voices. Yet, after some time, he wearied of them, and would sit in his box at the Opera, either alone or with Lord Henry, listening in rapt pleasure to "Tannhäuser," and seeing in the prelude to that great work of art a presentation of the tragedy of his own soul.

On one occasion he took up the study of jewels, and appeared at a costume ball as Anne de Joyeuse, Admiral of France, in a dress covered with five hundred and sixty pearls. This taste enthralled him for years, and, indeed, may be said never to have left him. He would often spend a whole day settling and resettling in their cases the various stones that he had collected, such as the olive-green chrysoberyl that turns red by lamplight, the cymophane with its wire-like line of silver, the pistachio-coloured peridot, rose-pink and wine-yellow topazes, carbuncles of fiery scarlet with tremulous four-rayed stars, flame-red cinnamon-stones, orange and violet spinels, and amethysts with their alternate layers of ruby and sapphire. He loved the red gold of the sunstone, and the moonstone's pearly whiteness, and the broken rainbow of the milky opal. He procured from Amsterdam three emeralds of extraordinary size and richness of colour, and had a turquoise *de la vieille roche* that was the envy of all the connoisseurs.

He discovered wonderful stories, also about jewels. In Alphonso's "Clericalis Disciplina" a serpent was mentioned with eyes of real jacinth, and in the romantic history of Alexander, the Conqueror of Emathia was said to have found in the vale of Jordan, snakes "with collars of real emeralds growing on their backs." There was a gem in the brain of the dragon, Philostratus told us, and "by the exhibition of golden letters and a scarlet robe" the monster could be thrown into a magical sleep, and slain. According to the great alchemist, Pierre de Boniface, the diamond rendered a man invisible, and the agate of India made him eloquent. The cornelian appeased anger, and the hyacinth provoked sleep, and the amethyst drove away the fumes of wine. The garnet cast out demons, and the hydropicus deprived the moon of her colour. The selenite waxed and waned with the moon, and the meloceus, that discovers thieves, could be affected only by the blood of kids. Leonardus Camillus had seen a white stone taken from the brain of a newly-killed toad, that was certain antidote against poison. The bezoar, that was found in the heart of the Arabian deer, was a charm that could cure the plague. In the nests of Arabian birds was the aspilates, that, according to Democritus, kept the wearer from any danger by fire.

The King of Ceilan rode through his city with a large ruby in his hand, at the ceremony of his coronation. The gates of the palace of John the Priest were "made of sardius, with the horn of the horned snake inwrought, so that no man might bring poison within." Over the gable were "two golden apples, in which were two carbuncles," so that the gold might shine by day, and the carbuncles by night. In Lodge's strange romance "A Margarite of America" it was stated that in the chamber of the queen one could behold "all the chaste ladies of the world, inchased out of silver, looking through fair mirrors of chrysolites, carbuncles, sapphires, and greene emeraults." Marco Polo had seen the inhabitants of Zipangu place rose-coloured pearls in the mouths of the dead. A sea monster had been enamoured of the pearl that the diver brought to King Perozes, and had slain the thief, and mourned for seven moons over its loss. When the Huns lured the king into the great pit, he flung it away–Procopius tells the story–nor was it ever found again, though the Emperor Anastasius offered five hundred-weight of gold pieces for it. The King of Malabar had shown to a certain Venetian a rosary of three hundred and four pearls, one for every god that he worshipped.

When the Duke de Valentinois, son of Alexander VI., visited Louis XII. of France, his horse was loaded with gold leaves, according to Brantôme, and his cap had double rows of rubies that threw out a great light. Charles of England had ridden in stirrups hung with four hundred and twenty-one diamonds. Richard II. had a coat, valued at thirty thousand marks, which was covered with balas rubies. Hall described Henry VIII., on his way to the Tower previous to his coronation, as wearing "a jacket of raised gold, the placard embroidered with diamonds and other rich stones, and a great bauderike about his neck of large balasses." The favourites of James I. wore earrings of emeralds set in gold filigrane. Edward II. gave to Piers Gaveston a suit of red-gold armour studded with jacinths, a collar of gold roses set with turquoise-stones, and a skull-cap *parsemé* with pearls. Henry II. wore jewelled gloves reaching to the elbow, and had a hawk-glove sewn with twelve rubies and fifty-two great orients. The ducal hat of Charles the Rash, the last Duke of Burgundy of his race, was hung with pear-shaped pearls, and studded with sapphires.

How exquisite life had once been! How gorgeous in its pomp and decoration! Even to read of the luxury of the dead was wonderful.

Then he turned his attention to embroideries, and to the tapestries that performed the office of frescoes in the chill rooms of the Northern nations of Europe. As he investigated the subject–and he always had an extraordinary faculty of becoming absolutely absorbed for the moment in whatever he took up–he was almost saddened by the reflection of the ruin that Time brought on beautiful and wonderful things. He, at any rate, had escaped that. Summer followed summer, and the yellow jonquils bloomed and died many times, and nights of horror repeated the story of their shame, but he was unchanged. No winter marred his face or stained his flower-like bloom. How different it was with material things! Where had they passed to? Where was the great crocus-coloured robe, on which the gods had fought against the giants, that had been worked by brown girls for the pleasure of Athena? Where, the huge velarium that Nero had stretched across the Colosseum at Rome, that Titan sail of purple on which was represented the starry sky, and Apollo driving a chariot drawn by white gilt-reined steeds? He longed to see the curious table-napkins wrought for the Priest of the Sun, on which were displayed all the dainties and viands that could be wanted for a feast; the mortuary cloth of King Chilperic, with its three hundred golden bees; the fantastic robes that excited the indignation of the Bishop of Pontus, and were figured with "lions, panthers, bears, dogs, forests, rocks, hunters–all, in fact, that a painter can copy from nature;"–and the coat that Charles of Orleans once wore, on the sleeves of which were embroidered the verses of a song beginning "*Madame, je suis tout joyeux*," the musical accompaniment of the words being wrought in gold thread, and each note, of square shape in those days, formed with four pearls. He read of the room that was prepared at the palace at Rheims for the use of Queen Joan of Burgundy, and was decorated with "thirteen hundred and twenty-one parrots, made in broidery, and blazoned with the king's arms, and five hundred and sixty-one butterflies, whose wings were similarly ornamented with the arms of the queen, the whole worked in gold." Catherine de Médicis had a mourning-bed made for her of black velvet powdered with crescents and suns. Its curtains were of damask, with leafy wreaths and garlands, figured upon a gold and silver ground, and fringed along the edges with broideries of pearls, and it stood in a room hung with rows of the queen's devices in cut black velvet upon cloth of silver. Louis XIV. had gold embroidered caryatides fifteen feet high in his apartment. The state bed of Sobieski, King of Poland, was made of Smyrna gold brocade embroidered in turquoises with verses from the Koran. Its supports were of silver gilt, beautifully chased, and profusely set with enamelled and jewelled medallions. It had been taken from the Turkish camp before Vienna, and the standard of Mohammed had stood beneath the tremulous gilt of its canopy.

And so, for a whole year, he sought to accumulate the most exquisite specimens that he could find of textile and embroidered work, getting the dainty Delhi muslines, finely wrought with gold with gold thread palmates, and stitched over with iridescent beetles' wings; the Dacca gauzes, that from their transparency are known in the East as "wovenair," and "running water," and "evening dew"; strange figured cloths from Java; elaborate yellow Chinese hangings; books bound in tawny satins or fair blue silks, and wrought with *fleurs de lys,* birds and images: veils of *lacis* worked in Hungary point; Sicilian brocades, and stiff Spanish velvets; Georgian work with its gilt coins, and Japanese *Foukousas* with their green-toned golds and their marvellously plumaged birds.

He had a special passion, also, for ecclesiastical vestments, as indeed he had for everything connected with the service of the Church. In the long cedar chests that lined the west gallery of his house he had stored away many rare and beautiful specimens of what is really the raiment of the Bride of Christ, who must wear purple and jewels and fine linen that she may hide the pallid macerated body that is worn by the suffering that she seeks for, and wounded by self-inflicted pain. He possessed a gorgeous cope of crimson silk and gold-thread damask, figured with a repeating pattern of golden pomegranates set in six-petalled formal blossoms, beyond which on either side was the pine-apple device wrought in seed-pearls. The orphreys were divided into panels representing scenes from the life of the Virgin, and the coronation of the Virgin was figured in coloured silks upon the hood. This was Italian work of the fifteenth century. Another cope was of green velvet, embroidered with heart-shaped groups of acanthus-leaves, from which spread long-stemmed white blossoms, the details of which were picked out with silver thread and coloured crystals. The morse bore a seraph's head in gold-thread raised work. The orphreys were woven in a diaper of red and gold silk, and were starred with medallions of many saints and martyrs, among whom was St. Sebastian. He has chasubles, also, of amber-coloured silk, and blue silk and gold brocade, and yellow silk damask and cloth of gold, figured with representations of the Passion and Crucifixion of Christ, and embroidered with lions and peacocks and other emblems; dalmatics of white satin and pink silk damask, decorated with tulips and dolphins and *fleurs de lys;* altar frontals of crimson velvet and blue linen; and many corporals, chalice-veils, and sudaria. In the mystic offices to which such things were put, there was something that quickened his imagination.

For these treasures, and everything that he collected in his lovely house, were to be to him means of forgetfulness, modes by which he could escape, for a season, from the fear that seemed to him at times to be almost too great to be borne. Upon the walls of the lonely locked room where he had spent so much of his boyhood, he had hung with his own hands the terrible portrait whose changing features showed him the real degradation of his life, and in front of it had draped the purple-and-gold pall as a curtain. For weeks he would not go there, would forget the hideous painted thing, and get back his light heart, his wonderful joyousness, his passionate absorption in mere existence. Then, suddenly, some night he would creep out of the house, go down to dreadful places near Blue Gate Fields, and stay there, day after day, until he was driven away. On his return he would sit in front of the picture, sometimes loathing it and himself, but filled, at other times, with that pride of individualism that is half the fascination of sin, and smiling, with secret pleasure, at the misshapen shadow that had to bear the burden that should have been his own.

After a few years he could not endure to be long out of England, and gave up the villa that he had shared at Trouville with Lord Henry, as well as the little white walled-in house at Algiers where they had more than once spent the winter. He hated to be separated from the picture that was such a part of his life, and was also afraid that during his absence some one might gain access to the room, in spite of the elaborate bars that he had caused to be placed upon the door.

He was quite conscious that this would tell them nothing. It was true that the portrait still preserved, under all the foulness and ugliness of the face, its marked likeness to himself; but what could they learn from that? He would laugh at any one who tried to taunt him. He had not painted it. What was it to him how vile and full of shame it looked? Even if he told them, would they believe it?

Yet he was afraid. Sometimes when he was down at his great house in Nottinghamshire, entertaining the fashionable young men of his own rank who were his chief companions, and astounding the county by the wanton luxury and gorgeous splendor of his mode of life, he would suddenly leave his guests and rush back to town to see that the door had not been tampered with, and that the picture was still there. What if it should be stolen? The mere thought made him cold with horror. Surely the world would know his secret then. Perhaps the world already suspected it.

For, while he fascinated many, there were not a few who distrusted him. He was very nearly blackballed at a West End club of which his birth and social position fully entitled him to become a member, and it was said that on one occasion, when he was brought by a friend into the smoking-room of the Churchill, the Duke of Berwick and another gentleman got up in a marked manner and went out. Curious stories became current about him after he had passed his twenty-fifth year. It was rumoured that he had been seen brawling with foreign sailors in a low den in the distant parts of Whitechapel, and that he consorted with thieves and coiners and knew the mysteries of their trade. His extraordinary absences became notorious, and, when he used to reappear again in society, men would whisper to each other in corners, or pass him with a sneer, or look at him with cold, searching eyes, as though they were determined to discover his secret.

Of such insolences and attempted slights, he, of course, took no notice, and in the opinion of most people his frank debonnair manner, his charming boyish smile, and the infinite grace of that wonderful youth that seemed never to leave him, were in themselves a sufficient answer to the calumnies, for so they termed them, that were circulated about him. It was remarked, however, that some of those who had been most intimate with him appeared, after a time, to shun him. Women who had wildly adored him, and for his sake had braved all social censure and set convention at defiance, were seen to grow pallid with shame or horror if Dorian Gray entered the room.

Yet these whispered scandals only increased in the eyes of many, his strange and dangerous charm. His great wealth was a certain element of security. Society, civilized society at least, is never very ready to believe anything to the detriment of those who are both rich and fascinating. It feels instinctively that manners are of more importance than morals, and, in its opinion, the highest respectability is of much less value than the possession of a good *chef.* And, after all, it is a very poor consolation to be told that the man who has given one a bad dinner, or poor wine, is irreproachable in his private life. Even the cardinal virtues cannot atone for half-cold *entrées,* as Lord Henry remarked once, in a discussion on the subject; and there is possibly a good deal to be said for his view. For the canons of good society are, or should be, the same as the canons of art. Form is absolutely essential to it. It should have the dignity of a ceremony, as well as its unreality, and should combine the insincere character of a romantic play with the wit and beauty that makes such plays delightful to us. Is insincerity such a terrible thing? I think not. It is merely a method by which we can multiply our personalities.

Such, at any rate, was Dorian Gray's opinion. He used to wonder at the shallow psychology of those who conceive the Ego in man as a thing simple, permanent, reliable, and of one essence. To him, man was a being with myriad lives and myriad sensations, a complex multiform creature that bore within itself strange legacies of thought and passion, and whose very flesh was tainted with the monstrous maladies of the dead. He loved to stroll through the gaunt cold picture-gallery of his country house and look at the various portraits of those whose blood flowed in his veins. Here was Philip Herbert, described by Francis Osborne, in his "Memoires on the Reigns of Queen Elizabeth and King James," as one who was "caressed by the Court for his handsome face, which kept him not long company." Was it young Herbert's life that he sometimes led? Had some strange poisonous germ crept from body to body till it had reached his own? Was it some dim sense of that ruined grace that had made him so suddenly, and almost without cause, give utterance, in Basil Hallward's studio, to the mad prayer that had so changed his life? Here, in gold-embroidered red doublet, jewelled surcoat, and gilt-edged ruff and wrist-bands, stood Sir Anthony Sherard, with his silver-and-black armour piled at his feet. What had this man's legacy been? Had the lover of Giovanna of Naples bequeathed him some inheritance of sin and shame? Were his own actions merely the dreams that the dead man had not dared to realize? Here, from the fading canvas, smiled Lady Elizabeth Devereux, in her gauze hood, pearl stomacher, and pink slashed sleeves. A flower was in her right hand, and her left clasped an enamelled collar of white and damask roses. On a table by her side lay a mandolin and an apple. There were large green rosettes upon her little pointed shoes. He knew her life, and the strange stories that were told about her lovers. Had he something of her temperament in him? These oval heavy-lidded eyes seemed to look curiously at him. What of George Willoughby, with his powdered hair and fantastic patches? How evil he looked! The face was saturnine and swarthy, and the sensual lips seemed to be twisted with disdain. Delicate lace ruffles fell over the lean yellow hands that were so overladen with rings. He had been a macaroni of the eighteenth century, and the friend, in his youth, of Lord Ferrars. What of the second Lord Beckenham, the companion of the Prince Regent in his wildest days, and one of the witnesses at the secret marriage with Mrs. Fitzherbert? How proud and handsome he was, with his chestnut curls and insolent pose! What passions had he bequeathed? The world had looked upon him as infamous. He had led the orgies at Carlton House. The star of the Garter glittered upon his breast. Beside him hung the portrait of his wife, a pallid, thin-lipped woman in black. Her blood, also, stirred within him. How curious it all seemed! And his mother with her Lady Hamilton face, and her moist wine-dashed lips—he knew what he had got from her. He had got from her his beauty, and his passion for the beauty of others. She laughed at him in her loose Bacchante dress. There were vine leaves in her hair. The purple spilled from the cup she was holding. The carnations of the painting had withered, but the eyes were still wonderful in their depth and brilliancy of colour. They seemed to follow him wherever he went.

Yet one had ancestors in literature, as well as in one's own race, nearer perhaps in type and temperament, many of them, and certainly with an influence of which one was more absolutely conscious. There were times when it appeared to Dorian Gray that the whole of history was merely the record of his own life, not as he had lived it in act and circumstance, but as his imagination had created it for him, as it had been in his brain and in his passions. He felt that he had known them all, those strange terrible figures that had passed across the stage of the world and made sin so marvellous and evil so full of subtlety. It seemed to him that in some mysterious way their lives had been his own.

The hero of the wonderful novel that had so influenced his life had himself known this curious fancy. In the seventh chapter he tells how, crowned with laurel, lest lightning might strike him, he had sat, as Tiberius, in a garden at Capri reading the shameful books of Elephantis, while dwarfs and peacocks strutted round him and the flute-player mocked the swagger of the censer; and, as Caligula, had caroused with the green-shirted jockeys in their stables, and supped in an ivory manger with a jewel-frontleted horse; and, as Domitian, had wandered through a corridor lined with marble mirrors, looking round with haggard eyes for the reflection of the dagger that was to end his days, and sick with that *ennui*, that terrible *tædium vitæ*, that comes on those to whom life denies nothing: and had peered through a clear emerald at the red shambles of the Circus, and then, in a litter of pearl and purple drawn by silver-shod mules, been carried through the Street of Pomegranates to a House of Gold, and heard men cry on Nero Cæsar as he passed by; and, as Elagabalus, had painted his face with colours, and plied the distaff among the women, and brought the Moon from Carthage, and given her in mystic marriage to the Sun.

Over and over again Dorian used to read this fantastic chapter, and the two chapters immediately following, in which, as in some curious tapestries or cunningly-wrought enamels, were pictured the awful and beautiful forms of those whom Vice and Blood and Weariness had made monstrous or mad: Filippo, Duke of Milan, who slew his wife, and painted her lips with a scarlet poison that her lover might suck death from the dead thing he fondled; Pietro Barbi, the Venetian, known as Paul the Second, who sought in his vanity to assume the title of Formosus, and whose tiara, valued at two hundred thousand florins, was bought at the price of a terrible sin; Gian Maria Visconti, who used hounds to chase living men, and whose murdered body was covered with roses by a harlot who had loved him; the Borgia on his white horse, with Fratricide riding beside him, and his mantle stained with the blood of Perotto; Pietro Riario, the young Cardinal Archbishop of Florence, child and minion of Sixtus IV., whose beauty was equalled only by his debauchery, and who received Leonora of Aragon in a pavilion of white and crimson silk, filled with nymphs and centaurs, and gilded a boy that he might serve at the feast as Ganymede or Hylas; Ezzelin, whose melancholy could be cured only by the spectacle of death, and who had a passion for red blood, as other men have for red wine—the son of the Fiend, as was reported, and one who had cheated his father at dice when gambling with him for his own soul: Giambattista Cibo, who in mockery took the name of Innocent, and into whose torpid veins the blood of three lads was infused by a Jewish doctor; Sigismondo Malatesta, the lover of Isotta, and the lord of Rimini, whose effigy was burned at Rome as the enemy of God and man, who strangled Polyssena with a napkin, and gave poison to Ginevra d'Este in a cup of emerald, and in honour of a shameful passion built a pagan church for Christian worship; Charles VI., who had so wildly adored his brother's wife that a leper had warned him of the insanity that was coming on him, and who, when his brain had sickened and grown strange, could only be soothed by Saracen cards painted with the images of Love and Death and Madness; and, in his trimmed jerkin and jewelled cap and acanthus-like curls, Grifonetto Baglioni, who slew Astorre with his bride, and Simonetto with his page, and whose comeliness was such that, as he lay dying in the yellow piazza of Perugia, those who had hated him could not choose but weep, and Atalanta, who had cursed him, blessed him.

There was a horrible fascination in them all. He saw them at night, and they troubled his imagination in the day. The Renaissance knew of strange manners of poisoning—poisoning by a helmet and a lighted torch, by an embroidered glove and a jewelled fan, by a gilded pomander and by an amber chain. Dorian Gray had been poisoned by a book. There were moments when he looked on evil simply as a mode through which he could realize his conception of the beautiful.

CHAPTER XII

It was on the ninth of November, the eve of his own thirty-eighth birthday, as he often remembered afterwards.

He was walking home about eleven o'clock from Lord Henry's, where he had been dining, and was wrapped in heavy furs, as the night was cold and foggy. At the corner of Grosvenor Square and South Audley Street a man passed him in the mist, walking very fast, and with the collar of his grey ulster turned up. He had a bag in his hand. Dorian recognized him. It was Basil Hallward. A strange sense of fear, for which he could not account, came over him. He made no sign of recognition, and went on quickly, in the direction of his own house.

But Hallward had seen him. Dorian heard him first stopping on the pavement and then hurrying after him. In a few moments his hand was on his arm.

"Dorian! What an extraordinary piece of luck! I have been waiting for you in your library ever since nine o'clock. Finally I took pity on your tired servant, and told him to go to bed, as he let me out. I am off to Paris by the midnight train, and I particularly wanted to see you, before I left. I thought it was you, or rather your fur coat, as you passed me. But I wasn't quite sure. Didn't you recognize me?"

"In this fog, my dear Basil? Why, I can't even recognize Grosvenor Square. I believe my house is somewhere about here, but I don't feel at all certain about it. I am sorry you are going away, as I have not seen you for ages. But I suppose you will be back soon?"

"No: I am going to be out of England for six months. I intend to take a studio in Paris, and shut myself up till I have finished a great picture I have in my head. However, it wasn't about myself I wanted to talk. Here we are at your door. Let me come in for a moment. I have something to say to you."

"I shall be charmed. But won't you miss your train?" said Dorian Gray, languidly, as he passed up the steps and opened the door with his latch-key.

The lamp-light struggled out through the fog, and Hallward looked at his watch.

"I have heaps of time," he answered. "The train doesn't go till twelve-fifteen, and it is only just eleven. In fact, I was on my way to the club to look for you, when I met you. You see, I sha'n't have any delay about luggage, as I have sent on my heavy things. All I have with me is in this bag, and I can easily get to Victoria in twenty minutes."

Dorian looked at him and smiled. "What a way for a fashionable painter to travel! A Gladstone bag and an ulster! Come in, or the fog will get into the house. And mind you don't talk about anything serious. Nothing is serious nowadays. At least nothing should be."

Hallward shook his head, as he entered, and followed Dorian into the library. There was a bright wood fire blazing in the large open hearth. The lamps were lit, and an open Dutch silver spirit-case stood, with some siphons of soda-water and large cut-glass tumblers, on a little marqueterie table.

"You see your servant made me quite at home, Dorian. He gave me everything I wanted, including you best gold-tipped cigarettes. He is a most hospitable creature. I like him much better than the Frenchman you used to have. What has become of the Frenchman, by the bye?"

Dorian shrugged his shoulders. "I believe he married Lady Radley's maid, and has established her in Paris as an English dressmaker. *Anglomanie* is very fashionable over there now, I hear. It seems silly of the French, doesn't it? But—do you know?—he was not at all a bad servant. I never liked him, but I had nothing to complain about. One often imagines things that are quite absurd. He was really very devoted to me, and seemed quite sorry when he went away. Have another brandy-and-soda? Or would you like hock-and-seltzer? I always take hock-and-seltzer myself. There is sure to be some in the next room."

"Thanks, I won't have anything more," said the painter, taking his cap and coat off, and throwing them on the bag that he had placed in the corner. "And now, my dear fellow, I want to speak to you seriously. Don't frown like that. You make it so much more difficult for me."

"What is it all about?" cried Dorian, in his petulant way, flinging himself down on the sofa. "I hope it is not about myself. I am tired of myself to-night. I should like to be somebody else."

"It is about yourself," answered Hallward, in his grave, deep voice, "and I must say it to you. I shall only keep you half an hour."

Dorian sighed, and lit a cigarette. "Half an hour!" he murmured.

"It is not much to ask of you, Dorian, and it is entirely for your own sake that I am speaking. I think it right that you should know that the most dreadful things are being said against you in London."

"I don't wish to know anything about them. I love scandals about other people, but scandals about myself don't interest me. They have not got the charm of novelty."

"They must interest you, Dorian. Every gentleman is interested in his good name. You don't want people to talk of you as something vile and degraded. Of course you have your position, and your wealth, and all that kind of thing. But position and wealth are not everything. Mind you, I don't believe these rumours at all. At least, I can't believe them when I see you. Sin is a thing that writes itself across a man's face. It cannot be concealed. People talk sometimes of secret vices. There are no such things. If a wretched man has a vice, it shows itself in the lines of his mouth, the droop of his eyelids, the moulding of his hands even. Somebody—I won't mention his name, but you know him—came to me last year to have his portrait done. I had never seen him before, and had never heard anything about him at the time, though I have heard a good deal since. He offered an extravagant price. I refused him. There was something in the shape of his fingers that I hated. I know now that I was quite right in what I fancied about him. His life is dreadful. But you, Dorian, with your pure, bright, innocent face, and your marvellous untroubled youth—I can't believe anything against you. And yet I see you very seldom, and you never come down to the studio now, and when I am away from you, and I hear all these hideous things that people are whispering about you, I don't know what to say. Why is it, Dorian, that a man like the Duke of Berwick leaves the room of a club when you enter it? Why is it that so many gentlemen in London will neither go to your house nor invite you to theirs? You used to be a friend of Lord Staveley. I met him at dinner last week. Your name happened to come up in conversation, in connection with the miniatures you have lent to the exhibition at the Dudley. Staveley curled his lip, and said that you might have the most artistic tastes, but that you were a man whom no pure-minded girl should be allowed to know, and whom no chaste woman would sit in the same room with. I reminded him that I was a friend of yours, and asked him what he meant. He told me. He told me right out before everybody. It was horrible! Why is your friendship so fatal to young men? There was that wretched boy in the Guards who committed suicide. You were his great friend. There was Sir Henry Ashton, who had to leave England, with a tarnished name. You and he were inseparable. What about Adrian Singleton, and his dreadful end? What about Lord Kent's only son, and his career? I met his father yesterday in St. James's Street. He seemed broken with shame and sorrow. What about the young Duke of Perth? What sort of life has he got now? What gentleman would associate with him?"

"Stop, Basil. You are talking about things of which you know nothing," said Dorian Gray, biting his lip, and with a note of infinite contempt in his voice. "You ask me why Berwick leaves a room when I enter it. It is because I know everything about his life, not because he knows anything about mine. With such blood as he has in his veins, how could his record be clean? You ask me about Henry Ashton and young Perth. Did I teach the one his vices, and the other his debauchery? If Kent's silly son takes his wife from the streets, what is that to me? If Adrian Singleton writes his friend's name across a bill, am I his keeper? I know how people chatter in England. The middle classes air their moral prejudices over their gross dinner-tables, and whisper about what they call the profligacies of their betters in order to try and pretend that they are in smart society, and on intimate terms with the people they slander. In this country it is enough for a man to have distinction and brains for every common tongue to wag against him. And what sort of lives do these people, who pose as being moral, lead themselves? My dear fellow, you forget that we are in the native land of the hypocrite."

"Dorian," cried Hallward, "that is not the question. England is bad enough I know, and English society is all wrong. That is the reason why I want you to be fine. You have not been fine. One has a right to judge of a man by the effect he has over his friends. Yours seem to lose all sense of honour, of goodness, of purity. You have filled them with a madness for pleasure. They have gone down into the depths. You led them there. Yes: you led them there, and yet you can smile, as you are smiling now. And there is worse behind. I know you and Harry are inseparable. Surely for that reason, if for none other, you should not have made his sister's name a byword."

"Take care, Basil. You go too far."

"I must speak, and you must listen. You shall listen. When you met Lady Gwendolyn, not a breath of scandal had ever touched her. Is there a single decent woman in London now who would drive with her in the Park? Why, even her children are not allowed to live with her. Then there are other stories—stories that you have been seen creeping at dawn out of dreadful houses and slinking in disguise into the foulest dens in London. Are they true? Can they be true? When I first heard them, I laughed. I hear them now, and they make me shudder. What about your country house, and the life that is led there? Dorian, you don't know what is said about you. I won't tell you that I don't want to preach to you. I remember Harry saying once that every man who turned himself into an amateur curate for the moment always began by saying that, and then proceeded to break his word. I do want to preach to you. I want you to lead such a life as will make the world respect you. I want you to have a clean name and a fair record. I want you to get rid of the dreadful people you associate with. Don't shrug your shoulders like that. Don't be so indifferent. You have a wonderful influence. Let it be for good, not for evil. They say that you corrupt every one with whom you become intimate, and that it is quite sufficient for you to enter a house, for shame of some kind to follow after. I don't know whether it is or not. How should I know? But it is said of you. I am told things that it seems impossible to doubt. Lord Gloucester was one of my greatest friends at Oxford. He showed me a letter that his wife had written to him when she was dying alone in her villa at Mentone. Your name was implicated in the most terrible confession I ever read. I told him that it was absurd—that I knew you thoroughly, and that you were incapable of anything of the kind. Know you? I wonder do I know you? Before I could answer that, I should have to see your soul."

"To see my soul!" muttered Dorian Gray, starting up from the sofa and turning almost white from fear.

"Yes," answered Hallward, gravely, and with deep-toned sorrow in his voice, "to see your soul. But only God can do that."

A bitter laugh of mockery broke from the lips of the younger man. "You shall see it yourself, to-night!" he cried, seizing a lamp from the table. "Come: it is your own handiwork. Why shouldn't you look at it? You can tell the world all about it afterwards, if you choose. Nobody would believe you. If they did believe you, they would like me all the better for it. I know the age better than you do, though you will prate about it so tediously. Come, I tell you. You have chattered enough about corruption. Now you shall look on it face to face."

There was the madness of pride in every word he uttered. He stamped his foot upon the ground in his boyish insolent manner. He felt a terrible joy at the thought that some one else was to share his secret, and that the man who had painted the portrait that was the origin of all his shame was to be burdened for the rest of his life with the hideous memory of what he had done.

"Yes," he continued, coming closer to him, and looking steadfastly into his stern eyes, "I shall show you my soul. You shall see the thing that you fancy only God can see."

Hallward started back. "This is blasphemy, Dorian!" he cried. "You must not say things like that. They are horrible, and they don't mean anything."

"You think so?" he laughed again.

"I know so. As for what I said to you to-night, I said it for your good. You know I have always been a staunch friend to you."

"Don't touch me. Finish what you have to say."

A twisted flash of pain shot across the painter's face. He paused for a moment, and a wild feeling of pity came over him. After all, what right had he to pry into the life of Dorian Gray? If he had done a tithe of what was rumoured about him, how much he must have suffered! Then he straightened himself up, and walked over to the fireplace, and stood there, looking at the burning logs with their frost-like ashes and their throbbing cores of flame.

"I am waiting, Basil," said the young man, in a hard, clear voice.

He turned round. "What I have to say is this," he cried. "You must give me some answer to these horrible charges that are made against you. If you tell me that they are absolutely untrue from beginning to end, I shall believe you. Deny them, Dorian, deny them! Can't you see what I am going through? My God! don't tell me that you are bad, and corrupt, and shameful."

Dorian Gray smiled. There was a curl of contempt in his lips. "Come upstairs, Basil," he said, quietly. "I keep a diary of my life from day to day, and it never leaves the room in which it is written. I shall show it to you if you come with me."

"I shall come with you, Dorian, if you wish it. I see I have missed my train. That makes no matter. I can go to-morrow. But don't ask me to read anything to-night. All I want is a plain answer to my question."

"That shall be given to you upstairs. I could not give it here. You will not have to read long."

CHAPTER XIII

He passed out of the room and began the ascent, Basil Hallward following close behind. They walked softly, as men do instinctively at night. The lamp cast fantastic shadows on the wall and staircase. A rising wind made some of the windows rattle.

When they reached the top landing, Dorian set the lamp down on the floor, and taking out the key turned it in the lock. "You insist on knowing, Basil?" he asked, in a low voice.

"Yes."

"I am delighted," he answered, smiling. Then he added, somewhat harshly: "You are the one man in the world who is entitled to know everything about me. You have had more to do with my life than you think:" and, taking up the lamp, he opened the door and went in. A cold current of air passed them, and the light shot up for a moment in a flame of murky orange. He shuddered. "Shut the door behind you," he whispered, as he placed the lamp on the table.

Hallward glanced around him, with a puzzled expression. The room looked as if it had not been lived in for years. A faded Flemish tapestry, a curtained picture, an old Italian *cassone*, and an almost empty bookcase—that was all that it seemed to contain, besides a chair and a table. As Dorian Gray was lighting a half-burned candle that was standing on the mantelshelf he saw that the whole place was covered with dust, and that the carpet was in holes. A mouse ran scuffling behind the wainscoting. There was a damp odour of mildew.

"So you think that it is only God who sees the soul, Basil? Draw that curtain back, and you will see mine."

The voice that spoke was cold and cruel. "You are mad, Dorian, or playing a part," muttered Hallward, frowning.

"You won't? Then I must do it myself," said the young man; and he tore the curtain from its rod, and flung it on the ground.

An exclamation of horror broke from the painter's lips as he saw in the dim light the hideous face on the canvas grinning at him. There was something in its expression that filled him with disgust and loathing. Good heavens! it was Dorian Gray's own face that he was looking at! The horror, whatever it was, had not yet entirely spoiled that marvellous beauty. There was still some gold in the thinning hair and some scarlet on the sensual mouth. The sodden eyes had kept something of the loveliness of their blue, the noble curves had not yet completely passed away from chiselled nostrils and from plastic throat. Yes, it was Dorian himself. But who had done it? He seemed to recognize his own brush-work, and the frame was his own design. The idea was monstrous, yet he felt afraid. He seized the lighted candle, and held it to the picture. In the left-hand corner was his own name, traced in long letters of bright vermilion.

It was some foul parody, some infamous, ignoble satire. He had never done that. Still, it was his own picture. He knew it, and he felt as if his blood had changed in a moment from fire to sluggish ice. His own picture! What did it mean? Why had it altered? He turned, and looked at Dorian Gray with the eyes of a sick man. His mouth twitched, and his parched tongue seemed unable to articulate. He passed his hand across his forehead. It was dank with clammy sweat.

The young man was leaning against the mantelshelf, watching him with that strange expression that one sees on the faces of those who are absorbed in a play when some great artist is acting. There was neither real sorrow in it nor real joy. There was simply the passion of the spectator, with perhaps a flicker of triumph in his eyes. He had taken the flower out of his coat, and was smelling it, or pretending to do so.

"What does this mean?" cried Hallward, at last. His own voice sounded shrill and curious in his ears.

"Years ago, when I was a boy," said Dorian Gray, crushing the flower in his hand, "you met me, flattered me, and taught me to be vain of my good looks. One day you introduced me to a friend of yours, who explained to me the wonder of youth, and you finished a portrait of me that revealed to me the wonder of beauty. In a mad moment, that, even now, I don't know whether I regret or not, I made a wish, perhaps you would call it a prayer. . . ."

"I remember it! Oh, how well I remember it! No! the thing is impossible. The room is damp. Mildew has got into the canvas. The paints I used had some wretched mineral poison in them. I tell you the thing is impossible."

"Ah, what is impossible?" murmured the young man, going over to the window, and leaning his forehead against the cold, mist-stained glass.

"You told me you had destroyed it."

"I was wrong. It has destroyed me."

"I don't believe it is my picture."

"Can't you see your ideal in it?" said Dorian, bitterly.

"My ideal, as you call it . . ."

"As you called it."

"There was nothing evil in it, nothing shameful. You were to me such an ideal as I shall never meet again. This is the face of a satyr."

"Is it the face of my soul."

"Christ! what a thing I must have worshipped! It has the eyes of a devil."

"Each of us has Heaven and Hell in him, Basil," cried Dorian, with a wild gesture of despair.

Hallward turned again to the portrait, and gazed at it. "My God! if it is true," he exclaimed, "and this is what you have done with your life, why, you must be worse even than those who talk against you fancy you to be!" He held the light up again to the canvas, and examined it. The surface seemed to be quite undisturbed, and as he had left it. It was from within, apparently, that the foulness and horror had come. Through some strange quickening of inner life the leprosies of sin were slowly eating the thing away. The rotting of a corpse in a watery grave was not so fearful.

His hand shook, and the candle fell from its socket on the floor, and lay there sputtering. He placed his foot on it and put it out. Then he flung himself into the rickety chair that was standing by the table and buried his face in his hands.

"Good God, Dorian, what a lesson! What an awful lesson!" There was no answer, but he could hear the young man sobbing at the window. "Pray, Dorian, pray," he murmured. "What is it that one was taught to say in one's boyhood? 'Lead us not into temptation. Forgive us our sins. Wash away our iniquities.' Let us say that together. The prayer of your pride has been answered. The prayer of your repentance will be answered also. I worshipped you too much. I am punished for it. You worshipped yourself too much. We are both punished."

Dorian Gray turned slowly around, and looked at him with tear-dimmed eyes. "It is too late, Basil," he faltered.

"It is never too late, Dorian. Let us kneel down and try if we cannot remember a prayer. Isn't there a verse somewhere, 'Though your sins be as scarlet, yet I will make them as white as snow'?"

"Those words mean nothing to me now."

"Hush! don't say that. You have done enough evil in your life. My God! Don't you see that accursed thing leering at us?"

Dorian Gray glanced at the picture, and suddenly an uncontrollable feeling of hatred for Basil Hallward came over him, as though it had been suggested to him by the image on the canvas, whispered into his ear by those grinning lips. The mad passions of a hunted animal stirred within him, and he loathed the man who was seated at the table, more than in his whole life he had ever loathed anything. He glanced wildly around. Something glimmered on the top of the painted chest that faced him. His eye fell on it. He knew what it was. It was a knife that he had brought up, some days before, to cut a piece of cord, and had forgotten to take away with him. He moved slowly towards it, passing Hallward as he did so. As soon as he got behind him, he seized it, and turned round. Hallward stirred in his chair as if he was going to rise. He rushed at him, and dug the knife into the great vein that is behind the ear, crushing the man's head down on the table, and stabbing again and again.

There was a stifled groan, and the horrible sound of some one choking with blood. Three times the outstretched arms shot up convulsively, waving grotesque stiff-fingered hands in the air. He stabbed him twice more, but the man did not move. Something began to trickle on the floor. He waited for a moment, still pressing the head down. Then he threw the knife on the table, and listened.

He could hear nothing, but the drip, drip on the threadbare carpet. He opened the door and went out on the landing. The house was absolutely quiet. No one was about. For a few seconds he stood bending over the balustrade, and peering down into the black seething well of darkness. Then he took out the key and returned to the room, locking himself in as he did so.

The thing was still seated in the chair, straining over the table with bowed head, and humped back, and long fantastic arms. Had it not been for the red, jagged tear in the neck, and the clotted black pool that was slowly widening on the table, one would have said that the man was simply asleep.

How quickly it had all been done! He felt strangely calm, and, walking over to the window, opened it and stepped out on the balcony. The wind had blown the fog away, and the sky was like a monstrous peacock's tail, starred with myriads of golden eyes. He looked down, and saw the policeman going his rounds and flashing the long beam of his lantern on the doors of the silent houses. The crimson spot of a prowling hansom gleamed at the corner, and then vanished. A woman in a fluttering shawl was creeping slowly by the railings, staggering as she went. Now and then she stopped, and peered back. Once, she began to sing in a hoarse voice. The policeman strolled over and said something to her. She stumbled away, laughing. A bitter blast swept across the Square. The gas lamps flickered, and became blue, and the leafless trees shook their black iron branches to and fro. He shivered, and went back, closing the window behind him.

Having reached the door, he turned the key, and opened it. He did not even glance at the murdered man. He felt that the secret of the whole thing was not to realize the situation. The friend who had painted the fatal portrait to which all his misery had been due, had gone out of his life. That was enough.

Then he remembered the lamp. It was a rather curious one of Moorish workmanship, made of dull silver inlaid with arabesques of burnished steel, and studded with coarse turquoises. Perhaps it might be missed by his servant, and questions would be asked. He hesitated for a moment, then he turned back and took it from the table. He could not help seeing the dead thing. How still it was! How horribly white the long hands looked! It was like a dreadful wax image.

Having locked the door behind him, he crept quietly downstairs. The woodwork creaked, and seemed to cry out as if in pain. He stopped several times, and waited. No: everything was still. It was merely the sound of his own footsteps.

When he reached the library, he saw the bag and coat in the corner. They must be hidden away somewhere. He unlocked a secret press that was in the wainscoting, a press in which he kept his own curious disguises, and put them into it. He could easily burn them afterwards. Then he pulled out his watch. It was twenty minutes to two.

He sat down and began to think. Every year—every month, almost—men were strangled in England for what he had done. There had been a madness of murder in the air. Some red star had come too close to the earth. . . . And yet what evidence was there against him? Basil Hallward had left the house at eleven. No one had seen him come in again. Most of the servants were at Selby Royal. His valet had gone to bed. . . . Paris? Yes. It was to Paris that Basil had gone, and by the midnight train, as he had intended. With his curious reserved habits, it would be months before any suspicions would be aroused. Months! Everything could be destroyed long before then.

A sudden thought struck him. He put on his fur coat and hat, and went out into the hall. There he paused, hearing the slow, heavy tread of the policeman on the pavement outside, and seeing the flash of the bull's-eye reflected in the window. He waited, and held his breath.

After a few moments he drew back the latch, and slipped out, shutting the door very gently behind him. Then he began ringing the bell. In about five minutes his valet appeared, half dressed, and looking very drowsy.

"I am sorry to have had to wake you up, Francis," he said, stepping in; "but I had forgotten my latchkey. What time is it?"

"Ten minutes past two, sir," answered the man, looking at the clock and blinking.

"Ten minutes past two? How horribly late! You must wake me at nine tomorrow. I have some work to do."

"All right, sir."

"Did any one call this evening?"

"Mr. Hallward, sir. He stayed here till eleven, and then he went away to catch his train."

"Oh! I am sorry I didn't see him. Did he leave any message?"

"No, sir, except that he would write to you from Paris, if he did not find you at the club."

"That will do, Francis. Don't forget to call me at nine to-morrow."

"No, sir."

The man shambled down the passage in his slippers.

Dorian Gray threw his hat and coat upon the table, and passed into the library. For a quarter of an hour he walked up and down the room biting his lip, and thinking. Then he took down the Blue Book from one of the shelves, and began to turn over the leaves. "Alan Campbell, 152, Hertford Street, Mayfair." Yes; that was the man he wanted.

CHAPTER XIV

At nine o'clock the next morning his servant came in with a cup of chocolate on a tray, and opened the shutters. Dorian was sleeping quite peacefully, lying on his right side, with one hand underneath his cheek. He looked like a boy who had been tired out with play, or study.

The man had to touch him twice on the shoulder before he woke, and as he opened his eyes a faint smile passed across his lips, as though he had been lost in some delightful dream. Yet he had not dreamed at all. His night had been untroubled by any images of pleasure or of pain. But youth smiles without any reason. It is one of its chiefest charms.

He turned round, and, leaning upon his elbow, began to sip his chocolate. The mellow November sun came streaming into the room. The sky was bright, and there was a genial warmth in the air. It was almost like a morning in May.

Gradually the events of the preceding night crept with silent bloodstained feet into his brain and reconstructed themselves there with terrible distinctness. He winced at the memory of all that he had suffered, and for a moment the same curious feeling of loathing for Basil Hallward, that had made him kill him as he sat in the chair, came back to him, and he grew cold with passion. The dead man was still sitting there, too, and in the sunlight now. How horrible that was! Such hideous things were for the darkness, not for the day.

He felt that if he brooded on what he had gone through he would sicken or grow mad. There were sins whose fascination was more in the memory than in the doing of them, strange triumphs that gratified the pride more than the passions, and gave to the intellect a quickened sense of joy, greater than any joy they brought, or could ever bring, to the senses. But this was not one of them. It was a thing to be driven out of the mind, to be drugged with poppies, to be strangled lest it might strangle one itself.

When the half-hour struck, he passed his hand across his forehead, and then got up hastily, and dressed himself with even more than his usual care, giving a good deal of attention to the choice of his necktie and scarf-pin, and changing his rings more than once. He spent a long time also over breakfast, tasting the various dishes, talking to his valet about some new liveries that he was thinking of getting made for the servants at Selby, and going through his correspondence. At some of the letters he smiled. Three of them bored him.

One he read several times over, and then tore up with a slight look of annoyance in his face. "That awful thing, a woman's memory!" as Lord Henry had once said.

After he had drunk his cup of black coffee, he wiped his lips slowly with a napkin, motioned to his servant to wait, and going over to the table sat down and wrote two letters. One he put in his pocket, the other he handed to the valet.

"Take this round to 152, Hertford Street, Francis, and if Mr. Campbell is out of town, get his address."

As soon as he was alone, he lit a cigarette, and began sketching upon a piece of paper, drawing first flowers, and bits of architecture, and then human faces. Suddenly he remarked that every face that he drew seemed to have a fantastic likeness to Basil Hallward. He frowned, and getting up, went over to the bookcase and took out a volume at hazard. He was determined that he would not think about what had happened until it became absolutely necessary that he should do so.

When he had stretched himself on the sofa, he looked at the title-page of the book. It was Gautier's "Emaux et Camées," Charpentier's Japanese-paper edition, with the Jacquemart etching. The binding was of citron-green leather, with a design of gilt trellis-work and dotted pomegranates. It had been given to him by Adrian Singleton. As he turned over the pages his eye fell on the poem about the hand of Lacenaire, the cold yellow hand "*du supplice encore mal lavée*," with its downy red hairs and its "doigts de faune." He glanced at his own white taper fingers, shuddering slightly in spite of himself, and passed on, till he came to those lovely stanzas upon Venice:

"*Sur une gamme chromatique,*
Le sein de perles ruisselant,
La Venus de l'Adriatique
Sort de l'eau son corps rose et blanc.

Les dômes, sur l'azur des ondes
Suivant la phrase au pur contour,
S'enflent comme des gorges rondes
Que soulève un soupir d'amour.

L'esquif aborde et me dépose,
Jetant son amarre au pilier,
Devant une façade rose,
Sur le marbre d'un escalier."

How exquisite they were! As one read them, one seemed to be floating down the green waterways of the pink and pearl city, seated in a black gondola with silver prow and trailing curtains. The mere lines looked to him like those straight lines of turquoise-blue that follow one as one pushes out to the Lido. The sudden flashes of colour reminded him of the gleam of the opal-and-iris-throated birds that flutter round the tall honey-combed Campanile, or stalk, with such stately grace, through the dim, dust-stained arcades. Leaning back with half-closed eyes, he kept saying over and over to himself:

"Devant une façade rose
Sur le marbre d'un escalier."

The whole of Venice was in those two lines. He remembered the autumn that he had passed there, and a wonderful love that had stirred him to mad, delightful follies. There was romance in every place. But Venice, like Oxford, had kept the background for romance, and, to the true romantic, background was everything, or almost everything. Basil had been with him part of the time, and had gone wild over Tintoret. Poor Basil! what a horrible way for a man to die!

He sighed, and took up the volume again, and tried to forget. He read of the swallows that fly in and out of the little café at Smyrna where the Hadjis sit counting their amber beads and the turbaned merchants smoke their long tasselled pipes and talk gravely to each other; he read of the Obelisk in the Place de la Concorde that weeps tears of granite in its lonely sunless exile, and longs to be back by the hot lotus-covered Nile, where there are Sphinxes, and rose-red ibises, and white vultures with gilded claws, and crocodiles, with small beryl eyes, that crawl over the green steaming mud; he began to brood over those verses which, drawing music from kiss-stained marble, tell of that curious statue that Gautier compares to a contralto voice, the "*monstre charmant*" that couches in the porphyry-room of the Louvre. But after a time the book fell from his hand. He grew nervous, and a horrible fit of terror came over him. What if Alan Campbell should be out of England? Days would elapse before he could come back. Perhaps he might refuse to come. What could he do then? Every moment was of vital importance.

They had been great friends once, five years before—almost inseparable, indeed. Then the intimacy had come suddenly to an end. When they met in society now, it was only Dorian Gray who smiled; Alan Campbell never did.

He was an extremely clever young man, though he had no real appreciation of the visible arts, and whatever little sense of the beauty of poetry he possessed he had gained entirely from Dorian. His dominant intellectual passion was for science. At Cambridge he had spent a great deal of his time working in the Laboratory, and had taken a good class in the Natural Science Tripos of his year. Indeed, he was still devoted to the study of chemistry, and had a laboratory of his own, in which he used to shut himself up all day long, greatly to the annoyance of his mother, who had set her heart on his standing for parliament and had a vague idea that a chemist was a person who made up prescriptions. He was an excellent musician, however, as well, and played both the violin and the piano better than most amateurs. In fact, it was music that had first brought him and Dorian Gray together—music and that indefinable attraction that Dorian seemed to be able to exercise whenever he wished, and indeed exercised often without being conscious of it. They had met at Lady Berkshire's the night that Rubinstein played there, and after that used to be always seen together at the Opera, and wherever good music was going on. For eighteen months their intimacy lasted. Campbell was always either at Selby Royal or in Grosvenor Square. To him, as to many others, Dorian Gray was the type of everything that is wonderful and fascinating in life. Whether or not a quarrel had taken place between them no one ever knew. But suddenly people remarked that they scarcely spoke when they met, and that Campbell seemed always to go away early from any party at which Dorian Gray was present. He had changed, too—was strangely melancholy at times, appeared almost to dislike hearing music, and would never himself play, giving as his excuse, when he was called upon, that he was so absorbed in science that he had no time left in which to practise. And this was certainly true. Every day he seemed to become more interested in biology, and his name appeared once or twice in some of the scientific reviews, in connection with certain curious experiments.

This was the man Dorian Gray was waiting for. Every second he kept glancing at the clock. As the minutes went by he became horribly agitated. At last he got up, and began to pace up and down the room, looking like a beautiful caged thing. He took long stealthy strides. His hands were curiously cold.

The suspense became unbearable. Time seemed to him to be crawling with feet of lead, while he by monstrous winds was being swept towards the jagged edge of some black cleft of precipice. He knew what was waiting for him there; saw it indeed, and, shuddering, crushed with dank hands his burning lids as though he would have robbed the very brain of sight, and driven the eyeballs back into their cave. It was useless. The brain had its own food on which it battened, and the imagination, made grotesque by terror, twisted and distorted as a living thing by pain, danced like some foul puppet on a stand, and grinned through moving masks. Then, suddenly, Time stopped for him. Yes: that blind, slow-breathing thing crawled no more, and horrible thoughts, Time being dead, raced nimbly on in front, and dragged a hideous future from its grave, and showed it to him. He stared at it. Its very horror made him stone.

At last the door opened, and his servant entered. He turned glazed eyes upon him.

"Mr. Campbell, sir," said the man.

A sigh of relief broke from his parched lips, and the colour came back to his cheeks.

"Ask him to come in at once, Francis." He felt that he was himself again His mood of cowardice had passed away.

The man bowed, and retired. In a few moments Alan Campbell walked in, looking very stern and rather pale, his pallor being intensified by his coal-black hair and dark eyebrows.

"Alan! this is kind of you. I thank you for coming."

"I had intended never to enter your house again, Gray. But you said it was a matter of life and death." His voice was hard and cold. He spoke with slow deliberation. There was a look of contempt in the steady searching gaze that he turned on Dorian. He kept his hands in the pockets of his Astrakhan coat, and seemed not to have noticed the gesture with which he had been greeted.

"Yes: it is a matter of life and death, Alan, and to more than one person. Sit down."

Campbell took a chair by the table, and Dorian sat opposite to him. The two men's eyes met. In Dorian's there was infinite pity. He knew that what he was going to do was dreadful.

After a strained moment of silence, he leaned across and said, very quietly, but watching the effect of each word upon the face of him he had sent for, "Alan, in a locked room at the top of this house, a room to which nobody but myself has access, a dead man is seated at a table. He has been dead ten hours now. Don't stir, and don't look at me like that. Who the man is, why he died, how he died, are matters that do not concern you. What you have to do is this——"

"Stop, Gray. I don't want to know anything further. Whether what you have told me is true or not true, doesn't concern me. I entirely decline to be mixed up in your life. Keep your horrible secrets to yourself. They don't interest me any more."

"Alan, they will have to interest you. This one will have to interest you. I am awfully sorry for you, Alan. But I can't help myself. You are the one man who is able to save me. I am forced to bring you into the matter. I have no option. Alan, you are scientific. You know about chemistry, and things of that kind. You have made experiments. What you have got to do is to destroy the thing that is upstairs–to destroy it so that not a vestige of it will be left. Nobody saw this person come into the house. Indeed, at the present moment he is supposed to be in Paris. He will not be missed for months. When he is missed, there must be no trace of him found here. You, Alan, you must change him, and everything that belongs to him, into a handful of ashes that I may scatter in the air."

"You are mad, Dorian."

"Ah! I was waiting for you to call me Dorian."

"You are mad, I tell you–mad to imagine that I would raise a finger to help you, mad to make this monstrous confession. I will have nothing to do with this matter, whatever it is. Do you think I am going to peril my reputation for you? What is it to me what devil's work you are up to?"

"It was suicide, Alan."

"I am glad of that. But who drove him to it? You, I should fancy."

"Do you still refuse to do this for me?"

"Of course I refuse. I will have absolutely nothing to do with it. I don't care what shame comes on you. You deserve it all. I should not be sorry to see you disgraced, publicly disgraced. How dare you ask me, of all men in the world, to mix myself up in this horror? I should have thought you knew more about people's characters. Your friend Lord Henry Wotton can't have taught you much about psychology, whatever else he has taught you. Nothing will induce me to stir a step to help you. You have come to the wrong man. Go to some of your friends. Don't come to me."

"Alan, it was murder. I killed him. You don't know what he had made me suffer. Whatever my life is, he had more to do with the making or marring of it than poor Harry has had. He may not have intended it, the result was the same."

"Murder! Good God, Dorian, is that what you have come to? I shall not inform upon you. It is not my business. Besides, without my stirring in the matter, you are certain to be arrested. Nobody ever commits a crime without doing something stupid. But I will have nothing to do with it."

"You must have something to do with it. Wait, wait a moment; listen to me Only listen, Alan. All I ask of you is to perform a certain scientific experiment. You go to hospitals and dead-houses, and the horrors that you do there don't affect you. If in some hideous dissecting-room or fetid laboratory you found this man lying on a leaden table with red gutters scooped out in it for the blood to flow through you would simply look upon him as an admirable subject. You would not turn a hair. You would not believe that you were doing anything wrong. On the contrary, you would probably feel that you were benefiting the human race, or increasing the sum of knowledge in the world, or gratifying intellectual curiosity, or something of that kind. What I want you to do is merely what you have often done before. Indeed, to destroy a body must be far less horrible than what you are accustomed to work at. And, remember, it is the only piece of evidence against me. If it is discovered, I am lost; and it is sure to be discovered unless you help me."

"I have no desire to help you. You forget that. I am simply indifferent to the whole thing. It has nothing to do with me."

"Alan, I entreat you. Think of the position I am in. Just before you came I almost fainted with terror. You may know terror yourself some day. No! don't think of that. Look at the matter purely from the scientific point of view. You don't inquire where the dead things on which you experiment come from. Don't inquire now. I have told you too much as it is. But I beg of you to do this. We were friends once, Alan."

"Don't speak about those days, Dorian: they are dead."

"The dead linger sometimes. The man upstairs will not go away. He is sitting at the table with bowed head and outstretched arms. Alan! Alan! if you don't come to my assistance I am ruined. Why, they will hang me, Alan! Don't you understand? They will hang me for what I have done."

"There is no good in prolonging this scene. I absolutely refuse to do anything in the matter. It is insane of you to ask me."

"You refuse?"

"Yes."

"I entreat you, Alan."

"It is useless."

The same look of pity came into Dorian Gray's eyes. Then he stretched out his hand, took a piece of paper, and wrote something on it. He read it over twice, folded it carefully, and pushed it across the table. Having done this, he got up, and went over to the window.

Campbell looked at him in surprise, and then took up the paper, and opened it. As he read it, his face became ghastly pale, and he fell back in his chair. A horrible sense of sickness came over him. He felt as if his heart was beating itself to death in some empty hollow.

After two or three minutes of terrible silence, Dorian turned round, and came and stood behind him, putting his hand upon his shoulder.

"I am so sorry for you, Alan," he murmured, "but you leave me no alternative. I have a letter written already. Here it is. You see the address. If you don't help me, I must send it. If you don't help me, I will send it. You know what the result will be. But you are going to help me. It is impossible for you to refuse now. I tried to spare you. You will do me the justice to admit that. You were stern, harsh, offensive. You treated me as no man has ever dared to treat me—no living man, at any rate. I bore it all. Now it is for me to dictate terms."

Campbell buried his face in his hands, and a shudder passed through him.

"Yes, it is my turn to dictate terms, Alan. You know what they are. The thing is quite simple. Come, don't work yourself into this fever. The thing has to be done. Face it, and do it."

A groan broke from Campbell's lips, and he shivered all over. The ticking of the clock on the mantel-piece seemed to him to be dividing time into separate atoms of agony, each of which was too terrible to be borne. He felt as if an iron ring was being slowly tightened round his forehead, as if the disgrace with which he was threatened had already come upon him. The hand upon his shoulder weighed like a band of lead. It was intolerable. It seemed to crush him.

"Come, Alan, you must decide at once."

"I cannot do it," he said mechanically, as though words could alter things.

"You must. You have no choice. Don't delay."

He hesitated a moment. "Is there a fire in the room upstairs?"

"Yes, there is a gas-fire with asbestos."

"I shall have to go home and get some things from the laboratory."

"No, Alan, you must not leave the house. Write out on a sheet of notepaper what you want, and my servant will take a cab and bring the things back to you."

Campbell scrawled a few lines, blotted them, and addressed an envelope to his assistant. Dorian took the note up and read it carefully. Then he rang the bell, and gave it to his valet, with orders to return as soon as possible, and to bring the things with him.

As the hall door shut, Campbell started nervously, and, having got up from the chair, went over to the chimney-piece. He was shivering with a kind of ague. For nearly twenty minutes, neither of the men spoke. A fly buzzed noisily about the room, and the ticking of the clock was like the beat of a hammer.

As the chime struck one, Campbell turned round, and, looking at Dorian Gray, saw that his eyes were filled with tears. There was something in the purity and refinement of that sad face that seemed to enrage him. "You are infamous, absolutely infamous!" he muttered.

"Hush, Alan: you have saved my life," said Dorian.

"Your life? Good heavens! what a life that is. You have gone from corruption to corruption, and you have culminated in crime. In doing what I am going to do, what you force me to do, it is not of your life that I am thinking."

"Ah, Alan," murmured Dorian, with a sigh, "I wish you had a thousandth part of the pity for me that I have for you." He turned away as he spoke, and stood looking out at the garden. Campbell made no answer.

After about ten minutes a knock came to the door, and the servant entered, carrying a large mahogany chest of chemicals, with a long coil of steel and platinum wire and two rather curiously-shaped iron clamps.

"Shall I leave the things here, sir?" he asked Campbell.

"Yes," said Dorian. And I am afraid, Francis, that I have another errand for you. What is the name of the man at Richmond who supplies Selby with orchids?"

"Harden, sir."

"Yes–Harden. You must go down to Richmond at once, see Harden personally, and tell him to send twice as many orchids as I ordered, and to have as few white ones as possible. In fact, I don't want any white ones. It is a lovely day, Francis, and Richmond is a very pretty place, otherwise I wouldn't bother you about it."

"No trouble, sir. At what time shall I be back?"

Dorian looked at Campbell. "How long will your experiment take, Alan?" he said, in a calm, indifferent voice. The presence of a third person in the room seemed to give him extraordinary courage.

Campbell frowned, and bit his lip. "It will take about five hours," he answered.

"It will be time enough, then, if you are back at half-past seven, Francis. Or stay: just leave my things out for dressing. You can have the evening to yourself. I am not dining at home, so I shall not want you."

"Thank you, sir," said the man, leaving the room.

"Now, Alan, there is not a moment to be lost. How heavy this chest is! I'll take it for you. You bring the other things." He spoke rapidly, and in an authoritative manner. Campbell felt dominated by him. They left the room together.

When they reached the top landing, Dorian took out the key and turned it in the lock. Then he stopped, and a troubled look came into his eyes. He shuddered. "I don't think I can go in, Alan," he murmured.

"It is nothing to me. I don't require you," said Campbell, coldly.

Dorian half opened the door. As he did so, he saw the face of his portrait leering in the sunlight. On the floor in front of it the torn curtain was lying. He remembered that the night before he had forgotten, for the first time in his life, to hide the fatal canvas, and was about to rush forward, when he drew back with a shudder.

What was that loathsome red dew that gleamed, wet and glistening, on one of the hands, as though the canvas had sweated blood? How horrible it was! –more horrible, it seemed to him for the moment, than the silent thing he knew was stretched across the table, the thing whose grotesque misshapen shadow on the spotted carpet showed him that it had not stirred, but was still there, as he had left it.

He heaved a deep breath, opened the door a little wider, and with half-closed eyes and averted head walked quickly in, determined that he would not look even once upon the dead man. Then, stooping down, and taking up the gold-and-purple hanging, he flung it right over the picture.

There he stopped, feeling afraid to turn round, and his eyes fixed themselves on the intricacies of the pattern before him. He heard Campbell bringing in the heavy chest, and the irons, and the other things that he had required for his dreadful work. He began to wonder if he and Basil Hallward had ever met, and, if so, what they had thought of each other.

"Leave me now," said a stern voice behind him.

He turned and hurried out, just conscious that the dead man had been thrust back into the chair, and that Campbell was gazing into a glistening yellow face. As he was going downstairs he heard the key being turned in the lock.

It was long after seven when Campbell came back into the library. He was pale, but absolutely calm. "I have done what you asked me to do," he muttered. "And now, good-bye. Let us never see each other again."

"You have saved me from ruin, Alan. I cannot forget that," said Dorian, simply.

As soon as Campbell had left, he went upstairs. There was a horrible smell of nitric acid in the room. But the thing that had been sitting at the table was gone.

CHAPTER XV

THAT evening, at eight-thirty, exquisitely dressed, and wearing a large buttonhole of Parma violets, Dorian Gray was ushered into Lady Narborough's drawing-room by bowing servants. His forehead was throbbing with maddened nerves, and he felt wildly excited, but his manner as he bent over his hostess's hand was as easy and graceful as ever. Perhaps one never seems so much at one's ease as when one has to play a part. Certainly no one looking at Dorian Gray that night could have believed that he had passed through a tragedy as horrible as any tragedy of our age. Those finely-shaped fingers could never have clutched a knife of sin, nor those smiling lips have cried out on God and goodness. He himself could not help wondering at the calm of his demeanour, and for a moment felt keenly the terrible pleasure of a double life.

It was a small party, got up rather in a hurry by Lady Narborough, who was a very clever woman, with what Lord Henry used to describe as the remains of really remarkable ugliness. She had proved an excellent wife to one of our most tedious ambassadors, and having buried her husband properly in a marble mausoleum, which she had herself designed, and married off her daughters to some rich, rather elderly men, she devoted herself now to the pleasures of French fiction, French cookery, and French *esprit* when she could get it.

Dorian was one of her especial favourites, and she always told him that she was extremely glad she had not met him in early life. "I know, my dear, I should have fallen madly in love with you," she used to say, "and thrown my bonnet right over the mills for your sake. It is most fortunate that you were not thought of at the time. As it was, our bonnets were so unbecoming, and the mills were so occupied in trying to raise the wind, that I never had even a flirtation with anybody. However, that was all Narborough's fault. He was dreadfully short-sighted, and there is no pleasure in taking in a husband who never sees anything."

Her guests this evening were rather tedious. The fact was, as she explained to Dorian, behind a very shabby fan, one of her married daughters had come up quite suddenly to stay with her, and, to make matters worse, had actually brought her husband with her. "I think it is most unkind of her, my dear," she whispered. "Of course I go and stay with them every summer after I come from Homburg, but then an old woman like me must have fresh air sometimes, and besides, I really wake them up. You don't know what an existence they lead down there. It is pure unadulterated country life. They get up early, because they have so much to do, and go to bed early because they have so little to think about. There has not been a scandal in the neighbourhood since the time of Queen Elizabeth, and consequently they all fall asleep after dinner. You sha'n't sit next either of them. You shall sit by me, and amuse me."

Dorian murmured a graceful compliment, and looked round the room. Yes: it was certainly a tedious party. Two of the people he had never seen before, and the others consisted of Ernest Harrowden, one of those middle-aged mediocrities so common in London clubs who have no enemies, but are thoroughly disliked by their friends; Lady Roxton, an overdressed woman of forty-seven, with a hooked nose, who was always trying to get herself compromised, but was so peculiarly plain that to her great disappointment no one would ever believe anything against her; Mrs. Erlynne, a pushing nobody, with a delightful lisp, and Venetian-red hair; Lady Alice Chapman, his hostess's daughter, a dowdy dull girl, with one of those characteristic British faces, that, once seen are never remembered; and her husband, a red-cheeked, white-whiskered creature who, like so many of his class, was under the impression that inordinate joviality can atone for an entire lack of ideas.

He was rather sorry he had come, till Lady Narborough, looking at the great ormolu gilt clock that sprawled in gaudy curves on the mauve-draped mantelshelf, exclaimed: "How horrid of Henry Wotton to be so late! I sent round to him this morning on chance, and he promised faithfully not to disappoint me."

It was some consolation that Harry was to be there, and when the door opened and he heard his slow musical voice lending charm to some insincere apology, he ceased to feel bored.

But at dinner he could not eat anything. Plate after plate went away untasted. Lady Narborough kept scolding him for what she called "an insult to poor Adolphe, who invented the *menu* specially for you," and now and then Lord Henry looked across at him, wondering at his silence and abstracted manner. From time to time the butler filled his glass with champagne. He drank eagerly, and his thirst seemed to increase.

"Dorian," said Lord Henry, at last, as the *chaudfroid* was being handed round, "what is the matter with you to-night? You are quite out of sorts."

"I believe he is in love," cried Lady Narborough, "and that he is afraid to tell me for fear I should be jealous. He is quite right. I certainly should."

"Dear Lady Narborough," murmured Dorian, smiling, "I have not been in love for a whole week–not, in fact, since Madame de Ferrol left town."

"How you men can fall in love with that woman!" exclaimed the old lady. "I really cannot understand it."

"It is simply because she remembers you when you were a little girl, Lady Narborough," said Lord Henry. "She is the one link between us and your short frocks."

"She does not remember my short frocks at all, Lord Henry. But I remember her very well at Vienna thirty years ago, and how *décolletée* she was then."

"She is still *décolletée*," he answered, taking an olive in his long fingers; "and when she is in a very smart gown she looks like an *édition de luxe* of a bad French novel. She is really wonderful, and full of surprises. Her capacity for family affection is extraordinary. When her third husband died, her hair turned quite gold from grief."

"How can you, Harry!" cried Dorian.

"It is a most romantic explanation," laughed the hostess. "But her third husband, Lord Henry! You don't mean to say Ferrol is the fourth?"

"Certainly, Lady Narborough."

"I don't believe a word of it."

"Well, ask Mr. Gray. He is one of her most intimate friends."

"Is it true, Mr. Gray?"

"She assures me so, Lady Narborough," said Dorian. "I asked her whether, like Marguerite de Navarre, she had their hearts embalmed and hung at her girdle. She told me she didn't, because none of them had had any hearts at all."

"Four husbands! Upon my word that is *trop de zêle*."

"*Trop d' audace*, I tell her," said Dorian.

"Oh! she is audacious enough for anything, my dear. And what is Ferrol like? I don't know him."

"The husbands of very beautiful women belong to the criminal classes," said Lord Henry, sipping his wine.

Lady Narborough hit him with her fan. "Lord Henry, I am not at all surprised that the world says that you are extremely wicked."

"But what world says that?" asked Lord Henry, elevating his eyebrows. "It can only be the next world. This world and I are on excellent terms."

"Everybody I know says you are very wicked," cried the old lady, shaking her head.

Lord Henry looked serious for some moments. "It is perfectly monstrous," he said, at last, "the way people go about nowadays saying things against one behind one's back that are absolutely and entirely true."

"Isn't he incorrigible?" cried Dorian, leaning forward in his chair.

"I hope so," said his hostess, laughing. "But really if you all worship Madame de Ferrol in this ridiculous way, I shall have to marry again so as to be in the fashion."

"You will never marry again, Lady Narborough," broke in Lord Henry. "You were far too happy. When a woman marries again it is because she detested her first husband. When a man marries again, it is because he adored his first wife. Women try their luck; men risk theirs."

"Narborough wasn't perfect," cried the old lady.

"If he had been, you would not have loved him, my dear lady," was the rejoinder. "Women love us for our defects. If we have enough of them they will forgive us everything, even our intellects. You will never ask me to dinner again, after saying this, I am afraid, Lady Narborough; but it is quite true."

"Of course it is true, Lord Henry. If we women did not love you for your defects, where would you all be? Not one of you would ever be married. You would be a set of unfortunate bachelors. Not, however, that that would alter you much. Nowadays all the married men live like bachelors, and all the bachelors like married men."

"*Fin de siècle*," murmured Lord Henry.

"*Fin du globe*," answered his hostess.

"I wish it were *fin du globe*," said Dorian, with a sigh. "Life is a great disappointment."

"Ah, my dear," cried Lady Narborough, putting on her gloves, "don't tell me that you have exhausted Life. When a man says that one knows that Life has exhausted him. Lord Henry is very wicked, and I sometimes wish that I had been; but you are made to be good—you look so good. I must find you a nice wife. Lord Henry, don't you think that Mr. Gray should get married?"

"I am always telling him so, Lady Narborough," said Lord Henry, with a bow.

"Well, we must look out for a suitable match for him. I shall go through Debrett carefully to-night, and draw out a list of all the eligible young ladies."

"With their ages, Lady Narborough?" asked Dorian.

"Of course, with their ages, slightly edited. But nothing must be done in a hurry. I want it to be what *The Morning Post* calls a suitable alliance, and I want you both to be happy."

"What nonsense people talk about happy marriages!" exclaimed Lord Henry. "A man can be happy with any woman, as long as he does not love her."

"Ah! what a cynic you are!" cried the old lady, pushing back her chair, and nodding to Lady Ruxton. "You must come and dine with me soon again. You are really an admirable tonic, much better than what Sir Andrew prescribes for me. You must tell me what people you would like to meet, though. I want it to be a delightful gathering."

"I like men who have a future, and women who have a past," he answered. "Or do you think that would make it a petticoat party?"

"I fear so," she said, laughing, as she stood up. "A thousand pardons, my dear Lady Ruxton," she added, "I didn't see you hadn't finished your cigarette."

"Never mind, Lady Narborough. I smoke a great deal too much. I am going to limit myself, for the future."

"Pray don't, Lady Ruxton," said Lord Henry. "Moderation is a fatal thing. Enough is as bad as a meal. More than enough is as good as a feast."

Lady Ruxton glanced at him curiously. "You must come and explain that to me some afternoon, Lord Henry. It sounds a fascinating theory," she murmured, as she swept out of the room.

"Now, mind you don't stay too long over your politics and scandal," cried Lady Narborough from the door. "If you do, we are sure to squabble upstairs."

The men laughed, and Mr. Chapman got up solemnly from the foot of the table and came up to the top. Dorian Gray changed his seat, and went and sat by Lord Henry. Mr. Chapman began to talk in a loud voice about the situation in the House of Commons. He guffawed at his adversaries. The word *doctrinaire*—word full of terror to the British mind—reappeared from time to time between his explosions. An alliterative prefix served as an ornament of oratory. He hoisted the Union Jack on the pinnacles of Thought. The inherited stupidity of the race—sound English common sense he jovially termed it—was shown to be the proper bulwark for Society.

A smile curved Lord Henry's lips, and he turned round and looked at Dorian.

"Are you better, my dear fellow?" he asked. "You seemed rather out of sorts at dinner."

"I am quite well, Harry. I am tired. That is all."

"You were charming last night. The little Duchess is quite devoted to you. She tells me she is going down to Selby."

"She has promised to come on the twentieth."

"Is Monmouth to be there too?"

"Oh, yes, Harry."

"He bores me dreadfully, almost as much as he bores her. She is very clever, too clever for a woman. She lacks the indefinable charm of weakness. It is the feet of clay that makes the gold of the image precious. Her feet are very pretty, but they are not feet of clay. White porcelain feet, if you like. They have been through the fire, and what fire does not destroy, it hardens. She has had experiences."

"How long has she been married?" asked Dorian.

"An eternity, she tells me. I believe, according to the peerage, it is ten years, but ten years with Monmouth must have been like eternity, with time thrown in. Who else is coming?"

"Oh, the Willoughbys, Lord Rugby and his wife, our hostess, Geoffrey Clouston, the usual set. I have asked Lord Grotrian."

"I like him," said Lord Henry. "A great many people don't, but I find him charming. He atones for being occasionally somewhat over-dressed, by being always absolutely over-educated. He is a very modern type."

"I don't know if he will be able to come, Harry. He may have to go to Monte Carlo with his father."

"Ah! what a nuisance people's people are! Try and make him come. By the way, Dorian, you ran off very early last night. You left before eleven. What did you do afterwards? Did you go straight home?"

Dorian glanced at him hurriedly, and frowned. "No, Harry," he said at last, "I did not get home till nearly three."

"Did you go to the club?"

"Yes," he answered. Then he bit his lip. "No, I don't mean that. I didn't go to the club. I walked about. I forget what I did. . . . How inquisitive you are, Harry! You always want to know what one has been doing. I always want to forget what I have been doing. I came in at half-past two, if you wish to know the exact time. I had left my latchkey at home, and my servant had to let me in. If you want any corroborative evidence on the subject you can ask him."

Lord Henry shrugged his shoulders. "My dear fellow, as if I cared! Let us go up to the drawing-room. No sherry, thank you, Mr. Chapman. Something has happened to you, Dorian. Tell me what it is. You are not yourself to-night."

"Don't mind me, Harry. I am irritable, and out of temper. I shall come round and see you to-morrow or next day. Make my excuses to Lady Narborough. I sha'n't go upstairs. I shall go home. I must go home."

"All right, Dorian. I dare say I shall see you to-morrow at tea-time. The Duchess is coming."

"I will try to be there, Harry," he said, leaving the room. As he drove back to his own house he was conscious that the sense of terror he thought he had strangled had come back to him. Lord Henry's casual questioning had made him lose his nerves for the moment, and he wanted his nerve still. Things that were dangerous had to be destroyed. He winced. He hated the idea of even touching them.

Yet it had to be done. He realized that, and when he had locked the door of his library, he opened the secret press into which he had thrust Basil Hallward's coat and bag. A huge fire was blazing. He piled another log on it. The smell of singeing clothes and burning leather was horrible. It took him three-quarters of an hour to consume everything. At the end he felt faint and sick, and having lit some Algerian pastilles in a pierced copper brazier, he bathed his hands and forehead with a cool musk-scented vinegar.

Suddenly he started. His eyes grew strangely bright and he gnawed nervously at his under-lip. Between two of the windows stood a large Florentine cabinet, made out of ebony, and inlaid with ivory and blue lapis. He watched it as though it were a thing that could fascinate and make afraid, as though it held something that he longed for and yet almost loathed. His breath quickened. A mad craving came over him. He lit a cigarette and then threw it away. His eyelids drooped till the long fringed lashes almost touched his cheek. But he still watched the cabinet. At last he got up from the sofa on which he had been lying, went over to it, and, having unlocked it, touched some hidden spring. A triangular drawer passed slowly out. His fingers moved instinctively towards it, dipped in, and closed on something. It was a small Chinese box of black and gold-dust lacquer, elaborately wrought, the sides patterned with curved waves, and the silken cords hung with round crystals and tasselled in plaited metal threads. He opened it. Inside was a green paste waxy in lustre, the odour curiously heavy and persistent.

He hesitated for some moments, with a strangely immobile smile upon his face. Then shivering, though the atmosphere of the room was terribly hot, he drew himself up, and glanced at the clock. It was twenty minutes to twelve. He put the box back, shutting the cabinet doors as he did so, and went into his bedroom.

As midnight was striking bronze blows upon the dusky air, Dorian Gray, dressed commonly, and with a muffler wrapped round his throat, crept quietly out of his house. In Bond Street he found a hansom with a good horse. He hailed it, and in a low voice gave the driver an address.

The man shook his head. "It is too far for me," he muttered.

"Here is a sovereign for you," said Dorian. "You shall have another if you drive fast."

"All right, sir," answered the man, "you will be there in an hour," and after his fare had got in he turned his horse round, and drove rapidly towards the river.

CHAPTER XVI

A cold rain began to fall, and the blurred street-lamps looked ghastly in the dripping mist. The public-houses were just closing, and dim men and women were clustering in broken groups round their doors. From some of the bars came the sound of horrible laughter. In others, drunkards brawled and screamed.

Lying back in the hansom, with his hat pulled over his forehead, Dorian Gray watched with listless eyes the sordid shame of the great city, and now and then he repeated to himself the words that Lord Henry had said to him on the first day they had met, "To cure the soul by means of the senses, and the senses by means of the soul." Yes, that was the secret. He had often tried it, and would try it again now. There were opium-dens, where one could buy oblivion, dens of horror where the memory of old sins could be destroyed by the madness of sins that were new.

The moon hung low in the sky like a yellow skull. From time to time a huge misshapen cloud stretched a long arm across and hid it. The gas-lamps grew fewer, and the streets more narrow and gloomy. Once the man lost his way, and had to drive back half a mile. A steam rose from the horse as it splashed up the puddles. The side-windows of the hansom were clogged with a grey-flannel mist.

"To cure the soul by means of the senses, and the senses by means of the soul!" How the words rang in his ears! His soul, certainly, was sick to death. Was it true that the senses could cure it? Innocent blood had been spilt. What could atone for that? Ah! for that there was no atonement; but though forgiveness was impossible, forgetfulness was possible still, and he was determined to forget, to stamp the thing out, to crush it as one would crush the adder that had stung one. Indeed, what right had Basil to have spoken to him as he had done? Who had made him a judge over others? He had said things that were dreadful, horrible, not to be endured.

On and on plodded the hansom, going slower, it seemed to him, at each step. He thrust up the trap, and called to the man to drive faster. The hideous hunger for opium began to gnaw at him. His throat burned, and his delicate hands twitched nervously together. He struck at the horse madly with his stick. The driver laughed, and whipped up. He laughed in answer, and the man was silent.

The way seemed interminable, and the streets like the black web of some sprawling spider. The monotony became unbearable, and, as the mist thickened, he felt afraid.

Then they passed by lonely brickfields. The fog was lighter here, and he could see the strange bottle-shaped kilns with their orange fan-like tongues of fire. A dog barked as they went by, and far away in the darkness some wandering seagull screamed. The horse stumbled in a rut, then swerved aside, and broke into a gallop.

After some time they left the clay road, and rattled again over rough-paven streets. Most of the windows were dark, but now and then fantastic shadows were silhouetted against some lamp-lit blind. He watched them curiously. They moved like monstrous marionettes, and made gestures like live things. He hated them. A dull rage was in his heart. As they turned a corner a woman yelled something at them from an open door, and two men ran after the hansom for about a hundred yards. The driver beat at them with his whip.

It is said that passion makes one think in a circle. Certainly with hideous iteration the bitten lips of Dorian Gray shaped and reshaped those subtle words that dealt with soul and sense, till he had found in them the full expression, as it were, of his mood, and justified, by intellectual approval, passions that without such justification would still have dominated his temper. From cell to cell of his brain crept the one thought; and the wild desire to live, most terrible of all man's appetites, quickened into force each trembling nerve and fibre. Ugliness that had once been hateful to him because it made things real, became dear to him now for that very reason. Ugliness was the one reality. The coarse brawl, the loathsome den, the crude vileness of disordered life, the very vileness of thief and outcast, were more vivid, in their intense actuality of impression, than all the gracious shapes of Art, the dreamy shadows of Song. They were what he needed for forgetfulness. In three days he would be free.

Suddenly the man drew up with a jerk at the top of a dark lane. Over the low roofs and jagged chimney-stacks of the houses rose the black masts of ships. Wreaths of white mist clung like ghostly sails to the yards.

"Somewhere about here, sir, ain't it?" he asked huskily through the trap.

Dorian started, and peered round. "This will do," he answered, and, having got out hastily, and given the driver the extra fare he had promised him, he walked quickly in the direction of the quay. Here and there a lantern gleamed at the stern of some huge merchantman. The light shook and splintered in the puddles. A red glare came from an outward-bound steamer that was coaling. The slimy pavement looked like a wet mackintosh.

He hurried on towards the left, glancing back now and then to see if he was being followed. In about seven or eight minutes he reached a small shabby house, that was wedged in between two gaunt factories. In one of the top windows stood a lamp. He stopped, and gave a peculiar knock.

After a little while he heard steps in the passage, and the chain being unhooked. The door opened quietly, and he went in without saying a word to the squat misshapen figure that flattened itself upon the shadow as he passed. At the end of the hall hung a tattered green curtain that swayed and shook in the gusty wind which had followed him in from the street. He dragged it aside, and entered a long, low room which looked as if it had once been a third-rate dancing-saloon. Shrill flaring gas-jets, dulled and distorted in the fly-blown mirrors that faced them, were ranged round the walls. Greasy reflectors of ribbed tin backed them, making quivering discs of light. The floor was covered with ochre-coloured sawdust, trampled here and there into mud, and stained with rings of spilt liquor. Some Malays were crouching by a little charcoal stove playing with bone counters, and showing their white teeth as they chattered. In one corner with his head buried in his arms, a sailor sprawled over a table, and by the tawdrily-painted bar that ran across one complete side stood two haggard women mocking an old man who was brushing the sleeves of his coat with an expression of disgust. "He thinks he's got red ants on him," laughed one of them, as Dorian passed by. The man looked at her in terror, and began to whimper.

At the end of the room there was a little staircase, leading to a darkened chamber. As Dorian hurried up its three rickety steps, the heavy odour of opium met him. He heaved a deep breath, and his nostrils quivered with pleasure. When he entered, a young man with smooth yellow hair, who was bending over a lamp lighting a long thin pipe, looked up at him, and nodded in a hesitating manner.

"You here, Adrian?" muttered Dorian.

"Where else should I be?" he answered, listlessly. "None of the chaps will speak to me now."

"I thought you had left England."

"Darlington is not going to do anything. My brother paid the bill at last. George doesn't speak to me either. . . . I don't care," he added, with a sigh. "As long as one has this stuff, one doesn't want friends. I think I have had too many friends."

Dorian winced, and looked around at the grotesque things that lay in such fantastic postures on the ragged mattresses. The twisted limbs, the gaping mouths, the staring lustreless eyes, fascinated him. He knew in what strange heavens they were suffering, and what dull hells were teaching them the secret of some new joy. They were better off than he was. He was prisoned in thought. Memory, like a horrible malady, was eating his soul away. From time to time he seemed to see the eyes of Basil Hallward looking at him. Yet he felt he could not stay. The presence of Adrian Singleton troubled him. He wanted to be where no one would know who he was. He wanted to escape from himself.

"I am going on to the other place," he said, after a pause.

"On the wharf?"

"Yes."

"That mad-cat is sure to be there. They won't have her in this place now."

Dorian shrugged his shoulders. "I am sick of women who love one. Women who hate one are much more interesting. Besides, the stuff is better."

"Much the same."

"I like it better. Come and have something to drink. I must have something."

"I don't want anything," murmured the young man.

"Never mind."

Adrian Singleton rose up wearily, and followed Dorian to the bar. A half caste, in a ragged turban and a shabby ulster, grinned a hideous greeting as he thrust a bottle of brandy and two tumblers in front of them. The women sidled up, and began to chatter. Dorian turned his back on them, and said something in a low voice to Adrian Singleton.

A crooked smile, like a Malay crease, writhed across the face of one of the women. "We're very proud to-night," she sneered.

"For God's sake don't talk to me," cried Dorian, stamping his foot on the ground. "What do you want? Money? Here it is. Don't ever talk to me again."

Two red sparks flashed for a moment in the woman's sodden eyes, then flickered out, and left them dull and glazed. She tossed her head, and raked the coins off the counter with greedy fingers. Her companion watched her enviously.

"It's no use," sighed Adrian Singleton. "I don't care to go back. What does it matter? I am quite happy here."

"You will write to me if you want anything, won't you?" said Dorian, after a pause.

"Perhaps."

"Good-night, then."

"Good-night," answered the young man, passing up the steps, and wiping his parched mouth with a handkerchief.

Dorian walked to the door with a look of pain in his face. As he drew the curtain aside a hideous laugh broke from the painted lips of the woman who had taken the money. "There goes the devil's bargain!" she hiccoughed, in a hoarse voice.

"Curse you," he answered, "don't call me that."

She snapped her fingers. "Prince Charming is what you like to be called, ain't it?" she yelled after him.

The drowsy sailor leapt to his feet as she spoke, and looked wildly round. The sound of the shutting of the hall door fell on his ear. He rushed out as if in pursuit.

Dorian Gray hurried along the quay through the drizzling rain. His meeting with Adrian Singleton had strangely moved him, and he wondered if the ruin of that young life was really to be laid at his door, as Basil Hallward had said to him with such infamy of insult. He bit his lip, and for a few seconds his eyes grew sad. Yet, after all, what did it matter to him? One's days were too brief to take the burden of another's errors on one's shoulders. Each man lived his own life, and paid his own price for living it. The only pity was one had to pay so often for a single fault. One had to pay over and over again, indeed. In her dealings with man Destiny never closed her accounts.

There are moments, psychologists tell us, when the passion for sin, or for what the world calls sin, so dominates a nature, that every fibre of the body, as every cell of the brain, seems to be instinct with fearful impulses. Men and women at such moments lose the freedom of their will. They move to their terrible end as automatons move. Choice is taken from them, and conscience is either killed, or, if it lives at all, lives but to give rebellion its fascination, and disobedience its charm. For all sins, as theologians weary not of reminding us, are sins of disobedience. When that high spirit, that morning-star of evil, fell from heaven, it was as a rebel that he fell.

Callous, concentrated on evil, with stained mind, and soul hungry for rebellion, Dorian Gray hastened on, quickening his steps as he went, but as he darted aside into a dim archway, that had served him often as a short cut to the ill-famed place where he was going, he felt himself suddenly seized from behind, and before he had time to defend himself he was thrust back against the wall, with a brutal hand round his throat.

He struggled madly for life, and by a terrible effort wrenched the tightening fingers away. In a second he heard the click of a revolver, and saw the gleam of a polished barrel pointing straight at his head, and the dusky form of a short thick-set man facing him.

"What do you want?" he gasped.

"Keep quiet," said the man. "If you stir, I shoot you."

"You are mad. What have I done to you?"

"You wrecked the life of Sibyl Vane," was the answer, "and Sibyl Vane was my sister. She killed herself. I know it. Her death is at your door. I swore I would kill you in return. For years I have sought you. I had no clue, no trace. The two people who could have described you were dead. I knew nothing of you but the pet name she used to call you. I heard it to-night by chance. Make your peace with God, for to-night you are going to die."

Dorian Gray grew sick with fear. "I never knew her," he stammered. "I never heard of her. You are mad."

"You had better confess your sin, for as sure as I am James Vane, you are going to die." There was a horrible moment. Dorian did not know what to say or do. "Down on your knees!" growled the man. "I give you one minute to make your peace–no more. I go on board to-night for India, and I must do my job first. One minute. That's all."

Dorian's arms fell to his side. Paralyzed with terror, he did not know what to do. Suddenly a wild hope flashed across his brain. "Stop," he cried. "How long ago is it since your sister died? Quick, tell me!"

"Eighteen years," said the man. "Why do you ask me? What do years matter?"

"Eighteen years," laughed Dorian Gray, with a touch of triumph in his voice. "Eighteen years! Set me under the lamp and look at my face."

James Vane hesitated for a moment, not understanding what was meant. Then he seized Dorian Gray and dragged him from the archway.

Dim and wavering as was the wind-blown light, yet it served to show him the hideous error, as it seemed, into which he had fallen, for the face of the man he had sought to kill had all the bloom of boyhood, all the unstained purity of youth. He seemed little more than a lad of twenty summers, hardly older, if older indeed at all, than his sister had been when they had parted so many years ago. It was obvious that this was not the man who had destroyed her life.

He loosened his hold and reeled back. "My God! my God!" he cried, "and I would have murdered you!"

Dorian Gray drew a long breath. "You have been on the brink of committing a terrible crime, my man," he said, looking at him sternly. "Let this be a warning to you not to take vengeance into your own hands."

"Forgive me, sir," muttered James Vane. "I was deceived. A chance word I heard in that damned den set me on the wrong track."

"You had better go home, and put that pistol away, or you may get into trouble," said Dorian, turning on his heel, and going slowly down the street.

James Vane stood on the pavement in horror. He was trembling from head to foot. After a little while a black shadow that had been creeping along the dripping wall, moved out into the light and came close to him with stealthy footsteps. He felt a hand laid on his arm and looked round with a start. It was one of the women who had been drinking at the bar.

"Why didn't you kill him?" she hissed out, putting her haggard face quite close to his. "I knew you were following him when you rushed out from Daly's. You fool! You should have killed him. He has lots of money, and he's as bad as bad."

"He is not the man I am looking for," he answered, "and I want no man's money. I want a man's life. The man whose life I want must be nearly forty now. This one is little more than a boy. Thank God, I have not got his blood upon my hands."

The woman gave a bitter laugh. "Little more than a boy!" she sneered. "Why, man, it's nigh on eighteen years since Prince Charming made me what I am."

"You lie!" cried James Vane.

She raised her hand up to heaven. "Before God I am telling the truth," she cried.

"Before God?"

"Strike me dumb if it ain't so. He is the worst one that comes here. They say he has sold himself to the devil for a pretty face. It's nigh on eighteen years since I met him. He hasn't changed much since then. I have though," she added, with a sickly leer.

"You swear this?"

"I swear it," came in hoarse echo from her flat mouth. "But don't give me away to him," she whined; "I am afraid of him. Let me have some money for my night's lodging."

He broke from her with an oath, and rushed to the corner of the street, but Dorian Gray had disappeared. When he looked back, the woman had vanished also.

CHAPTER XVII

A WEEK later Dorian Gray was sitting in the conservatory at Selby Royal talking to the pretty Duchess of Monmouth, who with her husband, a jaded-looking man of sixty, was amongst his guests. It was tea-time, and the mellow light of the huge lace-covered lamp that stood on the table lit up the delicate china and hammered silver of the service at which the Duchess was presiding. Her white hands were moving daintily among the cups, and her full red lips were smiling at something that Dorian had whispered to her. Lord Henry was lying back in a silk-draped wicker chair looking at them. On a peach-coloured divan sat Lady Narborough pretending to listen to the Duke's description of the last Brazilian beetle that he had added to his collection. Three young men in elaborate smoking-suits were handing tea-cakes to some of the women. The house-party consisted of twelve people, and there were more expected to arrive on the next day.

"What are you two talking about?" said Lord Henry, strolling over to the table, and putting his cup down. "I hope Dorian has told you about my plan for rechristening everything, Gladys. It is a delightful idea."

"But I don't want to be rechristened, Harry," rejoined the Duchess, looking up at him with her wonderful eyes. "I am quite satisfied with my own name, and I am sure Mr. Gray should be satisfied with his."

"My dear Gladys, I would not alter either name for the world. They are both perfect. I was thinking chiefly of flowers. Yesterday I cut an orchid, for my buttonhole. It was a marvellous spotted thing, as effective as the seven deadly sins. In a thoughtless moment I asked one of the gardeners what it was called. He told me that it was a fine specimen of *Rooinsoniana*, or something dreadful of that kind. It is a sad truth, but we have lost the faculty of giving lovely names to things. Names are everything. I never quarrel with actions. My one quarrel is with words. That is the reason I hate vulgar realism in literature. The man who could call a spade a spade should be compelled to use one. It is the only thing he is fit for."

"Then what should we call you, Harry?" she asked.

"His name is Prince Paradox," said Dorian.

"I recognize him in a flash," exclaimed the Duchess.

"I won't hear of it," laughed Lord Henry, sinking into a chair. "From a label there is no escape! I refuse the title."

"Royalties may not abdicate," fell as a warning from pretty lips.

"You wish me to defend my throne, then?"

"Yes."

"I give the truths of to-morrow."

"I prefer the mistakes of to-day," she answered.

"You disarm me, Gladys," he cried, catching the wilfulness of her mood.

"Of your shield, Harry: not of your spear."

"I never tilt against Beauty," he said, with a wave of his hand.

"That is your error, Harry, believe me. You value beauty far too much."

"How can you say that? I admit that I think that it is better to be beautiful than to be good. But on the other hand no one is more ready than I am to acknowledge that it is better to be good than to be ugly."

"Ugliness is one of the seven deadly sins, then?" cried the Duchess. "What becomes of your simile about the orchid?"

"Ugliness is one of the seven deadly virtues, Gladys. You, as a good Tory, must not underrate them. Beer, the Bible, and the seven deadly virtues have made our England what she is."

"You don't like your country, then?" she asked.

"I live in it."

"That you may censure it the better."

"Would you have me take the verdict of Europe on it?" he enquired.

"What do they say of us?"

"That Tartuffe has emigrated to England and opened a shop."

"Is that yours, Harry?"

"I give it to you."

"I could not use it. It is too true."

"You need not be afraid. Our countrymen never recognize a description."

"They are practical."

"They are more cunning than practical. When they make up their ledger, they balance stupidity by wealth, and vice by hypocrisy."

"Still, we have done great things."

"Great things have been thrust on us, Gladys."

"We have carried their burden."

"Only as far as the Stock Exchange."

She shook her head. "I believe in the race," she cried.

"It represents the survival of the pushing."

"It has development."

"Decay fascinates me more."

"What of Art?" she asked.

"It is a malady."

"Love?"

"An illusion."

"Religion?"

"The fashionable substitute for Belief."

"You are a sceptic."

"Never! Scepticism is the beginning of Faith."

"What are you?"

"To define is to limit."

"Give me a clue."

"Threads snap. You would lose your way in the labyrinth."

"You bewilder me. Let us talk of some one else."

"Our host is a delightful topic. Years ago he was christened Prince Charming."

"Ah! don't remind me of that," cried Dorian Gray.

"Our host is rather horrid this evening," answered the Duchess, colouring. "I believe he thinks that Monmouth married me on purely scientific principles as the best specimen he could find of a modern butterfly."

"Well, I hope he won't stick pins into you, Duchess," laughed Dorian.

"Oh! my maid does that already, Mr. Gray, when she is annoyed with me."

"And what does she get annoyed with you about, Duchess?"

"For the most trivial things, Mr. Gray, I assure you. Usually because I come in at ten minutes to nine and tell her that I must be dressed by half-past eight."

"How unreasonable of her! You should give her warning."

"I daren't, Mr. Gray. Why, she invents hats for me. You remember the one I wore at Lady Hilstone's garden-party? You don't, but it is nice of you to pretend that you do. Well, she made it out of nothing. All good hats are made out of nothing."

"Like all good reputations, Gladys," interrupted Lord Henry. "Every effect that one produces gives one an enemy. To be popular one must be a mediocrity."

"Not with women," said the Duchess, shaking her head, "and women rule the world. I assure you we can't bear mediocrities. We women, as some one says, love with our ears, just as you men love with your eyes, if you ever love at all."

"It seems to me that we never do anything else," murmured Dorian.

"Ah! then, you never really love, Mr. Gray," answered the Duchess, with mock sadness.

"My dear Gladys!" cried Lord Henry. "How can you say that? Romance lives by repetition, and repetition converts an appetite into an art. Besides, each time that one loves is the only time one has ever loved. Difference of object does not alter singleness of passion. It merely intensifies it. We can have in life but one great experience at best, and the secret of life is to reproduce that experience as often as possible."

"Even when one has been wounded by it, Harry?" asked the Duchess, after a pause.

"Especially when one has been wounded by it," answered Lord Henry.

The Duchess turned and looked at Dorian Gray with a curious expression in her eyes. "What do you say to that, Mr. Gray?" she enquired.

Dorian hesitated a moment. Then he threw back his head and laughed. "I always agree with Harry, Duchess."

"Even when he is wrong?"

"Harry is never wrong, Duchess."

"And does his philosophy make you happy?"

"I have never searched for happiness. Who wants happiness? I have searched for pleasure."

"And found it, Mr. Gray?"

"Often. Too often."

The Duchess sighed. "I am searching for peace," she said, "and if I don't go and dress, I shall have none this evening."

"Let me get you some orchids, Duchess," cried Dorian, starting to his feet, and walking down the conservatory.

"You are flirting disgracefully with him," said Lord Henry to his cousin. "You had better take care. He is very fascinating."

"If he were not, there would be no battle."

"Greek meets Greek then?"

"I am on the side of the Trojans. They fought for a woman."

"They were defeated."

"There are worse things than capture," she answered.

"You gallop with a loose rein."

"Pace gives life," was the *riposte*. "I shall write it in my diary to-night."

"What?"

"That a burnt child loves the fire."

"I am not even singed. My wings are untouched."

"You use them for everything, except flight."

"Courage has passed from men to women. It is a new experience for us."

"You have a rival."

"Who?"

He laughed. "Lady Narborough," he whispered. "She perfectly adores him."

"You fill me with apprehension. The appeal to Antiquity is fatal to us who are romanticists."

"Romanticists! You have all the methods of science."

"Men have educated us."

"But not explained you."

"Describe us as a sex," was her challenge.

"Sphinxes without secrets."

She looked at him, smiling. "How long Mr. Gray is!" she said. "Let us go and help him. I have not yet told him the colour of my frock."

"Ah! you must suit your frock to his flowers, Gladys."

"That would be a premature surrender."

"Romantic Art begins with its climax."

"I must keep an opportunity for retreat."

"In the Parthian manner?"

"They found safety in the desert. I could not do that."

"Women are not always allowed a choice," he answered, but hardly had he finished the sentence before from the far end of the conservatory came a stifled groan, followed by the dull sound of a heavy fall. Everybody started up. The Duchess stood motionless in horror. And with fear in his eyes Lord Henry rushed through the flapping palms, to find Dorian Gray lying face downwards on the tiled floor in a death-like swoon.

He was carried at once into the blue drawing-room, and laid upon one of the sofas. After a short time he came to himself, and looked round with a dazed expression.

"What has happened?" he asked. "Oh! I remember. Am I safe here, Harry?" He began to tremble.

"My dear Dorian," answered Lord Henry, "you merely fainted. That was all. You must have overtired yourself. You had better not come down to dinner. I will take your place."

"No, I will come down," he said, struggling to his feet. "I would rather come down. I must not be alone."

He went to his room and dressed. There was a wild recklessness of gaiety in his manner as he sat at table, but now and then a thrill of terror ran through him when he remembered that, pressed against the window of the conservatory, like a white handkerchief, he had seen the face of James Vane watching him.

CHAPTER XVIII

The next day he did not leave the house, and, indeed, spent most of the time in his own room, sick with a wild terror of dying, and yet indifferent to life itself. The consciousness of being hunted, snared, tracked down, had begun to dominate him. If the tapestry did but tremble in the wind, he shook. The dead leaves that were blown against the leaded panes seemed to him like his own wasted resolutions and wild regrets. When he closed his eyes, he saw again the sailor's face peering through the mist-stained glass, and horror seemed once more to lay its hand upon his heart.

But perhaps it had been only his fancy that had called vengeance out of the night, and set the hideous shapes of punishment before him. Actual life was chaos, but there was something terribly logical in the imagination. It was the imagination that set remorse to dog the feet of sin. It was the imagination that made each crime bear its missshapen brood. In the common world of fact the wicked were not punished, nor the good rewarded. Success was given to the strong, failure thrust upon the weak. That was all. Besides, had any stranger been prowling round the house he would have been seen by the servants or the keepers. Had any footmarks been found on the flower-beds, the gardeners would have reported it. Yes: it had been merely fancy. Sibyl Vane's brother had not come back to kill him. He had sailed away in his ship to founder in some winter sea. From him, at any rate, he was safe. Why, the man did not know who he was, could not know who he was. The mask of youth had saved him.

And yet if it had been merely an illusion, how terrible it was to think that conscience could raise such fearful phantoms, and give them visible form, and make them move before one! What sort of life would his be if, day and night, shadows of his crime were to peer at him from silent corners, to mock him from secret places, to whisper in his ear as he sat at the feast, to wake him with icy fingers as he lay asleep! As the thought crept through his brain, he grew pale with terror, and the air seemed to him to have become suddenly colder. Oh! in what a wild hour of madness he had killed his friend! How ghastly the mere memory of the scene! He saw it all again. Each hideous detail came back to him with added horror. Out of the black cave of Time, terrible and swathed in scarlet, rose the image of his sin. When Lord Henry came in at six o'clock, he found him crying as one whose heart will break.

It was not till the third day that he ventured to go out. There was something in the clear, pine-scented air of that winter morning that seemed to bring him back his joyousness and his ardour for life. But it was not merely the physical conditions of environment that had caused the change. His own nature had revolted against the excess of anguish that had sought to maim and mar the perfection of its calm. With subtle and finely-wrought temperaments it is always so. Their strong passions must either bruise or bend. They either slay the man, or themselves die. Shallow sorrows and shallow loves live on. The loves and sorrows that are great are destroyed by their own plenitude. Besides, he had convinced himself that he had been the victim of a terror-stricken imagination, and looked back now on his fears with something of pity and not a little of contempt.

After breakfast he walked with the Duchess for an hour in the garden, and then drove across the park to join the shooting-party. The crisp frost lay like salt upon the grass. The sky was an inverted cup of blue metal. A thin film of ice bordered the flat reed-grown lake.

At the corner of the pine wood he caught sight of Sir Geoffrey Clouston, the Duchess's brother, jerking two spent cartridges out of his gun. He jumped from the cart, and having told the groom to take the mare home, made his way towards his guest through the withered bracken and rough undergrowth.

"Have you had good sport, Geoffrey?" he asked.

"Not very good, Dorian. I think most of the birds have gone to the open. I dare say it will be better after lunch, when we get to new ground."

Dorian strolled along by his side. The keen aromatic air, the brown and red lights that glimmered in the wood, the hoarse cries of the beaters ringing out from time to time, and the sharp snaps of the guns that followed, fascinated him, and filled him with a sense of delightful freedom. He was dominated by the carelessness of happiness, by the high indifference of joy.

Suddenly from a lumpy tussock of old grass, some twenty yards in front of them, with black-tipped ears erect, and long hinder limbs throwing it forward, started a hare. It bolted for a thicket of alders. Sir Geoffrey put his gun to his shoulder, but there was something in the animal's grace of movement that strangely charmed Dorian Gray, and he cried out at once, "Don't shoot it, Geoffrey. Let it live."

"What nonsense, Dorian!" laughed his companion, and as the hare bounded into the thicket he fired. There were two cries heard, the cry of a hare in pain, which is dreadful, the cry of a man in agony, which is worse.

"Good heavens! I have hit a beater!" exclaimed Sir Geoffrey. "What an ass the man was to get in front of the guns! Stop shooting there!" he called out at the top of his voice. "A man is hurt."

The head-keeper came running up with a stick in his hand.

"Where, sir? Where is he?" he shouted. At the same time the firing ceased along the line.

"Here," answered Sir Geoffrey angrily, hurrying towards the thicket. "Why on earth don't you keep your men back? Spoiled my shooting for the day."

Dorian watched them as they plunged into the alder-clump, brushing the lithe, swinging branches aside. In a few moments they emerged, dragging a body after them into the sunlight. He turned away in horror. It seemed to him that misfortune followed wherever he went. He heard Sir Geoffrey ask if the man was really dead, and the affirmative answer of the keeper. The wood seemed to him to have become suddenly alive with faces. There was the trampling of myriad feet, and the low buzz of voices. A great copper-breasted pheasant came beating through the boughs overhead.

After a few moments, that were to him, in his perturbed state, like endless hours of pain, he felt a hand laid on his shoulder. He started, and looked round.

"Dorian," said Lord Henry, "I had better tell them that the shooting is stopped for to-day. It would not look well to go on."

"I wish it were stopped for ever, Harry," he answered, bitterly. "The whole thing is hideous and cruel. Is the man. . . ?"

He could not finish the sentence.

"I am afraid so," rejoined Lord Henry. "He got the whole charge of shot in his chest. He must have died almost instantaneously. Come; let us go home."

They walked side by side in the direction of the avenue for nearly fifty yards without speaking. Then Dorian looked at Lord Henry, and said, with a heavy sigh, "It is a bad omen, Harry, a very bad omen."

"What is?" asked Lord Henry. "Oh! this accident, I suppose. My dear fellow, it can't be helped. It was the man's own fault. Why did he get in front of the guns? Besides, it is nothing to us. It is rather awkward for Geoffrey, of course. It does not do to pepper beaters. It makes people think that one is a wild shot. And Geoffrey is not; he shoots very straight. But there is no use talking about the matter."

Dorian shook his head. "It is a bad omen, Harry. I feel as if something horrible were going to happen to some of us. To myself, perhaps," he added, passing his hand over his eyes, with a gesture of pain.

The elder man laughed. "The only horrible thing in the world is *ennui*, Dorian. That is the one sin for which there is no forgiveness. But we are not likely to suffer from it, unless these fellows keep chattering about this thing at dinner. I must tell them that the subject is to be tabooed. As for omens, there is no such thing as an omen. Destiny does not send us heralds. She is too wise or too cruel for that. Besides, what on earth could happen to you, Dorian? You have everything in the world that a man can want. There is no one who would not be delighted to change places with you."

"There is no one with whom I would not change places, Harry. Don't laugh like that. I am telling you the truth. The wretched peasant who has just died is better off than I am. I have no terror of Death. It is the coming of Death that terrifies me. Its monstrous wings seem to wheel in the leaden air around me. Good heavens! don't you see a man moving behind the trees there, watching me, waiting for me?"

Lord Henry looked in the direction in which the trembling gloved hand was pointing. "Yes," he said, smiling, "I see the gardener waiting for you. I suppose he wants to ask you what flowers you wish to have on the table to-night. How absurdly nervous you are, my dear fellow! You must come and see my doctor, when we get back to town."

Dorian heaved a sigh of relief as he saw the gardener approaching. The man touched his hat, glanced for a moment at Lord Henry in a hesitating manner, and then produced a letter, which he handed to his master. "Her Grace told me to wait for an answer," he murmured.

Dorian put the letter into his pocket. "Tell Her Grace that I am coming in," he said, coldly. The man turned round, and went rapidly in the direction of the house.

"How fond women are of doing dangerous things!" laughed Lord Henry. "It is one of the qualities in them that I admire most. A woman will flirt with anybody in the world as long as other people are looking on."

"How fond you are of saying dangerous things, Harry! In the present instance you are quite astray. I like the Duchess very much, but I don't love her."

"And the Duchess loves you very much, but she likes you less, as you are so excellently matched."

"You are talking scandal, Harry, and there is never any basis for scandal."

"The basis of every scandal is an immoral certainty," said Lord Henry, lighting a cigarette.

"You would sacrifice anybody, Harry, for the sake of an epigram."

"The world goes to the altar of its own accord," was the answer.

"I wish I could love," cried Dorian Gray, with a deep note of pathos in his voice. "But I seem to have lost the passion, and forgotten the desire. I am too much concentrated on myself. My own personality has become a burden to me. I want to escape, to go away, to forget. It was silly of me to come down here at all. I think I shall send a wire to Harvey to have the yacht got ready. On a yacht one is safe."

"Safe from what, Dorian? You are in some trouble. Why not tell me what it is? You know I would help you."

"I can't tell you, Harry," he answered, sadly. "And I dare say it is only a fancy of mine. This unfortunate accident has upset me. I have a horrible presentiment that something of the kind may happen to me."

"What nonsense!"

"I hope it is, but I can't help feeling it. Ah! here is the Duchess, looking the Artemis in a tailor-made gown. You see we have come back, Duchess."

"I have heard all about it, Mr. Gray," she answered. "Poor Geoffrey is terribly upset. And it seems that you asked him not to shoot the hare. How curious!"

"Yes, it was very curious. I don't know what made me say it. Some whim, I suppose. It looked the loveliest of little live things. But I am sorry they told you about the man. It is a hideous subject."

"It is an annoying subject," broke in Lord Henry. "It has no psychological value at all. Now if Geoffrey had done the thing on purpose, how interesting he would be! I should like to know some one who had committed a real murder."

"How horrid of you, Harry!" cried the Duchess. "Isn't it, Mr. Gray? Harry, Mr. Gray is ill again. He is going to faint."

Dorian drew himself up with an effort, and smiled. "It is nothing, Duchess," he murmured; "my nerves are dreadfully out of order. That is all. I am afraid I walked too far this morning. I didn't hear what Harry said. Was it very bad? You must tell me some other time. I think I must go and lie down. You will excuse me, won't you?"

They had reached the great flight of steps that led from the conservatory onto the terrace. As the glass door closed behind Dorian, Lord Henry turned and looked at the Duchess with his slumberous eyes. "Are you very much in love with him?" he asked.

She did not answer for some time, but stood gazing at the landscape. "I wish I knew," she said at last.

He shook his head. "Knowledge would be fatal. It is the uncertainty that charms one. A mist makes things wonderful."

"One may lose one's way."

"All ways end at the same point, my dear Gladys."

"What is that?"

"Disillusion."

"It was my *début* in life," she sighed.

"It came to you crowned."

"I am tired of strawberry leaves."

"They become you."

"Only in public."

"You would miss them," said Lord Henry.

"I will not part with a petal."

"Monmouth has ears."

"Old age is dull of hearing."

"Has he never been jealous?"

"I wish he had been."

He glanced about as if in search of something. "What are you looking for?" she enquired.

"The button from your foil," he answered. "You have dropped it."

She laughed. "I have still the mask."

"It makes your eyes lovelier," was his reply.

She laughed again. Her teeth showed like white seeds in a scarlet fruit.

Upstairs, in his own room, Dorian Gray was lying on a sofa, with terror in every tingling fibre of his body. Life had suddenly become too hideous a burden for him to bear. The dreadful death of the unlucky beater, shot in the thicket like a wild animal, had seemed to him to prefigure death for himself also. He had nearly swooned at what Lord Henry had said in a chance mood of cynical jesting.

At five o'clock he rang his bell for his servant, and gave him orders to pack his things for the night-express to town, and to have the brougham at the door by eight-thirty. He was determined not to sleep another night at Selby Royal. It was an ill-omened place. Death walked there in the sunlight. The grass of the forest had been spotted with blood.

Then he wrote a note to Lord Henry, telling him that he was going up to town to consult his doctor, and asking him to entertain his guests in his absence.

As he was putting it into the envelope, a knock came to the door, and his valet informed him that the head-keeper wished to see him. He frowned, and bit his lip. "Send him in," he muttered, after some moments' hesitation.

As soon as the man entered Dorian pulled his cheque-book out of a drawer, and spread it out before him.

"I suppose you have come about the unfortunate accident of this morning, Thornton?" he said, taking up a pen.

"Yes, sir," answered the game-keeper.

"Was the poor fellow married? Had he any people dependent on him?" asked Dorian, looking bored. "If so, I should not like them to be left in want, and will send them any sum of money you may think necessary."

"We don't know who he is, sir. That is what I took the liberty of coming to you about."

"Don't know who he is?" said Dorian, listlessly. "What do you mean? Wasn't he one of your men?"

"No, sir. Never saw him before. Seems like a sailor, sir."

The pen dropped from Dorian Gray's hand, and he felt as if his heart had suddenly stopped beating. "A sailor?" he cried out. "Did you say a sailor?"

"Yes, sir. He looks as if he had been a sort of sailor; tattooed on both arms, and that kind of thing."

"Was there anything found on him?" said Dorian, leaning forward and looking at the man with startled eyes. "Anything that would tell his name?"

"Some money, sir—not much, and a six-shooter. There was no name of any kind. A decent-looking man, sir, but rough-like. A sort of sailor we think."

Dorian started to his feet. A terrible hope fluttered past him. He clutched at it madly. "Where is the body?" he exclaimed. "Quick! I must see it at once."

"It is in an empty stable in the Home Farm, sir. The folk don't like to have that sort of thing in their houses. They say a corpse brings bad luck."

"The Home Farm! Go there at once and meet me. Tell one of the grooms to bring my horse round. No. Never mind. I'll go to the stables myself. It will save time."

In less than a quarter of an hour Dorian Gray was galloping down the long avenue as hard as he could go. The trees seemed to sweep past him in spectral procession, and wild shadows to fling themselves across his path. Once the mare swerved at a white gate-post and nearly threw him. He lashed her across the neck with his crop. She cleft the dusky air like an arrow. The stones flew from her hoofs.

At last he reached the Home Farm. Two men were loitering in the yard. He leapt from the saddle and threw the reins to one of them. In the farthest stable a light was glimmering. Something seemed to tell him that the body was there, and he hurried to the door, and put his hand upon the latch.

There he paused for a moment, feeling that he was on the brink of a discovery that would either make or mar his life. Then he thrust the door open, and entered.

On a heap of sacking in the far corner was lying the dead body of a man dressed in a coarse shirt and a pair of blue trousers. A spotted handkerchief had been placed over the face. A coarse candle, stuck in a bottle, sputtered beside it.

Dorian Gray shuddered. He felt that his could not be the hand to take the handkerchief away, and called out to one of the farm-servants to come to him.

"Take that thing off the face. I wish to see it," he said, clutching at the door-post for support.

When the farm-servant had done so, he stepped forward. A cry of joy broke from his lips. The man who had been shot in the thicket was James Vane.

He stood there for some minutes looking at the dead body. As he rode home, his eyes were full of tears, for he knew that he was safe.

CHAPTER XIX

"THERE is no use your telling me that you are going to be good," cried Lord Henry, dipping his white fingers into a red copper bowl filled with rose-water. "You are quite perfect. Pray, don't change."

Dorian Gray shook his head. "No, Harry, I have done too many dreadful things in my life. I am not going to do any more. I began my good actions yesterday."

"Where were you yesterday?"

"In the country, Harry. I was staying at a little inn by myself."

"My dear boy," said Lord Henry, smiling, "anybody can be good in the country. There are no temptations there. That is the reason why people who live out of town are so absolutely uncivilized. Civilization is not by any means an easy thing to attain to. There are only two ways by which man can reach it. One is by being cultured, the other by being corrupt. Country people have no opportunity of being either, so they stagnate."

"Culture and corruption," echoed Dorian. "I have known something of both. It seems terrible to me now that they should ever be found together. For I have a new ideal, Harry. I am going to alter. I think I have altered."

"You have not yet told me what your good action was. Or did you say you had done more than one?" asked his companion, as he spilt into his plate a little crimson pyramid of seeded strawberries, and through a perforated shell-shaped spoon snowed white sugar upon them.

"I can tell you, Harry. It is not a story I could tell to any one else. I spared somebody. It sounds vain, but you understand what I mean. She was quite beautiful, and wonderfully like Sibyl Vane. I think it was that which first attracted me to her. You remember Sibyl, don't you? How long ago that seems! Well, Hetty was not one of our own class, of course. She was simply a girl in a village. But I really loved her. I am quite sure that I loved her. All during this wonderful May that we have been having, I used to run down and see her two or three times a week. Yesterday she met me in a little orchard. The apple-blossoms kept tumbling down on her hair, and she was laughing. We were to have gone away together this morning at dawn. Suddenly I determined to leave her as flower-like as I had found her."

"I should think the novelty of the emotion must have given you a thrill of real pleasure, Dorian," interrupted Lord Henry. "But I can finish your idyll for you. You gave her good advice, and broke her heart. That was the beginning of your reformation."

"Harry, you are horrible! You mustn't say these dreadful things. Hetty's heart is not broken. Of course she cried, and all that. But there is no disgrace upon her. She can live, like Perdita, in her garden of mint and marigold."

"And weep over faithless Florizel," said Lord Henry, laughing, as he leant back in his chair. "My dear Dorian, you have the most curiously boyish moods. Do you think this girl will ever be really contented now with any one of her own rank? I suppose she will be married some day to a rough carter or a grinning ploughman. Well, the fact of having met you, and loved you, will teach her to despise her husband, and she will be wretched. From a moral point of view, I cannot say that I think much of your great renunciation. Even as a beginning, it is poor. Besides, how do you know that Hetty isn't floating at the present moment in some star-lit mill-pond, with lovely water-lilies round her, like Ophelia?"

"I can't bear this, Harry! You mock at everything, and then suggest the most serious tragedies. I am sorry I told you now. I don't care what you say to me. I know I was right in acting as I did. Poor Hetty! As I rode past the farm this morning, I saw her white face at the window, like a spray of jasmine. Don't let us talk about it any more, and don't try to persuade me that the first good action I have done for years, the first little bit of self-sacrifice I have ever known, is really a sort of sin. I want to be better. I am going to be better. Tell me something about yourself. What is going on in town? I have not been to the club for days."

"The people are still discussing poor Basil's disappearance."

"I should have thought they had got tired of that by this time," said Dorian, pouring himself out some wine, and frowning slightly.

"My dear boy, they have only been talking about it for six weeks, and the British public are really not equal to the mental strain of having more than one topic every three months. They have been very fortunate lately, however. They have had my own divorce-case, and Alan Campbell's suicide. Now they have got the mysterious disappearance of an artist. Scotland Yard still insists that the man in the grey ulster who left for Paris by the midnight train on the ninth of November was poor Basil, and the French police declare that Basil never arrived in Paris at all. I suppose in about a fortnight we shall be told that he has been seen in San Francisco. It is an odd thing, but every one who disappears is said to be seen at San Francisco. It must be a delightful city, and possess all the attractions of the next world."

"What do you think has happened to Basil?" asked Dorian, holding up his Burgundy against the light, and wondering how it was he could discuss the matter so calmly.

"I have not the slightest idea. If Basil chooses to hide himself, it is no business of mine. If he is dead, I don't want to think about him. Death is the only thing that ever terrifies me. I hate it."

"Why?" said the young man, wearily.

"Because," said Lord Henry, passing beneath his nostrils the gilt trellis of an open vinaigrette box, "one can survive everything nowadays except that. Death and vulgarity are the only two facts in the nineteenth century that one cannot explain away. Let us have our coffee in the music-room, Dorian. You must play Chopin to me. The man with whom my wife ran away played Chopin exquisitely. Poor Victoria! I was very fond of her. The house is rather lonely without her. Of course married life is merely a habit, a bad habit. But then one regrets the loss even of one's worst habits. Perhaps one regrets them the most. They are such an essential part of one's personality."

Dorian said nothing, but rose from the table, and, passing into the next room, sat down to the piano and let his fingers stray across the white and black ivory of the keys. After the coffee had been brought in, he stopped, and, looking over at Lord Henry, said, "Harry, did it ever occur to you that Basil was murdered?"

Lord Henry yawned. "Basil was very popular, and always wore a Waterbury watch. Why should he have been murdered? He was not clever enough to have enemies. Of course he had a wonderful genius for painting. But a man can paint like Velasquez and yet be as dull as possible. Basil was really rather dull. He only interested me once, and that was when he told me, years ago, that he had a wild adoration for you, and that you were the dominant motive of his art."

"I was very fond of Basil," said Dorian, with a note of sadness in his voice. "But don't people say that he was murdered?"

"Oh, some of the papers do. It does not seem to me to be at all probable. I know there are dreadful places in Paris, but Basil was not the sort of man to have gone to them. He had no curiosity. It was his chief defect."

"What would you say, Harry, if I told you that I had murdered Basil?" said the younger man. He watched him intently after he had spoken.

"I would say, my dear fellow, that you were posing for a character that doesn't suit you. All crime is vulgar, just as all vulgarity is crime. It is not in you, Dorian, to commit a murder. I am sorry if I hurt your vanity by saying so, but I assure you it is true. Crime belongs exclusively to the lower orders. I don't blame them in the smallest degree. I should fancy that crime was to them what art is to us, simply a method of procuring extraordinary sensations."

"A method of procuring sensations? Do you think, then, that a man who has once committed a murder could possibly do the same crime again? Don't tell me that."

"Oh! anything becomes a pleasure if one does it too often," cried Lord Henry, laughing. "That is one of the most important secrets of life. I should fancy, however, that murder is always a mistake. One should never do anything that one cannot talk about after dinner. But let us pass from poor Basil. I wish I could believe that he had come to such a really romantic end as you suggest; but I can't. I dare say he fell into the Seine off an omnibus, and that the conductor hushed up the scandal. Yes: I should fancy that was his end. I see him now lying on his back under those dull-green waters with the heavy barges floating over him, and long weeds catching in his hair. Do you know, I don't think he would have done much more good work. During the last ten years his painting had gone off very much."

Dorian heaved a sigh, and Lord Henry strolled across the room and began to stroke the head of a curious Java parrot, a large grey-plumaged bird, with pink crest and tail, that was balancing itself upon a bamboo perch. As his pointed fingers touched it, it dropped the white scurf of crinkled lids over black glass-like eyes, and began to sway backwards and forwards.

"Yes," he continued, turning round, and taking his handkerchief out of his pocket; "his painting had quite gone off. It seemed to me to have lost something. It had lost an ideal. When you and he ceased to be great friends, he ceased to be a great artist. What was it separated you? I suppose he bored you. If so, he never forgave you. It's a habit bores have. By the way, what has become of that wonderful portrait he did of you? I don't think I have ever seen it since he finished it. Oh! I remember your telling me years ago that you had sent it down to Selby, and that it had got mislaid or stolen on the way. You never got it back? What a pity! It was really a masterpiece. I remember I wanted to buy it. I wish I had now. It belonged to Basil's best period. Since then, his work was that curious mixture of bad painting and good intentions that always entitles a man to be called a representative British artist. Did you advertise for it? You should."

"I forget," said Dorian. "I suppose I did. But I never really liked it. I am sorry I sat for it. The memory of the thing is hateful to me. Why do you talk of it? It used to remind me of those curious lines in some play—'Hamlet,' I think—how do they run?—

"'*Like the painting of a sorrow,*
A face without a heart.'

Yes: that is what it was like."

Lord Henry laughed. "If a man treats life artistically, his brain is his heart," he answered, sinking into an arm-chair.

Dorian Gray shook his head, and struck some soft chords on the piano. "'Like the painting of a sorrow,'" he repeated, "'a face without a heart.'"

The elder man lay back and looked at him with half-closed eyes. "By the way, Dorian," he said, after a pause, "'what does it profit a man if he gain the whole world and lose'—how does the quotation run?—'his own soul?'"

The music jarred and Dorian Gray started, and stared at his friend. "Why do you ask me that, Harry?"

"My dear fellow," said Lord Henry, elevating his eyebrows in surprise, "I asked you because I thought you might be able to give me an answer. That is all. I was going through the Park last Sunday, and close by the Marble Arch there stood a little crowd of shabby-looking people listening to some vulgar street-preacher. As I passed by, I heard the man yelling out that question to his audience. It struck me as being rather dramatic. London is very rich in curious effects of that kind. A wet Sunday, an uncouth Christian in a mackintosh, a ring of sickly white faces under a broken roof of dripping umbrellas, and a wonderful phrase flung into the air by shrill, hysterical lips—it was really very good in its way, quite a suggestion. I thought of telling the prophet that Art had a soul, but that man had not. I am afraid, however, he would not have understood me."

"Don't, Harry. The soul is a terrible reality. It can be bought, and sold, and bartered away. It can be poisoned, or made perfect. There is a soul in each one of us. I know it."

"Do you feel quite sure of that, Dorian?"

"Quite sure."

"Ah! then it must be an illusion. The things one feels absolutely certain about are never true. That is the fatality of Faith, and the lesson of Romance. How grave you are! Don't be so serious. What have you or I to do with the superstitions of our age? No: we have given up our belief in the soul. Play me something. Play me a nocturne, Dorian, and, as you play, tell me, in a low voice, how you have kept your youth. You must have some secret. I am only ten years older than you are, and I am wrinkled, and worn, and yellow. You are really wonderful, Dorian. You have never looked more charming than you do to-night. You remind me of the day I saw you first. You were rather cheeky, very shy, and absolutely extraordinary. You have changed, of course, but not in appearance. I wish you would tell me your secret. To get back my youth I would do anything in the world, except take exercise, get up early, or be respectable. Youth! There is nothing like it. It's absurd to talk of the ignorance of youth. The only people to whose opinions I listen now with any respect are people much younger than myself. They seem in front of me. Life has revealed to them her latest wonder. As for the aged, I always contradict the aged. I do it on principle. If you ask them their opinion on something that happened yesterday, they solemnly give you the opinions current in 1820, when people wore high stocks, believed in everything, and knew absolutely nothing. How lovely that thing you are playing is! I wonder did Chopin write it at Majorca, with the sea weeping round the villa, and the salt spray dashing against the panes? It is marvellously romantic. What a blessing it is that there is one art left to us that is not imitative! Don't stop. I want music to-night. It seems to me that you are the young Apollo, and that I am Marsyas listening to you. I have sorrows, Dorian, of my own, that even you know nothing of. The tragedy of old age is not that one is old, but that one is young. I am amazed sometimes at my own sincerity. Ah, Dorian, how happy you are! What an exquisite life you have had! You have drunk deeply of everything. You have crushed the grapes against your palate. Nothing has been hidden from you. And it has all been to you no more than the sound of music. It has not marred you. You are still the same."

"I am not the same, Harry."

"Yes: you are the same. I wonder what the rest of your life will be. Don't spoil it by renunciations. At present you are a perfect type. Don't make yourself incomplete. You are quite flawless now. You need not shake your head: you know you are. Besides, Dorian, don't deceive yourself. Life is not governed by will or intention. Life is a question of nerves, and fibres, and slowly built-up cells in which thought hides itself and passion has its dreams. You may fancy yourself safe, and think yourself strong. But a chance tone of colour in a room or a morning sky, a particular perfume that you had once loved and that brings subtle memories with it, a line from a forgotten poem that you had come across again, a cadence from a piece of music that you had ceased to play—I tell you, Dorian, that it is on things like these that our lives depend. Browning writes about that somewhere; but our own senses will imagine them for us. There are moments when the odour of *lilas blanc* passes suddenly across me, and I have to live the strangest month of my life over again. I wish I could change places with you, Dorian. The world has cried out against us both, but it has always worshipped you. It always will worship you. You are the type of what the age is searching for, and what it is afraid it has found. I am so glad that you have never done anything, never carved a statue, or painted a picture, or produced anything outside yourself! Life has been your art. You have set yourself to music. Your days are your sonnets."

Dorian rose up from the piano, and passed his hand through his hair. "Yes, life has been exquisite," he murmured, "but I am not going to have the same life, Harry. And you must not say these extravagant things to me. You don't know everything about me. I think that if you did, even you would turn from me. You laugh. Don't laugh."

"Why have you stopped playing, Dorian? Go back and give me the nocturne over again. Look at that great honey-coloured moon that hangs in the dusky air. She is waiting for you to charm her, and if you play she will come closer to the earth. You won't? Let us go to the club, then. It has been a charming evening, and we must end it charmingly. There is some one at White's who wants immensely to know you—young Lord Poole, Bournemouth's eldest son. He has already copied your neckties, and has begged me to introduce him to you. He is quite delightful, and rather reminds me of you."

"I hope not," said Dorian, with a sad look in his eyes. "But I am tired to-night, Harry. I sha'n't go to the club. It is nearly eleven, and I want to go to bed early."

"Do stay. You have never played so well as to-night. There was something in your touch that was wonderful. It had more expression than I had ever heard from it before."

"It is because I am going to be good," he answered, smiling. "I am a little changed already."

"You cannot change to me, Dorian," said Lord Henry. "You and I will always be friends."

"Yet you poisoned me with a book once. I should not forgive that. Harry, promise me that you will never lend that book to any one. It does harm."

"My dear boy, you are really beginning to moralize. You will soon be going about like the converted, and the revivalist, warning people against all the sins of which you have grown tired. You are much too delightful to do that. Besides, it is no use. You and I are what we are, and will be what we will be. As for being poisoned by a book, there is no such thing as that. Art has no influence upon action. It annihilates the desire to act. It is superbly sterile. The books that the world calls immoral are books that show the world its own shame. That is all. But we won't discuss literature. Come round to-morrow. I am going to ride at eleven. We might go together, and I will take you to lunch afterwards with Lady Branksome. She is a charming woman, and wants to consult you about some tapestries she is thinking of buying. Mind you come. Or shall we lunch with our little Duchess? She says she never sees you now. Perhaps you are tired of Gladys? I thought you would be. Her clever tongue gets on one's nerves. Well, in any case, be here at eleven."

"Must I really come, Harry?"

"Certainly. The Park is quite lovely now. I don't think there have been such lilacs since the year I met you."

"Very well. I shall be here at eleven," said Dorian. "Good-night, Harry." As he reached the door he hesitated for a moment, as if he had something more to say. Then he sighed and went out.

CHAPTER XX

It was a lovely night, so warm that he threw his coat over his arm, and did not even put his silk scarf round his throat. As he strolled home, smoking his cigarette, two young men in evening dress passed him. He heard one of them whisper to the other, "That is Dorian Gray." He remembered how pleased he used to be when he was pointed out, or stared at, or talked about. He was tired of hearing his own name now. Half the charm of the little village where he had been so often lately was that no one knew who he was. He had often told the girl whom he had lured to love him that he was poor, and she had believed him. He had told her once that he was wicked, and she had laughed at him, and answered that wicked people were always very old and very ugly. What a laugh she had!—just like a thrush singing. And how pretty she had been in her cotton dresses and her large hats! She knew nothing, but she had everything that he had lost.

When he reached home, he found his servant waiting up for him. He sent him to bed, and threw himself down on the sofa in the library, and began to think over some of the things that Lord Henry had said to him.

Was it really true that one could never change? He felt a wild longing for the unstained purity of his boyhood—his rose-white boyhood, as Lord Henry had once called it. He knew that he had tarnished himself, filled his mind with corruption and given horror to his fancy; that he had been an evil influence to others and had experienced a terrible joy in being so; and that of the lives that had crossed his own it had been the fairest and the most full of promise that he had brought to shame. But was it all irretrievable? Was there no hope for him?

Ah! in what a monstrous moment of pride and passion he had prayed that the portrait should bear the burden of his days, and he keep the unsullied splendour of eternal youth! All his failure had been due to that. Better for him that each sin of his life had brought its sure, swift penalty along with it. There was purification in punishment. Not "Forgive us our sins" but "Smite us for our iniquities" should be the prayer of man to a most just God.

The curiously-carved mirror that Lord Henry had given to him, so many years ago now, was standing on the table, and the white-limbed Cupids laughed round it as of old. He took it up, as he had done on that night of horror, when he had first noted the change in the fatal picture, and with wild tear-dimmed eyes looked into its polished shield. Once, some one who had terribly loved him, had written to him a mad letter, ending with these idolatrous words: "The world is changed because you are made of ivory and gold. The curves of your lips rewrite history." The phrases came back to his memory, and he repeated them over and over to himself. Then he loathed his own beauty, and flinging the mirror to the floor crushed it into silver splinters beneath his heel. It was his beauty that had ruined him, his beauty and the youth that he had prayed for. But for these two things, his life might have been free from stain. His beauty had been to him but a mask, his youth but a mockery. What was youth at best? A green, an unripe time, a time of shallow moods, and sickly thoughts. Why had he worn its livery? Youth had spoiled him.

It was better not to think of the past. Nothing could alter that. It was of himself, and of his own future, that he had to think. James Vane was hidden in a nameless grave in Selby churchyard. Alan Campbell had shot himself one night in his laboratory, but had not revealed the secret that he had been forced to know. The excitement, such as it was, over Basil Hallward's disappearance would soon pass away. It was already waning. He was perfectly safe there. Nor, indeed, was it the death of Basil Hallward that weighed most upon his mind. It was the living death of his own soul that troubled him. Basil had painted the portrait that had marred his life. He could not forgive him that. It was the portrait that had done everything. Basil had said things to him that were unbearable, and that he had yet borne with patience. The murder had been simply the madness of a moment. As for Alan Campbell, his suicide had been his own act. He had chosen to do it. It was nothing to him.

A new life! That was what he wanted. That was what he was waiting for. Surely he had begun it already. He had spared one innocent thing, at any rate. He would never again tempt innocence. He would be good.

As he thought of Hetty Merton, he began to wonder if the portrait in the locked room had changed. Surely it was not still so horrible as it had been? Perhaps if his life became pure, he would be able to expel every sign of evil passion from the face. Perhaps the signs of evil had already gone away. He would go and look.

He took the lamp from the table and crept upstairs. As he unbarred the door, a smile of joy flitted across his strangely young-looking face and lingered for a moment about his lips. Yes, he would be good, and the hideous thing that he had hidden away would no longer be a terror to him. He felt as if the load had been lifted from him already.

He went in quietly, locking the door behind him, as was his custom, and dragged the purple hanging from the portrait. A cry of pain and indignation broke from him. He could see no change, save that in the eyes there was a look of cunning, and in the mouth the curved wrinkle of the hypocrite. The thing was still loathsome—more loathsome, if possible, than before—and the scarlet dew that spotted the hand seemed brighter, and more like blood newly spilt. Then he trembled. Had it been merely vanity that had made him do his one good deed? Or the desire for a new sensation, as Lord Henry had hinted, with his mocking laugh? Or that passion to act a part that sometimes makes us do things finer than we are ourselves? Or, perhaps, all these? And why was the red stain larger than it had been? It seemed to have crept like a horrible disease over the wrinkled fingers. There was blood on the painted feet, as though the thing had dripped—blood even on the hand that had not held the knife. Confess? Did it mean that he was to confess? To give himself up, and be put to death? He laughed. He felt that the idea was monstrous. Besides, even if he did confess, who would believe him? There was no trace of the murdered man anywhere. Everything belonging to him had been destroyed. He himself had burned what had been below-stairs. The world would simply say that he was mad. They would shut him up if he persisted in his story. . . . Yet it was his duty to confess, to suffer public shame, and to make public atonement. There was a God who called upon men to tell their sins to earth as well as to heaven. Nothing that he could do would cleanse him till he had told his own sin. His sin? He shrugged his shoulders. The death of Basil Hallward seemed very little to him. He was thinking of Hetty Merton. For it was an unjust mirror, this mirror of his soul that he was looking at. Vanity? Curiosity? Hypocrisy? Had there been nothing more in his renunciation than that? There had been something more. At least he thought so. But who could tell? . . . No. There had been nothing more. Through vanity he had spared her. In hypocrisy he had worn the mask of goodness. For curiosity's sake he had tried the denial of self. He recognized that now.

But this murder—was it to dog him all his life? Was he always to be burdened by his past? Was he really to confess? Never. There was only one bit of evidence left against him. The picture itself—that was evidence. He would destroy it. Why had he kept it so long? Once it had given him pleasure to watch it changing and growing old. Of late he had felt no such pleasure. It had kept him awake at night. When he had been away, he had been filled with terror lest other eyes should look upon it. It had brought melancholy across his passions. Its mere memory had marred many moments of joy. It had been like conscience to him. Yes, it had been conscience. He would destroy it.

He looked round, and saw the knife that had stabbed Basil Hallward. He had cleaned it many times, till there was no stain left upon it. It was bright, and glistened. As it had killed the painter, so it would kill the painter's work, and all that that meant. It would kill the past, and when that was dead he would be free. It would kill this monstrous soul-life, and without its hideous warnings, he would be at peace. He seized the thing, and stabbed the picture with it.

There was a cry heard, and a crash. The cry was so horrible in its agony that the frightened servants woke, and crept out of their rooms. Two gentlemen, who were passing in the Square below, stopped, and looked up at the great house. They walked on till they met a policeman, and brought him back. The man rang the bell several times, but there was no answer. Except for a light in one of the top windows, the house was all dark. After a time, he went away, and stood in an adjoining portico and watched.

"Whose house is that, constable?" asked the elder of the two gentlemen.

"Mr. Dorian Gray's, sir," answered the policeman.

They looked at each other, as they walked away, and sneered. One of them was Sir Henry Ashton's uncle.

Inside, in the servants' part of the house, the half-clad domestics were talking in low whispers to each other. Old Mrs. Leaf was crying, and wringing her hands. Francis was as pale as death.

After about a quarter of an hour, he got the coachman and one of the footmen and crept upstairs. They knocked, but there was no reply. They called out. Everything was still. Finally, after vainly trying to force the door, they got on the roof, and dropped down on to the balcony. The windows yielded easily: their bolts were old.

When they entered, they found hanging upon the wall a splendid portrait of their master as they had last seen him, in all the wonder of his exquisite youth and beauty. Lying on the floor was a dead man, in evening dress, with a knife in his heart. He was withered, wrinkled, and loathsome of visage. It was not till they had examined the rings that they recognized who it was.

PLAYS

LADY WINDERMERE'S FAN

The Persons of the Play

Lord Windermere
Lord Darlington
Lord Augustus Lorton
Mr. Dumby
Mr. Cecil Graham
Mr. Hopper
Parker, Butler
Lady Windermere
The Duchess of Berwick
Lady Agatha Carlisle
Lady Plymdale
Lady Stutfield
Lady Jedburgh
Mrs. Cowper-Cowper
Mrs. Erlynne
Rosalie, Maid

The Scenes of the Play

Act I. *Morning-room in Lord Windermere's House.* Act II. *Drawing-room in Lord Windermere's House.* Act III. *Lord Darlington's rooms.* Act IV. *Same as* Act I. *Time, The Present. Place, London. The Action of the Play takes place within twenty-four hours, beginning on a Tuesday afternoon at five o'clock, and ending the next day at 7.30 p. m.*

FIRST ACT

Scene—*Morning-room of Lord Windermere's house in Carlton House Terrace. Doors C. and R. Bureau with books and papers R. Sofa with small tea-table L. Window opening on to terrace L. Table R.*

[*Lady Windermere is at table R., arranging roses in a blue bowl.*]

[*Enter Parker.*]

Par. Is your ladyship at home this afternoon?

Lady Win. Yes—who has called?

Par. Lord Darlington, my lady.

Lady Win. [*Hesitates for a moment.*] Show him up—and I'm at home to any one who calls.

Par. Yes, my lady. [*Exit C.*]

LADY WIN. It's best for me to see him before to-night. I'm glad he's come.

[*Enter Parker C.*]

PAR. Lord Darlington.

[*Enter Lord Darlington C.*] [*Exit Parker.*]

LORD DAR. How do you do, Lady Windermere?

LADY WIN. How do you do, Lord Darlington? No, I can't shake hands with you. My hands are all wet with these roses. Aren't they lovely? They came up from Selby this morning.

LORD DAR. They are quite perfect. [*Sees a fan lying on the table.*] And what a wonderful fan! May I look at it?

LADY WIN. Do. Pretty, isn't it? It's got my name on it, and everything. I have only just seen it myself. It's my husband's birthday present to me. You know to-day is my birthday?

LORD DAR. No? Is it really?

LADY WIN. Yes; I'm of age to-day. Quite an important day in my life, isn't it? That is why I am giving this party to-night. Do sit down. [*Still arranging flowers.*]

LORD DAR. [*Sitting down.*] I wish I had known it was your birthday, Lady Windermere. I would have covered the whole street in front of your house with flowers for you to walk on. They are made for you. [*A short pause.*]

LADY WIN. Lord Darlington, you annoyed me last night at the Foreign Office. I am afraid you are going to annoy me again.

LORD DAR. I, Lady Windermere?

[*Enter Parker and Footman C. with tray and tea-things.*]

LADY WIN. Put it there, Parker. That will do. [*Wipes her hands with her pocket-handkerchief, goes to tea-table L. and sits down.*] Won't you come over, Lord Darlington? [*Exit Parker C.*]

LORD DAR. [*Takes chair and goes across L. C.*] I am quite miserable, Lady Windermere. You must tell me what I did. [*Sits down at table L.*]

LADY WIN. Well, you kept paying me elaborate compliments the whole evening.

LORD DAR. [*Smiling.*] Ah, now-a-days we are all of us so hard up, that the only pleasant things to pay *are* compliments. They're the only things we *can* pay.

LADY WIN. [*Shaking her head.*] No, I am talking very seriously. You mustn't laugh. I am quite serious. I don't like compliments, and I don't see why a man should think he is pleasing a woman enormously when he says to her a whole heap of things that he doesn't mean.

LORD DAR. Ah, but I did mean them. [*Takes tea which she offers him.*]

LADY WIN. [*Gravely.*] I hope not. I should be sorry to have to quarrel with you, Lord Darlington. I like you very much, you know that. But I shouldn't like you at all if I thought you were what most other men are. Believe me, you are better than most other men, and I sometimes think you pretend to be worse.

LORD DAR. We all have our little vanities, Lady Windermere.

LADY WIN. Why do you make that your special one? [*Still seated at table L.*]

LORD DAR. [*Still seated L. C.*] Oh, now-a-days so many conceited people go about Society pretending to be good, that I think it shows rather a sweet and modest disposition to pretend to be bad. Besides, there is this to be said. If you pretend to be good, the world takes you very seriously. If you pretend to be bad, it doesn't. Such is the astounding stupidity of optimism.

LADY WIN. Don't you *want* the world to take you seriously then, Lord Darlington?

LORD DAR. No, not the world. Who are the people the world takes seriously? All the dull people one can think of, from the Bishops down to the bores. I should like *you* to take me very seriously, Lady Windermere, *you* more than any one else in life.

LADY WIN. Why—why me?

LORD DAR. [*After a slight hesitation.*] Because I think we might be great friends. Let us be great friends. You may want a friend some day.

LADY WIN. Why do you say that?

LORD DAR. Oh!—we all want friends at times.

LADY WIN. I think we're very good friends already, Lord Darlington. We can always remain so as long as you don't——

LORD DAR. Don't what?

LADY WIN. Don't spoil it by saying extravagant silly things to me. You think I am a Puritan, I suppose? Well, I have something of the Puritan in me. I was brought up like that. I am glad of it. My mother died when I was a mere child. I lived always with Lady Julia, my father's eldest sister, you know. She was stern to me, but she taught me, what the world is forgetting, the difference that there is between what is right and what is wrong. *She* allowed of no compromise. I allow of none.

LORD DAR. My dear Lady Windermere!

LADY WIN. [*Leaning back on the sofa.*] You look on me as being behind the age. Well, I am! I should be sorry to be on the same level as an age like this.

LORD DAR. You think the age very bad?

LADY WIN. Yes. Now-a-days people seem to look on life as a speculation. It is not a speculation. It is a sacrament. Its ideal is Love. Its purification is sacrifice.

LORD DAR. [*Smiling.*] Oh, anything is better than being sacrificed!

LADY WIN. [*Leaning forward.*] Don't say that.

LORD DAR. I do say it. I feel it—I know it.

[*Enter Parker C.*]

PAR. The men want to know if they are to put the carpets on the terrace for to-night, my lady?

LADY WIN. You don't think it will rain, Lord Darlington, do you?

LORD DAR. I won't hear of its raining on your birthday!

LADY WIN. Tell them to do it at once, Parker. [*Exit Parker C.*]

LORD DAR. [*Still seated.*] Do you think then—of course I am only putting an imaginary instance—do you think, that in the case of a young married couple, say about two years married, if the husband suddenly becomes the intimate friend of a woman of—well, more than doubtful character, is always calling upon her, lunching with her, and probably paying her bills—do you think that the wife should not console herself?

LADY WIN. [*Frowning.*] Console herself?

LORD DAR. Yes, I think she should—I think she has the right.

LADY WIN. Because the husband is vile—should the wife be vile also?

LORD DAR. Vileness is a terrible word, Lady Windermere.

LADY WIN. It is a terrible thing, Lord Darlington.

LORD DAR. Do you know I am afraid that good people do a great deal of harm in this world. Certainly the greatest harm they do is that they make badness of such extraordinary importance. It is absurd to divide people into good and bad. People are either charming or tedious. I take the side of the charming, and you, Lady Windermere, can't help belonging to them.

LADY WIN. Now, Lord Darlington. [*Rising and crossing R., front of him.*] Don't stir, I am merely going to finish my flowers. [*Goes to table R. C.*]

LORD DAR. [*Rising and moving chair.*] And I must say I think you are very hard on modern life, Lady Windermere. Of course there is much against it, I admit. Most women, for instance, now-a-days, are rather mercenary.

LADY WIN. Don't talk about such people.

LORD DAR. Well then, setting mercenary people aside, who, of course, are dreadful, do you think seriously that women who have committed what the world calls a fault should never be forgiven?

LADY WIN. [*Standing at table.*] I think they should never be forgiven.

LORD DAR. And men? Do you think that there should be the same laws for men as there are for women?

LADY WIN. Certainly!

LORD DAR. I think life too complex a thing to be settled by these hard and fast rules.

LADY WIN. If we had "these hard and fast rules," we should find life much more simple.

LORD DAR. You allow of no exceptions?

LADY WIN. None!

LORD DAR. Ah, what a fascinating Puritan you are, Lady Windermere!

LADY WIN. The adjective was unnecessary, Lord Darlington.

LORD DAR. I couldn't help it. I can resist everything except temptation.

LADY WIN. You have the modern affectation of weakness.

LORD DAR. [*Looking at her.*] It's only an affectation, Lady Windermere. [*Enter Parker C.*]

PAR. The Duchess of Berwick and Lady Agatha Carlisle.

[*Enter the Duchess of Berwick and Lady Agatha Carlisle C.*]

[*Exit Parker C.*]

DUCH. [*Coming down C., and shaking hands.*] Dear Margaret, I am so pleased to see you. You remember Agatha, don't you? [*Crossing L. C.*] How do you do, Lord Darlington? I won't let you know my daughter, you are far too wicked.

LORD DAR. Don't say that, Duchess. As a wicked man I am a complete failure. Why, there are lots of people who say I have never really done anything wrong in the whole course of my life. Of course they only say it behind my back.

Duch. Isn't he dreadful? Agatha, this is Lord Darlington. Mind you don't believe a word he says. [*Lord Darlington crosses R. C.*] No, no tea, thank you, dear. [*Crosses and sits on sofa.*] We have just had tea at Lady Markby's. Such bad tea, too. It was quite undrinkable. I wasn't at all surprised. Her own son-in-law supplies it. Agatha is looking forward so much to your ball to-night, dear Margaret.

Lady Win. [*Seated L. C.*] Oh, you mustn't think it is going to be a ball, Duchess. It is only a dance in honour of my birthday. A small and early.

Lord Dar. [*Standing L. C.*] Very small, very early, and very select, Duchess.

Duch. [*On sofa L.*] Of course it's going to be select. But we know *that*, dear Margaret, about *your* house. It is really one of the few houses in London where I can take Agatha, and where I feel perfectly secure about poor Berwick. I don't know what Society is coming to. The most dreadful people seem to go everywhere. They certainly come to my parties—the men get quite furious if one doesn't ask them. Really, some one should make a stand against it.

Lady Win. *I* will, Duchess. I will have no one in my house about whom there is any scandal.

Lord Dar. [*R. C.*] Oh, don't say that, Lady Windermere. I should never be admitted! [*Sitting.*]

Duch. Oh, men don't matter. With women it is different. We're good. Some of us are, at least. But we are positively getting elbowed into the corner. Our husbands would really forget our existence if we didn't nag at them from time to time, just to remind them that we have a perfect legal right to do so.

Lord Dar. It's a curious thing, Duchess, about the game of marriage—a game, by the way, that is going out of fashion—the wives hold all the honours, and invariably lose the odd trick.

Duch. The odd trick? Is that the husband, Lord Darlington?

Lord Dar. It would be rather a good name for the modern husband.

Duch. Dear Lord Darlington, how thoroughly depraved you are!

Lady Win. Lord Darlington is trivial.

Lord Dar. Ah, don't say that, Lady Windermere.

Lady Win. Why do you *talk* so trivially about life, then?

Lord Dar. Because I think that life is far too important a thing ever to talk seriously about it. [*Moves up C.*]

Duch. What does he mean? Do, as a concession to my poor wits, Lord Darlington, just explain to me what you really mean?

Lord Dar. [*Coming down back of table.*] I think I had better not, Duchess. Now-a-days to be intelligible is to be found out. Good-bye! [*Shakes hands with Duchess.*] And now [*goes up stage*], Lady Windermere, good-bye. I may come to-night, mayn't I? Do let me come.

Lady Win. [*Standing up stage with Lord Darlington.*] Yes, certainly. But you are not to say foolish insincere things to people.

Lord Dar. [*Smiling.*] Ah! you are beginning to reform me. It is a dangerous thing to reform any one, Lady Windermere. [*Bows, and exit C.*]

DUCH. [*Who has risen, goes C.*] What a charming wicked creature! I like him so much. I'm quite delighted he's gone! How sweet you're looking! Where *do* you get your gowns? And now I must tell you how sorry I am for you, dear Margaret. [*Crosses to sofa and sits with Lady Windermere.*] Agatha darling!

LADY AGA. Yes mama. [*Rises.*]

DUCH. Will you go and look over the photograph album that I see there?

LADY AGA. Yes, mama. [*Goes to table L.*]

DUCH. Dear girl! She is so fond of photographs of Switzerland. Such a pure taste, I think. But I really am so sorry for you, Margaret.

LADY WIN. [*Smiling.*] Why, Duchess?

DUCH. Oh, on account of that horrid woman. She dresses so well, too, which makes it much worse, sets such a dreadful example. Augustus–you know my disreputable brother–such a trial to us all–well, Augustus is completely infatuated about her. It is quite scandalous, for she is absolutely inadmissable into society. Many a woman has a past, but I am told that she has at least a dozen, and that they all fit.

LADY WIN. Whom are you talking about, Duchess?

DUCH. About Mrs. Erlynne.

LADY WIN. Mrs. Erlynne? I never heard of her, Duchess. And what *has* she to do with me?

DUCH. My poor child! Agatha, darling!

LADY AGA. Yes, mama.

DUCH. Will you go out on the terrace and look at the sunset?

LADY AGA. Yes, mama. [*Exit through window L.*]

DUCH. Sweet girl! So devoted to sunsets! Shows such refinement of feeling, does it not? After all, there is nothing like nature, is there?

LADY WIN. But what is it, Duchess? Why do you talk to me about this person?

DUCH. Don't you really know? I assure you we're all so distressed about it. Only last night at dear Lady Fansen's every one was saying how extraordinary it was that, of all men in London, Windermere should behave in such a way.

LADY WIN. My husband–what has *he* got to do with any woman of that kind?

DUCH. Ah, what indeed, dear? That is the point. He goes to see her continually, and stops for hours at a time, and while he is there she is not at home to any one. Not that many ladies call on her, dear, but she has a great many disreputable men friends–my own brother in particular, as I told you–and that is what makes it so dreadful about Windermere. We looked upon *him* as being such a model husband, but I am afraid there is no doubt about it. My dear nieces–you know the Saville girls, don't you?–such nice domestic creatures–plain, dreadfully plain, but so good–well, they're always at the window doing fancy work, and making ugly things for the poor, which I think so useful of them in these dreadful socialistic days, and this terrible woman has taken a house in Curzon Street, right opposite them–such a respectable street, too. I don't know what we're coming to! And they tell me that Windermere goes there four and five times a week–they *see* him. They can't help it–and although they never talk scandal, they–well, of course–they remark on it to every one. And the worst of it all is, that I have been told that this woman has got a great deal of money out of somebody, for it seems that she came to London six months ago without anything at all to speak of, and now she has this charming house in Mayfair, drives her pony in the Park every afternoon, and all–well all–since she has known poor dear Windermere.

LADY WIN. Oh, I can't believe it!

DUCH. But it's quite true, my dear. The whole of London knows it. That is why I felt it was better to come and talk to you, and advise you to take Windermere away at once to Homburg or to Aix, where he'll have something to amuse him, and where you can watch him all day long. I assure you, my dear, that on several occasions after I was first married I had to pretend to be very ill, and was obliged to drink the most unpleasant mineral waters, merely to get Berwick out of town. He was so extremely susceptible. Though I am bound to say he never gave away any large sums of money to anybody. He is far too high-principled for that.

LADY WIN. [*Interrupting.*] Duchess, Duchess, it's impossible! [*Rising and crossing stage C.*] We are only married two years. Our child is but six months old. [*Sits in chair R. of L. table.*]

DUCH. Ah, the dear pretty baby! How is the little darling? Is it a boy or a girl? I hope a girl–Ah, no, I remember it's a boy! I'm so sorry. Boys are so wicked. My boy is excessively immoral. You wouldn't believe at what hours he comes home. And he's only left Oxford a few months–I really don't know what they teach them there.

LADY WIN. Are *all* men bad?

DUCH. Oh, all of them, my dear, all of them, without any exception. And they never grow any better. Men become old, but they never become good.

LADY WIN. Windermere and I married for love.

DUCH. Yes, we begin like that. It was only Berwick's brutal and incessant threats of suicide that made me accept him at all, and before the year was out he was running after all kinds of petticoats, every colour, every shape, every material. In fact, before the honeymoon was over, I caught him winking at my maid, a most pretty, respectable girl. I dismissed her at once without a character. No, I remember I passed her on to my sister; poor dear Sir George is so short-sighted, I thought it wouldn't matter. But it did, though it was most unfortunate. [*Rises.*] And now, my dear child, I must go, as we are dining out. And mind you don't take this little aberration of Windermere's too much to heart. Just take him abroad, and he'll come back to you all right.

LADY WIN. Come back to me? [*C.*]

DUCH. [*L. C.*] Yes, dear, these wicked women get our husbands away from us, but they always come back, slightly damaged, of course. And don't make scenes, men hate them!

LADY WIN. It is very kind of you, Duchess, to come and tell me all this. But I can't believe that my husband is untrue to me.

DUCH. Pretty child! I was like that once. Now I know that all men are monsters. [*Lady Windermere rings bell.*] The only thing to do is to feed the wretches well. A good cook does wonders, and that I know you have. My dear, Margaret, you are not going to cry?

Lady Win. You needn't be afraid, Duchess, I never cry.

Duch. That's quite right, dear. Crying is the refuge of plain women, but the ruin of pretty ones. Agatha, darling!

Lady Aga. [*Entering L.*] Yes, mama. [*Stands back of table L. C.*]

Duch. Come and bid good-bye to Lady Windermere, and thank her for your charming visit. [*Coming down again.*] And by the way, I must thank you for sending a card to Mr. Hopper—he's that rich young Australian people are taking such notice of just at present. His father made a great fortune by selling some kind of food in circular tins—most palatable, I believe—I fancy it is the thing the servants always refuse to eat. But the son is quite interesting. I think he's attracted by dear Agatha's clever talk. Of course, we should be very sorry to lose her, but I think that a mother who doesn't part with a daughter every season has no real affection. We're coming to-night, dear. [*Parker opens C. doors.*] And remember my advice, take the poor fellow out of town at once, it is the only thing to do. Good-bye, once more; come, Agatha. [*Exeunt Duchess and Lady Agatha C.*]

Lady Win. How horrible! I understand now what Lord Darlington meant by the imaginary instance of the couple not two years married. Oh! it can't be true—she spoke of enormous sums of money paid to this woman. I know where Arthur keeps his bank book—in one of the drawers of that desk. I might find out by that. I *will* find out. [*Opens drawer.*] No, it is some hideous mistake. [*Rises and goes C.*] Some silly scandal! He loves *me!* He loves *me!* But why should I not look! I am his wife, I have a right to look! [*Returns to bureau, takes out book and examines it, page by page, smiles and gives a sigh of relief*] I knew it, there is not a word of truth in this stupid story. [*Puts book back in drawer. As she does so, starts and takes out another book.*] A second book—private—locked! [*Tries to open it, but fails. Sees paper knife on bureau, and with it cuts cover from book. Begins to start at the first page.*] Mrs. Erlynne—£600—Mrs. Erlynne—£700—Mrs. Erlynne—£400. Oh! it is true! it is true! How horrible! [*Throws book on floor.*]

[*Enter Lord Windermere C.*]

Lord Win. Well, dear, has the fan been sent home yet? [*Going R. C. sees book.*] Margaret, you have cut open my bank book. You have no right to do such a thing!

Lady Win. You think it wrong that you are found out, don't you?

Lord Win. I think it wrong that a wife should spy on her husband.

Lady Win. I did not spy on you. I never knew of this woman's existence till half an hour ago. Some one who pitied me was kind enough to tell me what every one in London knows already—your daily visits to Curzon Street, your mad infatuation, the monstrous sums of money you squander on this infamous woman. [*Crossing L.*]

Lord Win. Margaret, don't talk like that of Mrs. Erlynne, you don't know how unjust it is!

LADY WIN. [*Turning to him.*] You are very jealous of Mrs. Erlynne's honour. I wish you had been as jealous of mine.

LORD WIN. Your honour is untouched, Margaret. You don't think for a moment that—— [*Puts book back into desk.*]

LADY WIN. I think that you spend your money strangely. That is all. Oh, don't imagine I mind about the money. As far as I am concerned, you may squander everything we have. But what I *do* mind is that you who have loved me, you who have taught me to love you, should pass from the love that is given to the love that is bought. Oh, it's horrible. [*Sits on sofa.*] And it is I who feel degraded. *You* don't feel anything. I feel stained, utterly stained. You can't realise how hideous the last six months seem to me now—every kiss you have given me is tainted in my memory.

LORD WIN. [*Crossing to her.*] Don't say that, Margaret. I never loved any one in the whole world but you.

LADY WIN. [*Rises.*] Who is this woman, then? Why do you take a house for her?

LORD WIN. I did not take a house for her.

LADY WIN. You gave her the money to do it, which is the same thing.

LORD WIN. Margaret, as far as I have known Mrs. Erlynne——

LADY WIN. Is there a Mr. Erlynne—or is he a myth?

LORD WIN. Her husband died many years ago. She is alone in the world.

LADY WIN. No relations? [*A pause.*]

LORD WIN. None.

LADY WIN. Rather curious, isn't it? [*L.*]

LORD WIN. [*L. C.*] Margaret, I was saying to you—and I beg you to listen to me—that as far as I have known Mrs. Erlynne, she has conducted herself well. If years ago——

LADY WIN. Oh! [*Crossing R. C.*] I don't want details about her life.

LORD WIN. I am not going to give you any details about her life. I tell you simply this—Mrs. Erlynne was once honoured, loved, respected. She was well born, she had a position—she lost everything—threw it away, if you like. That makes it all the more bitter. Misfortunes one can endure—they come from outside, they are accidents. But to suffer for one's own faults—ah! there is the sting of life. It was twenty years ago, too. She was little more than a girl then. She had been a wife for even less time than you have.

LADY WIN. I am not interested in her—and—you should not mention this woman and me in the same breath. It is an error of taste. [*Sitting R. at desk.*]

LORD WIN. Margaret, you could save this woman. She wants to get back into society, and she wants you to help her. [*Crossing to her.*]

LADY WIN. Me!

LORD WIN. Yes, you.

LADY WIN. How impertinent of her! [*A pause.*]

LORD WIN. Margaret, I came to ask you a great favour, and I still ask it of you, though you have discovered what I had intended you should never have known, that I have given Mrs. Erlynne a large sum of money. I want you to send her an invitation for our party to-night. [*Standing L. of her.*]

LADY WIN. You are mad! [*Rises.*]

LORD WIN. I entreat you. People may chatter about her, do chatter about her, of course, but they don't know anything definite against her. She has been to several houses—not to houses where you would go, I admit, but still to houses where women who are in what is called Society now-a-days do go. That does not content her. She wants you to receive her once.

LADY WIN. As a triumph for her, I suppose?

LORD WIN. No; but because she knows that you are a good woman—and that if she comes here once she will have a chance of a happier, a surer life, than she has had. She will make no further effort to know you. Won't you help a woman who is trying to get back?

LADY WIN. No! If a woman really repents, she never wishes to return to the society that has made or seen her ruin.

LORD WIN. I beg of you.

LADY WIN. [*Crossing to door R.*] I am going to dress for dinner, and don't mention the subject again this evening. Arthur [*going to him C.*], you fancy because I have no father or mother that I am alone in the world, and that you can treat me as you choose. You are wrong, I have friends, many friends.

LORD WIN. [*L. C.*] Margaret, you are talking foolishly, recklessly. I won't argue with you, but I insist upon your asking Mrs. Erlynne to-night.

LADY WIN. [*R. C.*] I shall do nothing of the kind. [*Crossing L. C.*]

LORD WIN. You refuse? [*C.*]

LADY WIN. Absolutely!

LORD WIN. Ah, Margaret, do this for my sake; it is her last chance.

LADY WIN. What has that to do with me?

LORD WIN. How hard good women are!

LADY WIN. How weak bad men are!

LORD WIN. Margaret, none of us men may be good enough for the women we marry—that is quite true—but you don't imagine I would ever—oh, the suggestion is monstrous!

LADY WIN. Why should *you* be different from other men? I am told there is hardly a husband in London who does not waste his life over *some* shameful passion.

LORD WIN. I am not one of them.

LADY WIN. I am not sure of that!

LORD WIN. You are sure in your heart. But don't make chasm after chasm between us. God knows the last few minutes have thrust us wide enough apart. Sit down and write the card.

LADY WIN. Nothing in the whole world would induce me.

LORD WIN. [*Crossing to the bureau.*] Then I will. [*Rings electric bell, sits and writes card.*]

LADY WIN. You are going to invite this woman? [*Crossing to him.*]

LORD WIN. Yes.

[*Pause. Enter Parker.*]

Parker!

PAR. Yes, my lord. [*Comes down L. C.*]

LORD WIN. Have this note sent to Mrs. Erlynne at No. 84A Curzon Street. [*Crossing to L. C. and giving note to Parker.*] There is no answer. [*Exit Parker C.*]

LADY WIN. Arthur, if that woman comes here, I shall insult her.

LORD WIN. Margaret, don't say that.

LADY WIN. I mean it.

LORD WIN. Child, if you did such a thing, there's not a woman in London who wouldn't pity you.

LADY WIN. There is not a *good* woman in London who would not applaud me. We have been too lax. We must make an example. I propose to begin to-night. [*Picking up fan.*] Yes, you gave me this fan to-day; it was your birthday present. If that woman crosses my threshold, I shall strike her across the face with it.

LORD WIN. Margaret, you couldn't do such a thing.

LADY WIN. You don't know me! [*Moves R.*]

[*Enter Parker.*]

Parker!

PAR. Yes, my lady.

LADY WIN. I shall dine in my own room. I don't want any dinner, in fact. See that everything is ready by half-past ten. And, Parker, be sure you pronounce the names of the guests very distinctly to-night. Sometimes you speak so fast that I miss them. I am particularly anxious to hear the names quite clearly, so as to make no mistake. You understand, Parker?

PAR. Yes, my lady.

LADY WIN. That will do! [*Exit Parker C.*]

[*Speaking to Lord Windermere.*] Arthur, if that woman comes here–I warn you——

LORD WIN. Margaret, you will ruin us!

LADY WIN. Us! From this moment my life is separate from yours. But if you wish to avoid a public scandal, write at once to this woman, and tell her that I forbid her to come here!

LORD WIN. I will not–I cannot–she must come!

LADY WIN. Then I shall do exactly as I have said. [*Goes R.*] You leave me no choice. [*Exit R.*]

LORD WIN. [*Calling after her.*] Margaret! Margaret! [*A pause.*] My God! What shall I do? I dare not tell her who this woman really is. The shame would kill her. [*Sinks down into a chair and buries his face in his hands.*]

ACT-DROP.

SECOND ACT

SCENE–*Drawing-room in Lord Windermere's house. Door R. U. opening into ball-room, where band is playing. Door L. through which guests are entering. Door L. U. opens on an illuminated terrace. Palms, flowers, and brilliant lights. Room crowded with guests. Lady Windermere is receiving them.*

DUCH. [*Up C.*] So strange Lord Windermere isn't here. Mr. Hopper is very late, too. You have kept those five dances for him, Agatha? [*Comes down.*]

LADY AGA. Yes, mama.

DUCH. [*Sitting on sofa.*] Just let me see your card. I'm so glad Lady Windermere has revived cards. They're a mother's only safeguard. You dear simple little thing! [*Scratches out two names.*] No nice girl should ever waltz with such particularly younger sons! It looks so fast! The last two dances you must pass on the terrace with Mr. Hopper.

[*Enter Mr. Dumby and Lady Plymdale from the ball-room.*]

LADY AGA. Yes, mama.

DUCH. [*Fanning herself.*] The air is so pleasant there.

PAR. Mrs. Cowper-Cowper. Lady Stutfield. Sir James Royston. Mr. Guy Berkeley.

[*These people enter as announced.*]

DUM. Good evening, Lady Stutfield. I suppose this will be the last ball of the season?

LADY STU. I suppose so, Mr. Dumby. It's been a delightful season, hasn't it?

DUM. Quite delightful! Good evening, Duchess. I suppose this will be the last ball of the season?

DUCH. I suppose so, Mr. Dumby. It has been a very dull season, hasn't it?

DUM. Dreadfully dull! Dreadfully dull!

MRS. COW. Good evening, Mr. Dumby. I suppose this will be the last ball of the season?

DUM. Oh, I think not. There'll probably be two more. [*Wanders back to Lady Plymdale.*]

PAR. Mr. Rufford. Lady Jedburgh and Miss Graham. Mr. Hopper.

[*These people enter as announced.*]

HOP. How do you do, Lady Windermere? How do you do, Duchess? [*Bows to Lady Agatha.*]

DUCH. Dear Mr. Hopper, how nice of you to come so early. We all know how you are run after in London.

HOP. Capital place, London! They are not nearly so exclusive in London as they are in Sydney.

DUCH. Ah, we know your value, Mr. Hopper. We wish there were more like you. It would make life so much easier. Do you know, Mr. Hopper, dear Agatha and I are so much interested in Australia. It must be so pretty with all the dear little kangaroos flying about. Agatha has found it on the map. What a curious shape it is! Just like a large packing case. However, it is a very young country, isn't it?

HOP. Wasn't it made at the same time as the others, Duchess?

DUCH. How clever you are, Mr. Hopper. You have a cleverness quite of your own. Now I mustn't keep you.

HOP. But I should like to dance with Lady Agatha, Duchess.

DUCH. Well, I *hope* she has a dance left. Have you got a dance left Agatha?

LADY AGA. Yes, mama.

DUCH. The next one?

LADY AGA. Yes, mama.

HOP. May I have the pleasure? [*Lady Agatha bows.*]

DUCH. Mind you take great care of my little chatterbox, Mr. Hopper.

[*Lady Agatha and Mr. Hopper pass into ball-room.*]

[*Enter Lord Windermere L.*]

LORD WIN. Margaret, I want to speak to you.

LADY WIN. In a moment. [*The music stops.*]

PAR. Lord Augustus Lorton.

[*Enter Lord Augustus.*]

LORD AUG. Good evening, Lady Windermere.

DUCH. Sir James, will you take me into the ball-room? Augustus has been dining with us to-night. I really have had quite enough of dear Augustus for the moment.

[*Sir James Royston gives the Duchess his arm and escorts her into the ball-room.*]

PAR. Mr. and Mrs. Arthur Bowden. Lord and Lady Paisley. Lord Darlington.

[*These people enter as announced.*]

LORD AUG. [*Coming up to Lord Windermere.*] Want to speak to you particularly, dear boy. I'm worn to a shadow. Know I don't look it. None of us men do look what we really are. Demmed good thing, too. What I want to know is this. Who is she? Where does she come from? Why hasn't she got any demmed relations? Demmed nuisance, relations! But they make one so demmed respectable.

LORD WIN. You are talking of Mrs. Erlynne, I suppose? I only met her six months ago. Till then I never knew of her existence.

LORD AUG. You have seen a good deal of her since then.

LORD WIN. [*Coldly.*] Yes, I have seen a good deal of her since then. I have just seen her.

LORD AUG. Egad! the women are very down on her. I have been dining with Arabella this evening! By Jove! you should have heard what she said about Mrs. Erlynne. She didn't leave a rag on her. . . . [*Aside.*] Berwick and I told her that didn't matter much, as the lady in question must have an extremely fine figure. You should have seen Arabella's expression! . . . But, look here, dear boy. I don't know what to do about Mrs. Erlynne. Egad! I might be married to her; she treats me with such demmed indifference. She's deuced clever, too! She explains everything. Egad! She explains you. She has got any amount of explanations for you–and all of them different.

LORD WIN. No explanations are necessary about my friendship with Mrs. Erlynne.

LORD AUG. Hem! Well, look here, dear old fellow. Do you think she will ever get into this demmed thing called Society? Would you introduce her to your wife? No use beating about the confounded bush. Would you do that?

LORD WIN. Mrs. Erlynne is coming here to-night.

LORD AUG. Your wife has sent her a card?

LORD WIN. Mrs. Erlynne has received a card.

LORD AUG. Then she's all right, dear boy. But why didn't you tell me that before? It would have saved me a heap of worry and demmed misunderstandings.

[*Lady Agatha and Mr. Hopper cross and exit on terrace L. U. E.*]

PAR. Mr. Cecil Graham!

[*Enter Mr. Cecil Graham.*]

CEC. [*Bows to Lady Windermere, passes over and shakes hands with Lord Windermere.*] Good evening, Arthur. Why don't you ask me how I am? I like people to ask me how I am. It shows a wide-spread interest in my health. Now to-night I am not at all well. Been dining with my people. Wonder why it is one's people are always so tedious? My father would talk morality after dinner. I told him he was old enough to know better. But my experience is that as soon as people are old enough to know better, they don't know anything at all. Hullo, Tuppy! Hear you are going to be married again; thought you were tired of that game.

LORD AUG. You're excessively trivial, my dear boy, excessively trivial!

CEC. By the way, Tuppy, which is it? Have you been twice married and once divorced, or twice divorced and once married? I say, you've been twice divorced and once married. It seems so much more probable.

LORD AUG. I have a very bad memory. I really don't remember which. [*Moves away R.*]

LADY PLY. Lord Windermere, I've something most particular to ask you.

LORD WIN. I am afraid—if you will excuse me—I must join my wife.

LADY PLY. Oh, you mustn't dream of such a thing. It's most dangerous nowa-days for a husband to pay any attention to his wife in public. It always makes people think that he beats her when they're alone. The world has grown so suspicious of anything that looks like a happy married life. But I'll tell you what it is at supper. [*Moves toward door of ball-room.*]

LORD WIN. [C.] Margaret, I *must* speak to you.

LADY WIN. Will you hold my fan for me, Lord Darlington? Thanks. [*Comes down to him.*]

LORD WIN. [*Crossing to her.*] Margaret, what you said before dinner was, of course, impossible?

LADY WIN. That woman is not coming here to-night!

LORD WIN. [*R. C.*] Mrs. Erlynne is coming here, and if you in any way annoy or wound her, you will bring shame and sorrow on us both. Remember that! Ah, Margaret! only trust me! A wife should trust her husband!

LADY WIN. [*C.*] London is full of women who trust their husbands. One can always recognise them. They look so thoroughly unhappy. I am not going to be one of them. [*Moves up.*] Lord Darlington, will you give me back my fan, please? Thanks. . . . A useful thing, a fan, isn't it? . . . I want a friend to-night, Lord Darlington. I didn't know I would want one so soon.

LORD DAR. Lady Windermere! I knew the time would come some day; but why to-night?

Lord Win. I *will* tell her. I must. It would be terrible if there were any scene. Margaret . . . .

Par. Mrs. Erlynne.

[*Lord Windermere starts. Mrs. Erlynne enters, very beautifully dressed, and very dignified. Lady Windermere clutches at her fan, then lets it drop on the floor. She bows coldly to Mrs. Erlynne, who bows to her sweetly in turn, and sails into the room.*]

Lord Dar. You have dropped your fan, Lady Windermere. [*Picks it up and hands it to her.*]

Mrs. Erl. [*C.*] How do you do again, Lord Windermere? How charming your sweet wife looks! Quite a picture!

Lord Win. [*In a low voice.*] It was terribly rash of you to come!

Mrs. Erl. [*Smiling.*] The wisest thing I ever did in my life. And, by the way, you must pay me a good deal of attention this evening. I am afraid of the women. You must introduce me to some of them. The men I can always manage. How do you do, Lord Augustus? You have quite neglected me lately. I have not seen you since yesterday. I am afraid you're faithless. Everyone told me so.

Lord Aug. [*R.*] Now really, Mrs. Erlynne, allow me to explain.

Mrs. Erl. [*R. C.*] No, dear Lord Augustus, you can't explain anything. It is your chief charm.

Lord Aug. Ah, if you find charm in me, Mrs. Erlynne——

[*They converse together. Lord Windermere moves uneasily about the room watching Mrs. Erlynne.*]

Lord Dar. [*To Lady Windermere.*] How pale you are!

Lady Win. Cowards are always pale.

Lord Dar. You look faint. Come out on the terrace.

Lady Win. Yes. [*To Parker.*] Parker, send my cloak out.

Mrs. Erl. [*Crossing to her.*] Lady Windermere, how beautifully your terrace is illuminated. Reminds me of Prince Doria's at Rome.

[*Lady Windermere bows coldly, and goes off with Lord Darlington.*]

Oh, how do you do, Mr. Graham? Isn't that your aunt, Lady Jedburgh? I should so much like to know her.

Cec. [*After a moment's hesitation and embarrassment.*] Oh, certainly, if you wish it. Aunt Caroline, allow me to introduce Mrs. Erlynne.

Mrs. Erl. So pleased to meet you, Lady Jedburgh. [*Sits beside her on the sofa.*] Your nephew and I are great friends. I am so much interested in his political career. I think he's sure to be a wonderful success. He thinks like a Tory, and talks like a radical, and that's so important now-a-days. He's such a brilliant talker, too. But we all know from whom he inherits that. Lord Allandale was saying to me only yesterday in the park, that Mr. Graham talks almost as well as his aunt.

Lady Jed. [*R.*] Most kind of you to say these charming things to me! [*Mrs. Erlynne smiles and continues conversation.*]

Dum. [*To Cecil Graham.*] Did you introduce Mrs. Erlynne to Lady Jedburgh?

CEC. Had to, my dear fellow. Couldn't help it. That woman can make one do anything she wants. How, I don't know.

DUM. Hope to goodness she won't speak to me!

[*Saunters towards Lady Plymdale.*]

MRS. ERL. [*C. to Lady Jedburgh.*] On Thursday? With great pleasure. [*Rises and speaks to Lord Windermere, laughing.*] What a bore it is to have to be civil to these old dowagers. But they always insist on it.

LADY PLY. [*To Mr. Dumby.*] Who is that well-dressed woman talking to Windermere?

DUM. Haven't got the slightest idea. Looks like an *edition de luxe* of a wicked French novel, meant specially for the English market.

MRS. ERL. So that is poor Dumby with Lady Plymdale? I hear she is frightfully jealous of him. He doesn't seem anxious to speak to me to-night. I suppose he is afraid of her. Those straw-coloured women have dreadful tempers. Do you know, I think I'll dance with you first, Windermere. [*Lord Windermere bites his lip and frowns.*] It will make Lord Augustus so jealous! Lord Augustus! [*Lord Augustus comes down.*] Lord Windermere insists on my dancing with him first, and, as it's his own house, I can't well refuse. You know I would much sooner dance with you.

LORD AUG. [*With a low bow.*] I wish I could think so, Mrs. Erlynne.

MRS. ERL. You know it far too well. I fancy a person dancing through life with you and finding it charming.

LORD AUG. [*Placing his hand on his white waistcoat.*] Oh, thank you, thank you. You are the most adorable of all ladies!

MRS. ERL. What a nice speech! So simple and so sincere! Just the sort of speech I like. Well, you shall hold my bouquet [*Goes towards ball-room on Lord Windermere's arm.*] Ah, Mr. Dumby, how are you? I am sorry I have been out the last three times you have called. Come and lunch on Friday.

DUM. [*With perfect nonchalance.*] Delighted.

[*Lady Plymdale glares with indignation at Mr. Dumby. Lord Augustus follows Mrs. Erlynne and Lord Windermere into the ball-room holding bouquet.*]

LADY PLY. [*To Mr. Dumby.*] What an absolute brute you are! I never can believe a word you say! Why did you tell me you didn't know her? What do you mean by calling on her three times running? You are not to go to lunch there; of course you understand that?

DUM. My dear Laura, I wouldn't dream of going!

LADY PLY. You haven't told me her name yet! Who is she?

DUM. [*Coughs slightly and smoothes his hair.*] She's a Mrs. Erlynne.

LADY PLY. *That* woman?

DUM. Yes, that is what every one calls her.

LADY PLY. How very interesting! How intensely interesting! I really must have a good stare at her. [*Goes to door of ball-room and looks in.*] I have heard the most shocking things about her. They say she is ruining poor Windermere. And Lady Windermere, who goes in for being so proper, invites her!

How extremely amusing! It takes a thoroughly good woman to do thoroughly stupid things. You are to lunch there on Friday!

Dum. Why?

Lady Ply. Because I want you to take my husband with you. He has been so attentive lately, that he has become a perfect nuisance. Now, this woman is just the thing for him. He'll dance attendance upon her as long as she lets him, and won't bother me. I assure you, women of that kind are most useful. They form the basis of other people's marriages.

Dum. What a mystery you are!

Lady Ply. [*Looking at him.*] I wish *you* were!

Dum. I am–to myself. I am the only person in the world I should like to know thoroughly; but I don't see any chance of it just at present.

[*They pass into the ball-room, and Lady Windermere and Lord Darlington enter from the terrace.*]

Lady Win. Yes. Her coming here is monstrous, unbearable. I know now what you meant to-day at tea-time. Why didn't you tell me right out? You should have!

Lord Dar. I couldn't! A man can't tell these things about another man! But if I had known he was going to make you ask her here to-night, I think I would have told you. That insult, at any rate, you would have been spared.

Lady Win. I did not ask her. He insisted on her coming–against my entreaties–against my commands. Oh! the house is tainted for me! I feel that every woman here sneers at me as she dances by with my husband. What have I done to deserve this? I gave him all my life. He took it–used it–spoiled it! I am degraded in my own eyes; and I lack courage–I am a coward! [*Sits down on sofa.*]

Lord Dar. If I know you at all, I know that you can't live with a man who treats you like this! What sort of life would you have with him? You would feel that he was lying to you every moment of the day. You would feel that the look in his eyes was false, his voice false, his touch false, his passion false. He would come to you when he was weary of others; you would have to comfort him. He would come to you when he was devoted to others; you would have to charm him. You would have to be to him the mask of his real life, the cloak to hide his secret.

Lady Win. You are right–you are terribly right. But where am I to turn? You said you would be my friend, Lord Darlington. Tell me, what am I to do? Be my friend now.

Lord Dar. Between men and women, there is no friendship possible. There is passion, enmity, worship, love, but no friendship. I love you––

Lady Win. No, no! [*Rises.*]

Lord Dar. Yes, I love you! You are more to me than anything in the whole world. What does your husband give you? Nothing. Whatever is in him he gives to this wretched woman, whom he has thrust into your society, into your home, to shame you before every one. I offer you my life––

Lady Win. Lord Darlington!

Lord Dar. My life–my whole life. Take it, and do with it what you will.

. . . I love you—love you as I have never loved any living thing. From the moment I met you I loved you, loved you blindly, adoringly, madly! You did not know it then—you know it now! Leave this house to-night. I won't tell you that the world matters nothing, or the world's voice, or the voice of society. They matter a good deal. They matter far too much. But there are moments when one has to choose between living one's own life, fully, entirely, completely—or dragging out some false, shallow, degrading existence that the world in its hypocrisy demands. You have that moment now. Choose! Oh, my love, choose!

LADY WIN. [*Moving slowly away from him, and looking at him with startled eyes.*] I have not the courage.

LORD DAR. [*Following her.*] Yes; you have the courage. There may be six months of pain, of disgrace even, but when you no longer bear his name, when you bear mine, all will be well. Margaret, my love, my wife that shall be some day—yes, my wife! You know it! What are you now? This woman has the place that belongs by right to you. Oh! go—go out of this house, with head erect, with a smile upon your lips, with courage in your eyes. All London will know why you did it; and who will blame you? No one. If they do, what matter? Wrong? What is wrong? It's wrong for a man to abandon his wife for a shameless woman. It is wrong for a wife to remain with a man who so dishonours her. You said once you would make no compromise with things. Make none now. Be brave! Be yourself!

LADY WIN. I am afraid of being myself. Let me think! Let me wait! My husband may return to me. [*Sits down on sofa.*]

LORD DAR. And you would take him back! You are not what I thought you were. You are just the same as every other woman. You would stand anything rather than face the censure of a world, whose praise you would despise. In a week you will be driving with this woman in the park. She will be your constant guest—your dearest friend. You would endure anything rather than break with one blow this monstrous tie. You are right. You have no courage; none!

LADY WIN. Ah, give me time to think. I cannot answer you now. [*Passes her hand nervously over her brow.*]

LORD DAR. It must be now or not at all.

LADY WIN. [*Rising from the sofa.*] Then not at all. [*A pause.*]

LORD DAR. You break my heart!

LADY WIN. Mine is already broken. [*A pause.*]

LORD DAR. To-morrow I leave England. This is the last time I shall ever look on you. You will never see me again. For one moment our lives met—our souls touched. They must never meet to touch again. Good-bye, Margaret. [*Exit.*]

LADY WIN. How alone I am in life! How terribly alone!

[*The music stops. Enter the Duchess of Berwick and Lord Paisley laughing and talking. Other guests come on from the ball-room.*]

DUCH. Dear Margaret, I've just been having such a delightful chat with Mrs. Erlynne. I am so sorry for what I said to you this afternoon about her.

Of course, she must be all right if *you* invite her. A most attractive woman, and has such sensible views of life. Told me she entirely disapproved of people marrying more than once, so I feel quite safe about poor Augustus. Can't imagine why people speak against her. It's those horrid nieces of mine—the Saville girls—they're always talking scandal. Still, I should go to Homburg, dear, I really should. She is just a little too attractive. But where is Agatha? Oh, there she is! [*Lady Agatha and Mr. Hopper enter from the terrace L. U. E.*] Mr. Hopper, I am very angry with you. You have taken Agatha out on the terrace, and she is so delicate.

HOP. [*L. C.*] Awfully sorry, Duchess. We went out for a moment and then got chatting together.

DUCH. [C.] Ah, about dear Australia, I suppose?

HOP. Yes.

DUCH. Agatha, darling! [*Beckons her over.*]

LADY AGA. Yes, mama.

DUCH. [*Aside.*] Did Mr. Hopper definitely——

LADY AGA. Yes, mama.

DUCH. And what answer did you give him, dear child?

LADY AGA. Yes, mama.

DUCH. [*Affectionately.*] My dear one! You always say the right thing. Mr. Hopper! James! Agatha has told me everything. How cleverly you have both kept your secret.

HOP. You don't mind my taking Agatha off to Australia, then, Duchess?

DUCH. [*Indignantly.*] To Australia? Oh! don't mention that dreadful vulgar place.

HOP. But she said she'd like to come with me.

DUCH. [*Severely.*] Did you say that, Agatha?

LADY AGA. Yes, mama.

DUCH. Agatha, you say the most silly things possible. I think on the whole that Grosvenor Square would be a more healthy place to reside in. There are lots of vulgar people live in Grosvenor Square, but at any rate there are no horrid kangaroos crawling about. But we'll talk about that to-morrow. James, you can take Agatha down. You'll come to lunch, of course, James. At half-past one instead of two. The Duke will wish to say a few words to you, I am sure.

HOP. I should like to have a chat with the Duke, Duchess. He has not said a single word to me yet.

DUCH. I think you'll find he will have a great deal to say to you to-morrow. [*Exit Lady Agatha with Mr. Hopper.*] And now good-night, Margaret. I'm afraid it's the old, old story, dear. Love—well, not love at first sight, but love at the end of the season, which is so much more satisfactory.

LADY WIN. Good-night, Duchess.

[*Exit the Duchess of Berwick on Lord Paisley's arm.*]

LADY PLY. My dear Margaret, what a handsome woman your husband has been dancing with! I should be quite jealous if I were you! Is she a great friend of yours?

Lady Win. No!

Lady Ply. Really? Good-night, dear. [*Looks at Mr. Dumby, and exit.*]

Dum. Awful manners young Hopper has.

Cec. Ah! Hopper is one of Nature's gentlemen, the worst type of gentleman I know.

Dum. Sensible woman, Lady Windermere. Lots of wives would have objected to Mrs. Erlynne coming. But Lady Windermere has that uncommon thing called common sense.

Cec. And Windermere knows that nothing looks so like innocence as an indiscretion.

Dum. Yes; dear Windermere is becoming almost modern. Never thought he would. [*Bows to Lady Windermere, and exit.*]

Lady Jed. Good-night, Lady Windermere. What a fascinating woman Mrs. Erlynne is! She is coming to lunch on Thursday, won't you come too? I expect the Bishop and dear Lady Merton.

Lady Win. I am afraid I am engaged, Lady Jedburgh.

Lady Jed. So sorry. Come, dear.

[*Exeunt Lady Jedburgh and Miss Graham.*]

[*Enter Mrs. Erlynne and Lord Windermere.*]

Mrs. Erl. Charming ball it has been! Quite reminds me of old days. [*Sits on the sofa.*] And I see that there are just as many fools in society as there used to be. So pleased to find that nothing has altered! Except Margaret. She's grown quite pretty. The last time I saw her—twenty years ago, she was a fright in flannel. Positive fright, I assure you. The dear Duchess! and that sweet Lady Agatha! Just the type of girl I like! Well, really, Windermere, if I am to be the Duchess' sister-in-law——

Lord Win. [*Sitting L. of her.*] But are you——?

[*Exit Mr. Cecil Graham with rest of guests. Lady Windermere watches, with a look of scorn and pain, Mrs. Erlynne and her husband. They are unconscious of her presence.*]

Mrs. Erl. Oh yes! He's to call to-morrow at twelve o'clock! He wanted to propose to-night. In fact he did. He kept on proposing. Poor Augustus, you know how he repeats himself. Such a bad habit! But I told him I wouldn't give him an answer till to-morrow. Of course I'm going to take him. And I dare say I'll make him an admirable wife, as wives go. And there is a great deal of good in Lord Augustus. Fortunately it is all on the surface. Just where good qualities should be. Of course you must help me in this matter.

Lord Win. I am not called upon to encourage Lord Augustus, I suppose?

Mrs. Erl. Oh, no! I do the encouraging. But you will make me a handsome settlement, Windermere, won't you?

Lord Win. [*Frowning.*] Is that what you want to talk to me about to-night?

Mrs. Erl. Yes.

Lord Win. [*With a gesture of impatience.*] I will not talk of it here.

Mrs. Erl. [*Laughing.*] Then we will talk of it on the terrace. Even business should have a picturesque background. Should it not, Windermere? With a proper background women can do anything.

LORD WIN. Won't to-morrow do as well?

MRS. ERL. No; you see, to-morrow I am going to accept him. And I think it would be a good thing if I was able to tell him that—well, what shall I say?—£2,000 a year left to me by a third cousin—or a second husband—or some distant relative of that kind. It would be an additional attraction, wouldn't it? You have a delightful opportunity now of paying me a compliment, Windermere. But you are not very clever at paying compliments. I am afraid Margaret doesn't encourage you in that excellent habit. It's a great mistake on her part. When men give up saying what is charming, they give up thinking what is charming. But seriously, what do you say to £2,000? £2,500, I think. In modern life margin is everything. Windermere, don't you think the world an intensely amusing place? I do!

[*Exit on terrace with Lord Windermere. Music strikes up in ball-room.*]

LADY WIN. To stay in this house any longer is impossible. To-night a man who loves me offered me his whole life. I refused it. It was foolish of me. I will offer him mine now. I will give him mine. I will go to him! [*Puts on cloak and goes to the door, then turns back. Sits down at table and writes a letter, puts it into an envelope, and leaves it on table.*] Arthur has never understood me. When he reads this, he will. He may do as he chooses now with his life. I have done with mine as I think best, as I think right. It is he who has broken the bond of marriage—not I. I only break its bondage. [*Exit.*]

[*Parker enters L., and crosses towards the ball-room R. Enter Mrs. Erlynne.*]

MRS. ERL. Is Lady Windermere in the ball-room?

PAR. Her ladyship has just gone out.

MRS. ERL. Gone out? She's not on the terrace?

PAR. No, madam. Her ladyship has just gone out of the house.

MRS. ERL. [*Starts, and looks at the servant with a puzzled expression on her face.*] Out of the house?

PAR. Yes, madam—her ladyship told me she had left a letter for his lordship on the table.

MRS. ERL. A letter for Lord Windermere?

PAR. Yes, madam.

MRS. ERL. Thank you.

[*Exit Parker. The music in the ball-room stops.*] Gone out of her house! A letter addressed to her husband! [*Goes over to bureau and looks at letter. Takes it up and lays it down again with a shudder of fear.*] No, no! It would be impossible! Life doesn't repeat its tragedies like that! Oh, why does this horrible fancy come across me? Why do I remember now the one moment of my life I most wish to forget? Does life repeat its tragedies? [*Tears letter open and reads it, then sinks down into a chair with a gesture of anguish.*] Oh, how terrible! The same words that twenty years ago I wrote to her father! and how bitterly I have been punished for it! No; my punishment, my real punishment is to-night, is now! [*Still seated R.*]

[*Enter Lord Windermere L. U. E.*]

LORD WIN. Have you said good-night to my wife? [*Comes C.*]

MRS. ERL. [*Crushing letter in her hand.*] Yes.

LORD WIN. Where is she?

MRS. ERL. She is very tired. She has gone to bed. She said she had a headache.

LORD WIN. I must go to her. You'll excuse me?

MRS. ERL. [*Rising hurriedly.*] Oh, no! It's nothing serious. She's only very tired, that is all. Besides, there are people still in the supper-room. She wants you to make her apologies to them. She said she didn't wish to be disturbed. [*Drops letter.*] She asked me to tell you.

LORD WIN. [*Picks up letter.*] You have dropped something.

MRS. ERL. Oh yes, thank you, that is mine. [*Puts out her hand to take it.*]

LORD WIN. [*Still looking at letter.*] But it's my wife's handwriting, isn't it?

MRS. ERL. [*Takes letter quickly.*] Yes, it's–an address. Will you ask them to call my carriage, please?

LORD WIN. Certainly. [*Goes L. and exit.*]

MRS. ERL. Thanks. What can I do? What can I do? I feel a passion awakening within me that I never felt before. What can it mean? The daughter must not be like the mother–that would be terrible. How can I save her? How can I save my child? A moment may ruin a life. Who knows that better than I? Windermere must be got out of the house; that is absolutely necessary. [*Goes L.*] But how shall I do it? It must be done somehow. Ah!

[*Enter Lord Augustus R. U. E. carrying bouquet.*]

LORD AUG. Dear lady, I am in such suspense! May I not have an answer to my request?

MRS. ERL. Lord Augustus, listen to me. You are to take Lord Windermere down to the club at once, and keep him there as long as possible. You understand?

LORD AUG. But you said you wished me to keep early hours!

MRS. ERL. [*Nervously.*] Do what I tell you. Do what I tell you.

LORD AUG. And my reward?

MRS. ERL. Your reward? Your reward? Oh! ask me that to-morrow. But don't let Windermere out of your sight to-night. If you do I will never forgive you. I will never speak to you again. I'll have nothing to do with you. Remember you are to keep Windermere at your club, and don't let him come back to-night. [*Exit L.*]

LORD AUG. Well, really, I might be her husband already. Positively I might. [*Follows her in a bewildered manner.*]

ACT-DROP.

THIRD ACT

SCENE–*Lord Darlington's Rooms. A large sofa is in front of fire-place R. At the back of the stage a curtain is drawn across the window. Doors L. and R. Table R. with writing materials. Table C. with syphons, glasses, and Tantalus frame. Table L. with cigar and cigarette box. Lamps lit.*

LADY WIN. [*Standing by the fire-place.*] Why doesn't he come? This waiting is horrible. He should be here. Why is he not here, to wake by passionate words some fire within me? I am cold—cold as a loveless thing. Arthur must have read my letter by this time. If he cared for me, he would have come after me, would have taken me back by force. But he doesn't care. He's entrammelled by this woman—fascinated by her—dominated by her. If a woman wants to hold a man, she has merely to appeal to what is worst in him. We make gods of men, and they leave us. Others make brutes of them and they fawn and are faithful. How hideous life is! . . . Oh! it was mad of me to come here, horribly mad. And yet which is the worst, I wonder, to be at the mercy of a man who loves me, or the wife of a man who in one's own house dishonours one? What woman knows? What woman in the whole world? But will he love me always, this man to whom I am giving my life? What do I bring him? Lips that have lost the note of joy, eyes that are blighted by tears, chill hands and icy heart. I bring him nothing. I must go back—no: I can't go back, my letter has put me in their power—Arthur would not take me back! That fatal letter! No! Lord Darlington leaves England to-morrow. I will go with him—I have no choice. [*Sits down for a few moments. Then starts up and puts on her cloak.*] No, no! I will go back, let Arthur do with me what he pleases. I can't wait here. It has been madness my coming. I must go at once. As for Lord Darlington—Oh! here he is! What shall I do? What can I say to him? Will he let me go away at all? I have heard that men are brutal, horrible. . . . Oh! [*Hides her face in her hands.*]

[*Enters Mrs. Erlynne L.*]

Mrs. Erl. Lady Windermere! [*Lady Windermere starts and looks up. Then recoils in contempt.*] Thank Heaven I am in time. You must go back to your husband's house immediately.

Lady Win. Must?

Mrs. Erl. [*Authoritatively.*] Yes, you must! There is not a second to be lost. Lord Darlington may return at any moment.

Lady Win. Don't come near me!

Mrs. Erl. Oh! You are on the brink of ruin; you are on the brink of a hideous precipice. You must leave this place at once, my carriage is waiting at the corner of the street. You must come with me and drive straight home.

[*Lady Windermere throws off her cloak and flings it on the sofa.*]

What are you doing?

Lady Win. Mrs. Erlynne—if you had not come here, I would have gone back. But now that I see you, I feel that nothing in the whole world would induce me to live under the same roof as Lord Windermere. You fill me with horror. There is something about you that stirs the wildest rage within me. And I know why you are here. My husband sent you to lure me back that I might serve as a blind to whatever relations exist between you and him.

Mrs. Erl. Oh! You don't think that—you can't.

Lady Win. Go back to my husband, Mrs. Erlynne. He belongs to you and not to me. I suppose he is afraid of a scandal. Men are such cowards. They outrage every law of the world, and are afraid of the world's tongue. But he had better prepare himself. He shall have a scandal. He shall have the worst scandal there has been in London for years. He shall see his name in every vile paper, mine on every hideous placard.

MRS. ERL. No—no——

LADY WIN. Yes! he shall. Had he come himself, I admit I would have gone back to the life of degradation you and he had prepared for me—I was going back—but to stay himself at home, and to send you as his messenger—oh! it was infamous—infamous.

MRS. ERL. [*C.*] Lady Windermere, you wrong me horribly—you wrong your husband horribly. He doesn't know you are here—he thinks you are safe in your own house. He thinks you are asleep in your own room. He never read the mad letter you wrote to him.

LADY WIN. [*R.*] Never read it!

MRS. ERL. No—he knows nothing about it.

LADY WIN. How simple you think me! [*Going to her.*] You are lying to me!

MRS. ERL. [*Restraining herself.*] I am not. I am telling you the truth.

LADY WIN. If my husband didn't read my letter, how is it that you are here? Who told you I had left the house you were shameless enough to enter? Who told you where I had gone to? My husband told you and sent you to decoy me back. [*Crosses L.*]

MRS. ERL. [*R. C.*] Your husband has never seen the letter. I—saw it, I opened it. I—read it.

LADY WIN. [*Turning to her.*] You opened a letter of mine to my husband. You wouldn't dare!

MRS. ERL. Dare! Oh! to save you from the abyss into which you are falling, there is nothing in the world I would not dare, nothing in the whole world. Here is the letter. Your husband has never read it. He never shall read it. [*Going to fire-place.*] It should never have been written. [*Tears it and throws it into the fire.*]

LADY WIN. [*With infinite contempt in her voice and look.*] How do I know that was my letter after all? You seem to think the commonest device can take me in!

MRS. ERL. Oh! why do you disbelieve everything I tell you? What object do you think I have in coming here, except to save you from utter ruin, to save you from the consequences of a hideous mistake? That letter that is burning now *was* your letter. I swear it to you!

LADY WIN. [*Slowly.*] You took good care to burn it before I had examined it. I cannot trust you. You, whose whole life is a lie, how could you speak the truth about anything? [*Sits down.*]

MRS. ERL. [*Hurriedly.*] Think as you like about me—say what you choose against me, but go back, go back to the husband you love.

LADY WIN. [*Sullenly.*] I do *not* love him!

MRS. ERL. You do, and you know that he loves you.

LADY WIN. He does not understand what love is. He understands it as little as you do—but I see what you want. It would be a great advantage for you to get me back. Dear Heaven! what a life I would have then! Living at the mercy of a woman who has neither mercy nor pity in her, a woman whom it is an infamy to meet, a degradation to know, a vile woman, a woman who comes between husband and wife!

Mrs. Erl. [*With a gesture of despair.*] Lady Windermere, Lady Windermere, don't say such terrible things. You don't know how terrible they are, how terrible and how unjust. Listen, you must listen! Only go back to your husband, and I promise you never to communicate with him again on any pretext—never to see him—never to have anything to do with his life or yours. The money that he gave me, he gave me not through love, but through hatred, not in worship, but in contempt. The hold I have over him——

Lady Win. [*Rising.*] Ah! you admit you have a hold!

Mrs. Erl. Yes, and I will tell you what it is. It is his love for you, Lady Windermere.

Lady Win. You expect me to believe that?

Mrs. Erl. You must believe it! It is true. It is his love for you that has made him submit to—oh! call it what you like, tyranny, threats, anything you choose. But it is his love for you. His desire to spare you—shame, yes, shame and disgrace.

Lady Win. What do you mean? You are insolent! What have I to do with you?

Mrs. Erl. [*Humbly.*] Nothing. I know it—but I tell you that your husband loves you—that you may never meet with such love again in your whole life—that such love you will never meet—and that if you throw it away, the day may come when you will starve for love, and it will not be given to you, beg for love and it will be denied you—Oh! Arthur loves you!

Lady Win. Arthur? And you tell me there is nothing between you?

Mrs. Erl. Lady Windermere, before Heaven your husband is guiltless of all offense towards you. And I—I tell you that had it ever occurred to me that such a monstrous suspicion would have entered your mind, I would have died rather than have crossed your life or his—oh! died, gladly died!

[*Moves away to sofa R.*]

Lady Win. You talk as if you had a heart. Women like you have no hearts. Heart is not in you. You are bought and sold. [*Sits L. C.*]

Mrs. Erl. [*Starts, with a gesture of pain. Then restrains herself, and comes over to where Lady Windermere is sitting. As she speaks, she stretches out her hands towards her, but does not dare to touch her.*] Believe what you choose about me. I am not worth a moment's sorrow. But don't spoil your beautiful young life on my account! You don't know what may be in store for you, unless you leave this house at once. You don't know what it is to fall into the pit, to be despised, mocked, abandoned, sneered at—to be an outcast! to find the door shut against one, to have to creep in by hideous byways, afraid every moment lest the mask should be stripped from one's face, and all the while to hear the laughter, the horrible laughter of the world, a thing more tragic than all the tears the world has ever shed. You don't know what it is. One pays for one's sin, and then one pays again, and all one's life one pays. You must never know that. As for me, if suffering be an expiation, then at this moment I have expiated all my faults, whatever they have been; for to-night you have made a heart in one who had it not, made it and broken it. But let that pass. I may have wrecked my own life, but I will not let you wreck yours. You—why, you are a mere girl, you would be lost. You haven't got the kind of brains that enables a woman to get back. You have neither the wit nor the courage. You couldn't stand dishonour. No! Go back, Lady Windermere, to the husband who loves you, whom you love. You have a child, Lady Windermere. Go back to that child who even now, in pain or in joy, may be calling to you. [*Lady Windermere rises.*] God gave you that child. He will require from you that you make his life fine, that you watch over him. What answer will you make to God if his life is ruined through you? Back to your house, Lady Windermere—your husband loves you. He has never swerved for a moment from the love he bears you. But even if he had a thousand loves, you must stay with your child. If he was harsh to you, you must stay with your child. If he ill-treated you, you must stay with your child. If he abandoned you, your place is with your child.

[*Lady Windermere bursts into tears and buries her face in her hands.*]

[*Rushing to her.*] Lady Windermere!

LADY WIN. [*Holding out her hands to her, helplessly, as a child might do.*] Take me home. Take me home.

MRS. ERL. [*Is about to embrace her. Then restrains herself. There is a look of wonderful joy in her face.*] Come! Where is your cloak? [*Getting it from sofa.*] Here. Put it on. Come at once!

[*They go to the door.*]

LADY WIN. Stop! Don't you hear voices?

MRS. ERL. No, no! There is no one!

LADY WIN. Yes, there is! Listen! Oh! that is my husband's voice! He is coming in! Save me! Oh, it's some plot! You have sent for him.

[*Voices outside.*]

MRS. ERL. Silence! I am here to save you if I can. But I fear it is too late! There! [*Points to the curtain across the window.*] The first chance you have, slip out, if you ever get a chance!

LADY WIN. But you!

MRS. ERL. Oh! never mind me. I'll face them.

[*Lady Windermere hides herself behind the curtain.*]

LORD AUG. [*Outside.*] Nonsense, dear Windermere, you must not leave me!

MRS. ERL. Lord Augustus! Then it is I who am lost! [*Hesitates for a moment, then looks round and sees door, R., and exit through it.*]

[*Enter Lord Darlington, Mr. Dumby, Lord Windermere, Lord Augustus Lorton, and Mr. Cecil Graham.*]

DUM. What a nuisance their turning us out of the club at this hour! It's only two o'clock. [*Sinks into a chair.*] The lively part of the evening is only just beginning. [*Yawns and closes his eyes.*]

LORD WIN. It is very good of you, Lord Darlington, allowing Augustus to force our company on you, but I'm afraid I can't stay long.

LORD DAR. Really! I am so sorry! You'll take a cigar, won't you?

LORD WIN. Thanks! [*Sits down.*]

LORD AUG. [*To Lord Windermere.*] My dear boy, you must not dream of going. I have a great deal to talk to you about, of demmed importance, too. [*Sits down with him at L. table.*]

CEC. Oh! We all know what that is! Tuppy can't talk about anything but Mrs. Erlynne!

LORD WIN. Well, that is no business of yours, is it, Cecil?

CEC. None. That is why it interests me. My own business always bores me to death. I prefer other people's.

LORD DAR. Have something to drink, you fellows. Cecil, you'll have a whisky and soda?

CEC. Thanks. [*Goes to the table with Lord Darlington.*] Mrs. Erlynne looked very handsome to-night, didn't she?

LORD DAR. I am not one of her admirers.

CEC. I usen't to be, but I am now. Why! she actually made me introduce her to poor dear Aunt Caroline. I believe she is going to lunch there.

LORD DAR. [*In surprise.*] No?

CEC. She is, really.

LORD DAR. Excuse me, you fellows. I'm going away to-morrow. And I have to write a few letters. [*Goes to writing table and sits down.*]

DUM. Clever woman, Mrs. Erlynne.

CEC. Hallo, Dumby! I thought you were asleep.

DUM. I am, I usually am!

LORD AUG. A very clever woman. Knows perfectly well what a demmed fool I am—knows it as well as I do myself.

[*Cecil Graham comes towards him laughing.*] Ah! you may laugh, my boy, but it is a great thing to come across a woman who thoroughly understands one.

DUM. It is an awfully dangerous thing. They always end by marrying one.

CEC. But I thought, Tuppy, you were never going to see her again. Yes! you told me so yesterday evening at the club. You said you'd heard—[*Whispering to him.*]

LORD AUG. Oh, she's explained that.

CEC. And the Wiesbaden affair?

LORD AUG. She's explained that too.

DUM. And her income, Tuppy? Has she explained that?

LORD AUG. [*In a very serious voice.*] She's going to explain that to-morrow.

[*Cecil Graham goes back to C. table.*]

DUM. Awfully commercial, women now-a-days. Our grandmothers threw their caps over the mills of course, but, by Jove, their granddaughters only throw their caps over mills that can raise the wind for them.

LORD AUG. You want to make her out a wicked woman. She is not!

CEC. Oh! Wicked women bother one. Good women bore one. That is the only difference between them.

LORD AUG. [*Puffing a cigar.*] Mrs. Erlynne has a future before her.

DUM. Mrs. Erlynne has a past before her.

LORD AUG. I prefer women with a past. They're always so demmed amusing to talk to.

CEC. Well, you'll have lots of topics of conversation with *her*, Tuppy. [*Rising and going to him.*]

LORD AUG. You're getting annoying, dear boy; you're getting demmed annoying.

CEC. [*Puts his hands on his shoulders.*] Now, Tuppy, you've lost your figure and you've lost your character. Don't lose your temper; you have only got one.

LORD AUG. My dear boy, if I wasn't the most good-natured man in London——

CEC. We'd treat you with more respect, wouldn't we, Tuppy? [*Strolls away.*]

DUM. The youth of the present day are quite monstrous. They have absolutely no respect for dyed hair. [*Lord Augustus looks round angrily.*]

CEC. Mrs. Erlynne has a very great respect for dear Tuppy.

DUM. Then Mrs. Erlynne sets an admirable example to the rest of her sex. It is perfectly brutal the way most women now-a-days behave to men who are not their husbands.

LORD WIN. Dumby, you are ridiculous, and Cecil, you let your tongue run away with you. You must leave Mrs. Erlynne alone. You don't really know anything about her, and you're always talking scandal against her.

CEC. [*Coming towards him L. C.*] My dear Arthur, *I* never talk scandal. *I* only talk gossip.

LORD WIN. What is the difference between scandal and gossip?

CEC. Oh! gossip is charming! History is merely gossip. . . . But scandal is gossip made tedious by morality. Now I never moralize. A man who moralises is usually a hypocrite, and a woman who moralises is invariably plain. There is nothing in the whole world so unbecoming to a man as a Nonconformist conscience. And most women know it, I'm glad to say.

LORD AUG. Just my sentiments, dear boy, just my sentiments.

CEC. Sorry to hear it, Tuppy; whenever people agree with me, I always feel I must be wrong.

LORD AUG. My dear boy, when I was your age——

CEC. But you never were, Tuppy, and you never will be. [*Goes up C.*] I say, Darlington, let us have some cards. You'll play, Arthur, won't you?

LORD WIN. No, thanks, Cecil.

DUM. [*With a sigh.*] Good heavens! how marriage ruins a man! It's as demoralising as cigarettes, and far more expensive.

CEC. You'll play, of course, Tuppy?

LORD AUG. [*Pouring himself out a brandy and soda at table.*] Can't, dear boy. Promised Mrs. Erlynne never to play or drink again.

CEC. Now, my dear Tuppy, don't be led astray into the paths of virtue. Reformed, you would be perfectly tedious. That is the worst of women. They always want one to be good. And if we are good, when they meet us, they don't love us at all. They like to find us quite irretrievably bad, and to leave us quite unattractively good.

LORD DAR. [*Rising from R. table, where he has been writing letters.*] They always do find us bad!

DUM. I don't think we are bad. I think we are all good except Tuppy.

LORD DAR. No, we are all in the gutter, but some of us are looking at the stars. [*Sits down at C. table.*]

DUM. We are all in the gutter, but some of us are looking at the stars? Upon my word, you are very romantic to-night, Darlington.

CEC. Too romantic! You must be in love. Who is the girl?

LORD DAR. The woman I love is not free, or thinks she isn't. [*Glances instinctively at Lord Windermere while he speaks.*]

CEC. A married woman, then! Well, there's nothing in the world like the devotion of a married woman. It's a thing no married man knows anything about.

LORD DAR. Oh! she doesn't love me. She is a good woman. She is the only good woman I have ever met in my life.

CEC. The only good woman you have ever met in your life?

LORD DAR. Yes!

CEC. [*Lighting a cigarette.*] Well, you are a lucky fellow! Why, I have met hundreds of good women. I never seem to meet any but good women. The world is perfectly packed with good women. To know them is a middle-class education.

LORD DAR. This woman has purity and innocence. She has everything we men have lost.

CEC. My dear fellow, what on earth should we men do going about with purity and innocence? A carefully thought-out buttonhole is much more effective.

DUM. She doesn't really love you then?

LORD DAR. No, she does not!

DUM. I congratulate you, my dear fellow. In this world there are only two tragedies. One is not getting what one wants, and the other is getting it. The last is much the worst, the last is a real tragedy! But I am interested to hear she does not love you. How long could you love a woman who didn't love you, Cecil?

CEC. A woman who didn't love me? Oh, all my life!

DUM. So could I. But it's so difficult to meet one.

LORD DAR. How can you be so conceited, Dumby?

DUM. I didn't say it as a matter of conceit. I said it as a matter of regret. I have been wildly, madly adored. I am sorry I have. It has been an immense nuisance. I should like to be allowed a little time to myself, now and then.

LORD AUG. [*Looking round.*] Time to educate yourself, I suppose.

DUM. No, time to forget all I have learned. That is much more important, dear Tuppy. [*Lord Augustus moves uneasily in his chair.*]

LORD DAR. What cynics you fellows are!

CEC. What is a cynic? [*Sitting on the back of the sofa.*]

LORD DAR. A man who knows the price of everything, and the value of nothing.

CEC. And a sentimentalist, my dear Darlington, is a man who sees an absurd value in everything, and doesn't know the market price of any single thing.

LORD DAR. You always amuse me, Cecil. You talk as if you were a man of experience.

CEC. I am. [*Moves up to front of fireplace.*]

LORD DAR. You are far too young!

CEC. That is a great error. Experience is a question of instinct about life. I have got it. Tuppy hasn't. Experience is the name Tuppy gives to his mistakes. That is all. [*Lord Augustus looks round indignantly.*]

DUM. Experience is the name everyone gives to their mistakes.

CEC. [*Standing with his back to fireplace.*] One shouldn't commit any. [*Sees Lady Windermere's fan on sofa.*]

DUM. Life would be very dull without them.

CEC. Of course you are quite faithful to this woman you are in love with, Darlington, to this good woman?

LORD DAR. Cecil, if one really loves a woman, all other women in the world become absolutely meaningless to one. Love changes one–I am changed.

CEC. Dear me! How very interesting! Tuppy, I want to talk to you. [*Lord Augustus takes no notice.*]

DUM. It's no use talking to Tuppy. You might just as well talk to a brick wall.

CEC. But I like talking to a brick wall–it's the only thing in the world that never contradicts me! Tuppy!

LORD AUG. Well, what is it? What is it? [*Rising and going over to Cecil Graham.*]

CEC. Come over here. I want you particularly. [*Aside.*] Darlington has been moralising and talking about the purity of love, and that sort of thing, and he has got some woman in his rooms all the time.

LORD AUG. No, really! really!

CEC. [*In a low voice.*] Yes, here is her fan. [*Points to her fan.*]

LORD AUG. [*Chuckling.*] By Jove! By Jove!

LORD WIN. [*Up by door.*] I am really off now, Lord Darlington. I am sorry you are leaving England so soon. Pray call on us when you come back! My wife and I will be charmed to see you!

LORD DAR. [*Up stage with Lord Windermere.*] I am afraid I shall be away for many years. Good-night!

CEC. Arthur!

LORD WIN. What?

CEC. I want to speak to you for a moment. No, do come!

LORD WIN. [*Putting on his coat.*] I can't–I'm off!

CEC. It is something very particular. It will interest you enormously.

LORD WIN. [*Smiling.*] It is some of your nonsense, Cecil.

CEC. It isn't! It isn't really!

LORD AUG. [*Going to him.*] My dear fellow, you mustn't go yet. I have a lot to talk to you about. And Cecil has something to show you.

LORD WIN. [*Walking over.*] Well, what is it?

CEC. Darlington has got a woman here in his rooms. Here is her fan. Amusing, isn't it? [*A pause.*]

LORD WIN. Good God! [*Seizes the fan—Dumby rises.*]

CEC. What is the matter?

LORD WIN. Lord Darlington!

LORD DAR. [*Turning round.*] Yes!

LORD WIN. What is my wife's fan doing here in your rooms? Hands off, Cecil. Don't touch me.

LORD DAR. Your wife's fan?

LORD WIN. Yes, here it is!

LORD DAR. [*Walking towards him.*] I don't know!

LORD WIN. You must know. I demand an explanation. Don't hold me, you fool. [*To Cecil Graham.*]

LORD DAR. [*Aside.*] She is here after all!

LORD WIN. Speak, sir! Why is my wife's fan here? Answer me! By God! I'll search your rooms and if my wife's here, I'll——[*Moves.*]

LORD DAR. You shall not search my rooms. You have no right to do so. I forbid you!

LORD WIN. You scoundrel! I'll not leave your room till I have searched every corner of it! What moves behind that curtain? [*Rushes towards the curtain C.*]

MRS. ERL. [*Enters behind R.*] Lord Windermere!

LORD WIN. Mrs. Erlynne!

[*Every one starts and turns round. Lady Windermere slips out from behind the curtain and glides from the room L.*]

MRS. ERL. I am afraid I took your wife's fan in mistake for my own when I was leaving your house to-night. I am so sorry. [*Takes fan from him. Lord Windermere looks at her in contempt. Lord Darlington in mingled astonishment and anger. Lord Augustus turns away. The other men smile at each other.*]

ACT-DROP.

FOURTH ACT

SCENE—*Same as in Act I.*

LADY WIN. [*Lying on sofa.*] How can I tell him? I can't tell him. It would kill me. I wonder what happened after I escaped from that horrible room. Perhaps she told them the true reason of her being there, and the real meaning of that—fatal fan of mine. Oh, if he knows—how can I look him in the face again? He would never forgive me. How securely one thinks one lives—out of reach of temptation, sin, folly. And then suddenly—Oh! Life is terrible. It rules us, we do not rule it.

[*Enter Rosalie R.*]

ROS. Did your ladyship ring for me?

LADY WIN. Yes. Have you found out at what time Lord Windermere came in last night?

Ros. His lordship did not come in till five o'clock.

Lady Win. Five o'clock? He knocked at my door this morning, didn't he?

Ros. Yes, my lady—at half-past nine. I told him your ladyship was not awake yet.

Lady Win. Did he say anything?

Ros. Something about your ladyship's fan. I didn't quite catch what his lordship said. Has the fan been lost, my lady? I can't find it, and Parker says it was not left in any of the rooms. He has looked in all of them and on the terrace as well.

Lady Win. It doesn't matter. Tell Parker not to trouble. That will do.

[*Exit Rosalie.*]

Lady Win. [*Rising.*] She is sure to tell him. I can fancy a person doing a wonderful act of self-sacrifice, doing it spontaneously, recklessly, nobly—and afterwards finding out that it costs too much. Why should she hesitate between her ruin and mine? . . . How strange! I would have publicly disgraced her in my own house. She accepts public disgrace in the house of another to save me. . . . There is a bitter irony in things, a bitter irony in the way we talk of good and bad women. . . . Oh, what a lesson! and what a pity that in life we only get our lessons when they are of no use to us! For even if she doesn't tell, I must. Oh! the shame of it, the shame of it. To tell it is to live through it all again. Actions are the first tragedy in life, words are the second. Words are perhaps the worst. Words are merciless. . . . Oh! [*Starts as Lord Windermere enters.*]

Lord Win. [*Kisses her.*] Margaret—how pale you look!

Lady Win. I slept very badly.

Lord Win. [*Sitting on the sofa with her.*] I am so sorry. I came in dreadfully late, and didn't like to wake you. You are crying, dear.

Lady Win. Yes, I am crying, for I have something to tell you, Arthur.

Lord Win. My dear child, you are not well. You've been doing too much. Let us go away to the country. You'll be all right at Selby. The season is almost over. There is no use staying on. Poor darling! We'll go away to-day, if you like. [*Rises.*] We can easily catch the 4:30. I'll send a wire to Fannen. [*Crosses and sits down at table to write a telegram.*]

Lady Win. Yes: let us go away to-day. No; I can't go to-day, Arthur. There is some one I must see before I leave town—some one who has been kind to me.

Lord Win. [*Rising and leaning over sofa.*] Kind to you?

Lady Win. Far more than that. [*Rises and goes to him.*] I will tell you, Arthur, but only love me, love me as you used to love me.

Lord Win. Used to? You are not thinking of that wretched woman who came here last night? [*Coming round and sitting R. of her.*] You don't still imagine—no, you couldn't.

Lady Win. I don't. I know now I was wrong and foolish.

Lord Win. It was very good of you to receive her last night—but you are never to see her again.

Lady Win. Why do you say that? [*A pause.*]

Lord Win. [*Holding her hand.*] Margaret, I thought Mrs. Erlynne was a woman more sinned against than sinning, as the phrase goes. I thought she wanted to be good, to get back into a place she had lost by a moment's folly, to lead again a decent life. I believed what she told me–I was mistaken in her. She is bad–as bad as a woman can be.

Lady Win. Arthur, Arthur, don't talk so bitterly about any woman. I don't think now that people can be divided into the good and the bad, as though they were two separate races or creations. What are called good women may have terrible things in them, mad moods of recklessness, assertion, jealousy, sin. Bad women, as they are termed, may have in them sorrow, repentance, pity, sacrifice. And I don't think Mrs. Erlynne a bad woman–I know she's not.

Lord Win. My dear child, the woman's impossible. No matter what harm she tries to do us, you must never see her again. She is inadmissable anywhere.

Lady Win. But I want to see her. I want her to come here.

Lord Win. Never!

Lady Win. She came here once as *your* guest. She must come now as *mine.* That is but fair.

Lord Win. She should never have come here.

Lady Win. [*Rising.*] It is too late, Arthur, to say that now. [*Moves away.*]

Lord Win. [*Rising.*] Margaret, if you knew where Mrs. Erlynne went last night, after she left this house, you would not sit in the same room with her. It was absolutely shameless, the whole thing .

Lady Win. Arthur, I can't bear it any longer. I must tell you. Last night——

[*Enter Parker with a tray on which lie Lady Windermere's fan and a card.*]

Par. Mrs. Erlynne has called to return your ladyship's fan which she took away by mistake last night. Mrs. Erlynne has written a message on the card.

Lady Win. Oh, ask Mrs. Erlynne to be kind enough to come up. [*Reads card.*] Say I shall be very glad to see her. [*Exit Parker.*] She wants to see me, Arthur.

Lord Win. [*Takes card and looks at it.*] Margaret, I *beg* you not to. Let me see her first, at any rate. She's a very dangerous woman. She is the most dangerous woman I know. You don't realize what you're doing.

Lady Win. It is right that I should see her.

Lord Win. My child, you may be on the brink of a great sorrow. Don't go to meet it. It is absolutely necessary that I should see her before you do.

Lady Win. Why should it be necessary?

[*Enter Parker.*]

Par. Mrs. Erlynne.

[*Enter Mrs. Erlynne.*] [*Exit Parker.*]

Mrs. Erl. How do you do, Lady Windermere? [*To Lord Windermere.*] How do you do? Do you know, Lady Windermere, I am so sorry about your fan. I can't imagine how I made such a silly mistake. Most stupid of me. And as I was driving in your direction, I thought I would take the opportunity of returning your property in person, with many apologies for my carelessness, and of bidding you good-bye.

Lady Win. Good-bye? [*Moves towards sofa with Mrs. Erlynne and sits down beside her.*] Are you going away, then, Mrs. Erlynne?

Mrs. Erl. Yes; I am going to live abroad again. The English climate doesn't suit me. My—heart is affected here, and that I don't like. I prefer living in the south. London is too full of fogs and—and serious people, Lord Windermere. Whether the fogs produce the serious people or whether the serious people produce the fogs, I don't know, but the whole thing rather gets on my nerves, and so I'm leaving this afternoon by the Club Train.

Lady Win. This afternoon? But I wanted so much to come and see you.

Mrs. Erl. How kind of you! But I am afraid I have to go.

Lady Win. Shall I never see you again, Mrs. Erlynne?

Mrs. Erl. I am afraid not. Our lives lie too far apart. But there is a little thing I would like you to do for me. I want a photograph of you, Lady Windermere—would you give me one? You don't know how gratified I should be.

Lady Win. Oh, with pleasure. There is one on that table. I'll show it to you. [*Goes across to the table.*]

Lord Win. [*Coming up to Mrs. Erlynne and speaking in a low voice.*] It is monstrous your intruding yourself here after your conduct last night.

Mrs. Erl. [*With an amused smile.*] My dear Windermere, manners before morals!

Lady Win. [*Returning.*] I'm afraid it is very flattering—I am not so pretty as that. [*Showing photograph.*]

Mrs. Erl. You are much prettier. But haven't you got one of yourself with your little boy?

Lady Win. I have. Would you prefer one of those?

Mr. Erl. Yes.

Lady Win. I'll go and get it for you, if you'll excuse me for a moment. I have one upstairs.

Mrs. Erl. So sorry, Lady Windermere, to give you so much trouble.

Lady Win. [*Moves to door R.*] No trouble at all, Mrs. Erlynne.

Mrs. Erl. Thanks so much. [*Exit Lady Windermere R.*] You seem rather out of temper this morning, Windermere. Why should you be? Margaret and I get on charmingly together.

Lord Win. I can't bear to see you with her. Besides, you have not told me the truth, Mrs. Erlynne.

Mrs. Erl. I have not told *her* the truth, you mean.

Lord Win. [*Standing C.*] I sometimes wish you had. I should have been spared then the misery, the anxiety, the annoyance of the last six months. But rather than my wife should know—that the mother whom she was taught to consider as dead, the mother whom she has mourned as dead, is living—a divorced woman going about under an assumed name, a bad woman preying upon life, as I know you now to be—rather than that, I was ready to supply you with money to pay bill after bill, extravagance after extravagance, to risk what occurred yesterday, the first quarrel I have ever had with my wife. You don't understand what that means to me. How could you? But I tell you that the only bitter words that ever came from those sweet lips of hers were on your account, and I hate to see you next to her. You sully the innocence that is in her. [*Moves L. C.*] And then I used to think that with all your faults you were frank and honest. You are not.

MRS. ERL. Why do you say that?

LORD WIN. You made me get you an invitation to my wife's ball.

MRS. ERL. For my daughter's ball—yes.

LORD WIN. You came, and within an hour of your leaving the house, you are found in a man's rooms—you are disgraced before every one. [*Goes up stage C.*]

MRS. ERL. Yes.

LORD WIN. [*Turning round on her.*] Therefore I have a right to look upon you as what you are—a worthless, vicious woman. I have the right to tell you never to enter this house, never to attempt to come near my wife——

MRS. ERL. [*Coldly.*] My daughter, you mean.

LORD WIN. You have no right to claim her as your daughter. You left her, abandoned her, when she was but a child in the cradle, abandoned her for your lover, who abandoned you in turn.

MRS. ERL. [*Rising.*] Do you count that to his credit, Lord Windermere—or to mine?

LORD WIN. To his, now that I know you.

MRS. ERL. Take care—you had better be careful.

LORD WIN. Oh, I am not going to mince words for you. I know you thoroughly.

MRS. ERL. [*Looking steadily at him.*] I question that.

LORD WIN. I *do* know you. For twenty years of your life you lived without your child, without a thought of your child. One day you read in the papers that she had married a rich man. You saw your hideous chance. You knew that to spare her the ignominy of learning that a woman like you was her mother, I would endure anything. You began your blackmailing.

MRS. ERL. [*Shrugging her shoulders.*] Don't use ugly words, Windermere. They are vulgar. I saw my chance, it is true, and took it.

LORD WIN. Yes, you took it—and spoiled it all last night, by being found out.

MRS. ERL. [*With a strange smile.*] You are quite right, I spoiled it all last night.

LORD WIN. And as for your blunder in taking my wife's fan from her, and then leaving it about in Darlington's rooms, it is unpardonable. I can't bear the sight of it now. I shall never let my wife use it again. The thing is soiled for me. You should have kept it, and not brought it back.

MRS. ERL. I think I *shall* keep it. [*Goes up.*] It's extremely pretty. [*Takes up fan.*] I shall ask Margaret to give it to me.

LORD WIN. I hope my wife will give it to you.

MRS. ERL. Oh, I'm sure she will have no objection.

LORD WIN. I wish at the same time she would give you a miniature she kisses every night before she prays—it's the miniature of a young, innocent-looking girl with beautiful dark hair.

MRS. ERL. Ah, yes, I remember. How long ago that seems! [*Goes to sofa and sits down.*] It was done before I was married. Dark hair and an innocent expression were the fashion then, Windermere! [*A pause.*]

Lord Win. What do you mean by coming here this morning? What is your object? [*Crossing L. C. and sitting.*]

Mrs. Erl. [*With a note of irony in her voice.*] To bid good-bye to my dear daughter, of course. [*Lord Windermere bites his underlip in anger. Mrs. Erlynne looks at him, and her voice and manner become serious. In her accents as she talks there is a note of deep tragedy. For a moment she reveals herself.*] Oh, don't imagine I am going to have a pathetic scene with her, weep on her neck and tell her who I am, and all that kind of thing. I have no ambition to play the part of a mother. Only once in my life have I known a mother's feelings. That was last night. They were terrible—they made me suffer—they made me suffer too much. For twenty years, as you say, I have lived childless—I want to live childless still. [*Hiding her feelings with a trivial laugh.*] Besides, my dear Windermere, how on earth could I pose as a mother with a grown up daughter? Margaret is twenty-one, and I have never admitted that I am more than twenty-nine, or thirty at the most. Twenty-nine when there are pink shades, thirty when there are not. So you see what difficulties it would involve. No, as far as I am concerned, let your wife cherish the memory of this dead, stainless mother. Why should I interfere with her illusions? I find it hard enough to keep my own. I lost one illusion last night. I thought I had no heart. I find I have, and a heart doesn't suit me, Windermere. Somehow it doesn't go with modern dress. It makes one look old. [*Takes up hand-mirror from table and looks into it.*] And it spoils one's career at critical moments.

Lord Win. You fill me with horror—with absolute horror.

Mrs. Erl. [*Rising.*] I suppose, Windermere, you would like me to retire into a convent or become a hospital nurse or something of that kind, as people do in silly modern novels. That is stupid of you, Arthur; in real life we don't do such things—not as long as we have any good looks left, at any rate. No—what consoles one now-a-days is not repentance, but pleasure. Repentance is quite out of date. And besides, if a woman really repents, she has to go to a bad dressmaker, otherwise no one believes in her. And nothing in the world would induce me to do that. No; I am going to pass entirely out of your two lives. My coming into them has been a mistake—I discovered that last night.

Lord Win. A fatal mistake.

Mrs. Erl. [*Smiling.*] Almost fatal.

Lord Win. I am sorry now I did not tell my wife the whole thing at once.

Mrs. Erl. I regret my bad actions. You regret your good ones—that is the difference between us.

Lord Win. I don't trust you. I *will* tell my wife. It's better for her to know, and from me. It will cause her infinite pain—it will humiliate her terribly, but it's right that she should know.

Mrs. Erl. You propose to tell her?

Lord Win. I am going to tell her.

Mrs. Erl. [*Going up to him*] If you do, I will make my name so infamous that it will mar every moment of her life. It will ruin her and make her wretched. If you dare to tell her, there is no depth of degradation I will not sink to, no pit of shame I will not enter. You shall not tell her—I forbid you.

LORD WIN. Why?

MRS. ERL. [*After a pause.*] If I said to you that I cared for her, perhaps loved her even—you would sneer at me, wouldn't you?

LORD WIN. I should feel it was not true. A mother's love means devotion, unselfishness, sacrifice. What could you know of such things?

MRS. ERL. You are right. What could I know of such things? Don't let us talk any more about *it;* as for telling my daughter who I am, that I do not allow. It is my secret, it is not yours. If I make up my mind to tell her, and I think I will, I shall tell her before I leave this house—if not, I shall never tell her.

LORD WIN. [*Angrily.*] Then let me beg of you to leave our house at once. I will make your excuses to Margaret.

[*Enter Lady Windermere R. She goes over to Mrs. Erlynne with the photograph in her hand. Lord Windermere moves to back of sofa, and anxiously watches Mrs. Erlynne as the scene progresses.*]

LADY WIN. I am so sorry, Mrs. Erlynne, to have kept you waiting. I couldn't find the photograph anywhere. At last I discovered it in my husband's dressing-room—he had stolen it.

MRS. ERL. [*Takes the photograph from her and looks at it.*] I am not surprised—it is charming. [*Goes over to sofa with Lady Windermere, and sits down beside her. Looks again at the photograph.*] And so that is your little boy! What is he called?

LADY WIN. Gerard, after my dear father.

MRS. ERL. [*Laying the photograph down.*] Really?

LADY WIN. Yes. If it had been a girl, I would have called it after my mother. My mother had the same name as myself, Margaret.

MRS. ERL. My name is Margaret, too.

LADY WIN. Indeed!

MRS. ERL. Yes. [*Pause.*] You are devoted to your mother's memory, Lady Windermere, your husband tells me.

LADY WIN. We all have ideals in life. At least we all should have. Mine is my mother.

MRS. ERL. Ideals are dangerous things. Realities are better. They wound, but they are better.

LADY WIN. [*Shaking her head.*] If I lost my ideals, I should lose everything.

MRS. ERL. Everything?

LADY WIN. Yes. [*Pause.*]

MRS. ERL. Did your father often speak to you of your mother?

LADY WIN. No, it gave him too much pain. He told me how my mother had died a few months after I was born. His eyes filled with tears as he spoke. Then he begged me never to mention her name to him again. It made him suffer even to hear it. My father—my father really died of a broken heart. His was the most ruined life I know.

MRS. ERL. [*Rising.*] I am afraid I must go now, Lady Windermere.

LADY WIN. [*Rising.*] Oh no, don't.

MRS. ERL. I think I had better. My carriage must have come back by this time. I sent it to Lady Jedburgh's with a note.

LADY WIN. Arthur, would you mind seeing if Mrs. Erlynne's carriage has come back?

MRS. ERL. Pray don't trouble Lord Windermere, Lady Windermere.

LADY WIN. Yes, Arthur, do go, please.

[*Lord Windermere hesitates for a moment and looks at Mrs. Erlynne. She remains quite impassive. He leaves the room.*]

[*To Mrs. Erlynne.*] Oh! What am I to say to you? You saved me last night! [*Goes towards her.*]

MRS. ERL. Hush—don't speak of it.

LADY WIN. I must speak of it. I can't let you think that I am going to accept this sacrifice. I am not. It is too great. I am going to tell my husband everything. It is my duty.

MRS. ERL. It is not your duty—at least you have duties to others besides him. You say you owe me something?

LADY WIN. I owe you everything.

MRS. ERL. Then pay your debt by silence. That is the only way in which it can be paid. Don't spoil the one good thing I have done in my life by telling it to anyone. Promise me that what passed last night will remain a secret between us. You must not bring misery into your husband's life. Why spoil his love? You must not spoil it. Love is easily killed. Oh, how easily love is killed! Pledge me your word, Lady Windermere, that you will *never* tell him. I insist upon it.

LADY WIN. [*With bowed head.*] It is your will, not mine.

MRS. ERL. Yes, it is my will. And never forget your child—I like to think of you as a mother. I like you to think of yourself as one.

LADY WIN. [*Looking up.*] I always will now. Only once in my life I have forgotten my own mother—that was last night. Oh, if I had remembered her, I should not have been so foolish, so wicked.

MRS. ERL. [*With a slight shudder.*] Hush, last night is quite over.

[*Enter Lord Windermere.*]

LORD WIN. Your carriage has not come back yet, Mrs. Erlynne.

MRS. ERL. It makes no matter. I'll take a hansom. There is nothing in the world so respectable as a good Shrewsbury and Talbot. And now, dear Lady Windermere, I am afraid it is really good-bye. [*Moves up C.*] Oh, I remember. You'll think me absurd, but, do you know, I've taken a great fancy to this fan that I was silly enough to run away with last night from your ball. Now, I wonder would you give it to me? Lord Windermere says you may. I know it is his present.

LADY WIN. Oh, certainly, if it will give you any pleasure. But it has my name on it. It has "Margaret" on it.

MRS. ERL. But we have the same Christian name.

LADY WIN. Oh, I forgot. Of course, do have it. What a wonderful chance our names being the same!

MRS. ERL. Quite wonderful. Thanks—it will always remind me of you. [*Shakes hands with her.*]

[*Enter Parker.*]

PAR. Lord Augustus Lorton. Mrs. Erlynne's carriage has come.

[*Enter Lord Augustus.*]

LORD AUG. Good morning, dear boy. Good morning, Lady Windermere. [*Sees Mrs. Erlynne.*] Mrs. Erlynne!

MRS. ERL. How do you do, Lord Augustus? Are you quite well this morning?

LORD AUG. [*Coldly.*] Quite well, thank you, Mrs Erlynne.

MRS. ERL. You don't look at all well, Lord Augustus. You stop up too late—it is so bad for you. You really should take more care of yourself. Good-bye, Lord Windermere. [*Goes towards door with a bow to Lord Augustus. Suddenly smiles, and looks back at him.*] Lord Augustus! Won't you see me to my carriage? You might carry the fan.

LORD WIN. Allow me!

MRS. ERL. No, I want Lord Augustus. I have a special message for the dear Duchess. Won't you carry the fan, Lord Augustus?

LORD AUG. If you really desire it, Mrs. Erlynne.

MRS. ERL. [*Laughing.*] Of course I do. You'll carry it so gracefully. You would carry off anything gracefully, dear Lord Augustus.

[*When she reaches the door she looks back for a moment at Lady Windermere. Their eyes meet. Then she turns, and exit C., followed by Lord Augustus.*]

LADY WIN. You will never speak against Mrs. Erlynne again, Arthur, will you?

LORD WIN. [*Gravely.*] She is better than one thought her.

LADY WIN. She is better than I am.

LORD WIN. [*Smiling as he strokes her hair.*] Child, you and she belong to different worlds. Into your world evil has never entered.

LADY WIN. Don't say that, Arthur. There is the same world for all of us, and good and evil, sin and innocence, go through it hand in hand. To shut one's eyes to half of life that one may live securely is as though one blinded oneself that one might walk with more safety in a land of pit and precipice.

LORD WIN. [*Moves down with her.*] Darling, why do you say that?

LADY WIN. [*Sits on sofa.*] Because I, who had shut my eyes to life, came to the brink. And one who had separated us——

LORD WIN. We were never parted.

LADY WIN. We never must be again. Oh, Arthur, don't love me less, and I will trust you more. I will trust you absolutely. Let us go to Selby. In the Rose Garden at Selby, the roses are white and red.

[*Enter Lord Augustus C.*]

LORD AUG. Arthur, she has explained everything!

[*Lady Windermere looks horribly frightened. Lord Windermere starts. Lord Augustus takes Lord Windermere by the arm, and brings him to front of stage.*] My dear fellow, she has explained every demmed thing. We all wronged her immensely. It was entirely for my sake she went to Darlington's rooms—called first at club. Fact is, she wanted to put me out of suspense, and being told I had gone on, followed—naturally—frightened when she heard a lot of men coming in—retired to another room—I assure you, most gratifying to me, the whole thing. We all behaved brutally to her. She is just the woman for me. Suits me down to the ground. All the condition she makes is that we live out of England—A very good thing, too!—Demmed clubs, demmed climate, demmed cooks, demmed everything! Sick of it all.

LADY WIN. [*Frightened.*] Has Mrs Erlynne——?

LORD AUG. [*Advancing towards her with bow.*] Yes, Lady Windermere, Mrs. Erlynne has done me the honour of accepting my hand.

LORD WIN. Well, you are certainly marrying a very clever woman.

LADY WIN. [*Taking her husband's hand.*] Ah, you're marrying a very good woman.

CURTAIN.

SALOME

THE PERSONS OF THE PLAY

HEROD ANTIPAS, Tetrarch of Judæa
IOKANAAN, The Prophet
THE YOUNG SYRIAN, Captain of the Guard
TIGELLINUS, A young Roman
A CAPPADOCIAN
A NUBIAN
FIRST SOLDIER
SECOND SOLDIER
THE PAGE OF HERODIAS
JEWS, NAZARENES, ETC.
A SLAVE
NAAMAN, The Executioner
HERODIAS, Wife of the Tetrarch
SALOME, Daughter of Herodias
THE SLAVES OF SALOME

SALOME

SCENE—*A great terrace in the Palace of Herod, set about the banqueting hall. Some soldiers are leaning over the balcony. To the right there is a gigantic staircase, to the left, at the back, an old cistern surrounded by a wall of green bronze. The moon is shining very brightly.*

THE YOUNG SYR. How beautiful is the Princess Salome to-night!

THE PAGE OF HER. Look at the moon. How strange the moon seems! She is like a woman rising from the tomb. She is like a dead woman. One might fancy she was looking for dead things.

THE YOUNG SYR. She has a strange look. She is like a little princess who wears a yellow veil, and whose feet are of silver. She is like a princess who has little white doves for feet. One might fancy she was dancing.

THE PAGE OF HER. She is like a woman who is dead. She moves very slowly.

[*Noise in the banqueting-hall.*]

FIRST SOL. What an uproar! Who are those wild beasts howling?

SECOND SOL. The Jews. They are always like that. They are disputing about their religion.

FIRST SOL. Why do they dispute about their religion?

SECOND SOL. I cannot tell. They are always doing it. The Pharisees, for instance, say that there are angels, and the Sadducees declare that angels do not exist.

FIRST SOL. I think it is ridiculous to dispute about such things.

THE YOUNG SYR. How beautiful is the Princess Salome to-night!

THE PAGE OF HER. You are always looking at her. You look at her too much. It is dangerous to look at people in such fashion. Something terrible may happen.

THE YOUNG SYR. She is very beautiful to-night.

FIRST SOL. The Tetrarch has a sombre aspect.

SECOND SOL. Yes; he has a sombre aspect.

FIRST SOL. He is looking at something.

SECOND SOL. He is looking at some one.

FIRST SOL. At whom is he looking?

SECOND SOL. I cannot tell.

THE YOUNG SYR. How pale the Princess is! Never have I seen her so pale. She is like the shadow of a white rose in a mirror of silver.

THE PAGE OF HER. You must not look at her. You look too much at her.

FIRST SOL. Herodias has filled the cup of the Tetrarch.

THE CAPPA. Is that the Queen Herodias, she who wears a black mitre sewed with pearls, and whose hair is powdered with blue dust?

FIRST SOL. Yes; that is Herodias, the Tetrarch's wife.

SECOND SOL. The Tetrarch is very fond of wine. He has wine of three sorts. One which is brought from the island of Samothrace, and is purple like the cloak of Cæsar.

THE CAPPA. I have never seen Cæsar.

SECOND SOL. Another that comes from a town called Cyprus, and is as yellow as gold.

THE CAPPA. I love gold.

SECOND SOL. And the third is a wine of Sicily. That wine is as red as blood.

THE NUB. The gods of my country are very fond of blood. Twice in the year we sacrifice to them young men and maidens: fifty young men and a hundred maidens. But I am afraid that we never give them quite enough, for they are very harsh to us.

THE CAPPA. In my country there are no gods left. The Romans have driven them out. There are some who say that they have hidden themselves in the mountains, but I do not believe it. Three nights I have been on the mountains seeking them everywhere. I did not find them, and at last I called them by their names, and they did not come. I think they are dead.

First Sol. The Jews worship a God that one cannot see.

The Cappa. I cannot understand that.

First Sol. In fact they only believe in things that one cannot see.

The Cappa. That seems to me altogether ridiculous.

The Voice of Iok. After me shall come another mightier than I. I am not worthy so much as to unloose the latchet of his shoes. When he cometh the solitary places shall be glad. They shall blossom like the rose. The eyes of the blind shall see the day, and the ears of the deaf shall be opened. The sucking child shall put his hand upon the dragon's lair, he shall lead the lions by their manes.

Second Sol. Make him be silent. He is always saying ridiculous things.

First Sol. No, no. He is a holy man. He is very gentle, too. Every day when I give him to eat he thanks me.

The Cappa. Who is he?

First Sol. A prophet.

The Cappa. What is his name?

First Sol. Iokanaan.

The Cappa. Whence comes he?

First Sol. From the desert, where he fed on locusts and wild honey. He was clothed in camel's hair, and round his loins he had a leathern belt. He was very terrible to look upon. A great multitude used to follow him. He even had disciples.

The Cappa. What is he talking about?

First Sol. We can never tell. Sometimes he says thing that affright one, but it is impossible to understand what he says.

The Cappa. May one see him?

First Sol. No. The Tetrarch has forbidden it.

The Young Syr. The Princess has hidden her face behind her fan! Her little white hands are fluttering like doves that fly to their dove-cots. They are like white butterflies. They are just white butterflies.

The Page of Her. What is that to you? Why do you look at her? You must not look at her. . . . Something terrible may happen.

The Cappa. [*Pointing to the cistern.*] What a strange prison!

Second Sol. It is an old cistern.

The Cappa. An old cistern! That must be a poisonous place in which to dwell!

Second Sol. Oh no! For instance, the Tetrarch's brother, his elder brother, the first husband of Herodias the Queen, was imprisoned there for twelve years. It did not kill him. At the end of the twelve years he had to be strangled.

The Cappa. Strangled? Who dared to do that?

Second Sol. [*Pointing to the Executioner, a huge negro.*] That man yonder, Naaman.

The Cappa. He was not afraid?

SECOND SOL. Oh no! The Tetrarch sent him the ring.

THE CAPPA. What ring?

SECOND SOL. The death ring. So he was not afraid.

THE CAPPA. Yet it is a terrible thing to strangle a king.

FIRST SOL. Why? Kings have but one neck, like other folk.

THE CAPPA. I think it terrible.

THE YOUNG SYR. The Princess is getting up! She is leaving the table! She looks very troubled. Ah, she is coming this way. Yes, she is coming towards us. How pale she is! Never have I seen her so pale.

THE PAGE OF HER. Do not look at her. I pray you not to look at her.

THE YOUNG SYR. She is like a dove that has strayed. . . . She is like a narcissus trembling in the wind. . . . She is like a silver flower.

[*Enter Salome.*]

SALOME. I will not stay. I cannot stay. Why does the Tetrarch look at me all the while with his mole's eyes under his shaking eyelids? It is strange that the husband of my mother looks at me like that. I know not what it means. Of a truth I know it too well.

THE YOUNG SYR. You have left the feast, Princess?

SALOME. How sweet is the air here! I can breathe here! Within there are Jews from Jerusalem who are tearing each other in pieces over their foolish ceremonies, and barbarians who drink and drink and spill their wine on the pavement, and Greeks from Smyrna with painted eyes and painted cheeks, and frizzed hair curled in columns, and Egyptians silent and subtle, with long nails of jade and russet cloaks, and Romans brutal and coarse, with their uncouth jargon. Ah! how I loathe the Romans! They are rough and common, and they give themselves the airs of noble lords.

THE YOUNG SYR. Will you be seated, Princess?

THE PAGE OF HER. Why do you speak to her? Oh! something terrible will happen. Why do you look at her?

SALOME. How good to see the moon! She is like a little piece of money, a little silver flower. She is cold and chaste. I am sure she is a virgin. She has the beauty of a virgin. Yes, she is a virgin. She has never defiled herself. She has never abandoned herself to men, like the other goddesses.

THE VOICE OF IOK. Behold! the Lord hath come. The Son of Man is at hand. The centaurs have hidden themselves in the rivers, and the nymphs have left the rivers, and are lying beneath the leaves in the forests.

SALOME. Who was that who cried out?

SECOND SOL. The prophet, Princess.

SALOME. Ah, the prophet! He of whom the Tetrarch is afraid?

SECOND SOL. We know nothing of that, Princess. It was the prophet Iokanaan who cried out.

THE YOUNG SYR. Is it your pleasure that I bid them bring your litter, Princess? The night is fair in the garden.

SALOME. He says terrible things about my mother, does he not?

SECOND SOL. We never understand what he says, Princess.

SALOME. Yes; he says terrible things about her.

[*Enter a Slave.*]

THE SLAVE. Princess, the Tetrarch prays you to return to the feast.

SALOME. I will not return.

THE YOUNG SYR. Pardon me, Princess, but if you return not some misfortune may happen.

SALOME. Is he an old man, this prophet?

THE YOUNG SYR. Princess, it were better to return. Suffer me to lead you in.

SALOME. This prophet . . . is he an old man?

FIRST SOL. No, Princess, he is quite young.

SECOND SOL. One cannot be sure. There are those who say that he is Elias.

SALOME. Who is Elias?

SECOND SOL. A prophet of this country in bygone days, Princess.

THE SLAVE. What answer may I give Tetrarch from the Princess?

THE VOICE OF IOK. Rejoice not, O land of Palestine, because the rod of him who smote thee is broken. For from the seed of the serpent shall come a basilisk, and that which is born of it shall devour the birds.

SALOME. What a strange voice! I would speak with him.

FIRST SOL. I fear it may not be, Princess. The Tetrarch does not suffer any one to speak with him. He has even forbidden the high priest to speak with him.

SALOME. I desire to speak with him.

FIRST SOL. It is impossible, Princess.

SALOME. I will speak with him.

THE YOUNG SYR. Would it not be better to return to the banquet?

SALOME. Bring forth this prophet.

[*Exit the Slave.*]

FIRST SOL. We dare not, Princess.

SALOME. [*Approaching the cistern and looking down into it.*] How black it is, down there! It must be terrible to be in so black a hole! It is like a tomb. . . . [*To the soldiers.*] Did you not hear me? Bring out the prophet. I would look on him.

SECOND SOL. Princess, I beg you, do not require this of us.

SALOME. You are making me wait upon your pleasure.

FIRST SOL. Princess, our lives belong to you, but we cannot do what you have asked of us. And indeed, it is not of us that you should ask this thing.

SALOME. [*Looking at the young Syrian.*] Ah!

THE PAGE OF HER. Oh! what is going to happen? I am sure that something terrible will happen.

SALOME. [*Going up to the young Syrian.*] Thou wilt do this thing for me, wilt thou not, Narraboth? Thou wilt do this thing for me. I have ever been kind towards thee. Thou wilt do it for me. I would but look at him, this strange prophet. Men have talked so much of him. Often I have heard the Tetrarch talk of him. I think he is afraid of him, the Tetrarch. Art thou, even thou, also afraid of him, Narraboth?

THE YOUNG SYR. I fear him not, Princess; there is no man I fear. But the

Tetrarch has formally forbidden that any man should raise the cover of this well.

SALOME. Thou wilt do this thing for me, Narraboth, and to-morrow when I pass in my litter beneath the gateway of the idol-sellers I will let fall for thee a little flower, a little green flower.

THE YOUNG SYR. Princess, I cannot, I cannot.

SALOME. [*Smiling.*] Thou wilt do this thing for me, Narraboth. Thou knowest that thou wilt do this thing for me. And on the morrow when I shall pass in my litter by the bridge of the idol-sellers, I will look at thee through the muslin veils, I will look at thee, Narraboth, it may be I will smile at thee. Look at me, Narraboth, look at me. Ah! thou knowest that thou wilt do what I ask of thee. Thou knowest it. . . . I know that thou wilt do this thing.

THE YOUNG SYR. [*Signing to the third soldier.*] Let the prophet come forth. . . . The Princess Salome desires to see him.

SALOME. Ah!

THE PAGE OF HER. Oh! How strange the moon looks! Like the hand of a dead woman who is seeking to cover herself with a shroud.

THE YOUNG SYR. She has a strange aspect! She is like a little princess, whose eyes are eyes of amber. Through the clouds of muslin she is smiling like a little princess. [*The prophet comes out of the cistern. Salome looks at him and steps slowly back.*]

IOKANAAN. Where is he whose cup of abominations is now full? Where is he, who in a robe of silver shall one day die in the face of all the people? Bid him come forth, that he may hear the voice of him who hath cried in the waste places and in the houses of kings.

SALOME. Of whom is he speaking?

THE YOUNG SYR. No one can tell, Princess.

IOKANAAN. Where is she who saw the images of men painted on the walls, even the images of the Chaldeans painted with colours, and gave herself up unto the lust in her eyes, and sent ambassadors into the land of Chaldea?

SALOME. It is of my mother that he is speaking.

THE YOUNG SYR. Oh no, Princess.

SALOME. Yes: it is of my mother that he is speaking.

IOKANAAN. Where is she who gave herself unto the Captains of Assyria, who have baldricks on their loins, and crowns of many colours on their heads? Where is she who hath given herself to the young men of the Egyptians, who are clothed in fine linen and hyacinth, whose shields are of gold, whose helmets are of silver, whose bodies are mighty? Go, bid her rise up from the bed of her abominations, from the bed of her incestuousness, that she may hear the words of him who prepareth the way of the Lord, that she may repent her of her iniquities. Though she will not repent, but will stick fast in her abominations, go bid her come, for the fan of the Lord is in His hand.

SALOME. Ah, but he is terrible, he is terrible!

THE YOUNG SYR. Do not stay here, Princess, I beseech you.

SALOME. It is his eyes above all that are terrible. They are like black holes burned by torches in a tapestry of Tyre. They are like the black caverns where the dragons live, the black caverns of Egypt in which the dragons make their lairs. They are like the black lakes troubled by fantastic moons. . . . Do you think he will speak again?

The Young Syr. Do not stay here, Princess. I pray you do not stay here.

Salome. How wasted he is! He is like a thin ivory statue. He is like an image of silver. I am sure he is chaste, as the moon is. He is like a moon-beam, like a shaft of silver. His flesh must be very cold, cold as ivory. . . . I would look closer at him.

The Young Syr. No, no, Princess!

Salome. I must look at him closer.

The Young Syr. Princess! Princess!

Iokanaan. Who is this woman who is looking at me? I will not have her look at me. Wherefore doth she look at me, with her golden eyes, under her gilded eyelids? I know not who she is. I do not desire to know who she is. Bid her begone. It is not to her that I would speak.

Salome. I am Salome, daughter of Herodias, Princess of Judæa.

Iokanaan. Back, daughter of Babylon! Come not near the chosen of the Lord. Thy mother hath filled the earth with the wine of her iniquities, and the cry of her sinning hath come up even to the ears of God.

Salome. Speak again, Iokanaan. Thy voice is as music to mine ear.

The Young Syr. Princess! Princess! Princess!

Salome. Speak again! Speak again, Iokanaan, and tell me what I must do.

Iokanaan. Daughter of Sodom, come not near me! But cover thy face with a veil, and scatter ashes upon thine head, and get thee to the desert, and seek out the Son of Man.

Salome. Who is he, the Son of Man? Is he as beautiful as thou art, Iokanaan?

Iokanaan. Get thee behind me! I hear in the palace the beating of the wings of the angel of death.

The Young Syr. Princess! I beseech thee to go within.

Iokanaan. Angel of the Lord God, what dost thou here with thy sword? Whom seekest thou in this palace? The day of him who shall die in a robe of silver has not yet come.

Salome. Iokanaan!

Iokanaan. Who speaketh?

Salome. I am amorous of thy body, Iokanaan! Thy body is white, like the lilies of a field that the mower hath never mowed. Thy body is white like the snows that lie on the mountains of Judæa, and come down into the valleys. The roses in the garden of the Queen of Arabia are not so white as thy body. Neither the roses of the garden of the Queen of Arabia, the garden of spices of the Queen of Arabia, nor the feet of the dawn when they light on the leaves, nor the breast of the moon when she lies on the breast of the sea. . . . There is nothing in the world so white as thy body. Suffer me to touch thy body.

Iokanaan. Back! daughter of Babylon! By woman came evil into the world. Speak not to me. I will not listen to thee. I listen but to the voice of the Lord God.

HEROD. I will stay here! Manasseh, lay carpets there. Light torches. Bring forth the ivory tables, and the tables of jasper. The air here is sweet. I will drink more wine with my guests. We must show all honours to the ambassadors of Cæsar.

HERODIAS. It is not because of them that you remain.

HEROD. Yes; the air is very sweet. Come, Herodias, our guests await us. Ah! I have slipped! I have slipped in blood! It is an ill omen. It is a very ill omen. Wherefore is there blood here? . . . and this body, what does this body here? Think you I am like the King of Egypt, who gives no feast to his guests but that he shows them a corpse? Whose is it? I will not look on it.

FIRST SOL. It is our captain, sire. It is the young Syrian whom you made captain of the guard but three days gone.

HEROD. I issued no order that he should be slain.

SECOND SOL. He slew himself, sire.

HEROD. For what reason? I had made him captain of my guard!

SECOND SOL. We do not know, sire. But with his own hand he slew himself.

HEROD. That seems strange to me. I had thought it was but the Roman philosophers who slew themselves. Is it not true, Tigellinus, that the philosophers at Rome slay themselves?

TIGELL. There be some who slay themselves, sire. They are the Stoics. The Stoics are people of no cultivation. They are ridiculous people. I myself regard them as being perfectly ridiculous.

HEROD. I also. It is ridiculous to kill oneself.

TIGELL. Everybody at Rome laughs at them. The Emperor has written a satire against them. It is recited everywhere.

HEROD. Ah! he has written a satire against them? Cæsar is wonderful. He can do everything. . . . It is strange that the young Syrian has slain himself. I am sorry he has slain himself. I am very sorry. For he was fair to look upon. He was even very fair. He had very langourous eyes. I remember that I saw that he looked languorously at Salome. Truly, I thought he looked too much at her.

HERODIAS. There are others who look too much at her.

HEROD. His father was a king. I drove him from his kingdom. And of his mother, who was a queen, you made a slave, Herodias. So he was here as my guest, as it were, and for that reason I made him my captain. I am sorry he is dead. Ho! why have you left the body here? It must be taken to some other place. I will not look at it—away with it! [*They take away the body.*] It is cold here. There is a wind blowing. Is there not a wind blowing?

HERODIAS. No; there is no wind.

HEROD. I tell you there is a wind that blows. . . . And I hear in the air something that is like the beating of wings, like the beating of vast wings. Do you not hear it?

HERODIAS. I hear nothing.

HEROD. I hear it no longer. But I heard it. It was the blowing of the wind. It has passed away. But no, I hear it again. Do you not hear it? It is just like a beating of wings.

HERODIAS. I tell you there is nothing. You are ill. Let us go within.

HEROD. I am not ill. It is your daughter who is sick to death. Never have I seen her so pale.

HERODIAS. I have told you not to look at her.

HEROD. Pour me forth wine. [*Wine is brought.*] Salome, come drink a little wine with me. I have here a wine that is exquisite. Cæsar himself sent it me. Dip into it thy little red lips, that I may drain the cup.

SALOME. I am not thirsty, Tetrarch.

HEROD. You hear how she answers me, this daughter of yours?

HERODIAS. She does right. Why are you always gazing at her?

HEROD. Bring me ripe fruits. [*Fruits are brought.*] Salome, come and eat fruits with me. I love to see in a fruit the mark of thy little teeth. Bite but a little of this fruit, that I may eat what is left.

SALOME. I am not hungry, Tetrarch.

HEROD. [*To Herodias.*] You see how you have brought up this daughter of yours.

HERODIAS. My daughter and I come of a royal race. As for thee, thy father was a camel driver! He was a thief and a robber to boot!

HEROD. Thou liest!

HERODIAS. Thou knowest well that it is true.

HEROD. Salome, come and sit next to me. I will give thee the throne of thy mother.

SALOME. I am not tired, Tetrarch.

HERODIAS. You see in what regard she holds you.

HEROD. Bring me—— What is it that I desire? I forget. Ah! ah! I remember.

THE VOICE OF IOKANAAN. Behold the time is come. That which I foretold has come to pass. The day that I spake of is at hand.

HERODIAS. Bid him be silent. I will not listen to his voice. This man is for ever hurling insults against me.

HEROD. He has said nothing against you. Besides, he is a very great prophet.

HERODIAS. I do not believe in prophets. Can a man tell what will come to pass? No man knows it. Also he is for ever insulting me. But I think you are afraid of him. . . . I know well that you are afraid of him.

HEROD. I am not afraid of him. I am afraid of no man.

HERODIAS. I tell you you are afraid of him. If you are not afraid of him why do you not deliver him to the Jews who for these six months past have been clamouring for him?

A JEW. Truly, my lord, it were better to deliver him into our hands.

HEROD. Enough on this subject. I have already given you my answer. I will not deliver him into your hands. He is a holy man. He is a man who has seen God.

A JEW. That cannot be. There is no man who hath seen God since the prophet Elias. He is the last man who saw God face to face. In these days God doth not show Himself. God hideth Himself. Therefore great evils have come upon the land.

ANOTHER J. Verily, no man knoweth if Elias the prophet did indeed see God. Peradventure it was but the shadow of God that he saw.

A THIRD J. God is at no time hidden. He showeth Himself at all times and in all places. God is in what is evil even as He is in what is good.

A FOURTH J. Thou shouldst not say that. It is a very dangerous doctrine. It is a doctrine that cometh from Alexandria, where men teach the philosophy of the Greeks. And the Greeks are Gentiles. They are not even circumcised.

A FIFTH J. No man can tell how God worketh. His ways are very dark. It may be that the things which we call evil are good, and that the things which we call good are evil. There is no knowledge of anything. We can but bow our heads to His will, for God is very strong. He breaketh in pieces the strong together with the weak, for He regardeth not any man.

FIRST J. Thou speakest truly. Verily, God is terrible. He breaketh in pieces the strong and the weak as men break corn in a mortar. But as for this man, he hath never seen God. No man hath seen God since the prophet Elias.

HERODIAS. Make them be silent. They weary me.

HEROD. But I have heard it said that Iokanaan is in very truth your prophet Elias.

THE JEW. That cannot be. It is more than three hundred years since the days of the prophet Elias.

HEROD. There be some who say that this man is Elias the prophet.

A NAZ. I am sure that he is Elias the prophet.

THE JEW. Nay, but he is not Elias the prophet.

THE VOICE OF IOK. Behold the day is at hand, the day of the Lord, and I hear upon the mountains the feet of Him who shall be the Saviour of the world.

HEROD. What does that mean? The Saviour of the world?

TIGELL. It is a title that Cæsar adopts.

HEROD. But Cæsar is not coming into Judæa. Only yesterday I received letters from Rome. They contained nothing concerning this matter. And you, Tigellinus, who were at Rome during the winter, you heard nothing concerning this matter, did you?

TIGELL. Sire, I heard nothing concerning the matter. I was but explaining the title. It is one of Cæsar's titles.

HEROD. But Cæsar cannot come. He is too gouty. They say that his feet are like the feet of an elephant. Also there are reasons of state. He who leaves Rome loses Rome. He will not come. Howbeit, Cæsar is lord, he will come if such be his pleasure. Nevertheless, I think he will not come.

FIRST NAZ. It was not concerning Cæsar that the prophet spake these words, sire.

HEROD. How?—it was not concerning Cæsar?

FIRST NAZ. No, my lord.

HEROD. Concerning whom then did he speak?

FIRST NAZ. Concerning Messias, who hath come.

A JEW. Messias hath not come.

FIRST NAZ. He hath come, and everywhere he worketh miracles!

HERODIAS. Ho! ho! miracles! I do not believe in miracles. I have seen too many. [*To the Page.*] My fan.

FIRST NAZ. This Man worketh true miracles. Thus, at a marriage which took place in a little town of Galilee, a town of some importance, He changed water into wine. Certain persons who were present related it to me. Also He healed two lepers that were seated before the Gate of Capernaum simply by touching them.

SECOND NAZ. Nay; it was two blind men that he healed at Capernaum.

FIRST NAZ. Nay; they were lepers. But He hath healed blind people also, and He was seen on a mountain talking with Angels.

A SAD. Angels do not exist.

A PHAR. Angels exist, but I do not believe that this Man has talked with them.

FIRST NAZ. He was seen by a great multitude of people talking with angels.

HERODIAS. How these men weary me! They are ridiculous! They are altogether ridiculous! [*To the Page.*] Well! my fan? [*The Page gives her the fan.*] You have a dreamer's look. You must not dream. It is only sick people who dream. [*She strikes the Page with her fan.*]

SECOND NAZ. There is also the miracle of the daughter of Jairus.

FIRST NAZ. Yea, that is sure. No man can gainsay it.

HERODIAS. Those men are mad. They have looked too long on the moon. Command them to be silent.

HEROD. What is this miracle of the daughter of Jairus?

FIRST NAZ. The daughter of Jairus was dead. This Man raised her from the dead.

HEROD. How! He raises people from the dead?

FIRST NAZ. Yea, sire; He raiseth the dead.

HEROD. I do not wish Him to do that. I forbid Him to do that. I suffer no man to raise the dead. This Man must be found and told that I forbid Him to raise the dead. Where is this Man at present?

SECOND NAZ. He is in every place, my lord, but it is hard to find Him.

FIRST NAZ. It is said that He is now in Samaria.

A JEW. It is easy to see that this is not Messias, if He is in Samaria. It is not to the Samaritans that Messias shall come. The Samaritans are accursed. They bring no offerings to the Temple.

SECOND NAZ. He left Samaria a few days since. I think that at the present moment He is in the neighborhood of Jerusalem.

FIRST NAZ. No; He is not there. I have just come from Jerusalem. For two months they have had no tidings of Him.

HEROD. No matter! But let them find Him, and tell Him, thus saith Herod the King, "I will not suffer Thee to raise the dead." To change water into wine, to heal the lepers and the blind. . . . He may do these things if He will. I say nothing against these things. In truth I hold it a kindly deed to heal a leper. But no man shall raise the dead. . . . It would be terrible if the dead came back.

THE VOICE OF IOK. Ah! The wanton one! The harlot! Ah! the daughter of

Babylon with her golden eyes and her gilded eyelids! Thus saith the Lord God, Let there come up against her a multitude of men. Let the people take stones and stone her. . . .

HERODIAS. Command him to be silent!

THE VOICE OF IOK. Let the captains of the hosts pierce her with their swords, let them crush her beneath their shields.

HERODIAS. Nay, but it is infamous.

THE VOICE OF IOK. It is thus that I will wipe out all wickedness from the earth, and that all women shall learn not to imitate her abominations.

HERODIAS. You hear what he says against me? You suffer him to revile her who is your wife!

HEROD. He did not speak your name.

HERODIAS. What does that matter? You know well that it is I whom he seeks to revile. And I am your wife, am I not?

HEROD. Of a truth, dear and noble Herodias, you are my wife, and before that you were the wife of my brother.

HERODIAS. It was thou didst snatch me from his arms.

HEROD. Of a truth I was stronger than he was. . . . But let us not talk of that matter. I do not desire to talk of it. It is the cause of the terrible words that the prophet has spoken. Peradventure on account of it a misfortune will come. Let us not speak of this matter. Noble Herodias, we are not mindful of our guests. Fill thou my cup, my well-beloved. Ho! fill with wine the great goblets of silver, and the great goblets of glass. I will drink to Cæsar. There are Romans here, we must drink to Cæsar.

ALL. Cæsar! Cæsar!

HEROD. Do you not see your daughter, how pale she is?

HERODIAS. What is it to you if she be pale or not?

HEROD. Never have I seen her so pale.

HERODIAS. You must not look at her.

THE VOICE OF IOK. In that day the sun shall become black like sackcloth of hair, and the moon shall become like blood, and the stars of the heaven shall fall upon the earth like unripe figs that fall from the fig-tree, and the kings of the earth shall be afraid.

HERODIAS. Ah! ah! I should like to see that day of which he speaks, when the moon shall become like blood, and when the stars shall fall upon the earth like unripe figs. This prophet talks like a drunken man . . . but I cannot suffer the sound of his voice. I hate his voice. Command him to be silent.

HEROD. I will not. I cannot understand what it is that he saith, but it may be an omen.

HERODIAS. I do not believe in omens. He speaks like a drunken man.

HEROD. It may be he is drunk with the wine of God.

HERODIAS. What wine is that, the wine of God? From what vineyards is it gathered? In what wine-press may one find it?

HEROD. [*From this point he looks all the while at Salome.*] Tigellinus, when you were at Rome of late, did the Emperor speak with you on the subject of . . . ?

Tigell. On what subject, my lord?

Herod. On what subject? Ah! I asked you a question, did I not? I have forgotten what I would have asked you.

Herodias. You are looking again at my daughter. You must not look at her I have already said so.

Herod. You say nothing else.

Herodias. I say it again.

Herod. And that restoration of the Temple about which they have talked so much, will anything be done? They say that the veil of the Sanctuary has disappeared, do they not?

Herodias. It was thyself didst steal it. Thou speakest at random and without wit. I will not stay here. Let us go within.

Herod. Dance for me, Salome.

Herodias. I will not have her dance.

Salome. I have no desire to dance, Tetrarch.

Herod. Salome, daughter of Herodias, dance for me.

Herodias. Peace. Let her alone.

Herod. I command thee to dance, Salome.

Salome. I will not dance, Tetrarch.

Herodias. [*Laughing.*] You see how she obeys you.

Herod. What is it to me whether she dance or not? It is nought to me. To-night I am happy. I am exceeding happy. Never have I been so happy.

First Sol. The Tetrarch has a sombre look. Has he not a sombre look?

Second Sol. Yes, he has a sombre look.

Herod. Wherefore should I not be happy? Cæsar, who is lord of the world, Cæsar, who is lord of all things, loves me well. He has just sent me most precious gifts. Also he has promised me to summon to Rome the King of Cappadocia, who is mine enemy. It may be that at Rome he will crucify him, for he is able to do all things that he has a mind to do. Verily, Cæsar is lord. Therefore I do well to be happy. I am very happy, never have I been so happy. There is nothing in the world that can mar my happiness.

The Voice of Iok. He shall be seated on his throne. He shall be clothed in scarlet and purple. In his hand he shall bear a golden cup full of his blasphemies. And the angel of the Lord shall smite him. He shall be eaten of worms.

Herodias. You hear what he says about you. He says that you shall be eaten of worms.

Herod. It is not of me that he speaks. He speaks never against me. It is of the King of Cappadocia that he speaks; the King of Cappadocia who is mine enemy. It is he who shall be eaten of worms. It is not I. Never has he spoken word against me, this prophet, save that I sinned in taking to wife the wife of my brother. It may be he is right. For, of a truth, you are sterile.

Herodias. I am sterile, I? You say that, you that are ever looking at my daughter, you that would have her dance for your pleasure? You speak as a fool. I have borne a child. You have gotten no child, no, not on one of your slaves. It is you who are sterile, not I.

Herod. Peace, woman! I say that you are sterile. You have borne me no child, and the prophet says that our marriage is not a true marriage. He says that it is a marriage of incest, a marriage that will bring evils. . . . I fear he is right; I am sure that he is right. But it is not the hour to speak of these things. I would be happy at this moment. Of a truth, I am happy. There is nothing I lack.

HERODIAS. I am glad you are of so fair a humour to-night. It is not your custom. But it is late. Let us go within. Do not forget that we hunt at sunrise. All honours must be shown to Cæsar's ambassadors, must they not?

SECOND SOL. The Tetrarch has a sombre look.

FIRST SOL. Yes, he has a sombre look.

HEROD. Salome, Salome, dance for me. I pray thee dance for me. I am sad to-night. Yes, I am passing sad to-night. When I came hither I slipped in blood, which is an ill omen; also I heard in the air a beating of wings, a beating of giant wings. I cannot tell what that they mean. . . . I am sad to-night. Therefore dance for me. Dance for me, Salome, I beseech thee. If thou dancest for me thou mayest ask of me what thou wilt, and I will give it thee. Yes, dance for me, Salome, and whatsoever thou shalt ask of me I will give it thee, even unto the half of my kingdom.

SALOME. [*Rising.*] Will you indeed give me whatsoever I shall ask of you, Tetrarch?

HERODIAS. Do not dance, my daughter.

HEROD. Whatsoever thou shalt ask of me, even unto the half of my kingdom.

SALOME. You swear it, Tetrarch?

HEROD. I swear it, Salome.

HERODIAS. Do not dance, my daughter.

SALOME. By what will you swear this thing, Tetrarch?

HEROD. By my life, by my crown, by my gods. Whatsoever thou shalt desire I will give it thee, even to the half of my kingdom, if thou wilt but dance for me. O Salome, Salome, dance for me!

SALOME. You have sworn an oath, Tetrarch.

HEROD. I have sworn an oath.

HERODIAS. My daughter, do not dance.

HEROD. Even to the half of my kingdom. Thou wilt be passing fair as a queen, Salome, if it please thee to ask for the half of my kingdom. Will she not be fair as a queen? Ah! it is cold here! There is an icy wind, and I hear . . . wherefore do I hear in the air this beating of wings? Ah! one might fancy a huge black bird that hovers over the terrace. Why can I not see it, this bird? The beat of its wings is terrible. The breath of the wind of its wings is terrible. It is a chill wind. Nay, but it is not cold, it is hot. I am choking. Pour water on my hands. Give me snow to eat. Loosen my mantle. Quick! quick! loosen my mantle. Nay, but leave it. It is my garland that hurts me, my garland of roses. The flowers are like fire. They have burned my forehead. [*He tears the wreath from his head, and throws it on the table.*] Ah! I can breathe now. How red those petals are! They are like stains of blood on the cloth. That does not matter. It is not wise to find symbols in everything that one sees. It makes life too full of terrors. It were better to say that stains of blood are as lovely as rose-petals. It were better far to say that. . . . But we will not speak of this. Now I am happy. I am passing happy. Have I not the right to be happy? Your daughter is going to dance for me. Wilt thou not dance for me, Salome? Thou hast promised to dance for me.

Herodias. I will not have her dance.

Salome. I will dance for you, Tetrarch.

Herod. You hear what your daughter says. She is going to dance for me. Thou doest well to dance for me, Salome. And when thou hast danced for me, forget not to ask of me whatsoever thou hast a mind to ask. Whatsoever thou shalt desire I will give it thee, even to the half of my kingdom. I have sworn it, have I not?

Salome. Thou hast sworn it, Tetrarch.

Herod. And I have never failed of my word. I am not of those who break their oaths. I know not how to lie. I am the slave of my word, and my word is the word of a king. The King of Cappadocia had ever a lying tongue, but he is no true king. He is a coward. Also he owes me money that he will not repay. He has even insulted my ambassadors. He has spoken words that were wounding. But Cæsar will crucify him when he comes to Rome. I know that Cæsar will crucify him. And if he crucify him not, yet will he die, being eaten of worms. The prophet has prophesied it. Well! Wherefore does thou tarry, Salome?

Salome. I am waiting until my slaves bring perfumes to me and the seven veils, and take from off my feet my sandals. [*Slaves bring perfumes and the seven veils, and take off the sandals of Salome.*]

Herod. Ah, thou art to dance with naked feet! 'Tis well! 'Tis well! Thy little feet will be like white doves. They will be like little white flowers that dance upon the trees. . . . No, no, she is going to dance on blood! There is blood spilt on the ground. She must not dance on blood. It were an evil omen.

Herodias. What is it to thee if she dance on blood? Thou hast waded deep enough in it. . . .

Herod. What is it to me? Ah! look at the moon! She has become red. She has become red as blood. Ah! the prophet prophesied truly. He prophesied that the moon would become as blood. Did he not prophesy it? All of ye heard him prophesying it. And now the moon has become as blood. Do ye not see it?

Herodias. Oh, yes, I see it well, and the stars are falling like unripe figs, are they not? and the sun is becoming black like sackcloth of hair, and the kings of the earth are afraid. That at least one can see. The prophet is justified of his words in that at least, for truly the kings of the earth are afraid. . . . Let us go within. You are sick. They will say at Rome that you are mad. Let us go within, I tell you.

The Voice of Iok. Who is this who cometh from Edom, who is this who cometh from Bozra, whose raiment is dyed with purple, who shineth in the beauty of his garments, who walketh mighty in his greatness? Wherefore is thy raiment stained with scarlet?

Herodias. Let us go within. The voice of that man maddens me. I will not have my daughter dance while he is continually crying out. I will not have her dance while you look at her in this fashion. In a word, I will not have her dance.

HEROD. Do not rise, my wife, my queen, it will avail thee nothing. I will not go within till she hath danced. Dance, Salome, dance for me.

HERODIAS. Do not dance, my daughter.

SALOME. I am ready, Tetrarch.

HEROD. [*Salome dances the dance of the seven veils.*] Ah! wonderful! wonderful! You see that she has danced for me, your daughter. Come near, Salome, come near, that I may give thee thy fee. Ah! I pay a royal price to those who dance for my pleasure. I will pay thee royally. I will give thee whatsoever thy soul desireth. What wouldst thou have? Speak.

SALOME. [*Kneeling.*] I would that they presently bring me in a silver charger . . .

HEROD. [*Laughing.*] In a silver charger? Surely yes, in a silver charger. She is charming, is she not? What is it that thou wouldst have in a silver charger, O sweet and fair Salome, thou that art fairer than all the daughters of Judæa? What wouldst thou have them bring thee in a silver charger? Tell me. Whatsoever it may be, thou shalt receive it. My treasures belong to thee. What is it that thou wouldst have, Salome?

SALOME. [*Rising.*] The head of Iokanaan.

HERODIAS. Ah! that is well said, my daughter.

HEROD. No, no!

HERODIAS. That is well said, my daughter.

HEROD. No, no, Salome. It is not that thou desirest. Do not listen to thy mother's voice. She is ever giving thee evil counsel. Do not heed her.

SALOME. It is not my mother's voice that I heed. It is for mine own pleasure that I ask the head of Iokanaan in a silver charger. You have sworn an oath, Herod. Forget not that you have sworn an oath.

HEROD. I know it. I have sworn an oath by my gods. I know it well. But I pray thee, Salome, ask of me something else. Ask of me the half of my kingdom, and I will give it thee. But ask not of me what thy lips have asked.

SALOME. I ask of you the head of Iokanaan.

HEROD. No, no, I will not give it thee.

SALOME. You have sworn an oath, Herod.

HERODIAS. Yes, you have sworn an oath. Everybody heard you. You swore it before everybody.

HEROD. Peace, woman! It is not to you I speak.

HERODIAS. My daughter has done well to ask the head of Iokanaan. He has covered me with insults. He has said unspeakable things against me. One can see that she loves her mother well. Do not yield, my daughter. He has sworn an oath, he has sworn an oath.

HEROD. Peace! Speak not to me! . . . Salome, I pray thee be not stubborn. I have ever been kind toward thee. I have ever loved thee. . . . It may be that I have loved thee too much. Therefore ask not this thing of me. This is a terrible thing, an awful thing to ask of me. Surely, I think thou art jesting. The head of a man that is cut from his body is ill to look upon, is it not?

It is not meet that the eyes of a virgin should look upon such a thing. What pleasure couldst thou have in it? There is no pleasure that thou couldst have in it. No, no, it is not that thou desirest. Hearken to me. I have an emerald, a great emerald and round, that the minion of Cæsar has sent unto me. When thou lookest through this emerald thou canst see that which passeth afar off. Cæsar himself carries such an emerald when he goes to the circus. But my emerald is the larger. I know well that it is the larger. It is the largest emerald in the whole world. Thou wilt take that, wilt thou not? Ask it of me and I will give it thee.

SALOME. I demand the head of Iokanaan.

HEROD. Thou art not listening. Thou art not listening. Suffer me to speak, Salome.

SALOME. The head of Iokanaan!

HEROD. No, no, thou wouldst not have that. Thou sayest that but to trouble me, because that I have looked at thee and ceased not this night. It is true, I have looked at thee and ceased not this night. Thy beauty has troubled me. Thy beauty has grievously troubled me, and I have looked at thee overmuch. Nay, but I will look at thee no more. One should not look at anything. Neither at things, nor at people should one look. Only in mirrors is it well to look, for mirrors do but show us masks. Oh! oh! bring wine. I thirst. . . . Salome, Salome, let us be as friends. Bethink thee . . . Ah! what would I say? What was't? Ah! I remember it! . . . Salome–nay but come nearer to me; I fear thou wilt not hear my words–Salome, thou knowest my white peacocks, my beautiful white peacocks, that walk in the garden between the myrtles and the tall cypress-trees. Their beaks are gilded with gold, and the grains that they eat are smeared with gold, and their feet are stained with purple. When they cry out the rain comes, and the moon shows herself in the heavens when they spread their tails. Two by two they walk between the cypress-trees and the black myrtles, and each has a slave to tend it. Sometimes they fly across the trees, and anon they couch in the grass, and round the pools of the water. There are not in all the world birds so wonderful. I know that Cæsar himself has no birds so fair as my birds. I will give thee fifty of my peacocks. They will follow thee whithersoever thou goest, and in the midst of them thou wilt be like unto the moon in the midst of a great white cloud. . . . I will give them to thee, all. I have but a hundred, and in the whole world there is no king who has peacocks like unto my peacocks. But I will give them all to thee. Only thou must loose me from my oath, and must not ask of me that which thy lips have asked of me.

[*He empties the cup of wine.*]

SALOME. Give me the head of Iokanaan!

HERODIAS. Well said, my daughter! As for you, you are ridiculous with your peacocks.

HEROD. Peace! you are always crying out. You cry out like a beast of prey. You must not cry in such fashion. Your voice wearies me. Peace, I tell you! . . . Salome, think on what thou art doing. It may be that this man comes from God. He is a holy man. The finger of God has touched him. God has put terrible words into his mouth. In the palace, as in the desert, God is ever with him. . . . It may be that He is, at least. One cannot tell, but it is possible that God is with him and for him. If he die also, peradventure some evil may befall me. Verily, he has said that evil will befall some one on the day whereon he dies. On whom should it fall if it fall not on me? Remember, I slipped in blood when I came hither. Also did I not hear a beating of wings in the air, a beating of vast wings? These are ill omens. And there were other things. I am sure that there were other things, though I saw them not. Thou wouldst not that some evil should befall me, Salome? Listen to me again.

SALOME. Give me the head of Iokanaan!

HEROD. Ah! thou art not listening to me. Be calm. As for me, am I not calm? I am altogether calm. Listen. I have jewels hidden in this place—jewels that thy mother even has never seen; jewels that are marvellous to look at. I have a collar of pearls, set in four rows. They are like unto moons chained with rays of silver. They are even as half a hundred moons caught in a golden net. On the ivory breast of a queen they have rested. Thou shalt be as fair as a queen when thou wearest them. I have amethysts of two kinds; one that is black like wine, and one that is red like wine that one has coloured with water. I have topazes yellow as are the eyes of tigers, and topazes that are pink as the eyes of a wood-pigeon, and green topazes that are as the eyes of cats. I have opals that burn always, with a flame that is cold as ice, opals that make sad men's minds, and are afraid of the shadows. I have onyxes like the eyeballs of a dead woman. I have moonstones that change when the moon changes, and are wan when they see the sun. I have sapphires big like eggs, and as blue as blue flowers. The sea wanders within them, and the moon comes never to trouble the blue of their waves. I have chrysolites and beryls, and chrysoprases and rubies; I have sardonyx and hyacinth stones, and stones of chalcedony, and I will give them all unto thee, all, and other things will I add to them. The King of the Indies has but even now sent me four fans fashioned from the feathers of parrots, and the King of Numidia a garment of ostrich feathers. I have a crystal, into which it is not lawful for a woman to look, nor may young men behold it until they have been beaten with rods. In a coffer of nacre I have three wondrous turquoises. He who wears them on his forehead can imagine things which are not, and he who carries them in his hand can turn the fruitful woman into a woman that is barren. These are great treasures. They are treasures above all price. But this is not all. In an ebony coffer I have two cups of amber that are like apples of pure gold. If an enemy pour poison into these cups they become like apples of silver. In a coffer incrusted with amber I have sandals incrusted with glass. I have mantles that have been brought from the land of the Seres, and bracelets decked about with carbuncles and with jade that come from the city of Euphrates. . . . What desirest thou more than this, Salome? Tell me the thing that thou desirest, and I will give it thee. All that thou askest I will give thee, save one thing only. I will give thee all that is mine, save only the life of one man. I will give thee the mantle of the high priest. I will give thee the veil of the sanctuary.

THE JEWS. Oh! oh!

SALOME. Give me the head of Iokanaan!

HEROD. [*Sinking back in his seat.*] Let her be given what she asks! Of a truth she is her mother's child. [*The first soldier approaches. Herodias draws from the hand of the Tetrarch the ring of death, and gives it to the soldier, who straightway bears it to the Executioner. The Executioner looks scared.*] Who has taken my ring? There was a ring on my right hand. Who has drunk my wine? There was wine in my cup. It was full of wine. Some one has drunk it! Oh! surely some evil will befall some one. [*The Executioner goes down into the cistern.*] Ah! wherefore did I give my oath? Hereafter let no king swear an oath. If he keep it not, it is terrible, and if he keep it, it is terrible also.

HERODIAS. My daughter has done well.

HEROD. I am sure that some misfortune will happen.

SALOME. [*She leans over the cistern and listens.*] There is no sound. I hear nothing. Why does he not cry out, this man? Ah! if any man sought to kill me, I would cry out, I would struggle, I would not suffer. . . . Strike, strike, Naaman, strike, I tell you. . . . No, I hear nothing. There is a silence, a terrible silence. Ah! something has fallen upon the ground. I heard something fall. It was the sword of the executioner. He is afraid, this slave. He has dropped his sword. He dares not kill him. He is a coward, this slave! Let soldiers be sent. [*She sees the Page of Herodias and addresses him.*] Come hither. Thou wert the friend of him who is dead, wert thou not? Well, I tell thee, there are not dead men enough. Go to the soldiers and bid them go down and bring me the thing I ask, the thing the Tetrarch has promised me, the thing that is mine. [*The Page recoils. She turns to the soldiers.*] Hither, ye soldiers. Get ye down into this cistern and bring me the head of this man. Tetrarch, Tetrarch, command your soldiers that they bring me the head of Iokanaan. [*A huge black arm, the arm of the Executioner, comes forth from the cistern, bearing on a silver shield the head of Iokanaan. Salome seizes it. Herod hides his face with his cloak. Herodias smiles and fans herself. The Nazarenes fall on their knees and begin to pray.*] Ah! thou wouldst not suffer me to kiss thy mouth, Iokanaan. Well! I will kiss it now. I will bite it with my teeth as one bites a ripe fruit. Yes, I will kiss thy mouth, Iokanaan. I said it; did I not say it? I said it. Ah! I will kiss it now. . . . But wherefore dost thou not look at me, Iokanaan? Thine eyes that were so terrible, so full of rage and scorn, are shut now. Wherefore are they shut? Open thine eyes! Lift up thine eyelids, Iokanaan! Wherefore dost thou not look at me? Art thou afraid of me, Iokanaan, that thou wilt not look at me? . . . And thy tongue, that was like a red snake darting poison, it moves no more, it speaks no words, Iokanaan, that scarlet viper that spat its venom upon me. It is strange, is it not? How is it that the red viper stirs no longer? . . . Thou wouldst have none of me, Iokanaan. Thou rejectedst me. Thou didst speak evil words against me. Thou didst bear thyself toward me as to a harlot, as to a woman that is a wanton, to me, Salome, daughter of Herodias, Princess of Judæa! Well, I still live, but thou art dead, and they head belongs tome. I can do with it what I will. I can throw it to the dogs and to the birds of the air. That which the dogs leave, the birds of the air shall devour. . . . Ah, Iokanaan, Iokanaan, thou wert the man that I loved alone among men! All other men were hateful to me. But thou wert beautiful! Thy body was a column of ivory set upon feet of silver. It was a garden full of doves and lilies of silver. It was a tower of silver decked with shields of ivory. There was nothing in the world so white as thy body. There was nothing in the world so black as thy hair. In the whole world there was nothing so red as thy mouth. Thy voice was a censer that scattered strange perfumes, and when I looked on thee I heard a strange music. Ah! wherefore didst thou not look at me, Iokanaan? With the cloak of thine hands, and with the cloak of thy blasphemies thou didst hide thy face. Thou didst put upon thine eyes the covering of him who would see his God. Well, thou hast seen thy God, Iokanaan, but me, me, thou didst never see. If thou hadst seen me thou hadst loved me. I saw thee, and I loved thee. Oh, how I loved thee! I love thee yet, Iokanaan. I love only thee. . . . I am athirst for thy beauty; I am hungry for thy body; and neither wine nor apples can appease my desire. What shall I do now, Iokanaan? Neither the floods nor the great waters can quench my passion. I was a princess, and thou didst scorn me. I was a virgin, and thou didst take my virginity from me. I was chaste, and thou didst fill my veins with fire. . . . Ah! ah! wherefore didst thou not look at me? If thou hadst looked at me thou hadst loved me. Well I know that thou wouldst have loved me, and the mystery of Love is greater than the mystery of Death.

HEROD. She is monstrous, thy daughter; I tell thee she is monstrous. In truth, what she has done is a great crime. I am sure that it is a crime against some unknown God.

HERODIAS. I am well pleased with my daughter. She has done well. And I would stay here now.

HEROD. [*Rising.*] Ah! There speaks my brother's wife! Come! I will not stay in this place. Come, I tell thee. Surely some terrible thing will befall. Manasseh, Issachar, Ozias, put out the torches. I will not look at things, I will not suffer things to look at me. Put out the torches! Hide the moon! Hide the stars! Let us hide ourselves in our palace, Herodias. I begin to be afraid.

[*The slaves put out the torches. The stars disappear. A great cloud crosses the moon and conceals it completely. The stage becomes quite dark. The Tetrarch begins to climb the staircase.*]

THE VOICE OF SAL. Ah! I have kissed thy mouth, Iokanaan, I have kissed thy mouth. There was a bitter taste on thy lips. Was it the taste of blood? . . . Nay; but perchance it was the taste of love. . . . They say that love hath a bitter taste. . . . But what matter? what matter? I have kissed thy mouth, Iokanaan, I have kissed thy mouth.

[*A ray of moonlight falls on Salome and illumines her.*]

HEROD. [*Turning round and seeing Salome.*] Kill that woman!

[*The soldiers rush forward and crush beneath their shields Salome, daughter of Herodias, Princess of Judæa.*]

CURTAIN.

A WOMAN OF NO IMPORTANCE

The Persons of the Play

Lord Illingworth
Sir John Pontefract
Lord Alfred Rufford
Mr. Kelvil, M.P.
The Ven. Archdeacon Daubeny, D.D.
Gerald Arbuthnot
Farquhar, Butler
Francis, Footman
Lady Hunstanton
Lady Caroline Pontefract
Lady Stutfield
Mrs. Allonby
Miss Hester Worsley
Alice, Maid
Mrs. Arbuthnot

The Scenes of the Play

Act I. *The Terrace at Hunstanton Chase.* Act II. *The Drawing-room at Hunstanton Chase.* Act III. *The Picture-gallery at Hunstanton Chase.* Act IV. *Sitting-room in Mrs. Arbuthnot's House at Wrockley. Time, the Present. Place, the Shires. The Action of the Play takes place within twenty-four hours.*

FIRST ACT

Scene—*Lawn in front of the terrace at Hunstanton.*

[*Sir John and Lady Caroline Pontefract, Miss Worsley, on chairs under large yew tree.*]

Lady Car. I believe this is the first English country house you have stayed at, Miss Worsley?

Hes. Yes, Lady Caroline.

Lady Car. You have no country houses, I am told, in America?

Hes. We have not many.

Lady Car. Have you any country? What we should call country?

Hes. [*Smiling.*] We have the largest country in the world, Lady Caroline They used to tell us at school that some of our states are as big as France and England put together.

Lady Car. Ah! you must find it very draughty, I should fancy. [*To Sir John.*] John, you should have your muffler. What is the use of my always knitting mufflers for you if you won't wear them?

Sir John. I am quite warm, I assure you.

Lady Car. I think not, John. Well, you couldn't come to a more charming place than this, Miss Worsley, though the house is excessively damp, quite unpardonably damp, and dear Lady Hunstanton is sometimes a little lax about the people she asks down here. [*To Sir John.*] Jane mixes too much. Lord Illingworth, of course, is a man of high distinction. It is a privilege to meet him. And that member of Parliament, Mr. Kettle——

Sir John. Kelvil, my love, Kelvil.

Lady Car. He must be quite respectable. One has never heard his name before in the whole course of one's life, which speaks volumes for a man, now-a-days. But Mrs. Allonby is hardly a very suitable person.

Hes. I dislike Mrs. Allonby. I dislike her more than I can say.

Lady Car. I am not sure, Miss Worsley, that foreigners like yourself should cultivate likes or dislikes about the people they are invited to meet. Mrs. Allonby is very well born. She is a niece of Lord Brancaster's. It is said, of course, that she ran away twice before she was married. But you know how unfair people often are. I myself don't believe she ran away more than once.

Hes. Mr. Arbuthnot is very charming.

Lady Car. Ah, yes! the young man who has a post in a bank. Lady Hunstanton is most kind in asking him here, and Lord Illingworth seems to have taken quite a fancy to him. I am not sure, however, that Jane is right in taking him out of his position. In my young days, Miss Worsley, one never met anyone in society who worked for their living. It was not considered the thing.

Hes. In America those are the people we respect most.

Lady Car. I have no doubt of it.

Hes. Mr. Arbuthnot has a beautiful nature! He is so simple, so sincere. He has one of the most beautiful natures I have ever come across. It is a privilege to meet *him.*

Lady Car. It is not customary in England, Miss Worsley, for a young lady to speak with such enthusiasm of any person of the opposite sex. English women conceal their feelings till after they are married. They show them then.

Hes. Do you, in England, allow no friendship to exist between a young man and a young girl?

[*Enter Lady Hunstanton followed by Footman with shawls and a cushion.*]

Lady Car. We think it very inadvisable. Jane, I was just saying what a pleasant party you have asked us to meet. You have a wonderful power of selection. It is quite a gift.

Lady Hun. Dear Caroline, how kind of you! I think we all do fit in very nicely together. And I hope our charming American visitor will carry back pleasant recollections of our English country life. [*To Footman.*] The cushion there, Francis. And my shawl. The Shetland. Get the Shetland.

[*Exit Footman for shawl.*]

[*Enter Gerald Arbuthnot.*]

Ger. Lady Hunstanton, I have such good news to tell you. Lord Illingworth has just offered to make me his secretary.

Lady Hun. His secretary? That is good news indeed, Gerald. It means a very brilliant future in store for you. Your dear mother will be delighted. I really must try and induce her to come up here to-night. Do you think she would, Gerald? I know how difficult it is to get her to go anywhere.

GER. Oh! I am sure she would, Lady Hunstanton, if she knew Lord Illingworth had made me such an offer.

[*Enter Footman with shawl.*]

LADY HUN. I will write and tell her about it, and ask her to come up and meet him. [*To Footman.*] Just wait, Francis. [*Writes letter.*]

LADY CAR. That is a very wonderful opening for so young a man as you are, Mr. Arbuthnot.

GER. It is indeed, Lady Caroline. I trust I shall be able to show myself worthy of it.

LADY CAR. I trust so.

GER. [*To Hester.*] *You* have not congratulated me yet, Miss Worsley.

HES. Are you very pleased about it?

GER. Of course I am. It means everything to me—things that were out of the reach of hope before may be within hope's reach now.

HES. Nothing should be out of the reach of hope. Life is a hope.

LADY HUN. I fancy, Caroline, that Diplomacy is what Lord Illingworth is aiming at. I heard that he was offered Vienna. But that may not be true.

LADY CAR. I don't think that England should be represented abroad by an unmarried man, Jane. It might lead to complications.

LADY HUN. You are too nervous, Caroline. Believe me, you are too nervous. Besides, Lord Illingworth may marry any day. I was in hopes he would have married Lady Kelso. But I believe he said her family was too large. Or was it her feet? I forget which. I regret it very much. She was made to be an ambassador's wife.

LADY CAR. She certainly has a wonderful faculty of remembering people's names, and forgetting their faces.

LADY HUN. Well, that is very natural, Caroline, is it not? [*To Footman.*] Tell Henry to wait for an answer. I have written a line to your dear mother, Gerald, to tell her your good news, and to say she really must come to dinner.

[*Exit Footman.*]

GER. That is awfully kind of you, Lady Hunstanton. [*To Hester.*] Will you come for a stroll, Miss Worsley?

HES. With pleasure.

[*Exit with Gerald.*]

LADY HUN. I am very much gratified at Gerald Arbuthnot's good fortune. He is quite a *protégé* of mine. And I am particularly pleased that Lord Illingworth should have made the offer of his own accord without my suggesting anything. Nobody likes to be asked favours. I remember poor Charlotte Pagden making herself quite unpopular one season, because she had a French governess she wanted to recommend to every one.

LADY CAR. I saw the governess, Jane. Lady Pagden sent her to me. It was before Eleanor came out. She was far too good-looking to be in any respectable household. I don't wonder Lady Pagden was so anxious to get rid of her.

LADY HUN. Ah, that explains it.

LADY CAR. John, the grass is too damp for you. You had better go and put on your overshoes at once.

SIR JOHN. I am quite comfortable, Caroline, I assure you.

LADY CAR. You must allow me to be the best judge of that, John. Pray, do as I tell you.

[*Sir John gets up and goes off.*]

LADY HUN. You spoil him, Caroline, you do, indeed.

[*Enter Mrs. Allonby and Lady Stutfield.*]

[*To Mrs. Allonby.*] Well, dear, I hope you like the park. It is said to be well timbered.

MRS. ALL. The trees are wonderful, Lady Hunstanton.

LADY STU. Quite, quite wonderful.

MRS. ALL. But somehow, I feel sure that if I lived in the country for six months, I should become so unsophisticated that no one would take the slightest notice of me.

LADY HUN. I assure you, dear, that the country has not that effect at all. Why, it was from Melthorpe, which is only two miles from here, that Lady Belton eloped with Lord Fethersdale. I remember the occurrence perfectly. Poor Lord Belton died three days afterwards of joy or gout. I forget which. We had a large party staying here at the time, so we were all very much interested in the whole affair.

MRS. ALL. I think to elope is cowardly. It's running away from danger. And danger has become so rare in modern life.

LADY CAR. As far as I can make out, the young women of the present day seem to make it the sole object of their lives to be always playing with fire.

MRS. ALL. The one advantage of playing with fire, Lady Caroline, is that one never gets even singed. It is the people who don't know how to play with it who get burned up.

LADY STU. Yes; I see that. It is very, very helpful.

LADY HUN. I don't know how the world would get on with such a theory as that, dear Mrs. Allonby.

LADY STU. Ah! The world was made for men and not for women.

MRS. ALL. Oh, don't say that, Lady Stutfield. We have a much better time than they have. There are far more things forbidden to us than are forbidden to them.

LADY STU. Yes; that is quite, quite true. I had not thought of that.

[*Enter Sir John and Mr. Kelvil.*]

LADY HUN. Well, Mr. Kelvil, have you got through your work?

KEL. I have finished my writing for the day, Lady Hunstanton. It has been an arduous task. The demands on the time of a public man are very heavy now-a-days, very heavy indeed. And I don't think they meet with adequate recognition.

LADY CAR. John, have you got your overshoes on?

SIR JOHN. Yes, my love.

LADY CAR. I think you had better come over here, John. It is more sheltered.

SIR JOHN. I am quite comfortable, Caroline.

LADY CAR. I think not, John. You had better sit beside me.

[*Sir John rises and goes across.*]

LADY STU. And what have you been writing about this morning, Mr. Kelvil?

KEL. On the usual subject, Lady Stutfield. On Purity.

LADY STU. That must be such a very, very interesting thing to write about.

KEL. It is the one subject of really national importance, now-a-days, Lady Stutfield. I purpose addressing my constituents on the question before Parliament meets. I find that the poorer classes of this country display a marked desire for a higher ethical standard.

LADY STU. How quite, quite nice of them.

LADY CAR. Are you in favour of women taking part in politics, Mr. Kettle?

SIR JOHN. Kelvil, my love, Kelvil.

KEL. The growing influence of women is the one reassuring thing in our political life, Lady Caroline. Women are always on the side of morality, public and private.

LADY STU. It is so very, very gratifying to hear you say that.

LADY HUN. Ah, yes! the moral qualities in women—that is the important thing. I am afraid, Caroline, that dear Lord Illingworth doesn't value the moral qualities in women as much as he should.

[*Enter Lord Illingworth.*]

LADY STU. The world says that Lord Illingworth is very, very wicked.

LORD ILL. But what world says that, Lady Stutfield? It must be the next world. This world and I are on excellent terms. [*Sits down beside Mrs. Allonby.*]

LADY STU. Every one *I* know says you are very, very wicked.

LORD ILL. It is perfectly monstrous the way people go about, now-a-days, saying things against one behind one's back that are absolutely and entirely true.

LADY HUN. Dear Lord Illingworth is quite hopeless, Lady Stutfield. I have given up trying to reform him. It would take a Public Company with a Board of Directors and a paid Secretary to do that. But you have the secretary already, Lord Illingworth, haven't you? Gerald Arbuthnot has told us of his good fortune; it is really most kind of you.

LORD ILL. Oh, don't say that, Lady Hunstanton. Kind is a dreadful word. I took a great fancy to young Arbuthnot the moment I met him, and he'll be of considerable use to me in something I am foolish enough to think of doing.

LADY HUN. He is an admirable young man. And his mother is one of my dearest friends. He has just gone for a walk with our pretty American. She is very pretty, is she not?

LADY CAR. Far too pretty. These American girls carry off all the good matches. Why can't they stay in their own country? They are always telling us it is the Paradise of women.

LORD ILL. It is, Lady Caroline. That is why, like Eve, they are so extremely anxious to get out of it.

LADY CAR. Who are Miss Worsley's parents?

LORD ILL. American women are wonderfully clever in concealing their parents.

LADY HUN. My dear Lord Illingworth, what do you mean? Miss Worsley, Caroline, is an orphan. Her father was a very wealthy millionaire, or philanthropist, or both, I believe, who entertained my son quite hospitably, when he visited Boston. I don't know how he made his money, originally.

KEL. I fancy in American dry goods.

LADY HUN. What are American dry goods?

LORD ILL. American novels.

LADY HUN. How very singular! . . . Well, from whatever source her large fortune came, I have a great esteem for Miss Worsley. She dresses exceedingly well. All Americans do dress well. They get their clothes in Paris.

MRS. ALL. They say, Lady Hunstanton, that when good Americans die they go to Paris.

LADY HUN. Indeed? And when bad Americans die where do they go?

LORD ILL. Oh, they go to America.

KEL. I am afraid you don't appreciate America, Lord Illingworth. It is a very remarkable country, especially considering its youth.

LORD ILL. The youth of America is their oldest tradition. It has been going on now for three hundred years. To hear them talk one would imagine they were in their first childhood. As far as civilisation goes they are in their second.

KEL. There is undoubtedly a great deal of corruption in American politics. I suppose you allude to that?

LORD ILL. I wonder.

LADY HUN. Politics are in a very sad way everywhere, I am told. They certainly are in England. Dear Mr. Cardew is ruining the country. I wonder Mrs. Cardew allows him. I am sure, Lord Illingworth, you don't think that uneducated people should be allowed to have votes?

LORD ILL. I think they are the only people who should.

KEL. Do you take no side then in modern politics, Lord Illingworth?

LORD ILL. One should never take sides in anything, Mr. Kelvil. Taking sides is the beginning of sincerity, and earnestness follows shortly afterwards, and the human being becomes a bore. However, the House of Commons really does very little harm. You can't make people good by Act of Parliament—that is something.

KEL. You cannot deny that the House of Commons has always shown great sympathy with the sufferings of the poor.

LORD ILL. That is its special vice. That is the special vice of the age. One should sympathise with the joy, the beauty, the colour of life. The less said about life's sores the better, Mr. Kelvil.

KEL. Still our East End is a very important problem.

LORD ILL. Quite so. It is the problem of slavery. And we are trying to solve it by amusing the slaves.

LADY HUN. Certainly, a great deal may be done by means of cheap entertainments, as you say, Lord Illingworth. Dear Dr. Daubeny, our rector here, provides with the assistance of his curates, really admirable recreations for the poor during the winter. And much good may be done by means of a magic lantern, or a missionary, or some popular amusement of that kind.

Lady Car. I am not at all in favour of amusements for the poor, Jane. Blankets and coals are sufficient. There is too much love of pleasure amongst the upper classes as it is. Health is what we want in modern life. The tone is not healthy, not healthy at all.

Kel. You are quite right, Lady Caroline.

Lady Car. I believe I am usually right.

Mrs. All. Horrid word "health."

Lord Ill. Silliest word in our language, and one knows so well the popular idea of health. The English country gentleman galloping after a fox—the unspeakable in full pursuit of the uneatable.

Kel. May I ask, Lord Illingworth, if you regard the House of Lords as a better institution than the House of Commons?

Lord Ill. A much better institution, of course. We in the House of Lords are never in touch with public opinion. That makes us a civilised body.

Kel. Are you serious in putting forward such a view?

Lord Ill. Quite serious, Mr. Kelvil. [*To Mrs. Allonby.*] Vulgar habit that is people have now-a-days of asking one, after one has given them an idea, whether one is serious or not. Nothing is serious except passion. The intellect is not a serious thing, and never has been. It is an instrument on which one plays, that is all. The only serious form of intellect I know is the British intellect. And on the British intellect the illiterates play the drum.

Lady Hun. What are you saying, Lord Illingworth, about the drum?

Lord Ill. I was merely talking to Mrs. Allonby about the leading articles in the London newspapers.

Lady Hun. But do you believe all that is written in the newspapers?

Lord Ill. I do. Now-a-days it is only the unreadable that occurs. [*Rises with Mrs. Allonby.*]

Lady Hun. Are you going, Mrs. Allonby?

Mrs. All. Just as far as the conservatory. Lord Illingworth told me this morning that there was an orchid there as beautiful as the seven deadly sins.

Lady Hun. My dear, I hope there is nothing of the kind. I will certainly speak to the gardener.

[*Exeunt Mrs. Allonby and Lord Illingworth.*]

Lady Car. Remarkable type, Mrs. Allonby.

Lady Hun. She lets her clever tongue run away with her sometimes.

Lady Car. Is that the only thing, Jane, Mrs. Allonby allows to run away with her?

Lady Hun. I hope so, Caroline, I am sure.

[*Enter Lord Alfred.*]

Dear Lord Alfred, do join us. [*Lord Alfred sits down beside Lady Stutfield.*]

Lady Car. You believe good of every one, Jane. It is a great fault.

Lady Stu. Do you really, really think, Lady Caroline, that one should believe evil of every one?

Lady Car. I think it is much safer to do so, Lady Stutfield. Until, of course.

people are found out to be good. But that requires a great deal of investigation, now-a-days.

Lady Stu. But there is so much unkind scandal in modern life.

Lady Car. Lord Illingworth remarked to me last night at dinner that the basis of every scandal is an absolutely immoral certainty.

Kel. Lord Illingworth is, of course, a very brilliant man, but he seems to me to be lacking in that fine faith in the nobility and purity of life which is so important in this country.

Lady Stu. Yes, quite, quite important, is it not?

Kel. He gives me the impression of a man who does not appreciate the beauty of our English home-life. I would say that he was tainted with foreign ideas on the subject.

Lady Stu. There is nothing, nothing like the beauty of home-life, is there?

Kel. It is the mainstay of our moral system in England, Lady Stutfield. Without it we would become like our neighbours.

Lady Stu. That would be so, so sad, would it not?

Kel. I am afraid, too, that Lord Illingworth regards woman simply as a toy. Now, I have never regarded woman as a toy. Woman is the intellectual help-meet of man in public as in private life. Without her we should forget the true ideals. [*Sits down beside Lady Stutfield.*]

Lady Stu. I am so very, very glad to hear you say that.

Lady Car. You a married man, Mr. Kettle?

Sir John. Kelvil, dear, Kelvil.

Kel. I am married, Lady Caroline.

Lady Car. Family?

Kel. Yes.

Lady Car. How many?

Kel. Eight.

[*Lady Stutfield turns her attention to Lord Alfred.*]

Lady Car. Mrs. Kettle and the children are, I suppose, at the seaside? [*Sir John shrugs his shoulders.*]

Kel. My wife is at the seaside with the children, Lady Caroline.

Lady Car. You will join them later on, no doubt?

Kel. If my public engagements permit me.

Lady Car. Your public life must be a great source of gratification to Mrs. Kettle.

Sir John. Kelvil, my love, Kelvil.

Lady Stu. [*To Lord Alfred.*] How very, very charming those gold-tipped cigarettes of yours are, Lord Alfred.

Lord Alf. They are awfully expensive. I can only afford them when I'm in debt.

Lady Stu. It must be terribly, terribly distressing to be in debt.

Lord Alf. One must have some occupation now-a-days. If I hadn't my debts I shouldn't have anything to think about. All the chaps I know are in debt.

Lady Stu. But don't the people to whom you owe the money give you a great, great deal of annoyance?

[*Enter Footman.*]

LORD ALF. Oh, no, they write; I don't.

LADY STU. How very, very strange.

LADY HUN. Ah, here is a letter, Caroline, from dear Mrs. Arbuthnot. She won't dine. I am so sorry. But she will come in the evening. I am very pleased indeed. She is one of the sweetest of women. Writes a beautiful hand too, so large, so firm. [*Hands letter to Lady Caroline.*]

LADY STU. [*Looking at it.*] A little lacking in femininity, Jane. Femininity is the quality I admire most in women.

LADY HUN. [*Taking back letter and leaving it on table.*] Oh! she is very feminine, Caroline, and so good too. You should hear what the Archdeacon says of her. He regards her as his right hand in the parish. [*Footman speaks to her.*] In the Yellow Drawing-room. Shall we all go in? Lady Stutfield, shall we go in to tea?

LADY STU. With pleasure, Lady Hunstanton. [*They rise and proceed to go off. Sir John offers to carry Lady Stutfield's cloak.*]

LADY CAR. John! If you would allow your nephew to look after Lady Stutfield's cloak, you might help me with my workbasket.

[*Enter Lord Illingworth and Mrs. Allonby.*]

SIR JOHN. Certainly my love. [*Exeunt.*]

MRS. ALL. Curious thing, plain women are always jealous of their husbands, beautiful women never are!

LORD ILL. Beautiful women never have time. They are always so occupied in being jealous of other people's husbands.

MRS. ALL. I should have thought Lady Caroline would have grown tired of conjugal anxiety by this time! Sir John is her fourth!

LORD ILL. So much marriage is certainly not becoming. Twenty years of romance make a woman look like a ruin; but twenty years of marriage make her something like a public building.

MRS. ALL. Twenty years of romance! Is there such a thing?

LORD ILL. Not in our day. Women have become too brilliant. Nothing spoils a romance so much as a sense of humour in the woman.

MRS. ALL. Or the want of it in the man.

LORD ILL. You are quite right. In a Temple every one should be serious, except the thing that is worshipped.

MRS. ALL. And that should be man?

LORD ILL. Women kneel so gracefully; men don't.

MRS. ALL. You are thinking of Lady Stutfield!

LORD ILL. I assure you I have not thought of Lady Stutfield for the last quarter of an hour.

MRS. ALL. Is she such a mystery?

LORD ILL. She is more than a mystery—she is a mood.

MRS. ALL. Moods don't last.

LORD ILL. It is their chief charm.

[*Enter Hester and Gerald.*]

GER. Lord Illingworth, every one has been congratulating me, Lady Hunstanton and Lady Caroline, and . . . every one. I hope I shall make a good secretary.

Lord Ill. You will be the pattern secretary, Gerald. [*Talks to him.*]

Mrs. All. You enjoy country life, Miss Worsley?

Hes. Very much indeed.

Mrs. All. Don't find yourself longing for a London dinner-party?

Hes. I dislike London dinner-parties.

Mrs. All. I adore them. The clever people never listen, and the stupid people never talk.

Hes. I think the stupid people talk a great deal.

Mrs. All. Ah, I never listen!

Lord Ill. My dear boy, if I didn't like you I wouldn't have made you the offer. It is because I like you so much that I want to have you with me. [*Exit Hester with Gerald.*] Charming fellow, Gerald Arbuthnot!

Mrs. All. He is very nice; very nice indeed. But I can't stand the American young lady.

Lord Ill. Why?

Mrs. All. She told me yesterday, and in quite a loud voice too, that she was only eighteen. It was most annoying.

Lord Ill. One should never trust a woman who tells one her real age. A woman who would tell one that would tell one anything.

Mrs. All. She is a Puritan besides——

Lord Ill. Ah, that is inexcusable. I don't mind plain women being Puritans. It is the only excuse they have for being plain. But she is decidedly pretty. I admire her immensely. [*Looks steadfastly at Mrs. Allonby.*]

Mrs. All. What a thoroughly bad man you must be!

Lord Ill. What do you call a bad man?

Mrs. All. The sort of man who admires innocence.

Lord Ill. And a bad woman?

Mrs. All. Oh! the sort of woman a man never gets tired of.

Lord Ill. You are severe—on yourself.

Mrs. All. Define us as a sex.

Lord Ill. Sphinxes without secrets.

Mrs. All. Does that include the Puritan women?

Lord Ill. Do you know, I don't believe in the existence of Puritan women? I don't think there is a woman in the world would not be a little flattered if one made love to her. It is that which makes women so irresistibly adorable.

Mrs. All. You think there is no woman in the world who would object to being kissed?

Lord Ill. Very few.

Mrs. All. Miss Worsley would not let you kiss her.

Lord Ill. Are you sure?

Mrs. All. Quite.

Lord Ill. What do you think she'd do if I kissed her?

Mrs. All. Either marry you, or strike you across the face with her glove. What would you do if she struck you across the face with her glove?

Lord Ill. Fall in love with her, probably.

Mrs. All. Then it is lucky you are not going to kiss her!

Lord Ill. Is that a challenge?

Mrs. All. It is an arrow shot into the air.

Lord Ill. Don't you know that I always succeed in whatever I try?

Mrs. All. I am sorry to hear it. We women adore failures. They lean on us.

Lord Ill. You worship successes. You cling to them.

Mrs. All. We are the laurels to hide their baldness.

Lord Ill. And they need you always, except at the moment of triumph.

Mrs. All. They are uninteresting then.

Lord Ill. How tantalising you are! [*A pause.*]

Mrs. All. Lord Illingworth, there is one thing I shall always like you for.

Lord Ill. Only one thing? And I have so many bad qualities.

Mrs. All. Ah, don't be too conceited about them. You may lose them as you grow old.

Lord Ill. I never intend to grow old. The soul is born old but grows young. That is the comedy of life.

Mrs. All. And the body is born young and grows old. That is life's tragedy.

Lord Ill. Its comedy also, sometimes. But what is the mysterious reason why you will always like me?

Mrs. All. It is that you have never made love to me.

Lord Ill. I have never done anything else.

Mrs. All. Really? I have not noticed it.

Lord Ill. How fortunate! It might have been a tragedy for both of us.

Mrs. All. We should each have survived.

Lord Ill. One can survive everything now-a-days, except death, and live down anything except a good reputation.

Mrs. All. Have you tried a good reputation?

Lord Ill. It is one of the many annoyances to which I have never been subjected.

Mrs. All. It may come.

Lord Ill. Why do you threaten me?

Mrs. All. I will tell you when you have kissed the Puritan.

[*Enter Footman.*]

Fran. Tea is served in the Yellow Drawing-room, my lord.

Lord Ill. Tell her ladyship we are coming in. [*Exit.*]

Fran. Yes, my lord.

Lord Ill. Shall we go in to tea?

Mrs. All. Do you like such simple pleasures?

Lord Ill. I adore simple pleasures. They are the last refuge of the complex. But, if you wish, let us stay here. Yes, let us stay here. The Book of Life begins with a man and a woman in a garden.

Mrs. All. It ends with Revelations.

Lord Ill. You fence divinely. But the button has come off your foil.

Mrs. All. I have still the mask.

Lord Ill. It makes your eyes lovelier.

MRS. ALL. Thank you. Come.

LORD ILL. [*Sees Mrs. Arbuthnot's letter on table, and takes it up and looks at envelope.*] What a curious handwriting! It reminds me of the handwriting of a woman I used to know years ago.

MRS. ALL. Who?

LORD ILL. Oh! no one. No one in particular. A woman of no importance. [*Throws letter down, and passes up the steps of the terrace with Mrs. Allonby. They smile at each other.*]

ACT-DROP.

SECOND ACT

SCENE–*Drawing-room at Hunstanton Chase after dinner, lamps lit. Door L. C. Door R. C.*

[*Ladies seated on sofas.*]

MRS. ALL. What a comfort it is to have got rid of the men for a little!

LADY STU. Yes; men persecute us dreadfully, don't they?

MRS. ALL. Persecute us? I wish they did.

LADY HUN. My dear!

MRS. ALL. The annoying thing is that the wretches can be perfectly happy without us. That is why I think it is every woman's duty never to leave them alone for a single moment, except during this short breathing space after dinner, without which I believe we poor women would be absolutely worn to shadows.

[*Enter Servants with coffee.*]

LADY HUN. Worn to shadows, dear?

MRS. ALL. Yes, Lady Hunstanton. It is such a strain keeping men up to the mark. They are always trying to escape from us.

LADY STU. It seems to me that it is we who are always trying to escape from them. Men are so very, very heartless. They know their power and use it.

LADY CAR. [*Takes coffee from Servant.*] What stuff and nonsense all this about men is! The thing to do is to keep men in their proper place.

MRS. ALL. But what is their proper place, Lady Caroline?

LADY CAR. Looking after their wives, Mrs. Allonby.

MRS. ALL. [*Takes coffee from Servant.*] Really? And if they're not married?

LADY CAR. If they are not married, they should be looking after a wife. It's perfectly scandalous the amount of bachelors who are going about society. There should be a law passed to compel them all to marry within twelve months.

LADY STU. [*Refuses coffee.*] But if they're in love with some one who, perhaps, is tied to another?

LADY CAR. In that case, Lady Stutfield, they should be married off in a week to some plain respectable girl, in order to teach them not to meddle with other people's property.

MRS. ALL. I don't think that we should ever be spoken of as other people's property. All men are married women's property. That is the only true definition of what married women's property really is. But we don't belong to any one.

Lady Stu. Oh, I am so very, very glad to hear you say so.

Lady Hun. But do you really think, dear Caroline, that legislation would improve matters in any way? I am told that, now-a-days, all the married men live like bachelors, and all the bachelors like married men.

Mrs. All. I certainly never know one from the other.

Lady Stu. Oh, I think one can always know at once whether a man has home claims upon his life or not. I have noticed a very, very sad expression in the eyes of so many married men.

Mrs. All. Ah, all that I have noticed is that they are horribly tedious when they are good husbands, and abominably conceited when they are not.

Lady Hun. Well, I suppose the type of husband has completely changed since my young days, but I'm bound to state that poor dear Hunstanton was the most delightful of creatures, and as good as gold.

Mrs. All. Ah, my husband is a sort of promissory note. I am tired of meeting him.

Lady Car. But you renew him from time to time, don't you?

Mrs. All. Oh, no, Lady Caroline. I have only had one husband as yet. I suppose you look upon me as quite an amateur.

Lady Car. With your views on life I wonder you married at all.

Mrs. All. So do I.

Lady Hun. My dear child, I believe you are really very happy in your married life, but that you like to hide your happiness from others.

Mrs. All. I assure you I was horribly deceived in Ernest.

Lady Hun. Oh, I hope not, dear. I knew his mother quite well. She was a Stratton, Caroline, one of Lord Crowland's daughters.

Lady Car. Victoria Stratton? I remember her perfectly. A silly fair-haired woman with no chin.

Mrs. All. Ah, Ernest has a chin. He has a very strong chin, a square chin. Ernest's chin is far too square.

Lady Stu. But do you really think a man's chin can be too square? I think a man should look very, very strong, and that his chin should be quite, quite square.

Mrs. All. Then you should certainly know Ernest, Lady Stutfield. It is only fair to tell you beforehand he has got no conversation at all.

Lady Stu. I adore silent men.

Mrs. All. Oh, Ernest isn't silent. He talks the whole time. But he has got no conversation. What he talks about I don't know. I haven't listened to him for years.

Lady Stu. Have you never forgiven him then? How sad that seems! But all life is very, very sad, is it not?

Mrs. All. Life, Lady Stutfield, is simply a *mauvais quart d'heure* made up of exquisite moments.

Lady Stu. Yes, there are moments, certainly. But was it something very, very wrong that Mr. Allonby did? Did he become angry with you, and say anything that was unkind or true?

Mrs. All. Oh dear, no. Ernest is invariably calm. That is one of the reasons he always gets on my nerves. Nothing is so aggravating as calmness. There is something positively brutal about the good temper of most modern men. I wonder we women stand it as well as we do.

Lady Stu. Yes: men's good temper shows they are not so sensitive as we are, not so finely strung. It makes a great barrier often between husband and wife, does it not? But I would so much like to know what was the wrong thing Mr. Allonby did.

Mrs. All. Well, I will tell you, if you solemnly promise to tell everybody else.

Lady Stu. Thank you, thank you. I will make a point of repeating it.

Mrs. All. When Ernest and I were engaged he swore to me positively on his knees that he never had loved any one before in the whole course of his life. I was very young at the time, so I didn't believe him, I needn't tell you. Unfortunately, however, I made no enquiries of any kind till after I had been actually married four or five months. I found out then that what he had told me was perfectly true. And that sort of thing makes a man so absolutely uninteresting.

Lady Hun. My dear!

Mrs. All. Men always want to be a woman's first love. That is their clumsy vanity. We women have a more subtle instinct about things. What we like is to be a man's last romance.

Lady Stu. I see what you mean. It's very, very beautiful.

Lady Hun. My dear child, you don't mean to tell me that you won't forgive your husband because he never loved any one else? Did you ever hear of such a thing, Caroline? I am quite surprised.

Lady Car. Oh, women have become so highly educated, Jane, that nothing should surprise us now-a-days, except happy marriages. They apparently are getting remarkably rare.

Mrs. All. Oh, they're quite out of date.

Lady Stu. Except amongst the middle classes, I have been told.

Mrs. All. How like the middle casses!

Lady Stu. Yes–is it not–very, very like them?

Lady Car. If what you tell us about the middle classes is true, Lady Stutfield, it redounds greatly to their credit. It is much to be regretted that in our rank of life the wife should be so persistently frivolous, under the impression apparently that it is the proper thing to be. It is to that I attribute the unhappiness of so many marriages we all know of in society.

Mrs. All. Do you know, Lady Caroline, I don't think the frivolity of the wife has ever anything to do with it. More marriages are ruined now-a-days by the common sense of the husband than by anything else. How can a woman be expected to be happy with a man who insists on treating her as if she were a perfectly rational being?

Lady Hun. My dear!

MRS. ALL. Man, poor, awkward, reliable, necessary man belongs to a sex that has been rational for millions and millions of years. He can't help himself. It is in his race. The History of Woman is very different. We have always been picturesque protests against the mere existence of common sense. We saw its dangers from the first.

LADY STU. Yes, the common sense of husbands is certainly most, most trying. Do tell me your conception of the Ideal Husband. I think it would be so very, very helpful.

MRS. ALL. The Ideal Husband? There couldn't be such a thing. The institution is wrong.

LADY STU. The Ideal Man, then, in his relations to *us*.

LADY CAR. He would probably be extremely realistic.

MRS. ALL. The Ideal Man! Oh, the Ideal Man should talk to us as if we were goddesses, and treat us as if we were children. He should refuse all our serious requests, and gratify every one of our whims. He should encourage us to have caprices, and forbid us to have missions. He should always say much more than he means, and always mean much more than he says.

LADY HUN. But how could he do both, dear?

MRS. ALL. He should never run down other pretty women. That would show he had no taste, or make one suspect that he had too much. No; he should be nice about them all, but say that somehow they don't attract him.

LADY STU. Yes, that is always very, very pleasant to hear about other women.

MRS. ALL. If we ask him a question about anything, he should give us an answer all about ourselves. He should invariably praise us for whatever qualities he knows we haven't got. But he should be pitiless, quite pitiless, in reproaching us for the virtues that we have never dreamed of possessing. He should never believe that we know the use of useful things. That would be unforgivable. But he should shower on us everything we don't want.

LADY CAR. As far as I can see, he is to do nothing but pay bills and compliments.

MRS. ALL. He should persistently compromise us in public, and treat us with absolute respect when we are alone. And yet he should be always ready to have a perfectly terrible scene, whenever we want one, and to become miserable, absolutely miserable, at a moment's notice, and to overwhelm us with just reproaches in less than twenty minutes, and to be positively violent at the end of half an hour, and to leave us for ever at a quarter to eight, when we have to go and dress for dinner. And when, after that, one has seen him for really the last time, and he has refused to take back the little things he has given one, and promised never to communicate with one again, or to write one any foolish letters, he should be perfectly broken-hearted, and telegraph to one all day long, and send one little notes every half-hour by a private hansom, and dine quite alone at the club, so that every one should know how unhappy he was. And after a whole dreadful week, during which one has gone about everywhere with one's husband, just to show how absolutely lonely one was, he may be given a third last parting, in the evening, and then, if his conduct has been quite irreproachable, and one has behaved really badly to him, he should be allowed to admit that he has been entirely in the wrong, and when he has admitted that, it becomes a woman's duty to forgive, and one can do it all over again from the beginning, with variations.

LADY HUN. How clever you are, my dear! You never mean a single word you say.

LADY STU. Thank you, thank you. It has been quite, quite entrancing. I must try and remember it all. There are such a number of details that are so very, very important.

LADY CAR. But you have not told us yet what the reward of the Ideal Man is to be.

MRS. ALL. His reward? Oh, infinite expectation. That is quite enough for him.

LADY STU. But men are so terribly, terribly exacting, are they not?

MRS. ALL. That makes no matter. One should never surrender.

LADY STU. Not even to the Ideal Man?

MRS. ALL. Certainly not to him. Unless, of course, one wants to grow tired of him.

LADY STU. Oh! . . . yes. I see that. It is very, very helpful. Do you think, Mrs. Allonby, I shall ever meet the Ideal Man? Or are there more than one?

MRS. ALL. There are just four in London, Lady Stutfield.

LADY HUN. Oh, my dear!

MRS. ALL. [*Going over to her.*] What has happened? Do tell me.

LADY HUN. [*In a low voice.*] I had completely forgotten that the American young lady has been in the room all the time. I am afraid some of this clever talk may have shocked her a little.

MRS. ALL. Ah, that will do her so much good!

LADY HUN. Let us hope she didn't understand much. I think I had better go over and talk to her. [*Rises and goes across to Hester Worsley.*] Well, dear Miss Worsley. [*Sitting down beside her.*] How quiet you have been in your nice little corner all this time! I suppose you have been reading a book? There are so many books here in the library.

HES. No, I have been listening to the conversation.

LADY HUN. You mustn't believe everything that was said, you know, dear.

HES. I didn't believe any of it.

LADY HUN. That is quite right, dear.

HES. [*Continuing.*] I couldn't believe that any women could really hold such views of life as I have heard to-night from some of your guests. [*An awkward pause.*]

LADY HUN. I hear you have such pleasant society in America. Quite like our own in places, my son wrote to me.

HES. There are cliques in America as elsewhere, Lady Hunstanton. But true American society consists simply of all the good women and good men we have in our country.

LADY HUN. What a sensible system, and I dare say quite pleasant, too. I am afraid in England we have too many artificial social barriers. We don't see as much as we should of the middle and lower classes.

HES. In America we have no lower classes.

LADY HUN. Really? What a very strange arrangement!

MRS. ALL. What is that dreadful girl talking about?

LADY STU. She is painfully natural, is she not?

LADY CAR. There are a great many things you haven't got in America, I am told, Miss Worsley. They say you have no ruins, and no curiosities.

MRS. ALL. [*To Lady Stutfield.*] What nonsense! They have their mothers and their manners.

HES. The English aristocracy supply us with our curiosities, Lady Caroline. They are sent over to us every summer, regularly, in the steamers, and propose to us the day after they land. As for ruins, we are trying to build up something that will last longer than brick and stone. [*Gets up to take her fan from table.*]

LADY HUN. What is that, dear? Ah, yes, an iron Exhibition, is it not, at that place that has the curious name?

HES. [*Standing by table.*] We are trying to build up life, Lady Hunstanton, on a better, truer, purer basis than life rests on here. This sounds strange to you all, no doubt. How could it sound other than strange? You rich people in England, you don't know how you are living. How could you know? You shut out from your society the gentle and the good. You laugh at the simple and the pure. Living, as you all do, on others and by them, you sneer at self-sacrifice, and if you throw bread to the poor, it is merely to keep them quiet for a season. With all your pomp and wealth and art you don't know how to live–you don't even know that. You love the beauty that you can see and touch and handle, the beauty that you can destroy, and do destroy, but of the unseen beauty of life, of the unseen beauty of a higher life, you know nothing. You have lost life's secret. Oh, your English society seems to me shallow, selfish, foolish. It has blinded its eyes, and stopped its ears. It lies like a leper in purple. It sits like a dead thing smeared with gold. It is all wrong, all wrong.

LADY STU. I don't think one should know of these things. It is not very, very nice, is it?

LADY HUN. My dear Miss Worsley, I thought you liked English society so much. You were such a success in it. And you were so much admired by the best people. I quite forget what Lord Henry Weston said of you–but it was most complimentary, and you know what an authority he is on beauty.

HES. Lord Henry Weston! I remember him, Lady Hunstanton. A man with a hideous smile and a hideous past. He is asked everywhere. No dinner-party is complete without him. What of those whose ruin is due to him? They are outcasts. They are nameless. If you met them in the street you would turn your head away. I don't complain of their punishment. Let all women who have sinned be punished.

[*Mrs. Arbuthnot enters from terrace behind in a cloak with a lace veil over her head. She hears the last words and starts.*]

LADY HUN. My dear young lady!

HES. It is right that they should be punished, but don't let them be the only ones to suffer. If a man and woman have sinned, let them both go forth into the desert to love or loathe each other there. Let them both be branded. Set a mark, if you wish, on each, but don't punish the one and let the other go free. Don't have one law for men and another for women. You are unjust to women in England. And till you count what is a shame in a woman to be an infamy in a man, you will always be unjust, and Right, that pillar of fire, and Wrong, that pillar of cloud, will be made dim to your eyes, or be not seen at all, or if seen, not regarded.

LADY CAR. Might I, dear Miss Worsley, as you are standing up, ask you for my cotton that is just behind you? Thank you.

LADY HUN. My dear Mrs. Arbuthnot! I am so pleased you have come up. But I didn't hear you announced.

MRS. ARB. Oh, I came straight in from the terrace, Lady Hunstanton, just as I was. You didn't tell me you had a party.

LADY HUN. Not a party. Only a few guests who are staying in the house, and whom you must know. Allow me. [*Tries to help her. Rings bell.*] Caroline, this is Mrs. Arbuthnot, one of my sweetest friends. Lady Caroline Pontefract, Lady Stutfield, Mrs. Allonby, and my young American friend, Miss Worsley, who has just been telling us all how wicked we are.

HES. I am afraid you think I spoke too strongly, Lady Hunstanton. But there are some things in England——

LADY HUN. My dear young lady, there was a great deal of truth, I dare say, in what you said, and you looked very pretty while you said it, which is much more important, Lord Illingworth would tell us. The only point where I thought you were a little hard was about Lady Caroline's brother, about poor Lord Henry. He is really such good company.

[*Enter Footman.*]

Take Mrs. Arbuthnot's things. [*Exit Footman with wraps.*]

HES. Lady Caroline, I had no idea it was your brother. I am sorry for the pain I must have caused you—I——

LADY CAR. My dear Miss Worsley, the only part of your little speech, if I may so term it, with which I thoroughly agreed, was the part about my brother. Nothing that you could possibly say could be too bad for him. I regard Henry as infamous, absolutely infamous. But I am bound to state, as you were remarking, Jane, that he is excellent company, and he has one of the best cooks in London, and after a good dinner one can forgive anybody, even one's own relations.

LADY HUN. [*To Miss Worsley.*] Now, do come, dear, and make friends with Mrs. Arbuthnot. She is one of the good, sweet, simple people you told us we never admitted into society. I am sorry to say Mrs. Arbuthnot comes very rarely to me. But that is not my fault.

MRS. ALL. What a bore it is the men staying so long after dinner! I expect they are saying the most dreadful things about us.

LADY STU. Do you really think so?

MRS. ALL. I am sure of it.

LADY STU. How very, very horrid of them! Shall we go on to the terrace?

MRS. ALL. Oh, anything to get away from the dowagers and the dowdies.

[*Rises and goes with Lady Stutfield to door L. C.*] We are only going to look at the stars, Lady Hunstanton.

LADY HUN. You will find a great many, dear, a great many. But don't catch cold. [*To Mrs. Arbuthnot.*] We shall all miss Gerald so much, dear Mrs. Arbuthnot.

MRS. ARB. But has Lord Illingworth really offered to make Gerald his secretary?

LADY HUN. Oh, yes! He has been most charming about it. He has the highest possible opinion of your boy. You don't know Lord Illingworth, I believe, dear.

MRS. ARB. I have never met him.

LADY HUN. You know him by name, no doubt?

MRS. ARB. I am afraid I don't. I live so much out of the world, and see so few people. I remember hearing years ago of an old Lord Illingworth who lived in Yorkshire, I think.

LADY HUN. Ah, yes. That would be the last Earl but one. He was a very curious man. He wanted to marry beneath him. Or wouldn't, I believe. There was some scandal about it. The present Lord Illingworth is quite different. He is very distinguished. He does—well, he does nothing, which I am afraid our pretty American visitor here thinks very wrong of anybody, and I don't know that he cares much for the subjects in which you are so interested, dear Mrs. Arbuthnot. Do you think, Caroline, that Lord Illingworth is interested in the Housing of the Poor?

LADY CAR. I should fancy not at all, Jane.

LADY HUN. We all have our different tastes, have we not? But Lord Illingworth has a very high position, and there is nothing he couldn't get if he chose to ask for it. Of course, he is comparatively a young man still, and he has only come to his title within—how long exactly is it, Caroline, since Lord Illingworth succeeded?

LADY CAR. About four years, I think, Jane. I know it was the same year in which my brother had his last exposure in the evening newspapers.

LADY HUN. Ah, I remember. That would be about four years ago. Of course, there were a great many people between the present Lord Illingworth and the title, Mrs. Arbuthnot. There was—who was there, Caroline?

LADY CAR. There was poor Margaret's baby. You remember how anxious she was to have a boy, and it was a boy, but it died, and her husband died shortly afterwards, and she married almost immediately one of Lord Ascot's sons, who, I am told, beats her.

LADY HUN. Ah, that is in the family, dear, that is in the family. And there was also, I remember, a clergyman who wanted to be a lunatic, or a lunatic who wanted to be a clergyman, I forget which, but I know the Court of Chancery investigated the matter, and decided that he was quite sane. And I saw him afterwards at poor Lord Plumstead's with straws in his hair, or something very odd about him. I can't recall what. I often regret, Lady Caroline, that dear Lady Cecilia never lived to see her son get the title.

MRS. ARB. Lady Cecilia?

LADY HUN. Lord Illingworth's mother, dear Mrs. Arbuthnot, was one of the Duchess of Jerningham's pretty daughters, and she married Sir Thomas Harford, who wasn't considered a very good match for her at the time, though he was said to be the handsomest man in London. I knew them all quite intimately, and both the sons, Arthur and George.

MRS. ARB. It was the eldest son who succeeded, of course, Lady Hunstanton?

LADY HUN. No, dear, he was killed in the hunting field. Or was it fishing, Caroline? I forget. But George came in for everything. I always tell him no younger son has ever had such good luck as he has had.

MRS. ARB. Lady Hunstanton, I want to speak to Gerald at once. Might I see him? Can he be sent for?

LADY HUN. Certainly, dear. I will send one of the servants into the dining-room to fetch him. I don't know what keeps the gentlemen so long. [*Rings bell.*] When I knew Lord Illingworth first as plain George Harford, he was simply a very brilliant young man about town, with not a penny of money except what poor dear Lady Cecilia gave him. She was quite devoted to him. Chiefly, I fancy, because he was on bad terms with his father. Oh, here is the dear Archdeacon. [*To Servant.*] It doesn't matter.

[*Enter Sir John and Doctor Daubeny. Sir John goes over to Lady Stutfield, Doctor Daubeny to Lady Hunstanton.*]

THE ARCHD. Lord Illingworth has been most entertaining. I have never enjoyed myself more. [*Sees Mrs. Arbuthnot.*] Ah, Mrs. Arbuthnot.

LADY HUN. [*To Doctor Daubeny.*] You see I have got Mrs. Arbuthnot to come to me at last.

THE ARCHD. That is a great honour, Lady Hunstanton. Mrs. Daubeny will be quite jealous of you.

LADY HUN. Ah, I am so sorry Mrs. Daubeny could not come with you to-night. Headache as usual, I suppose.

THE ARCHD. Yes, Lady Hunstanton; a perfect martyr. But she is happiest alone. She is happiest alone.

LADY CAR. [*To her husband.*] John! [*Sir John goes over to his wife. Doctor Daubeny talks to Lady Hunstanton and Mrs. Arbuthnot.*]

[*Mrs. Arbuthnot watches Lord Illingworth the whole time. He has passed across the room without noticing her, and approaches Mrs. Allonby, who with Lady Stutfield is standing by the door looking on to the terrace.*]

LORD ILL. How is the most charming woman in the world?

MRS. ALL. [*Taking Lady Stutfield by the hand.*] We are both quite well, thank you, Lord Illingworth. But what a short time you have been in the dining-room. It seems as if we had only just left.

LORD ILL. I was bored to death. Never opened my lips the whole time. Absolutely longing to come in to you.

MRS. ALL. You should have. The American girl has been giving us a lecture.

LORD ILL. Really? All Americans lecture, I believe. I suppose it is something in their climate. What did she lecture about?

MRS. ALL. Oh, Puritanism, of course.

LORD ILL. I am going to convert her, am I not? How long do you give me?

MRS. ALL. A week.

LORD ILL. A week is more than enough.

[*Enter Gerald and Lord Alfred.*]

GER. [*Going to Mrs. Arbuthnot.*] Dear mother!

MRS. ARB. Gerald, I don't feel at all well. See me home, Gerald. I shouldn't have come.

GER. I am so sorry, mother. Certainly. But you must know Lord Illingworth first. [*Goes across room.*]

MRS. ARB. Not to-night, Gerald.

GER. Lord Illingworth, I want you so much to know my mother.

LORD ILL. With the greatest pleasure. [*To Mrs. Allonby.*] I'll be back in a moment. People's mothers always bore me to death. All women become like their mothers. That is their tragedy.

MRS. ALL. No man does. That is his.

LORD ILL. What a delightful mood you are in to-night! [*Turns round and goes across with Gerald to Mrs. Arbuthnot. When he sees her, he starts back in wonder. Then slowly his eyes turn towards Gerald.*]

GER. Mother, this is Lord Illingworth, who has offered to take me as his private secretary. [*Mrs. Arbuthnot bows coldly.*] It is a wonderful opening for me, isn't it? I hope he won't be disappointed in me, that is all. You'll thank Lord Illingworth, mother, won't you?

MRS. ARB. Lord Illingworth is very good, I am sure, to interest himself in you for the moment.

LORD ILL. [*Putting his hand on Gerald's shoulder.*] Oh, Gerald and I are great friends already, Mrs. . . . Arbuthnot.

MRS. ARB. There can be nothing in common between you and my son, Lord Illingworth.

GER. Dear mother, how can you say so? Of course, Lord Illingworth is awfully clever and that sort of thing. There is nothing Lord Illingworth doesn't know.

LORD ILL. My dear boy!

GER. He knows more about life than any one I have ever met. I feel an awful duffer when I am with you, Lord Illingworth. Of course, I have had so few advantages. I have not been to Eton or Oxford like other chaps. But Lord Illingworth doesn't seem to mind that. He has been awfully good to me, mother.

MRS. ARB. Lord Illingworth may change his mind. He may not really want you as his secretary.

GER. Mother!

MRS. ARB. You must remember, as you said yourself, you have had so few advantages.

MRS. ALL. Lord Illingworth, I want to speak to you for a moment. Do come over.

LORD ILL. Will you excuse me, Mrs. Arbuthnot? Now, don't let your charming mother make any more difficulties, Gerald. The thing is quite settled, isn't it?

GER. I hope so. [*Lord Illingworth goes across to Mrs. Allonby.*]

MRS. ALL. I thought you were never going to leave the lady in black velvet.

LORD ILL. She is excessively handsome. [*Looks at Mrs. Arbuthnot.*]

LADY HUN. Caroline, shall we all make a move to the music-room? Miss Worsley is going to play. You'll come too, dear Mrs. Arbuthnot, won't you? You don't know what a treat is in store for you. [*To Doctor Daubeny.*] I must really take Miss Worsley down some afternoon to the rectory. I should so much like dear Mrs. Daubeny to hear on the violin. Ah, I forgot. Dear Mrs. Daubeny's hearing is a little defective, is it not?

THE ARCHD. Her deafness is a great privation to her. She can't even hear my sermons now. She reads them at home. But she has many resources in herself, many resources.

LADY HUN. She reads a good deal, I suppose?

THE ARCHD. Just the very largest print. The eyesight is rapidly going. But she's never morbid, never morbid.

GER. [*To Lord Illingworth.*] Do speak to my mother, Lord Illingworth, before you go into the music-room. She seems to think, somehow, you don't mean what you said to me.

MRS. ALL. Aren't you coming?

LORD ILL. In a few moments. Lady Hunstanton, if Mrs. Arbuthnot would allow me, I would like to say a few words to her, and we will join you later on.

LADY HUN. Ah, of course. You will have a great deal to say to her, and she will have a great deal to thank you for. It is not every son who gets such an offer, Mrs. Arbuthnot. But I know you appreciate that, dear.

LADY CAR. John!

LADY HUN. Now, don't keep Mrs. Arbuthnot too long, Lord Illingworth. We can't spare her.

[*Exit following the other guests. Sound of violin heard from music-room.*]

LORD ILL. So that is our son, Rachel! Well, I am very proud of him. He is a Harford, every inch of him. By the way, why Arbuthnot, Rachel?

MRS. ARB. One name is as good as another, when one has no right to any name.

LORD ILL. I suppose so—but why Gerald?

MRS. ARB. After a man whose heart I broke—after my father.

LORD ILL. Well, Rachel, what is over is over. All I have got to say now is that I am very, very much pleased with our boy. The world will know him merely as my private secretary, but to me he will be something very near, and very dear. It is a curious thing, Rachel; my life seemed to be quite complete. It was not so. It lacked something, it lacked a son. I have found my son now, I am glad I have found him.

MRS. ARB. You have no right to claim him, or the smallest part of him. The boy is entirely mine, and shall remain mine.

LORD ILL. My dear Rachel, you have had him to yourself for over twenty years. Why not let me have him for a little now? He is quite as much mine as yours.

MRS. ARB. Are you talking of the child you abandoned? Of the child who, as far as you are concerned, might have died of hunger and want?

LORD ILL. You forget, Rachel, it was you who left me. It was not I who left you.

MRS. ARB. I left you because you refused to give the child a name. Before my son was born, I implored you to marry me.

LORD ILL. I had no expectations then. And besides, Rachel, I wasn't much older than you were. I was only twenty-two. I was twenty-one, I believe, when the whole thing began in your father's garden.

MRS. ARB. When a man is old enough to do wrong he should be old enough to do right also.

LORD ILL. My dear Rachel, intellectual generalities are always interesting, but generalities in morals mean absolutely nothing. As for saying I left our child to starve, that, of course, is untrue and silly. My mother offered you six hundred a year. But you wouldn't take anything. You simply disappeared, and carried the child away with you.

MRS. ARB. I wouldn't have accepted a penny from her. Your father was different. He told you, in my presence, when we were in Paris, that it was your duty to marry me.

LORD ILL. Oh, duty is what one expects from others, it is not what one does oneself. Of course, I was influenced by my mother. Every man is when he is young.

MRS. ARB. I am glad to hear you say so. Gerald shall certainly not go away with you.

LORD ILL. What nonsense, Rachel!

MRS. ARB. Do you think I would allow my son——

LORD ILL. *Our* son.

MRS. ARB. My son [*Lord Illingworth shrugs his shoulders*]—to go away with the man who spoiled my youth, who ruined my life, who has tainted every moment of my days? You don't realise what my past has been in suffering and in shame.

LORD ILL. My dear Rachel, I must candidly say that I think Gerald's future considerably more important than your past.

MRS. ARB. Gerald cannot separate his future from my past.

LORD ILL. That is exactly what he should do. That is exactly what you should help him to do. What a typical woman you are! You talk sentimentally, and you are thoroughly selfish the whole time. But don't let us have a scene. Rachel, I want you to look at this matter from the common-sense point of view, from the point of view of what is best for our son, leaving you and me out of the question. What is our son at present? An underpaid clerk in a small Provincial Bank in a third-rate English town. If you imagine he is quite happy in such a position, you are mistaken. He is thoroughly discontented.

MRS. ARB. He was not discontented till he met you. You have made him so.

LORD ILL. Of course, I made him so. Discontent is the first step in the progress of a man or a nation. But I did not leave him with a mere longing for things he could not get. No, I made him a charming offer. He jumped at it, I need hardly say. Any young man would. And now, simply because it turns out that

I am the boy's own father, and he my own son, you propose practically to ruin his career. That is to say, if I were a perfect stranger, you would allow Gerald to go away with me, but as he is my own flesh and blood you won't. How utterly illogical you are!

MRS. ARB. I will not allow him to go.

LORD ILL. How can you prevent it? What excuse can you give to him for making him decline such an offer as mine? I won't tell him in what relations I stand to him, I need hardly say. But you daren't tell him. You know that. Look how you have brought him up.

MRS. ARB. I have brought him up to be a good man.

LORD ILL. Quite so. And what is the result? You have educated him to be your judge if he ever finds you out. And a bitter, an unjust judge he will be to you. Don't be deceived, Rachel. Children begin by loving their parents. After a time they judge them. Rarely, if ever, do they forgive them.

MRS. ARB. George, don't take my son away from me. I have had twenty years of sorrow, and I have only had one thing to love me, only one thing to love. You have had a life of joy, and pleasure, and success. You have been quite happy, you have never thought of us. There was no reason, according to your views of life, why you should have remembered us at all. Your meeting us was a mere accident, a horrible accident. Forget it. Don't come now, and rob me of . . . of all I have, of all I have in the whole world. You are so rich in other things. Leave me the little vineyard of my life; leave me the walled-in garden and the well of water; the ewe-lamb God sent me, in pity or in wrath, oh! leave me that. George, don't take Gerald from me.

LORD ILL. Rachel, at the present moment you are not necessary to Gerald's career; I am. There is nothing more to be said on the subject.

MRS. ARB. I will not let him go.

LORD ILL. Here is Gerald. He has a right to decide for himself.

[*Enter Gerald.*]

GER. Well, dear mother, I hope you have settled it all with Lord Illingworth?

MRS. ARB. I have not, Gerald.

LORD ILL. Your mother seems not to like your coming with me, for some reason.

GER. Why, mother?

MRS. ARB. I thought you were quite happy here with me, Gerald. I didn't know you were so anxious to leave me.

GER. Mother, how can you talk like that? Of course I have been quite happy with you. But a man can't always stay with his mother. No chap does. I want to make myself a position, to do something. I thought you would have been proud to see me Lord Illingworth's secretary.

MRS. ARB. I do not think you would be suitable as a private secretary to Lord Illingworth. You have no qualifications.

LORD ILL. I don't wish to seem to interfere for a moment, Mrs. Arbuthnot, but as far as your last objection is concerned, I surely am the best judge. And I can only tell you that your son has all the qualifications I had hoped for. He has more, in fact, than I had even thought of. Far more. [*Mrs. Arbuthnot remains silent.*] Have you any other reason, Mrs. Arbuthnot, why you don't wish your son to accept this post?

GER. Have you, mother? Do answer.

LORD ILL. If you have, Mrs. Arbuthnot, pray, pray say it. We are quite by ourselves here. Whatever it is, I need not say I will not repeat it.

GER. Mother?

LORD ILL. If you would like to be alone with your son, I will leave you. You may have some other reason you don't wish me to hear.

MRS. ARB. I have no other reason.

LORD ILL. Then, my dear boy, we may look on the thing as settled. Come, you and I will smoke a cigarette on the terrace together. And Mrs. Arbuthnot, pray let me tell you, that I think you have acted very, very wisely.

[*Exit with Gerald. Mrs. Arbuthnot is left alone. She stands immobile, with a look of unutterable sorrow on her face.*]

ACT-DROP.

THIRD ACT

SCENE—*The Picture-gallery at Hunstanton Chase. Door at back leading on to terrace.*

[*Lord Illingworth and Gerald, R. C. Lord Illingworth lolling on a sofa. Gerald in a chair.*]

LORD ILL. Thoroughly sensible woman, your mother, Gerald. I knew she would come round in the end.

GER. My mother is awfully conscientious, Lord Illingworth, and I know she doesn't think I am educated enough to be your secretary. She is perfectly right, too. I was fearfully idle when I was at school, and I couldn't pass an examination now to save my life.

LORD ILL. My dear Gerald, examinations are of no value whatsoever. If a man is a gentleman, he knows quite enough, and if he is not a gentleman, whatever he knows is bad for him.

GER. But I am so ignorant of the world, Lord Illingworth.

LORD ILL. Don't be afraid, Gerald. Remember that you've got on your side the most wonderful thing in the world—youth! There is nothing like youth. The middle-aged are mortgaged to Life. The old are in Life's lumber-room. But youth is the Lord of Life. Youth has a kingdom waiting for it. Every one is born a king, and most people die in exile, like most kings. To win back my youth, Gerald, there is nothing I wouldn't do—except take exercise, get up early, or be a useful member of the community.

GER. But you don't call yourself old, Lord Illingworth?

LORD ILL. I am old enough to be your father, Gerald.

GER. I don't remember my father; he died years ago.

LORD ILL. So Lady Hunstanton told me.

GER. It is very curious, my mother never talks to me about my father. I sometimes think she must have married beneath her.

LORD ILL. [*Winces slightly.*] Really? [*Goes over and puts his hand on Gerald's shoulder.*] You have missed not having a father, I suppose, Gerald?

GER. Oh, no; my mother has been so good to me. No one ever had such a mother as I have had.

LORD ILL. I am quite sure of that. Still I should imagine that most mothers don't quite understand their sons. Don't realise, I mean, that a son has ambitions, a desire to see life, to make himself a name. After all, Gerald, you couldn't be expected to pass all your life in such a hole as Wrockley, could you?

GER. Oh, no! It would be dreadful!

LORD ILL. A mother's love is very touching, of course, but it is often curiously selfish. I mean, there is a good deal of selfishness in it.

GER. [*Slowly.*] I suppose there is.

LORD ILL. Your mother is a thoroughly good woman. But good women have such limited views of life, their horizon is so small, their interests are so petty, aren't they?

GER. They are awfully interested, certainly, in things we don't care much about.

LORD ILL. I suppose your mother is very religious, and that sort of thing.

GER. Oh, yes, she's always going to church.

LORD ILL. Ah! she is not modern, and to be modern is the only thing worth being now-a-days. You want to be modern, don't you, Gerald? You want to know life as it really is. Not to be put off with any old-fashioned theories about life. Well, what you have to do at present is simply to fit yourself for the best society. A man who can dominate a London dinner-table can dominate the world. The future belongs to the dandy. It is the exquisites who are going to rule.

GER. I should like to wear nice things awfully, but I have always been told that a man should not think too much about his clothes.

LORD ILL. People now-a-days are so absolutely superficial that they don't understand the philosophy of the superficial. By the way, Gerald, you should learn how to tie your tie better. Sentiment is all very well for the button-hole. But the essential thing for a necktie is style. A well-tied tie is the first serious step in life.

GER. [*Laughing.*] I might be able to learn how to tie a tie, Lord Illingworth, but I should never be able to talk as you do. I don't know how to talk.

LORD ILL. Oh! talk to every woman as if you loved her, and to every man as if he bored you, and at the end of your first season you will have the reputation of possessing the most perfect social tact.

GER. But it is very difficult to get into society, isn't it?

LORD ILL. To get into the best society, now-a-days, one has either to feed people, amuse people, or shock people—that is all.

GER. I suppose society is wonderfully delightful!

LORD ILL. To be in it is merely a bore. But to be out of it simply a tragedy.

Society is a necessary thing. No man has any real success in this world unless he has got women to back him, and women rule society. If you have not got women on your side you are quite over. You might as well be a barrister, or a stockbroker, or a journalist at once.

GER. It is very difficult to understand women, is it not?

LORD ILL. You should never try to understand them. Women are pictures. Men are problems. If you want to know what a woman really means–which, by the way, is always a dangerous thing to do–look at her, don't listen to her.

GER. But women are awfully clever, aren't they?

LORD ILL. One should always tell them so. But, to the philosopher, my dear Gerald, women represent the triumph of matter over mind–just as men represent the triumph of mind over morals.

GER. How then can women have so much power as you say they have?

LORD ILL. The history of women is the history of the worst form of tyranny the world has ever known. The tyranny of the weak over the strong. It is the only tyranny that lasts.

GER. But haven't women got a refining influence?

LORD ILL. Nothing refines but the intellect.

GER. Still, there are many different kinds of women, aren't there?

LORD ILL. Only two kinds in society: the plain and the coloured.

GER. But there are good women in society, aren't there?

LORD ILL. Far too many.

GER. But do you think women shouldn't be good?

LORD ILL. One should never tell them so, they'd all become good at once. Women are a fascinatingly wilful sex. Every woman is a rebel, and usually in wild revolt against herself.

GER. You have never been married, Lord Illingworth, have you?

LORD ILL. Men marry because they are tired; women because they are curious. Both are disappointed.

GER. But don't you think one can be happy when one is married?

LORD ILL. Perfectly happy. But the happiness of a married man, my dear Gerald, depends on the people he has not married.

GER. But if one is in love?

LORD ILL. One should always be in love. That is the reason one should never marry.

GER. Love is a very wonderful thing, isn't it?

LORD ILL. When one is in love one begins by deceiving oneself. And one ends by deceiving others. That is what the world calls a romance. But a really *grande passion* is comparatively rare now-a-days. It is the privilege of people who have nothing to do. That is the one use of the idle classes in a country, and the only possible explanation of us Harfords.

GER. Harfords, Lord Illingworth?

LORD ILL. That is my family name. You should study the Peerage, Gerald. It is the one book a young man about town should know thoroughly, and it is the best thing in fiction the English have ever done. And now, Gerald, you are going now into a perfectly new life with me, and I want you to know how to live. [*Mrs. Arbuthnot appears on terrace behind.*] For the world has been made by fools that wise men should live in it!

[*Enter L. C. Lady Hunstanton and Dr. Daubeny.*]

Lady Hun. Ah! here you are, dear Lord Illingworth. Well, I suppose you have been telling our young friend, Gerald, what his new duties are to be, and giving him a great deal of good advice over a pleasant cigarette.

Lord Ill. I have been giving him the best of advice, Lady Hunstanton, and the best of cigarettes.

Lady Hun. I am so sorry I was not here to listen to you, but I suppose I am too old now to learn. Except from you, dear Archdeacon, when you are in your nice pulpit. But then I always know what you are going to say, so I don't feel alarmed. [*Sees Mrs. Arbuthnot.*] Ah! dear Mrs. Arbuthnot, do come and join us. Come, dear. [*Enter Mrs. Arbuthnot.*] Gerald has been having such a long talk with Lord Illingworth; I am sure you must feel very much flattered at the pleasant way in which everything has turned out for him. Let us sit down. [*They sit down.*] And how is your beautiful embroidery going on?

Mrs. Arb. I am always at work, Lady Hunstanton.

Lady Hun. Mrs. Daubeny embroiders a little, too, doesn't she?

The Archd. She was very deft with her needle once, quite a Dorcas. But the gout has crippled her fingers a good deal. She has not touched the tambour frame for nine or ten years. But she has many other amusements. She is very much interested in her own health.

Lady Hun. Ah! that is always a nice distraction, is it not? Now, what are you talking about, Lord Illingworth? Do tell us.

Lord Ill. I was on the point of explaining to Gerald that the world has always laughed at its own tragedies, that being the only way in which it has been able to bear them. And that, consequently, whatever the world has treated seriously belongs to the comedy side of things.

Lady Hun. Now I am quite out of my depth. I usually am when Lord Illingworth says anything. And the Humane Society is most careless. They never rescue me. I am left to sink. I have a dim idea, dear Lord Illingworth, that you are always on the side of the sinners, and I know I always try to be on the side of the saints, but that is as far as I get. And after all, it may be merely the fancy of a drowning person.

Lord Ill. The only difference between the saint and the sinner is that every saint has a past, and every sinner has a future.

Lady Hun. Ah! that quite does for me. I haven't a word to say. You and I, dear Mrs. Arbuthnot, are behind the age. We can't follow Lord Illingworth. Too much care was taken with our education, I am afraid. To have been well brought up is a great drawback now-a-days. It shuts one out from so much.

Mrs. Arb. I should be sorry to follow Lord Illingworth in any of his opinions.

Lady Hun. You are quite right, dear.

[*Gerald shrugs his shoulders and looks irritably over at his mother. Enters Lady Caroline.*]

Lady Car. Jane, have you seen John anywhere?

LADY HUN. You needn't be anxious about him, dear. He is with Lady Stutfield; I saw them some time ago, in the Yellow Drawing-room. They seem quite happy together. You are not going, Caroline? Pray sit down.

LADY CAR. I think I had better look after John.

[*Exit Lady Caroline.*]

LADY HUN. It doesn't do to pay men so much attention. And Caroline has really nothing to be anxious about. Lady Stutfield is very sympathetic. She is just as sympathetic about one thing as she is about another. A beautiful nature. [*Enter Sir John and Mrs. Allonby.*] Ah! here is Sir John! And with Mrs. Allonby too! I suppose it was Mrs. Allonby I saw him with. Sir John, Caroline has been looking everywhere for you.

MRS. ALL. We have been waiting for her in the Music-room, dear Lady Hunstanton.

LADY HUN. Ah! the Music-room, of course. I thought it was the Yellow Drawing-room, my memory is getting so defective. [*To the Archdeacon.*] Mrs. Daubeny has a wonderful memory, hasn't she?

THE ARCHD. She used to be quite remarkable for her memory, but since her last attack she recalls chiefly the events of her early childhood. But she finds great pleasure in such retrospections, great pleasure.

[*Enter Lady Stutfield and Mr. Kelvil.*]

LADY HUN. Ah! dear Lady Stutfield! and what has Mr. Kelvil been talking to you about?

LADY STU. About Bimetallism, as well as I remember.

LADY HUN. Bimetallism! Is that quite a nice subject? However, I know people discuss everything very freely now-a-days. What did Sir John talk to you about, dear Mrs. Allonby?

MRS. ALL. About Patagonia.

LADY HUN. Really? What a remote topic! But very improving, I have no doubt.

MRS. ALL. He has been most interesting on the subject of Patagonia. Savages seem to have quite the same views as cultured people on almost all subjects. They are excessively advanced.

LADY HUN. What do they do?

MRS. ALL. Apparently everything.

LADY HUN. Well, it is very gratifying, dear Archdeacon, is it not, to find that Human Nature is permanently one. On the whole, the world is the same world, is it not?

LORD ILL. The world is simply divided into two classes—those who believe the incredible, like the public—and those who do the improbable——

MRS. ALL. Like yourself?

LORD ILL. Yes; I am always astonishing myself. It is the only thing that makes life worth living.

LADY STU. And what have you been doing lately that astonishes you?

LORD ILL. I have been discovering all kinds of beautiful qualities in my own nature.

MRS. ALL. Ah! don't become quite perfect all at once. Do it gradually!

LORD ILL. I don't intend to grow perfect at all. At least, I hope I sha'n't. It would be most inconvenient. Women love us for our defects. If we have enough of them, they will forgive us everything, even our gigantic intellects.

MRS. ALL. It is premature to ask us to forgive analysis. We forgive adoration; that is quite as much as should be expected from us.

[*Enter Lord Alfred. He joins Lady Stutfield.*]

LADY HUN. Ah! we women should forgive everything, shouldn't we, dear Mrs. Arbuthnot? I am sure you agree with me in that.

MRS. ARB. I do not, Lady Hunstanton. I think there are many things women should never forgive.

LADY HUN. What sort of things?

MRS. ARB. The ruin of another woman's life.

[*Moves slowly away to back of stage.*]

LADY HUN. Ah! those things are very sad, no doubt, but I believe there are admirable homes where people of that kind are looked after and reformed, and I think on the whole that the secret of life is to take things very, very easily.

MRS. ALL. The secret of life is never to have an emotion that is unbecoming.

LADY STU. The secret of life is to appreciate the pleasure of being terribly. terribly deceived.

KEL. The secret of life is to resist temptation, Lady Stutfield.

LORD ILL. There is no secret of life. Life's aim, if it has one, is simply to be always looking for temptations. There are not nearly enough. I sometimes pass a whole day without coming across a single one. It is quite dreadful. It makes one so nervous about the future.

LADY HUN. [*Shakes her fan at him.*] I don't know how it is, dear Lord Illingworth, but everything you have said to-day seems to me excessively immoral. It has been most interesting, listening to you.

LORD ILL. All thought is immoral. Its very essence is destruction. If you think of anything, you kill it. Nothing survives being thought of.

LADY HUN. I don't understand a word, Lord Illingworth. But I have no doubt it is all quite true. Personally, I have very little to reproach myself with, on the score of thinking. I don't believe in women thinking too much. Women should think in moderation, as they should do all things in moderation.

LORD ILL. Moderation is a fatal thing, Lady Hunstanton. Nothing succeeds like excess.

LADY HUN. I hope I shall remember that. It sounds an admirable maxim. But I'm beginning to forget everything. It's a great misfortune.

LORD ILL. It is one of your most fascinating qualities, Lady Hunstanton. No woman should have a memory. Memory in a woman is the beginning of dowdiness. One can always tell from a woman's bonnet whether she has got a memory or not.

LADY HUN. How charming you are, dear Lord Illingworth. You always find out that one's most glaring fault is one's most important virtue. You have the most comforting views of life.

[*Enter Farquhar.*]

FARQ. Doctor Daubeny's carriage!

Lady Hun. My dear Archdeacon! It is only half-past ten.

The Archd. [*Rising.*] I am afraid I must go, Lady Hunstanton. Tuesday is always one of Mrs. Daubeny's bad nights.

Lady Hun. [*Rising.*] Well, I won't keep you from her. [*Goes with him towards door.*] I have told Farquhar to put a brace of partridge into the carriage. Mrs. Daubeny may fancy them.

The Archd. It is very kind of you, but Mrs. Daubeny never touches solids now. Lives entirely on jellies. But she is wonderfully cheerful, wonderfully cheerful. She has nothing to complain of. [*Exit with Lady Hunstanton.*]

Mrs. All. [*Goes over to Lord Illingworth.*] There is a beautiful moon tonight.

Lord Ill. Let us go and look at it. To look at anything that is inconstant is charming now-a-days.

Mrs. All. You have your looking-glass.

Lord Ill. It is unkind. It merely shows me my wrinkles.

Mrs. All. Mine is better behaved. It never tells me the truth.

Lord Ill. Then it is in love with you.

[*Exeunt Sir John, Lady Stutfield, Mr. Kelvil, and Lord Alfred.*]

Ger. [*to Lord Illingworth.*] May I come too?

Lord Ill. Do, my dear boy. [*Moves towards door with Mrs. Allonby and Gerald.*]

[*Lady Caroline enters, looks rapidly round and goes out in opposite direction to that taken by Sir John and Lady Stutfield.*]

Mrs. Arb. Gerald!

Ger. What, mother?

[*Exit Lord Illingworth with Mrs. Allonby.*]

Mrs. Arb. It is getting late. Let us go home.

Ger. My dear mother. Do let us wait a little longer. Lord Illingworth is so delightful, and, by the way, mother, I have a great surprise for you. We are starting for India at the end of this month.

Mrs. Arb. Let us go home.

Ger. If you really want to, of course, mother, but I must bid good-bye to Lord Illingworth first. I'll be back in five minutes. [*Exit.*]

Mrs. Arb. Let him leave me if he chooses, but not with him—not with him! I couldn't bear it. [*Walks up and down.*]

[*Enter Hester.*]

Hes. What a lovely night it is, Mrs. Arbuthnot.

Mrs. Arb. Is it?

Hes. Mrs. Arbuthnot, I wish you would let us be friends. You are so different from the other women here. When you came into the Drawing-room this evening, somehow you brought with you a sense of what is good and pure in life. I had been foolish. There are things that are right to say, but that may be said at the wrong time and to the wrong people.

Mrs. Arb. I heard what you said. I agree with it, Miss Worsley.

Hes. I didn't know you had heard it. But I knew you would agree with me. A woman who has sinned should be punished, shouldn't she?

Mrs. Arb. Yes.

Hes. She shouldn't be allowed to come into the society of good men and women?

Mrs. Arb. She should not.

Hes. And the man should be punished in the same way?

Mrs. Arb. In the same way. And the children, if there are children, in the same way also?

Hes. Yes, it is right that the sins of the parents should be visited on the children. It is a just law. It is God's law.

Mrs. Arb. It is one of God's terrible laws. [*Moves away to fireplace.*]

Hes. You are distressed about your son leaving you, Mrs. Arbuthnot?

Mrs. Arb. Yes.

Hes. Do you like him going away with Lord Illingworth? Of course there is position, no doubt, and money, but position and money are not everything, are they?

Mrs. Arb. They are nothing; they bring misery.

Hes. Then why do you let your son go with him?

Mrs. Arb. He wishes it himself.

Hes. But if you asked him he would stay, would he not?

Mrs. Arb. He has set his heart on going.

Hes. He couldn't refuse you anything. He loves you too much. Ask him to stay. Let me send him in to you. He is on the terrace at this moment with Lord Illingworth. I heard them laughing together as I passed through the Music-room.

Mrs. Arb. Don't trouble, Miss Worsley, I can wait. It is of no consequence.

Hes. No, I'll tell him you want him. Do–do ask him to stay.

[*Exit Hester*]

Mrs. Arb. He won't come–I know he won't come.

[*Enter Lady Caroline. She looks round anxiously. Enter Gerald.*]

Lady Car. Mr. Arbuthnot, may I ask you is Sir John anywhere on the terrace?

Ger. No, Lady Caroline, he is not on the terrace.

Lady Car. It is very curious. It is time for him to retire

[*Exit Lady Caroline.*]

Ger. Dear mother, I am afraid I kept you waiting. I forgot all about it. I am so happy to-night, mother; I have never been so happy.

Mrs. Arb. At the prospect of going away?

Ger. Don't put it like that, mother. Of course I am sorry to leave you. Why, you are the best mother in the whole world. But after all, as Lord Illingworth says, it is impossible to live in such a place as Wrockley. You don't mind it. But I'm ambitious; I want something more than that. I want to have a career. I want to do something that will make you proud of me, and Lord Illingworth is going to help me. He is going to do everything for me.

Mrs. Arb. Gerald, don't go away with Lord Illingworth. I implore you not to. Gerald, I beg you!

Ger. Mother, how changeable you are! You don't seem to know your own mind for a single moment. An hour and a half ago in the Drawing-room you agreed to the whole thing; now you turn round and make objections, and try to force me to give up my one chance in life. Yes, my one chance. You don't suppose that men like Lord Illingworth are to be found every day, do you, mother? It is very strange that when I have had such a wonderful piece of good luck, the one person to put difficulties in my way should be my own mother. Besides, you know, mother, I love Hester Worsley. Who could help loving her? I love her more than I have ever told you, far more. And if I had a position, if I had prospects, I could–I could ask her to——Don't you understand now, mother, what it means to me to be Lord Illingworth's secretary? To start like that is to find a career ready for one–before one–waiting for one. If I were Lord Illingworth's secretary I could ask Hester to be my wife. As a wretched bank clerk with a hundred a year it would be an impertinence.

MRS. ARB. I fear you need have no hopes of Miss Worsley. I know her views on life. She has just told them to me. [*A pause.*]

GER. Then I have my ambition left, at any rate. That is something–I am glad I have that! You have always tried to crush my ambition, mother–haven't you? You have told me that the world is a wicked place, that success is not worth having, that society is shallow, and all that sort of thing–well, I don't believe it, mother. I think the world must be delightful. I think society must be exquisite. I think success is a thing worth having. You have been wrong in all that you taught me, mother, quite wrong. Lord Illingworth is a successful man. He is a fashionable man. He is a man who lives in the world and for it. Well, I would give anything to be just like Lord Illingworth.

MRS. ARB. I would sooner see you dead.

GER. Mother, what is your objection to Lord Illingworth? Tell me–tell me right out. What is it?

MRS. ARB. He is a bad man.

GER. In what way bad? I don't understand what you mean.

MRS. ARB. I will tell you.

GER. I suppose you think him bad because he doesn't believe the same things as you do. Well, men are different from women, mother. It is natural that they should have different views.

MRS. ARB. It is not what Lord Illingworth believes, or what he does not believe, that makes him bad. It is what he is.

GER. Mother, is it something you know of him? Something you actually know?

MRS. ARB. It is something I know.

GER. Something you are quite sure of?

MRS. ARB. Quite sure of.

GER. How long have you known it?

MRS. ARB. For twenty years.

GER. Is it fair to go back twenty years in any man's career? And what have you or I to do with Lord Illingworth's early life? What business is it of ours?

MRS. ARB. What this man has been, he is now, and will be always.

GER. Mother, tell me what Lord Illingworth did? If he did anything shameful, I will not go away with him. Surely you know me well enough for that?

MRS. ARB. Gerald, come near to me. Quite close to me, as you used to do when you were a little boy, when you were your mother's own boy. [*Gerald sits down beside his mother. She runs her fingers through his hair, and strokes his hands.*] Gerald, there was a girl once, she was very young, she was a little over eighteen at the time. George Harford—that was Lord Illingworth's name then—George Harford met her. She knew nothing about life. He—knew everything. He made this girl love him. He made her love him so much that she left her father's house with him one morning. She loved him so much, and he had promised to marry her! He had solemnly promised to marry her, and she had believed him. She was very young, and—and ignorant of what life really is. But he put the marriage off from week to week, and month to month. She trusted in him all the while. She loved him. Before her child was born—for she had a child—she implored him for the child's sake to marry her, that the child might have a name, that her sin might not be visited on the child, who was innocent. He refused. After the child was born she left him, taking the child away and her life was ruined, and her soul ruined, and all that was sweet, and good, and pure in her ruined also. She suffered terribly—she suffers now. She will always suffer. For her there is no joy, no peace, no atonement. She is a woman who drags a chain like a guilty thing. She is a woman who wears a mask, like a thing that is a leper. The fire cannot purify her. The waters cannot quench her anguish. Nothing can heal her! no anodyne can give her sleep! no poppies forgetfulness! She is lost! She is a lost soul! That is why I call Lord Illingworth a bad man. That is why I don't want my boy to be with him.

GER. My dear mother, it all sounds very tragic, of course. But I dare say the girl was just as much to blame as Lord Illingworth was. After all, would a really nice girl, a girl with any nice feelings at all, go away from her home with a man to whom she was not married, and live with him as his wife? No nice girl would.

MRS. ARB. [*After a pause.*] Gerald, I withdraw all my objections. You are at liberty to go away with Lord Illingworth, when and where you choose.

GER. Dear mother, I knew you wouldn't stand in my way. You are the best woman God ever made. And, as for Lord Illingworth, I don't believe he is capable of anything infamous or base. I can't believe it of him—I can't.

HES. [*Outside.*] Let me go! Let me go!

[*Enter Hester in terror, and rushes over to Gerald and flings herself in his arms.*]

HES. Oh! save me—save me from him!

GER. From whom?

HES. He has insulted me! Horribly insulted me! Save me!

GER. Who? Who has dared——?

[*Lord Illingworth enters at back of stage. Hester breaks from Gerald's arms and points to him.*]

GER. [*He is quite beside himself with rage and indignation.*] Lord Illingworth, you have insulted the purest thing on God's earth, a thing as pure as your own mother. You have insulted the woman I love most in the world with my own mother. As there is a God in heaven, I will kill you.

MRS. ARB. [*Rushing across and catching hold of him.*] No! no!

GER. [*Thrusting her back.*] Don't hold me, mother. Don't hold me—I'll kill him!

MRS. ARB. Gerald!

GER. Let me go, I say!

MRS. ARB. Stop, Gerald, stop! He is your own father!

[*Gerald clutches his mother's hand and looks into her face. She sinks slowly on the ground in shame. Hester steals towards the door. Lord Illingworth frowns and bites his lip. After a time Gerald raises his mother up, puts his arm around her, and leads her from the room.*]

ACT-DROP.

FOURTH ACT

SCENE—*Sitting-room at Mrs. Arbuthnot's House. Large open French window at back, looking onto garden. Doors R.C. and L.C.*

[*Gerald Arbuthnot writing at table.*]

[*Enter Alice R.C. followed by Lady Hunstanton and Mrs. Allonby.*]

ALICE. Lady Hunstanton and Mrs. Allonby. [*Exit L.C.*]

LADY HUN. Good morning, Gerald.

GER. [*Rising.*] Good morning, Lady Hunstanton. Good morning, Mrs. Allonby.

LADY HUN. [*Sitting down.*] We came to inquire for your dear mother, Gerald. I hope she is better?

GER. My mother has not come down yet, Lady Hunstanton.

LADY HUN. Ah, I am afraid the heat was too much for her last night. I think there must have been thunder in the air. Or perhaps it was the music. Music makes one feel so romantic—at least it always gets on one's nerves.

MRS. ALL. It's the same thing, now-a-days.

LADY HUN. I am so glad I don't know what you mean, dear. I am afraid you mean something wrong. Ah, I see you're examining Mrs. Arbuthnot's pretty room. Isn't it nice and old-fashioned?

MRS. ALL. [*Surveying the room through her lorgnette.*] It looks quite the happy English home.

LADY HUN. That's just the word, dear; that just describes it. One feels your mother's good influence in everything she has about her, Gerald.

MRS. ALL. Lord Illingworth says that all influence is bad, but that a good influence is the worst in the world.

LADY HUN. When Lord Illingworth knows Mrs. Arbuthnot better, he will change his mind. I must certainly bring him here.

MRS. ALL. I should like to see Lord Illingworth in a happy English home.

LADY HUN. It would do him a great deal of good, dear. Most women in

London, now-a-days, seem to furnish their rooms with nothing but orchids, foreigners, and French novels. But here we have the room of a sweet saint. Fresh natural flowers, books that don't shock one, pictures that one can look at without blushing.

MRS. ALL. But I like blushing.

LADY HUN. Well, there *is* a good deal to be said for blushing, if one can do it at the proper moment. Poor dear Hunstanton used to tell me I didn't blush nearly often enough. But then he was so very particular. He wouldn't let me know any of his men friends, except those who were over seventy, like poor Lord Ashton; who afterwards, by the way, was brought into the Divorce Court. A most unfortunate case.

MRS. ALL. I delight in men over seventy. They always offer one the devotion of a lifetime. I think seventy an ideal age for a man.

LADY HUN. She is quite incorrigible, Gerald, isn't she? By-the-by, Gerald, I hope your dear mother will come and see me more often now. You and Lord Illingworth start almost immediately, don't you?

GER. I have given up my intention of being Lord Illingworth's secretary.

LADY HUN. Surely not, Gerald! It would be most unwise of you. What reason can you have?

GER. I don't think I should be suitable for the post.

MRS. ALL. I wish Lord Illingworth would ask me to be his secretary. But he says I am not serious enough.

LADY HUN. My dear, you really mustn't talk like that in this house. Mrs. Arbuthnot doesn't know anything about the wicked society in which we all live. She won't go into it. She is far too good. I consider it was a great honour her coming to me last night. It gave quite an atmosphere of respectability to the party.

MRS. ALL. Ah, that must have been what you thought was thunder in the air.

LADY HUN. My dear, how can you say that? There is no resemblance between the two things at all. But really, Gerald, what do you mean by not being suitable?

GER. Lord Illingworth's views of life and mine are too different.

LADY HUN. But, my dear Gerald, at your age you shouldn't have any views of life. They are quite out of place. You must be guided by others in this matter. Lord Illingworth has made you the most flattering offer, and travelling with him you would see the world—as much of it, at least, as one should look at—under the best auspices possible, and stay with all the right people, which is so important at this solemn moment in your career.

GER. I don't want to see the world; I've seen enough of it.

MRS. ALL. I hope you don't think you have exhausted life, Mr. Arbuthnot. When a man says that one knows that life has exhausted him.

GER. I don't wish to leave my mother.

LADY HUN. Now, Gerald, that is pure laziness on your part. Not leave your mother! If I were your mother I would insist on your going.

[*Enter Alice L.C.*]

Alice. Mrs. Arbuthnot's compliments, my lady, but she has a bad headache, and cannot see any one this morning. [*Exit R.C.*]

Lady Hun. [*Rising.*] A bad headache! I am so sorry! Perhaps you'll bring her up to Hunstanton this afternoon, if she is better, Gerald.

Ger. I am afraid not this afternoon, Lady Hunstanton.

Lady Hun. Well, to-morrow, then. Ah, if you had a father, Gerald, he wouldn't let you waste your life here. He would send you off with Lord Illingworth at once. But mothers are so weak. They give up to their sons in everything. We are all heart, all heart. Come dear, I must call at the rectory and inquire for Mrs. Daubeny, who, I am afraid, is far from well. It is wonderful how the Archdeacon bears up, quite wonderful. He is the most sympathetic of husbands. Quite a model. Good-bye, Gerald, give my fondest love to your mother.

Mrs. All. Good-bye, Mr. Arbuthnot.

Ger. Good-bye.

[*Exit Lady Hunstanton and Mrs. Allonby. Gerald sits down and reads over his letter.*]

Ger. What name can I sign? I, who have no right to any name. [*Signs name, puts letter into envelope, addresses it, and is about to seal it, when Door L.C. opens and Mrs. Arbuthnot enters. Gerald lays down sealing-wax. Mother and son look at each other.*]

Lady Hun. [*Through French window at the back.*] Good-bye again, Gerald. We are taking the short cut across your pretty garden. Now, remember my advice to you–start at once with Lord Illingworth.

Mrs. All. *Au revoir*, Mr. Arbuthnot. Mind you bring me back something nice from your travels–not an Indian shawl–on no account an Indian shawl. [*Exeunt.*]

Ger. Mother, I have just written to him.

Mrs. Arb. To whom?

Ger. To my father. I have written to tell him to come here at four o'clock this afternoon.

Mrs. Arb. He shall not come here. He shall not cross the threshold of my house.

Ger. He must come.

Mrs. Arb. Gerald, if you are going away with Lord Illingworth, go at once. Go before it kills me; but don't ask me to meet him.

Ger. Mother, you don't understand. Nothing in the world would induce me to go away with Lord Illingworth, or to leave you. Surely you know me well enough for that. No; I have written to him to say——

Mrs. Arb. What can you have to say to him?

Ger. Can't you guess, mother, what I have written in this letter?

Mrs. Arb. No.

Ger. Mother, surely you can. Think, think what must be done, now, at once, within the next few days.

Mrs. Arb. There is nothing to be done.

Ger. I have written to Lord Illingworth to tell him that he must marry you.

Mrs. Arb. Marry me?

Ger. Mother, I will force him to do it. The wrong that has been done you must be repaired. Atonement must be made. Justice may be slow, mother, but it comes in the end. In a few days you shall be Lord Illingworth's lawful wife.

Mrs. Arb. But, Gerald——

Ger. I will insist upon his doing it. I will make him do it; he will not dare to refuse.

Mrs. Arb. But, Gerald, it is I who refuse. I will not marry Lord Illingworth.

Ger. Not marry him? Mother!

Mrs. Arb. I will not marry him.

Ger. But you don't understand; it is for your sake I am talking, not for mine. This marriage, this necessary marriage, this marriage, that, for obvious reasons, must inevitably take place, will not help me, will not give me a name that will be really, rightly mine to bear. But surely it will be something for you, that you, my mother, should, however late, become the wife of the man who is my father. Will not that be something?

Mrs. Arb. I will not marry him.

Ger. Mother, you must.

Mrs. Arb. I will not. You talk of atonement for a wrong done. What atonement can be made to me? There is no atonement possible. I am disgraced: he is not. That is all. It is the usual history of a man and a woman as it usually happens, as it always happens. And the ending is the ordinary ending. The woman suffers. The man goes free.

Ger. I don't know if that is the ordinary ending, mother: I hope it is not. but your life, at any rate, shall not end like that. The man shall make whatever reparation is possible. It is not enough. It does not wipe out the past, I know that. But at least it makes the future better, better for you, mother.

Mrs. Arb. I refuse to marry Lord Illingworth.

Ger. If he came to you himself and asked you to be his wife you would give him a different answer. Remember, he is my father.

Mrs. Arb. If he came himself, which he will not do, my answer would be the same. Remember I am your mother.

Ger. Mother, you make it terribly difficult for me by talking like that, and I can't understand why you won't look at this matter from the right, from the only proper standpoint. It is to take away the bitterness out of your life, to take away the shadow that lies on your name, that this marriage must take place. There is no alternative: and after the marriage you and I can go away together. But the marriage must take place first. It is a duty that you owe, not merely to yourself, but to all other women–yes: to all the other women in the world, lest he betray more.

Mrs. Arb. I owe nothing to other women. There is not one of them to help me. There is not one woman in the world to whom I could go for pity, if I would take it, or for sympathy, if I could win it. Women are hard on each other. That girl, last night, good though she is, fled from the room as though I were a tainted thing. She was right. I am a tainted thing. But my wrongs are my own, and I will bear them alone. I must bear them alone. What have women who have not sinned to do with me, or I with them? We do not understand each other.

[*Enter Hester behind.*]

GER. I implore you to do what I ask you.

MRS. ARB. What son has ever asked of his mother to make so hideous a sacrifice? None.

GER. What mother has ever refused to marry the father of her own child? None.

MRS. ARB. Let me be the first, then. I will not do it.

GER. Mother, you believe in religion, and you brought me up to believe in it also. Well, surely your religion, the religion that you taught me when I was a boy, mother, must tell you that I am right. You know it, you feel it.

MRS. ARB. I do not know it. I do not feel it, nor will I ever stand before God's altar and ask God's blessing on so hideous a mockery as a marriage between me and George Harford. I will not say the words the Church bids us to say. I will not say them. I dare not. How could I swear to love the man I loathe, to honour him who brought you dishonour, to obey him who, in his mastery, made me to sin? No; marriage is a sacrament for those who love each other. It is not for such as him or such as me. Gerald, to save you from the world's sneers and taunts I have lied to the world. For twenty years I have lied to the world. I could not tell the world the truth. Who can, ever? But not for my own sake will I lie to God, and in God's presence. No, Gerald, no ceremony, Church-hallowed or State-made, shall ever bind me to George Harford. It may be that I am too bound to him already, who, robbing me, yet left me richer, so that in the mire of my life, I found the pearl of price, or what I thought would be so.

GER. I don't understand you now.

MRS. ARB. Men don't understand what mothers are. I am no different from other women except in the wrong done me and the wrong I did, and my very heavy punishments and great disgrace. And yet, to bear you I had to look on death. To nurture you I had to wrestle with it. Death fought with me for you. All women have to fight with death to keep their children. Death, being childless, wants our children from us. Gerald, when you were naked I clothed you, when you were hungry I gave you food. Night and day all that long winter I tended you. No office is too mean, no care too lowly for the thing we women love–and oh! how *I* loved *you*. Not Hannah Samuel more. And you needed love, for you were weakly, and only love could have kept you alive. Only love can keep any one alive. And boys are careless often and without thinking give pain, and we always fancy that when they come to man's estate and know us better, they will repay us. But it is not so. The world draws them from our side, and they make friends with whom they are happier than they are with us, and have amusements from which we are barred, and interests that are not ours: and they are unjust to us often, for when they find life bitter they blame us for it, and when they find it sweet we do not taste its sweetness with them. . . . You made many friends and went into their houses and were glad with them, and I, knowing my secret did not dare to follow, but stayed at home and closed the door, shut out the sun and sat in darkness. What should I have done in honest households? My past was ever with me. . . . And you thought I didn't care for the pleasant things of life. I tell you I longed for them, but did not dare to touch them, feeling I had no right. You thought I was happier working amongst the poor. That was my mission, you imagined. It was not, but where else was I to go? The sick do not ask if the hand that smoothes their pillow is pure, nor the dying care if the lips that touch their brow have known the kiss of sin. It was you I thought of all the time; I gave to them the love you did not need: lavished on them a love that was not theirs. . . . And you thought I spent too much of my time going to Church, and in Church duties. But where else could I turn? God's house is the only house where sinners are made welcome, and you were always in my heart, Gerald, too much in my heart. For, though day after day, at morn or evensong, I have knelt in God's house, I have never repented of my sin. How could I repent of my sin when you, my love, were its fruit! Even now that you are bitter to me I cannot repent. I do not. You are more to me than innocence. I would rather be your mother—oh! much rather!—than have been always pure. . . . Oh, don't you see? don't you understand? It is my dishonour that has made you so dear to me. It is my disgrace that has bound you so closely to me. It is the price I paid for you—the price of soul and body—that makes me love you as I do. Oh, don't ask me to do this horrible thing. Child of my shame, be still the child of my shame!

GER. Mother, I didn't know you loved me so much as that. And I will be a better son to you than I have been. And you and I must never leave each other . . . but, mother . . . I can't help it . . . you must become my father's wife. You must marry him. It is your duty.

HES. [*Running forward and embracing Mrs. Arbuthnot.*] No, no; you shall not. That would be real dishonour, the first you have ever known. That would be real disgrace: the first to touch you. Leave him and come with me. There are other countries than England. . . . Oh! other countries over sea, better, wiser, and less unjust lands. The world is very wide and very big.

MRS. ARB. No, not for me. For me the world is shrivelled to a palm's breadth, and where I walk there are thorns.

HES. It shall not be so. We shall somewhere find green valleys and fresh waters, and if we weep, well, we shall weep together. Have we not both loved him?

GER. Hester!

HES. [*Waving him back.*] Don't, don't! You cannot love me at all, unless you love her also. You cannot honour me, unless she's holier to you. In her all womanhood is martyred. Not she alone, but all of us are stricken in her house.

GER. Hester, Hester, what shall I do?

HES. Do you respect the man who is your father?

GER. Respect him? I despise him! He is infamous!

HES. I thank you for saving me from him last night.

GER. Ah, that is nothing. I would die to save you. But you don't tell me what to do now!

HES. Have I not thanked you for saving *me?*

GER. But what should I do?

HES. Ask your own heart, not mine. I never had a mother to save, or shame.

MRS. ARB. He is hard—he is hard. Let me go away.

GER. [*Rushes over and kneels down beside his mother.*] Mother, forgive me: I have been to blame.

MRS. ARB. Don't kiss my hands: they are cold. My heart is cold: something has broken it.

HES. Ah, don't say that. Hearts live by being wounded. Pleasure may turn a heart to stone, riches may make it callous, but sorrow—oh, sorrow cannot break it. Besides, what sorrows have you now? Why at this moment you are more dear to him than ever, *dear* though you have *been*, and oh! how dear you *have* been always. Ah! be kind to him.

GER. You are my mother and my father all in one. I need no second parent. It was for you I spoke, for you alone. Oh, say something, mother. Have I but found one love to lose another? Don't tell me that. O mother, you are cruel. [*Gets up and flings himself sobbing on a sofa.*]

MRS. ARB. [*To Hester.*] But has he found indeed another love?

HES. You know I have loved him always.

MRS. ARB. But we are very poor.

HES. Who, being loved, is poor? Oh, no one. I hate my riches. They are a burden. Let him share it with me.

MRS. ARB. But we are disgraced. We rank among the outcasts. Gerald is nameless. The sins of the parents should be visited on the children. It is God's law.

HES. I was wrong. God's law is only Love.

MRS. ARB. [*Rises, and taking Hester by the hand, goes slowly over to where Gerald is lying on the sofa with his head buried in his hands. She touches him and he looks up.*] Gerald, I cannot give you a father, but I have brought you a wife.

GER. Mother, I am not worthy either of her or you.

MRS. ARB. So she comes first, you are worthy. And when you are away, Gerald . . . with . . . her—oh, think of me sometimes. Don't forget me. And when you pray, pray for me. We should pray when we are happiest, and you will be happy, Gerald.

HES. Oh, you don't think of leaving us?

GER. Mother, you won't leave us?

MRS. ARB. I might bring shame upon you!

GER. Mother!

MRS. ARB. For a little then: and if you let me, near you always.

HES. [*To Mrs. Arbuthnot.*] Come out with us to the garden.

MRS. ARB. Later on, later on. [*Exeunt Hester and Gerald.*]

[*Mrs. Arbuthnot goes toward door L.C. Stops at looking-glass over mantelpiece and looks into it.*]

[*Enter Alice R.C.*]

ALICE. A gentleman to see you, ma'am.

MRS. ARB. Say I am not at home. Show me the card. [*Takes card from salver and looks at it.*] Say I will not see him.

[*Lord Illingworth enters. Mrs. Arbuthnot sees him in the glass and starts, but does not turn round. Exit Alice.*]

What can you have to say to me to-day, George Harford? You can have nothing to say to me. You must leave this house.

LORD ILL. Rachel, Gerald knows everything about you and me now, so some arrangement must be come to that will suit us all three. I assure you, he will find in me the most charming and generous of fathers.

MRS. ARB. My son may come in at any moment. I saved you last night. I may not be able to save you again. My son feels my dishonour strongly, terribly strongly. I beg you to go.

LORD ILL. [*Sitting down.*] Last night was excessively unfortunate. That silly Puritan girl making a scene merely because I wanted to kiss her. What harm is there in a kiss?

MRS. ARB. [*Turning round.*] A kiss may ruin a human life, George Harford. *I* know that. *I* know that too well.

LORD ILL. We won't discuss that at present. What is of importance to-day, as yesterday, is still our son. I am extremely fond of him, as you know, and odd though it may seem to you, I admired his conduct last night immensely. He took up the cudgels for that pretty prude with wonderful promptitude. He is just what I should have liked a son of mine to be. Except that no son of mine should ever take the side of the Puritans: that is always an error. Now, what I propose is this.

MRS. ARB. Lord Illingworth, no proposition of yours interests me.

LORD ILL. According to our ridiculous English laws, I can't legitimise Gerald. But I can leave him my property. Illingworth is entailed, of course, but it is a tedious barrack of a place. He can have Ashby, which is much prettier, Harborough, which has the best shooting in the north of England, and the house in St. James Square. What more can a gentleman desire in this world?

MRS. ARB. Nothing more, I am quite sure.

LORD ILL. As for the title, a title is really rather a nuisance in these democratic days. As George Harford I had everything I wanted. Now I have merely everything that other people want, which isn't nearly so pleasant. Well, my proposal is this.

MRS. ARB. I told you I was not interested, and I beg you to go.

LORD ILL. The boy is to be with you for six months in the year, and with me for the other six. That is perfectly fair, is it not? You can have whatever allowance you like, and live where you choose. As for your past, no one knows anything about it except myself and Gerald. There is the Puritan, of course, the Puritan in white muslin, but she doesn't count. She couldn't tell the story without explaining that she objected to being kissed, could she? And all the women would think her a fool and the men think her a bore. And you need not be afraid that Gerald won't be my heir. I needn't tell you I have not the slightest intention of marrying.

MRS. ARB. You come too late. My son has no need of you. You are not necessary.

LORD ILL. What do you mean, Rachel?

MRS. ARB. That you are not necessary to Gerald's career. He does not require you.

LORD ILL. I do not understand you.

MRS. ARB. Look into the garden. [*Lord Illingworth rises and goes towards window.*] You had better not let them see you: you bring unpleasant memories. [*Lord Illingworth looks out and starts.*] She loves him. They love each other. We are safe from you, and we are going away.

LORD ILL. Where?

MRS. ARB. We will not tell you, and if you find us we will not know you. You seem surprised. What welcome would you get from the girl whose lips you tried to soil, from the boy whose life you have shamed, from the mother whose dishonour comes from you.

LORD ILL. You have grown hard, Rachel.

MRS. ARB. I was too weak once. It is well for me that I have changed.

LORD ILL. I was very young at the time. We men know life too early.

MRS. ARB. And we women know life too late. That is the difference between men and women. [*A pause.*]

LORD ILL. Rachel, I want my son. My money may be of no use to him now. I may be of no use to him, but I want my son. Bring us together, Rachel. You can do it if you choose. [*Sees letter on table.*]

MRS. ARB. There is no room in my boy's life for *you*. He is not interested in *you*.

LORD ILL. Then why does he write to me?

MRS. ARB. What do you mean?

LORD ILL. What letter is this? [*Takes up letter.*]

MRS. ARB. That–is nothing. Give it to me.

LORD ILL. It is addressed to *me*.

MRS. ARB. You are not to open it. I forbid you to open it.

LORD ILL. And in Gerald's handwriting.

MRS. ARB. It was not to have been sent. It is a letter he wrote to you this morning before he saw me. But he is sorry now he wrote it, very sorry. You are not to open it. Give it to me.

LORD ILL. It belongs to me. [*Opens it, sits down and reads it slowly. Mrs. Arbuthnot watches him all the time.*] You have read this letter, I suppose, Rachel?

MRS. ARB. No.

LORD ILL. You know what is in it?

MRS. ARB. Yes!

LORD ILL. I don't admit for a moment that the boy is right in what he says. I don't admit it is any duty of mine to marry you. I deny it entirely. But to get my son back I am ready–yes, I am ready to marry you, Rachel–and to treat you always with the deference and respect due to my wife. I will marry you as soon as you choose. I give you my word of honour.

Mrs. Arb. You made that promise to me once before and broke it.

Lord Ill. I will keep it now. And that will show you that I love my son, at least as much as you love him. For when I marry you, Rachel, there are some ambitions I shall have to surrender. High ambitions too, if any ambition is high.

Mrs. Arb. I decline to marry you, Lord Illingworth.

Lord Ill. Are you serious?

Mrs. Arb. Yes.

Lord Ill. Do tell me your reasons. They would interest me enormously.

Mrs. Arb. I have already explained them to my son.

Lord Ill. I suppose they were intensely sentimental, weren't they? You women live by your emotions and for them. You have no philosophy of life.

Mrs. Arb. You are right. We women live by our emotions and for them. By our passions, and for them, if you will. I have two passions, Lord Illingworth: my love of him, my hate of you. You cannot kill those. They feed each other.

Lord Ill. What sort of love is that which needs to have hate as its brother?

Mrs. Arb. It is the sort of love I have for Gerald. Do you think that terrible? Well, it is terrible. All love is terrible. All love is a tragedy. I loved you once, Lord Illingworth. Oh, what a tragedy for a woman to have loved you!

Lord Ill. So you really refuse to marry me?

Mrs. Arb. Yes.

Lord Ill. Because you hate me?

Mrs. Arb. Yes.

Lord Ill. And does my son hate me as you do?

Mrs. Arb. No.

Lord Ill. I am glad of that, Rachel.

Mrs. Arb. He merely despises you.

Lord Ill. What a pity! What a pity for him, I mean.

Mrs. Arb. Don't be deceived, George. Children begin by loving their parents. After a time they judge them. Rarely if ever do they forgive them.

Lord Ill. [*Reads letter over again, very slowly.*] May I ask by what arguments you made the boy who wrote this letter, this beautiful, passionate letter, believe that you should not marry his father, the father of your own child?

Mrs. Arb. It was not I who made him see it. It was another.

Lord Ill. What *fin-de-siècle* person?

Mrs. Arb. The Puritan, Lord Illingworth.[*A pause.*]

Lord Ill. [*Winces, then rises slowly and goes over to table where his hat and gloves are. Mrs. Arbuthnot is standing close to the table. He picks up one of the gloves and begins putting it on.*] There is not much then for me to do here, Rachel?

Mrs. Arb. Nothing.

Lord Ill. It is good-bye, is it?

Mrs. Arb. For ever, I hope, this time, Lord Illingworth.

Lord Ill. How curious! At this moment you look exactly as you looked the night you left me twenty years ago. You have just the same expression in your mouth. Upon my word, Rachel, no woman ever loved me as you did.

Why, you gave yourself to me like a flower, to do anything I liked with. You were the prettiest of playthings, the most fascinating of small romances. . . . [*Pulls out watch.*] Quarter to two! Must be strolling back to Hunstanton. Don't suppose I shall see you there again. I'm sorry, I am, really. It's been an amusing experience to have met amongst people of one's own rank, and treated quite seriously too, one's mistress and one's—

[*Mrs. Arbuthnot snatches up glove and strikes Lord Illingworth across the face with it. Lord Illingworth starts. He is dazed by the insult of his punishment. Then he controls himself, and goes to window and looks out at his son. Sighs, and leaves the room.*]

MRS. ARB. [*Falls sobbing on the sofa.*] He would have said it. He would have said it.

[*Enter Gerald and Hester from the garden.*]

GER. Well, dear mother. You never came out after all. So we have come in to fetch you. Mother, you have not been crying? [*Kneels down beside her.*]

MRS. ARB. My boy! My boy! My boy! [*Running her fingers through his hair.*]

HES. [*Coming over.*] But you have two children now. You'll let me be your daughter?

MRS. ARB. [*Looking up.*] Would you choose me for a mother?

HES. You of all women I have ever known.

[*They move towards the door leading into garden with their arms round each other's waists. Gerald goes to table L.C. for his hat. On turning round he sees Lord Illingworth's glove lying on the floor, and picks it up.*]

GER. Hallo, mother, whose glove is this? You have had a visitor. Who was it?

MRS. ARB. [*Turning round.*] Oh! no one. No one in particular. A man of no importance.

CURTAIN.

AN IDEAL HUSBAND

THE PERSONS OF THE PLAY

THE EARL OF CAVERSHAM, K. G.
VISCOUNT GORING, his son
SIR ROBERT CHILTERN, Bart., Under-secretary for Foreign Affairs
VICOMTE DE NANJAC, Attaché at the French Embassy in London
MR. MONTFORD
MASON, Butler to Sir Robert Chiltern
PHIPPS, Lord Goring's Servant
HAROLD
JAMES
footmen
LADY CHILTERN
LADY MARKBY
THE COUNTESS OF BASILDON
MRS. MARCHMONT
MISS MABEL CHILTERN, Sir Robert Chiltern's sister
MRS. CHEVELEY

THE SCENES OF THE PLAY

ACT I, *The Octagon Room in Sir Robert Chiltern's House in Grosvenor Square.* ACT II, *Morning-room in Sir Robert Chiltern's House.* ACT III, *The Library of Lord Goring's House in Curzon Street.* ACT IV, *Same as in* ACT II. *Time, The Present. Place, London. The Action of the Play is completed within twenty-four hours.*

FIRST ACT

SCENE—*The octagon room at Sir Robert Chiltern's house in Grosvenor Square.*

[*The room is brilliantly lighted and full of guests. At the top of the staircase stands Lady Chiltern, a woman of grave Greek beauty, about twenty-seven years of age. She receives the guests as they come up. Over the well of the staircase hangs a great chandelier with wax lights, which illumine a large eighteenth-century French tapestry—representing the Triumph of Love, from a design by Boucher—that is stretched on the staircase wall. On the right is the entrance to the music-room. The sound of a string quartette is faintly heard. The entrance on the left leads to other reception-rooms. Mrs. Marchmont and Lady Basildon, two very pretty women, are seated together on a Louis Seize sofa. They are types of exquisite fragility. Their affectation of manner has a delicate charm. Watteau would have loved to paint them.*]

MRS. MAR. Going on to the Hartlocks' to-night, Margaret?

LADY BAS. I suppose so. Are you?

MRS. MAR. Yes. Horribly tedious parties they give, don't they?

LADY BAS. Horribly tedious! Never know why I go. Never know why I go anywhere.

MRS. MAR. I come here to be educated.

LADY BAS. Ah! I hate being educated.

MRS. MAR. So do I. It puts one almost on a level with the commercial classes, doesn't it? But dear Gertrude Chiltern is always telling me that I should have some serious purpose in life. So I come here to try to find one.

LADY BAS. [*Looking round through her lorgnette.*] I don't see anybody here to-night whom one could possibly call a serious purpose. The man who took me in to dinner talked to me about his wife the whole time.

MRS. MAR. How very trivial of him!

LADY BAS. Terribly trivial! What did your man talk about?

MRS. MAR. About myself.

LADY BAS. [*Languidly.*] And were you interested?

MRS. MAR. [*Shaking her head.*] Not in the smallest degree.

LADY BAS. What martyrs we are, dear Margaret!

MRS. MAR. [*Rising.*] And how well it becomes us, Olivia!

[*They rise and go towards the music-room. The Vicomte de Nanjac, a young attaché known for his neckties and his Anglomania, approaches with a low bow, and enters into conversation.*]

MASON. [*Announcing guests from the top of the staircase.*] Mr. and Lady Jane Barford. Lord Caversham.

[*Enter Lord Caversham, an old gentleman of seventy, wearing the riband and star of the Garter. A fine Whig type. Rather like a portrait by Lawrence.*]

LORD CAV. Good evening, Lady Chiltern! Has my good-for-nothing young son been here?

LADY CHI. [*Smiling.*] I don't think Lord Goring has arrived yet.

MABEL. [*Coming up to Lord Caversham.*] Why do you call Lord Goring good-for-nothing?

[*Mabel Chiltern is a perfect example of the English type of prettiness, the apple-blossom type. She has all the fragrance and freedom of a flower. There is ripple after ripple of sunlight in her hair, and the little mouth, with its parted lips, is expectant, like the mouth of a child. She has the fascinating tyranny of youth, and the astonishing courage of innocence. To sane people she is not reminiscent of any work of art. But she is really like a Tanagra statuette, and would be rather annoyed if she were told so.*]

LORD CAV. Because he leads such an idle life.

MABEL. How can you say such a thing? Why, he rides in the Row at ten o'clock in the morning, goes to the Opera three times a week, changes his clothes at least five times a day, and dines out every night of the season. You don't call that leading an idle life, do you?

LORD CAV. [*Looking at her with a kindly twinkle in his eyes.*] You are a very charming young lady!

MABEL. How sweet of you to say that, Lord Caversham. Do come to us more often. You know we are always at home on Wednesdays, and you look so well with your star!

LORD CAV. Never go anywhere now. Sick of London Society. Shouldn't mind being introduced to my own tailor; he always votes on the right side. But object strongly to being sent down to dinner with my wife's milliner. Never could stand Lady Caversham's bonnets!

LADY CHI. Oh, I love London Society! I think it has immensely improved. It is entirely composed now of beautiful idiots and brilliant lunatics. Just what Society should be.

LORD CAV. Hum! Which is Goring? Beautiful idiot, or the other thing?

MABEL. [*Gravely.*] I have been obliged for the present to put Lord Goring into a class quite by himself. But he is developing charmingly.

LORD CAV. Into what?

MABEL. [*With a little curtsey.*] I hope to let you know very soon, Lord Caversham!

MASON. [*Announcing guests.*] Lady Markby. Mrs. Cheveley.

[*Enter Lady Markby and Mrs. Cheveley. Lady Markby is a pleasant, kindly, popular woman, with gray hair à la marquise and good lace. Mrs. Cheveley, who accompanies her, is tall and rather slight. Lips very thin and highly coloured, a line of scarlet on a pallid face. Venetian red hair, aquiline nose, and long throat. Rouge accentuates the natural paleness of her complexion. Grey-green eyes that move restlessly. She is in heliotrope, with diamonds. She looks rather like an orchid, and makes great demands on one's curiosity. A work of art, on the whole, but showing the influence of too many schools.*]

LADY MAR. Good evening, dear Gertrude! So kind of you to let me bring my friend, Mrs. Cheveley. Two such charming women should know each other!

LADY CHI. [*Advances towards Mrs. Cheveley with a sweet smile. Then suddenly stops, and bows rather distantly.*] I think Mrs. Cheveley and I have met before. I did not know she had married a second time.

LADY MAR. [*Genially.*] Ah, nowadays people marry as often as they can, don't they? It is most fashionable. [*To Duchess of Maryborough.*] Dear Duchess, and how is the Duke? Brain still weak, I suppose? Well, that is only to be expected, is it not? His good father was just the same. There is nothing like race, is there?

MRS. CHEV. [*Playing with her fan.*] But have we really met before, Lady Chiltern? I can't remember where. I have been out of England for so long.

LADY CHI. We were at school together, Mrs. Cheveley.

MRS. CHEV. [*Superciliously.*] Indeed? I have forgotten all about my schooldays. I have a vague impression that they were detestable.

LADY CHI. [*Coldly.*] I am not surprised!

MRS. CHEV. [*In her sweetest manner.*] Do you know, I am quite looking forward to meeting your clever husband, Lady Chiltern. Since he has been at the Foreign Office, he has been so much talked of in Vienna. They actually succeed in spelling his name right in the newspapers. That in itself is fame, on the continent.

LADY CHI. I hardly think there will be much in common between you and my husband, Mrs. Cheveley. [*Moves away.*]

VICOMTE. Ah! chère Madame, quelle surprise! I have not seen you since Berlin!

MRS. CHEV. Not since Berlin, Vicomte. Five years ago!

VICOMTE. And you are younger and more beautiful than ever. How do you manage it?

MRS. CHEV. By making it a rule only to talk to perfectly charming people like yourself.

VICOMTE. Ah! you flatter me. You butter me, as they say here.

MRS. CHEV. Do they say that here? How dreadful of them!

VICOMTE. Yes, they have a wonderful language. It should be more widely known.

[*Sir Robert Chiltern enters. A man of forty, but looking somewhat younger. Clean-shaven, with finely-cut features, dark-haired and dark-eyed. A personality of mark. Not popular—few personalities are. But intensely admired by the few, and deeply respected by the many. The note of his manner that of perfect distinction, with a slight touch of pride. One feels that he is conscious of the success he has made in life. A nervous temperament, with a tired look. The firmly-chiselled mouth and chin contrast strikingly with the romantic expression in the deep-set eyes. The variance is suggestive of an almost complete separation of passion and intellect, as though thought and emotion were each isolated in its own sphere through some violence of will-power. There is nervousness in the nostrils, and in the pale, thin, pointed hands. It would be inaccurate to call him picturesque. Picturesqueness cannot survive the House of Commons. But Vandyck would have liked to have painted his head.*]

SIR ROBERT. Good evening, Lady Markby! I hope you have brought Sir John with you?

LADY MAR. Oh! I have brought a much more charming person than Sir John. Sir John's temper since he has taken seriously to politics has become quite unbearable. Really, now that the House of Commons is trying to become useful, it does a great deal of harm.

SIR ROBERT. I hope not, Lady Markby. At any rate we do our best to waste the public time, don't we? But who is this charming person you have been kind enough to bring to us?

LADY MAR. Her name is Mrs. Cheveley! One of the Dorsetshire Cheveleys, I suppose. But I really don't know. Families are so mixed now-a-days. Indeed, as a rule, everybody turns out to be somebody else.

SIR ROBERT. Mrs. Cheveley? I seem to know the name.

LADY MAR. She has just arrived from Vienna.

SIR ROBERT. Ah! yes. I think I know whom you mean.

LADY MAR. Oh! she goes everywhere there, and has such pleasant scandals about all her friends. I really must go to Vienna next winter. I hope there is a good chef at the Embassy.

SIR ROBERT. If there is not, the Ambassador will certainly have to be recalled. Pray point out Mrs. Cheveley to me. I should like to see her.

LADY MAR. Let me introduce you. [*To Mrs. Cheveley.*] My dear, Sir Robert is dying to know you.

SIR ROBERT. [*Bowing.*] Everyone is dying to know the brilliant Mrs Cheveley. Our attachés at Vienna write to us about nothing else.

MRS. CHEV. Thank you, Sir Robert. An acquaintance that begins with a compliment is sure to develop into a real friendship. It starts in the right manner. And I find that I know Lady Chiltern already.

SIR ROBERT. Really?

MRS. CHEV. Yes. She has just reminded me that we were at school together. I remember it perfectly now. She always got the good conduct prize. I have a distinct recollection of Lady Chiltern always getting the good conduct prize!

SIR ROBERT. [*Smiling.*] And what prizes did you get, Mrs. Cheveley?

MRS. CHEV. My prizes came a little later on in life. I don't think any of them were for good conduct. I forget!

SIR ROBERT. I am sure they were for something charming!

MRS. CHEV. I don't know that women are always rewarded for being charming. I think they are usually punished for it! Certainly, more women grow old now-a-days through the faithfulness of their admirers than through anything else! At least that is the only way I can account for the terribly haggard look of most of your pretty women in London!

SIR ROBERT. What an appalling philosophy that sounds! To attempt to classify you, Mrs. Cheveley, would be an impertinence. But may I ask, at heart, are you an optimist or a pessimist? Those seem to be the only two fashionable religions left to us nowadays.

MRS. CHEV. Oh, I'm neither. Optimism begins in a broad grin, and Pessimism ends with blue spectacles. Besides, they are both of them merely poses.

SIR ROBERT. You prefer to be natural?

MRS. CHEV. Sometimes. But it is such a very difficult pose to keep up.

SIR ROBERT. What would those modern psychological novelists, of whom we hear so much, say to such a theory as that?

MRS. CHEV. Ah! the strength of women comes from the fact that psychology cannot explain us. Men can be analyzed, women . . . merely adored.

SIR ROBERT. You think science cannot grapple with the problem of women?

MRS. CHEV. Science can never grapple with the irrational. That is why it has no future before it, in this world.

SIR ROBERT. And women represent the irrational.

MRS. CHEV. Well-dressed women do.

SIR ROBERT. [*With a polite bow.*] I fear I could hardly agree with you there. But do sit down. And now tell me, what makes you leave your brilliant Vienna for our bloomy London—or perhaps the question is indiscreet?

MRS. CHEV. Questions are never indiscreet. Answers sometimes are.

SIR ROBERT. Well, at any rate, may I know if it is politics or pleasure?

MRS. CHEV. Politics are my only pleasure. You see now-a-days it is not fashionable to flirt till one is forty, or to be romantic till one is forty-five, so we poor women who are under thirty, or say we are, have nothing open to us but politics or philanthropy. And philanthropy seems to me to have become simply the refuge of people who wish to annoy their fellow-creatures. I prefer politics. I think they are more . . . becoming!

Sir Robert. A political life is a noble career!

Mrs. Chev. Sometimes. And sometimes it is a clever game, Sir Robert. And sometimes it is a great nuisance.

Sir Robert. Which do you find it?

Mrs. Chev. I? A combination of all three. [*Drops her fan.*]

Sir Robert. [*Picks up fan.*] Allow me!

Mrs. Chev. Thanks.

Sir Robert. But you have not told me yet what makes you honour London so suddenly. Our season is almost over.

Mrs. Chev. Oh! I don't care about the London season! It is too matrimonial. People are either hunting for husbands, or hiding from them. I wanted to meet you. It is quite true. You know what a woman's curiosity is. Almost as great as a man's! I wanted immensely to meet you, and . . . to ask you to do something for me.

Sir Robert. I hope it is not a little thing, Mrs. Cheveley. I find that little things are so very difficult to do.

Mrs. Chev. [*After a moment's reflection.*] No, I don't think it is quite a little thing.

Sir Robert. I am so glad. Do tell me what it is.

Mrs. Chev. Later on. [*Rises.*] And now may I walk through your beautiful house? I hear your pictures are charming. Poor Baron Arnheim—you remember the Baron?—used to tell me you had some wonderful Corots.

Sir Robert. [*With an almost imperceptible start.*] Did you know Baron Arnheim well?

Mrs. Chev. [*Smiling.*] Intimately. Did you?

Sir Robert. At one time.

Mrs. Chev. Wonderful man, wasn't he?

Sir Robert. [*After a pause.*] He was very remarkable, in many ways.

Mrs. Chev. I often think it such a pity he never wrote his memoirs. They would have been most interesting.

Sir Robert. Yes; he knew men and cities well, like the old Greek.

Mrs. Chev. Without the dreadful disadvantage of having a Penelope waiting at home for him.

Mason. Lord Goring.

[*Enter Lord Goring. Thirty-four, but always says he is younger. A well-bred, expressionless face. He is clever, but would not like to be thought so. A flawless dandy, he would be annoyed if he were considered romantic. He plays with life, and is on perfectly good terms with the world. He is fond of being misunderstood. It gives him a post of vantage.*]

Sir Robert. Good evening, my dear Arthur! Mrs. Cheveley, allow me to introduce to you Lord Goring, the idlest man in London.

Mrs. Chev. I have met Lord Goring before.

Lord Gor. [*Bowing.*] I did not think you would remember me, Mrs. Cheveley.

MRS. CHEV. My memory is under admirable control. And are you still a bachelor?

LORD GOR. I . . . believe so.

MRS. CHEV. How very romantic!

LORD GOR. Oh! I am not at all romantic. I am not old enough. I leave romance to my seniors.

SIR ROBERT. Lord Goring is the result of Boodle's Club, Mrs. Cheveley.

MRS. CHEV. He reflects every credit on the institution.

LORD GOR. May I ask are you staying in London long?

MRS. CHEV. That depends partly on the weather, partly on the cooking, and partly on Sir Robert.

SIR ROBERT. You are not going to plunge us into a European war, I hope?

MRS. CHEV. There is no danger, at present!

[*She nods to Lord Goring, with a look of amusement in her eyes, and goes out with Sir Robert Chiltern. Lord Goring saunters over to Mabel Chiltern.*]

MABEL. You are very late!

LORD GOR. Have you missed me?

MABEL. Awfully!

LORD GOR. Then I am sorry I did not stay away longer. I like being missed.

MABEL. How very selfish of you!

LORD GOR. I am very selfish.

MABEL. You are always telling me of your bad qualities, Lord Goring.

LORD GOR. I have only told you half of them as yet, Miss Mabel!

MABEL. Are the others very bad?

LORD GOR. Quite dreadful! When I think of them at night I go to sleep at once.

MABEL. Well, I delight in your bad qualities. I wouldn't have you part with one of them.

LORD GOR. How very nice of you! But then you are always nice. By the way, I want to ask you a question, Miss Mabel. Who brought Mrs. Cheveley here? That woman in heliotrope, who has just gone out of the room with your brother?

MABEL. Oh, I think Lady Markby brought her. Why do you ask?

LORD GOR. I hadn't seen her for years, that is all.

MABEL. What an absurd reason!

LORD GOR. All reasons are absurd.

MABEL. What sort of woman is she?

LORD GOR. Oh! a genius in the daytime and a beauty at night!

MABEL. I dislike her already.

LORD GOR. That shows your admirable good taste.

VICOMTE. [*Approaching.*] Ah, the English young lady is the dragon of good taste, is she not? Quite the dragon of good taste.

LORD GOR. So the newspapers are always telling us.

VICOMTE. I read all your English newspapers. I find them so amusing.

LORD GOR. Then, my dear Nanjac, you must certainly read between the lines.

VICOMTE. I should like to, but my professor objects. [*To Mabel Chiltern.*] May I have the pleasure of escorting you to the music-room, Mademoiselle?

MABEL. [*Looking very disappointed.*] Delighted, Vicomte, quite delighted! [*Turning to Lord Goring.*] Aren't you coming to the music-room?

LORD GOR. Not if there is any music going on, Miss Mabel.

MABEL. [*Severely.*] The music is in German. You would not understand it.

[*Goes out with the Vicomte de Nanjac. Lord Caversham comes up to his son.*]

LORD CAV. Well, sir! what are you doing here? Wasting your life as usual! You should be in bed, sir. You keep too late hours! I heard of you the other night at Lady Rufford's dancing till four o'clock in the morning!

LORD GOR. Only a quarter to four, father.

LORD CAV. Can't make out how you stand London Society. The thing has gone to the dogs, a lot of damned nobodies talking about nothing.

LORD GOR. I love talking about nothing, father. It is the only thing I know anything about.

LORD CAV. You seem to me to be living entirely for pleasure.

LORD GOR. What else is there to live for, father? Nothing ages like happiness.

LORD CAV. You are heartless, sir, very heartless!

LORD GOR. I hope not, father. Good evening, Lady Basildon!

LADY BAS. [*Arching two pretty eyebrows.*] Are you here? I had no idea you ever came to political parties!

LORD GOR. I adore political parties. They are the only place left to us where people don't talk politics.

LADY BAS. I delight in talking politics. I talk them all day long. But I can't bear listening to them. I don't know how the unfortunate men in the House stand these long debates.

LORD GOR. By never listening.

LADY BAS. Really?

LORD GOR. [*In his most serious manner.*] Of course. You see, it is a very dangerous thing to listen. If one listens one may be convinced; and a man who allows himself to be convinced by an argument is a thoroughly unreasonable person.

LADY BAS. Ah! that accounts for so much in men that I have never understood, and so much in women that their husbands never appreciate in them!

MRS. MAR. [*With a sigh.*] Our husbands never appreciate anything in us. We have to go to others for that!

LADY BAS. [*Emphatically.*] Yes, always to others, have we not?

LORD GOR. [*Smiling.*] And those are the views of the two ladies who are known to have the most admirable husbands in London.

MRS. MAR. That is exactly what we can't stand. My Reginald is quite hopelessly faultless. He is really unendurably so, at times! There is not the smallest element of excitement in knowing him.

LORD GOR. How terrible! Really, the thing should be more widely known!

LADY BAS. Basildon is quite as bad; he is as domestic as if he was a bachelor.

Mrs. Mar. [*Pressing Lady Basildon's hand.*] My poor Olivia! We have married perfect husbands, and we are well punished for it.

Lord Gor. I should have thought it was the husbands who were punished.

Mrs. Mar. [*Drawing herself up.*] Oh, dear, no! They are as happy as possible! And as for trusting us, it is tragic how much they trust us.

Lady Bas. Perfectly tragic!

Lord Gor. Or comic, Lady Basildon?

Lady Bas. Certainly not comic, Lord Goring. How unkind of you to suggest such a thing!

Mrs. Mar. I am afraid Lord Goring is in the camp of the enemy, as usual. I saw him talking to that Mrs. Cheveley when he came in.

Lord Gor. Handsome woman, Mrs. Cheveley!

Lady Bas. [*Stiffly.*] Please don't praise other women in our presence. You might wait for us to do that!

Lord Gor. I did wait.

Mrs. Mar. Well, we are not going to praise her. I hear she went to the Opera on Monday night, and told Tommy Rufford at supper that, as far as she could see, London Society was entirely made up of dowdies and dandies.

Lord Gor. She is quite right, too. The men are all dowdies and the women are all dandies, aren't they? [*After a pause.*] Oh! do you really think that is what Mrs. Cheveley meant?

Mrs. Mar. Of course. And a very sensible remark for Mrs. Cheveley to make, too.

[*Enter Mabel Chiltern. She joins the group.*]

Mabel. Why are you talking about Mrs. Cheveley? Everybody is talking about Mrs. Cheveley! Lord Goring says–what did you say, Lord Goring, about Mrs. Cheveley? Oh! I remember, that she was a genius in the daytime and a beauty at night.

Lady Bas. What a horrid combination! So very unnatural!

Mrs. Mar. [*In her most dreamy manner.*] I like looking at genuises, and listening to beautiful people.

Lord Gor. Ah! that is morbid of you, Mrs. Marchmont!

Mrs. Mar. [*Brightening to a look of real pleasure.*] I am so glad to hear you say that. Marchmont and I have been married for seven years, and he has never once told me that I was morbid. Men are so painfully unobservant!

Lady Bas. [*Turning to her.*] I have always said, dear Margaret, that you were the most morbid person in London.

Mrs. Mar. Ah! but you are always sympathetic, Olivia!

Mabel. Is it morbid to have a desire for food? I have a great desire for food. Lord Goring, will you give me some supper?

Lord Gor. With pleasure, Miss Mabel. [*Moves away with her.*]

Mabel. How horrid you have been! You have never talked to me the whole evening.

Lord Gor. How could I? You went away with the child-diplomatist.

Mabel. You might have followed us. Pursuit would have been only polite. I don't think I like you at all this evening!

Lord Gor. I like you immensely.

Mabel. Well, I wish you'd show it in a more marked way!

[They go aownstairs.]

Mrs. Mar. Olivia, I have a curious feeling of absolute faintness. I think I should like some supper very much. I know I should like some supper.

Lady Bas. I am positively dying for supper, Margaret!

Mrs. Mar. Men are so horribly selfish, they never think of these things.

Lady Bas. Men are grossly material, grossly material!

[The Vicomte de Nanjac enters from the music-room with some other guests. After having carefully examined all the people present, he approaches Lady Basildon.]

Vicomte. May I have the honour of taking you down to supper, Comtesse?

Lady Bas. [*Coldly.*] I never take supper, thank you, Vicomte. [*The Vicomte is about to retire. Lady Basildon, seeing this, rises at once and takes his arm.*] But I will come down with you with pleasure.

Vicomte. I am so fond of eating! I am very English in all my tastes.

Lady Bas. You look quite English, Vicomte, quite English.

[They pass out. Mr. Montford, a perfectly-groomed young dandy, approaches Mrs. Marchmont.]

Mr. Mon. Like some supper, Mrs. Marchmont?

Mrs. Mar. [*Languidly.*] Thank you, Mr. Montford, I never touch supper. [*Rises hastily and takes his arm.*] But I will sit beside you, and watch you.

Mr. Mon. I don't know that I like being watched when I am eating.

Mrs. Mar. Then I will watch some one else.

Mr. Mon. I don't know that I should like that either.

Mrs. Mar. [*Severely.*] Pray, Mr. Montford, do not make these painful scenes of jealousy in public!

[They go downstairs with the other guests, passing Sir Robert Chiltern and Mrs. Cheveley, who now enter.]

Sir Robert. And are you going to any of our country houses before you leave England, Mrs. Cheveley?

Mrs. Chev. Oh, no! I can't stand your English house-parties. In England people actually try to be brilliant at breakfast. That is so dreadful of them! Only dull people are brilliant at breakfast. And then the family skeleton is always reading family prayers. My stay in England really depends on you, Sir Robert. [*Sits down on the sofa.*]

Sir Robert. [*Taking a seat beside her.*] Seriously?

Mrs. Chev. Quite seriously. I want to talk to you about a great political and financial scheme, about this Argentine Canal Company, in fact.

Sir Robert. What a tedious, practical subject for you to talk about, Mrs. Cheveley!

Mrs. Chev. Oh, I like tedious, practical subjects. What I don't like are tedious, practical people. There is a wide difference. Besides, you are interested, I know, in International Canal schemes. You were Lord Radley's secretary, weren't you, when the Government bought the Suez Canal shares?

Sir Robert. Yes. But the Suez Canal was a very great and splendid undertaking. It gave us our direct route to India. It had imperial value. It was necessary that we should have control. This Argentine scheme is a commonplace Stock Exchange swindle.

Mrs. Chev. A speculation, Sir Robert! A brilliant, daring speculation.

Sir Robert. Believe me, Mrs. Cheveley, it is a swindle. Let us call things by their proper names. It makes matters simpler. We have all the information about it at the Foreign Office. In fact, I sent out a special Commission to inquire into the matter privately, and they report that the works are hardly begun, and as for the money already subscribed, no one seems to know what has become of it. The whole thing is a second Panama, and with not a quarter of the chance of success that miserable affair ever had. I hope you have not invested in it. I am sure you are far too clever to have done that.

Mrs. Chev. I have invested very largely in it.

Sir Robert. Who could have advised you to do such a foolish thing?

Mrs. Chev. Your old friend—and mine.

Sir Robert. Who?

Mrs. Chev. Baron Arnheim.

Sir Robert. [*Frowning.*] Ah! yes. I remember hearing, at the time of his death, that he had been mixed up in the whole affair.

Mrs. Chev. It was his last romance. His last but one, to do him justice.

Sir Robert. [*Rising.*] But you have not seen my Corots yet. They are in the music-room. Corots seem to go with music, don't they? May I show them to you?

Mrs. Chev. [*Shaking her head.*] I am not in a mood to-night for silver twilights, or rose-pink dawns. I want to talk business. [*Motions to him with her fan to sit down again beside her.*]

Sir Robert. I fear I have no advice to give you, Mrs. Cheveley, except to interest yourself in something less dangerous. The success of the Canal depends, of course, upon the attitude of England, and I am going to lay the report of the Commissioners before the House to-morrow night.

Mrs. Chev. That you must not do. In your own interests, Sir Robert, to say nothing of mine, you must not do that.

Sir Robert. [*Looking at her in wonder.*] In my own interests? My dear Mrs. Cheveley, what do you mean? [*Sits down beside her.*]

Mrs. Chev. Sir Robert, I will be quite frank with you. I want you to withdraw the report that you had intended to lay before the House, on the ground that you have reasons to believe that the Commissioners have been prejudiced or misinformed, or something. Then I want you to say a few words to the effect that the Government is going to reconsider the question, and that you have reason to believe that the Canal, if completed, will be of great international value. You know the sort of things ministers say in cases of this kind. A few ordinary platitudes will do. In modern life nothing produces such an effect as a good platitude. It makes the whole world kin. Will you do that for me?

Sir Robert. Mrs. Cheveley, you cannot be serious in making me such a proposition!

MRS. CHEV. I am quite serious.

SIR ROBERT. [*Coldly.*] Pray allow me to believe that you are not!

MRS. CHEV. [*Speaking with great deliberation and emphasis.*] Ah! but I am. And, if you do what I ask you, I . . . will pay you very handsomely!

SIR ROBERT. Pay me!

MRS. CHEV. Yes.

SIR ROBERT. I am afraid I don't quite understand what you mean.

MRS. CHEV. [*Leaning back on the sofa and looking at him.*] How very disappointing! And I have come all the way from Vienna in order that you should thoroughly understand me.

SIR ROBERT. I fear I don't.

MRS. CHEV. [*In her most nonchalant manner.*] My dear Sir Robert, you are a man of the world, and you have your price, I suppose. Everybody has nowadays. The drawback is that most people are so dreadfully expensive. I know I am. I hope you will be more reasonable in your terms.

SIR ROBERT. [*Rises indignantly.*] If you will allow me, I will call your carriage for you. You have lived so long abroad, Mrs. Cheveley, that you seem to be unable to realize that you are talking to an English gentleman.

MRS. CHEV. [*Detains him by touching his arm with her fan, and keeping it there while she is talking.*] I realise that I am talking to a man who laid the foundation of his fortune by selling to a Stock Exchange speculator a Cabinet secret.

SIR ROBERT. [*Biting his lip.*] What do you mean?

MRS. CHEV. [*Rising and facing him.*] I mean that I know the real origin of your wealth and your career, and I have got your letter, too.

SIR ROBERT. What letter?

MRS. CHEV. [*Contemptuously.*] The letter you wrote to Baron Arnheim, when you were Lord Radley's secretary, telling the Baron to buy Suez Canal shares—a letter written three days before the Government announced its own purchase.

SIR ROBERT. [*Hoarsely.*] It is not true.

MRS. CHEV. You thought that letter had been destroyed. How foolish of you! It is in my possession.

SIR ROBERT. The affair to which you allude was no more than a speculation. The House of Commons had not yet passed the bill; it might have been rejected.

MRS. CHEV. It was a swindle, Sir Robert. Let us call things by their proper names. It makes everything simpler. And now I am going to sell you that letter, and the price I ask for it is your public support of the Argentine scheme. You made your own fortune out of one canal. You must help me and my friends to make our fortunes out of another!

SIR ROBERT. It is infamous, what you propose—infamous!

MRS CHEV. Oh, no! This is the game of life as we all have to play it, Sir Robert, sooner or later.

SIR ROBERT. I cannot do what you ask me.

MRS. CHEV. You mean you cannot help doing it. You know you are standing on the edge of a precipice. And it is not for you to make terms. It is for you to accept them. Suppose you refuse——

SIR ROBERT. What then?

MRS. CHEV. My dear Sir Robert, what then! You are ruined, that is all! Remember to what a point your Puritanism in England has brought you. In old days nobody pretended to be a bit better than his neighbours. In fact, to be a bit better than one's neighbour was considered excessively vulgar and middle-class. Nowadays, with our modern mania for morality, everyone has to pose as a paragon of purity, incorruptibility, and all the other seven deadly virtues—and what is the result? You all go over like ninepins—one after the other. Not a year passes in England without somebody disappearing. Scandals used to lend charm, or at least interest, to a man—now they crush him. And yours is a very nasty scandal. You couldn't survive it. If it were known that as a young man, secretary to a great and important minister, you sold a Cabinet secret for a large sum of money, and that that was the origin of your wealth and career, you would be hounded out of public life, you would disappear completely. And after all, Sir Robert, why should you sacrifice your entire future rather than deal diplomatically with your enemy? For the moment I am your enemy. I admit it! And I am much stronger than you are. The big battalions are on my side. You have a splendid position, but it is your splendid position that makes you so vulnerable. You can't defend it. And I am in attack. Of course I have not talked morality to you. You must admit in fairness that I have spared you that. Years ago you did a clever, unscrupulous thing; it turned out a great success. You owe to it your fortune and position. And now you have got to pay for it. Sooner or later we all have to pay for what we do. You have to pay now. Before I leave you to-night, you have got to promise me to suppress your report, and to speak in the House in favour of this scheme.

SIR ROBERT. What you ask is impossible.

MRS. CHEV. You must make it possible. You are going to make it possible. Sir Robert, you know what your English newspapers are like. Suppose that when I leave this house I drive down to some newspaper office, and give them this scandal and the proofs of it! Think of their loathsome joy, of the delight they would have in dragging you down, of the mud and mire they would plunge you in. Think of the hypocrite with his greasy smile penning his leading article, and arranging the foulness of the public placard.

SIR ROBERT. Stop! You want me to withdraw the report and to make a short speech stating that I believe there are possibilities in the scheme?

MRS. CHEV. [*Sitting down on the sofa.*] Those are my terms.

SIR ROBERT. [*In a low voice.*] I will give you any sum of money you want.

MRS. CHEV. Even you are not rich enough, Sir Robert, to buy back your past. No man is.

SIR ROBERT. I will not do what you ask me. I will not.

MRS. CHEV. You have to. If you don't . . . [*Rises from the sofa.*]

SIR ROBERT. [*Bewildered and unnerved.*] Wait a moment! What did you propose? You said that you would give me back my letter, didn't you?

MRS. CHEV. Yes. That is agreed. I will be in the Ladies' Gallery to-morrow night at half-past eleven. If by that time—and you will have had heaps of opportunity—you have made an announcement to the House in the terms I wish, I shall hand you back your letter with the prettiest thanks, and the best, or at any rate the most suitable, compliment I can think of. I intend to play quite fairly with you. One should always play fairly . . . when one has the winning cards. The Baron taught me that . . . amongst other things.

SIR ROBERT. You must let me have time to consider your proposal.

MRS. CHEV. No; you must settle now!

SIR ROBERT. Give me a week—three days!

MRS. CHEV. Impossible! I have got to telegraph to Vienna to-night.

SIR ROBERT. My God! what brought you into my life?

MRS. CHEV. Circumstances. [*Moves towards the door.*]

SIR ROBERT. Don't go. I consent. The report shall be withdrawn. I will arrange for a question to be put to me on the subject.

MRS. CHEV. Thank you. I knew we should come to an amicable agreement. I understood your nature from the first. I analyzed you, though you did not adore me. And now you can get my carriage for me, Sir Robert. I see the people coming up from supper, and Englishmen always get romantic after a meal, and that bores me dreadfully. [*Exit Sir Robert Chiltern.*]

[*Enter Guests, Lady Chiltern, Lady Markby, Lord Caversham, Lady Basildon, Mrs. Marchmont, Vicomte de Nanjac, Mr. Montford.*]

LADY MAR. Well, dear Mrs. Cheveley, I hope you have enjoyed yourself. Sir Robert is very entertaining, is he not?

MRS. CHEV. Most entertaining! I have enjoyed my talk with him immensely.

LADY MAR. He has had a very interesting and brilliant career. And he has married a most admirable wife. Lady Chiltern is a woman of the very highest principles, I am glad to say. I am a little too old now, myself, to trouble about setting a good example, but I always admire people who do. And Lady Chiltern has a very ennobling effect on life, though her dinner-parties are rather dull sometimes. But one can't have everything, can one? And now I must go, dear. Shall I call for you to-morrow?

MRS. CHEV. Thanks.

LADY MAR. We might drive in the Park at five. Everything looks so fresh in the Park now!

MRS. CHEV. Except the people!

LADY MAR. Perhaps the people are a little jaded. I have often observed that the Season as it goes on produces a kind of softening of the brain. However, I think anything is better than high intellectual pressure. That is the most unbecoming thing there is. It makes the noses of the young girls so particularly large. And there is nothing so difficult to marry as a large nose, men don't like them. Good-night, dear! [*To Lady Chiltern.*] Good-night, Gertrude! [*Goes out on Lord Caversham's arm.*]

MRS. CHEV. What a charming house you have, Lady Chiltern! I have spent a delightful evening. It has been so interesting getting to know your husband.

LADY CHI. Why did you wish to meet my husband, Mrs. Cheveley?

MRS. CHEV. Oh, I will tell you. I wanted to interest him in this Argentine

Canal scheme, of which I dare say you have heard. And I found him most susceptible—susceptible to reason, I mean. A rare thing in a man. I converted him in ten minutes. He is going to make a speech in the House to-morrow night in favour of the idea. We must go to the Ladies' Gallery and hear him! It will be a great occasion!

Lady Chi. There must be some mistake. That scheme could never have my husband's support.

Mrs. Chev. Oh, I assure you it's all settled. I don't regret my tedious journey from Vienna now. It has been a great success. But, of course, for the next twenty-four hours the whole thing is a dead secret.

Lady Chi. [*Gently.*] A secret? Between whom?

Mrs. Chev. [*With a flash of amusement in her eyes.*] Between your husband and myself.

Sir Robert. [*Entering.*] Your carriage is here, Mrs. Cheveley!

Mrs. Chev. Thanks! Good evening, Lady Chiltern! Good-night, Lord Goring! I am at Claridge's. Don't you think you might leave a card?

Lord Gor. If you wish it, Mrs. Cheveley!

Mrs. Chev. Oh, don't be so solemn about it, or I shall be obliged to leave a card on you. In England I suppose that would be hardly considered *en règle*. Abroad, we are more civilized. Will you see me down, Sir Robert? Now that we have both the same interests at heart we shall be great friends, I hope!

[*Sails out on Sir Robert Chiltern's arm. Lady Chiltern goes to the top of the staircase and looks down at them as they descend. Her expression is troubled. After a little time she is joined by some of the guests, and passes with them into another reception-room.*]

Mabel. What a horrid woman!

Lord Gor. You should go to bed, Miss Mabel.

Mabel. Lord Goring!

Lord Gor. My father told me to go to bed an hour ago. I don't see why I shouldn't give you the same advice. I always pass on good advice. It is the only thing to do with it. It is never of any use to oneself.

Mabel. Lord Goring, you are always ordering me out of the room. I think it most courageous of you. Especially as I am not going to bed for hours. [*Goes over to the sofa.*] You can come and sit down if you like, and talk about anything in the world, except the Royal Academy, Mrs. Cheveley, or novels in the Scotch dialect. They are not improving subjects. [*Catches sight of something that is lying on the sofa half-hidden by the cushions.*] What is this? Some one has dropped a diamond brooch! Quite beautiful, isn't it? [*Shows it to him.*] I wish it was mine, but Gertrude won't let me wear anything but pearls, and I am thoroughly sick of pearls. They make me look so plain, so good and so intellectual. I wonder whom the brooch belongs to.

Lord Gor. I wonder who dropped it.

Mabel. It is a beautiful brooch.

Lord Gor. It is a handsome bracelet.

Mabel. It isn't a bracelet. It's a brooch.

Lord Gor. It can be used as a bracelet. [*Takes it from her, and, pulling out a green letter-case, puts the ornament carefully in it, and replaces the whole thing in his breast-pocket with the most perfect sang-froid.*]

MABEL. What are you doing?

LORD GOR. Miss Mabel, I am going to make a rather strange request to you.

MABEL. [*Eagerly.*] Oh, pray do! I have been waiting for it all the evening.

LORD GOR. [*Is a little taken aback, but recovers himself.*] Don't mention to anybody that I have taken charge of this brooch. Should anyone write and claim it, let me know at once.

MABEL. That is a strange request.

LORD GOR. Well, you see I gave this brooch to somebody once, years ago.

MABEL. You did?

LORD GOR. Yes.

[*Lady Chiltern enters alone. The other guests have gone.*]

MABEL. Then I shall certainly bid you good-night. Good-night, Gertrude! [*Exit.*]

LADY CHI. Good-night, dear! [*To Lord Goring.*] You saw whom Lady Markby brought here to-night.

LORD GOR. Yes. It was an unpleasant surprise. What did she come here for?

LADY CHI. Apparently to try and lure Robert to uphold some fraudulent scheme in which she is interested. The Argentine Canal, in fact.

LORD GOR. She has mistaken her man, hasn't she?

LADY CHI. She is incapable of understanding an upright nature like my husband's!

LORD GOR. Yes. I should fancy she came to grief if she tried to get Robert into her toils. It is extraordinary what astounding mistakes clever women make.

LADY CHI. I don't call women of that kind clever. I call them stupid!

LORD GOR. Same thing often. Good-night, Lady Chiltern!

LADY CHI. Good-night!

[*Enter Sir Robert Chiltern.*]

SIR ROBERT. My dear Arthur, you are not going? Do stop a little!

LORD GOR. Afraid I can't, thanks. I have promised to look in at the Hartlocks. I believe they have got a mauve Hungarian band that plays mauve Hungarian music. See you soon. Good-bye! [*Exit.*]

SIR ROBERT. How beautiful you look to-night, Gertrude!

LADY CHI. Robert, it is not true, is it? You are not going to lend your support to this Argentine speculation? You couldn't!

SIR ROBERT. [*Starting.*] Who told you I intended to do so?

LADY CHI. That woman who has just gone out, Mrs. Cheveley, as she calls herself now. She seemed to taunt me with it. Robert, I know this woman. You don't. We were at school together. She was untruthful, dishonest, an evil influence on everyone whose trust or friendship she could win. I hated, I despised her. She stole things, she was a thief. She was sent away for being a thief. Why do you let her influence you?

SIR ROBERT. Gertrude, what you tell me may be true, but it happened many years ago. It is best forgotten! Mrs. Cheveley may have changed since then. No one should be entirely judged by their past.

LADY CHI. [*Sadly.*] One's past is what one is. It is the only way by which people should be judged.

SIR ROBERT. That is a hard saying, Gertrude!

LADY CHI. It is a true saying, Robert. And what did she mean by boasting that she had got you to lend your support, your name to a thing I have heard you describe as the most dishonest and fraudulent scheme there has ever been in political life?

SIR ROBERT. [*Biting his lip.*] I was mistaken in the view I took. We all may make mistakes.

LADY CHI. But you told me yesterday that you had received the report from the Commission, and that it entirely condemned the whole thing.

SIR ROBERT. [*Walking up and down.*] I have reasons now to believe that the Commission was prejudiced, or, at any rate, misinformed. Besides, Gertrude, public and private life are different things. They have different laws and move on different lines.

LADY CHI. They should both represent man at his highest. I see no difference between them.

SIR ROBERT. [*Stopping.*] In the present case, on a matter of practical politics, I have changed my mind. That is all.

LADY CHI. All!

SIR ROBERT. [*Sternly.*] Yes!

LADY CHI. Robert! Oh! it is horrible that I should have to ask you such a question–Robert, are you telling me the whole truth?

SIR ROBERT. Why do you ask me such a question?

LADY CHI. [*After a pause.*] Why do you not answer it?

SIR ROBERT. [*Sitting down.*] Gertrude, truth is a very complex thing, and politics is a very complex business. There are wheels within wheels. One may be under certain obligations to people that one must pay. Sooner or later in political life one has to compromise. Everyone does.

LADY CHI. Compromise? Robert, why do you talk so differently to-night from the way I have always heard you talk? Why are you changed?

SIR ROBERT. I am not changed. But circumstances alter things.

LADY CHI. Circumstances should never alter principles.

SIR ROBERT. But if I told you––

LADY CHI. What?

SIR ROBERT. That it was necessary, vitally necessary.

LADY CHI. It can never be necessary to do what is not honourable. Or if it be necessary, then what is it that I have loved! But it is not, Robert; tell me it is not. Why should it be? What gain would you get? Money? We have no need of that! And money that comes from a tainted source is a degradation. Power? But power is nothing in itself. It is power to do good that is fine–that, and that only. What is it, then? Robert, tell me why you are going to do this dishonourable thing!

SIR ROBERT. Gertrude, you have no right to use that word. I told you it was a question of rational compromise. It is no more than that.

LADY CHI. Robert, that is all very well for other men, for men who treat life simply as a sordid speculation; but not for you, Robert, not for you. You are different. All your life you have stood apart from others. You have never let the world soil you. To the world, as to myself, you have been an ideal always. Oh! be that ideal still. That great inheritance throw not away—that tower of ivory do not destroy. Robert, men can love what is beneath them—things unworthy, stained, dishonoured. We women worship when we love; and when we lose our worship, we lose everything. Oh! don't kill my love for you, don't kill that!

SIR ROBERT. Gertrude!

LADY CHI. I know that there are men with horrible secrets in their lives—men who have done some shameful thing, and who in some critical moment have to pay for it, by doing some other act of shame—oh! don't tell me you are such as they are! Robert, is there in your life any secret dishonour or disgrace? Tell me, tell me at once, that——

SIR ROBERT. That what?

LADY CHI. [*Speaking very slowly.*] That our lives may drift apart.

SIR ROBERT. Drift apart?

LADY CHI. That they may be entirely separate. It would be better for us both.

SIR ROBERT. Gertrude, there is nothing in my past life that you might not know.

LADY CHI. I was sure of it, Robert. I was sure of it. But why did you say those dreadful things, things so unlike your real self? Don't let us ever talk about the subject again. You will write, won't you, to Mrs. Cheveley, and tell her that you cannot support this scandalous scheme of hers? If you have given her any promise you must take it back, that is all!

SIR ROBERT. Must I write and tell her that?

LADY CHI. Surely, Robert! What else is there to do?

SIR ROBERT. I might see her personally. It would be better.

LADY CHI. You must never see her again, Robert. She is not a woman you should ever speak to. She is not worthy to talk to a man like you. No; you must write to her at once, now, this moment, and let your letter show her that your decision is quite irrevocable!

SIR ROBERT. Write this moment!

LADY CHI. Yes.

SIR ROBERT. But it is so late. It is close on twelve.

LADY CHI. That makes no matter. She must know at once that she has been mistaken in you—and that you are not a man to do anything base or underhand or dishonourable. Write her, Robert. Write that you decline to support this scheme of hers, as you hold it to be a dishonest scheme. Yes—write the word dishonest. She knows what that word means. [*Sir Robert Chiltern sits down and writes a letter. His wife takes it up and reads it.*] Yes; that will do. [*Rings bell.*] And now the envelope. [*He writes the envelope slowly. Enter Mason.*] Have this letter sent at once to Claridge's Hotel. There is no answer. [*Exit Mason. Lady Chiltern kneels down beside her husband and puts her arms round him.*] Robert, love gives one a sort of instinct to things. I feel to-night that I have saved you from something that might have been a danger to you, from something that might have made men honour you less than they do. I don't think you realize sufficiently, Robert, that you have brought into the political life of our time a nobler atmosphere, a finer attitude towards life, a freer air of purer aims and higher ideals–I know it, and for that I love you, Robert.

SIR ROBERT. Oh, love me always, Gertrude, love me always!

LADY CHI. I will love you always, because you will always be worthy of love. We needs must love the highest when we see it! [*Kisses him and rises and goes out.*]

[*Sir Robert Chiltern walks up and down for a moment; then sits down and buries his face in his hands. The servant enters and begins putting out the lights. Sir Robert Chiltern looks up.*]

SIR ROBERT. Put out the lights, Mason, put out the lights.

[*The servant puts out the light. The room becomes almost dark. The only light there is comes from the great chandelier that hangs over the staircase and illumines the tapestry of the Triumph of Love.*]

ACT-DROP.

SECOND ACT

SCENE–*Morning-room in Sir Robert Chiltern's house.*

[*Lord Goring, dressed in the height of fashion, is lounging in an armchair. Sir Robert Chiltern is standing in front of the fireplace. He is evidently in a state of great mental excitement and distress. As the scene progresses he paces nervously up and down the room.*]

LORD GOR. My dear Robert, it's a very awkward business, very awkward indeed. You should have told your wife the whole thing. Secrets from other people's wives are a necessary luxury in modern life. So, at least, I am always told at the club by people who are bald enough to know better. But no man should have a secret from his own wife. She invariably finds it out. Women have a wonderful instinct about things. They can discover everything except the obvious.

SIR ROBERT. Arthur, I couldn't tell my wife. When could I have told her? Not last night. It would have made a life-long separation between us, and I would have lost the love of the one woman in the world I worship, of the only woman who has ever stirred love within me. Last night it would have been quite impossible. She would have turned from me in horror . . . in horror and in contempt.

LORD GOR. Is Lady Chiltern as perfect as all that?

SIR ROBERT. Yes; my wife is as perfect as all that.

LORD GOR. [*Taking off his left-hand glove.*] What a pity! I beg your pardon, my dear fellow, I didn't quite mean that. But if what you tell me is true, I should like to have a serious talk about life with Lady Chiltern.

Sir Robert. It would be quite useless.

Lord Gor. May I try?

Sir Robert. Yes; but nothing could make her alter her views.

Lord Gor. Well, at the worst it would simply be a psychological experiment.

Sir Robert. All such experiments are terribly dangerous.

Lord Gor. Everything is dangerous, my dear fellow. If it wasn't so, life wouldn't be worth living. . . . Well, I am bound to say that I think you should have told her years ago.

Sir Robert. When? When we were engaged? Do you think she would have married me if she had known that the origin of my fortune is such as it is, the basis of my career such as it is, and that I had done a thing that I suppose most men would call shameful and dishonourable?

Lord Gor. [*Slowly.*] Yes; most men would call it ugly names. There is no doubt of that.

Sir Robert. [*Bitterly.*] Men who every day do something of the same kind themselves. Men who, each one of them, have worse secrets in their own lives.

Lord Gor. That is the reason they are so pleased to find out other people's secrets. It distracts public attention from their own.

Sir Robert. And, after all, whom did I wrong by what I did? No one.

Lord Gor. [*Looking at him steadily.*] Except yourself, Robert.

Sir Robert. [*After a pause.*] Of course I had private information about a certain transaction contemplated by the Government of the day, and I acted on it. Private information is practically the source of every large modern fortune.

Lord Gor. [*Tapping his boot with his cane.*] And public scandal invariably the result.

Sir Robert. [*Pacing up and down the room.*] Arthur, do you think that what I did nearly eighteen years ago should be brought up against me now? Do you think it fair that a man's whole career should be ruined for a fault done in one's boyhood almost? I was twenty-two at the time, and I had the double misfortune of being well-born and poor, two unforgivable things nowadays. Is it fair that the folly, the sin of one's youth, if men choose to call it a sin, should wreck a life like mine, should place me in the pillory, should shatter all that I have worked for, all that I have built up? Is it fair, Arthur?

Lord Gor. Life is never fair, Robert. And perhaps it is a good thing for most of us that it is not.

Sir Robert. Every man of ambition has to fight his century with its own weapons. What this century worships is wealth. To succeed one must achieve wealth. At all costs one must have wealth.

Lord Gor. You underrate yourself, Robert. Believe me, without wealth you could have succeeded just as well.

Sir Robert. When I was old, perhaps. When I had lost my passion for power, or could not use it. When I was tired, worn out, disappointed. I wanted my success when I was young. Youth is the time for success. I couldn't wait.

Lord Gor. Well, you certainly have had your success while you are still young. No one in our day has had such a brilliant success. Under-Secretary for Foreign Affairs at the age of forty—that's good enough for anyone, I should think.

Sir Robert. And if it is all taken away from me now? If I lose everything over a horrible scandal? If I am hounded from public life?

Lord Gor. Robert, how could you have sold yourself for money?

Sir Robert. [*Excitedly.*] I did not sell myself for money. I bought success at a great price. That is all.

Lord Gor. [*Gravely.*] Yes; you certainly paid a great price for it. But what first made you think of doing such a thing?

Sir Robert. Baron Arnheim.

Lord Gor. Damned scoundrel!

Sir Robert. No; he was a man of a most subtle and refined intellect. A man of culture, charm, and distinction. One of the most intellectual men I ever met.

Lord Gor. Ah! I prefer a gentlemanly fool any day. There is more to be said for stupidity than people imagine. Personally, I have a great admiration for stupidity. It is a sort of fellow-feeling, I suppose. But how did he do it? Tell me the whole thing.

Sir Robert. [*Throws himself into an armchair by the writing-table.*] One night after dinner at Lord Radley's the Baron began talking about success in modern life as something that one could reduce to an absolutely definite science. With that wonderfully fascinating quiet voice of his he expounded to us the most terrible of all philosophies, the philosophy of power, preached to us the most marvellous of all gospels, the gospel of gold. I think he saw the effect he had produced on me, for some days afterward he wrote and asked me to come and see him. He was living then in Park Lane, in the house Lord Woolcomb has now. I remember so well how, with a strange smile on his pale curved lips, he led me through his wonderful picture gallery, showed me his tapestries, his enamels, his jewels, his carved ivories, made me wonder at the strange loveliness of the luxury in which he lived; and then told me that luxury was nothing but a background, a painted scene in a play, and that power, power over other men, power over the world was the one thing worth having, the one supreme pleasure worth knowing, the one toy one never tired of, and that in our century only the rich possessed it.

Lord Gor. [*With great deliberation.*] A thoroughly shallow creed.

Sir Robert. [*Rising.*] I didn't think so then. I don't think so now. Wealth has given me enormous power. It gave me at the very outset of my life freedom, and freedom is everything. You have never been poor, and never known what ambition is. You cannot understand what a wonderful chance the Baron gave me. Such a chance as few men get.

Lord Gor. Fortunately for them, if one is to judge by results. But tell me definitely, how did the Baron finally persuade you to—well, to do what you did?

Sir Robert. When I was going away he said to me that if I ever could give him any private information of real value he would make me a very rich man. I was dazed at the prospect he held out to me, and my ambition and my desire for power were at that time boundless. Six weeks later certain private documents passed through my hands.

Lord Gor. [*Keeping his eyes steadily fixed on the carpet.*] State documents?

Sir Robert. Yes. [*Lord Goring sighs, then passes his hand across his forehead and looks up.*]

Lord Gor. I had no idea that you, of all men in the world, could have been so weak, Robert, as to yield to such a temptation as Baron Arnheim held out to you.

Sir Robert. Weak? Oh, I am sick of hearing that phrase. Sick of using it about others. Weak? Do you really think, Arthur, that it is weakness that yields to temptation? I tell you that there are terrible temptations that it requires strength, strength and courage, to yield to. To stake all one's life on a single moment, to risk everything on one throw, whether the stakes be power or pleasure, I care not–there is no weakness in that. There is a horrible, a terrible courage. I had that courage. I sat down the same afternoon and wrote Baron Arnheim the letter this woman now holds. He made three-quarters of a million over the transaction.

Lord Gor. And you?

Sir Robert. I received from the Baron £110,000.

Lord Gor. You were worth more, Robert.

Sir Robert. No; that money gave me exactly what I wanted, power over others. I went into the House immediately. The Baron advised me in finance from time to time. Before five years I had almost trebled my fortune. Since then everything I have touched has turned out a success. In all things connected with money I have had a luck so extraordinary that sometimes it has made me almost afraid. I remember having read somewhere, in some strange book, that when the gods wish to punish us they answer our prayers.

Lord Gor. But tell me, Robert, did you never suffer any regret for what you had done?

Sir Robert. No. I felt that I had fought the century with its own weapons, and won.

Lord Gor. [*Sadly.*] You thought you had won.

Sir Robert. I thought so. [*After a long pause.*] Arthur, do you despise me for what I have told you?

Lord Gor. [*With deep feeling in his voice.*] I am very sorry for you, Robert, very sorry indeed.

Sir Robert. I don't say that I suffered any remorse. I didn't. Not remorse in the ordinary, rather silly sense of the word. But I have paid conscience money many times. I had a wild hope that I might disarm destiny. The sum Baron Arnheim gave me I have distributed twice over in public charities since then.

Lord Gor. [*Looking up.*] In public charities? Dear me! what a lot of harm you must have done, Robert!

Sir Robert. Oh, don't say that, Arthur; don't talk like that.

Lord Gor. Never mind what I say, Robert. I am always saying what I shouldn't say. In fact, I usually say what I really think. A great mistake nowadays. It makes one so liable to be misunderstood. As regards this dreadful business, I will help you in whatever way I can. Of course you know that.

SIR ROBERT. Thank you, Arthur, thank you. But what is to be done? What can be done?

LORD GOR. [*Leaning back with his hands in his pockets.*] Well, the English can't stand a man who is always saying he is in the right, but they are very fond of a man who admits that he has been in the wrong. It is one of the best things in them. However, in your case, Robert, a confession would not do. The money, if you will allow me to say so is . . . awkward. Besides, if you did make a clean breast of the whole affair, you would never be able to talk morality again. And in England a man who can't talk morality twice a week to a large, popular, immoral audience is quite over as a serious politician. There would be nothing left for him as a profession except Botany or the Church. A confession would be of no use. It would ruin you.

SIR ROBERT. It would ruin me. Arthur, the only thing for me to do now is to fight the thing out.

LORD GOR. [*Rising from his chair.*] I was waiting for you to say that, Robert. It is the only thing to do now. And you must begin by telling your wife the whole story.

SIR ROBERT. That I will not do.

LORD GOR. Robert, believe me, you are wrong.

SIR ROBERT. I couldn't do it. It would kill her love for me. And now about this woman, this Mrs. Cheveley. How can I defend myself against her? You knew her before, Arthur, apparently.

LORD GOR. Yes.

SIR ROBERT. Did you know her well?

LORD GOR. [*Arranging his necktie.*] So little that I got engaged to be married to her once, when I was staying at the Tenbys'. The affair lasted for three days . . . nearly.

SIR ROBERT. Why was it broken off?

LORD GOR. [*Airily.*] Oh, I forget. At least, it makes no matter. By the way, have you tried her with money? She used to be confoundedly fond of money.

SIR ROBERT. I offered her any sum she wanted. She refused.

LORD GOR. Then the marvellous gospel of gold breaks down sometimes. The rich can't do everything, after all.

SIR ROBERT. Not everything. I suppose you are right. Arthur, I feel that public disgrace is in store for me. I feel certain of it. I never knew what terror was before. I know it now. It is as if a hand of ice were laid upon one's heart. It is as if one's heart were beating itself to death in some empty hollow.

LORD GOR. [*Striking the table.*] Robert, you must fight her. You must fight her.

SIR ROBERT. But how?

LORD GOR. I can't tell you how, at present. I have not the smallest idea. But everyone has some weak point. There is some flaw in each one of us. [*Strolls over to the fireplace and looks at himself in the glass.*] My father tells me that even I have faults. Perhaps I have. I don't know.

Sir Robert. In defending myself against Mrs. Cheveley, I have a right to use any weapon I can find, have I not?

Lord Gor. [*Still looking in the glass.*] In your place I don't think I should have the smallest scruple in doing so. She is thoroughly well able to take care of herself.

Sir Robert. [*Sits down at the table and takes a pen in his hand.*] Well, I shall send a cipher telegram to the embassy at Vienna, to inquire if there is anything known against her. There may be some secret scandal she might be afraid of.

Lord Gor. [*Settling his buttonhole.*] Oh, I should fancy Mrs. Cheveley is one of those very modern women of our time who find a new scandal as becoming as a new bonnet, and air them both in the Park every afternoon at five-thirty. I am sure she adores scandals, and that the sorrow of her life at present is that she can't manage to have enough of them.

Sir Robert. [*Writing.*] Why do you say that?

Lord Gor. [*Turning round.*] Well, she wore far too much rouge last night, and not quite enough clothes. That is always a sign of despair in a woman.

Sir Robert. [*Striking a bell.*] But it is worth while my writing to Vienna, is it not?

Lord Gor. It is always worth while asking a question, though it is not always worth while answering one.

[*Enter Mason.*]

Sir Robert. Is Mr. Trafford in his room?

Mason. Yes, Sir Robert.

Sir Robert. [*Puts what he has written into an envelope, which he then carefully closes.*] Tell him to have this sent off in cipher at once. There must not be a moment's delay.

Mason. Yes, Sir Robert.

Sir Robert. Oh, just give that back to me again.

[*Writes something on the envelope. Mason then goes out with the letter.*]

Sir Robert. She must have had some curious hold over Baron Arnheim. I wonder what it was.

Lord Gor. [*Smiling.*] I wonder.

Sir Robert. I will fight her to the death, as long as my wife knows nothing.

Lord Gor. [*Strongly.*] Oh, fight in any case—in any case.

Sir Robert. [*With a gesture of despair.*] If my wife found out, there would be little left to fight for. Well, as soon as I hear from Vienna, I shall let you know the result. It is a chance, just a chance, but I believe in it. And as I fought the age with its own weapons, I will fight her with her weapons. It is only fair, and she looks like a woman with a past, doesn't she?

Lord Gor. Most pretty women do. But there is a fashion in pasts just as there is a fashion in frocks. Perhaps Mrs. Cheveley's past is merely a slightly *décolleté* one, and they are excessively popular nowadays. Besides, my dear Robert, I should not build too high hopes on frightening Mrs. Cheveley. I should not fancy Mrs. Cheveley is a woman who would be easily frightened. She has survived all her creditors, and she shows wonderful presence of mind.

Sir Robert. Oh! I live on hopes now. I clutch at every chance. I feel like a man on a ship that is sinking. The water is round my feet, and the very air is bitter with storm. Hush! I hear my wife's voice.

[*Enter Lady Chiltern in walking dress.*]

Lady Chi. Good afternoon, Lord Goring!

Lord Gor. Good afternoon, Lady Chiltern! Have you been in the Park?

Lady Chi. No: I have just come from the Woman's Liberal Association, where, by the way, Robert, your name was received with loud applause, and now I have come in to have my tea. [*To Lord Goring.*] You will wait and have some tea, won't you?

Lord Gor. I'll wait for a short time, thanks.

Lady Chi. I will be back in a moment. I am only going to take my hat off.

Lord Gor. [*In his most earnest manner.*] Oh! please don't. It is so pretty. One of the prettiest hats I ever saw. I hope the Woman's Liberal Association received it with loud applause.

Lady Chi. [*With a smile.*] We have much more important work to do than to look at each other's bonnets, Lord Goring.

Lord Gor. Really? What sort of work?

Lady Chi. Oh! dull, useful, delightful things, Factory Acts, Female Inspectors, the Eight Hours' Bill, the Parliamentary Franchise. . . . Everything, in fact, that you would find thoroughly uninteresting.

Lord Gor. And never bonnets?

Lady Chi. [*With mock indignation.*] Never bonnets, never.

[*Lady Chiltern goes out through the door leading to her boudoir.*]

Sir Robert. [*Takes Lord Goring's hand.*] You have been a good friend to me, Arthur, a thoroughly good friend.

Lord Gor. I don't know that I have been able to do much for you, Robert, as yet. In fact, I have not been able to do anything for you, as far as I can see. I am thoroughly disappointed with myself.

Sir Robert. You have enabled me to tell you the truth. That is something. The truth has always stifled me.

Lord Gor. Ah! the truth is a thing I get rid of as soon as possible! Bad habit, by the way. Makes one very unpopular at the club . . . with the older members. They call it being conceited. Perhaps it is.

Sir Robert. I would to God that I had been able to tell the truth . . . to live the truth. Ah! that is the great thing in life, to live the truth. [*Sighs and goes towards the door.*] I'll see you soon again, Arthur, sha'n't I?

Lord Gor. Certainly. Whenever you like. I'm going to look in at the Bachelors' Ball to-night, unless I find something better to do. But I'll come round to-morrow morning. If you should want me to-night by any chance, send round a note to Curzon Street.

Sir Robert. Thank you.

[*As he reaches the door, Lady Chiltern enters from her boudoir.*]

Lady Chi. You are not going, Robert?

SIR ROBERT. I have some letters to write, dear.

LADY CHI. [*Going to him.*] You work too hard, Robert. You seem never to think of yourself, and you are looking so tired.

SIR ROBERT. It is nothing, dear, nothing. [*He kisses her and goes out.*]

LADY CHI. [*To Lord Goring.*] Do sit down. I am so glad you have called. I want to talk to you about . . . well, not about bonnets, or the Woman's Liberal Association. You take far too much interest in the first subject, and not nearly enough in the second.

LORD GOR. You want to talk to me about Mrs. Cheveley?

LADY CHI. Yes. You have guessed it. After you left last night I found out that what she had said was really true. Of course I made Robert write her a letter at once, withdrawing his promise.

LORD GOR. So he gave me to understand.

LADY CHI. To have kept it would have been the first stain on a career that has been stainless always. Robert must be above reproach. He is not like other men. He cannot afford to do what other men do. [*She looks at Lord Goring, who remains silent.*] Don't you agree with me? You are Robert's greatest friend. You are our greatest friend, Lord Goring. No one, except myself, knows Robert better than you do. He has no secrets from me, and I don't think he has any from you.

LORD GOR. He certainly has no secrets from me. At least I don't think so.

LADY CHI. Then am I not right in my estimate of him? I know I am right. But speak to me frankly.

LORD GOR. [*Looking straight at her.*] Quite frankly?

LADY CHI. Surely. You have nothing to conceal, have you?

LORD GOR. Nothing. But, my dear Lady Chiltern, I think, if you will allow me to say so, that in practical life——

LADY CHI. [*Smiling.*] Of which you know so little, Lord Goring——

LORD GOR. Of which I know nothing by experience, though I know something by observation. I think that in practical life there is something about success, actual success, that is a little unscrupulous, something about ambition that is unscrupulous always. Once a man has set his heart and soul on getting to a certain point, if he has to climb the crag, he climbs the crag; if he has to walk in the mire——

LADY CHI. Well?

LORD GOR. He walks in the mire. Of course I am only talking generally about life.

LADY CHI. [*Gravely.*] I hope so. Why do you look at me so strangely, Lord Goring?

LORD GOR. Lady Chiltern, I have sometimes thought that . . . perhaps you are a little hard in your views on life. I think that . . . often you don't make sufficient allowances. In every nature there are elements of weakness, or worse than weakness. Supposing, for instance, that–that any public man, my father, or Lord Merton, or Robert, say, had, years ago, written some foolish letter to some one . . .

LADY CHI. What do you mean by a foolish letter?

LORD GOR. A letter gravely compromising one's position. I am only putting an imaginary case.

LADY CHI. Robert is as incapable of doing a foolish thing as he is of doing a wrong thing.

LORD GOR. [*After a long pause.*] Nobody is incapable of doing a foolish thing. Nobody is incapable of doing a wrong thing.

LADY CHI. Are you a Pessimist? What will the other dandies say? They will all have to go into mourning.

LORD GOR. [*Rising.*] No, Lady Chiltern, I am not a Pessimist. Indeed I am not sure that I quite know what Pessimism really means. All I do know is that life cannot be understood without much charity, cannot be lived without much charity. It is love, and not German philosophy, that is the true explanation of this world, whatever may be the explanation of the next. And if you are ever in trouble, Lady Chiltern, trust me absolutely, and I will help you in every way I can. If you ever want me, come to me for my assistance, and you shall have it. Come at once to me.

LADY CHI. [*Looking at him in surprise.*] Lord Goring, you are talking quite seriously. I don't think I ever heard you talk seriously before.

LORD GOR. [*Laughing.*] You must excuse me, Lady Chiltern. It won't occur again, if I can help it.

LADY CHI. But I like you to be serious.

[*Enter Mabel Chiltern, in the most ravishing frock.*]

MABEL. Dear Gertrude, don't say such a dreadful thing to Lord Goring. Seriousness would be very unbecoming to him. Good afternoon, Lord Goring! Pray be as trivial as you can.

LORD GOR. I should like to, Miss Mabel, but I am afraid I am . . . a little out of practice this morning; and besides, I have to be going now.

MABEL. Just when I have come in! What dreadful manners you have! I am sure you were very badly brought up.

LORD GOR. I was.

MABEL. I wish I had brought you up!

LORD GOR. I am so sorry you didn't.

MABEL. It is too late now, I suppose?

LORD GOR. [*Smiling.*] I am not so sure.

MABEL. Will you ride to-morrow morning?

LORD GOR. Yes, at ten.

MABEL. Don't forget.

LORD GOR. Of course I sha'n't. By the way, Lady Chiltern, there is no list of your guests in "The Morning Post" of to-day. It has apparently been crowded out by the County Council, or the Lambeth Conference, or something equally boring. Could you let me have a list? I have a particular reason for asking you.

LADY CHI. I am sure Mr. Trafford will be able to give you one.

LORD GOR. Thanks, so much.

MABEL. Tommy is the most useful person in London.

LORD GOR. [*Turning to her.*] And who is the most ornamental?

Mabel. [*Triumphantly.*] I am.

Lord Gor. How clever of you to guess it! [*Takes up his hat and cane.*] Good-bye, Lady Chiltern! You will remember what I said to you, won't you?

Lady Chi. Yes; but I don't know why you said it to me.

Lord Gor. I hardly know myself. Good-bye, Miss Mabel!

Mabel. [*With a little move of disappointment.*] I wish you were not going. I have had four wonderful adventures this morning; four and a half, in fact. You might stop and listen to some of them.

Lord Gor. How very selfish of you to have four and a half! There won't be any left for me.

Mabel. I don't want you to have any. They would not be good for you.

Lord Gor. That is the first unkind thing you have ever said to me. How charmingly you said it! Ten to-morrow.

Mabel. Sharp.

Lord Gor. Quite sharp. But don't bring Mr. Trafford.

Mabel. [*With a little toss of her head.*] Of course I sha'n't bring Tommy Trafford. Tommy Trafford is in great disgrace.

Lord Gor. I am delighted to hear it. [*Bows and goes out.*]

Mabel. Gertrude, I wish you would speak to Tommy Trafford.

Lady Chi. What has poor Mr. Trafford done this time? Robert says he is the best secretary he has ever had.

Mabel. Well, Tommy has proposed to me again. Tommy really does nothing but propose to me. He proposed to me last night in the music-room, when I was quite unprotected, as there was an elaborate trio going on. I didn't dare to make the smallest repartee, I need hardly tell you. If I had, it would have stopped the music at once. Musical people are so absurdly unreasonable. They always want one to be perfectly dumb at the very moment when one is longing to be absolutely deaf. Then he proposed to me in broad daylight this morning in front of that dreadful statue of Achilles. Really, the things that go on in front of that work of art are quite appalling. The police should interfere. At luncheon I saw by the glare in his eye that he was going to propose again, and I just managed to check him in time by assuring him that I was a bimetallist. Fortunately I don't know what bimetallism means. And I don't believe anybody else does either. But the observation crushed Tommy for ten minutes. He looked quite shocked. And then Tommy is so annoying in the way he proposes. If he proposed at the top of his voice, I should not mind so much. That might produce some effect on the public. But he does it in a horrid confidential way. When Tommy wants to be romantic he talks to one just like a doctor. I am very fond of Tommy, but his methods of proposing are quite out of date. I wish, Gertrude, you would speak to him, and tell him that once a week is quite often enough to propose to anyone, and that it should always be done in a manner that attracts some attention.

Lady Chi. Dear Mabel, don't talk like that. Besides, Robert thinks very highly of Mr. Trafford. He believes he has a brilliant future before him.

Mabel. Oh! I wouldn't marry a man with a future before him for anything under the sun.

LADY CHI. Mabel!

MABEL. I know, dear. You married a man with a future, didn't you? But then Robert was a genius, and you have a noble, self-sacrificing character. You can stand geniuses. I have no character at all, and Robert is the only genius I could ever bear. As a rule, I think they are quite impossible. Geniuses talk so much, don't they? Such a bad habit! And they are always thinking about themselves, when I want them to be thinking about me. I must go round now and rehearse at Lady Basildon's. You remember, we are having tableaux, don't you? The Triumph of something, I don't know what! I hope it will be triumph of me. Only triumph I am really interested in at present. [*Kisses Lady Chiltern and goes out; then comes running back.*] Oh, Gertrude, do you know who is coming to see you? That dreadful Mrs. Cheveley, in a most lovely gown. Did you ask her?

LADY CHI. [*Rising.*] Mrs. Cheveley! Coming to see me? Impossible!

MABEL. I assure you she is coming upstairs, as large as life and not nearly so natural.

LADY CHI. You need not wait, Mabel. Remember, Lady Basildon is expecting you.

MABEL. Oh! I must shake hands with Lady Markby. She is delightful. I love being scolded by her.

[*Enter Mason.*]

MASON. Lady Markby. Mrs. Cheveley.

[*Enter Lady Markby and Mrs. Cheveley.*]

LADY CHI. [*Advancing to meet them.*] Dear Lady Markby, how nice of you to come and see me! [*Shakes hands with her, and bows somewhat distantly to Mrs. Cheveley.*] Won't you sit down, Mrs. Cheveley?

MRS. CHEV. Thanks. Isn't that Miss Chiltern? I should like so much to know her.

LADY CHI. Mabel, Mrs. Cheveley wishes to know you. [*Mabel Chiltern gives a little nod.*]

MRS. CHEV. [*Sitting down.*] I thought your frock so charming last night, Miss Chiltern. So simple and . . . suitable.

MABEL. Really? I must tell my dressmaker. It will be such a surprise to her. Good-bye, Lady Markby!

LADY MAR. Going already?

MABEL. I am so sorry but I am obliged to. I am just off to rehearsal. I have got to stand on my head in some tableaux.

LADY MAR. On your head, child? Oh, I hope not. I believe it is most unhealthy. [*Takes a seat on the sofa next Lady Chiltern.*]

MABEL. But it is for an excellent charity; in aid of the Undeserving, the only people I am really interested in. I am the secretary, and Tommy Trafford is treasurer.

MRS. CHEV. And what is Lord Goring?

MABEL. Oh! Lord Goring is president.

MRS. CHEV. The post should suit him admirably, unless he has deteriorated since I knew him first.

LADY MAR. [*Reflecting.*] You are remarkably modern, Mabel. A little too modern, perhaps. Nothing is so dangerous as being too modern. One is apt to grow old-fashioned quite suddenly. I have known many instances of it.

MABEL. What a dreadful prospect!

LADY MAR. Ah, my dear, you need not be nervous. You will always be as pretty as possible. That is the best fashion there is, and the only fashion that England succeeds in setting.

MABEL. [*With a curtsey.*] Thank you so much, Lady Markby, for England . . . and myself. [*Goes out.*]

LADY MAR. [*Turning to Lady Chiltern.*] Dear Gertrude, we just called to know if Mrs. Cheveley's diamond brooch has been found.

LADY CHI. Here?

MRS. CHEV. Yes. I missed it when I got back to Claridge's, and I thought I might possibly have dropped it here.

LADY CHI. I have heard nothing about it. But I will send for the butler and ask. [*Touches the bell.*]

MRS. CHEV. Oh, pray don't trouble, Lady Chiltern. I daresay I lost it at the Opera before we came on here.

LADY MAR. Ah yes, I suppose it must have been at the Opera. The fact is, we all scramble and jostle so much nowadays that I wonder we have anything at all left on us at the end of an evening. I know myself that, when I am coming back from the drawing-room, I always feel as if I hadn't a shred on me, except a small shred of decent reputation, just enough to prevent the lower classes making painful observations through the windows of the carriage. The fact is that our Society is terribly overpopulated. Really, some one should arrange a proper scheme of assisted emigration. It would do a great deal of good.

MRS. CHEV. I quite agree with you, Lady Markby. It is nearly six years since I have been in London for the season, and I must say Society has become dreadfully mixed. One sees the oddest people everywhere.

LADY MAR. That is quite true, dear. But one needn't know them. I'm sure I don't know half the people who come to my house. Indeed, from all I hear, I shouldn't like to.

[*Enter Mason.*]

LADY CHI. What sort of a brooch was it that you lost, Mrs. Cheveley?

MRS. CHEV. A diamond snake-brooch, with a ruby, a rather large ruby.

LADY MAR. I thought you said there was a sapphire on the head, dear?

MRS. CHEV. [*Smiling.*] No, Lady Markby—a ruby.

LADY MAR. [*Nodding her head.*] And very becoming, I am quite sure.

LADY CHI. Has a ruby and diamond brooch been found in any of the rooms this morning, Mason?

MASON. No, my lady.

MRS. CHEV. It really is of no consequence, Lady Chiltern. I am so sorry to have put you to any inconvenience.

LADY CHI. [*Coldly.*] Oh, it has been no inconvenience. That will do, Mason. You can bring tea. [*Exit Mason.*]

LADY MAR. Well, I must say it is most annoying to lose anything. I remember once at Bath, years ago, losing in the Pump Room an exceedingly handsome cameo bracelet that Sir John had given me. I don't think he has ever given me anything since, I am sorry to say. He has sadly degenerated. Really, this horrid House of Commons quite ruins our husbands for us. I think the Lower House by far the greatest blow to a happy married life that there has been since that terrible thing called the Higher Education of Women was invented.

LADY CHI. Ah, it is heresy to say that in this house, Lady Markby. Robert is a great champion of the Higher Education of Women, and so, I am afraid, am I.

MRS. CHEV. The higher education of men is what I should like to see. Men need it so sadly.

LADY MAR. They do, dear. But I am afraid such a scheme would be quite unpractical. I don't think man has much capacity for development. He has got as far as he can, and that is not far, is it? With regard to women, well, dear Gertrude, you belong to the younger generation, and I am sure it is all right if you approve of it. In my time, of course, we were taught not to understand anything. That was the old system, and wonderfully interesting it was. I assure you that the amount of things I and my poor dear sister were taught not to understand was quite extraordinary. But modern women understand everything, I am told.

MRS. CHEV. Except their husbands. That is the one thing the modern woman never understands.

LADY MAR. And a very good thing, too, dear, I daresay. It might break up many a happy home if they did. Not yours, I need hardly say, Gertrude. You have married a pattern husband. I wish I could say as much for myself. But since Sir John has taken to attending the debates regularly, which he never used to do in the good old days, his language has become quite impossible. He always seems to think that he is addressing the House and consequently whenever he discusses the state of the agricultural labourer, or the Welsh Church, or something quite improper of that kind, I am obliged to send all the servants out of the room. It is not pleasant to see one's own butler, who has been with one for twenty-three years, actually blushing at the sideboard, and the footmen making contortions in corners like persons in circuses. I assure you my life will be quite ruined unless they send John at once to the Upper House. He won't take any interest in politics then, will he? The House of Lords is so sensible. An assembly of gentlemen. But in his present state, Sir John is really a great trial. Why, this morning before breakfast was half over, he stood up on the hearthrug, put his hands in his pockets, and appealed to the country at the top of his voice. I left the table as soon as I had my second cup of tea, I need hardly say. But his violent language could be heard all over the house! I trust, Gertrude, that Sir Robert is not like that?

LADY CHI. But I am very much interested in politics, Lady Markby. I love to hear Robert talk about them.

LADY MAR. Well, I hope he is not as devoted to Blue Books as Sir John is. I don't think they can be quite improving reading for anyone.

MRS. CHEV. [*Languidly.*] I have never read a Blue Book. I prefer books . . . in yellow covers.

LADY MAR. [*Genuinely unconscious.*] Yellow is a gayer colour, is it not? I used to wear yellow a good deal in my early days, and would do so now if Sir John was not so painfully personal in his observations, and a man on the question of dress is always ridiculous, is he not?

MRS. CHEV. Oh, no! I think men are the only authorities on dress.

LADY MAR. Really? One wouldn't say so from the sort of hats they wear, would one?

[*The butler enters, followed by the footman. Tea is set on a small table close to Lady Chiltern.*]

LADY CHI. May I give you some tea, Mrs. Cheveley?

MRS. CHEV. Thanks. [*The butler hands Mrs. Cheveley a cup of tea on a salver.*]

LADY CHI. Some tea, Lady Markby?

LADY MAR. No thanks, dear. [*The servants go out.*] The fact is, I have promised to go round for ten minutes to see poor Lady Brancaster, who is in very great trouble. Her daughter, quite a well-brought-up girl, too, has actually become engaged to be married to a curate in Shropshire. It is very sad, very sad indeed. I can't understand this modern mania for curates. In my time we girls saw them, of course, running about the place like rabbits. But we never took any notice of them, I need hardly say. But I am told that nowadays country society is quite honeycombed with them. I think it most irreligious. And then the eldest son has quarrelled with his father, and it is said that when they meet at the club Lord Brancaster always hides himself behind the money article in "The Times." However, I believe that is quite a common occurrence nowadays and that they have to take in extra copies of "The Times" at all the clubs in St. James's Street; there are so many sons who won't have anything to do with their fathers, and so many fathers who won't speak to their sons. I think myself, it is very much to be regretted.

MRS. CHEV. So do I. Fathers have so much to learn from their sons nowadays.

LADY MAR. Really, dear? What?

MRS. CHEV. The art of living. The only really Fine Art we have produced in modern times.

LADY MAR. [*Shaking her head.*] Ah! I am afraid Lord Brancaster knew a good deal about that. More than his poor wife ever did. [*Turning to Lady Chiltern.*] You know Lady Brancaster, don't you, dear?

LADY CHI. Just slightly. She was staying at Langston last autumn, when we were there.

LADY MAR. Well, like all stout women, she looks the very picture of happiness, as no doubt you noticed. But there are many tragedies in her family, besides this affair of the curate. Her own sister, Mrs. Jekyll, had a most unhappy life; through no fault of her own, I am sorry to say. She ultimately was so broken-hearted that she went into a convent, or on to the operatic stage, I forget which. No; I think it was decorative art-needlework she took up. I know she had lost all sense of pleasure in life. [*Rising.*] And now, Gertrude, if you will allow me, I shall leave Mrs. Cheveley in your charge and call back for her in a quarter of an hour. Or perhaps, dear Mrs. Cheveley, you wouldn't mind waiting in the carriage while I am with Lady Brancaster. As I intend it to be a visit of condolence, I sha'n't stay long.

Mrs. Chev. [*Rising.*] I don't mind waiting in the carriage at all, provided there is somebody to look at one.

Lady Mar. Well, I hear the curate is always prowling about the house.

Mrs. Chev. I am afraid I am not fond of girl friends.

Lady Chi. [*Rising.*] Oh, I hope Mrs. Cheveley will stay here a little. I should like to have a few minutes' conversation with her.

Mrs. Chev. How very kind of you, Lady Chiltern! Believe me, nothing would give me greater pleasure.

Lady Mar. Ah! no doubt you both have many pleasant reminiscences of your schooldays to talk over together. Good-bye, dear Gertrude! Shall I see you at Lady Bonar's to-night? She has discovered a wonderful new genius. He does . . . nothing at all, I believe. That is a great comfort, is it not?

Lady Chi. Robert and I are dining at home by ourselves to-night, and I don't think I shall go anywhere afterwards. Robert, of course, will have to be in the House. But there is nothing interesting on.

Lady Mar. Dining at home by yourselves? Is that quite prudent? Ah, I forgot, your husband is an exception. Mine is the general rule, and nothing ages a woman so rapidly as having married the general rule.

[*Exit Lady Markby.*]

Mrs. Chev. Wonderful woman, Lady Markby, isn't she? Talks more and says less than anybody I ever met. She is made to be a public speaker. Much more so than her husband, though he is a typical Englishman, always dull and usually violent.

Lady Chi. [*Makes no answer, but remains standing. There is a pause. Then the eyes of the two women meet. Lady Chiltern looks stern and pale. Mrs. Cheveley seems rather amused.*] Mrs. Cheveley, I think it is right to tell you quite frankly that, had I known who you really were, I should not have invited you to my house last night.

Mrs. Chev. [*With an impertinent smile.*] Really?

Lady Chi. I could not have done so.

Mrs. Chev. I see that after all these years you have not changed a bit, Gertrude.

Lady Chi. I never change.

Mrs. Chev. [*Elevating her eyebrows.*] Then life has taught you nothing?

Lady Chi. It has taught me that a person who has once been guilty of a dishonest and dishonourable action may be guilty of it a second time, and should be shunned.

Mrs. Chev. Would you apply that rule to everyone?

Lady Chi. Yes, to everyone, without exception.

Mrs. Chev. Then I am sorry for you, Gertrude, very sorry for you.

Lady Chi. You see now, I am sure, that for many reasons any further acquaintance between us during your stay in London is quite impossible?

MRS. CHEV. [*Leaning back in her chair.*] Do you know, Gertrude, I don't mind your talking morality a bit. Morality is simply the attitude we adopt towards people whom we personally dislike. You dislike me. I am quite aware of that. And I have always detested you. And yet I have come here to do you a service.

LADY CHI. [*Contemptuously.*] Like the service you wished to render my husband last night, I suppose. Thank heaven, I saved him from that.

MRS. CHEV. [*Starting to her feet.*] It was you who made him write that insolent letter to me? It was you who made him break his promise?

LADY CHI. Yes.

MRS. CHEV. Then you must make him keep it. I give you till to-morrow morning–no more. If by that time your husband does not solemnly bind himself to help me in this great scheme in which I am interested——

LADY CHI. This fraudulent speculation——

MRS. CHEV. Call it what you choose. I hold your husband in the hollow of my hand, and if you are wise you will make him do what I tell him.

LADY CHI. [*Rising and going towards her.*] You are impertinent. What has my husband to do with you? With a woman like you?

MRS. CHEV. [*With a bitter laugh.*] In this world like meets with like. It is because your husband is himself fraudulent and dishonest that we pair so well together. Between you and him there are chasms. He and I are closer than friends. We are enemies linked together. The same sin binds us.

LADY CHI. How dare you class my husband with yourself? How dare you threaten him or me? Leave my house. You are unfit to enter it.

[*Sir Robert Chiltern enters from behind. He hears his wife's last words, and sees to whom they are addressed. He grows deadly pale.*]

MRS. CHEV. Your house! A house bought with the price of dishonour. A house, everything in which has been paid for by fraud. [*Turns round and sees Sir Robert Chiltern.*] Ask him what the origin of his fortune is! Get him to tell you how he sold to a stockbroker a Cabinet secret. Learn from him to what you owe your position.

LADY CHI. It is not true! Robert! It is not true!

MRS. CHEV. [*Pointing at him with outstretched finger.*] Look at him! Can he deny it? Does he dare to?

SIR ROBERT. Go! Go at once! You have done your worst now.

MRS. CHEV. My worst? I have not yet finished with you, with either of you. I give you both till to-morrow at noon. If by then you don't do what I bid you to do, the whole world shall know the origin of Robert Chiltern.

[*Sir Robert Chiltern strikes the bell. Enter Mason.*]

SIR ROBERT. Show Mrs. Cheveley out.

[*Mrs. Cheveley starts; then bows with somewhat exaggerated politeness to Lady Chiltern, who makes no sign of response. As she passes by Sir Robert Chiltern, who is standing close to the door, she pauses for a moment and looks him straight in the face. She then goes out, followed by the servant, who closes the door after him. The husband and wife are left alone. Lady Chiltern stands like some one in a dreadful dream. Then she turns round and looks at her husband. She looks at him with strange eyes, as though she was seeing him for the first time.*]

LADY CHI. You sold a Cabinet secret for money! You began your life with fraud! You built up your career on dishonour! Oh, tell me it is not true! Lie to me! Lie to me! Tell me it is not true!

SIR ROBERT. What this woman said is quite true. But, Gertrude, listen to me. You don't realize how I was tempted. Let me tell you the whole thing. [*Goes towards her.*]

LADY CHI. Don't come near me. Don't touch me. I feel as if you had soiled me for ever. Oh! what a mask you have been wearing all these years! A horrible painted mask! You sold yourself for money. Oh! a common thief were better! You put yourself up to sale to the highest bidder! You were bought in the market. You lied to the whole world. And yet you will not lie to me.

SIR ROBERT. [*Rushing towards her.*] Gertrude! Gertrude!

LADY CHI. [*Thrusting him back with outstretched hands.*] No, don't speak! Say nothing! Your voice wakes terrible memories—memories of things that made me love you—memories of words that made me love you—memories that now are horrible to me. And how I worshipped you! You were to me something apart from common life, a thing pure, noble, honest, without stain. The world seemed to me finer because you were in it, and goodness more real because you lived. And now—oh, when I think that I made of a man like you my ideal! the ideal of my life!

SIR ROBERT. There was your mistake. There was your error. The error all women commit. Why can't you women love us, faults and all? Why do you place us on monstrous pedestals? We have all feet of clay, women as well as men; but when we men love women, we love them knowing their weaknesses, their follies, their imperfections, love them all the more, it may be, for that reason. It is not the perfect, but the imperfect, who have need of love. It is when we are wounded by our own hands, or by the hands of others, that love should come to cure us—else what use is love at all? All sins, except a sin against itself, Love should forgive. All lives, save loveless lives, true Love should pardon. A man's love is like that. It is wider, larger, more human than a woman's. Women think that they are making ideals of men. What they are making of us are false idols merely. You made your false idol of me, and I had not the courage to come down, show you my wounds, tell you my weaknesses. I was afraid that I might lose your love, as I have lost it now. And so, last night you ruined my life for me—yes, ruined it! What this woman asked of me was nothing compared to what she offered to me. She offered security, peace, stability. The sin of my youth, that I had thought was buried, rose up in front of me, hideous, horrible, with its hands at my throat. I could have killed it for ever, sent it back into its tomb, destroyed its record, burned the one witness against me. You prevented me. No one but you, you know it. And now what is there before me but public disgrace, ruin, terrible shame, the mockery of the world, a lonely dishonoured life, a lonely dishonoured death, it may be, some day? Let women make no more ideals of men! let them not put them on altars and bow before them, or they may ruin other lives as completely as you—you whom I have so wildly loved—have ruined mine!

[*He passes from the room. Lady Chiltern rushes towards him, but the door is closed when she reaches it. Pale with anguish, bewildered, helpless, she sways like a plant in the water. Her hands, outstretched, seem to tremble in the air like blossoms in the wind. Then she flings herself down beside the sofa and buries her face. Her sobs are like the sobs of a child.*]

ACT-DROP.

THIRD ACT

SCENE—*The library in Lord Goring's house. An Adams room. On the right is the door leading into the hall. On the left, the door of the smoking-room. A pair of folding doors at the back open into the drawing-room. The fire is lit. Phipps, the butler, is arranging some newspapers on the writing-table. The distinction of Phipps is his impassivity. He has been termed by enthusiasts the Ideal Butler. The Sphinx is not so incommunicable. He is a mask with a manner. Of his intellectual or emotional life history knows nothing. He represents the dominance of form.*

[*Enter Lord Goring in evening dress with a buttonhole. He is wearing a silk hat and Inverness cape. White-gloved, he carries a Louis Seize cane. His are all the delicate fopperies of Fashion. One sees that he stands in immediate relation to modern life, makes it indeed, and so masters it. He is the first well-dressed philosopher in the history of thought.*]

LORD GOR. Got my second buttonhole for me, Phipps?

PHIPPS. Yes, my lord. [*Takes his hat, cane and cape, and presents new buttonhole on salver.*]

LORD GOR. Rather distinguished thing, Phipps. I am the only person of the smallest importance in London at present who wears a buttonhole.

PHIPPS. Yes, my lord, I have observed that.

LORD GOR. [*Taking out old buttonhole.*] You see, Phipps, Fashion is what one wears oneself. What is unfashionable is what other people wear.

PHIPPS. Yes, my lord.

LORD GOR. Just as vulgarity is simply the conduct of other people.

PHIPPS. Yes, my lord.

LORD GOR. [*Putting in new buttonhole.*] And falsehoods the truths of other people.

PHIPPS. Yes, my lord.

LORD GOR. Other people are quite dreadful. The only possible society is oneself.

PHIPPS. Yes, my lord.

LORD GOR. To love oneself is the beginning of a lifelong romance, Phipps.

PHIPPS. Yes, my lord.

LORD GOR. [*Looking at himself in the glass.*] Don't think I quite like this buttonhole, Phipps. Makes me look a little too old. Makes me almost in the prime of life, eh, Phipps?

PHIPPS. I don't observe any alteration in your lordship's appearance.

LORD GOR. You don't, Phipps?

PHIPPS. No, my lord.

LORD GOR. I am not quite sure. For the future a more trivial buttonhole, Phipps, on Thursday evenings.

PHIPPS. I will speak to the florist, my lord. She has had a loss in her family lately, which perhaps accounts for the lack of triviality your lordship complains of in the buttonhole.

LORD GOR. Extraordinary thing about the lower classes in England–they are always losing their relations.

PHIPPS. Yes, my lord! they are extremely fortunate in that respect.

LORD GOR. [*Turns round and looks at him. Phipps remains impassive.*] Hum! Any letters, Phipps?

PHIPPS. Three, my lord.[*Hands letters on a salver.*]

LORD GOR. [*Takes letters.*] Want my cab round in twenty minutes.

PHIPPS. Yes, my lord. [*Goes toward door.*]

LORD GOR. [*Holds up letter in pink envelope*] Ahem! Phipps, when did this letter arrive?

PHIPPS. It was brought by hand just after your lordship went to the Club.

LORD GOR. That will do. [*Exit Phipps.*] Lady Chiltern's handwriting on Lady Chiltern's pink notepaper. That is rather curious. I thought Robert was to write. Wonder what Lady Chiltern has got so say to me? [*Sits at bureau and opens letter, and reads it.*] "I want you. I trust you. I am coming to you. Gertrude." [*Puts down the letter with a puzzled look. Then takes it up, and reads it again slowly.*] "I want you. I trust you. I am coming to you." So she has found out everything! Poor woman! Poor woman! [*Pulls out watch and looks at it.*] But what an hour to call! Ten o'clock! I shall have to give up going to the Berkshires'. However, it is always nice to be expected, and not to arrive. I am not expected at the Bachelors', so I shall certainly go there. Well, I will make her stand by her husband. That is the only thing for her to do. That is the only thing for any women to do. It is the growth of the moral sense in women that makes marriage such a hopeless, one-sided institution. Ten o'clock. She should be here soon. I must tell Phipps I am not in to anyone else. [*Goes towards bell.*]

[*Enter Phipps.*]

PHIPPS. Lord Caversham.

LORD GOR. Oh, why will parents always appear at the wrong time? Some extraordinary mistake in nature, I suppose. [*Enter Lord Caversham.*] Delighted to see you, my dear father. [*Goes to meet him.*]

LORD CAV. Take my cloak off.

LORD GOR. Is it worth while, father?

LORD CAV. Of course it is worth while, sir. Which is the most comfortable chair?

Lord Gor. This one, father. It is the chair I use myself, when I have visitors.

Lord Cav. Thank ye. No draught I hope, in this room?

Lord Gor. No, father.

Lord Cav. [*Sitting down.*] Glad to hear it. Can't stand draughts. No draughts at home.

Lord Gor. Good many breezes, father.

Lord Cav. Eh? Eh? Don't understand what you mean. Want to have a serious conversation with you, sir.

Lord Gor. My dear father! At this hour?

Lord Cav. Well, sir, it is only ten o'clock. What is your objection to the hour? I think the hour is an admirable hour!

Lord Gor. Well, the fact is, father, this is not my day for talking seriously. I am very sorry, but it is not my day.

Lord Cav. What do you mean, sir?

Lord Gor. During the season, father, I only talk seriously on the first Tuesday in every month, from four to seven.

Lord Cav. Well, make it Tuesday, sir, make it Tuesday.

Lord Gor. But it is after seven, father, and my doctor says I must not have any serious conversation after seven. It makes me talk in my sleep.

Lord Cav. Talk in your sleep, sir? What does that matter? You are not married.

Lord Gor. No, father, I am not married.

Lord Cav. Hum! That is what I have come to talk to you about, sir. You have got to get married, and at once. Why, when I was your age, sir, I had been an inconsolable widower for three months, and was already paying my addresses to your admirable mother. Damme, sir, it is your duty to get married You can't be always living for pleasure. Every man of position is married nowadays. Bachelors are not fashionable any more. They are a damaged lot. Too much is known about them. You must get a wife, sir. Look where your friend Robert Chiltern has got to by probity, hard work, and a sensible marriage with a good woman. Why don't you imitate him, sir? Why don't you take him for your model?

Lord Gor. I think I shall, father.

Lord Cav. I wish you would, sir. Then I should be happy. At present I make your mother's life miserable on your account. You are heartless, sir, quite heartless.

Lord Gor. I hope not, father.

Lord Cav. And it is high time for you to get married. You are thirty-four years of age, sir.

Lord Gor. Yes, father, but I only admit to thirty-two—thirty-one and a half when I have a really good buttonhole. This buttonhole is not . . . trivial enough.

Lord Cav. I tell you you are thirty-four, sir. And there is a draught in your room, besides, which makes your conduct worse. Why did you tell me there was no draught, sir? I feel a draught, sir, I feel it distinctly.

Lord Gor. So do I, father. It is a dreadful draught. I will come and see you to-morrow, father. We can talk over anything you like. Let me help you on with your cloak, father.

Lord Cav. No, sir; I have called this evening for a definite purpose, and I am going to see it through at all cost to my health or yours. Put down my cloak, sir.

Lord Gor. Certainly, father. But let us go into another room. [*Rings bell.*] There is a dreadful draught here. [*Enter Phipps.*] Phipps, is there a good fire in the smoking-room?

Phipps. Yes, my lord.

Lord Gor. Come in there, father. Your sneezes are quite heart-rending.

Lord Cav. Well, sir, I suppose I have a right to sneeze when I choose?

Lord Gor. [*Apologetically.*] Quite so, father. I was merely expressing sympathy.

Lord Cav. Oh, damn sympathy. There is a great deal too much of that sort of thing going on nowadays.

Lord Gor. I quite agree with you, father. If there was less sympathy in the world there would be less trouble in the world.

Lord Cav. [*Going towards the smoking-room.*] That is a paradox, sir. I hate paradoxes.

Lord Gor. So do I, father. Everybody one meets is a paradox nowadays. It is a great bore. It makes society so obvious.

Lord Cav. [*Turning round and looking at his son beneath his bushy eyebrows.*] Do you always really understand what you say, sir?

Lord Gor. [*After some hesitation.*] Yes, father, if I listen attentively.

Lord Cav. [*Indignantly.*] If you listen attentively! . . . Conceited young puppy!

[*Goes off grumbling into the smoking-room. Phipps enters.*]

Lord Gor. Phipps, there is a lady coming to see me this evening on particular business. Show her into the drawing-room when she arrives. You understand?

Phipps. Yes, my lord.

Lord Gor. It is a matter of the gravest importance, Phipps.

Phipps. I understand, my lord.

Lord Gor. No one else is to be admitted, under any circumstances.

Phipps. I understand, my lord. [*Bell rings.*]

Lord Gor. Ah, that is probably the lady. I shall see her myself.

[*Just as he is going towards the door Lord Caversham enters from the smoking-room.*]

Lord Cav. Well, sir? am I to wait attendance on you?

Lord Gor. [*Considerably perplexed.*] In a moment, father. Do excuse me. [*Lord Caversham goes back.*] Well, remember my instructions, Phipps–into that room.

Phipps. Yes, my lord.

[*Lord Goring goes into the smoking-room. Harold, the footman, shows Mrs. Cheveley in. Lamia-like, she is in green and silver. She has a cloak of black satin, lined with dead rose-leaf silk.*]

Harold. What name, madam?

MRS. CHEV. [*To Phipps, who advances towards her.*] Is Lord Goring not here? I was told he was at home.

PHIPPS. His lordship is engaged at present with Lord Caversham, madam.

[*Turns a cold, glassy eye on Harold, who at once retires.*]

MRS. CHEV. [*To herself.*] How very filial!

PHIPPS. His lordship told me to ask you, madam, to be kind enough to wait in the drawing-room for him. His lordship will come to you there.

MRS. CHEV. [*With a look of surprise.*] Lord Goring expects me?

PHIPPS. Yes, madam.

MRS. CHEV. Are you quite sure?

PHIPPS. His lordship told me that if a lady called I was to ask her to wait in the drawing-room. [*Goes to the door of the drawing-room and opens it.*] His lordship's directions on the subject were very precise.

MRS. CHEV. [*To herself.*] How thoughtful of him! To expect the unexpected shows a thoroughly modern intellect.[*Goes towards the drawing-room and looks in.*] Ugh! How dreary a bachelor's drawing-room always looks. I shall have to alter all this. [*Phipps brings the lamp from the writing-table.*] No, I don't care for that lamp. It is far too glaring. Light some candles.

PHIPPS. [*Replaces lamp.*] Certainly, madam.

MRS. CHEV. I hope the candles have very becoming shades.

PHIPPS. We have had no complaints about them, madam, as yet.

[*Passes into the drawing-room and begins to light the candles.*]

MRS. CHEV. [*To herself.*] I wonder what woman he is waiting for to-night. It will be delightful to catch him. Men always look so silly when they are caught. And they are always being caught. [*Looks about room and approaches the writing-table.*] What a very interesting room! What a very interesting picture! Wonder what his correspondence is like. [*Takes up letters.*] Oh, what a very uninteresting correspondence! Bills and cards, debts and dowagers! Who on earth writes to him on pink paper! How silly to write on pink paper! It looks like the beginning of a middle-class romance. Romance should never begin with sentiment. It should begin with science and end with a settlement. [*Puts letter down, then takes it up again.*] I know that handwriting. That is Gertrude Chiltern's. I remember it perfectly. The ten commandments in every stroke of the pen, and the moral law all over the page. Wonder what Gertrude is writing to him about? Something horrid about me, I suppose. How I detest that woman! [*Reads it.*] "I trust you. I want you. I am coming to you. Gertrude." "I trust you. I want you. I am coming to you."

[*A look of triumph comes over her face. She is just about to steal the letter, when Phipps comes in.*]

PHIPPS. The candles in the drawing-room are lit, madam, as you directed.

MRS. CHEV. Thank you. [*Rises hastily, and slips the letter under a large silver-cased blotting-book that is lying on the table.*]

PHIPPS. I trust the shades will be to your liking, madam. They are the most becoming we have. They are the same as his lordship uses himself when he is dressing for dinner.

MRS. CHEV. [*With a smile.*] Then I am sure they will be perfectly right.

PHIPPS. [*Gravely.*] Thank you, madam.

[*Mrs. Cheveley goes into the drawing-room. Phipps closes the door and retires. The door is then slowly opened, and Mrs. Cheveley comes out and creeps stealthily towards the writing-table. Suddenly voices are heard from the smoking-room. Mrs. Cheveley grows pale and stops. The voices grow louder, and she goes back into the drawing-room, biting her lip.*]

[*Enter Lord Goring and Lord Caversham.*]

LORD GOR. [*Expostulating.*] My dear father, if I am to get married, surely you will allow me to choose the time, place and person? Particularly the person.

LORD CAV. [*Testily.*] That is a matter for me, sir. You would probably make a very poor choice. It is I who should be consulted, not you. There is property at stake. It is not a matter for affection. Affection comes later on in married life.

LORD GOR. Yes. In married life affection comes when people thoroughly dislike each other, father, doesn't it? [*Puts on Lord Caversham's cloak for him.*]

LORD CAV. Certainly, sir. I mean certainly not, sir. You are talking very foolishly to-night. What I say is that marriage is a matter for common sense.

LORD GOR. But women who have common sense are so curiously plain, father, aren't they? Of course I only speak from heresay.

LORD CAV. No woman, plain or pretty, has any common sense at all, sir. Common sense is the privilege of our own sex.

LORD GOR. Quite so. And we men are so self-sacrificing that we never use it, do we, father?

LORD CAV. I use it, sir. I use nothing else.

LORD GOR. So my mother tells me.

LORD CAV. It is the secret of your mother's happiness. You are very heartless, sir, very heartless.

LORD GOR. I hope not, father.

[*Goes out for a moment. Then returns, looking rather put out, with Sir Robert Chiltern.*]

SIR ROBERT. My dear Arthur, what a piece of good luck meeting you on the doorstep! Your servant had just told me you were not at home. How extraordinary!

LORD GOR. The fact is, I am horribly busy to-night, Robert, and I gave orders I was not at home to anyone. Even my father had a comparatively cold reception. He complained of a draught the whole time.

SIR ROBERT. Ah! you must be at home to me, Arthur. You are my best friend. Perhaps by to-morrow you will be my only friend. My wife has discovered everything.

LORD GOR. Ah! I guessed as much!

SIR ROBERT. [*Looking at him.*] Really! How?

LORD GOR. [*After some hesitation.*] Oh, merely by something in the expression of your face as you came in. Who told her?

SIR ROBERT. Mrs. Cheveley herself. And the woman I love knows that I began my career with an act of low dishonesty, that I built up my life upon sands of shame—that I sold, like a common huckster, the secret that had been intrusted to me as a man of honour. I thank heaven poor Lord Radley died without knowing that I betrayed him. I would to God I had died before I had been so horribly tempted, or had fallen so low. [*Burying his face in his hands.*]

LORD GOR. [*After a pause.*] You have heard nothing from Vienna yet, in answer to your wire?

SIR ROBERT. [*Looking up.*] Yes; I got a telegram from the first secretary at eight o'clock to-night.

LORD GOR. Well?

SIR ROBERT. Nothing is absolutely known against her. On the contrary, she occupies a rather high position in society. It is a sort of open secret that Baron Arnheim left her the greater portion of his immense fortune. Beyond that I can learn nothing.

LORD GOR. She doesn't turn out to be a spy, then?

SIR ROBERT. Oh! spies are of no use nowadays. Their profession is over. The newspapers do their work instead.

LORD GOR. And thunderingly well they do it.

SIR ROBERT. Arthur, I am parched with thirst. May I ring for something? Some hock and seltzer?

LORD GOR. Certainly. Let me. [*Rings the bell.*]

SIR ROBERT. Thanks! I don't know what to do, Arthur, I don't know what to do, and you are my only friend. But what a friend you are—the one friend I can trust. I can trust you absolutely, can't I?

[*Enter Phipps.*]

LORD GOR. My dear Robert, of course. Oh! [*To Phipps.*] Bring some hock and seltzer.

PHIPPS. Yes, my lord.

LORD GOR. And Phipps!

PHIPPS. Yes, my lord.

LORD GOR. Will you excuse me for a moment, Robert? I want to give some directions to my servant.

SIR ROBERT. Certainly.

LORD GOR. When that lady calls, tell her that I am not expected home this evening. Tell her that I have been suddenly called out of town. You understand?

PHIPPS. The lady is in that room, my lord. You told me to show her into that room, my lord.

LORD GOR. You did perfectly right.[*Exit Phipps.*] What a mess I am in. No; I think I shall get through it. I'll give her a lecture through the door. Awkward thing to manage, though.

SIR ROBERT. Arthur, tell me what I should do. My life seems to have crumbled about me. I am a ship without a rudder in a night without a star.

LORD GOR. Robert, you love your wife, don't you?

SIR ROBERT. I love her more than anything in the world. I used to think ambition the great thing. It is not. Love is the great thing in the world. There is nothing but love, and I love her. But I am defamed in her eyes. I am ignoble in her eyes. There is a wide gulf between us now. She has found me out, Arthur, she has found me out.

Lord Gor. Has she never in her life done some folly—some indiscretion—that she should not forgive your sin?

Sir Robert. My wife! Never! She does not know what weakness or temptation is. I am of clay like other men. She stands apart as good women do—pitiless in her perfection—cold and stern and without mercy. But I love her, Arthur. We are childless, and I have no one else to love, no one else to love me. Perhaps if God had sent us children she might have been kinder to me. But God has given us a lonely house. And she has cut my heart in two. Don't let us talk of it. I was brutal to her this evening. But I suppose when sinners talk to saints they are brutal always. I said to her things that were hideously true, on my side, from my standpoint, from the standpoint of men. But don't let us talk of that.

Lord Gor. Your wife will forgive you. Perhaps at this moment she is forgiving you. She loves you, Robert. Why should she not forgive?

Sir Robert. God grant it! God grant it! [*Buries his face in his hands.*] But there is something more I have to tell you, Arthur.

[*Enter Phipps with drinks.*]

Phipps. [*Hands hock and seltzer to Sir Robert Chiltern.*] Hock and seltzer, sir.

Sir Robert. Thank you.

Lord Gor. Is your carriage here, Robert?

Sir Robert. No; I walked from the club.

Lord Gor. Sir Robert will take my cab, Phipps.

Phipps. Yes, my lord.

Lord Gor. Robert, you don't mind my sending you away?

Sir Robert. Arthur, you must let me stay for five minutes. I have made up my mind what I am going to do to-night in the House. The debate on the Argentine Canal is to begin at eleven. [*A chair falls in the drawing-room.*] What is that?

Lord Gor. Nothing.

Sir Robert. I heard a chair fall in the next room. Some one has been listening.

Lord Gor. No, no; there is no one there.

Sir Robert. There is some one. There are lights in the room, and the door is ajar. Some one has been listening to every secret of my life. Arthur, what does this mean?

Lord Gor. Robert, you are excited, unnerved. I tell you there is no one in that room. Sit down, Robert.

Sir Robert. Do you give me your word that there is no one there?

Lord Gor. Yes.

Sir Robert. Your word of honour? [*Sits down.*]

Lord Gor. Yes.

Sir Robert. [*Rises.*] Arthur, let me see for myself.

Lord Gor. No, no.

Sir Robert. If there is no one there why should I not look in that room? Arthur, you must let me go into that room and satisfy myself. Let me know that no eavesdropper has heard my life's secret. Arthur, you don't realize what I am going through.

Lord Gor. Robert, this must stop. I have told you that there is no one in that room—that is enough.

Sir Robert. [*Rushes to the door of the room.*] It is not enough. I insist on going into this room. You have told me there is no one there, so what reason can you have for refusing me?

Lord Gor. For God's sake, don't! There is some one there. Some one whom you must not see.

Sir Robert. Ah, I thought so!

Lord Gor. I forbid you to enter that room.

Sir Robert. Stand back. My life is at stake. And I don't care who is there. I I will know who it is to whom I have told my secret and my shame. [*Enters room.*]

Lord Gor. Great Heavens! his own wife!

[*Sir Robert Chiltern comes back, with a look of scorn and anger on his face.*]

Sir Robert. What explanation have you to give me for the presence of that woman here?

Lord Gor. Robert, I swear to you on my honour that that lady is stainless and guiltless of all offence towards you.

Sir Robert. She is a vile, an infamous thing!

Lord Gor. Don't say that, Robert! It was for your sake she came here. It was to try and save you she came here. She loves you and no one else.

Sir Robert. You are mad. What have I to do with her intrigues with you? Let her remain your mistress! You are well suited to each other. She, corrupt and shameful—you, false as a friend, treacherous as an enemy even——

Lord Gor. It is not true, Robert. Before heaven, it is not true. In her presence and in yours I will explain all.

Sir Robert. Let me pass, sir. You have lied enough upon your word of honour.

[*Sir Robert Chiltern goes out. Lord Goring rushes to the door of the drawing-room, when Mrs. Cheveley comes out, looking radiant and much amused.*]

Mrs. Chev. [*With a mock curtsey.*] Good evening, Lord Goring!

Lord Gor. Mrs. Cheveley! Great Heavens! May I ask what you were doing in my drawing-room?

Mrs. Chev. Merely listening. I have a perfect passion for listening through keyholes. One always hears such wonderful things through them.

Lord Gor. Doesn't that sound rather like tempting Providence?

Mrs. Chev. Oh, surely Providence can resist temptation by this time. [*Makes a sign to him to take her cloak off, which he does.*]

Lord Gor. I am glad you have called. I am going to give you some good advice.

Mrs. Chev. Oh! pray don't. One should never give a woman anything that she can't wear in the evening.

Lord Gor. I see you are quite as wilful as you used to be.

Mrs. Chev. Far more! I have greatly improved. I have had more experience.

Lord Gor. Too much experience is a dangerous thing. Pray have a cigarette. Half the pretty women in London smoke cigarettes. Personally I prefer the other half.

Mrs. Chev. Thanks. I never smoke. My dressmaker wouldn't like it, and a woman's first duty in life is to her dressmaker, isn't it? What the second duty is, no one has as yet discovered.

Lord Gor. You have come here to sell me Robert Chiltern's letter, haven't you?

Mrs. Chev. To offer it to you on conditions. How did you guess that?

Lord Gor. Because you haven't mentioned the subject. Have you got it with you?

Mrs. Chev. [*Sitting down.*] Oh, no! A well-made dress has no pockets.

Lord Gor. What is your price for it?

Mrs. Chev. How absurdly English you are! The English think that a cheque-book can solve every problem in life. Why, my dear Arthur, I have very much more money than you have, and quite as much as Robert Chiltern has got hold of. Money is not what I want.

Lord Gor. What do you want then, Mrs. Cheveley?

Mrs. Chev. Why don't you call me Laura?

Lord Gor. I don't like the name.

Mrs. Chev. You used to adore it.

Lord Gor. Yes: that's why. [*Mrs. Cheveley motions to him to sit down beside her. He smiles, and does so.*]

Mrs. Chev. Arthur, you loved me once.

Lord Gor. Yes.

Mrs. Chev. And you asked me to be your wife.

Lord Gor. That was the natural result of my loving you.

Mrs. Chev. And you threw me over because you saw, or said you saw, poor old Lord Mortlake trying to have a violent flirtation with me in the conservatory at Tenby.

Lord Gor. I am under the impression that my lawyer settled that matter with you on certain terms . . . dictated by yourself.

Mrs. Chev. At that time I was poor; you were rich.

Lord Gor. Quite so. That is why you pretended to love me.

Mrs. Chev. [*Shrugging her shoulders.*] Poor old Lord Mortlake, who had only two topics of conversation, his gout and his wife! I never could quite make out which of the two he was talking about. He used the most horrible language about them both. Well, you were silly, Arthur. Why, Lord Mortlake was never anything more to me than an amusement. One of those utterly tedious amusements one only finds at an English country house on an English country Sunday. I don't think anyone at all morally responsible for what he or she does at an English country house.

LORD GOR. Yes. I know lots of people think that.

MRS. CHEV. I loved you, Arthur.

LORD GOR. My dear Mrs. Cheveley, you have always been far too clever to know anything about love.

MRS. CHEV. I did love you. And you loved me. You know you loved me, and love is a very wonderful thing. I suppose that when a man has once loved a woman, he will do anything for her, except continue to love her? [*Puts her hand on his.*]

LORD GOR. [*Taking hand away quietly.*] Yes; except that.

MRS. CHEV. [*After a pause.*] I am tired of living abroad. I want to come back to London. I want to have a charming house here. I want to have a salon. If one could only teach the English how to talk, and the Irish how to listen, society here would be quite civilized. Besides, I have arrived at the romantic stage. When I saw you last night at the Chilterns', I knew you were the only person I had ever cared for, if I ever have cared for anybody, Arthur. And so, on the morning of the day you marry me, I will give you Robert Chiltern's letter. That is my offer. I will give it to you now, if you promise to marry me.

LORD GOR. Now?

MRS. CHEV. [*Smiling.*] To-morrow.

LORD GOR. Are you really serious?

MRS. CHEV. Yes, quite serious.

LORD GOR. I should make you a very bad husband.

MRS. CHEV. I don't mind bad husbands. I have had two. They amused me immensely.

LORD GOR. You mean that you amused yourself immensely, don't you?

MRS. CHEV. What do you know about my married life?

LORD GOR. Nothing: but I can read it like a book.

MRS. CHEV. What book?

LORD GOR. [*Rising.*] The Book of Numbers.

MRS. CHEV. Do you think it quite charming of you to be so rude to a woman in your own house?

LORD GOR. In the case of very fascinating women, sex is a challenge, not a defense.

MRS. CHEV. I suppose that is meant for a compliment. My dear Arthur, women are never disarmed by compliments. Men always are. That is the difference between the two sexes.

LORD GOR. Women are never disarmed by anything, as far as I know them.

MRS. CHEV. [*After a pause.*] Then you are going to allow your greatest friend, Robert Chiltern, to be ruined, rather than marry some one who really has considerable attractions left. I thought you would have risen to some great height of self-sacrifice, Arthur, I think you should. And the rest of your life you could spend in contemplating your own perfections.

LORD GOR. Oh! I do that as it is. And self-sacrifice is a thing that should be put down by law. It is so demoralizing to the people for whom one sacrifices oneself. They always go to the bad.

MRS. CHEV. As if anything could demoralize Robert Chiltern! You seem to forget that I know his real character.

LORD GOR. What you know about him is not his real character. It was an act of folly done in his youth, dishonourable, I admit, shameful, I admit, unworthy of him, I admit, and therefore . . . not his true character.

MRS. CHEV. How you men stand up for each other!

LORD GOR. How you women war against each other!

MRS. CHEV. [*Bitterly.*] I only war against one woman, against Gertrude Chiltern. I hate her. I hate her now more than ever.

LORD GOR. Because you have brought a real tragedy into her life, I suppose.

MRS. CHEV. [*With a sneer.*] Oh, there is only one real tragedy in a woman's life. The fact that her past is always her lover, and her future invariably her husband.

LORD GOR. Lady Chiltern knows nothing of the kind of life to which you are alluding.

MRS. CHEV. A woman whose size in gloves is seven and three-quarters never knows much about anything. You know Gertrude has always worn seven and three-quarters? That is one of the reasons why there was never any moral sympathy between us . . . Well, Arthur, I suppose this romantic interview may be regarded as at an end. You admit it was romantic, don't you? For the privilege of being your wife I was ready to surrender a great prize, the climax of my diplomatic career. You declined. Very well. If Sir Robert doesn't uphold my Argentine scheme, I expose him. *Voilà tout.*

LORD GOR. You mustn't do that. It would be vile, horrible, infamous.

MRS. CHEV. [*Shrugging her shoulders.*] Oh! don't use big words. They mean so little. It is a commercial transaction. That is all. There is no good mixing up sentimentality in it. I offered to sell Robert Chiltern a certain thing. If he won't pay me my price, he will have to pay the world a greater price. There is no more to be said. I must go. Good-bye. Won't you shake hands?

LORD GOR. With you? No. Your transaction with Robert Chiltern may pass as a loathsome commercial transaction of a loathsome commercial age; but you seem to have forgotten that you who came here to-night to talk of love, you whose lips desecrated the word love, you to whom the thing is a book closely sealed, went this afternoon to the house of one of the most noble and gentle women in the world to degrade her husband in her eyes, to try and kill her love for him, to put poison in her heart, and bitterness in her life, to break her idol and, it may be, spoil her soul. That I cannot forgive you. That was horrible. For that there can be no forgiveness.

MRS. CHEV. Arthur, you are unjust to me. Believe me, you are quite unjust to me. I didn't go to taunt Gertrude at all. I had no idea of doing anything of the kind when I entered. I called with Lady Markby simply to ask whether an ornament, a jewel, that I lost somewhere last night, had been found at the Chilterns'. If you don't believe me, you can ask Lady Markby. She will tell you it is true. The scene that occurred happened after Lady Markby had left, and was really forced on me by Gertrude's rudeness and sneers. I called, oh!—a little out of malice if you like—but really to ask if a diamond brooch of mine had been found. That was the origin of the whole thing.

LORD GOR. A diamond snake-brooch with a ruby?

MRS. CHEV. Yes. How do you know?

LORD GOR. Because it is found. In point of fact, I found it myself, and stupidly forgot to tell the butler anything about it as I was leaving. [*Goes over to the writing-table and pulls out the drawers.*] It is in this drawer. No, that one. This is the brooch, isn't it? [*Holds up the brooch.*]

MRS. CHEV. Yes. I am so glad to get it back. It was . . . a present.

LORD GOR. Won't you wear it?

MRS. CHEV. Certainly, if you pin it in. [*Lord Goring suddenly clasps it on her arm.*] Why do you put it on as a bracelet? I never knew it could be worn as a bracelet.

LORD GOR. Really?

MRS. CHEV. [*Holding out her handsome arm.*] No; but it looks very well on me as a bracelet, doesn't it?

LORD GOR. Yes; much better than when I saw it last.

MRS. CHEV. When did you see it last?

LORD GOR. [*Calmly.*] Oh, ten years ago, on Lady Berkshire, from whom you stole it.

MRS. CHEV. [*Starting.*] What do you mean?

LORD GOR. I mean that you stole that ornament from my cousin, Mary Berkshire, to whom I gave it when she was married. Suspicion fell on a wretched servant, who was sent away in disgrace. I recognized it last night. I determined to say nothing about it till I had found the thief. I have found the thief now, and I have heard her own confession.

MRS. CHEV. [*Tossing her head.*] It is not true.

LORD GOR. You know it is true. Why, thief is written across your face at this moment.

MRS. CHEV. I will deny the whole affair from beginning to end. I will say that I have never seen this wretched thing, that it was never in my possession.

[*Mrs. Cheveley tries to get the bracelet off her arm, but fails. Lord Goring looks on amused. Her thin fingers tear at the jewel to no purpose. A curse breaks from her.*]

LORD GOR. The drawback of stealing a thing, Mrs. Cheveley, is that one never knows how wonderful the thing that one steals is. You can't get that bracelet off, unless you know where the spring is. And I see you don't know where the spring is. It is rather difficult to find.

MRS. CHEV. You brute! You coward! [*She tries again to unclasp the bracelet, but fails.*]

LORD GOR. Oh! don't use big words. They mean so little.

MRS. CHEV. [*Again tears at the bracelet in a paroxysm of rage, with inarticulate sounds. Then stops, and looks at Lord Goring.*] What are you going to do?

LORD GOR. I am going to ring for my servant. He is an admirable servant. Always comes in the moment one rings for him. When he comes I will tell him to fetch the police.

MRS. CHEV. [*Trembling.*] The police? What for?

LORD GOR. To-morrow the Berkshires will prosecute you. That is what the police are for.

MRS. CHEV. [*Is now in an agony of physical terror. . . . Her face is distorted. Her mouth awry. A mask has fallen from her. She is, for the moment, dreadful to look at.*] Don't do that. I will do anything you want. Anything in the world you want.

LORD GOR. Give me Robert Chiltern's letter.

MRS. CHEV. Stop! Stop! Let me have time to think.

LORD GOR. Give me Robert Chiltern's letter.

MRS. CHEV. I have not got it with me. I will give it to you to-morrow.

LORD GOR. You know you are lying. Give it to me at once. [*Mrs. Cheveley pulls the letter out, and hands it to him. She is horribly pale.*] This is it?

MRS. CHEV. [*In a hoarse voice.*] Yes.

LORD GOR. [*Takes the letter, examines it, sighs, and burns it over the lamp.*] For so well-dressed a woman, Mrs. Cheveley, you have moments of admirable common sense. I congratulate you.

MRS. CHEV. [*Catches sight of Lady Chiltern's letter, the cover of which is just showing from under the blotting-book.*] Please get me a glass of water.

LORD GOR. Certainly. [*Goes to the corner of the room and pours out a glass of water. While his back is turned Mrs. Cheveley steals Lady Chiltern's letter. When Lord Goring returns with the glass she refuses it with a gesture.*]

MRS. CHEV. Thank you. Will you help me on with my cloak?

LORD GOR. With pleasure. [*Puts her cloak on.*]

MRS. CHEV. Thanks. I am never going to try to harm Robert Chiltern again.

LORD GOR. Fortunately you have not the chance, Mrs. Cheveley.

MRS. CHEV. Well, if even I had the chance, I wouldn't. On the contrary, I am going to render him a great service.

LORD GOR. I am charmed to hear it. It is a reformation.

MRS. CHEV. Yes. I can't bear so upright a gentleman, so honourable an English gentleman, being so shamefully deceived, and so——

LORD GOR. Well?

MRS. CHEV. I find that somehow Gertrude Chiltern's dying speech and confession has strayed into my pocket.

LORD GOR. What do you mean?

MRS. CHEV. [*With a bitter note of triumph in her voice.*] I mean that I am going to send Robert Chiltern the love letter his wife wrote to you to-night.

LORD GOR. Love letter?

MRS. CHEV. [*Laughing.*] "I want you. I trust you. I am coming to you. Gertrude."

[*Lord Goring rushes to the bureau and takes the envelope, finds it empty, and turns round.*]

LORD GOR. You wretched woman, must you always be thieving? Give me back that letter. I'll take it from you by force. You shall not leave my room till I have got it.

[*He rushes towards her, but Mrs Cheveley at once puts her hand on the elec-*

tric bell that is on the table. The bell sounds with shrill reverberations, and Phipps enters.]

MRS. CHEV. [*After a pause.*] Lord Goring merely rang that you should show me out. Good-night, Lord Goring!

[*Goes out, followed by Phipps. Her face is illumined with evil triumph. There is joy in her eyes. Youth seems to have come back to her. Her last glance is like a swift arrow. Lord Goring bites his lip, and lights a cigarette.*]

ACT-DROP.

FOURTH ACT

SCENE—*Same as Act II.*

[*Lord Goring is standing by the fireplace with his hands in his pockets. He is looking rather bored.*]

LORD GOR. [*Pulls out his watch, inspects it, and rings the bell.*] It is a great nuisance. I can't find anyone in this house to talk to. And I am full of interesting information. I feel like the latest edition of something or other.

[*Enter servant.*]

JAMES. Sir Robert is still at the Foreign Office, my lord.

LORD GOR. Lady Chiltern not down yet?

JAMES. Her ladyship has not yet left her room. Miss Chiltern has just come in from riding.

LORD GOR. [*To himself.*] Ah! that is something.

JAMES. Lord Caversham has been waiting some time in the library for Sir Robert. I told him your lordship was here.

LORD GOR. Thank you. Would you kindly tell him I've gone?

JAMES. [*Bowing.*] I shall do so, my lord. [*Exit servant.*]

LORD GOR. Really, I don't want to meet my father three days running. It is a great deal too much excitement for any son. I hope to goodness he won't come up. Fathers should be neither seen nor heard. That is the only proper basis for family life. Mothers are different. Mothers are darlings. [*Throws himself down into a chair, picks up a paper and begins to read it.*]

[*Enter Lord Caversham.*]

LORD CAV. Well, sir, what are you doing here? Wasting your time as usual, I suppose?

LORD GOR. [*Throws down paper and rises.*] My dear father, when one pays a visit it is for the purpose of wasting other people's time, not one's own.

LORD CAV. Have you been thinking over what I spoke to you about last night?

LORD GOR. I have been thinking about nothing else.

LORD CAV. Engaged to be married yet?

LORD GOR. [*Genially.*] Not yet: but I hope to be before lunch-time.

LORD CAV. [*Caustically.*] You can have till dinner-time if it would be of any convenience to you.

LORD GOR. Thanks awfully, but I think I'd sooner be engaged before lunch.

LORD CAV. Humph! Never know when you are serious or not.

LORD GOR. Neither do I, father.

[*A pause.*]

LORD CAV. I suppose you have read "The Times" this morning?

LORD GOR. [*Airily.*] "The Times"? Certainly not. I only read "The Morning Post." All that one should know about modern life is where the Duchesses are; anything else is quite demoralizing.

LORD CAV. Do you mean to say you have not read "The Times" leading article on Robert Chiltern's career?

LORD GOR. Good Heavens! No. What does it say?

LORD CAV. What should it say, sir? Everything complimentary, of course. Chiltern's speech last night on this Argentine Canal Scheme was one of the finest pieces of oratory ever delivered in the House since Canning.

LORD GOR. Ah! Never heard of Canning. Never wanted to. And did . . . did Chiltern uphold the scheme?

LORD CAV. Uphold it, sir? How little you know him! Why he denounced it roundly, and the whole system of modern political finance. This speech is the turning-point in his career, as "The Times" points out. You should read this article, sir. [*Opens "The Times."*] "Sir Robert Chiltern . . . most rising of all our young statesmen . . . Brilliant orator . . . Unblemished career . . . Well-known integrity of character . . . Represents what is best in English public life . . . Noble contrast to the lax morality so common among foreign politicians." They will never say that of you, sir.

LORD GOR. I sincerely hope not, father. However, I am delighted at what you tell me about Robert, thoroughly delighted. It shows he has got pluck.

LORD CAV. He has got more than pluck, sir, he has got genius.

LORD GOR. Ah! I prefer pluck. It is not so common, nowadays, as genius is.

LORD CAV. I wish you would go into Parliament.

LORD GOR. My dear father, only people who look dull ever get into the House of Commons, and only people who are dull ever succeed there.

LORD CAV. Why don't you try to do something useful in life?

LORD GOR. I am far too young.

LORD CAV. [*Testily.*] I hate this affectation of youth, sir. It is a great deal too prevalent nowadays.

LORD GOR. Youth isn't an affectation. Youth is an art.

LORD CAV. Why don't you propose to that pretty Miss Chiltern?

LORD GOR. I am of a very nervous disposition, especially in the morning.

LORD CAV. I don't suppose there is the smallest chance of her accepting you.

LORD GOR. I don't know how the betting stands to-day.

LORD CAV. If she did accept you she would be the prettiest fool in England.

LORD GOR. That is just what I should like to marry. A thoroughly sensible wife would reduce me to a condition of absolute idiocy in less than six months.

LORD CAV. You don't deserve her, sir.

LORD GOR. My dear father, if we men married the women we deserved, we should have a very bad time of it.

[*Enter Mabel Chiltern.*]

MABEL. Oh! . . . How do you do, Lord Caversham? I hope Lady Caversham is quite well?

LORD CAV. Lady Caversham is as usual, as usual.

LORD GOR. Good morning, Miss Mabel!

MABEL. [*Taking no notice at all of Lord Goring, and addressing herself exclusively to Lord Caversham.*] And Lady Caversham's bonnets . . . are they at all better?

LORD CAV. They have had a serious relapse, I am sorry to say.

LORD GOR. Good morning, Miss Mabel!

MABEL. [*To Lord Caversham.*] I hope an operation will not be necessary.

LORD CAV. [*Smiling at her pertness.*] If it is we shall have to give Lady Caversham a narcotic. Otherwise she would never consent to have a feather touched.

LORD GOR. [*With increased emphasis.*] Good morning, Miss Mabel!

MABEL. [*Turning round with feigned surprise.*] Oh, are you here? Of course you understand that after breaking your appointment I am never going to speak to you again.

LORD GOR. Oh, please don't say such a thing. You are the one person in London I really like to have to listen to me.

MABEL. Lord Goring, I never believe a single word that either you or I say to each other.

LORD CAV. You are quite right, my dear, quite right . . . as far as he is concerned, I mean.

MABEL. Do you think you could possibly make your son behave a little better occasionally? Just as a change.

LORD CAV. I regret to say, Miss Chiltern, that I have no influence at all over my son. I wish I had. If I had, I know what I would make him do.

MABEL. I am afraid that he has one of those terribly weak natures that are not susceptible to influence.

LORD CAV. He is very heartless, very heartless.

LORD GOR. It seems to me that I am a little in the way here.

MABEL. It is very good for you to be in the way, and to know what people say of you behind your back.

LORD GOR. I don't at all like knowing what people say of me behind my back. It makes me far too conceited.

LORD CAV. After that, my dear, I really must bid you good morning.

MABEL. Oh! I hope you are not going to leave me all alone with Lord Goring? Especially at such an early hour in the day.

LORD CAV. I am afraid I can't take him with me to Downing Street. It is not the Prime Minister's day for seeing the unemployed.

[*Shakes hands with Mabel Chiltern, takes up his hat and stick, and goes out, with a parting glare of indignation at Lord Goring.*]

MABEL. [*Takes up roses and begins to arrange them in a bowl on the table.*] People who don't keep their appointments in the Park are horrid.

LORD GOR. Detestable.

MABEL. I am glad you admit it. But I wish you wouldn't look so pleased about it.

LORD GOR. I can't help it. I always look pleased when I am with you.

MABEL. [*Sadly.*] Then I suppose it is my duty to remain with you?

LORD GOR. Of course it is.

MABEL. Well, my duty is a thing I never do, on principle. It always depresses me. So I am afraid I must leave you.

LORD GOR. Please don't, Miss Mabel. I have something very particular to say to you.

MABEL. [*Rapturously.*] Oh! is it a proposal?

LORD GOR. [*Somewhat taken aback.*] Well, yes, it is–I am bound to say it is.

MABEL. [*With a sigh of pleasure.*] I am so glad. That makes the second to-day.

LORD GOR. [*Indignantly.*] The second to-day? What conceited ass has been impertinent enough to dare to propose to you before I had proposed to you?

MABEL. Tommy Trafford, of course. It is one of Tommy's days for proposing. He always proposes on Tuesdays and Thursdays, during the season.

LORD GOR. You didn't accept him, I hope?

MABEL. I make it a rule never to accept Tommy. That is why he goes on proposing. Of course, as you didn't turn up this morning, I very nearly said yes. It would have been an excellent lesson both for him and for you if I had. It would have taught you both better manners.

LORD GOR. Oh! bother Tommy Trafford. Tommy is a silly little ass. I love you.

MABEL. I know. And I think you might have mentioned it before. I am sure I have given you heaps of opportunities.

LORD GOR. Mabel, do be serious. Please be serious.

MABEL. Ah! that is the sort of thing a man always says to a girl before he has been married to her. He never says it afterwards.

LORD GOR. [*Taking hold of her hand.*] Mabel, I have told you that I love you. Can't you love me a little in return?

MABEL. You silly Arthur! If you knew anything about . . . anything, which you don't, you would know that I adore you. Everyone in London knows it except you. It is a public scandal the way I adore you. I have been going about for the last six months telling the whole of society that I adore you. I wonder you consent to have anything to say to me. I have no character left at all. At least, I feel so happy that I am quite sure I have no character left at all.

LORD GOR. [*Catches her in his arms and kisses her. Then there is a pause of bliss.*] Dear! Do you know I was awfully afraid of being refused!

MABEL. [*Looking up at him.*] But you never have been refused yet by anybody, have you, Arthur? I can't imagine anyone refusing you.

LORD GOR. [*After kissing her again.*] Of course I'm not nearly good enough for you, Mabel.

MABEL. [*Nestling close to him.*] I am so glad, darling. I was afraid you were.

LORD GOR. [*After some hesitation.*] And I'm . . . I'm a little over thirty.

MABEL. Dear, you look weeks younger than that.

LORD GOR. [*Enthusiastically.*] How sweet of you to say so! . . . And it is only fair to tell you frankly that I am fearfully extravagant.

MABEL. But so am I, Arthur. So we're sure to agree. And now I must go and see Gertrude.

LORD GOR. Must you really? [*Kisses her.*]

MABEL. Yes.

LORD GOR. Then do tell her I want to talk to her particularly. I have been waiting here all the morning to see either her or Robert.

MABEL. Do you mean to say you didn't come here expressly to propose to me?

LORD GOR. [*Triumphantly.*] No, that was a flash of genius.

MABEL. Your first.

LORD GOR. [*With determination.*] My last.

MABEL. I am delighted to hear it. Now don't stir. I'll be back in five minutes. And don't fall into any temptations while I am away.

LORD GOR. Dear Mabel, while you are away, there are none. It makes me horribly dependent on you.

[*Enter Lady Chiltern.*]

LADY CHI. Good morning, dear. How pretty you are looking!

MABEL. How pale you are looking, Gertrude! It is most becoming!

LADY CHI. Good morning, Lord Goring!

LORD GOR. [*Bowing.*] Good morning, Lady Chiltern!

MABEL. [*Aside to Lord Goring.*] I shall be in the conservatory, under the second palm tree on the left.

LORD GOR. Second on the left?

MABEL. [*With a look of mock surprise.*] Yes; the usual palm tree.

[*Blows a kiss to him, unobserved by Lady Chiltern, and goes out.*]

LORD GOR. Lady Chiltern, I have a certain amount of very good news to tell you. Mrs. Cheveley gave me up Robert's letter last night, and I burned it. Robert is safe.

LADY CHI. [*Sinking on the sofa.*] Safe! Oh! I am so glad of that. What a good friend you are to him—to us!

LORD GOR. There is only one person now that could be said to be in any danger.

LADY CHI. Who is that?

LORD GOR. [*Sitting down beside her.*] Yourself.

LADY CHI. I! In danger? What do you mean?

LORD GOR. Danger is too great a word. It is a word I should not have used. But I admit I have something to tell you that may distress you, that terribly distresses me. Yesterday evening you wrote me a very beautiful, womanly letter, asking me for my help. You wrote to me as one of your oldest friends, one of your husband's oldest friends. Mrs. Cheveley stole that letter from my rooms.

LADY CHI. Well, what use is it to her? Why should she not have it?

LORD GOR. [*Rising.*] Lady Chiltern, I will be quite frank with you. Mrs.

Cheveley puts a certain construction on that letter and proposes to send it to your husband.

LADY CHI. But what construction could she put on it? . . . Oh! not that! not that! If I in—in trouble, and wanting your help, trusting you, propose to come to you . . . that you may advise me . . . assist me . . . Oh! are there women so horrible as that . . . ? And she proposes to send it to my husband? Tell me what happened. Tell me all that happened.

LORD GOR. Mrs. Cheveley was concealed in a room adjoining my library, without my knowledge. I thought that the person who was waiting in that room to see me was yourself. Robert came in unexpectedly. A chair or something fell in the room. He forced his way in, and he discovered her. We had a terrible scene. I still thought it was you. He left me in anger. At the end of everything Mrs. Cheveley got possession of your letter—she stole it, when or how, I don't know.

LADY CHI. At what hour did this happen?

LORD GOR. At half-past ten. And now I propose that we tell Robert the whole thing at once.

LADY CHI. [*Looking at him with amazement that is almost terror.*] You want me to tell Robert that the woman you expected was not Mrs. Cheveley, but myself? That it was I whom you thought was concealed in a room in your house, at half-past ten o'clock at night? You want me to tell him that?

LORD GOR. I think it is better that he should know the exact truth.

LADY CHI. [*Rising.*] Oh, I couldn't, I couldn't!

LORD GOR. May I do it?

LADY CHI. No.

LORD GOR. [*Gravely.*] You are wrong, Lady Chiltern.

LADY CHI. No. The letter must be intercepted. That is all. But how can I do it? Letters arrive for him every moment of the day. His secretaries open them and hand them to him. I dare not ask the servants to bring me his letters. It would be impossible. Oh! why don't you tell me what to do?

LORD GOR. Pray be calm, Lady Chiltern, and answer the questions I am going to put to you. You said his secretaries open his letters.

LADY CHI. Yes.

LORD GOR. Who is with him to-day? Mr. Trafford, isn't it?

LADY CHI. No. Mr. Montfort, I think.

LORD GOR. You can trust him?

LADY CHI. [*With a gesture of despair.*] Oh! how do I know?

LORD GOR. He would do what you asked him, wouldn't he?

LADY CHI. I think so.

LORD GOR. Your letter was on pink paper. He could recognize it without reading it, couldn't he? By the colour?

LADY CHI. I suppose so.

LORD GOR. Is he in the house now?

LADY CHI. Yes.

LORD GOR. Then I will go and see him myself, and tell him that a certain letter, written on pink paper, is to be forwarded to Robert to-day, and that at all costs it must not reach him. [*Goes to the door, and opens it.*] *Oh!* Robert is coming upstairs with the letter in his hand. It has reached him already.

LADY CHI. [*With a cry of pain.*] Oh! you have saved his life; what have you done with mine!

[*Enter Sir Robert Chiltern. He has the letter in his hand, and is reading it. He comes towards his wife, not noticing Lord Goring's presence.*]

SIR ROBERT. "I want you. I trust you. I am coming to you. Gertrude." Oh, my love! Is this true? Do you indeed trust me, and want me? If so, it was for me to come to you, not for you to write of coming to me. This letter of yours, Gertrude, makes me feel that nothing that the world may do can hurt me now. You want me, Gertrude?

[*Lord Goring, unseen by Sir Robert Chiltern, makes an imploring sign to Lady Chiltern to accept the situation and Sir Robert's error.*]

LADY CHI. Yes.

SIR ROBERT. You trust me, Gertrude?

LADY CHI. Yes.

SIR ROBERT. Ah! why did you not add you loved me?

LADY CHI. [*Taking his hand.*] Because I loved you.

[*Lord Goring passes into the conservatory.*]

SIR ROBERT. [*Kisses her.*] Gertrude, you don't know what I feel. When Montfort passed me your letter across the table—he had opened it by mistake, I suppose, without looking at the handwriting on the envelope—and I read it—oh! I did not care what disgrace or punishment was in store for me, I only thought you loved me still.

LADY CHI. There is no disgrace in store for you, nor any public shame. Mrs. Cheveley has handed over to Lord Goring the document that was in her possession, and he has destroyed it.

SIR ROBERT. Are you sure of this, Gertrude?

LADY CHI. Yes; Lord Goring has just told me.

SIR ROBERT. Then I am safe! Oh! what a wonderful thing to be safe! For two days I have been in terror. I am safe now. How did Arthur destroy my letter? Tell me.

LADY CHI. He burned it.

SIR ROBERT. I wish I had seen that one sin of my youth burning to ashes. How many men there are in modern life who would like to see their past burning to white ashes before them! Is Arthur still here?

LADY CHI. Yes; he is in the conservatory.

SIR ROBERT. I am so glad now I made that speech last night in the House, so glad. I made it thinking that public disgrace might be the result. But it has not been so.

LADY CHI. Public honour has been the result.

SIR ROBERT. I think so. I fear so, almost. For although I am safe from detection, although every proof against me is destroyed, I suppose, Gertrude . . . I suppose I should retire from public life? [*He looks anxiously at his wife.*]

LADY CHI. [*Eagerly.*] Oh yes, Robert, you should do that. It is your duty to do that.

SIR ROBERT. It is much to surrender.

LADY CHI. No; it will be much to gain.

[*Sir Robert Chiltern walks up and down the room with a troubled expression. Then comes over to his wife, and puts his hand on her shoulder.*]

SIR ROBERT. And you would be happy living somewhere alone with me, abroad perhaps, or in the country away from London, away from public life? You would have no regrets?

LADY CHI. Oh! none, Robert.

SIR ROBERT. [*Sadly.*] And your ambition for me? You used to be ambitious for me.

LADY CHI. Oh! my ambition! I have none now, but that we two may love each other. It was your ambition that led you astray. Let us not talk about ambition.

[*Lord Goring returns from the conservatory, looking very pleased with himself, and with an entirely new buttonhole that some one has made for him.*]

SIR ROBERT. [*Going towards him.*] Arthur, I have to thank you for what you have done for me. I don't know how I can repay you. [*Shakes hands with him.*]

LORD GOR. My dear fellow,. I'll tell you at once. At the present moment, under the usual palm tree . . . I mean in the conservatory . . .

[*Enter Mason.*]

MASON. Lord Caversham.

LORD GOR. That admirable father of mine really makes a habit of turning up at the wrong moment. It is very heartless of him, very heartless indeed.

[*Enter Lord Caversham. Mason goes out.*]

LORD CAV. Good morning, Lady Chiltern! Warmest congratulations to you, Chiltern, on your brilliant speech last night. I have just left the Prime Minister, and you are to have the vacant seat in the Cabinet.

SIR ROBERT. [*With a look of joy and triumph.*] A seat in the Cabinet?

LORD CAV. Yes; here is the Prime Minister's letter. [*Hands letter.*]

SIR ROBERT. [*Takes letter and reads.*] A seat in the Cabinet!

LORD CAV. Certainly, and you well deserve it too. You have got what we want so much in political life nowadays–high character, high moral tone, high principles. [*To Lord Goring.*] Everything that you have not got, sir, and never will have.

LORD GOR. I don't like principles, father, I prefer prejudices.

[*Sir Robert Chiltern is on the brink of accepting the Prime Minister's offer, when he sees his wife looking at him with her clear, candid eyes. He then realizes that it is impossible.*]

SIR ROBERT. I cannot accept this offer, Lord Caversham. I have made up my mind to decline it.

LORD CAV. Decline it, sir!

SIR ROBERT. My intention is to retire at once from public life.

LORD CAV. [*Angrily.*] Decline a seat in the Cabinet, and retire from public life? Never heard such damned nonsense in the whole course of my existence. I beg your pardon, Lady Chiltern. Chiltern. Chiltern, I beg your pardon. [*To Lord Goring.*] Don't grin like that, sir.

LORD GOR. No, father.

LORD CAV. Lady Chiltern, you are a sensible woman, the most sensible woman in London, the most sensible woman I know. Will you kindly prevent your husband from making such a . . . from taking such . . . Will you kindly do that, Lady Chiltern?

LADY CHI. I think my husband is right in his determination, Lord Caversham. I approve of it.

LORD CAV. You approve of it? Good Heavens!

LADY CHI. [*Taking her husband's hand.*] I admire him for it. I admire him immensely for it. I have never admired him so much before. He is finer than even I thought him. [*To Sir Robert Chiltern.*] You will go and write your letter to the Prime Minister now, won't you? Don't hesitate about it, Robert.

SIR ROBERT. [*With a touch of bitterness.*] I suppose I had better write it at once. Such offers are not repeated. I will ask you to excuse me for a moment, Lord Caversham.

LADY CHI. I may come with you, Robert, may I not?

SIR ROBERT. Yes, Gertrude.

[*Lady Chiltern goes out with him.*]

LORD CAV. What is the matter with this family? Something wrong here, eh? [*Tapping his forehead.*] Idiocy? Hereditary, I suppose. Both of them, too. Wife as well as husband. Very sad. Very sad indeed! And they are not an old family. Can't understand it.

LORD GOR. It is not idiocy, father, I assure you.

LORD CAV. What is it then, sir?

LORD GOR. [*After some hesitation.*] Well, it is what is called nowadays a high moral tone, father. That is all.

LORD CAV. Hate these new-fangled names. Same thing as we used to call idiocy fifty years ago. Sha'n't stay in this house any longer.

LORD GOR. [*Taking his arm.*] Oh! just go in here for a moment, father. Third palm tree to the left, the usual palm tree.

LORD CAV. What, sir?

LORD GOR. I beg your pardon, father, I forgot. The conservatory, father, the conservatory—there is some one there I want you to talk to.

LORD CAV. What about, sir?

LORD GOR. About me, father.

LORD CAV. [*Grimly.*] Not a subject on which much eloquence is possible.

LORD GOR. No, father; but the lady is like me. She doesn't care much for eloquence in others. She thinks it a little loud.

[*Lord Caversham goes into the conservatory. Lady Chiltern enters.*]

LORD GOR. Lady Chiltern, why are you playing Mrs. Cheveley's cards?

LADY CHI. [*Startled.*] I don't understand you.

LORD GOR. Mrs. Cheveley made an attempt to ruin your husband. Either to drive him from public life, or to make him adopt a dishonourable position. From the latter tragedy you saved him. The former you are now thrusting on him. Why should you do him the wrong Mrs. Cheveley tried to do and failed?

LADY CHI. Lord Goring?

LORD GOR. [*Pulling himself together with a great effort, and showing the philosopher that underlies the dandy.*] Lady Chiltern, allow me. You wrote me a letter last night in which you said you trusted me and wanted my help. Now is the moment when you really want my help, now is the time when you have got to trust me, to trust in my counsel and judgment. You love Robert. Do you want to kill his love for you? What sort of existence will he have if you rob him of the fruits of his ambition, if you take from him the splendour of a great political career, if you close the doors of public life against him, if you condemn him to sterile failure, he who was made for triumph and success? Women are not meant to judge us, but to forgive us when we need forgiveness. Pardon, not punishment, is their mission. Why should you scourge him with rods for a sin done in his youth, before he knew you, before he knew himself? A man's life is of more value than a woman's. It has larger issues, wider scope, greater ambitions. A woman's life revolves in curves of emotions. It is upon lines of intellect that a man's life progresses. Don't make any terrible mistake, Lady Chiltern. A woman who can keep a man's love, and love him in return, has done all the world wants of women, or should want of them.

LADY CHI. [*Troubled and hesitating.*] But it is my husband himself who wishes to retire from public life. He feels it is his duty. It was he who first said so.

LORD GOR. Rather than lose your love, Robert would do anything, wreck his whole career, as he is on the brink of doing now. He is making for you a terrible sacrifice. Take my advice, Lady Chiltern, and do not accept a sacrifice so great. If you do, you will live to repent it bitterly. We men and women are not made to accept such sacrifices from each other. We are not worthy of them. Besides, Robert has been punished enough.

LADY CHI. We have both been punished. I set him up too high.

LORD GOR. [*With deep feeling in his voice.*] Do not for that reason set him down now too low. If he has fallen from his altar, do not thrust him into the mire. Failure to Robert would be the very mire of shame. Power is his passion. He would lose everything, even his power to feel love. Your husband's life is at this moment in your hands, your husband's love is in your hands. Don't mar both for him.

[*Enter Sir Robert Chiltern.*]

SIR ROBERT. Gertrude, here is the draft of my letter. Shall I read it to you?

LADY CHI. Let me see it.

[*Sir Robert hands her the letter. She reads it, and then, with a gesture of passion, tears it up.*]

SIR ROBERT. What are you doing?

LADY CHI. A man's life is of more value than a woman's. It has larger issues, wider scope, greater ambitions. Our lives revolve in curves of emotions. It is upon lines of intellect that a man's life progresses. I have just learnt this, and much else with it, from Lord Goring. And I will not spoil your life for you, nor see you spoil it as a sacrifice to me, a useless sacrifice!

SIR ROBERT. Gertrude! Gertrude!

Lady Chi. You can forget. Men easily forget. And I forgive. That is how women help the world. I see that now.

Sir Robert. [*Deeply overcome by emotion, embraces her.*] My wife! my wife! [*To Lord Goring.*] Arthur, it seems that I am always to be in your debt.

Lord Gor. Oh, dear no, Robert! Your debt is to Lady Chiltern, not to me!

Sir Robert. I owe you much. And now tell me what you were going to ask me just now as Lord Caversham came in.

Lord Gor. Robert, you are your sister's guardian, and I want your consent to my marriage with her. That is all.

Lady Chi. Oh, I am so glad! I am so glad! [*Shakes hands with Lord Goring.*]

Lord Gor. Thank you, Lady Chiltern.

Sir Robert. [*With a troubled look.*] My sister to be your wife?

Lord Gor. Yes.

Sir Robert. [*Speaking with great firmness.*] Arthur, I am very sorry, but the thing is quite out of the question. I have to think of Mabel's future happiness. And I don't think her happiness would be safe in your hands. And I cannot have her sacrificed!

Lord Gor. Sacrificed!

Sir Robert. Yes, utterly sacrificed. Loveless marriages are horrible. But there is one thing worse than an absolutely loveless marriage. A marriage in which there is love, but on one side only; faith, but on one side only; devotion, but on one side only, and in which of the two hearts one is sure to be broken.

Lord Gor. But I love Mabel. No other woman has any place in my life.

Lady Chi. Robert, if they love each other, why should they not be married?

Sir Robert. Arthur cannot bring Mabel the love that she deserves.

Lord Gor. What reason have you for saying that?

Sir Robert. [*After a pause.*] Do you really require me to tell you?

Lord Gor. Certainly I do.

Sir Robert. As you choose. When I called on you yesterday evening I found Mrs. Cheveley concealed in your rooms. It was between ten and eleven o'clock at night. I do not wish to say anything more. Your relations with Mrs. Cheveley have, as I said to you last night, nothing whatsoever to do with me. I know you were engaged to be married to her once. The fascination she exercised over you then seems to have returned. You spoke to me last night of her as of a woman pure and stainless, a woman whom you respected and honoured. That may be so. But I cannot give my sister's life into your hands. It would be wrong of me. It would be unjust, infamously unjust to her.

Lord Gor. I have nothing more to say.

Lady Chi. Robert, it was not Mrs. Cheveley whom Lord Goring expected last night.

Sir Robert. Not Mrs. Cheveley! Who was it then?

Lord Gor. Lady Chiltern.

Lady Chi. It was your own wife. Robert, yesterday afternoon Lord Goring told me that if ever I was in trouble I could come to him for help, as he was our oldest and best friend. Later on, after that terrible scene in this room, I wrote to him telling him that I trusted him, that I had need of him, that I was coming to him for help and advice. [*Sir Robert Chiltern takes the letter out of his pocket.*] Yes, that letter. I didn't go to Lord Goring's after all. I felt that it is from ourselves alone that help can come. Pride made me think that. Mrs. Cheveley went. She stole my letter and sent it anonymously to you this morning, that you should think . . . Oh! Robert, I cannot tell you what she wished you to think. . . .

SIR ROBERT. What! Had I fallen so low in your eyes that you thought that even for a moment I could have doubted your goodness? Gertrude, Gertrude, you are to me the white image of all good things, and sin can never touch you. Arthur, you can go to Mabel, and you have my best wishes! Oh! stop a moment. There is no name at the beginning of this letter. The brilliant Mrs. Cheveley does not seem to have noticed that. There should be a name.

LADY CHI. Let me write yours. It is you I trust and need. You and none else.

LORD GOR. Well, really, Lady Chiltern, I think I should have back my own letter.

LADY CHI. [*Smiling.*] No; you shall have Mabel. [*Takes the letter and writes her husband's name on it.*]

LORD GOR. Well, I hope she hasn't changed her mind. It's nearly twenty minutes since I saw her last.

[*Enter Mabel Chiltern and Lord Caversham.*]

MABEL. Lord Goring, I think your father's conversation much more improving than yours. I am only going to talk to Lord Caversham in the future, and always under the usual palm tree.

LORD GOR. Darling! [*Kisses her.*]

LORD CAV. [*Considerably taken aback.*] What does this mean, sir? You don't mean to say that this charming, clever young lady has been so foolish as to accept you?

LORD GOR. Certainly, father! And Chiltern's been wise enough to accept the seat in the Cabinet.

LORD CAV. I am very glad to hear that, Chiltern . . . I congratulate you, sir. If the country doesn't go to the dogs or the Radicals, we shall have you Prime Minister, some day.

[*Enter Mason.*]

MASON. Luncheon is on the table, my lady! [*Mason goes out.*]

LADY CHI. You'll stop to luncheon, Lord Caversham, won't you?

LORD CAV. With pleasure, and I'll drive you down to Downing Street afterwards, Chiltern. You have a great future before you, a great future. Wish I could say the same for you, sir. [*To Lord Goring.*] But your career will have to be entirely domestic.

LORD GOR. Yes, father, I prefer it domestic.

LORD CAV. And if you don't make this young lady an ideal husband, I'll cut you off with a shilling.

MABEL. An ideal husband! Oh, I don't think I should like that. It sounds like something in the next world.

LORD CAV. What do you want him to be then, dear?

MABEL. He can be what he chooses. All I want is to be . . . to be . . . oh! a real wife to him.

LORD CAV. Upon my word, there is a good deal of common sense in that, Lady Chiltern.

[*They all go out except Sir Robert Chiltern. He sinks into a chair, wrapt in thought. After a little time Lady Chiltern returns to look for him.*]

LADY CHI. [*Leaning over the back of the chair.*] Aren't you coming in, Robert?

SIR ROBERT. [*Taking her hand.*] Gertrude, is it love you feel for me, or is it pity merely?

LADY CHI. [*Kisses him.*] It is love, Robert. Love, and only love. For both of us a new life is beginning.

CURTAIN.

THE IMPORTANCE OF BEING EARNEST

THE PERSONS OF THE PLAY

JOHN WORTHING, J.P.
ALGERNON MONCRIEFF
REV. CANON CHASUBLE, D.D.
MERRIMAN, BUTLER
LANE, MANSERVANT
LADY BRACKNELL
HON. GWENDOLEN FAIRFAX
CECILY CARDEW
MISS PRISM, GOVERNESS

THE SCENES OF THE PLAY

ACT. I, *Algernon Moncrieff's Flat in Half-Moon Street, W.* ACT II, *The Garden at the Manor House, Woolton.* ACT III, *Morning-room at the Manor House, Woolton. Time, The Present.*

FIRST ACT

SCENE—*Morning-room in Algernon's flat in Half-Moon Street. The room is luxuriously and artistically furnished. The sound of a piano is heard in the adjoining room.*

[*Lane is arranging afternoon tea on the table, and after the music has ceased, Algernon enters.*]

ALG. Did you hear what I was playing, Lane?

LANE. I didn't think it polite to listen, sir.

ALG. I'm sorry for that, for your sake. I don't play accurately—anyone can play accurately—but I play with wonderful expression. As far as the piano is concerned, sentiment is my forte. I keep science for Life.

LANE. Yes, sir.

ALG. And, speaking of the science of Life, have you got the cucumber sandwiches cut for Lady Bracknell?

LANE. Yes, sir. [*Hands them on a salver.*]

ALG. [*Inspects them, takes two, and sits down on the sofa.*] Oh! . . . by the way, Lane, I see from your book that on Thursday night, when Lord Shoreman and Mr. Worthing were dining with me, eight bottles of champagne are entered as having been consumed.

LANE. Yes, sir; eight bottles and a pint.

ALG. Why is it that at a bachelor's establishment the servants invariably drink the champagne? I ask merely for information.

LANE. I attribute it to the superior quality of the wine, sir. I have often observed that in married households the champagne is rarely of a first-rate brand.

ALG. Good Heavens! Is marriage so demoralising as that?

LANE. I believe it *is* a very pleasant state, sir. I have had very little experience of it myself up to the present. I have only been married once. That was in consequence of a misunderstanding between myself and a young person.

ALG. [*Languidly.*] I don't know that I am much interested in your family life, Lane.

LANE. No, sir; it is not a very interesting subject. I never think of it myself.

ALG. Very natural, I am sure. That will do, Lane, thank you.

LANE. Thank you, sir. [*Lane goes out.*]

ALG. Lane's views on marriage seem somewhat lax. Really, if the lower orders don't set us a good example, what on earth is the use of them? They seem, as a class, to have absolutely no sense of moral responsibility.

[*Enter Lane.*]

LANE. Mr. Ernest Worthing.

[*Enter Jack.*] [*Lane goes out.*]

ALG. How are you, my dear Ernest? What brings you up to town?

JACK. Oh, pleasure, pleasure! What else should bring one anywhere? Eating as usual, I see, Algy!

ALG. [*Stiffly.*] I believe it is customary in good society to take some slight refreshment at five o'clock. Where have you been since last Thursday?

JACK. [*Sitting down on the sofa.*] In the country.

ALG. What on earth do you do there?

JACK. [*Pulling off his gloves.*] When one is in town one amuses oneself. When one is in the country one amuses other people. It is excessively boring.

ALG. And who are the people you amuse?

JACK. [*Airily.*] Oh, neighbours, neighbours.

ALG. Got nice neighbours in your part of Shropshire?

JACK. Perfectly horrid! Never speak to one of them.

ALG. How immensely you must amuse them! [*Goes over and takes sandwich.*] By the way, Shropshire is your county, is it not?

JACK. Eh? Shropshire? Yes, of course. Hallo! Why all these cups? Why cucumber sandwiches? Why such reckless extravagance in one so young? Who is coming to tea?

ALG. Oh! merely Aunt Augusta and Gwendolen.

JACK. How perfectly delightful!

ALG. Yes, that is all very well; but I am afraid Aunt Augusta won't quite approve of your being here.

JACK. May I ask why?

ALG. My dear fellow, the way you flirt with Gwendolen is perfectly disgraceful. It is almost as bad as the way Gwendolen flirts with you.

JACK. I am in love with Gwendolen. I have come up to town expressly to propose to her.

ALG. I thought you had come up for pleasure? . . . I call that business.

JACK. How utterly unromantic you are!

ALG. I really don't see anything romantic in proposing. It is very romantic to be in love. But there is nothing romantic about a definite proposal. Why, one may be accepted. One usually is, I believe. Then the excitement is all over. The very essence of romance is uncertainty. If ever I get married, I'll certainly try to forget the fact.

JACK. I have no doubt about that, dear Algy. The Divorce Court was specially invented for people whose memories are so curiously constituted.

ALG. Oh! there is no use speculating on that subject. Divorces are made in Heaven— [*Jack puts out his hand to take a sandwich. Algernon at once interferes.*] Please don't touch the cucumber sandwiches. They are ordered specially for Aunt Augusta. [*Takes one and eats it.*]

JACK. Well, you have been eating them all the time.

ALG. That is quite a different matter. She is my aunt. [*Takes plate from below.*] Have some bread and butter. The bread and butter is for Gwendolen. Gwendolen is devoted to bread and butter.

JACK. [*Advancing to table and helping himself.*] And very good bread and butter it is too.

ALG. Well, my dear fellow, you need not eat as if you were going to eat it all. You behave as if you were married to her already. You are not married to her already, and I don't think you ever will be.

JACK. Why on earth do you say that?

ALG. Well, in the first place girls never marry the men they flirt with. Girls don't think it right.

JACK. Oh, that is nonsense!

ALG. It isn't. It is a great truth. It accounts for the extraordinary number of bachelors that one sees all over the place. In the second place, I don't give my consent.

JACK. Your consent!

ALG. My dear fellow, Gwendolen is my first cousin. And before I allow you to marry her, you will have to clear up the whole question of Cecily. [*Rings bell.*]

JACK. Cecily! What on earth do you mean? What do you mean, Algy, by Cecily? I don't know anyone of the name of Cecily.

[*Enter Lane.*]

ALG. Bring me that cigarette case Mr. Worthing left in the smoking-room the last time he dined here.

LANE. Yes, sir. [*Lane goes out.*]

JACK. Do you mean to say you have had my cigarette case all this time? I wish to goodness you had let me know. I have been writing frantic letters to Scotland Yard about it. I was very nearly offering a large reward.

ALG. Well, I wish you would offer one. I happen to be more than usually hard up.

JACK. There is no good offering a large reward now that the thing is found.

[*Enter Lane with the cigarette case on a salver. Algernon takes it at once. Lane goes out.*]

ALG. I think that is rather mean of you, Ernest, I must say. [*Opens case and examines it.*] However, it makes no matter, for, now that I look at the inscription inside, I find that the thing isn't yours after all.

JACK. Of course it's mine. [*Moving to him.*] You have seen me with it a hundred times, and you have no right whatsoever to read what is written inside. It is a very ungentlemanly thing to read a private cigarette case.

ALG. Oh! it is absurd to have a hard-and-fast rule about what one should read and what one shouldn't. More than half of modern culture depends on what one shouldn't read.

JACK. I am quite aware of the fact, and I don't propose to discuss modern culture. It isn't the sort of thing one should talk of in private. I simply want my cigarette case back.

ALG. Yes; but this isn't your cigarette case. This cigarette case is a present from someone of the name of Cecily, and you said you didn't know anyone of that name.

JACK. Well, if you want to know, Cecily happens to be my aunt.

ALG. Your aunt!

JACK. Yes. Charming old lady she is, too. Lives at Tunbridge Wells. Just give it back to me, Algy.

ALG. [*Retreating to back of sofa.*] But why does she call herself Cecily if she is your aunt and lives at Tunbridge Wells? [*Reading.*] "From little Cecily with her fondest love."

JACK. [*Moving to sofa and kneeling upon it.*] My dear fellow, what on earth is there in that? Some aunts are tall, some aunts are not tall. That is a matter that surely an aunt may be allowed to decide for herself. You seem to think that every aunt should be exactly like your aunt! That is absurd! For Heaven's sake give me back my cigarette case. [*Follows Algy round the room.*]

ALG. Yes. But why does your aunt call you her uncle? "From little Cecily, with her fondest love to her dear Uncle Jack." There is no objection, I admit, to an aunt being a small aunt, but why an aunt, no matter what her size may be, should call her own nephew her uncle, I can't quite make out. Besides, your name isn't Jack at all; it is Ernest.

JACK. It isn't Ernest; it's Jack.

ALG. You have always told me it was Ernest. I have introduced you to everyone as Ernest. You answer to the name of Ernest. You look as if your name was Ernest. You are the most earnest looking person I ever saw in my life. It is perfectly absurd your saying that your name isn't Ernest. It's on your cards. Here is one of them. [*Taking it from case.*] "Mr. Ernest Worthing, B. 4, The Albany." I'll keep this as a proof that your name is Ernest if ever you attempt to deny it to me, or to Gwendolen, or to anyone else. [*Puts the card in his pocket.*]

JACK. Well, my name is Ernest in town and Jack in the country, and the cigarette case was given to me in the country.

ALG. Yes, but that does not account for the fact that your small Aunt Cecily, who lives at Tunbridge Wells, calls you her dear uncle. Come, old boy, you had much better have the thing out at once.

JACK. My dear Algy, you talk exactly as if you were a dentist. It is very vulgar to talk like a dentist when one isn't a dentist. It produces a false impression.

ALG. Well, that is exactly what dentists always do. Now, go on! Tell me the whole thing. I may mention that I have always suspected you of being a confirmed and secret Bunburyist; and I am quite sure of it now.

JACK. Bunburyist! What on earth do you mean by a Bunburyist?

ALG. I'll reveal to you the meaning of that incomparable expression as soon as you are kind enough to inform me why you are Ernest in town and Jack in the country.

JACK. Well, produce my cigarette case first.

ALG. Here it is. [*Hands cigarette case.*] Now produce your explanation, and pray make it improbable. [*Sits on sofa.*]

JACK. My dear fellow, there is nothing improbable about my explanation at all. In fact it's perfectly ordinary. Old Mr. Thomas Cardew, who adopted me when I was a little boy, made me in his will guardian to his granddaughter, Miss Cecily Cardew. Cecily, who addresses me as her uncle from motives of respect that you could not possibly appreciate, lives at my place in the country under the charge of her admirable governess, Miss Prism.

ALG. Where is that place in the country, by the way?

JACK. That is nothing to you, dear boy. You are not going to be invited. . . . I may tell you candidly that the place is not in Shropshire.

ALG. I suspected that, my dear fellow! I have Bunburyed all over Shropshire on two separate occasions. Now go on. Why are you Ernest in town and Jack in the country?

JACK. My dear Algy, I don't know whether you will be able to understand my real motives. You are hardly serious enough. When one is placed in the position of guardian, one has to adopt a very high moral tone on all subjects. It's one's duty to do so. And as a high moral tone can hardly be said to conduce very much to either one's health or one's happiness, in order to get up to town I have always pretended to have a younger brother of the name of Ernest, who lives in the Albany, and gets into the most dreadful scrapes. That, my dear Algy, is the whole truth pure and simple.

ALG. The truth is rarely pure and never simple. Modern life would be very tedious if it were either, and modern literature a complete impossibility!

JACK. That wouldn't be at all a bad thing.

ALG. Literary criticism is not your forte, my dear fellow. Don't try it. You should leave that to people who haven't been at a University. They do it so well in the daily papers. What you really are is a Bunburyist. I was quite right in saying you were a Bunburyist. You are one of the most advanced Bunburyists I know.

JACK. What on earth do you mean?

ALG. You have invented a very useful young brother called Ernest, in order that you may be able to come up to town as often as you like. I have invented an invaluable permanent invalid called Bunbury, in order that I may be able to go down into the country whenever I choose. Bunbury is perfectly invaluable. If it wasn't for Bunbury's extraordinary bad health, for instance, I wouldn't be able to dine with you at Willis's to-night, for I have been really engaged to Aunt Augusta for more than a week.

JACK. I haven't asked you to dine with me anywhere to-night.

ALG. I know. You are absurdly careless about sending out invitations. It is very foolish of you. Nothing annoys people so much as not receiving invitations.

JACK. You had much better dine with your Aunt Augusta.

ALG. I haven't the smallest intention of doing anything of the kind. To begin with, I dined there on Monday, and once a week is quite enough to dine with one's own relations. In the second place, whenever I do dine there I am always treated as a member of the family, and sent down with either no woman at all, or two. In the third place, I know perfectly well whom she will place me next to, to-night. She will place me next Mary Farquhar, who always flirts with her own husband across the dinner-table. That is not very pleasant. Indeed, it is not even decent . . . and that sort of thing is enormously on the increase. The amount of women in London who flirt with their own husbands is perfectly scandalous. It looks so bad. It is simply washing one's clean linen in public. Besides, now that I know you to be a confirmed Bunburyist, I naturally want to talk to you about Bunburying. I want to tell you the rules.

JACK. I'm not a Bunburyist at all. If Gwendolen accepts me, I am going to kill my brother, indeed I think I'll kill him in any case. Cecily is a little too much interested in him. It is rather a bore. So I am going to get rid of Ernest. And I strongly advise you to do the same with Mr. . . . with your invalid friend who has the absurd name.

ALG. Nothing will induce me to part with Bunbury, and if you ever get married, which seems to me extremely problematic, you will be very glad to know Bunbury. A man who marries without knowing Bunbury has a very tedious time of it.

JACK. That is nonsense. If I marry a charming girl like Gwendolen, and she is the only girl I ever saw in my life that I would marry, I certainly won't want to know Bunbury.

ALG. Then your wife will. You don't seem to realize, that in married life three is company and two is none.

JACK. [*Sententiously.*] That, my dear young friend, is the theory that the corrupt French Drama has been propounding for the last fifty years.

ALG. Yes; and that the happy English home has proved in half the time.

JACK. For Heaven's sake, don't try to be cynical. It's perfectly easy to be cynical.

ALG. My dear fellow, it isn't easy to be anything now-a-days. There's such a lot of beastly competition about. [*The sound of an electric bell is heard.*] Ah! that must be Aunt Augusta. Only relatives, or creditors, ever ring in that Wagnerian manner. Now, if I get her out of the way for ten minutes, so that you can have an opportunity for proposing to Gwendolen, may I dine with you to-night at Willis's?

JACK. I suppose so, if you want to.

ALG. Yes, but you must be serious about it. I hate people who are not serious about meals. It is so shallow of them.

[*Enter Lane.*]

LANE. Lady Bracknell and Miss Fairfax.

[*Algernon goes forward to meet them. Enter Lady Bracknell and Gwendolen.*]

LADY BRA. Good afternoon, dear Algernon. I hope you are behaving very well.

ALG. I'm feeling very well, Aunt Augusta.

LADY BRA. That's not quite the same thing. In fact the two things rarely go together. [*Sees Jack and bows to him with icy coldness.*]

ALG. [*To Gwendolen.*] Dear me, you are smart!

GWEN. I am always smart! Aren't I, Mr. Worthing?

JACK. You are quite perfect, Miss Fairfax.

GWEN. Oh! I hope I am not that. It would leave no room for developments, and I intend to develop in many directions. [*Gwendolen and Jack sit down together in the corner.*]

LADY BRA. I'm sorry if we are a little late, Algernon, but I was obliged to call on dear Lady Harbury. I hadn't been there since her poor husband's death. I never saw a woman so altered; she looks quite twenty years younger. And now I'll have a cup of tea, and one of those nice cucumber sandwiches you promised me.

ALG. Certainly, Aunt Augusta. [*Goes over to tea-table.*]

LADY BRA. Won't you come and sit here, Gwendolen?

GWEN. Thanks, mamma, I'm quite comfortable where I am.

ALG. [*Picking up empty plate in horror.*] Good Heavens! Lane! Why are there no cucumber sandwiches? I ordered them specially.

LANE. [*Gravely.*] There were no cucumbers in the market this morning, sir I went down twice.

ALG. No cucumbers!

LANE. No, sir. Not even for ready money.

ALG. That will do, Lane, thank you.

LANE. Thank you, sir.

ALG. I am greatly distressed, Aunt Augusta, about there being no cucumbers, not even for ready money.

LADY BRA. It really makes no matter, Algernon. I had some crumpets with Lady Harbury, who seems to me to be living entirely for pleasure now.

ALG. I hear her hair has turned quite gold from grief.

LADY BRA. It certainly has changed its color. From what cause I, of course, cannot say. [*Algernon crosses and hands tea.*] Thank you. I've quite a treat for you to-night, Algernon. I am going to send you down with Mary Farquhar. She is such a nice woman, and so attentive to her husband. It's delightful to watch them.

ALG. I am afraid, Aunt Augusta, I shall have to give up the pleasure of dining with you to-night after all.

LADY BRA. [*Frowning.*] I hope not, Algernon. It would put my table completely out. Your uncle would have to dine upstairs. Fortunately he is accustomed to that.

ALG. It's a great bore, and, I need hardly say, a terrible disappointment to me, but the fact is I have just had a telegram to say that my poor friend Bunbury is very ill again. [*Exchanges glances with Jack.*] They seem to think I should be with him.

LADY BRA. It is very strange. This Mr. Bunbury seems to suffer from curiously bad health.

ALG. Yes; poor Bunbury is a dreadful invalid.

LADY BRA. Well, I must say, Algernon, that I think it is high time that Mr. Bunbury made up his mind whether he was going to live or to die. This shilly-shallying with the question is absurd. Nor do I in any way approve of the modern sympathy with invalids. I consider it morbid. Illness of any kind is hardly a thing to be encouraged in others. Health is the primary duty of life. I am always telling that to your poor uncle, but he never seems to take much notice . . . as far as any improvement in his ailments goes. I should be obliged if you would ask Mr. Bunbury, from me, to be kind enough not to have a relapse on Saturday, for I rely on you to arrange my music for me. It is my last reception, and one wants something that will encourage conversation, particularly at the end of the season when everyone has practically said whatever they had to say, which, in most cases, was probably not much.

ALG. I'll speak to Bunbury, Aunt Augusta, if he is still conscious, and I think I can promise you he'll be all right by Saturday. Of course the music is a great difficulty. You see, if one plays good music, people don't listen, and if one plays bad music, people don't talk. But I'll run over the programme I've drawn out, if you will kindly come into the next room for a moment.

LADY BRA. Thank you, Algernon. It is very thoughtful of you. [*Rising, and following Algernon.*] I'm sure the programme will be delightful, after a few expurgations. French songs I cannot possibly allow. People always seem to think that they are improper, and either look shocked, which is vulgar, or laugh, which is worse. But German sounds a thoroughly respectable language, and indeed, I believe is so. Gwendolen, you will accompany me.

GWEN. Certainly, mamma.

[*Lady Bracknell and Algernon go into the music-room, Gwendolen remains behind.*]

JACK. Charming day it has been, Miss Fairfax.

GWEN. Pray don't talk to me about the weather, Mr. Worthing. Whenever people talk to me about the weather, I always feel quite certain that they mean something else. And that makes me so nervous.

JACK. I do mean something else.

GWEN. I thought so. In fact, I am never wrong.

JACK. And I would like to be allowed to take advantage of Lady Bracknell's temporary absence . . .

GWEN. I would certainly advise you to do so. Mamma has a way of coming back suddenly into a room that I have often had to speak to her about.

JACK. [*Nervously.*] Miss Fairfax, ever since I met you I have admired you more than any girl . . . I have ever met since . . . I met you.

GWEN. Yes, I am quite aware of the fact. And I often wish that in public, at any rate, you had been more demonstrative. For me you have always had an irresistible fascination. Even before I met you I was far from indifferent to you. [*Jack looks at her in amazement.*] We live, as I hope you know, Mr. Worthing, in an age of ideals. The fact is constantly mentioned in the more expensive monthly magazines, and has reached the provincial pulpits I am told: and my ideal has always been to love some one of the name of Ernest. There is something in that name that inspires absolute confidence. The moment Algernon first mentioned to me that he had a friend called Ernest, I knew I was destined to love you.

JACK. You really love me, Gwendolen?

GWEN. Passionately!

JACK. Darling! You don't know how happy you've made me.

GWEN. My own Ernest!

JACK. But you don't really mean to say that you couldn't love me if my name wasn't Ernest?

GWEN. But your name is Ernest.

JACK. Yes, I know it is. But supposing it was something else? Do you mean to say you couldn't love me then?

GWEN. [*Glibly.*] Ah! that is clearly a metaphysical speculation, and like most metaphysical speculations has very little reference at all to the actual facts of real life, as we know them.

JACK. Personally, darling, to speak quite candidly, I don't much care about the name of Ernest . . . I don't think the name suits me at all.

GWEN. It suits you perfectly. It is a divine name. It has a music of its own. It produces vibrations.

JACK. Well, really, Gwendolen, I must say that I think there are lots of other much nicer names. I think Jack, for instance, a charming name.

GWEN. Jack? . . . No, there is very little music in the name Jack, if any at all, indeed. It does not thrill. It produces absolutely no vibrations. . . . I have known several Jacks, and they all, without exception, were more than usually plain. Besides, Jack is a notorious domesticity for John! And I pity any woman who is married to a man called John. She would probably never be allowed to know the entrancing pleasure of a single moment's solitude. The only really safe name is Ernest.

JACK. Gwendolen, I must get christened at once—I mean we must get married at once. There is no time to be lost.

GWEN. Married, Mr. Worthing?

JACK. [*Astounded.*] Well . . . surely. You know that I love you, and you led me to believe, Miss Fairfax, that you were not absolutely indifferent to me.

GWEN. I adore you. But you haven't proposed to me yet. Nothing has been said at all about marriage. The subject has not even been touched on.

JACK. Well . . . may I propose to you now?

GWEN. I think it would be an admirable opportunity. And to spare you any possible disappointment, Mr. Worthing, I think it only fair to tell you quite frankly beforehand that I am fully determined to accept you.

JACK. Gwendolen!

GWEN. Yes, Mr. Worthing, what have you got to say to me?

JACK. You know what I have got to say to you.

GWEN. Yes, but you don't say it.

JACK. Gwendolen, will you marry me? [*Goes on his knees.*]

GWEN. Of course I will, darling. How long you have been about it! I am afraid you have had very little experience in how to propose.

JACK. My own one, I have never loved anyone in the world but you.

GWEN. Yes, but men often propose for practice. I know my brother Gerald does. All my girl-friends tell me so. What wonderfully blue eyes you have, Ernest! They are quite, quite blue. I hope you will always look at me just like that, especially when there are other people present.

[*Enter Lady Bracknell.*]

LADY BRA. Mr. Worthing! Rise, sir, from this semi-recumbent posture. It is most indecorous.

GWEN. Mamma! [*He tries to rise; she restrains him.*] I must beg you to retire. This is no place for you. Besides, Mr. Worthing has not quite finished yet.

LADY BRA. Finished what, may I ask?

GWEN. I am engaged to Mr. Worthing, mamma. [*They rise together.*]

LADY BRA. Pardon me, you are not engaged to anyone. When you do become engaged to some one, I, or your father, should his health permit him, will inform you of the fact. An engagement should come on a young girl as a surprise, pleasant or unpleasant, as the case may be. It is hardly a matter that she could be allowed to arrange for herself. . . . And now I have a few questions to put to you, Mr. Worthing. While I am making these inquiries, you, Gwendolen, will wait for me below in the carriage.

GWEN. [*Reproachfully.*] Mamma!

LADY BRA. In the carriage, Gwendolen! [*Gwendolen goes to the door. She and Jack blow kisses to each other behind Lady Bracknell's back. Lady Bracknell looks vaguely about as if she could not understand what the noise was. Finally turns round.*] Gwendolen, the carriage!

GWEN. Yes, mamma. [*Goes out, looking back at Jack.*]

LADY BRA. [*Sitting down.*] You can take a seat, Mr. Worthing.

[*Looks in her pocket for note-book and pencil.*]

JACK. Thank you, Lady Bracknell, I prefer standing.

LADY BRA. [*Pencil and note-book in hand.*] I feel bound to tell you that you are not down on my list of eligible young men, although I have the same list as the dear Duchess of Bolton has. We work together, in fact. However, I am quite ready to enter your name, should your answers be what a really affectionate mother requires. Do you smoke?

JACK. Well, yes, I must admit I smoke.

LADY BRA. I am glad to hear it. A man should always have an occupation of some kind. There are far too many idle men in London as it is. How old are you?

JACK Twenty-nine.

LADY BRA. A very good age to be married at. I have always been of opinion that a man who desires to get married should know either everything or nothing. Which do you know?

JACK. [*After some hesitation.*] I know nothing, Lady Bracknell.

LADY BRA. I am pleased to hear it. I do not approve of anything that tampers with natural ignorance. Ignorance is like a delicate exotic fruit; touch it and the bloom is gone. The whole theory of modern education is radically unsound. Fortunately in England, at any rate, education produces no effect whatsoever. If it did, it would prove a serious danger to the upper classes, and probably lead to acts of violence in Grosvenor Square. What is your income?

JACK. Between seven and eight thousand a year.

LADY BRA. [*Makes a note in her book.*] In land, or in investments?

JACK. In investments, chiefly.

LADY BRA. That is satisfactory. What between the duties expected of one during one's lifetime, and the duties exacted from one after one's death, land has ceased to be either a profit or a pleasure. It gives one position, and prevents one from keeping it up. That's all that can be said about land.

JACK. I have a country house with some land, of course, attached to it, about fifteen hundred acres, I believe; but I don't depend on that for my real income. In fact, as far as I can make out, the poachers are the only people who make anything out of it.

LADY BRA. A country house! How many bedrooms? Well, that point can be cleared up afterwards. You have a town house, I hope? A girl with a simple, unspoiled nature, like Gwendolen, could hardly be expected to reside in the country.

JACK. Well, I own a house in Belgrave Square, but it is let by the year to Lady Bloxham. Of course, I can get it back whenever I like, at six months' notice.

LADY BRA. Lady Bloxham? I don't know her.

JACK. Oh, she goes about very little. She is a lady considerably advanced in years.

LADY BRA. Ah, now-a-days that is no guarantee of respectability of character. What number in Belgrave Square?

JACK. 149.

LADY BRA. [*Shaking her head.*] The unfashionable side. I thought there was something. However, that could easily be altered.

JACK. Do you mean the fashion, or the side?

LADY BRA. [*Sternly.*] Both, if necessary, I presume. What are your politics?

JACK. Well, I am afraid I really have none. I am a Liberal Unionist.

LADY BRA. Oh, they count as Tories. They dine with us. Or come in the evening, at any rate. Now to minor matters. Are your parents living?

JACK. I have lost both my parents.

LADY BRA. Both? . . . That seems like carelessness. Who was your father? He was evidently a man of some wealth. Was he born in what the Radical papers call the purple of commerce, or did he rise from the ranks of aristocracy?

JACK. I am afraid I really don't know. The fact is, Lady Bracknell, I said I had lost my parents. It would be nearer the truth to say that my parents seem to have lost me. . . . I don't actually know who I am by birth. I was . . . well, I was found.

LADY BRA. Found!

JACK. The late Mr. Thomas Cardew, an old gentleman of a very charitable and kindly disposition, found me, and gave me the name of Worthing, because he happened to have a first-class ticket for Worthing in his pocket at the time. Worthing is a place in Sussex. It is a seaside resort.

LADY BRA. Where did the charitable gentleman who had a first-class ticket for this seaside resort find you?

JACK. [*Gravely.*] In a hand-bag.

LADY BRA. A hand-bag?

JACK. [*Very seriously.*] Yes, Lady Bracknell. I was in a hand-bag—a somewhat large, black leather hand-bag, with handles to it—an ordinary hand-bag, in fact.

LADY BRA. In what locality did this Mr. James, or Thomas, Cardew come across this ordinary hand-bag?

JACK. In the cloak-room at Victoria Station. It was given to him in mistake for his own.

LADY BRA. The cloak-room at Victoria Station?

JACK. Yes. The Brighton line.

LADY BRA. The line is immaterial. Mr. Worthing, I confess I feel somewhat bewildered by what you have just told me. To be born, or at any rate, bred in a hand-bag, whether it had handles or not, seems to me to display a contempt for the ordinary decencies of family life that remind one of the worst excesses of the French Revolution. And I presume you know what that unfortunate movement led to? As for the particular locality in which the hand-bag was found, a cloak-room at a railway station might serve to conceal a social indiscretion—has probably, indeed, been used for that purpose before now—but it could hardly be regarded as an assured basis for a recognized position in good society.

JACK. May I ask you then what you would advise me to do? I need hardly say I would do anything in the world to ensure Gwendolen's happiness.

LADY BRA. I would strongly advise you, Mr. Worthing, to try and acquire some relations as soon as possible, and to make a definite effort to produce at any rate one parent, of either sex, before the season is quite over.

JACK. I don't see how I could possibly manage to do that. I can produce the hand-bag at any moment. It is in my dressing-room at home. I really think that should satisfy you, Lady Bracknell.

LADY BRA. Me, sir! What has it to do with me? You can hardly imagine that I and Lord Bracknell would dream of allowing our only daughter—a girl brought up with the utmost care—to marry into a cloak-room, and form an alliance with a parcel? Good morning, Mr. Worthing!

[*Lady Bracknell sweeps out in majestic indignation.*]

JACK. Good morning! [*Algernon, from the other room, strikes up the Wedding March. Jack looks perfectly furious, and goes to the door.*] For goodness' sake don't play that ghastly tune, Algy! How idiotic you are!

[*The music stops, and Algernon enters cheerily.*]

ALG. Didn't it go off all right, old boy? You don't mean to say Gwendolen refused you? I know it is a way she has. She is always refusing people. I think it is most ill-natured of her.

JACK. Oh, Gwendolen is as right as a trivet. As far as she is concerned, we are engaged. Her mother is perfectly unbearable. Never met such a Gorgon . . . I don't really know what a Gorgon is like, but I am quite sure that Lady Bracknell is one. In any case, she is a monster, without being a myth, which is rather unfair . . . I beg your pardon, Algy, I suppose I shouldn't talk about your own aunt in that way before you.

ALG. My dear boy, I love hearing my relations abused. It is the only thing that makes me put up with them at all. Relations are simply a tedious pack of people who haven't got the remotest knowledge of how to live, nor the smallest instinct about when to die.

JACK. Oh, that is nonsense!

ALG. It isn't!

JACK. Well, I won't argue about the matter. You always want to argue about things.

ALG. That is exactly what things were originally made for.

JACK. Upon my word, if I thought that, I'd shoot myself . . . [*A pause.*] You don't think there is any chance of Gwendolen becoming like her mother in about a hundred and fifty years, do you, Algy?

ALG. All women become like their mothers. That is their tragedy. No man does. That's his.

JACK. Is that clever?

ALG. It is perfectly phrased! and quite as true as any observation in civilized life should be.

JACK. I am sick to death of cleverness. Everybody is clever now-a-days. You can't go anywhere without meeting clever people. The thing has become an absolute public nuisance. I wish to goodness we had a few fools left.

ALG. We have.

JACK. I should extremely like to meet them. What do they talk about?

ALG. The fools? Oh! about the clever people, of course.

JACK. What fools!

ALG. By the way, did you tell Gwendolen the truth about your being Ernest in town, and Jack in the country?

JACK. [*In a very patronising manner.*] My dear fellow, the truth isn't quite the sort of thing one tells to a nice sweet refined girl. What extraordinary ideas you have about the way to behave to a woman!

ALG. The only way to behave to a woman is to make love to her, if she is pretty, and to someone else if she is plain.

JACK. Oh, that is nonsense.

ALG. What about your brother? What about the profligate Ernest?

JACK. Oh, before the end of the week I shall have got rid of him. I'll say he died in Paris of apoplexy. Lots of people die of apoplexy, quite suddenly, don't they?

ALG. Yes, but it's hereditary, my dear fellow. It's a sort of thing that runs in families. You had much better say a severe chill.

JACK. You are sure a severe chill isn't hereditary, or anything of that kind?

ALG. Of course is isn't!

JACK. Very well, then. My poor brother Ernest is carried off suddenly in Paris, by a severe chill. That gets rid of him.

ALG. But I thought you said that . . . Miss Cardew was a little too much interested in your poor brother, Ernest? Won't she feel his loss a good deal?

JACK. Oh, that is all right. Cecily is not a silly romantic girl, I am glad to say. She has got a capital appetite, goes long walks, and pays no attention at all to her lessons.

ALG. I would rather like to see Cecily.

JACK. I will take very good care you never do. She is excessively pretty, and she is only just eighteen.

ALG. Have you told Gwendolen yet that you have an excessively pretty ward who is only just eighteen?

JACK. Oh! one doesn't blurt these things out to people. Cecily and Gwendolen are perfectly certain to be extremely great friends. I'll bet you anything you like that half an hour after they have met, they will be calling each other sister.

ALG. Women only do that when they have called each other a lot of other things first. Now, my dear boy, if we want to get a good table at Willis's, we really must go and dress. Do you know it is nearly seven?

JACK. [*Irritably.*] Oh! it always is nearly seven.

ALG. Well, I'm hungry.

JACK. I never knew you when you weren't. . . .

ALG. What shall we do after dinner? Go to the theatre?

JACK. Oh no! I loathe listening.

ALG. Well, let us go to the club?

JACK. Oh no! I hate talking.

ALG. Well, we might trot round to the Empire at ten?

JACK. Oh no! I can't bear looking at things. It is so silly.

ALG. Well, what shall we do?

JACK. Nothing!

ALG. It is awfully hard work doing nothing. However, I don't mind hard work where there is no definite object of any kind.

[*Enter Lane.*]

LANE. Miss Fairfax.

[*Enter Gwendolen. Lane goes out.*]

ALG. Gwendolen, upon my word!

GWEN. Algy, kindly turn your back. I have something very particular to say to Mr. Worthing.

ALG. Really, Gwendolen, I don't think I can allow this at all.

GWEN. Algy, you always adopt a strictly immoral attitude towards life. You are not quite old enough to do that. [*Algernon retires to the fireplace.*]

JACK. My own darling!

GWEN. Ernest, we may never be married. From the expression on mamma's face I fear we never shall. Few parents now-a-days pay any regard to what their children say to them. The old-fashioned respect for the young is fast dying out. Whatever influence I ever had over mamma, I lost at the age of three. But although she may prevent us from becoming man and wife, and I may marry someone else, and marry often, nothing that she can possibly do can alter my eternal devotion to you.

JACK. Dear Gwendolen!

GWEN. The story of your romantic origin, as related to me by mamma, with unpleasing comments, has naturally stirred the deeper fibres of my nature. Your Christian name has an irresistible fascination. The simplicity of your character makes you exquisitely incomprehensible to me. Your town address at the Albany I have. What is your address in the country?

JACK. The Manor House, Woolton, Hertfordshire.

[*Algernon, who has been carefully listening, smiles to himself, and writes the address on his shirt-cuff. Then picks up the Railway Guide.*]

GWEN. There is a good postal service, I suppose? It may be necessary to do something desperate. That of course will require serious consideration. I will communicate with you daily.

JACK. My own one!

GWEN. How long do you remain in town?

JACK. Till Monday.

GWEN. Good! Algy, you may turn round now.

ALG. Thanks, I've turned round already.

GWEN. You may also ring the bell.

JACK. You will let me see you to your carriage, my own darling?

GWEN. Certainly.

JACK. [*To Lane, who now enters.*] I will see Miss Fairfax out.

LANE. Yes. sir. [*Jack and Gwendolen go off.*]

[*Lane presents several letters on a salver to Algernon. It is to be surmised that they are bills, as Algernon, after looking at the envelopes, tears them up.*]

Alg. A glass of sherry, Lane.

Lane. Yes, sir.

Alg. To-morrow, Lane, I'm going Bunburying.

Lane. Yes, sir.

Alg. I shall probably not be back till Monday. You can put up my dress clothes, my smoking jacket, and all the Bunbury suits. . . .

Lane. Yes, sir. [*Handing sherry.*]

Alg. I hope to-morrow will be a fine day, Lane.

Lane. It never is, sir.

Alg. Lane, you're a perfect pessimist.

Lane. I do my best to give satisfaction, sir.

[*Enter Jack. Lane goes off.*]

Jack. There's a sensible, intellectual girl! the only girl I ever cared for in my life. [*Algernon is laughing immoderately.*] What on earth are you so amused at?

Alg. Oh, I'm a little anxious about poor Bunbury, that is all.

Jack. If you don't take care, your friend Bunbury will get you into a serious scrape some day.

Alg. I love scrapes. They are the only things that are never serious.

Jack. Oh, that's nonsense, Algy. You never talk anything but nonsense.

Alg. Nobody ever does.

[*Jack looks indignantly at him, and leaves the room. Algernon lights a cigarette, reads his shirt-cuff, and smiles.*]

Act-Drop.

SECOND ACT

Scene—*Garden at the Manor House. A flight of gray stone steps leads up to the house. The garden, an old-fashioned one, full of roses. Time of year, July. Basket chairs, and a table covered with books, are set under a large yew tree.*

[*Miss Prism discovered seated at the table. Cecily is at the back watering flowers.*]

Miss Pri. [*Calling.*] Cecily, Cecily! Surely such a utilitarian occupation as the watering of flowers is rather Moulton's duty than yours? Especially at a moment when intellectual pleasures await you. Your German grammar is on the table. Pray open it at page fifteen. We will repeat yesterday's lesson.

Cec. [*Coming over very slowly.*] But I don't like German. It isn't at all a becoming language. I know perfectly well that I look quite plain after my German lesson.

Miss Pri. Child, you know how anxious your guardian is that you should improve yourself in every way. He laid particular stress on your German, as he was leaving for town yesterday. Indeed, he always lays stress on your German when he is leaving for town.

CEC. Dear Uncle Jack is so very serious! Sometimes he is so serious that I think he cannot be quite well.

MISS PRI. [*Drawing herself up.*] Your guardian enjoys the best of health, and his gravity of demeanour is especially to be commended in one so comparatively young as he is. I know no one who has a higher sense of duty and responsibility.

CEC. I suppose that is why he often looks a little bored when we three are together.

MISS PRI. Cecily! I am surprised at you. Mr. Worthing has many troubles in his life. Idle merriment and triviality would be out of place in his conversation. You must remember his constant anxiety about that unfortunate young man his brother.

CEC. I wish Uncle Jack would allow that unfortunate young man, his brother, to come down here sometimes. We might have a good influence over him, Miss Prism. I am sure you certainly would. You know German, and geology, and things of that kind influence a man very much. [*Cecily begins to write in her diary.*]

MISS PRI. [*Shaking her head.*] I do not think that even I could produce any effect on a character that according to his own brother's admission is irretrievably weak and vacillating. Indeed I am not sure that I would desire to reclaim him. I am not in favour of this modern mania for turning bad people into good people at a moment's notice. As a man sows so let him reap. You must put away your diary, Cecily. I really don't see why you should keep a diary at all.

CEC. I keep a diary in order to enter the wonderful secrets of my life. If I didn't write them down I should probably forget all about them.

MISS PRI. Memory, my dear Cecily, is the diary that we all carry about with us.

CEC. Yes, but it usually chronicles the things that have never happened, and couldn't possibly have happened. I believe that Memory is responsible for nearly all the three-volume novels that Mudie sends us.

MISS PRI. Do not speak slightingly of the three-volume novel, Cecily. I wrote one myself in earlier days.

CEC. Did you really, Miss Prism? How wonderfully clever you are! I hope it did not end happily? I don't like novels that end happily. They depress me so much.

MISS PRI. The good ended happily, and the bad unhappily. That is what Fiction means.

CEC. I suppose so. But it seems very unfair. And was your novel ever published?

MISS PRI. Alas! no. The manuscript unfortunately was abandoned. I use the word in the sense of lost or mislaid. To your work, child, these speculations are profitless.

CEC. [*Smiling.*] But I see dear Dr. Chasuble coming up through the garden.

MISS PRI. [*Rising and advancing.*] Dr. Chasuble! This is indeed a pleasure.

[*Enter Canon Chasuble.*]

CHAS. And how are we this morning? Miss Prism, you are, I trust, well?

CEC. Miss Prism has just been complaining of a slight headache. I think it would do her so much good to have a short stroll with you in the Park, Dr. Chasuble.

MISS PRI. Cecily, I have not mentioned anything about a headache.

CEC. No, dear Miss Prism, I know that, but I felt instinctively that you had a headache. Indeed I was thinking about that, and not about my German lesson, when the Rector came in.

CHAS. I hope Cecily, you are not inattentive.

CEC. Oh, I am afraid I am.

CHAS. That is strange. Were I fortunate enough to be Miss Prism's pupil, I would hang upon her lips. [*Miss Prism glares.*] I spoke metaphorically. My metaphor was drawn from bees. Ahem! Mr. Worthing, I suppose, has not returned from town yet?

MISS PRI. We do not expect him till Monday afternoon.

CHAS. Ah yes, he usually likes to spend his Sunday in London. He is not one of those whose sole aim is enjoyment, as, by all accounts, that unfortunate young man his brother seems to be. But I must not disturb Egeria and her pupil any longer.

MISS PRI. Egeria? My name is Laetitia, Doctor.

CHAS. [*Bowing.*] A classical allusion merely, drawn from the Pagan authors. I shall see you both no doubt at Evensong?

MISS PRI. I think, dear Doctor, I will have a stroll with you. I find I have a headache after all, and a walk might do it good.

CHAS. With pleasure, Miss Prism, with pleasure. We might go as far as the schools and back.

MISS PRI. That would be delightful. Cecily, you will read your Political Economy in my absence. The chapter on the Fall of the Rupee you may omit. It is somewhat too sensational. Even these metallic problems have their melodramatic side.

[*Goes down the garden with Dr. Chasuble.*]

CEC. [*Picks up books and throws them back on table.*] Horrid Political Economy! Horrid Geography! Horrid, horrid German!

[*Enter Merriman with a card on a salver.*]

MERR. Mr. Ernest Worthing has just driven over from the station. He has brought his luggage with him.

CEC. [*Takes the card and reads it.*] "Mr. Ernest Worthing, B. 4 The Albany, W." Uncle Jack's brother! Did you tell him Mr. Worthing was in town?

MERR. Yes, Miss. He seemed very much disappointed. I mentioned that you and Miss Prism were in the garden. He said he was anxious to speak to you privately for a moment.

CEC. Ask Mr. Ernest Worthing to come here. I suppose you had better talk to the housekeeper about a room for him.

MERR. Yes, Miss. [*Merriman goes off.*]

Cec. I have never met any really wicked person before. I feel rather frightened. I am so afraid he will look just like everyone else.

[*Enter Algernon, very gay and debonnair.*]

He does!

Alg. [*Raising his hat.*] You are my little cousin Cecily, I'm sure.

Cec. You are under some strange mistake. I am not little. In fact, I believe I am more than usually tall for my age. [*Algernon is rather taken aback.*] But I am your cousin Cecily. You, I see from your card, are Uncle Jack's brother, my cousin Ernest, my wicked cousin Ernest.

Alg. Oh! I am not really wicked at all, Cousin Cecily. You mustn't think that I am wicked.

Cec. If you are not, then you have certainly been deceiving us all in a very inexcusable manner. I hope you have not been leading a double life, pretending to be wicked and being really good all the time. That would be hypocrisy.

Alg. [*Looks at her in amazement.*] Oh! Of course I have been rather reckless.

Cec. I am glad to hear it.

Alg. In fact, now you mention the subject, I have been very bad in my own small way.

Cec. I don't think you should be so proud of that, though I am sure it must have been very pleasant.

Alg. It is much pleasanter being here with you.

Cec. I can't understand how you are here at all. Uncle Jack won't be back till Monday afternoon.

Alg. That is a great disappointment. I am obliged to go up by the first train on Monday morning. I have a business appointment that I am anxious . . . to miss.

Cec. Couldn't you miss it anywhere but in London?

Alg. No: the appointment is in London.

Cec. Well, I know, of course, how important it is not to keep a business engagement, if one wants to retain any sense of the beauty of life, but still I think you had better wait till Uncle Jack arrives. I know he wants to speak to you about your emigrating.

Alg. About my what?

Cec. Your emigrating. He has gone up to buy your outfit.

Alg. I certainly wouldn't let Jack buy my outfit. He has no taste in neckties at all.

Cec. I don't think you will require neckties. Uncle Jack is sending you to Australia.

Alg. Australia? I'd sooner die.

Cec. Well, he said at dinner on Wednesday night, that you would have to choose between this world, the next world, and Australia.

Alg. Oh, well! The accounts I have received of Australia and the next world are not particularly encouraging. This world is good enough for me, Cousin Cecily.

Cec. Yes, but are you good enough for it?

ALG. I'm afraid I'm not that. That is why I want you to reform me. You might make that your mission, if you don't mind, Cousin Cecily.

CEC. I'm afraid I've no time, this afternoon.

ALG. Well, would you mind my reforming myself this afternoon?

CEC. It is rather Quixotic of you. But I think you should try.

ALG. I will. I feel better already.

CEC. You are looking a little worse.

ALG. That is because I am hungry.

CEC. How thoughtless of me. I should have remembered that when one is going to lead an entirely new life, one requires regular and wholesome meals. Won't you come in?

ALG. Thank you. Might I have a buttonhole first? I never have any appetite unless I have a buttonhole first.

CEC. A Maréchale Niel? [*Picks up scissors.*]

ALG. No, I'd sooner have a pink rose.

CEC. Why? [*Cuts a flower.*]

ALG. Because you are like a pink rose, Cousin Cecily.

CEC. I don't think it can be right for you to talk to me like that. Miss Prism never says such things to me.

ALG. Then Miss Prism is a shortsighted old lady. [*Cecily puts the rose in his buttonhole.*] You are the prettiest girl I ever saw.

CEC. Miss Prism says that all good looks are a snare.

ALG. They are a snare that every sensible man would like to be caught in.

CEC. Oh! I don't think I would care to catch a sensible man. I shouldn't know what to talk to him about.

[*They pass into the house. Miss Prism and Dr. Chasuble return.*]

MISS PRI. You are too much alone, dear Dr. Chasuble. You should get married. A misanthrope I can understand—a womanthrope, never!

CHAS. [*With a scholar's shudder.*] Believe me, I do not deserve so neologistic a phrase. The precept as well as the practice of the Primitive Church was distinctly against matrimony.

MISS PRI. [*Sententiously.*] That is obviously the reason why the Primitive Church has not lasted up to the present day. And you do not seem to realize, dear Doctor, that by persistently remaining single, a man converts himself into a permanent public temptation. Men should be more careful; this very celibacy leads weaker vessels astray.

CHAS. But is a man not equally attractive when married?

MISS PRI. No married man is ever attractive except to his wife.

CHAS. And often, I've been told, not even to her.

MISS PRI. That depends on the intellectual sympathies of the woman. Maturity can always be depended on. Ripeness can be trusted. Young women are green. [*Dr. Chasuble starts.*] I spoke horticulturally. My metaphor was drawn from fruits. But where is Cecily?

CHAS. Perhaps she followed us to the schools.

[*Enter Jack slowly from the back of the garden. He is dressed in the deepest mourning, with crape hatband and black gloves.*]

MISS PRI. Mr. Worthing!

CHAS. Mr. Worthing!

MISS PRI. This is indeed a surprise. We did not look for you till Monday afternoon.

JACK. [*Shakes Miss Prism's hand in a tragic manner.*] I have returned sooner than I expected. Dr. Chasuble, I hope you are well?

CHAS. Dear Mr. Worthing, I trust this garb of woe does not betoken some terrible calamity?

JACK. My brother.

MISS PRI. More shameful debts and extravagance?

CHAS. Still leading his life of pleasure?

JACK. [*Shaking his head.*] Dead!

CHAS. Your brother Ernest dead?

JACK. Quite dead.

MISS PRI. What a lesson for him! I trust he will profit by it.

CHAS. Mr. Worthing, I offer you my sincere condolence. You have at least the consolation of knowing that you were always the most generous and forgiving of brothers.

JACK. Poor Ernest! He had many faults, but it is a sad, sad blow.

CHAS. Very sad indeed. Were you with him at the end?

JACK. No. He died abroad; in Paris, in fact. I had a telegram last night from the manager of the Grand Hotel.

CHAS. Was the cause of death mentioned?

JACK. A severe chill, it seems.

MISS. PRI. As a man sows, so shall he reap.

CHAS. [*Raising his hand.*] Charity, dear Miss Prism, charity! None of us are perfect. I myself am peculiarly susceptible to draughts. Will the interment take place here?

JACK. No. He seemed to have expressed a desire to be buried in Paris.

CHAS. In Paris! [*Shakes his head.*] I fear that hardly points to any very serious state of mind at the last. You would no doubt wish me to make some slight allusion to this tragic domestic affliction next Sunday. [*Jack presses his hand convulsively.*] My sermon on the meaning of the manna in the wilderness can be adapted to almost any occasion, joyful, or, as in the present case, distressing. [*All sigh.*] I have preached it at harvest celebrations, christenings, confirmations, on days of humiliation and festal days. The last time I delivered it was in the Cathedral, as a charity sermon on behalf of the Society for the Prevention of Discontent among the Upper Orders. The Bishop, who was present, was much struck by some of the analogies I drew.

JACK. Ah! that reminds me, you mentioned christenings, I think, Dr. Chasuble? I suppose you know how to christen all right? [*Dr. Chasuble looks astounded.*] I mean, of course, you are continually christening, aren't you?

MISS PRI. It is, I regret to say, one of the Rector's most constant duties in this parish. I have often spoken to the poorer classes on the subject. But they don't seem to know what thrift is.

CHAS. But is there any particular infant in whom you are interested, Mr. Worthing? Your brother was, I believe, unmarried, was he not?

JACK. Oh yes.

MISS. PRI. [*Bitterly.*] People who live entirely for pleasure usually are.

JACK. But it is not for any child, dear Doctor. I am very fond of children. No! the fact is, I would like to be christened myself, this afternoon, if you have nothing better to do.

CHAS. But surely, Mr. Worthing, you have been christened already?

JACK. I don't remember anything about it.

CHAS. But have you any grave doubts on the subject?

JACK. I certainly intend to have. Of course I don't know if the thing would bother you in any way, or if you think I am a little too old now.

CHAS. Not at all. The sprinkling, and, indeed, the immersion of adults is a perfectly canonical practice.

JACK. Immersion!

CHAS. You need have no apprehensions. Sprinkling is all that is necessary, or indeed I think advisable. Our weather is so changeable. At what hour would you wish the ceremony performed?

JACK. Oh, I might trot round about five if that would suit you.

CHAS. Perfectly, perfectly! In fact I have two similar ceremonies to perform at that time. A case of twins that occurred recently in one of the outlying cottages on your own estate. Poor Jenkins the carter, a most hard-working man.

JACK. Oh! I don't see much fun in being christened along with other babies. It would be childish. Would half-past five do?

CHAS. Admirably! Admirably! [*Takes out watch.*] And now, dear Mr. Worthing, I will not intrude any longer into a house of sorrow. I would merely beg you not to be too much bowed down by grief. What seem to us bitter trials are often blessings in disguise.

MISS PRI. This seems to me a blessing of an extremely obvious kind.

[*Enter Cecily from the house.*]

CEC. Uncle Jack! Oh, I am pleased to see you back. But what horrid clothes you have got on! Do go and change them.

MISS PRI. Cecily!

CHAS. My child! my child! [*Cecily goes towards Jack; he kisses her brow in a melancholy manner.*]

CEC. What is the matter, Uncle Jack? Do look happy! You look as if you had a toothache, and I have got such a surprise for you. Who do you think is in the dining-room? Your brother!

JACK. Who?

CEC. Your brother Ernest. He arrived about half an hour ago.

JACK. What nonsense! I haven't got a brother!

CEC. Oh, don't say that. However badly he may have behaved to you in the past he is still your brother. You couldn't be so heartless as to disown him. I'll tell him to come out. And you will shake hands with him, won't you, Uncle Jack? [*Runs back into the house.*]

CHAS. These are very joyful tidings.

MISS PRI. After we had all been resigned to his loss, his sudden return seems to me peculiarly distressing.

JACK. My brother is in the dining-room? I don't know what it all means. I think it is perfectly absurd.

[*Enter Algernon and Cecily hand in hand. They come slowly up to Jack.*]

JACK. Good Heavens! [*Motions Algernon away.*]

ALG. Brother John, I have come down from town to tell you that I am very sorry for all the trouble I have given you, and that I intend to lead a better life in the future. [*Jack glares at him and does not take his hand.*]

CEC. Uncle Jack, you are not going to refuse your own brother's hand?

JACK. Nothing will induce me to take his hand. I think his coming down here disgraceful. He knows perfectly well why.

CEC. Uncle Jack, do be nice. There is some good in everyone. Ernest has just been telling me about his poor invalid friend Mr. Bunbury whom he goes to visit so often. And surely there must be much good in one who is kind to an invalid, and leaves the pleasures of London to sit by a bed of pain.

JACK. Oh! he has been talking about Bunbury, has he?

CEC. Yes, he has told me all about poor Mr. Bunbury, and his terrible state of health.

JACK. Bunbury! Well, I won't have him talk to you about Bunbury or about anything else. It is enough to drive one perfectly frantic.

ALG. Of course I admit that the faults were all on my side. But I must say that I think Brother John's coldness to me is peculiarly painful. I expected a more enthusiastic welcome, especially considering it is the first time I have come here.

CEC. Uncle Jack, if you don't shake hands with Ernest, I will never forgive you.

JACK. Never forgive me?

CEC. Never, never, never!

JACK. Well, this is the last time I shall ever do it.

[*Shakes hands with Algernon and glares.*]

CHAS. It is pleasant, is it not, to see so perfect a reconciliation? I think we might leave the two brothers together.

MISS PRI. Cecily, you will come with us.

CEC. Certainly, Miss Prism. My little task of reconciliation is over.

CHAS. You have done a beautiful action to-day, dear child.

MISS PRI. We must not be premature in our judgments.

CEC. I feel very happy. [*They all go off.*]

JACK. You young scoundrel, Algy, you must get out of this place as soon as possible. I don't allow any Bunburying here.

[*Enter Merriman.*]

MERR. I have put Mr. Ernest's things in the room next to yours, sir. I suppose that is all right?

JACK. What?

MERR. Mr. Ernest's luggage, sir. I have unpacked it and put it in the room next to your own.

JACK. His luggage?

MERR. Yes, sir. Three portmanteaus, a dressing-case, two hat boxes, and a large luncheon-basket.

ALG. I am afraid I can't stay more than a week this time.

JACK. Merriman, order the dog-cart at once. Mr. Ernest has been suddenly called back to town.

MERR. Yes, sir. [*Goes back into the house.*]

ALG. What a fearful liar you are, Jack. I have not been called back to town at all.

JACK. Yes, you have.

ALG. I haven't heard anyone call me.

JACK. Your duty as a gentleman calls you back.

ALG. My duty as a gentleman has never interfered with my pleasures in the smallest degree.

JACK. I can quite understand that.

ALG. Well, Cecily is a darling.

JACK. You are not to talk of Miss Cardew like that. I don't like it.

ALG. Well, I don't like your clothes. You look perfectly ridiculous in them. Why on earth don't you go up and change? It is perfectly childish to be in deep mourning for a man who is actually staying for a whole week with you in your house as a guest. I call it grotesque.

JACK. You are certainly not staying with me for a whole week as a guest or anything else. You have got to leave . . . by the four-five train.

ALG. I certainly won't leave you so long as you are in mourning. It would be most unfriendly. If I were in mourning you would stay with me, I suppose. I should think it very unkind if you didn't.

JACK. Well, will you go if I change my clothes?

ALG. Yes, if you are not too long. I never saw anybody take so long to dress, and with such little result.

JACK. Well, at any rate, that is better than being always over-dressed as you are.

ALG. If I am occasionally a little over-dressed, I make up for it by being always immensely over-educated.

JACK. Your vanity is ridiculous, your conduct an outrage, and your presence in my garden utterly absurd. However, you have got to catch the four-five, and I hope you will have a pleasant journey back to town. This Bunburying, as you call it, has not been a great success for you. [*Goes into the house.*]

ALG. I think it has been a great success. I'm in love with Cecily, and that is everything.

[*Enter Cecily at the back of the garden. She picks up the can and begins to water the flowers.*]

But I must see her before I go, and make arrangements for another Bunbury. Ah, there she is.

CEC. Oh, I merely came back to water the roses. I thought you were with Uncle Jack.

ALG. He's gone to order the dog-cart for me.

CEC. Oh, is he going to take you for a nice drive?

ALG. He's going to send me away.

CEC. Then have we got to part?

ALG. I am afraid so. It's very painful parting.

CEC. It is always painful to part from people whom one has known for a very brief space of time. The absence of old friends one can endure with equanimity. But even a momentary separation from anyone to whom one has just been introduced is almost unbearable.

ALG. Thank you.

[*Enter Merriman.*]

MERR. The dog-cart is at the door, sir. [*Algernon looks appealingly at Cecily.*]

CEC. It can wait, Merriman . . . for . . . five minutes.

MERR. Yes, Miss. [*Exit Merriman.*]

ALG. I hope, Cecily, I shall not offend you if I state quite frankly and openly that you seem to me to be in every way the visible personification of absolute perfection.

CEC. I think your frankness does you great credit, Ernest. If you will allow me I will copy your remarks into my diary. [*Goes over to table and begins writing in diary.*]

ALG. Do you really keep a diary? I'd give anything to look at it. May I?

CEC. Oh no. [*Puts her hand over it.*] You see, it is simply a very young girl's record of her own thoughts and impressions, and consequently meant for publication. When it appears in volume form I hope you will order a copy. But pray, Ernest, don't stop. I delight in taking down from dictation. I have reached "absolute perfection." You can go on. I am quite ready for more.

ALG. [*Somewhat taken aback.*] Ahem! Ahem!

CEC. Oh, don't cough, Ernest. When one is dictating one should speak fluently and not cough. Besides, I don't know how to spell a cough.

[*Writes as Algernon speaks.*]

ALG. [*Speaking very rapidly.*] Cecily, ever since I first looked upon your wonderful and incomparable beauty, I have dared to love you wildly, passionately, devotedly, hopelessly.

CEC. I don't think that you should tell me that you love me wildly, passionately, devotedly, hopelessly. Hopelessly doesn't seem to make much sense, does it?

ALG. Cecily!

[*Enter Merriman.*]

MERR. The dog-cart is waiting, sir.

ALG. Tell it to come round next week, at the same hour.

MERR. [*Looks at Cecily, who makes no sign.*] Yes, sir. [*Merriman retires.*]

CEC. Uncle Jack would be very much annoyed if he knew you were staying on till next week, at the same hour.

ALG. Oh, I don't care about Jack. I don't care for anybody in the whole world but you. I love you, Cecily. You will marry me, won't you?

CEC. You silly boy! Of course. Why, we have been engaged for the last three months.

ALG. For the last three months?

CEC. Yes, it will be exactly three months on Thursday.

ALG. But how did we become engaged?

CEC. Well, ever since dear Uncle Jack first confessed to us that he had a younger brother who was very wicked and bad, you of course have formed the chief topic of conversation between myself and Miss Prism. And of course a man who is much talked about is always very attractive. One feels there must be something in him after all. I daresay it was foolish of me, but I fell in love with you, Ernest.

ALG. Darling! And when was the engagement actually settled?

CEC. On the 14th of February last. Worn out by your entire ignorance of my existence, I determined to end the matter one way or the other, and after a long struggle with myself I accepted you under this dear told tree here. The next day I bought this little ring in your name, and this is the little bangle with the true lovers' knot I promised you always to wear.

ALG. Did I give you this? It's very pretty, isn't it?

CEC. Yes, you've wonderfully good taste, Ernest. It's the excuse I've always given for your leading such a bad life. And this is the box in which I keep all your dear letters. [*Kneels at table, opens box, and produces letters tied up with blue ribbon.*]

ALG. My letters! But my own sweet Cecily, I have never written you any letters.

CEC. You need hardly remind me of that, Ernest. I remember only too well that I was forced to write your letters for you. I always wrote three times a week, and sometimes oftener.

ALG. Oh, do let me read them, Cecily?

CEC. Oh, I couldn't possibly. They would make you far too conceited. [*Replaces box.*] The three you wrote me after I had broken off the engagement are so beautiful, and so badly spelled, that even now I can hardly read them without crying a little.

ALG. But was our engagement ever broken off?

CEC. Of course it was. On the 22nd of last March. You can see the entry if you like. [*Shows diary.*] "To-day I broke off my engagement with Ernest. I feel it is better to do so. The weather still continues charming."

ALG. But why on earth did you break it off? What had I done? I had done nothing at all. Cecily, I am very much hurt indeed to hear you broke it off. Particularly when the weather was so charming.

CEC. It would hardly have been a really serious engagement if it hadn't been broken off at least once. But I forgave you before the week was out.

ALG. [*Crossing to her, and kneeling.*] What a perfect angel you are, Cecily.

CEC. You dear romantic boy. [*He kisses her, she puts her fingers through his hair.*] I hope your hair curls naturally, does it?

ALG. Yes, darling, with a little help from others.

CEC. I am so glad.

ALG. You'll never break off our engagement again, Cecily?

CEC. I don't think I could break it off now that I have actually met you. Besides, of course, there is the question of your name.

ALG. Yes, of course. [*Nervously.*]

CEC. You must not laugh at me, darling, but it had always been a girlish dream of mine to love some one whose name was Ernest. [*Algernon rises, Cecily also.*] There is something in that name that seems to inspire absolute confidence. I pity any poor married woman whose husband is not called Ernest.

ALG. But, my dear child, do you mean to say you could not love me if I had some other name?

CEC. But what name?

ALG. Oh, any name you like–Algernon–for instance . . .

CEC. But I don't like the name of Algernon.

ALG. Well, my own dear, sweet, loving little darling, I really can't see why you should object to the name of Algernon. It is not at all a bad name. In fact, it is rather an artistocratic name. Half of the chaps who get into the Bankruptcy Court are called Algernon. But seriously, Cecily . . . [*Moving to her.*] . . . if my name was Algy, couldn't you love me?

CEC. [*Rising.*] I might respect you, Ernest, I might admire your character, but I fear that I should not be able to give you my undivided attention.

ALG. Ahem! Cecily! [*Picking up hat.*] Your Rector here is, I suppose, thoroughly experienced in the practice of all the rites and ceremonials of the Church?

CEC. Oh, yes. Dr. Chasuble is a most learned man. He has never written a single book, so you can imagine how much he knows.

ALG. I must see him at once on a most important christening–I mean on most important business.

CEC. Oh!

ALG. I sha'n't be away more than half an hour.

CEC. Considering that we have been engaged since February the 14th, and that I only met you to-day for the first time, I think it is rather hard that you should leave me for so long a period as half an hour. Couldn't you make it twenty minutes?

ALG. I'll be back in no time.

[*Kisses her and rushes down the garden.*]

CEC. What an impetuous boy he is! I like his hair so much. I must enter his proposal in my diary.

[*Enter Merriman.*]

MERR. A Miss Fairfax has just called to see Mr. Worthing. On very important business Miss Fairfax states.

CEC. Isn't Mr. Worthing in his library?

MERR. Mr. Worthing went over in the direction of the Rectory some time ago.

CEC. Pray ask the lady to come out here; Mr. Worthing is sure to be back soon. And you can bring tea.

MERR. Yes, Miss. [*Goes out.*]

CEC. Miss Fairfax! I suppose one of the many good elderly women who are associated with Uncle Jack in some of his philanthropic work in London. I don't quite like women who are interested in philanthropic work. I think it is so forward of them.

[*Enter Merriman.*]

MERR. Miss Fairfax.

[*Enter Gwendolen.*] [*Exit Merriman.*]

CEC. [*Advancing to meet her.*] Pray let me introduce myself to you. My name is Cecily Cardew.

GWEN. Cecily Cardew? [*Moving to her and shaking hands.*] What a very sweet name! Something tells me that we are going to be great friends. I like you already more than I can say. My first impressions of people are never wrong.

CEC. How nice of you to like me so much after we have known each other such a comparatively short time. Pray sit down.

GWEN. [*Still standing up.*] I may call you Cecily, may I not?

CEC. With pleasure!

GWEN. And you will always call me Gwendolen, won't you?

CEC. If you wish.

GWEN. Then that is all quite settled, is it not?

CEC. I hope so. [*A pause. They both sit down together.*]

GWEN. Perhaps this might be a favourable opportunity for my mentioning who I am. My father is Lord Bracknell. You have never heard of papa, I suppose?

CEC. I don't think so.

GWEN. Outside the family circle, papa, I am glad to say, is entirely unknown. I think that is quite as it should be. The home seems to me to be the proper sphere for the man. And certainly once a man begins to neglect his domestic duties he becomes painfully effeminate, does he not? And I don't like that. It makes men so very attractive. Cecily, mamma, whose views on education are remarkably strict, has brought me up to be extremely short-sighted; it is part of her system; so do you mind my looking at you through my glasses?

CEC. Oh! not at all, Gwendolen. I am very fond of being looked at.

GWEN. [*After examinging Cecily carefully through a lorgnette.*] You are here on a short visit, I suppose.

CEC. Oh no! I live here.

GWEN. [*Severely.*] Really? Your mother, no doubt, or some female relative of advanced years, resides here also?

CEC. Oh no! I have no mother, nor, in fact, any relations.

GWEN. Indeed?

CEC. My dear guardian, with the assistance of Miss Prism, has the arduous task of looking after me.

GWEN. Your guardian?

CEC. Yes, I am Mr. Worthing's ward.

GWEN. Oh! It is strange he never mentioned to me that he had a ward. How secretive of him! He grows more interesting hourly. I am not sure, however, that the news inspires me with feelings of unmixed delight. [*Rising and going to her.*] I am very fond of you, Cecily; I have liked you ever since I met you! But I am bound to state that now that I know that you are Mr. Worthing's ward, I cannot help expressing a wish you were—well just a little older than you seem to be—and not quite so very alluring in appearance. In fact, if I may speak candidly——

CEC. Pray do! I think that whenever one has anything unpleasant to say, one should always be quite candid.

GWEN. Well, to speak with perfect candour, Cecily, I wish that you were fully forty-two, and more than usually plain for your age. Ernest has a strong, upright nature. He is the very soul of truth and honour. Disloyalty would be as impossible to him as deception. But even men of the noblest possible moral character are extremely susceptible to the influence of the physical charms of others. Modern, no less than Ancient History, supplies us with many most painful examples of what I refer to. If it were not so, indeed, History would be quite unreadable.

CEC. I beg your pardon, Gwendolen, did you say Ernest?

GWEN. Yes.

CEC. Oh, but it is not Mr. Ernest Worthing who is my guardian. It is his brother—his elder brother.

GWEN. [*Sitting down again.*] Ernest never mentioned to me that he had a brother.

CEC. I am sorry to say they have not been on good terms for a long time.

GWEN. Ah! that accounts for it. And now that I think of it I have never heard any man mention his brother. The subject seems distasteful to most men. Cecily, you have lifted a load from my mind. I was growing almost anxious. It would have been terrible if any cloud had come across a friendship like ours, would it not? Of course you are quite, quite sure that it is not Mr. Ernest Worthing who is your guardian?

CEC. Quite sure. [*A pause.*] In fact, I am going to be his.

GWEN. [*Enquiringly.*] I beg your pardon?

CEC. [*Rather shy and confidingly.*] Dearest Gwendolen, there is no reason why I should make a secret of it to you. Our little county newspaper is sure to chronicle the fact next week. Mr. Ernest Worthing and I are engaged to be married.

GWEN. [*Quite politely, rising.*] My darling Cecily, I think there must be some slight error. Mr. Ernest Worthing is engaged to me. The announcement will appear in "The Morning Post" on Saturday at the latest.

CEC. [*Very politely, rising.*] I am afraid you must be under some misconception. Ernest proposed to me exactly ten minutes ago. [*Shows diary.*]

GWEN. [*Examines diary through her lorgnette carefully.*] It is certainly very curious, for he asked me to be his wife yesterday afternoon at 5:30. If you would care to verify the incident, pray do so. [*Produces diary of her own.*] I never travel without my diary. One should always have something sensational to read in the train. I am so sorry, dear Cecily, if it is any disappointment to you, but I am afraid *I* have the prior claim.

CEC. It would distress me more than I can tell you, dear Gwendolen, if it caused you any mental or physical anguish, but I feel bound to point out that since Ernest proposed to you he clearly has changed his mind.

GWEN. [*Meditatively.*] If the poor fellow has been entrapped into any foolish promise I shall consider it my duty to rescue him at once, and with a firm hand.

CEC. [*Thoughtfully and sadly.*] Whatever unfortunate entanglement my dear boy may have got into, I will never reproach him with it after we are married.

GWEN. Do you allude to me, Miss Cardew, as an entanglement? You are presumptuous. On an occasion of this kind it becomes more than a moral duty to speak one's mind. It becomes a pleasure.

CEC. Do you suggest, Miss Fairfax, that I entrapped Ernest into an engagement? How dare you? This is no time for wearing the shallow mask of manners. When I see a spade I call it a spade.

GWEN. [*Satirically.*] I am glad to say that I have never seen a spade. It is obvious that our social spheres have been widely different.

[*Enter Merriman, followed by the footman. He carries a salver, table cloth, and plate stand. Cecily is about to retort. The presence of the servants exercises a restraining influence, under which both girls chafe.*]

MERR. Shall I lay tea here as usual, Miss?

CEC. [*Sternly, in a calm voice.*] Yes, as usual. [*Merriman begins to clear table and lay cloth. A long pause. Cecily and Gwendolen glare at each other.*]

GWEN. Are there many interesting walks in the vicinity, Miss Cardew?

CEC. Oh! yes! a great many. From the top of one of the hills quite close one can see five counties.

GWEN. Five counties! I don't think I should like that. I hate crowds.

CEC. [*Sweetly.*] I suppose that is why you live in town? [*Gwendolen bites her lip, and beats her foot nervously with her parasol.*]

GWEN. [*Looking round.*] Quite a well-kept garden this is, Miss Cardew.

CEC. So glad you like it, Miss Fairfax.

GWEN. I had no idea there were any flowers in the country.

CEC. Oh, flowers are as common here, Miss Fairfax, as people are in London.

GWEN. Personally I cannot understand how anybody manages to exist in the country, if anybody who is anybody does. The country always bores me to death.

CEC. Ah! This is what the newspapers call agricultural depression, is it not? I believe the aristocracy are suffering very much from it just at present. It is almost an epidemic amongst them, I have been told. May I offer you some tea, Miss Fairfax?

GWEN. [*With elaborate politeness.*] Thank you. [*Aside.*] Detestable girl! But I require tea!

CEC. [*Sweetly.*] Sugar?

GWEN. [*Superciliously.*] No, thank you. Sugar is not fashionable any more. [*Cecily looks angrily at her, takes up the tongs and puts four lumps of sugar into the cup.*]

CEC. [*Severely.*]Cake or bread and butter?

GWEN. [*In a bored manner.*] Bread and butter, please. Cake is rarely seen at the best houses nowadays.

CEC. [*Cuts a very large slice of cake, and puts it on the tray.*] Hand that to Miss Fairfax.

[*Merriman does so, and goes out with footman. Gwendolen drinks the tea and makes a grimace. Puts down cup at once, reaches out her hand to the bread and butter, looks at it, and finds it is cake. Rises in indignation.*]

GWEN. You have filled my tea with lumps of sugar, and though I asked most distinctly for bread and butter, you have given me cake. I am known for the gentleness of my disposition, and the extraordinary sweetness of my nature, but I warn you, Miss Cardew, you may go too far.

CEC. [*Rising.*]To save my poor, innocent, trusting boy from the machinations of any other girl there are no lengths to which I would not go.

GWEN. From the moment I saw you I distrusted you. I felt that you were false and deceitful. I am never deceived in such matters. My first impressions of people are invariably right.

CEC. It seems to me, Miss Fairfax, that I am trespassing on your valuable time. No doubt you have many other calls of a similar character to make in the neighbourhood.

[*Enter Jack.*]

GWEN. [*Catching sight of him.*] Ernest! My own Ernest!

JACK. Gwendolen! Darling! [*Offers to kiss her.*]

GWEN. [*Drawing back.*] A moment! May I ask if you are engaged to be married to this young lady? [*Points to Cecily.*]

JACK. [*Laughing.*] To dear little Cecily! Of course not! What could have put such an idea into your pretty little head?

GWEN. Thank you. You may! [*Offers her cheek.*]

CEC. [*Very sweetly.*] I knew there must be some misunderstanding, Miss Fairfax. The gentleman whose arm is at present round your waist is my dear guardian, Mr. John Worthing.

GWEN. I beg your pardon?

CEC. This is Uncle Jack.

GWEN. [*Receding.*] Jack! Oh! [*Enter Algernon.*]

CEC. Here is Ernest.

ALG. [*Goes straight over to Cecily without noticing anyone else.*] My own love! [*Offers to kiss her.*]

CEC. [*Drawing back.*] A moment, Ernest! May I ask you–are you engaged to be married to this young lady?

ALG. [*Looking round.*] To what young lady? Good Heavens! Gwendolen!

CEC. Yes! to good Heavens, Gwendolen, I mean to Gwendolen.

ALG. [*Laughing.*] Of course not! What could have put such an idea into your pretty little head?

CEC. Thank you. [*Presenting her cheek to be kissed.*] You may. [*Algernon kisses her.*]

GWEN. I felt there was some slight error, Miss Cardew. The gentleman who is now embracing you is my cousin, Mr. Algernon Moncrieff.

CEC. [*Breaking away from Algernon.*] Algernon Moncrieff! Oh! [*The two girls move towards each other and put their arms round each other's waists as if for protection.*]

CEC. Are you called Algernon?

ALG. I cannot deny it.

CEC. Oh!

GWEN. Is your name really John?

JACK. [*Standing rather proudly.*] I could deny it if I liked. I could deny anything if I liked. But my name certainly is John. It has been John for years.

CEC. [*To Gwendolen.*] A gross deception has been practiced on both of us.

GWEN. My poor wounded Cecily!

CEC. My sweet wronged Gwendolen!

GWEN. [*Slowly and seriously.*] You will call me sister, will you not? [*They embrace. Jack and Algernon groan and walk up and down.*]

CEC. [*Rather brightly.*] There is just one question I would like to be allowed to ask my guardian.

GWEN. An admirable idea! Mr. Worthing, there is just one question I would like to be permitted to put to you. Where is your brother Ernest? We are both engaged to be married to your brother Ernest, so it is a matter of some importance to us to know where your brother Ernest is at present.

JACK. [*Slowly and hesitatingly.*] Gwendolen–Cecily–it is very painful for me to be forced to speak the truth. It is the first time in my life that I have ever been reduced to such a painful position, and I am really quite inexperienced in doing anything of the kind. However I will tell you quite frankly that I have no brother Ernest. I have no brother at all. I never had a brother in my life, and I certainly have not the smallest intention of ever having one in the future.

CEC. [*Surprised.*] No brother at all?

JACK. [*Cheerily.*] None!

GWEN. [*Severely.*]Had you never a brother of any kind?

JACK. [*Pleasantly.*] Never. Not even of any kind.

GWEN. I am afraid it is quite clear, Cecily, that neither of us is engaged to be married to anyone.

CEC. It is not a very pleasant position for a young girl suddenly to find herself in. Is it?

GWEN. Let us go into the house. They will hardly venture to come after us there.

CEC. No, men are so cowardly, aren't they?

[*They retire into the house with scornful looks.*]

JACK. This ghastly state of things is what you call Bunburying, I suppose?

ALG. Yes, and a perfectly wonderful Bunbury it is. The most wonderful Bunbury I have ever had in my life.

JACK. Well, you've no right whatsoever to Bunbury here.

ALG. That is absurd. One has a right to Bunbury anywhere one chooses. Every serious Bunburyist knows that.

JACK. Serious Bunburyist! Good Heavens!

ALG. Well, one must be serious about something, if one wants to have any amusement in life. I happen to be serious about Bunburying. What on earth you are serious about I haven't got the remotest idea. About everything, I should fancy. You have such an absolutely trivial nature.

JACK. Well, the only small satisfaction I have in the whole of this wretched business is that your friend Bunbury is quite exploded. You won't be able to run down to the country quite so often as you used to do, dear Algy. And a very good thing too.

ALG. Your brother is a little off colour, isn't he, dear Jack? You won't be able to disappear to London quite so frequently as your wicked custom was. And not a bad thing either.

JACK. As for your conduct towards Miss Cardew, I must say that your taking in a sweet, simple, innocent girl like that was quite inexcusable. To say nothing of the fact that she is my ward.

ALG. I can see no possible defence at all for your deceiving a brilliant, clever, thoroughly experienced young lady like Miss Fairfax. To say nothing of the fact that she is my cousin.

JACK. I wanted to be engaged to Gwendolen, that is all. I love her.

ALG. Well, I simply wanted to be engaged to Cecily. I adore her.

JACK. There is certainly no chance of your marrying Miss Cardew.

ALG. I don't think there is much likelihood, Jack, of you and Miss Fairfax being united.

JACK. Well, that is no business of yours.

ALG. If it was my business, I wouldn't talk about it. [*Begins to eat muffins.*] It is very vulgar to talk about one's business. Only people like stockbrokers do that, and then merely at dinner-parties.

JACK. How you can sit there, calmly eating muffins when we are in this horrible trouble, I can't make out. You seem to me to be perfectly heartless.

ALG. Well, I can't eat muffins in an agitated manner. The butter would probably get on my cuffs. One should always eat muffins quite calmly. It is the only way to eat them.

JACK. I say it's perfectly heartless your eating muffins at all, under the circumstances.

ALG. When I am in trouble, eating is the only thing that consoles me. Indeed, when I am in really great trouble, as anyone who knows me intimately will tell you, I refuse everything except food and drink. At the present moment I am eating muffins because I am unhappy. Besides, I am particularly fond of muffins. [*Rising.*]

JACK. [*Rising.*] Well, that is no reason why you should eat them all in that greedy way. [*Takes muffins from Algernon.*]

ALG. [*Offering tea-cake.*] I wish you would have tea-cake instead. I don't like tea-cake.

JACK. Good Heavens! I suppose a man may eat his own muffins in his own garden.

ALG. But you have just said it was perfectly heartless to eat muffins.

JACK. I said it was perfectly heartless of you, under the circumstances. That is a very different thing.

ALG. That may be. But the muffins are the same. [*He seizes the muffin-dish from Jack.*]

JACK. Algy, I wish to goodness you would go.

ALG. You can't possibly ask me to go without having some dinner. It's absurd. I never go without my dinner. No one ever does, except vegetarians and people like that. Besides I have just made arrangements with Dr. Chasuble to be christened at a quarter to six under the name of Ernest.

JACK. My dear fellow, the sooner you give up that nonsense the better. I made arrangements this morning with Dr. Chasuble to be christened myself at 5:30, and I naturally will take the name of Ernest. Gwendolen would wish it. We can't both be christened Ernest. It's absurd. Besides, I have a perfect right to be christened if I like. There is no evidence at all that I ever have been christened by anybody. I should think it extremely probable I never was, and so does Dr. Chasuble. It is entirely different in your case. You have been christened already.

ALG. Yes, but I have not been christened for years.

JACK. Yes, but you have been christened. That is the important thing.

ALG. Quite so. So I know my constitution can stand it. If you are not quite sure about your ever having been christened, I must say I think it rather dangerous your venturing on it now. It might make you very unwell. You can hardly have forgotten that someone very closely connected with you was very nearly carried off this week in Paris by a severe chill.

JACK. Yes, but you said yourself that a severe chill was not hereditary.

ALG. It usen't to be, I know—but I daresay it is now. Science is always making wonderful improvements in things.

JACK. [*Picking up the muffin-dish.*] Oh, that is nonsense; you are always talking nonsense.

ALG. Jack, you are at the muffins again. I wish you wouldn't. There are only two left. [*Takes them.*] I told you I was particularly fond of muffins.

JACK. But I hate tea-cake.

ALG. Why on earth then do you allow tea-cake to be served up for your guests? What ideas you have of hospitality!

JACK. Algernon! I have already told you to go. I don't want you here. Why don't you go?

ALG. I haven't quite finished my tea yet! and there is still one muffin left [*Jack groans, and sinks into a chair. Algernon still continues eating.*]

ACT-DROP.

THIRD ACT

SCENE—*Morning-room at the Manor House.*

[*Gwendolen and Cecily are at the window, looking out into the garden.*]

GWEN. The fact that they did not follow us at once into the house, as anyone else would have done, seems to me to show that they have some sense of shame left.

CEC. They have been eating muffins. That looks like repentance.

GWEN. [*After a pause.*] They don't seem to notice us at all. Couldn't you cough?

CEC. But I haven't got a cough.

GWEN. They're looking at us. What effrontery!

CEC. They're approaching. That's very forward of them.

GWEN. Let us preserve a dignified silence.

CEC. Certainly. It's the only thing to do now.

[*Enter Jack followed by Algernon. They whistle some dreadful popular air from a British Opera.*]

GWEN. This dignified silence seems to produce an unpleasant effect.

CEC. A most distasteful one.

GWEN. But we will not be the first to speak.

CEC. Certainly not.

GWEN. Mr. Worthing, I have something very particular to ask you. Much depends on your reply.

CEC. Gwendolen, your common sense is invaluable. Mr. Moncrieff, kindly answer me the following question. Why did you pretend to be my guardian's brother?

ALG. In order that I might have an opportunity of meeting you.

CEC. [*To Gwendolen.*] That certainly seems a satisfactory explanation, does it not?

GWEN. Yes, dear, if you can believe him.

CEC. I don't. But that does not affect the wonderful beauty of his answer.

GWEN. True. In matters of grave importance, style, not sincerity is the vital thing. Mr. Worthing, what explanation can you offer to me for pretending to have a brother? Was it in order that you might have an opportunity of coming up to town to see me as often as possible?

JACK. Can you doubt it, Miss Fairfax?

GWEN. I have the gravest doubts upon the subject. But I intend to crush them. This is not the moment for German scepticism. [*Moving to Cecily.*] Their explanations appear to be quite satisfactory, especially Mr. Worthing's. That seems to me to have the stamp of truth upon it.

CEC. I am more than content with what Mr. Moncrieff said. His voice alone inspires one with absolute credulity.

GWEN. Then you think we should forgive them?

CEC. Yes. I mean no.

GWEN. True! I had forgotten. There are principles at stake that one cannot surrender. Which of us should tell them? The task is not a pleasant one.

CEC. Could we not both speak at the same time?

GWEN. An excellent idea! I nearly always speak at the same time as other people. Will you take the time from me?

CEC. Certainly. [*Gwendolen beats time with uplifted finger.*]

GWEN. AND CEC. [*Speaking together.*] Your Christian names are still an insuperable barrier. That is all!

JACK AND ALG. [*Speaking together.*] Our Christian names! Is that all? But we are going to be christened this afternoon.

GWEN. [*To Jack.*] For my sake you are prepared to do this terrible thing?

JACK. I am.

CEC. [*To Algernon.*] To please me you are ready to face this fearful ordeal?

ALG. I am!

GWEN. How absurd to talk of the equality of the sexes! Where questions of self-sacrifice are concerned, men are infinitely beyond us.

JACK. We are. [*Clasps hands with Algernon.*]

CEC. They have moments of physical courage of which we women know absolutely nothing.

GWEN. [*To Jack.*] Darling!

ALG. [*To Cecily.*] Darling! [*They fall into each other's arms.*]

[*Enter Merriman. When he enters he coughs loudly, seeing the situation.*]

MERR. Ahem! Ahem! Lady Bracknell!

JACK. Good Heavens!

[*Enter Lady Bracknell. The couples separate in alarm. Exit Merriman.*]

LADY BRA. Gwendolen! What does this mean?

GWEN. Merely that I am engaged to be married to Mr. Worthing, mamma.

LADY BRA. Come here. Sit down. Sit down immediately. Hesitation of any kind is a sign of mental decay in the young, of physical weakness in the old. [*Turns to Jack.*] Apprised, sir, of my daughter's sudden flight by her trusty maid, whose confidence I purchased by means of a small coin, I followed her at once by a luggage train. Her unhappy father is, I am glad to say, under the impression that she is attending a more than usually lengthy lecture by the University Extension Scheme on the Influence of a permanent income on Thought. I do not propose to undeceive him. Indeed I have never undeceived him on any question. I would consider it wrong. But of course, you will clearly understand that all communication between yourself and my daughter must cease immediately from this moment. On this point, as indeed on all points, I am firm.

JACK. I am engaged to be married to Gwendolen, Lady Bracknell!

LADY BRA. You are nothing of the kind, so. And now, as regards Algernon! . . . Algernon!

ALG. Yes, Aunt Augusta.

LADY BRA. May I ask if it is in this house that your invalid friend Mr. Bunbury resides?

ALG. [*Stammering.*] *Oh! No!* Bunbury doesn't live here. Bunbury is somewhere else at present. In fact, Bunbury is dead.

LADY BRA. Dead! When did Mr. Bunbury die? His death must have been extremely sudden.

ALG. [*Airily.*] Oh! I killed Bunbury this afternoon. I mean poor Bunbury died this afternoon.

LADY BRA. What did he die of?

ALG. Bunbury? Oh, he was quite exploded.

LADY BRA. Exploded! Was he the victim of a revolutionary outrage? I was not aware that Mr. Bunbury was interested in social legislation. If so, he is well punished for his morbidity.

ALG. My dear Aunt Augusta, I mean he was found out! The doctors found out that Bunbury could not live, that is what I mean—so Bunbury died.

LADY BRA. He seems to have had great confidence in the opinion of his physicians. I am glad, however, that he made up his mind at the last to some definite course of action, and acted under proper medical advice. And now that we have finally got rid of this Mr. Bunbury, may I ask, Mr. Worthing, who is that young person whose hand my nephew Algernon is now holding in what seems to me a peculiarly unnecessary manner?

JACK. That lady is Miss Cecily Cardew, my ward. [*Lady Bracknell bows coldly to Cecily.*]

ALG. I am engaged to be married to Cecily, Aunt Augusta.

LADY BRA. I beg your pardon?

CEC. Mr. Moncrieff and I are engaged to be married, Lady Bracknell.

LADY BRA. [*With a shiver, crossing to the sofa and sitting down.*] I do not know whether there is anything peculiarly exciting in the air of this particular part of Hertfordshire, but the number of engagements that go on seems to me considerably above the proper average that statistics have laid down for our guidance. I think some preliminary enquiry on my part would not be out of place. Mr. Worthing, is Miss Cardew at all connected with any of the larger railway stations in London? I merely desire information. Until yesterday I had no idea that there were any families or persons whose origin was a Terminus. [*Jack looks perfectly furious, but restrains himself.*]

JACK. [*In a clear, cold voice.*] Miss Cardew is the granddaughter of the late Mr. Thomas Cardew of 149, Belgrave Square, S.W.; Gervase Park, Dorking, Surrey; and the Sporran, Fifeshire, N.B.

LADY BRA. That sounds not unsatisfactory. Three addresses always inspire confidence, even in tradesmen. But what proof have I of their authenticity.

JACK. I have carefully preserved the Court Guides of the period. They are open to your inspection, Lady Bracknell.

LADY BRA. [*Grimly.*] I have known strange errors in that publication.

JACK. Miss Cardew's family solicitors are Messrs. Markby, Markby, and Markby.

LADY BRA. Markby, Markby, and Markby? A firm of the very highest position in their profession. Indeed I am told that one of the Mr. Markbys is occasionally to be seen at dinner parties. So far I am satisfied.

JACK. [*Very irritably.*] How extremely kind of you, Lady Bracknell! I have also in my possession, you will be pleased to hear, certificates of Miss Cardew's birth, baptism, whooping cough, registration, vaccination, confirmation, and the measles; both the German and the English variety.

LADY BRA. Ah! A life crowded with incident, I see; though perhaps somewhat too exciting for a young girl. I am not myself in favour of premature experiences. [*Rises, looks at her watch.*] Gwendolen! the time approaches for our departure. We have not a moment to lose. As a matter of form, Mr. Worthing, I had better ask you if Miss Cardew has any little fortune.

JACK. Oh! about a hundred and thirty thousand pounds in the Funds. That is all. Good-bye, Lady Bracknell. So pleased to have seen you.

LADY BRA. [*Sitting down again.*] A moment, Mr. Worthing. A hundred and thirty thousand pounds! And in the Funds! Miss Cardew seems to me a most attractive young lady, now that I look at her. Few girls of the present day have any really solid qualities, any of the qualities that last, and improve with time. We live, I regret to say, in an age of surfaces. [*To Cecily.*] Come over here, dear. [*Cecily goes across.*] Pretty child! your dress is sadly simple, and your hair seems almost as Nature might have left it. But we can soon alter all that. A thoroughly experienced French maid produces a really marvellous result in a very brief space of time. I remember recommending one to young Lady Lancing, and after three months her own husband did not know her.

JACK. [*Aside.*] And after six months nobody knew her.

LADY BRA. [*Glares at Jack for a few moments. Then bends, with a practised smile, to Cecily.*] Kindly turn round, sweet child. [*Cecily turns completely round.*] No, the side view is what I want. [*Cecily presents her profile.*] Yes, quite as I expected. There are distinct social possibilities in your profile. The two weak points in our age are its want of principle and its want of profile. The chin a little higher, dear. Style largely depends on the way the chin is worn. They are worn very high, just at present. Algernon!

ALG. Yes, Aunt Augusta!

LADY BRA. There are distinct social possibilities in Miss Cardew's profile.

ALG. Cecily is the sweetest, dearest, prettiest girl in the whole world. And I don't care twopence about social possibilities.

LADY BRA. Never speak disrespectfully of Society, Algernon. Only people who can't get into it do that. [*To Cecily.*] Dear child, of course you know that Algernon has nothing but his debts to depend upon. But I do not approve of mercenary marriages. When I married Lord Bracknell I had no fortune of any kind. But I never dreamed for a moment of allowing that to stand in my way. Well, I suppose I must give my consent.

ALG. Thank you, Aunt Augusta.

LADY BRA. Cecily, you may kiss me!

CEC. [*Kisses her.*] Thank you, Lady Bracknell.

LADY BRA. You may also address me as Aunt Augusta for the future.

CEC. Thank you, Aunt Augusta.

LADY BRA. The marriage, I think, had better take place quite soon.

ALG. Thank you, Aunt Augusta.

CEC. Thank you, Aunt Augusta.

LADY BRA. To speak frankly, I am not in favour of long engagements. They give people the opportunity of finding out each other's character before marriage, which I think is never advisable.

JACK. I beg your pardon for interrupting you, Lady Bracknell, but this engagement is quite out of the question. I am Miss Cardew's guardian, and she cannot marry without my consent until she comes of age. That consent I absolutely decline to give.

LADY BRA. Upon what grounds, may I ask? Algernon is an extremely, I may almost say an ostentatiously, eligible young man. He has nothing, but he looks everything. What more can one desire?

JACK. It pains me very much to have to speak frankly to you, Lady Bracknell, about your nephew, but the fact is that I do not approve at all of his moral character. I suspect him of being untruthful. [*Algernon and Cecily look at him in indignant amazement.*]

LADY BRA. Untruthful! My nephew Algernon? Impossible! He is an Oxonian.

JACK. I fear there can be no possible doubt about the matter. This afternoon, during my temporary absence in London on an important question of romance, he obtained admission to my house by means of the false pretense of being my brother. Under an assumed name he drank, I've just been informed by my butler, an entire pint bottle of my Perrier-Jouet, Brut, '89; a wine I was specially reserving for myself. Continuing his disgraceful deception, he succeeded in the course of the afternoon in alienating the affections of my only ward. He subsequently stayed to tea, and devoured every single muffin. And what makes his conduct all the more heartless is, that he was perfectly well aware from the first that I have no brother, that I never had a brother, and that I don't intend to have a brother, not even of any kind. I distinctly told him so myself yesterday afternoon.

LADY BRA. Ahem! Mr. Worthing, after careful consideration I have decided entirely to overlook my nephew's conduct to you.

JACK. That is very generous of you, Lady Bracknell. My own decision, however, is unalterable. I decline to give my consent.

LADY BRA. [*To Cecily.*] Come here, sweet child. [*Cecily goes over.*] How old are you, dear?

CEC. Well, I am really only eighteen, but I always admit to twenty when I go to evening parties.

LADY BRA. You are perfectly right in making some slight alteration. Indeed, no woman should ever be quite accurate about her age. It looks so calculating. . . . [*In a meditative manner.*] Eighteen, but admitting to twenty at evening parties. Well, it will not be very long before you are of age and free from the restraints of tutelage. So I don't think your guardian's consent is, after all, a matter of any importance.

JACK. Pray excuse me, Lady Bracknell, for interrupting you again, but it is only fair to tell you that according to the terms of her grandfather's will Miss Cardew does not come legally of age till she is thirty-five.

LADY BRA. That does not seem to me to be a grave objection. Thirty-five is a very attractive age. London society is full of women of the very highest birth who have, of their own free choice, remained thirty-five for years. Lady Dumbleton is an instance in point. To my own knowledge she has been thirty-five ever since she arrived at the age of forty, which was many years ago now. I see no reason why our dear Cecily should not be even still more attractive at the age you mention than she is at present. There will be a large accumulation of property.

CEC. Algy, could you wait for me till I was thirty-five?

ALG. Of course I could, Cecily. You know I could.

CEC. Yes, I felt it instinctively, but I couldn't wait all that time. I hate waiting even five minutes for anybody. It always makes me rather cross. I am not punctual myself, I know, but I do like punctuality in others, and waiting, even to be married, is quite out of the question.

ALG. Then what is to be done, Cecily?

CEC. I don't know, Mr. Moncrieff.

LADY BRA. My dear Mr. Worthing, as Miss Cardew states positively that she cannot wait till she is thirty-five–a remark which I am bound to say seems to me to show a somewhat impatient nature–I would beg of you to reconsider your decision.

JACK. But, my dear Lady Bracknell, the matter is entirely in your own hands. The moment you consent to my marriage with Gwendolen, I will most gladly allow your nephew to form an alliance with my ward.

LADY BRA. [*Rising and drawing herself up.*] You must be quite aware that what you propose is out of the question.

JACK. Then a passionate celibacy is all that any of us can look forward to.

LADY BRA. That is not the destiny I propose for Gwendolen. Algernon, of course, can choose for himself. [*Pulls out her watch.*] Come, dear; [*Gwendolen rises.*] we have already missed five, if not six, trains. To miss any more might expose us to comment on the platform.

[*Enter Dr. Chasuble.*]

CHAS. Everything is quite ready for the christenings.

LADY BRA. The christenings, sir! Is not that somewhat premature?

CHAS. [*Looking rather puzzled, and pointing to Jack and Algernon.*] Both these gentlemen have expressed a desire for immediate baptism.

LADY BRA. At their age? The idea is grotesque and irreligious! Algernon, I forbid you to be baptised. I will not hear of such excesses. Lord Bracknell would be highly displeased if he learned that that was the way in which you wasted your time and money.

CHAS. Am I to understand then that there are to be no christenings at all this afternoon?

JACK. I don't think that, as things are now, it would be of much practical value to either of us, Dr. Chasuble.

CHAS. I am grieved to hear such sentiments from you, Mr. Worthing. They savour of the heretical views of the Anabaptists, views that I have completely refuted in four of my unpublished sermons. However, as your present mood seems to be one peculiarly secular, I will return to the church at once. Indeed,

I have just been informed by the pew-opener that for the last hour and a half Miss Prism has been waiting for me in the vestry.

LADY BRA. [*Starting.*] Miss Prism! Did I hear you mention a Miss Prism?

CHAS. Yes, Lady Bracknell. I am on my way to join her.

LADY BRA. Pray, allow me to detain you for a moment. This matter may prove to be one of vital importance to Lord Bracknell and myself. Is this Miss Prism a female of repellent aspect, remotely connected with education?

CHAS. [*Somewhat indignantly.*] She is the most cultivated of ladies, and the very picture of respectability.

LADY BRA. It is obviously the same person. May I ask what position she holds in your household?

CHAS. [*Severely.*] I am a celibate, madam.

JACK. [*Interposing.*] Miss Prism, Lady Bracknell, has been for the last three years Miss Cardew's esteemed governess and valued companion.

LADY BRA. In spite of what I hear of her, I must see her at once. Let her be sent for.

CHAS. [*Looking off.*] She approaches; she is nigh.

[*Enter Miss Prism hurriedly.*]

MISS PRI. I was told you expected me in the vestry, dear Canon. I have been waiting for you there for an hour and three quarters. [*Catches sight of Lady Bracknell who has fixed her with a stony glare. Miss Prism grows pale and quails. She looks anxiously round as if desirous to escape.*]

LADY BRA. [*In a severe, judicial voice.*] Prism! [*Miss Prism bows her head in shame.*] Come here, Prism! [*Miss Prism approaches in a humble manner.*] Prism! Where is that baby? [*General consternation. The Canon starts back in horror. Algernon and Jack pretend to be anxious to shield Cecily and Gwendolen from hearing the details of a terrible public scandal.*] Twenty-eight years ago, Prism, you left Lord Bracknell's house, Number 104, Upper Grosvenor Street, in charge of a perambulator that contained a baby, of the male sex. You never returned. A few weeks later, through the elaborate investigations of the Metropolitan police, the perambulator was discovered at midnight, standing by itself in a remote corner of Bayswater. It contained the manuscript of a three-volume novel of more than usually revolting sentimentality. [*Miss Prism starts in involuntary indignation.*] But the baby was not there! [*Everyone looks at Miss Prism.*] Prism! Where is that baby? [*A pause.*]

MISS PRI. Lady Bracknell, I admit with shame that I do not know. I only wish I did. The plain facts of the case are these. On the morning of the day you mention, a day that is forever branded on my memory, I prepared as usual to take the baby out in its perambulator. I had also with me a somewhat old, but capacious hand-bag, in which I had intended to place the manuscript of a work of fiction that I had written during my few unoccupied hours. In a moment of mental abstraction, for which I can never forgive myself, I deposited the manuscript in the bassinette, and placed the baby in the hand-bag.

JACK. [*Who has been listening attentively.*] But where did you deposit the hand-bag?

MISS PRI. Do not ask me, Mr. Worthing.

JACK. Miss Prism, this is a matter of no small importance to me. I insist on knowing where you deposited the hand-bag that contained that infant.

MISS PRI. I left it in the cloak room of one of the larger railway stations in London.

JACK. What railway station?

MISS PRI. [*Quite crushed.*] Victoria. The Brighton line. [*Sinks into a chair.*]

JACK. I must retire to my room for a moment. Gwendolen, wait for me here.

GWEN. If you are not too long, I will wait here for you all my life.

[*Exit Jack in great excitement.*]

CHAS. What do you think this means, Lady Bracknell?

LADY BRA. I dare not even suspect, Dr. Chasuble. I need hardly tell you that in families of high position strange coincidences are not supposed to occur. They are hardly considered the thing.

[*Noises heard overhead as if someone was throwing trunks about. Everyone looks up.*]

CEC. Uncle Jack seems strangely agitated.

CHAS. Your guardian has a very emotional nature.

LADY BRA. This noise is extremely unpleasant. It sounds as if he was having an argument. I dislike arguments of any kind. They are always vulgar, and often convincing.

CHAS. [*Looking up.*] It has stopped now. [*The noise is redoubled.*]

LADY BRA. I wish he would arrive at some conclusion.

GWEN. This suspense is terrible. I hope it will last.

[*Enter Jack with a hand-bag of black leather in his hand.*]

JACK. [*Rushing over to Miss Prism.*] Is this the hand-bag, Miss Prism? Examine it carefully before you speak. The happiness of more than one life depends on your answer.

MISS PRI. [*Calmly.*] It seems to be mine. Yes, here is the injury it received through the upsetting of a Gower Street omnibus in younger and happier days. Here is the stain on the lining caused by the explosion of a temperance beverage, an incident that occurred at Leamington. And here, on the lock, are my initials. I had forgotten that in an extravagant mood I had had them placed there. The bag is undoubtedly mine. I am delighted to have it so unexpectedly restored to me. It has been a great inconvenience being without it all these years.

JACK. [*In a pathetic voice.*] Miss Prism. more is restored to you than this hand-bag. I was the baby you placed in it.

MISS PRI. [*Amazed.*] You?

JACK. [*Embracing her.*] Yes . . . Mother!

MISS PRI. [*Recoiling in indignant astonishment.*] Mr. Worthing! I am unmarried!

JACK. Unmarried! I do not deny that is a serious blow. But after all, who has a right to cast a stone against one who has suffered? Cannot repentance wipe out an act of folly? Why should there be one law for men, and another for women? Mother, I forgive you. [*Tries to embrace her again.*]

MISS PRI. [*Still more indignant.*] Mr. Worthing, there is some error. [*Point-*

ing to Lady Bracknell.] There is the lady who can tell you who you really are.

JACK. [*After a pause.*] Lady Bracknell, I hate to seem inquisitive, but would you kindly inform me who I am?

LADY BRA. I am afraid that the news I have to give you will not altogether please you. You are the son of my poor sister, Mrs. Moncrieff, and consequently Algernon's elder brother.

JACK. Algy's elder brother! Then I have a brother after all. I knew I had a brother! I always said I had a brother! Cecily, how could you have ever doubted that I had a brother? [*Seizes hold of Algernon.*] Dr. Chasuble, my unfortunate brother. Miss Prism, my unfortunate brother. Gwendolen, my unfortunate brother. Algy, you young scoundrel, you will have to treat me with more respect in the future. You have never behaved to me like a brother in all your life.

ALG. Well, not till today, old boy, I admit. I did my best, however, though I was out of practise. [*Shakes hands.*]

GWEN. [*To Jack.*] My own! But what own are you? What is your Christian name, now that you have become someone else?

JACK. Good Heavens! . . . I had quite forgotten that point. Your decision on the subject of my name is irrevocable, I suppose?

GWEN. I never change, except in my affections.

CEC. What a noble nature you have, Gwendolen!

JACK. Then the question had better be cleared up at once. Aunt Augusta, a moment. At the time when Miss Prism left me in the hand-bag, had I been christened already?

LADY BRA. Every luxury that money could buy, including christening, had been lavished on you by your fond and doting parents.

JACK. Then I was christened! That is settled. Now, what name was I given? Let me know the worst.

LADY BRA. Being the eldest son you were naturally christened after your father.

JACK. [*Irritably.*] Yes, but what was my father's Christian name?

LADY BRA. [*Meditatively.*] I cannot at the present moment recall what the General's Christian name was. But I have no doubt he had one. He was eccentric, I admit. But only in later years. And that was the result of the Indian climate, and marriage, and indigestion, and other things of that kind.

JACK. Algy! Can't you recollect what our father's Christian name was?

ALG. My dear boy, we were never even on speaking terms. He died before I was a year old.

JACK. His name would appear in the Army Lists of the period, I suppose, Aunt Augusta?

LADY BRA. The General was essentially a man of peace, except in his domestic life. But I have no doubt his name would appear in any military directory.

JACK. The Army Lists of the last forty years are here. These delightful records should have been my constant study. [*Rushes to bookcase and tears the books out.*] M. Generals . . . Mallam, Maxbohm, Magley, what ghastly names they have—Markby, Migsby, Mobbs, Moncrieff! Lieutenant 1840, Captain, Lieutenant-Colonel, Colonel, General 1869, Christian names, Ernest, John. [*Puts book very quietly down and speaks quite calmly.*] I always told you, Gwendolen, my name was Ernest, didn't I? Well, it is Ernest after all. I mean it naturally is Ernest.

LADY BRA. Yes, I remember now that the General was called Ernest. I knew I had some particular reason for disliking the name.

GWEN. Ernest! My own Ernest! I felt from the first that you could have no other name!

JACK. Gwendolen, it is a terrible thing for a man to find out suddenly that all his life he has been speaking nothing but the truth. Can you forgive me?

GWEN. I can. For I feel that you are sure to change.

JACK. My own one!

CHAS. [*To Miss Prism.*] Laetitia! [*Embraces her.*]

MISS PRI. [*Enthusiastically.*] Frederick! At last!

ALG. *Cecily!* [*Embraces her.*] At last!

JACK. Gwendolen! [*Embraces her.*] At last!

LADY BRA. My nephew, you seem to be displaying signs of triviality.

JACK. On the contrary, Aunt Augusta, I've now realized for the first time in my life the vital Importance of Being Ernest.

CURTAIN.

ESSAYS AND FAIRY TALES

ESSAYS AND FAIRY TALES

PEN, PENCIL, AND POISON

A STUDY IN GREEN

It has constantly been made a subject of reproach against artists and men of letters that they are lacking in wholeness and completeness of nature. As a rule, this must necessarily be so. That very concentration of vision and intensity of purpose which is the characteristic of the artistic temperament, is in itself a mode of limitation. To those who are preoccupied with the beauty of form, nothing else seems of much importance. Yet there are many exceptions to this rule. Rubens served as ambassador, and Goethe as state councillor, and Milton as Latin secretary to Cromwell. Sophocles held civic office in his own city; the humourists, essayists, and novelists of modern America seem to desire nothing better than to become the diplomatic representatives of their country; and Charles Lamb's friend, Thomas Griffiths Wainewright, the subject of this brief memoir, though of an extremely artistic temperament, followed many masters other than art, being not merely a poet and a painter, an art critic, an antiquarian, and a writer of prose, an amateur of beautiful things, and a dilettante of things delightful, but also a forger of no mean or ordinary capabilities, and as a subtle and secret poisoner almost without a rival in this or any age.

This remarkable man, so powerful with "pen, pencil, and poison," as a great poet of our own day has finely said of him, was born at Chiswick, in 1794. His father was the son of a distinguished solicitor of Gray's Inn and Hatton Garden. His mother was the daughter of the celebrated Dr. Griffiths, the editor and founder of the *Monthly Review*, the partner in another literary speculation of Thomas Davies, that famous bookseller of whom Johnson said that he was not a bookseller, but "a gentleman who dealt in books," the friend of Goldsmith and Wedgwood, and one of the most well-known men of his day. Mrs. Wainewright died, in giving him birth, at the early age of twenty-one, and an obituary notice in the *Gentleman's Magazine* tells us of her "amiable disposition and numerous accomplishments," and adds, somewhat quaintly, that "she is supposed to have understood the writings of Mr. Locke as well as perhaps any person of either sex now living." His father did not long survive his young wife, and the little child seems to have been brought up by his grandfather, and, on the death of the latter, in 1803, by his uncle, George Edward Griffiths, whom he subsequently poisoned. His boyhood was passed at Linden House, Turnham Green, one of those many fine Georgian mansions that have, unfortunately, disappeared before the inroads of the suburban builder, and to its lovely gardens and well timbered park he owed that simple and impassioned love of nature which never left him all through his life, and which made him so peculiarly susceptible to the spiritual influence of Wordsworth's poetry.

He went to school at Charles Burney's academy at Hammersmith. Mr. Burney was the son of the historian of music, and the near kinsman of the artistic lad who was destined to turn out his most remarkable pupil. He seems to have been a man of a good deal of culture, and in after years Mr. Wainewright often spoke of him with much affection as a philosopher, an archæologist, and an admirable teacher, who, while he valued the intellectual side of education, did not forget the importance of early moral training. It was under Mr. Burney that he first developed his talent as an artist, and Mr. Hazlitt tells us that a drawing-book which he used at school is still extant, and displays great talent and natural feeling. Indeed, painting was the first art that fascinated him. It was not till much later that he sought to find expression by pen or poison.

Before this, however, he seems to have been carried away by boyish dreams of the romance and chivalry of a soldier's life, and to have become a young guardsman. But the reckless, dissipated life of his companions failed to satisfy the refined, artistic temperament of one who was made for other things. In a short time he wearied of the service. "Art," he tells us, in words that still move by their ardent sincerity and strange fervour, "Art touched her renegade; by her pure and high influences the noisome mists were purged; my feelings, parched hot and tarnished, were renovated with cool, fresh bloom, simple, beautiful to the simple-hearted." But Art was not the only cause of the change. "The writings of Wordsworth," he goes on to say, "did much towards calming the confusing whirl necessarily incident to sudden mutations. I wept over them tears of happiness and gratitude." He accordingly left the army, with its rough barrack life and coarse mess-room tittle-tattle, and returned to Linden House, full of this new-born enthusiasm for culture. A severe illness, in which, to use his own words, he was "broken like a vessel of clay," prostrated him for a time. His delicately strung organisation, however indifferent it might have been to inflicting pain on others, was itself most keenly sensitive to pain. He shrank from suffering as a thing that mars and maims human life, and seems to have wandered through that terrible valley of melancholia from which so many great, perhaps greater, spirits have never emerged. But he was young—only twenty-five years of age—and he soon passed out of the "dead black waters," as he called them, into the larger air of humanistic culture. As he was recovering from the illness that had led him almost to the gates of death, he conceived the idea of taking up literature as an art. "I said with John Woodvill," he cries, "it were a life of gods to dwell in such an element," to see, and hear, and write brave things:

> "These high and gusty relishes of life
> Have no allayings of mortality."

It is impossible not to feel that in this passage we have the utterance of a man who had a true passion for letters. "To see, and hear, and write brave things," this was his aim.

Scott, the editor of the *London Magazine*, struck by the young man's genius, or under the influence of the strange fascination that he exercised on every one who knew him, invited him to write a series of articles on artistic subjects, and under a series of fanciful pseudonyms he began to contribute to the literature of his day. *Janus Weathercock*, *Egomet Bonmot*, and *Van Vinkbooms*, were some of the grotesque masks under which he chose to hide his seriousness, or to reveal his levity. A mask tells us more than a face. These disguises intensified his personality. In an incredibly short time he seems to have made his mark. Charles Lamb speaks of "kind, light-hearted Wainewright," whose prose is "capital." We hear of him entertaining Macready, John Forster, Maginn, Talfourd, Sir Wentworth Dilke, the poet John Clare, and others, at a *petit-dîner*. Like Disraeli, he determined to startle the town as a dandy, and his beautiful rings, his antique cameo breastpin, and his pale lemon-coloured kid gloves, were well known, and indeed were regarded by Hazlitt as being the signs of a new manner in literature: while his rich, curly hair, fine eyes, and exquisite white hands, gave him the dangerous and delightful distinction of being different from others. There was something in him of Balzac's Lucien de Rubempré. At times he reminds us of Julien Sorel. De Quincey saw him once. It was at a dinner at Charles Lamb's. "Amongst the company, all literary men, sat a murderer," he tells us, and he goes on to describe how on that day he had been ill, and had hated the face of man and woman, and yet found himself looking with intellectual interest across the table at the young writer beneath whose affectations of manner there seemed to him to lie so much unaffected sensibility, and speculates on "what sudden growth of another interest" would have changed his mood, had he known of what terrible sin the guest to whom Lamb paid so much attention was even then guilty.

His life-work falls naturally under the three heads suggested by Mr. Swinburne, and it may be partly admitted that, if we set aside his achievements in the sphere of poison, what he has actually left to us hardly justifies his reputation.

But then it is only the Philistine who seeks to estimate a personality by the vulgar test of production. This young dandy sought to be somebody, rather than to do something. He recognised that Life itself is an art, and has its modes of style no less than the arts that seek to express it. Nor is his work without interest. We hear of William Blake stopping in the Royal Academy before one of his pictures and pronouncing it to be "very fine." His essays are prefiguring of much that has since been realised. He seems to have anticipated some of those accidents of modern culture that are regarded by many as true essentials. He writes about La Gioconda, and early French poets, and the Italian Renaissance. He loves Greek gems, and Persian carpets, and Elizabethan translations of *Cupid and Psyche*, and the *Hypnerotomachia*, and book-bindings, and early editions, and wide-margined proofs. He is keenly sensitive to the value of beautiful surroundings, and never wearies of describing to us the rooms in which he lived, or would have liked to live. He had that curious love of green which, in individuals, is always the sign of a subtle artistic temperament, and in nations is said to denote a laxity, if not a decadence of morals. Like Baudelaire, he was extremely fond of cats, and with Gautier, he was fascinated by that "sweet marble monster" of both sexes that we can still see at Florence and in the Louvre.

There is, of course, much in his descriptions, and his suggestions for decoration, that shows that he did not entirely free himself from the false taste of his time. But it is clear that he was one of the first to recognise what is, indeed, the very keynote of æsthetic eclecticism, I mean the true harmony of all really beautiful things, irrespective of age or place, of school or manner. He saw that in decorating a room, which is to be, not a room for show, but a room to live in, we should never aim at any archæological reconstruction of the past, nor burden ourselves with any fanciful necessity for historical accuracy. In this artistic perception he was perfectly right. All beautiful things belong to the same age.

And so, in his own library, as he describes it, we find the delicate fictile vase of the Greek, with its exquisitely painted figures and the faint KALOS (Gr.) finely traced upon its side, and behind it hangs an engraving of the "Delphic Sibyl" of Michael Angelo, or of the "Pastoral" of Giorgione. Here is a bit of Florentine majolica, and here a rude lamp from some old Roman tomb. On the table lies a book of Hours, "cased in a cover of solid silver gilt, wrought with qaint devices and studded with small brilliants and rubies," and close by it "squats a little ugly monster, a Lar, perhaps, dug up in the sunny fields of corn-bearing Sicily." Some dark antique bronzes contrast "with the pale gleam of two noble *Christi Crucifixi*, one carved in ivory, the other moulded in wax." He has his trays of Tassie's gems, his tiny Louis-Quatorze *bonbonnière* with a miniature by Petitot, his highly prized "brown-biscuit teapots, filigree-worked," his citron morocco letter-case, and his "pomona-green" chair.

One can fancy him lying there in the midst of his books and casts and engravings, a true virtuoso, a subtle connoisseur, turning over his fine collection of Marc Antonios, and his Turner's "Liber Studiorum," of which he was a warm admirer, or examining with a magnifier some of his antique gems and cameos, "the head of Alexander on an onyx of two strata," or "that superb *altissimo relievo* on cornelian, Jupiter Ægiochus." He was always a great amateur of engravings, and gives some very useful suggestions as to the best means of forming a collection. Indeed, while fully appreciating modern art, he never lost sight of the importance of reproductions of the great masterpieces of the past, and all that he says about the value of plaster casts is quite admirable.

As an art critic he concerned himself primarily with the complex impressions produced by a work of art, and certainly the first step in æsthetic criticism is to realise one's own impressions. He cared nothing for abstract discussions on the nature of the Beautiful, and the historical method, which has since yielded such rich fruit, did not belong to his day, but he never lost sight of the great truth that Art's first appeal is neither to the intellect nor to the emotions, but purely to the artistic temperament, and he more than once points out that this temperament, this "taste," as he calls it, being unconsciously guided and made perfect by frequent contact with the best work, becomes in the end a form of right judgment. Of course, there are fashions in art just as there are fashions in dress, and perhaps none of us can ever quite free ourselves from the influence of custom and the influence of novelty. He certainly could not, and he frankly acknowledges how difficult it is to form any fair estimate of contemporary work. But, on the whole, his taste was good and sound. He admired Turner and Constable at a time when they were not so much thought of as they are now, and saw that for the highest landscape art we require more than "mere industry and accurate transcription." Of Crome's "Heath Scene near Norwich" he remarks that it shows "how much a subtle observation of the elements, in their wild moods, does for a most uninteresting flat," and of the popular type of landscape of his day he says that it is "simply an enumeration of hill and dale, stumps of trees, shrubs, water, meadows, cottages, and houses; little more than topography, a kind of pictorial mapwork; in which rainbows, showers, mists, haloes, large beams shooting through rifted clouds, storms, starlight, all the most valued materials of the real painter, are not." He had a thorough dislike of what is obvious or commonplace in art, and while he was charmed to entertain Wilkie at dinner, he cared as little for Sir David's pictures as he did for Mr. Crabbe's poems. With the imitative and realistic tendencies of his day he had no sympathy, and he tells us frankly that his great admiration for Fuseli was largely due to the fact that the little Swiss did not consider it necessary that an artist should only paint what he sees. The qualities that he sought for in a picture were composition, beauty and dignity of line, richness of colour, and imaginative power. Upon the other hand, he was not a doctrinaire. "I hold that no work of art can be tried otherwise than by laws deduced from itself: whether or not it be consistent with itself is the question." This is one of his excellent aphorisms. And in criticising painters so different as Landseer and Martin, Stothard and Etty, he shows that, to use a phrase now classical, he is trying "to see the object as in itself it really is."

However, as I pointed out before, he never feels quite at his ease in his criticisms of contemporary work. "The present," he says, "is about as agreeable a confusion to me as Ariosto on the first perusal. . . . Modern things dazzle me. I must look at them through Time's telescope. Elia complains that to him the merit of a MS. poem is uncertain; 'print,' as he excellently says, 'settles it.' Fifty years' toning does the same thing to a picture." He is happier when he is writing about Watteau and Lancret, about Rubens and Giorgione, about Rembrandt, Correggio, and Michael Angelo; happiest of all when he is writing about Greek things. What is Gothic touched him very little, but classical art and the art of the Renaissance were always dear to him. He saw what our English school could gain from a study of Greek models, and never wearies of pointing out to the young student the artistic possibilities that lie dormant in Hellenic marbles and Hellenic methods of work. In his judgments on the great Italian Masters, says De Quincey, "There seemed a tone of sincerity and of native sensibility, as in one who spoke for himself, and was not merely a copier from books." The highest praise that we can give to him is that he tried to revive style as a conscious tradition. But he saw that no amount of art lectures or art congresses, or "plans for advancing the fine arts," will ever produce this result. The people, he says very wisely, and in the true spirit of Toynbee Hall, must always have "the best models constantly before their eyes."

As is to be expected from one who was a painter, he is often extremely technical in his art criticisms. Of Tintoret's "St. George delivering the Egyptian Princess from the Dragon" he remarks:

"The robe of Sabra, warmly glazed with Prussian blue, is relieved from the pale greenish background by a vermilion scarf; and the full hues of both are beautifully echoed, as it were, in a lower key by the purple-lake coloured stuffs and bluish iron armour of the saint, besides an ample balance to the vivid azure drapery on the foreground in the indigo shades of the wild wood surrounding the castle."

And elsewhere he talks learnedly of "a delicate Schiavone, various as a tulip bed, with rich broken tints," of "a glowing portrait, remarkable for *morbidezza*, by the scarce Moroni," and of another picture being "pulpy in the carnations."

But as a rule, he deals with his impressions of the work as an artistic whole, and tries to translate those impressions into words, to give, as is were, the literary equivalent for the imaginative and mental effect. He was one of the first to develop what has been called the art-literature of the nineteenth century, that form of literature which has found in Mr. Ruskin and Mr. Browning its two most perfect exponents. His description of Lancret's *Repas Italien*, in which "a dark-haired girl, 'amorous of mischief,' lies on the daisy-powdered grass," is in some respects very charming. Here is his account of "The Crucifixion," by Rembrandt. It is extremely characteristic of his style:

"Darkness–sooty, portentious darkness–shrouds the whole scene: only above the accursed wood, as if through a horrid rift in the murky ceiling, a rainy deluge–'sleety-flaw, discoloured water'–streams down amain, spreading a grisly, spectral light, even more horrible than that palpable night. Already the Earth pants thick and fast! the darkened Cross trembles! the winds are dropt–the air is stagnant–a muttering rumble growls underneath their feet, and some of that miserable crowd begin to fly down the hill. The horses snuff the coming terror, and become unmanageable through fear. The moment rapidly approaches when, nearly torn asunder by His own weight, fainting with loss of blood, which now runs in narrow rivulets from His slit veins, His temples and breast drowned in sweat, and His black tongue parched with the fiery death-fever, Jesus cries, 'I thirst.' The deadly vinegar is elevated to Him.

"His head sinks, and the sacred corpse 'swings senseless of the cross.' A sheet of vermilion flame shoots sheer through the air and vanishes; the rocks of Carmel and Lebanon cleave asunder; the sea rolls on high from the sands its black, weltering waves. Earth yawns, and the graves give up their dwellers. The dead and the living are mingled together in unnatural conjunction and hurry through the holy city. New prodigies await them there. The veil of the temple–the unpiercable veil–is rent asunder from top to bottom, and that dreaded recess containing the Hebrew mysteries–the fatal ark with the tables and seven-branched candelabrum–is disclosed by the light of unearthly flames to the God-deserted multitude.

"Rembrandt never *painted* this sketch, and he was quite right. It would have lost nearly all its charms in losing that perplexing veil of indistinctness which affords such ample range wherein the doubting imagination may speculate. At present it is like a thing in another world. A dark gulf is betwixt us. It is not tangible by the body. We can only approach it in the spirit."

In this passage, written, the author tells us, "in awe and reverence," there is much that is terrible, and very much that is quite horrible, but it is not without a certain crude form of power, or, at any rate, a certain crude violence of words, a quality which this age should highly appreciate, as it is its chief defect. It is pleasanter, however, to pass to this description of Giulio Romano's "Cephalus and Procris":

"We should read Moschus's lament for Bion, the sweet shepherd, before looking at this picture, or study the picture as a preparation for the lament. We have nearly the same images in both. For either victim the high groves and the forest dells murmur; the flowers exhale sad perfume from their buds; the nightingale mourns on the craggy lands, and the swallow in the long-winding veils; 'the satyrs, too, and fauns dark-veiled groan,' and the fountain nymphs within the wood melt into tearful waters. The sheep and goats leave their pasture; and oreads, 'who love to scale the most inaccessible tops of all uprightest rocks, hurry down from the song of their wind-courting pines; while the dryads bend from the branches of the meeting trees, and the rivers moan for white Procris, 'with many-sobbing streams,'

'Filling the far-seen ocean with a voice.'

The golden bees are silent on the thymy Hymettus; and the knelling horn of Aurora's love no more shall scatter away the cold twilight on the top of Hymettus. The foreground of our subject is a grassy, sunburnt bank, broken into swells and hollows like waves (a sort of land-breakers), rendered more uneven by many foot-tripping roots and stumps of trees stocked untimely by the axe, which are again throwing out light green shoots. This bank rises rather suddenly on the right to a clustering grove, penetrable to no star, at the entrance of which sits the stunned Thessalian king, holding between his knees that ivory-bright body which was, but an instant agone, parting the rough boughs with her smooth forehead, and treading alike on thorns and flowers with jealousy-stung foot—now helpless, heavy, void of all motion, save when the breeze lifts her thick hair in mockery.

"From between the closely-neighboured boles astonished nymphs press forward with loud cries—

'And deerskin-vested satyrs, crowned with ivy twists, advance;
And put strange pity in their horned countenance.'

"Laelaps lies beneath, and shows by his panting the rapid pace of death. On the other side of the group, Virtuous Love with 'vans dejected' holds forth the arrow to an approaching troop of sylvan people, fauns, rams, goats, satyrs, and satyr-mothers, pressing their children tighter with their fearful hands, who hurry along from the left in a sunken path between the foreground and a rocky wall, on whose lowest ridge a brook-guardian pours from her urn her grief-telling waters. Above, and more remote than the Ephidryad, another female, rending her locks, appears among the vine-festooned pillars of an unshorn grove. The centre of the picture is filled by shady meadows, sinking down to a river-mouth; beyond is 'the vast strength of the ocean stream,' from whose floor the extinguisher of stars, rosy Aurora, drives furiously up her brine-washed steeds to behold the death-pangs of her rival."

Were this description carefully rewritten, it would be quite admirable. The conception of making a prose-poem out of paint is excellent. Much of the best modern literature springs from the same aim. In a very ugly and sensible age, the arts borrow, not from life, but from each other.

His sympathies, too, were wonderfully varied. In everything connected with the stage, for instance, he was always extremely interested, and strongly upheld the necessity for archæological accuracy in costume and scene-painting. "In art," he says in one of his essays, "whatever is worth doing at all is worth doing well"; and he points out that once we allow the intrusion of anachronisms, it becomes difficult to say where the line is to be drawn. In literature, again, like Lord Beaconsfield on a famous occasion, he was, "on the side of the angels." He was one of the first to admire Keats and Shelley—"the tremulously sensitive and poetical Shelley," as he calls him. His admiration for Wordsworth was sincere and profound. He thoroughly appreciated William Blake. One of the best copies of the "Songs of Innocence and Experience" that is now in existence was wrought specially for him. He loved Alain Chartier, and Ronsard, and the Elizabethan dramatists, and Chaucer and Chapman, and Petrarch. And to him all the arts were one. "Art critics," he remarks with much wisdom, "seem hardly aware of the identity of the primal seeds of poetry and painting, nor that any true advancement in the serious study of one art co-generates a proportionate perfection in the other"; and he says elsewhere that if a man who does not admire Michael Angelo talks of his love for Milton, he is deceiving either himself or his listeners. To his fellow-contributors in the *London Magazine* he was always most generous, and praises Barry Cornwall, Allan Cunningham, Hazlitt, Elton, and Leigh Hunt without anything of the malice of a friend. Some of his sketches of Charles Lamb are admirable in their way, and, with the art of the true comedian, borrow their style from their subject:

"What can I say of thee more than all know? that thou hadst the gaiety of a boy with the knowledge of a man: as gentle a heart as ever sent tears to the eyes.

"How wittily would he mistake your meaning, and put in a conceit most seasonably out of season. His talk, without affectation, was compressed, like his beloved Elizabethans, even unto obscurity. Like grains of fine gold, his sentences would beat out into whole sheets. He had small mercy on spurious fame, and a caustic observation on the *fashion for men of genius* was a standing dish. Sir Thomas Browne was a 'bosom cronie' of his; so was Burton, and old Fuller. In his amorous vein he dallied with that peerless Duchess of many-folio odour; and with the heyday comedies of Beaumont and Fletcher he induced light dreams. He would deliver critical touches on these, like one inspired, but it was good to let him choose his own game; if another began even on the acknowledged pets he was liable to interrupt, or rather append, in a mode difficult to define whether as misapprehensive or mischievous. One night at

C——'s, the above dramatic partners were the temporary subject of chat. Mr. X. commended the passion and haughty style of a tragedy (I don't know which of them), but was instantly taken up by Elia, who told him '*That* was nothing; the lyrics were the high things—the lyrics!' "

One side of his literary career deserves special notice. Modern journalism may be said to owe almost as much to him as to any man of the early part of this century. He was the pioneer of Asiatic prose, and delighted in pictorial epithets and pompous exaggerations. To have a style so gorgeous that it conceals the subject is one of the highest achievements of an important and much admired school of Fleet Street leader-writers, and this school *Janus Weathercock* may be said to have invented. He also saw that it was quite easy by continued reiteration to make the public interested in his own personality, and in his purely journalistic articles this extraordinary young man tells the world what he had for dinner, where he gets his clothes, what wines he likes, and in what state of health he is, just as if he were writing weekly notes for some popular newspaper of our own time. This being the least valuable side of his work, is the one that has had the most obvious influence. A publicist, nowadays, is a man who bores the community with the details of the illegalities of his private life.

Like most artificial people he had a great love of nature. "I hold three things in high estimation," he says somewhere: "to sit lazily on an eminence that commands a rich prospect; to be shadowed by thick trees while the sun shines around me; and to enjoy solitude with the consciousness of neighbourhood. The country gives them all to me." He writes about his wandering over fragrant furze and heath repeating Collin's "Ode to Evening," just to catch the fine quality of the moment; about smothering his face "in a watery bed of cowslips, wet with May dews"; and about the pleasure of seeing the sweet-breathed kine "pass slowly homeward through the twilight," and hearing "the distant clank of the sheep-bell." One phrase of his, "the polyanthus glowed in its cold bed of earth, like a solitary picture of Giorgione on a dark oaken panel," is curiously characteristic of his temperament, and this passage is rather pretty in its way—

"The short, tender grass was covered with marguerites—'such that men called *daisies* in our town'—thick as stars on a summer's night. The harsh caw of the busy rooks came, pleasantly mellowed, from a high, dusky grove of elms at some distance off, and at intervals was heard the voice of a boy scaring away the birds from the newly-sown seeds. The blue depths were the colour of the darkest ultramarine; not a cloud streaked the calm æther; only round the horizon's edge streamed a light, warm film of misty vapour, against which the near village, with its ancient stone church, showed sharply out with blinding whiteness. I thought of Wordsworth's 'Lines Written in March.' "

However, we must not forget that the cultivated young man who penned these lines, and who was so susceptible to Wordsworthian influences, was also, as I said at the beginning of this memoir, one of the most subtle and secret poisoners of this or any age. How he first became fascinated by this strange sin he does not tell us, and the diary in which he carefully noted the results of his terrible experiments and the methods that he adopted, has unfortunately been lost to us. Even in later days, too, he was always reticent on the matter, and preferred to speak about "The Excursion," and the "Poems founded on the Affections." There is no doubt, however, that the poison that he used was strychnine. In one of the beautiful rings of which he was so proud, and which served to show off the fine modelling of his delicate ivory hands, he used to carry crystals of the Indian *nux vomica*, a poison, one of his biographers tells us, "nearly tasteless, difficult of discovery, and capable of almost infinite dilution." His murders, says De Quincey, were more than were ever made known judicially. This is no doubt so, and some of them are worthy of mention. His first victim was his uncle, Mr. Thomas Griffiths. He poisoned him in 1829 to gain possession of Linden House, a place to which he had always been very much attached. In the August of the next year he poisoned Mrs. Abercrombie, his wife's mother, and in the following December he poisoned the lovely Helen Abercrombie, his sister-in-law. Why he murdered Mrs. Abercrombie is not ascertained. It may have been for a caprice, or to quicken some hideous sense of power that was in him, or because she suspected something, or for no reason. But the murder of Helen Abercrombie was carried out by himself and his wife for the sake of a sum of about 18,000*l*, for which they had insured her life in various offices. The circumstances were as follows: On the 12th of December, he and his wife and child came up to London from Linden House, and took lodgings at No. 12, Conduit Street, Regent Street. With them were the two sisters, Helen and Madeleine Abercrombie. On the evening of the 14th they all went to the play, and at supper that night Helen sickened. The next day she was extremely ill, and Dr. Locock, of Hanover Square, was called in to attend her. She lived till Monday, the 20th, when, after the doctor's morning visit, Mr. and Mrs. Wainewright brought her some poisoned jelly, and then went out for a walk. When they returned Helen Abercrombie was dead. She was about twenty years of age, a tall, graceful girl with fair hair. A very charming red-chalk drawing of her by her brother-in-law is still in existence, and shows how much his style as an artist was influenced by Sir Thomas Lawrence, a painter for whose work he had always entertained a great admiration. De Quincey says that Mrs. Wainewright was not really privy to the murder. Let us hope that she was not. Sin should be solitary, and have no accomplices.

The insurance companies, suspecting the real facts of the case, declined to pay the policy on the technical ground of misrepresentation and want of interest, and, with curious courage, the poisoner entered an action in the Court of Chancery against the Imperial, it being agreed that one decision should govern all the cases. The trial, however, did not come on for five years, when, after one disagreement, a verdict was ultimately given in the companies' favour. The judge on the occasion was Lord Abinger. *Egomet Bonmot* was represented by Mr. Erle and Sir William Follet, and the Attorney-General and Sir Frederick Pollock appeared for the other side. The plaintiff, unfortunately, was unable to be present at either of the trials. The refusal of the companies to give him the 18,000*l* had placed him in a position of most painful pecuniary embarrassment. Indeed, a few months after the murder of Helen Abercrombie, he had been actually arrested for debt in the streets of London while he was serenading the pretty daughter of one of his friends. This difficulty was got over at the time, but shortly afterwards he thought it better to go abroad till he could come to some practical arrangement with his creditors. He accordingly went to Boulogne on a visit to the father of the young lady in question, and while he was there induced him to insure his life with the Pelican Company for 3000*l*. As soon as the necessary formalities had been gone through and the policy executed, he dropped some crystals of strychnine into his coffee as they sat together one evening after dinner. He himself did not gain any monetary advantage by doing this. His aim was simply to revenge himself on the first office that had refused to pay him the price of his sin. His friend died the next day in his presence, and he left Boulogne at once for a sketching tour through the most picturesque parts of Brittany, and was for some time the guest of an old French gentleman, who had a beautiful country house at St. Omer. From this he moved to Paris, where he remained for several years, living in luxury, some say, while others talk of his "skulking with poison in his pocket, and being dreaded by all who knew him." In 1837 he returned to England privately. Some strange mad fascination brought him back. He followed a woman whom he loved.

It was the month of June, and he was staying at one of the hotels in Covent Garden. His sitting-room was on the ground floor, and he prudently kept the blinds down, for fear of being seen. Thirteen years before, when he was making his fine collection of majolicas and Marc Antonios, he had forged the names of his trustees to a power of attorney, which enabled him to get possession of some of the money which he had inherited from his mother, and had brought into marriage settlement. He knew that this forgery had been discovered, and that by returning to England he was imperilling his life. Yet he returned. Should one wonder? It was said that the woman was very beautiful. Besides, she did not love him.

It was by mere accident that he was discovered. A noise in the street attracted his attention, and, in his artistic interest in modern life, he pushed aside the blind for a moment. Some one outside called out: "That's Wainewright, the Bank-forger." It was Forrester, the Bow Street runner.

On the fifth of July he was brought up at the Old Bailey. The following report of the proceedings appeared in the *Times:*

"Before Mr. Justice Vaughan and Mr. Baron Alderson, Thomas Griffiths Wainewright, aged forty-two, a man of gentlemanly appearance, wearing mustachios, was indicted for forging and uttering a certain power of attorney for 2259*l*, with intent to defraud the Governor and Company of the Bank of England.

"There were five indictments against the prisoner, to all of which he pleaded not guilty, when he was arraigned before Mr. Serjeant Arabin in the course of the morning. On being brought before the judges, however, he begged to be allowed to withdraw the former plea, and then pleaded guilty to two of the indictments which were not of a capital nature.

"The counsel for the Bank having explained that there were three other indictments, but that the Bank did not desire to shed blood, the plea of guilty on the two minor charges was recorded, and the prisoner, at the close of the session, sentenced by the Recorder to transportation for life."

He was taken back to Newgate, preparatory to his removal to the colonies. In a fanciful passage in one of his early essays he had fancied himself "lying in Horsemonger Gaol under sentence of death" for having been unable to resist the temptation of stealing some Marc Antonios from the British Museum in order to complete his collection. The sentence now passed on him was to a man of his culture a form of death. He complained bitterly of it to his friends, and pointed out, with a good deal of reason, some people may fancy, that the money was practically his own, having come to him from his mother, and that the forgery, such as it was, had been committed thirteen years before, which, to use his own phrase, was at least a *circonstance attenuante*. The permanence of personality is a very subtle metaphysical problem, and certainly the English law solves the question in an extremely rough and ready manner. There is, however, something dramatic in the fact that this heavy punishment was inflicted on him for what, if we remember his fatal influence on the prose of modern journalism, was certainly not the worst of all his sins.

While he was in gaol, Dickens, Macready, and Hablot Browne came across him by chance. They had been going over the prisons of London, searching for artistic effects, and in Newgate they suddenly caught sight of Wainewright. He met them with a defiant stare, Forster tells us, but Macready was "horrified to recognise a man familiarly known to him in former years, and at whose table he had dined."

Others had more curiosity, and his cell was for some time a kind of fashionable lounge. Many men of letters went down to visit their old literary comrade. But he was no longer the kind light-hearted Janus whom Charles Lamb admired. He seemed to have grown quite cynical.

To the agent of an insurance company who was visiting him one afternoon, and thought he would improve the occasion by pointing out that, after all, crime was a bad speculation, he replied: "Sir, you City men enter on your speculations and take the chances of them. Some of your speculations succeed, some fail. Mine happen to have failed, yours happen to have succeeded. That is the only difference, sir, between my visitor and me. But, sir, I will tell you one thing in which I have succeeded to the last. I have been determined through life to hold the position of a gentleman. I have always done so. I do so still. It is the custom of this place that each of the inmates of a cell shall take his morning's turn of sweeping it out. I occupy a cell with a bricklayer and a sweep, but they never offer me the broom!" When a friend reproached him with the murder of Helen Abercrombie he shrugged his shoulders and said, "Yes; it was a dreadful thing to do, but she had very thick ankles."

From Newgate he was brought to the hulks at Portsmouth, and sent from there in the *Susan* to Van Diemen's Land along with three hundred other convicts. The voyage seems to have been most distasteful to him, and in a letter written to a friend he spoke bitterly about the ignominy of "the companion of poets and artists" being compelled to associate with "country bumpkins." The phrase that he applies to his companions need not surprise us. Crime in England is rarely the result of sin. It is nearly always the result of starvation. There was probably no one on board in whom he would have found a sympathetic listener, or even a psychologically interesting nature.

His love of art, however, never deserted him. At Hobart Town he started a studio, and returned to sketching and portrait-painting, and his conversation and manners seem not to have lost their charm. Nor did he give up his habit of poisoning, and there are two cases on record in which he tried to make away with people who had offended him. But his hand seems to have lost its cunning. Both of his attempts were complete failures, and in 1844, being thoroughly dissatisfied with Tasmanian society, he presented a memorial to the governor of the settlement, Sir John Eardley Wilmot, praying for a ticket-of-leave. In it he speaks of himself as being "tormented by ideas struggling for outward form and realisation, barred up from increase of knowledge, and deprived of the exercise of profitable or even of decorous speech." His request, however, was refused, and the associate of Coleridge consoled himself by making those marvellous *Paradis Artificiels* whose secret is only known to the eaters of opium. In 1852 he died of apoplexy, his sole living companion being a cat, for which he had evinced an extraordinary affection.

His crimes seem to have had an important effect upon his art. They gave a strong personality to his style, a quality that his early work certainly lacked. In a note to the Life of Dickens, Forster mentions that in 1847 Lady Blessington received from her brother, Major Power, who held a military appointment at Hobart Town, an oil portrait of a young lady from his clever brush; and it is said that "he contrived to put the expression of his own wickedness into the portrait of a nice, kind-hearted girl." M. Zola, in one of his novels, tells us of a young man who, having committed a murder, takes to art, and paints greenish impressionist portraits of perfectly respectable people, all of which bear a curious resemblance to his victim. The development of Mr. Wainewright's style seems to me far more subtle and suggestive. One can fancy an intense personality being created out of sin.

This strange and fascinating figure that for a few years dazzled literary London, and made so brilliant a *début* in life and letters, is undoubtedly a most interesting study. Mr. W. Carew Hazlitt, his latest biographer, to whom I am indebted for many of the facts contained in this memoir, and whose little book is, indeed, quite invaluable in its way, is of opinion that his love of art and nature was a mere pretence and assumption, and others have denied to him all literary power. This seems to me a shallow, or at least a mistaken, view. The fact of a man being a poisoner is nothing against his prose. The domestic virtues are not the true basis of art, though they may serve as an excellent advertisement for second-rate artists. It is possible that De Quincey exaggerated his critical powers, and I cannot help saying again that there is much in his published works that is too familiar, too common, too journalistic, in the bad sense of that bad word. Here and there he is distinctly vulgar in expression, and he is always lacking in the self-restraint of the true artist. But for some of his faults we must blame the time in which he lived, and, after all, prose that Charles Lamb thought "capital" has no small historic interest. That he had a sincere love of art and nature seems to me quite certain. There is no essential incongruity between crime and culture. We cannot re-write the whole of history for the purpose of gratifying our moral sense of what should be.

Of course, he is far too close to our own time for us to be able to form any purely artistic judgment about him. It is impossible not to feel a strong prejudice against a man who might have poisoned Lord Tennyson, or Mr. Gladstone, or the Master of Balliol. But had the man worn a costume and spoken a language different from our own, had he lived in imperial Rome, or at the time of the Italian Renaissance, or in Spain in the seventeenth century, or in any land or any century but this century and this land, we would be quite able to arrive at a perfectly unprejudiced estimate of his position and value. I know that there are many historians, or at least writers on historical subjects, who still think it necessary to apply moral judgments to history, and who distribute their praise or blame with the solemn complacency of a successful schoolmaster. This, however, is a foolish habit, and merely shows that the moral insinct can be brought to such a pitch of perfection that it will make its appearance wherever it is not required. Nobody with the true historical sense ever dreams of blaming Nero, or scolding Tiberius or censuring Cæsar Borgia. These personages have become like the puppets of a play. They may fill us with terror, or horror, or wonder, but they do not harm us. They are not in immediate relation to us. We have nothing to fear from them. They have passed into the sphere of art and science, and neither art nor science knows anything of moral approval or disapproval. And so it may be some day with Charles Lamb's friend. At present I feel that he is just a little too modern to be treated in that fine spirit of disinterested curiosity to which we owe so many charming studies of the great criminals of the Italian Renaissance from the pens of Mr. John Addington Symonds, Miss A. Mary F. Robinson, Miss Vernon Lee, and other distinguished writers. However, Art has not forgotten him. He is the hero of Dickens's *Hunted Down*, the Varney of Bulwer's *Lucretia;* and it is gratifying to note that fiction has paid some homage to one who was so powerful with "pen, pencil, and poison." To be suggestive for fiction is to be of more importance than a fact.

THE SOUL OF MAN UNDER SOCIALISM

THE chief advantage that would result from the establishment of Socialism is, undoubtedly, the fact that Socialism would relieve us from that sordid necessity of living for others which, in the present condition of things, presses so hardly upon almost everybody. In fact, scarcely any one at all escapes.

Now and then, in the course of the century, a great man of science, like Darwin; a great poet, like Keats; a fine critical spirit, like M. Renan; a supreme artist, like Flaubert, has been able to isolate himself, to keep himself out of reach of the clamorous claims of others, to stand "under the shelter of the wall," as Plato puts it, and so to realise the perfection of what was in him, to his own incomparable gain, and to the incomparable and lasting gain of the whole world. These, however, are exceptions. The majority of people spoil their lives by an unhealthy and exaggerated altruism—are forced, indeed, so to spoil them. They find themselves surrounded by hideous poverty, by hideous ugliness, by hideous starvation. It is inevitable that they should be strongly moved by all this. The emotions of man are stirred more quickly than man's intelligence; and, as I pointed out some time ago in an article on the function of criticism, it is much more easy to have sympathy with suffering than it is to have sympathy with thought. Accordingly, with admirable though misdirected intentions, they very seriously and very sentimentally set themselves to the task of remedying the evils that they see. But their remedies do not cure the disease: they merely prolong it. Inded, their remedies are part of the disease.

They try to solve the problem of poverty, for instance, by keeping the poor alive; or, in the case of a very advanced school, by amusing the poor.

But this is not a solution: it is an aggravation of the difficulty. *The proper aim is to try and reconstruct society on such a basis that poverty will be impossible.* And the altruistic virtues have really prevented the carrying out of this aim. Just as the worst slave-owners were those who were kind to their slaves, and so prevented the horror of the system being realised by those who suffered from it, and understood by those who contemplated it, so, in the present state of things in England, the people who do most harm are the people who try to do most good; and at last we have had the spectacle of men who have really studied the problem and know the life—educated men who live in the East End—coming forward and imploring the cummunity to restrain its altruistic impulses of charity, benevolence, and the like. They do so on the ground that such charity degrades and demoralises. They are perfectly right. Charity creates a multitude of sins.

There is also this to be said. It is immoral to use private property in order to alleviate the horrible evils that result from the institution of private property. It is both immoral and unfair.

Under Socialism all this will, of course, be altered. There will be no people living in fetid dens and fetid rags, and bringing up unhealthy, hunger-pinched children in the midst of impossible and absolutely repulsive surroundings. The security of society will not depend, as it does now, on the state of the weather. If a frost comes we shall not have a hundred thousand men out of work, tramping about the streets in a state of disgusting misery, or whining to their neighbours for alms, or crowding round the doors of loathsome shelters to try and secure a hunch of bread and a night's unclean lodging. Each member of the society will share in the general prosperity and happiness of the society, and if a frost comes no one will practically be anything the worse.

Upon the other hand, *Socialism itself will be of value simply because it will lead to Individualism.*

Socialism, Communism, or whatever one chooses to call it, by converting private property into public wealth, and substituting co-operation for competition, will restore society to its proper condition of a thoroughly healthy organism, and insure the material well-being of each member of the community. It will, in fact, give Life its proper basis and its proper environment. But for the full development of Life to its highest mode of perfection, something more is needed. What is needed is Individualism. If the Socialism is Authoritarian; if there are Governments armed with economic power as they are now with political power; if, in a word, we are to have Industrial Tyrannies, then the last state of man will be worse than the first. At present, in consequence of the existence of private property, a great many people are enabled to develop a certain very limited amount of Individualism. They are either under no necessity to work for their living, or are enabled to choose the sphere of activity that is really congenial to them and gives them pleasure. These are the poets, the philosophers, the men of science, the men of culture–in a word, the real men, the men who have realised themselves, and in whom all Humanity gains a partial realisation. Upon the other hand, there are a great many people who, having no private property of their own, and being always on the brink of sheer starvation, are compelled to do the work of beasts of burden, to do work that is quite uncongenial to them, and to which they are forced by the peremptory, unreasonable, degrading Tyranny of want. These are the poor, and amongst them there is no grace of manner, or charm of speech, or civilisation, or culture, or refinement in pleasures, or joy of life. From their collective force Humanity gains much in material prosperity. But it is only the material result that it gains, and the man who is poor is in himself absolutely of no importance. He is merely the infinitesimal atom of a force that, so far from regarding him, crushes him: indeed, prefers him crushed, as in that case he is far more obedient.

Of course, it might be said that the Individualism generated under conditions of private property is not always, or even as a rule, of a fine or wonderful type, and that the poor, if they have not culture and charm, have still many virtues. Both these statements would be quite true. The possession of private property is very often extremely demoralising, and that is, of course, one of the reasons why Socialism wants to get rid of the institution. In fact, property is really a nuisance. Some years ago people went about the country saying that property has duties. They said it so often and to tediously that, at last, the Church has begun to say it. One hears it now from every pulpit. It is perfectly true. Property not merely has duties, but has so many duties that its possession to any large extent is a bore. It involves endless claims upon one, endless attention to business, endless bother. If property had simply pleasures, we could stand it; but its duties make it unbearable. In the interest of the rich we must get rid of it. The virtues of the poor may be readily admitted, and are much to be regretted. We are often told that the poor are grateful for charity. Some of them are, no doubt, *but the best amongst the poor are never grateful.* They are ungrateful, discontented, disobedient, and rebellious. They are quite right to be so. Charity they feel to be a ridiculously inadequate mode of partial restitution, or a sentimental dole, usually accompanied by some impertinent attempt on the part of the sentimentalist to tryrannise over their private lives. Why should they be grateful for the crumbs that fall from the rich man's table? They should be seated at the board, and are beginning to know it. As for being discontented, a man who would not be discontented with such surroundings and such a low mode of life would be a perfect brute. Disobedience, in the eyes of any one who has read history, is man's original virtue. It is through disobedience that progress has been made, through disobedience and through rebellion. Sometimes the poor are praised for being thrifty. But to recommend thrift to the poor is both grotesque and insulting. It is like advising a man who is starving to eat less. For a town or country labourer to practise thrift would be absolutely immoral. Man should not be ready to show that he can live like a badly-fed animal. He should decline to live like that, and should either steal or go on the rates, which is considered by many to be a form of stealing. As for begging, it is safer to beg than to take, but it is finer to take than to beg. No; a poor man who is ungrateful, unthrifty, discontented, and rebellious is probably a real personality, and has much in him. He is at any rate a healthy protest. As for the virtuous poor, one can pity them, of course, but one cannot possibly admire them. They have made private terms with the enemy and sold their birthright for very bad pottage. They must also be extraordinarily stupid. I can quite understand a man accepting laws that protect private property, and admit of its accumulation, as long as he himself is able under these conditions to realise some form of beautiful and intellectual life. But it is almost incredible to me how a man whose life is marred and made hideous by such laws can possibly asquiesce in their continuance.

However, the explanation is not really so difficult to find. It is simply this. Misery and poverty are so absolutely degrading, and exercise such a paralysing effect over the nature of men, that no class is ever really conscious of its own suffering. They have to be told of it by other people, and they often entirely disbelieve them. What is said by great employers of labour against agitators is unquestionably true. Agitators are a set of interfering, meddling people, who come down to some perfectly contented class of the community, and sow the seeds of discontent amongst them. That is the reason why agitators are so absolutely necessary. Without them, in our incomplete state, there would be no advance towards civilisation. Slavery was put down in America, not in consequence of any action on the part of the slaves, or even any express desire on their part that they should be free. It was put down entirely through the grossly illegal conduct of certain agitators in Boston and elsewhere, who were not slaves themselves, nor owners of slaves, nor had anything to do with the question really. It was, undoubtedly, the Abolitionists who set the torch alight, who began the whole thing. And it is curious to note that from the slaves themselves they received, not merely very little assistance, but hardly any sympathy even; and when at the close of the war the slaves found themselves free, found themselves indeed so absolutely free that they were free to starve, many of them bitterly regretted the new state of things. To the thinker, the most tragic fact in the whole of the French Revolution is not that Marie Antoinette was killed for being a queen, but that the starved peasant of the Vendée voluntarily went out to die for the hideous cause of feudalism.

It is clear, then, that no Authoritarian Socialism will do. For while under the present system a very large number of people can lead lives of a certain amount of freedom and expression and happiness, under an industrial barrack system, or a system of economic tyranny, nobody would be able to have any such freedom at all. It is to be regretted that a portion of our community should be practically in slavery, but to propose to solve the problem by enslaving the entire community is childish. Every man must be left quite free to choose his own work. No form of compulsion must be exercised over him. If there is, his work will not be good for him, will not be good in itself, and will not be good for others. And by work I simply mean activity of any kind.

I hardly think that any Socialist, nowadays, would seriously propose that an inspector should call every morning at each house to see that each citizen rose up and did manual labour for eight hours. Humanity has got beyond that stage, and reserves such a form of life for the people whom, in a very arbitrary manner, it chooses to call criminals. But I confess that many of the socialistic views that I have come across seem to me to be tainted with ideas of authority, if not of actual compulsion. Of course, authority and compulsion are out of the question. All association must be quite voluntary. *It is only in voluntary associations that man is fine.*

But it may be asked how Individualism, which is now more or less dependent on the existence of private property for its development, will benefit by the abolition of such private property. The answer is very simple. It is true that, under existing conditions, a few men who have had private means of their own, such as Byron, Shelley, Browning, Victor Hugo, Baudelaire, and others, have been able to realise their personality more or less completely. Not one of these men ever did a single day's work for hire. They were relieved from poverity. They had an immense advantage. The question is whether it would be for the good of Individualism that such an advantage should be taken away. Let us suppose that it is taken away. What happens then to Individualism? How will it benefit?

It will benefit in this way. Under the new conditions Individualism will be far freer, far finer, and far more intensified than it is now. I am not talking of the great imaginatively-realised Individualism of such poets as I have mentioned, but of the great actual Individualism latent and potential in mankind generally. For the recognition of private property has really harmed Individualism, and obscured it, by confusing a man with what he possesses. It has led Individualism entirely astray. It has made gain not growth its aim. So that man thought that the important thing was to have, and did not know that the important thing is to be. *The true perfection of man lies, not in what man has, but in what man is.* Private property has crushed true Individualism, and set up an Individualism that is false. It has debarred one part of the community from being individual by starving them. It has debarred the other part of the community from being individual by putting them on the wrong road and encumbering them. Indeed, so completely has man's personality been absorbed by his possessions that the English law has always treated offences against a man's property with far more severity than offences against his person, and property is still the test of complete citizenship. The industry necessary for the making of money is also very demoralising. In a community like ours, where property confers immense distinction, social position, honour, respect, titles, and other pleasant things of the kind, man, being naturally ambitious, makes it his aim to accumulate this property, and goes on wearily and tediously accumulating it long after he has got far more than he wants, or can use, or enjoy, or perhaps even know of. Man will kill himself by overwork in order to secure property, and really, considering the enormous advantages that property brings, one is hardly surprised. One's regret is that society should be constructed on such a basis that man has been forced into a groove in which he cannot freely develop what is wonderful, and fascinating, and delightful in him—in which, in fact, he misses the true pleasure and joy of living. He is also, under existing conditions, very insecure. An enormously wealthy merchant may be—often is—at every moment of his life at the mercy of things that are not under his control. If the wind blows an extra point or so, or the weather suddenly changes, or some trivial thing happens, his ship may go down, his speculations may go wrong, and he finds himself a poor man, with his social position quite gone. Now, nothing should be able to harm a man except himself. Nothing should be able to rob a man at all. What a man really has, is what is in him. What is outside of him should be a matter of no importance.

With the abolition of private property, then, we shall have true, beautiful, healthy Individualism. Nobody will waste his life in accumulating things, and the symbols for things. One will live. To live is the rarest thing in the world. Most people exist, that is all.

It is a question whether we have ever seen the full expression of a personality, except on the imaginative plane of art. In action, we never have. Cæsar, says Mommsen, was the complete and perfect man. But how tragically insecure was Cæsar! Wherever there is a man who exercises authority, there is a man who resists authority. Cæsar was very perfect, but his perfection travelled by too dangerous a road. Marcus Aurelius was the perfect man, says Renan. Yes; the great emporer was a perfect man. But how intolerable were the endless claims upon him! He staggered under the burden of the empire. He was conscious how inadequate one man was to bear the weight of that Titan and too vast orb. What I mean by a perfect man is one who develops under perfect conditions; one who is not wounded, or worried, or maimed, or in danger. *Most personalities have been obliged to be rebels. Half their strength has been wasted in friction.* Byron's personality, for instance, was terribly wasted in its battle with the stupidity, and hypocrisy, and Philistinism of the English. Such battles do not always intensify strength: they often exaggerate weakness. Byron was never able to give us what he might have given us. Shelley escaped better. Like Byron, he got out of England as soon as possible. But he was not so well known. If the English had had any idea of what a great poet he really was, they would have fallen on him with tooth and nail, and made his life as unbearable for him as they possibly could. But he was not a remarkable figure in society, and consequently he escaped, to a certain degree. Still, even in Shelley the note of rebellion is sometimes too strong. The note of the perfect personality is not rebellion, but peace.

It will be a marvellous thing—the true personality of man—when we see it. It will grow naturally and simply, flower-like, or as a tree grows. It will not be at discord. It will never argue or dispute. It will not prove things. It will know everything. And yet it will not busy itself about knowledge. It will have wisdom. Its value will not be measured by material things. It will have nothing. And yet it will have everything, and whatever one takes from it, it will still have, so rich will it be. It will not be always meddling with others, or asking them to be like itself. It will love them because they will be different. And yet, while it will not meddle with others, it will help all, as a beautiful thing helps us by being what it is. The personality of man will be very wonderful. It will be as wonderful as the personality of a child.

In its development it will be assisted by Christianity, if men desire that; but if men do not desire that, it will develop none the less surely. For it will not worry itself about the past, nor care whether things happened or did not happen. Nor will it admit any laws but its own laws; nor any authority but its own authority. Yet it will love those who sought to intensify it, and speak often of them. And of these Christ was one.

"Know Thyself" was written over the portal of the antique world. Over the portal of the new world, "Be Thyself" shall be written. And the message of Christ to man was simply "Be Thyself." That is the secret of Christ.

When Jesus talks about the poor He simply means personalities, just as when He talks about the rich He simply means people who have not developed their personalities. Jesus moved in a community that allowed the accumulation of private property just as ours does, and the gospel that He preached was not that in such a community it is an advantage for a man to live on scanty, unwholesome food, to wear ragged, unwholesome clothes, to sleep in horrid, unwholesome dwellings, and a disadvantage for a man to live under healthy, pleasant, and decent conditions. Such a view would have been wrong there and then, and would, of course, be still more wrong now and in England; for as man moves northwards the material necessities of life become of more vital importance, and our society is infinitely more complex, and displays far greater extremes of luxury and pauperism than any society of the antique world. What Jesus meant was this. He said to man, "You have a wonderful personality. Develop it. Be yourself. Don't imagine that your perfection lies in accumulating or possessing external things. Your perfection is inside of you. If only you could realise that, you would not want to be rich. Ordinary riches can be stolen from a man. Real riches cannot. In the treasury-house of your soul there are infinitely precious things, that may not be taken from you. And so, try to so shape your life that external things will not harm you. And try also to get rid of personal property. It involves sordid preoccupation, endless industry, continual wrong. Personal property hinders Individualism at every step." It is to be noted that Jesus never says that impoverished people are necessarily good, or wealthy people necessarily bad. That would not have been true. Wealthy people are, as a class, better than impoverished people, more moral, more intellectual, more well-behaved. *There is only one class in the community that thinks more about money than the rich, and that is the poor.* The poor can think of nothing else. That is the misery of being poor. What Jesus does say is that man reaches his perfection, not through what he has, not even through what he does, but entirely through what he is. And so the wealthy young man who comes to Jesus is represented as a thoroughly good citizen, who has broken none of the laws of his state, none of the commandments of his religion. He is quite respectable, in the ordinary sense of that extraordinary word. Jesus says to him, "You should give up private property. It hinders you from realising your perfection. It is a drag upon you. It is a burden. Your personality does not need it. It is within you, and not outside of you, that you will find what you really are, and what you really want." To his own friends he says the same thing. He tells them to be themselves, and not to be always worrying about other things. What do other things matter? Man is complete in himself. When they go into the world, the world will disagree with them. That is inevitable. The world hates Individualism. But this is not to trouble them. They are to be calm and self-centred. If a man takes their cloak, they are to give him their coat, just to show that material things are of no importance. If people abuse them, they are not to answer back. What does it signify? The things people say of a man do not alter a man. He is what he is. Public opinion is of no value whatsoever. Even if people employ actual violence, they are not to be violent in turn. That would be to fall to the same level. After all, even in prison, a man can be quite free. His soul can be free. His personality can be untroubled. He can be at peace. And, above all things, they are not to interfere with other people or judge them in any way. Personality is a very mysterious thing. A man cannot always be estimated by what he does. He may keep the law, and yet be worthless. He may break the law, and yet be fine. He may be bad, without ever doing anything bad. He may commit a sin against society, and yet realise through that sin his true perfection.

There was a woman who was taken in adultery. We are not told the history of her love, but that love must have been very great; for Jesus said that her sins were forgiven her, not because she had repented, but because her love was so intense and wonderful. Later on, a short time before His death, as He sat at a feast, the woman came in and poured costly perfumes on His hair. His friends tried to interfere with her, and said that it was an extravagance, and that the money that the perfume cost should have been expended on charitable relief of people in want, or something of that kind. Jesus did not accept that view. He pointed out that the material needs of Man were great and very permanent, but that the spiritual needs of Man were greater still, and that in one divine moment, and by selecting its own mode of expression, a personality might make itself perfect. The world worships the woman, even now, as a saint.

Yes; there are suggestive things in Individualism. Socialism annihilates family life, for instance. With the abolition of private property, marriage in its present form must disappear. This is part of the programme. Individualism accepts this and makes it fine. It converts the abolition of legal restraint into a form of of freedom that will help the full development of personality, and make the love of man and woman more wonderful, more beautiful, and more ennobling. Jesus knew this. He rejected the claims of family life, although they existed in His day and community in a very marked form. "Who is my mother? Who are my brothers?" He said, when He was told that they wished to speak to Him. When one of His followers asked leave to go and bury his father, "Let the dead bury the dead," was His terrible answer. He would allow no claim whatsoever to be made on personality.

And so he would lead a Christ-like life is he who is perfectly and absolutely himself. He may be a great poet, or a great man of science; or a young student at a University, or one who watches sheep upon a moor; or a maker of dramas, like Shakespeare, or a thinker about God, like Spinoza; or a child who plays in a garden, or a fisherman who throws his nets into the sea. It does not matter what he is, as long as he realises the perfection of the soul that is within him. All imitation in morals and in life is wrong. Through the streets of Jerusalem at the present day crawls one who is mad and carries a wooden cross on his shoulders. He is a symbol of the lives that are marred by imitation. Father Damien was Christ-like when he went out to live with the lepers, because in such service he realised fully what was best in him. But he was not more Christ-like than Wagner, when he realised his soul in music; or than Shelley, when he realised his soul in song. There is no one type for man. There are as many perfections as there are imperfect men. And while to the claims of charity a man may yield and yet be free, to the claims of conformity no man may yield and remain free at all.

Individualism, then, is what through Socialism we are to attain to. As a natural result the State must give up all idea of government. It must give it up because, as a wise man once said many centuries before Christ, there is such a thing as leaving mankind alone; there is no such thing as governing mankind. *All modes of government are failures.* Despotism is unjust to everybody, including the despot, who was probably made for better things. Oligarchies are unjust to the many, and ochlocracies are unjust to the few. High hopes were once formed of democracy; but democracy means simply the bludgeoning of the people by the people for the people. It has been found out. I must say that it was high time, for all authority is quite degrading. It degrades those who exercise it, and degrades those over whom it is exercised. When it is violently, grossly, and cruelly used, it produces a good effect, by creating, or at any rate bringing out, the spirit of revolt and individualism that is to kill it. When it is used with a certain amount of kindness, and accompanied by prizes and rewards, it is dreadfully demoralising. People, in that case, are less conscious of the horrible pressure that is being put on them, and so go through their lives in a sort of coarse comfort, like petted animals, without ever realising that they are probably thinking other people's thoughts, living by other people's standards, wearing practically what one may call other people's second-hand clothes, and never being themselves for a single moment. "He who would be free," says a fine thinker, "must not conform." And authority, by bribing people to conform, produces a very gross kind of overfed barbarism amongst us.

With authority, punishment will pass away. This will be a great gain—a gain, in fact, of incalculable value. As one reads history, not in the expurgated editions written for schoolboys and passmen, but in the original authorities of each time, one is absolutely sickened, not by the crimes that the wicked have committed, but by the punishments that the good have inflicted; *and a community is infinitely more brutalised by the habitual employment of punishment than it is by the occasional occurrence of crime.* It obviously follows that the more punishment is inflicted the more crime is produced, and most modern legislation has recognised this, and has made it its task to diminish punishment as far as it thinks it can. Wherever it has really diminished it the results have always been extremely good. The less punishment the less crime. When there is no punishment at all, crime will either cease to exist, or, if it occurs, will be treated by physicians as a very distressing form of dementia, to be cured by care and kindness. For what are called criminals nowadays are not criminals at all. Starvation, and not sin, is the parent of modern crime. That indeed is the reason why our criminals are, as a class, so absolutely uninteresting from any psychological point of view. They are not marvellous Macbeths and terrible Vautrins. They are merely what ordinary, respectable, commonplace people would be if they had not got enough to eat. When private property is abolished there will be no necessity for crime, no demand for it; it will cease to exist. Of course, all crimes are not crimes against property, though such are the crimes that the English law, valuing what a man has more than what a man is, punishes with the harshest and most horrible severity, if we except the crime of murder, and regard death as worse than penal servitude, a point on which our criminals, I believe, disagree. But though a crime may not be against property, it may spring from the misery and rage and depression produced by our wrong system of property-holding, and so, when that system is abolished, will disappear. When each member of the community has sufficient for his wants, and is not interfered with by his neighbour, it will not be an object of any interest to him to interfere with any one else. Jealousy, which is an extraordinary source of crime in modern life, is an emotion closely bound up with our conceptions of property, and under Socialism and Individualism will die out. It is remarkable that in communistic tribes jealousy is entirely unknown.

Now, as the State is not to govern, it may be asked what the State is to do. The State is to be a voluntary association that will organise labour, and be the manufacturer and distributor of necessary commodities. *The State is to make what is useful. The individual is to make what is beautiful.* And as I have mentioned the word labour, I cannot help saying that a great deal of nonsense is being written and talked nowadays about the dignity of manual labour. There is nothing necessarily dignified about manual labour at all, and most of it is absolutely degrading. It is mentally and morally injurious to man to do anything in which he does not find pleasure, and many forms of labour are quite pleasureless activities, and should be regarded as such. To sweep a slushy crossing for eight hours on a day when the east wind is blowing is a disgusting occupation. To sweep it with mental, moral, or physical dignity seems to me to be impossible. To sweep it with joy would be appalling. Man is made for something better than disturbing dirt. All work of that kind should be done by a machine.

And I have no doubt that it will be so. Up to the present, man has been, to a certain extent, the slave of machinery, and there is something tragic in the fact that as soon as man had invented a machine to do his work he began to starve. This, however, is, of course, the result of our property system and our system of competition. One man owns a machine which does the work of five hundred men. Five hundred men are, in consequence, thrown out of employment, and, having no work to do, become hungry and take to thieving. The one man secures the produce of the machine and keeps it, and has five hundred times as much as he should have, and probably, which is of much more importance, a great deal more than he really wants. Were that machine the property of all, every one would benefit by it. It would be an immense advantage to the community. All unintellectual labour, all monotonous, dull labour, all labour that deals with dreadful things, and involves unpleasant conditions, must be done by machinery. Machinery must work for us in the coal mines, and do all sanitary services, and be the stokers of steamers, and clean the streets, and run messages on wet days, and do anything that is tedious or distressing. *At present machinery competes against man. Under proper conditions machinery will serve man.* There is no doubt at all that this is the future of machinery, and just as trees grow while the country gentleman is asleep, so while Humanity will be amusing itself, or enjoying cultivated leisure—which, and not labour, is the aim of man—or making beautiful things, or reading beautiful things, or simply contemplating the world with admiration and delight, machinery will be doing all the necessary and unpleasant work. The fact is, that civilisation requires slaves. The Greeks were quite right there. Unless there are slaves to do the ugly, horrible, uninteresting work, culture and contemplation become almost impossible. Human slavery is wrong, insecure, and demoralising. On mechanical slavery, on the slavery of the machine, the future of the world depends. And when scientific men are no longer called upon to go down to a depressing East End and distribute bad cocoa and worse blankets to starving people, they will have delightful leisure in which to devise wonderful and marvellous things for their own joy and the joy of every one else. There will be great storages of force for every city, and for every house if required, and this force man will convert into heat, light, or motion, according to his needs. Is this Utopia? A map of the world that does not include Utopia is not worth even glancing at, for it leaves out the one country at which Humanity is always landing. And when Humanity lands there, it looks out, and, seeing a better country, sets sail. Progress is the realisation of Utopias.

Now, I have said that the community by means of organisation of machinery will supply the useful things, and that the beautiful things will be made by the individual. This is not merely necessary, but it is the only possible way by which we can get either the one or the other. An individual who has to make things for the use of others, and with reference to their wants and their wishes, does not work with interest, and consequently cannot put into his work what is best in him. Upon the other hand, whenever a community or a powerful section of a community, or a government of any kind, attempts to dictate to the artist what he is to do, Art either entirely vanishes, or becomes stereotyped, or degenerates into a low and ignoble form of craft. *A work of art is the unique result of a unique temperament. Its beauty comes from the fact that the author is what he is. It has nothing to do with the fact that other people want what they want.* Indeed, the moment that an artist takes notice of what other people want, and tries to supply the demand, he ceases to be an artist, and becomes a dull or an amusing craftsman, an honest or a dishonest tradesman. He has no further claim to be considered as an artist. *Art is the most intense mode of individualism that the world has known.* I am inclined to say that it is the only real mode of individualism that the world has known. Crime, which, under certain conditions, may seem to have created individualism, must take cognisance of other people and interfere with them. It belongs to the sphere of action. But alone, without any reference to his neighbours, without any interference, the artist can fashion a beautiful thing; and if he does not do it solely for his own pleasure, he is not an artist at all.

And it is to be noted that it is the fact that Art is this intense form of individualism that makes the public try to exercise over it an authority that is as immoral as it is ridiculous, and as corrupting as it is contemptible. It is not quite their fault. The public have always, and in every age, been badly brought up. They are continually asking Art to be popular, to please their want of taste, to flatter their absurd vanity, to tell them what they have been told before, to show them what they ought to be tired of seeing, to amuse them when they feel heavy after eating too much, and to distract their thoughts when they are wearied of their own stupidity. *Now Art should never try to be popular. The public should try to make itself artistic.* There is a very wide difference. If a man of science were told that the results of his experiments, and the conclusions that he arrived at, should be of such a character that they would not upset the received popular notions on the subject, or disturb popular prejudice, or hurt the sensibilities of people who knew nothing about science; if a philosopher were told that he had a perfect right to speculate in the highest spheres of thought, provided that he arrived at the same conclusions as were held by those who had never thought in any sphere at all—well, nowadays the man of science and the philosopher would be considerably amused. Yet it is really a very few years since both philosophy and science were subjected to brutal popular control, to authority in fact—the authority of either the general ignorance of the community, or the terror and greed for power of an ecclesiastical or governmental class. Of course, we have to a very great extent got rid of any attempt on the part of the community or the Church, or the Government, to interfere with the individualism of speculative thought, but the attempt to interfere with the individualism of imaginative art still lingers. In fact, it does more than linger: it is aggressive, offensive, and brutalising.

In England, the arts that have escaped best are the arts in which the public take no interest. Poetry is an instance of what I mean. We have been able to have fine poetry in England because the public do not read it, and consequently do not influence it. The public like to insult poets because they are individual, but once they have insulted them they leave them alone. In the case of the novel and the drama, arts in which the public do take an interest, the result of the exercise of popular authority has been absolutely ridiculous.

No country produces such badly written fiction, such tedious, common work in the novel form, such silly, vulgar plays as England. It must necessarily be so. The popular standard is of such a character that no artist can get to it. It is at once too easy and too difficult to be a popular novelist. It is too easy, because the requirements of the public as far as plot, style, psychology, treatment of life, and treatment of literature are concerned, are within the reach of the very meanest capacity and the most uncultivated mind. It is too difficult, because to meet such requirements the artist would have to do violence to his temperament, would have to write not for the artistic joy of writing, but for the amusement of half-educated people, and so would have to suppress his individualism, forget his culture, annihilate his style, and surrender everything that is valuable in him. In the case of the drama, things are a little better: the theatre-going public like the obvious, it is true, but they do not like the tedious; and burlesque and farcical comedy, the two most popular forms, are distinct forms of art. Delightful work may be produced under burlesque and farcical conditions, and in work of this kind the artist in England is allowed very great freedom. It is when one comes to the higher forms of the drama that the result of popular control is seen. The one thing that the public dislike is novelty. Any attempt to extend the subject-matter of art is extremely distasteful to the public; and yet the vitality and progress of art depend in a large measure on the continual extension of subject-matter. The public dislike novelty because they are afraid of it. It represents to them a mode of Individualism, an assertion on the part of the artist that he selects his own subject, and treats it as he chooses. The public are quite right in their attitude. Art is Individualism, and Individualism is a disturbing and disintegrating force. Therein lies its immense value. For what it seeks to disturb is monotony of type, slavery of custom, tyranny of habit, and the reduction of man to the level of a machine. In Art, the public accept what has been, because they cannot alter it, not because they appreciate it. They swallow their classics whole, and never taste them. They endure them as the inevitable, and, as they cannot mar them, they mouth about them. Strangely enough, or not strangely, according to one's own views, this acceptance of the classics does a great deal of harm. The uncritical admiration of the Bible and Shakespeare in England is an instance of what I mean. With regard to the Bible, considerations of ecclesiastical authority enter into the matter, so that I need not dwell upon the point.

But in the case of Shakespeare it is quite obvious that the public really see neither the beauties nor the defects of his plays. If they saw the beauties, they would not object to the development of the drama; and if they saw the defects, they would not object to the development of the drama either. *The fact is, the public make use of the classics of a country as a means of checking the progress of Art.* They degrade the classics into authorities. They use them as bludgeons for preventing the free expression of Beauty in new forms. They are always asking a writer why he does not write like somebody else, or a painter why he does not paint like somebody else, quite oblivious of the fact that if either of them did anything of the kind he would cease to be an artist. A fresh mode of Beauty is absolutely distasteful to them, and whenever it appears they get so angry and bewildered that they always use two stupid expressions—one is that the work of art is grossly unintelligible; the other, that the work of art is grossly immoral. What they mean by these words seems to me to be this. When they say a work is grossly unintelligible, they mean that the artist has said or made a beautiful thing that is new; when they describe a work as grossly immoral, they mean that the artist has said or made a beautiful thing that is true. The former expression has reference to style; the latter to subject-matter. But they probably use the words very vaguely, as an ordinary mob will use ready-made paving-stones. *There is not a single real poet or prose writer of this century, for instance, on whom the British public have not solemnly conferred diplomas of immorality*, and these diplomas practically take the place, with us, of what in France is the formal recognition of an Academy of Letters, and fortunately make the establishment of such an institution quite unnecessary in England. Of course, the public are very reckless in their use of the word. That they should have called Wordsworth an immoral poet was only to be expected. Wordsworth was a poet. But that they should have called Charles Kingsley an immoral novelist is extraordinary. Kingsley's prose was not of a very fine quality. Still, there is the word, and they use it as best they can. An artist is, of course, not disturbed by it. The true artist is a man who believes absolutely in himself, because he is absolutely himself. But I can fancy that if an artist produced a work of art in England that immediately on its appearance was recognised by the public, through their medium, which is the public press, as a work that was quite intelligible and highly moral, he would begin to seriously question whether in its creation he had really been himself at all, and consequently whether the work was not quite unworthy of him, and either of a thoroughly second-rate order, or of no artistic value whatsoever.

Perhaps, however, I have wronged the public in limiting them to such words as "immoral," "unintelligible," "exotic," and "unhealthy." There is one other word that they use. That word is "morbid." They do not use it often. The meaning of the word is so simple that they are afraid of using it. Still, they use it sometimes, and, now and then, one comes across it in popular newspapers. It is, of course, a ridiculous word to apply to a work of art. For what is morbidity but a mood of emotion or a mode of thought that one cannot express? The public are all morbid, because the public can never find expression for anything. *The artist is never morbid. He expresses everything.* He stands outside his subject, and through its medium produces incomparable and artistic effects. To call an artist morbid because he deals with morbidity as a subject-matter is as silly as if one called Shakespeare mad because he wrote *King Lear*.

On the whole, an artist in England gains something by being attacked. His individuality is intensified. He becomes more completely himself. Of course, the attacks are very gross, very impertinent, and very contemptible. But then no artist expects grace from the vulgar mind, or style from the suburban intellect. Vulgarity and stupidity are two very vivid facts in modern life. One regrets them, naturally. But there they are. They are subjects for study, like everything else. And it is only fair to state, with regard to modern journalists, that they always apologise to one in private for what they have written against one in public.

Within the last few years two other adjectives, it may be mentioned, have been added to the very limited vocabulary of art abuse that is at the disposal of the public. One is the word "unhealthy," the other is the word "exotic." The latter merely expresses the rage of the momentary mushroom against the immortal, entrancing, and exquisitely lovely orchid. It is a tribute, but a tribute of no importance. The word "unhealthy," however, admits of analysis. It is a rather interesting word. In fact, it is so interesting that the people who use it do not know what it means.

What does it mean? What is a healthy or an unhealthy work of art? All terms that one applies to a work of art, provided that one applies them rationally, have reference to either its style or its subject, or to both together. From the point of view of style, a healthy work of art is one whose style recognises the beauty of the material it employs, be that material one of words or of bronze, or colour or of ivory, and uses that beauty as a factor in producing the aesthetic effect. From the point of view of subject, a healthy work of art is one the choice of whose subject is conditioned by the temperament of the artist, and comes directly out of it. In fine, a healthy work of art is one that has both perfection and personality. Of course, form and substance cannot be separated in a work of art; they are always one. But for purposes of analysis, and setting the wholeness of aesthetic impression aside for a moment, we can intellectually so separate them. An unhealthy work of art, on the other hand, is a work whose style is obvious, old-fashioned, and common, and whose subject is deliberately chosen, not because the artist has any pleasure in it, but because he thinks that the public will pay him for it. *In fact, the popular novel that the public calls healthy is always a thoroughly unhealthy production; and what the public call an unhealthy novel is always a beautiful and healthy work of art.*

I need hardly say that I am not, for a single moment, complaining that the public and the public press misuse these words. I do not see how, with their lack of comprehension of what Art is, they could possibly use them in the proper sense. I am merely pointing out the misuse; and as for the origin of the misuse and the meaning that lies behind it all, the explanation is very simple. It comes from the barbarous conception of authority. It comes from the natural inability of a community corrupted by authority to understand or appreciate Individualism. In a word, it comes from that monstrous and ignorant thing that is called Public Opinion, which, bad and well-meaning as it is when it tries to control action, is infamous and of evil meaning when it tries to control Thought or Art.

Indeed, there is much more to be said in favour of the physical force of the public than there is in favour of the public's opinion. The former may be fine. The latter must be foolish. It is often said that force is no argument. That, however, entirely depends on what one wants to prove. Many of the most important problems of the last few centuries, such as the continuance of personal government in England, or feudalism in France, have been solved entirely by means of physical force. The very violence of a revolution may make the public grand and splendid for a moment. It was a fatal day when the public discovered that the pen is mightier than the paving-stone, and can be made as offensive as the brick-bat. They at once sought for the journalist, found him, developed him, and made him their industrious and well-paid servant. It is greatly to be regretted, for both their sakes. Behind the barricade there may be much that is noble and heroic. But what is there behind the leading article but prejudice, stupidity, cant, and twaddle? And when these four are joined together they make a terrible force, and constitute the new authority.

In old days men had the rack. Now they have the press. That is an improvement certainly. But still it is very bad, and wrong, and demoralizing. Somebody—was it Burke?—called journalism the fourth estate. That was true at the time, no doubt. But at the present moment it really is the only estate. It has eaten up the other three. The Lords Temporal say nothing, the Lords Spiritual have nothing to say, and the House of Commons has nothing to say and says it. We are dominated by Journalism. In America the President reigns for four years, and Journalism governs for ever and ever. Fortunately, in America journalism has carried its authority to the grossest and most brutal extreme. As a natural consequence it has begun to create a spirit of revolt. People are amused by it, or disgusted by it, according to their temperaments. But it is no longer the real force it was. It is not seriously treated. In England, Journalism, not, except in a few well-known instances, having been carried to such excesses of brutality, is still a great factor, a really remarkable power. The tyranny that it proposes to exercise over people's private lives seems to me to be quite extraordinary. *The fact is, that the public have an insatiable curiosity to know everything, except what is worth knowing.* Journalism, conscious of this, and having tradesmanlike habits, supplies their demands. In centuries before ours the public nailed the ears of journalists to the pump. That was quite hideous. In this century journalists have nailed their own ears to the keyhole. That is much worse. And what aggravates the mischief is that the journalists who are most to blame are not the amusing journalists who write for what are called Society papers. The harm is done by the serious, thoughtful, earnest journalists, who solemnly, as they are doing at present, will drag before the eyes of the public some incident in the private life of a great statesman, of a man who is a leader of political thought as he is a creator of political force, and invite the public to discuss the incident, to exercise authority in the matter, to give their views, and not merely to give their views, but to carry them into action, to dictate to the man upon all other points, to dictate to his party, to dictate to his country; in fact, to make themselves ridiculous, offensive, and harmful. The private lives of men and women should not be told to the public. The public have nothing to do with them at all. In France they manage these things better. There they do not allow the details of the trials that take place in the divorce courts to be published for the amusement or criticism of the public. All that the public are allowed to know is that the divorce has taken place and was granted on petition of one or other or both of the married parties concerned. In France, in fact, they limit the journalist, and allow the artist almost perfect freedom. *Here we allow absolute freedom to the journalist, and entirely limit the artist.* English public opinion, that is to say, tries to constrain and impede and warp the man who makes things that are beautiful in effect, and compels the journalist to retail things that are ugly, or disgusting, or revolting in fact, so that we have the most serious journalists in the world, and the most indecent newspapers. It is no exaggeration to talk of compulsion. There are possibly some journalists who take a real pleasure in publishing horrible things, or who, being poor, look to scandals as forming a sort of permanent basis for an income. But there are other journalists, I feel certain, men of education and cultivation, who really dislike publishing these things, who know that it is wrong to do so, and only do it because the unhealthy conditions under which their occupation is carried on oblige them to supply the public with what the public wants, and to compete with other journalists in making that supply as full and satisfying to the gross popular appetite as possible. It is a very degrading position for any body of educated men to be placed in, and I have no doubt that most of them feel it acutely.

However, let us leave what is really a very sordid side of the subject, and return to the question of popular control in the matter of Art, by which I mean Public Opinion dictating to the artist the form which he is to use, the mode in which he is to use it, and the materals with which he is to work. I have pointed out that the arts which have escaped best in England are the arts in which the public have not been interested. They are, however, interested in the drama, and as a certain advance has been made in the drama within the last ten or fifteen years, it is important to point out that this advance is entirely due to a few individual artists refusing to accept the popular want of taste as their standard, and refusing to regard Art as a mere matter of demand and supply. With his marvellous and vivid personality, with a style that has really a true colour-element in it, with his extraordinary power, not over mere mimicry, but over imaginative and intellectual creation, Mr. Irving, had his sole object been to give the public what they wanted, could have produced the commonest plays in the commonest manner, and made as much success and money as a man could possibly desire. But his object was not that. His object was to realise his own perfection as an artist, under certain conditions, and in certain forms of Art. At first he appealed to the few: now he has educated the many. He has created in the public both taste and temperament. The public appreciate his artistic success immensely. I often wonder, however, whether the public understand that that success is entirely due to the fact that he did not accept their standard, but realised his own. With their standard the Lyceum would have been a sort of second-rate booth, as some of the popular theatres in London are at present. Whether they understand it or not, the fact, however, remains, that taste and temperament have to a certain extent been created in the public, and that the public are capable of developing these qualities. The problem then is, Why do not the public become more civilised? They have the capacity. What stops them?

The thing that stops them, it must be said again, is their desire to exercise authority over the artist and over works of art. To certain theatres, such as the

Lyceum and the Haymarket, the public seem to come in a proper mood. In both of these theatres there have been individual artists, who have succeeded in creating in their audiences—and every theatre in London has its own audience—the temperament to which Art appeals. And what is that temperament? It is the temperament of receptivity. That is all.

If a man approaches a work of art with any desire to exercise authority over it and the artist, he approaches it in such a spirit that he cannot receive any artistic impression from it at all. *The work of art is to dominate the spectator: the spectator is not to dominate the work of art.* The spectator is to be receptive. He is to be the violin on which the master is to play. And the more completely he can suppress his own silly views, his own foolish prejudices, his own absurd ideas of what Art should be or should not be, the more likely he is to understand and appreciate the work of art in question. This is, of course, quite obvious in the case of the vulgar theatre-going public of English men and women. But it is equally true of what are called educated people. For an educated person's ideas of Art are drawn naturally from what Art has been, whereas the new work of art is beautiful by being what Art has never been; and to measure it by the standard of the past is to measure it by a standard on the rejection of which its real perfection depends. A temperament capable of receiving, through an imaginative medium, and under imaginative conditions, new and beautiful impressions is the only temperament that can appreciate a work of art. And true as this is in the case of the appreciation of sculpture and painting, it is still more true of the appreciation of such arts as the drama. For a picture and a statue are not at war with Time. They take no count of its succession. In one moment their unity may be apprehended. In the case of literature it is different. Time must be traversed before the unity of effect is realised. And so, in the drama, there may occur in the first act of the play something whose real artistic value may not be evident to the spectator till the third or fourth act is reached. Is the silly fellow to get angry and call out, and disturb the play, and annoy the artists? No. The honest man is to sit quietly, and know the delightful emotions of wonder, curiosity, and suspense. He is not to go to the play to lose a vulgar temper. He is to go to the play to realise an artistic temperament. He is to go to the play to gain an artistic temperament. He is not the arbiter of the work of art. He is one who is admitted to contemplate the work of art, and, if the work be fine, to forget in its contemplation all the egotism that mars him—the egotism of his ignorance, or the egotism of his information. This point about the drama is hardly, I think, sufficiently recognised. I can quite understand that were *Macbeth* produced for the first time before a modern London audience, many of the people present would strongly and vigorously object to the introduction of the witches in the first act, with their grotesque phrases and their ridiculous words. But when the play is over one realises that the laughter of the witches in *Macbeth* is as terrible as the laughter of madness in *Lear*, more terrible than the laughter of Iago in the tragedy of the Moor. No spectator of art needs a more perfect mood of receptivity than the spectator of a play. The moment he seeks to exercise authority he becomes the avowed enemy of Art and of himself. Art does not mind. It is he who suffers.

With the novel it is the same thing. Popular authority and the recognition of popular authority are fatal. Thackeray's *Esmond* is a beautiful work of art because he wrote it to please himself. In his other novels, in *Pendennis*, in *Philip*, in *Vanity Fair* even, at times, he is too conscious of the public, and spoils his work by appealing directly to the sympathies of the public, or by directly mocking at them. *A true artist takes no notice whatever of the public. The public are to him non-existent.* He has no poppied or honeyed cakes through which to give the monster sleep or sustenance. He leaves that to the popular novelist. One incomparable novelist we have now in England, Mr. George Meredith. There are better artists in France, but France has no one whose view of life is so large, so varied, so imaginatively true. There are tellers of stories in Russia who have a more vivid sense of what pain in fiction may be. But to him belongs philosophy in fiction. His people not merely live, but they live in thought. One can see them from myriad points of view. They are suggestive. There is soul in them and around them. They are interpretative and symbolic. And he who made them, those wonderful quickly moving figures, made them for his own pleasure, and has never asked the public what they wanted, has never cared to know what they wanted, has never allowed the public to dictate to him or influence him in any way, but has gone on intensifying his own personality, and producing his own individual work. At first none came to him. That did not matter. Then the few came to him. That did not change him. The many have come now. He is still the same. He is an incomparable novelist.

With the decorative arts it is not different. The public clung with really pathetic tenacity to what I believe were the direct traditions of the Great Exhibition of international vulgarity, traditions that were so appalling that the houses in which people lived were only fit for blind people to live in. Beautiful things began to be made, beautiful colours came from the dyer's hand, beautiful patterns from the artist's brain, and the use of beautiful things and their value and importance were set forth. The public were really very indignant. They lost their temper. They said silly things. No one minded. No one was a whit the worse. No one accepted the authority of public opinion. And now it is almost impossible to enter any modern house without seeing some recognition of good taste, some recognition of the value of lovely surroundings, some sign of appreciation of beauty. In fact, people's houses are, as a rule, quite charming nowadays. People have been to a very great extent civilised. It is only fair to state, however, that the extraordinary success of the revolution in house decoration and furniture and the like has not really been due to the majority of the public developing a very fine taste in such matters. It has been chiefly due to the fact that the craftsmen of things so appreciated the pleasure of making what was beautiful, and woke to such a vivid consciousness of the hideousness and vulgarity of what the public had previously wanted, that they simply starved the public out. It would be quite impossible at the present moment to furnish a room as rooms were furnished a few years ago, without going for everything to an auction of second-hand furniture from some third-rate lodging-house. The things are no longer made. However they may object to it, people must nowadays have something charming in their surroundings.

Fortunately for them, their assumption of authority in these art matters came to entire grief.

It is evident, then, that all authority in such things is bad. People sometimes inquire what form of government is most suitable for an artist to live under. To this question there is only one answer. *The form of government that is most suitable to the artist is no government at all.* Authority over him and his art is ridiculous. It has been stated that under despotisms artists have produced lovely work. This is not quite so. Artists have visited despots, not as subjects to be tyrannised over, but as wandering wonder-makers, as fascinating vagrant personalities, to be entertained and charmed and suffered to be at peace, and allowed to create. There is this to be said in favour of the despot, that he, being an individual, may have culture, while the mob being a monster, has none. One who is an Emperor and King may stoop down to pick up a brush for a painter, but when the democracy stoops down it is merely to throw mud. And yet the democracy have not so far to stoop as the Emperor. In fact, when they want to throw mud they have not to stoop at all. But there is no necessity to separate the monarch from the mob; all authority is equally bad.

There are three kinds of despots. There is the despot who tyrannises over the body. There is the despot who tyrannises over the soul. There is the despot who tyrannises over soul and body alike. The first is called the Prince. The second is called the Pope. The third is called the people. The Prince may be cultivated. Many Princes have been. Yet in the Prince there is danger. One thinks of Dante at the bitter feast in Verona, of Tasso in Ferrara's madman's cell. It is better for the artist not to live with Princes. The Pope may be cultivated. Many Popes have been; the bad Popes have been. The bad Popes loved Beauty almost as passionately, nay, with as much passion as the good Popes hated Thought. To the wickedness of the Papacy humanity owes much. The goodness of the Papacy owes a terrible debt to Humanity. Yet, though the Vatican has kept the rhetoric of its thunders and lost the rod of its lightning, it is better for the artist not to live with Popes. It was a Pope who said of Cellini to a conclave of Cardinals that common laws and common authority were not made for men such as he; but it was a Pope who thrust Cellini into prison, and kept him there till he sickened with rage, and created unreal visions for himself, and saw the gilded sun enter his room, and grew so enamoured of it that he sought to escape, and crept out from tower to tower, and falling through dizzy air at dawn, maimed himself, and was by a vine-dresser covered with vine leaves, and carried in a cart to one who, loving beautiful things, had care of him. There is danger in Popes. And as for the People, what of them and their authority? Perhaps of them and their authority one has spoken enough. Their authority is a thing blind, deaf, hideous, grotesque, tragic, amusing, serious, and obscene. It is impossible for the artist to live with the People. All despots bribe. The people bribe and brutalise. Who told them to exercise authority? They were made to live, to listen, and to love. Some one has done them a great wrong. They have marred themselves by imitation of their inferiors. They have taken the sceptre of the Prince. How should they use it? They have taken the triple tiara of the Pope. How should they carry its burden? They are as a clown whose heart is broken. They are as a priest whose soul is not yet born. Let all who love Beauty pity them. Though they themselves love not Beauty, yet let them pity themselves. Who taught them the trick of tyranny?

There are many other things that one might point out. One might point out how the Renaissance was great, because it sought to solve no social problem, and busied itself not about such things, but suffered the individual to develop freely, beautifully, and naturally, and so had great and individual artists, and great and individual men. One might point out how Louis XIV, by creating the modern state, destroyed the individualism of the artist, and made things monstrous in their monotony of repetition, and contemptible in their conformity to rule, and destroyed throughout all France all those fine freedoms of expression that had made tradition new in beauty, and new modes one with antique form. But the past is of no importance. The present is of no importance. It is with the future that we have to deal. For the past is what man should not have been. The present is what man ought not to be. The future is what artists are.

It will, of course, be said that such a scheme as is set forth here is quite unpractical, and goes against human nature. This is perfectly true. It is impractical, and it goes against human nature. This is why it is worth carrying out, and that is why one proposes it. For what is a practical scheme? *A practical scheme is either a scheme that is already in existence, or a scheme that could be carried out under existing conditions.* But it is exactly the existing conditions that one objects to; and any scheme that could accept these conditions is wrong and foolish. The conditions will be done away with, and human nature will change. The only thing that one really knows about human nature is that it changes. Change is the one quality we can predicate of it. The systems that fail are those that rely on the permanency of human nature, and not on its growth and development. The error of Louis XIV was that he thought human nature would always be the same. The result of his error was the French Revolution. It was an admirable result. All the results of mistakes of governments are quite admirable.

It is to be noted also that Individualism does not come to man with any sickly cant about duty, which merely means doing what other people want, because they want it; or any hideous cant about self-sacrifice, which is merely a survival of savage mutilation. *In fact, it does not come to man with any claims upon him at all. It comes naturally and inevitably out of man.* It is the point to which all development tends. It is the differentiation to which all organisms grow. It is the perfectioin that is inherent in every mode of life, and towards which every mode of life quickens. And so Individualism exercises no compulsion over man. On the contrary, it says to man that he should suffer no compulsion to be exercised over him. It does not try to force people to be good. It knows that people are good when they are let alone. Man will develop Individualism out of himself. Man is now so developing Individualism. To ask whether Individualism is practical is like asking whether Evolution is practical. *Evolution is the law of life*, and there is no evolution except *towards Individ-*

ualism. Where this tendency is not expressed, it is a case of artificially arrested growth, or of disease, or of death.

Individualism will also be unselfish and unaffected. It has been pointed out that one of the results of the extraordinary tyranny of authority is that words are absolutely distorted from their proper and simple meaning, and are used to express the obverse of their right signification. What is true about Art is true about Life. A man is called affected, nowadays, if he dresses as he likes to dress. But in doing that he is acting in a perfectly natural manner. Affectation, in such matters, consists in dressing according to the views of one's neighbour, whose views, as they are the views of the majority, will probably be extremely stupid. Or a man is called selfish if he lives in the manner that seems to him most suitable for the full realisation of his own personality; if, in fact, the primary aim of his life is self-development. But this is the way in which every one should live. *Selfishness is not living as one wishes to live, it is asking others to live as one wishes to live.* And unselfishness is letting other people's lives alone, not interfering with them. Selfishness always aims at creating around it an absolute uniformity of type. Unselfishness recognises infinite variety of type as a delightful thing, accepts it, acquiesces in it, enjoys it. It is not selfish to think for oneself. A man who does not think for himself does not think at all. It is grossly selfish to require of one's neighbour that he should think in the same way, and hold the same opinions. Why should he? If he can think, he will probably think differently. If he cannot think, it is monstrous to require thought of any kind from him. A red rose is not selfish because it wants to be a red rose. It would be horribly selfish if it wanted all the other flowers in the garden to be both red and roses. Under Individualism people will be quite natural and absolutely unselfish, and will know the meanings of the words, and realise them in their free, beautiful lives. Nor will men be egotistic as they are now. For the egotist is he who makes claims upon others, and the Individualist will not desire to do that. It will not give him pleasure. When man has realised Individualism, he will also realise sympathy and exercise it freely and spontaneously. Up to the present man has hardly cultivated sympathy at all. He has merely sympathy with pain, and sympathy with pain is not the highest form of sympathy. *All sympathy is fine, but sympathy with suffering is the least fine mode.* It is tainted with egotism. It is apt to become morbid. There is in it a certain element of terror for our own safety. We become afraid that we ourselves might be as the leper or as the blind, and that no man would have care of us. It is curiously limiting, too. One should sympathise with the entirety of life, not with life's sores and maladies merely, but with life's joy and beauty and energy and health and freedom. The wider sympathy is, of course, the more difficult. It requires more unselfishness. Anybody can sympathise with the sufferings of a friend, but it requires a very fine nature–it requires, in fact, the nature of a true Individualist–to sympathise with a friend's success. In the modern stress of competition and struggle for place, such sympathy is naturally rare, and is also very much stifled by the immoral ideal of uniformity of type and conformity to rule which is so prevalent everywhere, and is perhaps most obnoxious in England.

Sympathy with pain there will, of course, always be. It is one of the first instincts of man. The animals which are individual, the higher animals that is to say, share it with us. But it must be remembered that while sympathy with joy intensifies the sum of joy in the world, sympathy with pain does not really diminish the amount of pain. It may make man better able to endure evil, but the evil remains. Sympathy with consumption does not cure consumption; that is what Science does. And when Socialism has solved the problem of poverty, and Science solved the problem of disease, the area of the sentimentalists will be lessened, and the sympathy of man will be large, healthy, and spontaneous. Man will have joy in the contemplation of the joyous lives of others.

For it is through joy that the Individualism of the future will develop itself. *Christ made no attempt to reconstruct society, and consequently the Individualism that He preached to man could be realised only through pain or in solitude.* The ideals that we owe to Christ are the ideals of the man who abandons society entirely, or of the man who resists society absolutely. But man is naturally social. Even the Thebaid became people at last. And though the cenobite realises his personality, it is often an impoverished personality that he so realises. Upon the other hand, the terrible truth that pain is a mode through which man may realise himself exercised a wonderful fascination over the world. Shallow speakers and shallow thinkers in pulpits and on platforms often talk about the world's worship of pleasure, and whine against it. But it is rarely in the world's history that its ideal has been one of joy and beauty. The worship of pain has far more often dominated the world. Mediævalism, with its saints and martyrs, its love of self-torture, its wild passion for wounding itself, its gashing with knives, and its whipping with rods—Mediævalism is real Christianity, and the mediæval Christ is the real Christ. When the Renaissance dawned upon the world, and brought with it the new ideals of the beauty of life and the joy of living, men could not understand Christ. Even Art shows us that. The painters of the Renaissance drew Christ as a little boy playing with another boy in a palace or a garden, or lying back in His mother's arms, smiling at her, or at a flower, or at a bright bird; or as a noble, stately figure moving nobly through the world; or as a wonderful figure rising in a sort of ecstasy from death to life. Even when they drew Him crucified, they drew Him as a beautiful God on whom evil men had inflicted suffering. But He did not preoccupy them much. What delighted them was to paint the men and women whom they admired, and to show the loveliness of this lovely earth. They painted many religious pictures; in fact, they painted far too many, and the monotony of type and motive is wearisome and was bad for art. It was the result of the authority of the public in art matters, and it is to be deplored. But their soul was not in the subject. Raphael was a great artist when he painted his portrait of the Pope. When he painted his Madonnas and infant Christs, he is not a great artist at all. Christ had no message for the Renaissance, which was wonderful because it brought an ideal at variance with His, and to find the presentation of the real Christ we must go to mediæval art. There He is one maimed and marred; one who is not comely to look on, because Beauty is a joy; one who is not in fair raiment, because that may be a joy also; He is a beggar who has a marvellous soul; He is a leper whose soul is divine; He needs neither property nor health; He is a God realising His perfection through pain.

The evolution of man is slow. The injustice of men is great. It was necessary that pain should be put forward as a mode of self-realisation. Even now in some places in the world, the message of Christ is necessary. No one who lived in modern Russia could possibly realise his perfection except by pain. A few Russian artists have realised themselves in Art, in a fiction that is mediæval in character, because its dominent note is the realisation of men through suffering. But for those who are not artists, and to whom there is no mode of life but the actual life of fact, pain is the only door to perfection. A Russian who lives happily under the present system of government in Russia must either believe that man has no soul, or that, if he has, it is not worth while developing. A Nihilist who rejects all authority, because he knows authority to be evil, and who welcomes all pain, because through that he realises his personality, is a real Christian. To him the Christian ideal is a true thing.

And yet, Christ did not revolt against authority. He accepted the imperial authority of the Roman Empire and paid tribute. He endured the ecclesiastical authority of the Jewish Church, and would not repel its violence by any violence of His own. He had, as I said before, no scheme for the reconstruction of society. But the modern world has schemes. It proposes to do away with poverty and the suffering that it entails. It desires to get rid of pain, and the suffering that pain entails. It trusts to Socialism and to Science as its methods. What it aims at is an Individualism expressing itself through joy. This Individualism will be larger, fuller, lovelier than any Individualism has ever been. Pain is not the ultimate mode of perfection. It is merely provisional and a protest. It has reference to wrong, unhealthy, unjust surroundings. When the wrong, and the disease, and the injustice are removed, it will have no further place. It will have done its work. It was a great work, but it is almost over. Its sphere lessens every day.

Nor will man miss it. *For what man has sought for is, indeed, neither pain nor pleasure, but simply Life.* Man has sought to live intensely, fully, perfectly. When he can do so without exercising restraint on others, or suffering it ever, and his activities are all pleasurable to him, he will be saner, healthier, more civilised, more himself. Pleasure is Nature's test, her sign of approval. When man is happy, he is in harmony with himself and his environment. The new Individualism, for whose service Socialism, whether it wills it or not, is working, will be perfect harmony. It will be what the Greeks sought for, but could not, except in Thought, realise completely, because they had slaves, and fed them; it will be what the Renaissance sought for, but could not realise completely except in Art, because it had slaves, and starved them. It will be complete, and through it each man will attain to his perfection. The new Individualism is the new Hellenism.

FAIRY TALES

THE HAPPY PRINCE

HIGH above the city, on a tall column, stood the statue of the Happy Prince. He was gilded all over with thin leaves of fine gold; for eyes he had two bright sapphires, and a large red ruby glowed on his sword-hilt.

He was very much admired indeed. "He is as beautiful as a weathercock," remarked one of the Town Councillors who wished to gain a reputation for having artistic tastes; "only not quite so useful," he added, fearing lest people should think him unpractical, which he really was not.

"Why can't you be like the Happy Prince?" asked a sensible mother of her little boy who was crying for the moon. "The Happy Prince never dreams of crying for anything."

"I am glad there is some one in the world who is quite happy," muttered a disappointed man as he gazed at the wonderful statue.

"He looks just like an angel," said the Charity Children as they came out of the cathedral in their bright scarlet cloaks, and their clean white pinafores.

"How do you know?" said the Mathematical Master, "you have never seen one."

"Ah! but we have, in our dreams," answered the children; and the Mathematical Master frowned and looked very severe, for he did not approve of children dreaming.

One night there flew over the city a little Swallow. His friends had gone away to Egypt six weeks before, but he had stayed behind, for he was in love with the most beautiful Reed. He had met her early in the spring as he was flying down the river after a big yellow moth, and had been so attracted by her slender waist that he had stopped to talk to her.

"Shall I love you?" said the Swallow, who liked to come to the point at once, and the Reed made him a low bow. So he flew round and round her, touching the water with his wings, and making silver ripples. This was his courtship, and it lasted all through the summer.

"It is a ridiculous attachment," twittered the other Swallows, "she has no money, and far too many relations"; and indeed the river was quite full of Reeds. Then, when the autumn came, they all flew away.

After they had gone he felt lonely, and began to tire of his lady-love. "She has no conversation," he said, "and I am afraid that she is a coquette, for she is always flirting with the wind." And certainly, whenever the wind blew, the Reed made the most graceful curtsies. "I admit that she is domestic," he continued, "but I love travelling, and my wife, consequently, should love travelling also."

"Will you come away with me?" he said finally to her; but the Reed shook her head, she was so attached to her home.

"You have been trifling with me," he cried. "I am off to the Pyramids. Good-bye!" and he flew away.

All day long he flew, and at night-time he arrived at the city. "Where shall I put up?" he said; "I hope the town has made preparations."

Then he saw the statue on the tall column. "I will put up there," he cried; "it is a fine position with plenty of fresh air." So he alighted just between the feet of the Happy Prince.

"I have a golden bedroom," he said softly to himself as he looked round, and he prepared to go to sleep; but just as he was putting his head under his wing a large drop of water fell on him. "What a curious thing!" he cried, "there is not a single cloud in the sky, the stars are quite clear and bright, and yet it is raining. The climate in the north of Europe is really dreadful. The Reed used to like the rain, but that was merely her selfishness."

Then another drop fell.

"What is the use of a statue if it cannot keep the rain off?" he said; "I must look for a good chimney-pot," and he determined to fly away.

But before he had opened his wings, a third drop fell, and he looked up, and saw—Ah! what did he see?

The eyes of the Happy Prince were filled with tears, and tears were running down his golden cheeks. His face was so beautiful in the moonlight that the little Swallow was filled with pity.

"Who are you?" he said.

"I am the Happy Prince."

"Why are you weeping then?" asked the Swallow; "you have quite drenched me."

"When I was alive and had a human heart," answered the statue, "I did not know what tears were, for I lived in the Palace of Sans Souci, where sorrow is not allowed to enter. In the day time I played with my companions in the garden, and in the evening I led the dance in the Great Hall. Round the garden ran a very lofty wall, but I never cared to ask what lay beyond it, everything about me was so beautiful. My courtiers called me the Happy Prince, and happy indeed I was, if pleasure be happiness. So I lived, and so I died. And now that I am dead they have set me up here so high that I can see all the ugliness and all the misery of my city, and though my heart is made of lead yet I cannot choose but weep."

"What, is he not solid gold?" said the Swallow to himself. He was too polite to make any personal remarks out loud.

"Far away," continued the statue in a low musical voice, "far away in a little street there is a poor house. One of the windows is open, and through it I can see a woman seated at a table. Her face is thin and worn, and she has coarse red hands, all pricked by the needle, for she is a seamstress. She is embroidering passion-flowers on a satin gown for the loveliest of the Queen's maids-of-honour to wear at the next Court-ball. In a bed in the corner of the room her little boy is lying ill. He has a fever, and is asking for oranges. His mother has nothing to give him but river water, so he is crying. Swallow, Swallow, little

Swallow, will you not bring her the ruby out of my sword-hilt? My feet are fastened to this pedestal and I cannot move."

"I am waited for in Egypt," said the Swallow. "My friends are flying up and down the Nile, and talking to the large lotus-flowers. Soon they will be going to sleep in the tomb of the great King. The King is there himself in his painted coffin. He is wrapped in yellow linen, and embalmed with spices. Round his neck is a chain of pale green jade, and his hands are like withered leaves."

"Swallow, Swallow, little Swallow," said the Prince, "will you not stay with me for one night, and be my messenger? The boy is so thirsty, and the mother so sad."

"I don't think I like boys," answered the Swallow. "Last summer, when I was staying on the river, there were two rude boys, the miller's sons, who were always throwing stones at me. They never hit me, of course; we swallows fly far too well for that, and besides, I come of a family famous for its agility; but still, it was a mark of disrespect."

But the Happy Prince looked so sad that the little Swallow was sorry. "It is very cold here," he said; "but I will stay with you for one night, and be your messenger."

"Thank you, little Swallow," said the Prince.

So the Swallow picked out the great ruby from the Prince's sword, and flew away with it in his beak over the roofs of the town.

He passed by the cathedral tower, where the white marble angels were sculptured. He passed by the palace and heard the sound of dancing. A beautiful girl came out on the balcony with her lover. "How wonderful the stars are," he said to her, "and how wonderful is the power of love!" "I hope my dress will be ready in time for the State-ball," she answered; "I have ordered passion-flowers to be embroidered on it; but the seamstresses are so lazy."

He passed over the river, and saw the lanterns hanging to the masts of the ships. He passed over the Ghetto, and saw the old Jews bargaining with each other, and weighing out money in copper scales. At last he came to the poor house and looked in. The boy was tossing feverishly on his bed, and the mother had fallen asleep, she was so tired. In he hopped, and laid the great ruby on the table beside the woman's thimble. Then he flew gently round the bed, fanning the boy's forehead with his wings. "How cool I feel," said the boy, "I must be getting better"; and he sank into a delicious slumber.

Then the Swallow flew back to the Happy Prince, and told him what he had done. "It is curious," he remarked, "but I feel quite warm now, although it is so cold."

"That is because you have done a good action," said the Prince. And the little Swallow began to think, and then he fell asleep. Thinking always made him sleepy.

When day broke he flew down to the river and had a bath. "What a remarkable phenomenon," said the Professor of Ornithology as he was passing over the bridge. "A swallow in winter!" And he wrote a long letter about it to the local newspaper. Every one quoted it, it was full of so many words that they could not understand.

"To-night I go to Egypt," said the Swallow, and he was in high spirits at the prospect. He visited all the public monuments, and sat a long time on top of the church steeple. Wherever he went the Sparrows chirruped, and said to each other, "What a distinguished stranger!" so he enjoyed himself very much.

When the moon rose he flew back to the Happy Prince. "Have you any commissions for Egypt?" he cried. "I am just starting."

"Swallow, Swallow, little Swallow," said the Prince, "will you not stay with me one night longer?"

"I am waited for in Egypt," answered the Swallow. "To-morrow my friends will fly up to the Second Cataract. The river-horse couches there among the bulrushes, and on a great granite throne sits the God Memnon. All night long he watches the stars, and when the morning star shines he utters one cry of joy, and then he is silent. At noon the yellow lions come down to the water's edge to drink. They have eyes like green beryls, and their roar is louder than the roar of the cataract."

"Swallow, Swallow, little Swallow," said the Prince, "far away across the city I see a young man in a garret. He is leaning over a desk covered with papers, and in a tumbler by his side there is a bunch of withered violets. His hair is brown and crisp, and his lips are red as a pomegranate, and he has large and dreamy eyes. He is trying to finish a play for the Director of the Theatre, but he is too cold to write any more. There is no fire in the grate, and hunger has made him faint."

"I will wait with you one night longer," said the Swallow, who really had a good heart. "Shall I take him another ruby?"

"Alas! I have no ruby now," said the Prince; "my eyes are all that I have left. They are made of rare sapphires, which were brought out of India a thousand years ago. Pluck out one of them and take it to him. He will sell it to the jeweller, and buy food and firewood, and finish his play."

"Dear Prince," said the Swallow, "I cannot do that"; and he began to weep.

"Swallow, Swallow, little Swallow," said the Prince, "do as I command you."

So the Swallow plucked out the Prince's eye, and flew away to the student's garret. It was easy enough to get in, as there was a hole in the roof. Through this he darted, and came into the room. The young man had his head buried in his hands, so he did not hear the flutter of the bird's wings, and when he looked up he found the beautiful sapphire lying on the withered violets.

"I am beginning to be appreciated," he cried; "this is from some great admirer. Now I can finish my play," and he looked quite happy.

The next day the Swallow flew down to the harbour. He sat on the mast of a large vessel and watched the sailors hauling big chests out of the hold with ropes. "Heave a-hoy!" they shouted as each chest came up. "I am going to Egypt!" cried the Swallow, but nobody minded, and when the moon rose he flew back to the Happy Prince.

"I am come to bid you good-bye," he cried.

"Swallow, Swallow, little Swallow," said the Prince, "will you not stay with me one night longer?"

"It is winter," answered the Swallow, "and the chill snow will soon be here.

In Egypt the sun is warm on the green palm-trees, and the crocodiles lie in the mud and look lazily about them. My companions are building a nest in the Temple of Baalbec, and the pink and white doves are watching them, and cooing to each other. Dear Prince, I must leave you, but I will never forget you, and next spring I will bring you back two beautiful jewels in place of those you have given away. The ruby shall be redder than a red rose, and the sapphire shall be as blue as the great sea."

"In the square below," said the Happy Prince, "there stands a little match-girl. She has let her matches fall in the gutter, and they are all spoiled. Her father will beat her if she does not bring home some money, and she is crying. She has no shoes or stockings, and her little head is bare. Pluck out my other eye, and give it to her, and her father will not beat her."

"I will stay with you one night longer," said the Swallow, "but I cannot pluck out your eye. You would be quite blind then."

"Swallow, Swallow, little Swallow," said the Prince, "do as I command you."

So he plucked out the Prince's other eye, and darted down with it. He swooped past the match-girl, and slipped the jewel into the palm of her hand. "What a lovely bit of glass," cried the little girl; and she ran home, laughing.

Then the Swallow came back to the Prince. "You are blind now," he said, "so I will stay with you always."

"No, little Swallow," said the poor Prince, "you must go away to Egypt."

"I will stay with you always," said the Swallow, and he slept at the Prince's feet.

All the next day he sat on the Prince's shoulder, and told him stories of what he had seen in strange lands. He told him of the red ibises, who stand in long rows on the banks of the Nile, and catch gold fish in their beaks; of the Sphinx, who is as old as the world itself, and lives in the desert, and knows everything; of the merchants, who walk slowly by the side of their camels, and carry amber beads in their hands; of the King of the Mountains of the Moon, who is as black as ebony, and worships a large crystal; of the great green snake that sleeps in a palm-tree, and has twenty priests to feed it with honey-cakes; and of the pygmies who sail over a big lake on large flat leaves, and are always at war with the butterflies.

"Dear little Swallow," said the Prince, "you tell me of marvellous things, but more marvellous than anything is the suffering of men and of women. There is no Mystery so great as Misery. Fly over my city, little Swallow, and tell me what you see there."

So the Swallow flew over the great city, and saw the rich making merry in their beautiful houses, while the beggars were sitting at the gates. He flew into dark lanes, and saw the white faces of starving children looking out listlessly at the black streets. Under the archway of a bridge two little boys were lying in one another's arms to try and keep themselves warm. "How hungry we are!" they said. "You must not lie here," shouted the Watchman, and they wandered out into the rain.

Then he flew back and told the Prince what he had seen.

"I am covered with fine gold," said the Prince, "you must take it off, leaf by leaf, and give it to my poor; the living always think that gold can make them happy."

Leaf after leaf of the fine gold the Swallow picked off, till the Happy Prince looked quite dull and grey. Leaf after leaf of the fine gold he brought to the poor, and the children's faces grew rosier, and they laughed and played games in the street. "We have bread now!" they cried.

Then the snow came, and after the snow came the frost. The streets looked as if they were made of silver, they were so bright and glistening; long icicles like crystal daggers hung down from the eaves of the houses, everybody went about in furs, and the little boys wore scarlet caps and skated on the ice.

The poor little Swallow grew colder and colder, but he would not leave the Prince, he loved him too well. He picked up crumbs outside the baker's door when the baker was not looking, and tried to keep himself warm by flapping his wings.

But at last he knew that he was going to die. He had just strength to fly up to the Prince's shoulder once more. "Good-bye, dear Prince!" he murmured, "will you let me kiss your hand?"

"I am glad that you are going to Egypt at last, little Swallow," said the Prince, "you have stayed too long here; but you must kiss me on the lips, for I love you."

"It is not to Egypt that I am going," said the Swallow. "I am going to the House of Death. Death is the brother of Sleep, is he not?"

And he kissed the Happy Prince on the lips, and fell down dead at his feet.

At that moment a curious crack sounded inside the statue, as if something had broken. The fact is that the leaden heart had snapped right in two. It certainly was a dreadfully hard frost.

Early the next morning the Mayor was walking in the square below in company with the Town Councillors. As they passed the column he looked up at the statue: "Dear me! how shabby the Happy Prince looks!" he said.

"How shabby indeed!" cried the Town Councillors, who always agreed with the Mayor, and they went up to look at it.

"The ruby has fallen out of his sword, his eyes are gone, and he is golden no longer," said the Mayor; "in fact, he is little better than a beggar!"

"Little better than a beggar," said the Town Councillors.

"And here is actually a dead bird at his feet!" continued the Mayor. "We must really issue a proclamation that birds are not to be allowed to die here." And the Town Clerk made a note of the suggestion.

So they pulled down the statue of the Happy Prince. "As he is no longer beautiful he is no longer useful," said the Art Professor at the University.

Then they melted the statue in a furnace, and the Mayor held a meeting of the Corporation to decide what was to be done with the metal. "We must have another statue, of course," he said, "and it shall be a statue of myself."

"Of myself," said each of the Town Councillors, and they quarrelled. When I last heard of them they were quarrelling still.

"What a strange thing," said the overseer of the workmen at the foundry. "This broken lead heart will not melt in the furnace. We must throw it away." So they threw it on a dust heap where the dead Swallow was also lying.

"Bring me the two most precious things in the city," said God to one of His Angels; and the Angel brought Him the leaden heart and the dead bird.

"You have rightly chosen," said God, "for in my garden of Paradise this little bird shall sing for evermore, and in my city of gold the Happy Prince shall praise me."

THE NIGHTINGALE AND THE ROSE

"SHE said that she would dance with me if I brought her red roses," cried the young Student; "but in all my garden there is no red rose."

From her nest in the holm-oak tree the Nightingale heard him, and she looked out through the leaves, and wondered.

"No red rose in all my garden!" he cried, and his beautiful eyes filled with tears. "Ah, on what little things does happiness depend! I have read all that the wise men have written, and all the secrets of philosophy are mine, yet for want of a red rose is my life made wretched."

"Here at last is a true lover," said the Nightingale. "Night after night have I sung of him, though I knew him not; night after night have I told his story to the stars, and now I see him. His hair is dark as the hyacinth-blossom, and his lips are red as the rose of his desire; but passion has made his face like pale ivory, and sorrow has set her seal upon his brow."

"The Prince gives a ball to-morrow night," murmured the young Student, "and my love will be of the company. If I bring her a red rose she will dance with me till dawn. If I bring her a red rose, I shall hold her in my arms, and she will lean her head upon my shoulder, and her hand will be clasped in mine. But there is no red rose in my garden, so I shall sit lonely, and she will pass me by. She will have no heed of me, and my heart will break."

"Here indeed is the true lover," said the Nightingale. "What I sing of, he suffers: what is joy to me, to him is pain. Surely Love is a wonderful thing. It is more precious than emeralds, and dearer than fine opals. Pearls and pomegranates cannot buy it, nor is it set forth in the market-place. It may not be purchased of the merchants, nor can it be weighed out in the balance for gold."

"The musicians will sit in their gallery," said the young Student, "and play upon their stringed instruments, and my love will dance to the sound of the harp and the violin. She will dance so lightly that her feet will not touch the floor, and the courtiers in their gay dresses will throng around her. But with me she will not dance, for I have no red rose to give her"; and he flung himself down on the grass, and buried his face in his hands, and wept.

"Why is he weeping?" asked a little Green Lizard, as he ran past him with his tail in the air.

"Why, indeed?" said a Butterfly, who was fluttering about after a sunbeam.

"Why, indeed?" whispered a Daisy to his neighbour, in a soft, low voice.

"He is weeping for a red rose," said the Nightingale.

"For a red rose!" they cried; "how very ridiculous!" and the little Lizard, who was something of a cynic, laughed outright.

But the Nightingale understood the secret of the Student's sorrow, and she sat silent in the oak-tree, and thought about the mystery of Love.

Suddenly she spread her brown wings for flight, and soared into the air. She passed through the grove like a shadow, and like a shadow she sailed across the garden.

In the centre of the grass-plot was standing a beautiful Rose-tree, and when she saw it, she flew over to it, and lit upon a spray.

"Give me a red rose," she cried, "and I will sing you my sweetest song."

But the Tree shook its head.

"My roses are white," it answered; "as white as the foam of the sea, and whiter than the snow upon the mountain. But go to my brother who grows round the old sun-dial, and perhaps he will give you what you want."

So the Nightingale flew over to the Rose-tree that was growing round the old sun-dial.

"Give me a red rose," she cried, "and I will sing you my sweetest song."

But the Tree shook its head.

"My roses are yellow," it answered; "as yellow as the hair of the mermaiden who sits upon an amber throne, and yellower than the daffodil that blooms in the meadow before the mower comes with his scythe. But go to my brother who grows beneath the Student's window, and perhaps he will give you what you want."

So the Nightingale flew over to the Rose-tree that was growing beneath the Student's window.

"Give me a red rose," she cried, "and I will sing you my sweetest song."

But the Tree shook its head.

"My roses are red," it answered; "as red as the feet of the dove, and redder than the great fans of coral that wave and wave in the ocean cavern. But the winter has chilled my veins, and the frost has nipped my buds, and the storm has broken my branches, and I shall have no roses at all this year."

"One red rose is all I want," cried the Nightingale. "Only one red rose! Is there any way by which I can get it?"

"There is a way," answered the Tree; "but it is so terrible that I dare not tell it to you."

"Tell it to me," said the Nightingale, "I am not afraid."

"If you want a red rose," said the Tree, "you must build it out of music by moonlight, and stain it with your own heart's-blood. You must sing to me with your breast against a thorn. All night long you must sing to me, and the thorn must pierce your heart, and your life-blood must flow into my veins, and become mine."

"Death is a great price to pay for a red rose," cried the Nightingale, "and Life is very dear to all. It is pleasant to sit in the green wood, and to watch the Sun in his chariot of gold, and the Moon in her chariot of pearl. Sweet is the scent of the hawthorn, and sweet are the bluebells that hide in the valley.

and the heather that blows on the hill. Yet Love is better than Life, and what is the heart of a bird compared to the heart of a man?"

So she spread her brown wings for flight, and soared into the air. She swept over the garden like a shadow, and like a shadow she sailed through the grove.

The young Student was still lying on the grass, where she had left him, and the tears were not yet dry on his beautiful eyes.

"Be happy," cried the Nightingale, "be happy; you shall have your red rose. I will build it out of music by moonlight, and stain it with my own heart's-blood. All that I ask of you in return is that you will be a true lover, for Love is wiser than Philosophy, though she is wise, and mightier than Power, though he is mighty. Flame-coloured are his wings, and coloured like flame is his body. His lips are sweet as honey, and his breath is like frankincense."

The Student looked up from the grass, and listened, but he could not understand what the Nightingale was saying to him, for he only knew the things that are written down in books.

But the Oak-tree understood, and felt sad, for he was very fond of the little nightingale who had built her nest in his branches.

"Sing me one last song," he whispered; "I shall feel very lonely when you are gone."

So the Nightingale sang to the Oak-tree, and her voice was like water bubbling from a silver jar.

When she had finished her song the Student got up, and pulled a note-book and a lead-pencil out of his pocket.

"She has form," he said to himself, as he walked away through the grove, "that cannot be denied her; but has she got feeling? I am afraid not. In fact, she is like most artists; she is all style, without any sincerity. She would not sacrifice herself for others. She thinks merely of music, and everybody knows that the arts are selfish. Still, it must be admitted that she has some beautiful notes in her voice. What a pity it is that they do not mean anything, or do any practical good." And he went into his room, and lay down on his little pallet-bed, and began to think of his love; and, after a time, he fell asleep.

And when the Moon shone in the heavens the Nightingale flew to the Rose-tree, and set her breast against the thorn. All night long she sang with her breast against the thorn, and the cold, crystal Moon leaned down and listened. All night long she sang, and the thorn went deeper and deeper into her breast, and her life-blood ebbed away from her.

She sang first of the birth of love in the heart of a boy and a girl. And on the topmost spray of the Rose-tree there blossomed a marvellous rose, petal followed petal, as song followed song. Pale was it, as first, as the mist that hangs over the river—pale as the feet of the morning, and silver as the wings of the dawn. As the shadow of a rose in a mirror of silver, as the shadow of a rose in a water-pool, so was the rose that blossomed on the topmost spray of the Tree.

But the Tree cried to the Nightingale to press closer against the thorn. "Press closer, little Nightingale," cried the Tree, "or the Day will come before the rose is finished."

So the Nightingale pressed closer against the thorn, and louder and louder grew her song, for she sang of the birth of passion in the soul of a man and a maid.

And a delicate flush of pink came into the leaves of the rose, like the flush in the face of the bridegroom when he kisses the lips of the bride. But the thorn had not yet reached her heart, so the rose's heart remained white, for only a Nightingale's heart's-blood can crimson the heart of a rose.

And the Tree cried to the Nightingale to press closer against the thorn. "Press closer, little Nightingale," cried the Tree, "or the Day will come before the rose is finished."

So the Nightingale pressed closer against the thorn, and the thorn touched her heart, and a fierce pang of pain shot through her. Bitter, bitter was the pain, and wilder and wilder grew her song, for she sang of the Love that is perfected by Death, of the Love that dies not in the tomb.

And the marvellous rose became crimson, like the rose of the eastern sky. Crimson was the girdle of petals, and crimson as a ruby was the heart.

But the Nightingale's voice grew fainter, and her little wings began to beat, and a film came over her eyes. Fainter and fainter grew her song, and she felt something choking her in her throat.

Then she gave one last burst of music. The White Moon heard it, and she forgot the dawn, and lingered on in the sky. The red rose heard it and it trembled all over with ecstasy, and opened it petals to the cold morning air. Echo bore it to her purple cavern in the hills, and woke the sleeping shepherds from their dreams. It floated through the reeds of the river, and they carried its message to the sea.

"Look, look!" cried the Tree, "the rose is finished now"; but the Nightingale made no answer, for she was lying dead in the long grass, with the thorn in her heart.

And at noon the Student opened his window and looked out.

"Why, what a wonderful piece of luck!" he cried; "here is a red rose! I have never seen any rose like it in all my life. It is so beautiful that I am sure it has a long Latin name"; and he leaned down and plucked it.

Then he put on his hat, and ran up to the Professor's house with the rose in his hand.

The daughter of the Professor was sitting in the doorway winding blue silk on a reel, and her little dog was lying at her feet.

"You said that you would dance with me if I brought you a red rose," cried the Student. "Here is the reddest rose in all the world. You will wear it to-night next your heart, and as we dance together it will tell you how I love you."

But the girl frowned.

"I am afraid it will not go with my dress," she answered; "and, besides, the Chamberlain's nephew has sent me some real jewels, and everybody knows that jewels cost far more than flowers."

"Well, upon my word, you are very ungrateful," said the Student, angrily; and he threw the rose into the street. where it fell into the gutter, and a cart-wheel went over it.

"Ungrateful!" said the girl. "I tell you what, you are very rude; and, after all, who are you? Only a Student. Why, I don't believe you have even got silver buckles to your shoes as the Chamberlain's nephew has"; and she got up from her chair and went into the house.

"What a silly thing Love is," said the Student as he walked away. "It is not half as useful as Logic, for it does not prove anything, and it is always telling one of things that are not going to happen, and making one believe things that are not true. In fact, it is quite unpractical, and, as in this age to be practical is everything, I shall go back to Philosophy and study Metaphysics."

So he returned to his room and pulled out a great dusty book, and began to read.

THE SELFISH GIANT

Every afternoon, as they were coming from school, the children used to go and play in the Giant's garden.

It was a large, lovely garden, with soft green grass. Here and there over the grass stood beautiful flowers like stars, and there were twelve peach-trees that in the spring-time broke out into delicate blossoms of pink and pearl, and in the autumn bore rich fruit. The birds sat on the trees and sang so sweetly that the children used to stop their games in order to listen to them. "How happy we are here!" they cried to each other.

One day the Giant came back. He had been to visit his friend the Cornish ogre, and had stayed with him for seven years. After the seven years were over he had said all that he had to say, for his conversation was limited, and he determined to return to his own castle. When he arrived he saw the children playing in the garden.

"What are you doing there?" he cried in a very gruff voice, and the children ran away.

"My own garden is my own garden," said the Giant; "any one can understand that, and I will allow nobody to play in it but myself." So he built a high wall all around it, and put up a notice-board.

TRESPASSERS
WILL BE
PROSECUTED.

He was a very selfish Giant.

The poor children had now nowhere to play. They tried to play on the road, but the road was very dusty and full of hard stones, and they did not like it. They used to wander round the high wall when their lessons were over, and talk about the beautiful garden inside. "How happy we were there," they said to each other.

Then the Spring came, and all over the country there were little blossoms and little birds. Only in the garden of the Selfish Giant it was still winter. The birds did not care to sing in it as there were no children, and the trees forgot to blossom. Once a beautiful flower put its head out from the grass, but when it saw the notice-board it was so sorry for the children that it slipped back into the ground again, and went off to sleep. The only people who were pleased were the Snow and the Frost. "Spring has forgotten this garden," they cried, "so we will live here all the year round." The Snow covered up the grass with her great white cloak, and the Frost painted all the trees silver. Then they invited the North Wind to stay with them, and he came. He was wrapped in furs, and he roared all day about the garden, and blew the chimney-pots down. "This is a delightful spot," he said, "we must ask the Hail on a visit." So the Hail came. Every day for three hours he rattled on the roof of the castle till he broke most of the slates, and then he ran round and round the garden as fast as he could go. He was dressed in grey, and his breath was like ice.

"I cannot understand why the Spring is so late in coming," said the Selfish Giant, as he sat at the window and looked out at his cold white garden. "I hope there will be a change in the weather."

But the Spring never came, nor the Summer. The Autumn gave golden fruit to every garden, but to the Giant's garden she gave none. "He is too selfish," she said. So it was always Winter there, and the North Wind, and the Hail, and the Frost, and the Snow danced about through the trees.

One morning the Giant was lying awake in bed when he heard some lovely music. It sounded so sweet to his ears that he thought it must be the King's musicians passing by. It was really only a little linnet singing outside his window, but it was so long since he had heard a bird sing in his garden that it seemed to him to be the most beautiful music in the world. Then the Hail stopped dancing over his head, and the North Wind ceased roaring, and a delicious perfume came to him through the open casement. "I believe the Spring has come at last," said the Giant; and he jumped out of bed and looked out.

What did he see?

He saw a most wonderful sight. Through a little hole in the wall the children had crept in, and they were sitting in the branches of the trees. In every tree that he could see there was a little child. And the trees were so glad to have the children back again that they had covered themselves with blossoms, and were waving their arms gently above the children's heads. The birds were flying about and twittering with delight, and the flowers were looking up through the green grass and laughing. It was a lovely scene, only in one corner it was still winter. It was the farthest corner of the garden, and in it was standing a little boy. He was so small that he could not reach up to the branches of the tree, and he was wandering all round it, crying bitterly. The poor tree was still quite covered with frost and snow, and the North Wind was blowing and roaring above it. "Climb up! little boy," said the Tree, and it bent its branches down as low as it could; but the boy was too tiny.

And the Giant's heart melted as he looked out. "How selfish I have been!" he said; "now I know why the Spring would not come here. I will put the poor little boy on the top of the tree, and then I will knock down the wall, and my garden shall be the children's playground for ever and ever." He was really very sorry for what he had done.

So he crept downstairs and opened the front door quite softly, and went out into the garden. But when the children saw him they were so frightened that they all ran away, and the garden became winter again. Only the little boy did not run, for his eyes were so full of tears that he did not see the Giant coming. And the Giant stole up behind him and took him gently in his hand, and put him up into the tree. And the tree broke at once into blossom, and the birds came and sang on it, and the little boy stretched out his two arms and flung them around the Giant's neck, and kissed him. And the other children, when they saw that the Giant was not wicked any longer, came running back, and with them came the Spring. "It is your garden now, little children," said the Giant, and he took a great axe and knocked down the wall. And when the people were going to market at twelve o'clock they found the Giant playing with the children in the most beautiful garden they had ever seen.

All day long they played, and in the evening they came to the Giant to bid him good-bye.

"But where is your little companion?" he said: "the boy I put into the tree." The Giant loved him the best because he had kissed him.

"We don't know," answered the children; "he has gone away."

"You must tell him to be sure and come here to-morrow," said the Giant. But the children said that they did not know where he lived, and had never seen him before; and the Giant felt very sad.

Every afternoon, when school was over, the children came and played with the Giant. But the little boy whom the Giant loved was never seen again. The Giant was very kind to all the children, yet he longed for his first little friend, and often spoke of him. "How I would like to see him!" he used to say.

Years went over, and the Giant grew very old and feeble. He could not play about any more, so he sat in a huge armchair, and watched the children at their games, and admired his garden. "I have many beautiful flowers," he said; "but the children are the most beautiful flowers of all."

One winter morning he looked out of his window as he was dressing. He did not hate the Winter now, for he knew that it was merely the Spring asleep, and that the flowers were resting.

Suddenly he rubbed his eyes in wonder, and looked and looked. It certainly was a marvellous sight. In the farthest corner of the garden was a tree quite covered with lovely white blossoms. Its branches were all golden, and silver fruit hung down from them, and underneath it stood the little boy he had loved.

Downstairs ran the Giant in great joy, and out into the garden. He hastened across the grass, and came near to the child. And when he came quite close his face grew red with anger, and he said, "Who hath dared to wound thee?" For on the palms of the child's hands were the prints of two nails, and the prints of two nails were on the little feet.

"Who hath dared to wound thee?" cried the Giant; "tell me, that I may take my big sword and slay him."

"Nay!" answered the child; "but these are the wounds of Love."

"Who art thou?" said the Giant, and a strange awe fell on him, and he knelt before the little child.

And the child smiled on the Giant, and said to him, "You let me play once in your garden, to-day you shall come with me to my garden, which is Paradise."

And when the children ran in that afternoon, they found the Giant lying dead under the tree, all covered with white blossoms.

THE DEVOTED FRIEND

ONE morning the old Water-rat put his head out of his hole. He had bright beady eyes and stiff grey whiskers, and his tail was like a long bit of black india-rubber. The little ducks were swimming about in the pond, looking just like a lot of yellow canaries, and their mother, who was pure white with real red legs, was trying to teach them how to stand on their heads in the water.

"You will never be in the best society unless you can stand on your heads," she kept saying to them; and every now and then she showed them how it was done. But the little ducks paid no attention to her. They were so young that they did not know what an advantage it is to be in society at all.

"What disobedient children!" cried the old Water-rat; "they really deserve to be drowned."

"Nothing of the kind," answered the Duck; "every one must make a beginning, and parents cannot be too patient."

"Ah! I know nothing about the feelings of parents," said the Water-rat; "I am not a family man. In fact, I have never been married, and I never intend to be. Love is all very well in its way, but friendship is much higher. Indeed, I know of nothing in the world that is either nobler or rarer than a devoted friendship."

"And what, pray, is your idea of the duties of a devoted friend?" asked a Green Linnet, who was sitting in a willow-tree hard by, and had overheard the conversation.

"Yes, that is just what I want to know," said the Duck, and she swam away to the end of the pond, and stood upon her head, in order to give her children a good example.

"What a silly question!" cried the Water-rat. "I should expect my devoted friend to be devoted to me, of course."

"And what would you do in return?" said the little bird, swinging upon a silver spray, and flapping his tiny wings.

"I don't understand you," answered the Water-rat.

"Let me tell you a story on the subject," said the Linnet.

"Is the story about me?" asked the Water-rat. "If so, I will listen to it, for I am extremely fond of fiction."

"It is applicable to you," answered the Linnet; and he flew down, and alighting upon the bank, he told the story of The Devoted Friend.

"Once upon a time," said the Linnet, "there was an honest little fellow named Hans."

"Was he very distinguished?" asked the Water-rat.

"No," answered the Linnet, "I don't think he was distinguished at all, except for his kind heart, and his funny round good-humoured face. He lived in a tiny cottage all by himself, and every day he worked in his garden. In all the country-side there was no garden so lovely as his. Sweet-william grew there, and Gilly-flowers, and Shepherd's-purses, and Fair-maids of France. There were damask Roses, and yellow Roses, lilac Crocuses, and gold, purple Violets and white. Columbine and Lady smock, Marjoram and Wild Basil, the Cowslip and the Flower-de-luce, the Daffodil and the Clove-Pink bloomed or blossomed in their proper order as the months went by, one flower taking another flower's place, so that there were always beautiful things to look at, and pleasant odours to smell.

"Little Hans had a great many friends, but the most devoted friend of all was big Hugh the Miller. Indeed, so devoted was the rich Miller to little Hans, that he would never go by his garden without leaning over the wall and plucking a large nose-gay, or a handful of sweet herbs, or filling his pockets with plums and cherries if it was the fruit season.

" 'Real friends should have everything in common,' the Miller used to say, and little Hans nodded and smiled, and felt very proud of having a friend with such noble ideas.

"Sometimes, indeed, the neighbours thought it strange that the rich Miller never gave little Hans anything in return, though he had a hundred sacks of flour stored away in his mill, and six milch cows, and a large flock of woolly sheep; but Hans never troubled his head about these things, and nothing gave him greater pleasure than to listen to all the wonderful things the Miller used to say about the unselfishness of true friendship.

"So little Hans worked away in his garden. During the spring, the summer, and the autumn he was very happy, but when the winter came, and he had no fruit or flowers to bring to the market, he suffered a good deal from cold and hunger, and often had to go to bed without any supper but a few dried pears or some hard nuts. In the winter, also, he was extremely lonely, as the Miller never came to see him then.

" 'There is no good in my going to see little Hans as long as the snow lasts,' the Miller used to say to his wife, 'for when people are in trouble they should be left alone, and not be bothered by visitors. That at least is my idea about friendship, and I am sure I am right. So I shall wait till the spring comes, and then I shall pay him a visit, and he will be able to give me a large basket of primroses, and that will make him so happy.'

" 'You are certainly very thoughtful about others,' answered the Wife, as she sat in her comfortable arm-chair by the big pinewood fire; 'very thoughtful indeed. It is quite a treat to hear you talk about friendship. I am sure the clergyman himself could not say such beautiful things as you do, though he does live in a three-storied house, and wear a gold ring on his little finger.'

" 'But could we not ask little Hans up here?' said the Miller's youngest son.

'If poor Hans is in trouble I will give him half my porridge, and show him my white rabbits.'

" 'What a silly boy you are!' cried the Miller; 'I really don't know what is the use of sending you to school. You seem not to learn anything. Why, if little Hans came up here, and saw our warm fire, and our good supper, and our great cask of red wine, he might get envious, and envy is a most terrible thing, and would spoil anybody's nature. I certainly will not allow Hans's nature to be spoiled. I am his best friend, and I will always watch over him, and see that he is not led into any temptations. Besides, if Hans came here, he might ask me to let him have some flour on credit, and that I could not do. Flour is one thing, and friendship is another, and they should not be confused. Why, the words are spelt differently, and mean quite different things. Everybody can see that.'

" 'How well you talk!' said the Miller's Wife, pouring herself out a large glass of warm ale; 'really I feel quite drowsy. It is just like being in church.'

" 'Lots of people act well,' answered the Miller; 'but very few people talk well, which shows that talking is much the more difficult thing of the two, and much the finer thing also'; and he looked sternly across the table at his little son, who felt so ashamed of himself that he hung his head down, and grew quite scarlet, and began to cry into his tea. However, he was so young that you must excuse him."

"Is that the end of the story?" asked the Water-rat.

"Certainly not," answered the Linnet, "that is the beginning."

"Then you are quite behind the age," said the Water-rat. "Every good story-teller nowadays starts with the end, and then goes on to the beginning, and concludes with the middle. That is the new method. I heard all about it the other day from a critic who was walking round the pond with a young man. He spoke of the matter at great length, and I am sure he must have been right, for he had blue spectacles and a bald head, and whenever the young man made any remark, he always answered 'Pooh!' But pray go on with your story. I like the Miller immensely. I have all kinds of beautiful sentiments myself, so there is a great sympathy between us."

"Well," said the Linnet, hopping now on one leg and now on the other, "as soon as the winter was over, and the primroses began to open their pale yellow stars, the Miller said to his wife that he would go down and see little Hans.

" 'Why, what a good heart you have!' cried his Wife; 'you are always thinking of others. And mind you take the big basket with you for the flowers.'

"So the Miller tied the sails of the windmill together with a strong iron chain, and went down the hill with the basket on his arm.

" 'Good morning, little Hans,' said the Miller.

" 'Good morning,' said Hans, leaning on his spade, and smiling from ear to ear.

" 'And how have you been all the winter?' said the Miller.

" 'Well, really,' cried Hans, 'it is very good of you to ask, very good indeed. I am afraid I had rather a hard time of it, but now the spring has come, and I am quite happy, and all my flowers are doing well.'

" 'We often talked of you during the winter, Hans,' said the Miller, 'and wondered how you were getting on.'

" 'That was kind of you,' said Hans; 'I was half afraid you had forgotten me.'

" 'Hans, I am surprised at you,' said the Miller; 'friendship never forgets. That is the wonderful thing about it, but I am afraid you don't understand the poetry of life. How lovely your primroses are looking, by-the-bye!'

" 'They are certainly very lovely,' said Hans, 'and it is a most lucky thing for me that I have so many. I am going to bring them into the market and sell them to the Burgomaster's daughter, and buy back my wheelbarrow with the money.'

" 'Buy back your wheelbarrow? You don't mean to say you have sold it? What a very stupid thing to do!'

" 'Well, the fact is,' said Hans, 'that I was obliged to. You see the winter was a very bad time for me, and I really had no money at all to buy bread with. So I first sold the silver buttons off my Sunday coat, and then I sold my silver chain, and then I sold my big pipe, and at last I sold my wheelbarrow. But I am going to buy them all back again now.'

" 'Hans,' said the Miller, 'I will give you my wheelbarrow. It is not in very good repair; indeed, one side is gone, and there is something wrong with the wheel-spokes; but in spite of that I will give it to you. I know it is very generous of me, and a great many people would think me extremely foolish for parting with it, but I am not like the rest of the world. I think that generosity is the essence of friendship, and, besides I have got a new wheelbarrow for myself. Yes, you may set your mind at ease, I will give you my wheelbarrow.'

" 'Well, really, that is generous of you,' said little Hans, and his funny round face glowed all over with pleasure. 'I can easily put it in repair, as I have a plank of wood in the house.'

" 'A plank of wood!' said the Miller, 'why, that is just what I want for the roof of my barn. There is a very large hole in it, and the corn will all get damp if I don't stop it up. How lucky you mentioned it! It is quite remarkable how one good action always breeds another. I have given you my wheelbarrow, and now you are going to give me your plank. Of course, the wheelbarrow is worth far more than the plank, but true friendship never notices things like that. Pray get it at once, and I will set to work at my barn this very day.'

" 'Certainly,' cried little Hans, and he ran into the shed and dragged the plank out.

" 'It is not a very big plank,' said the Miller, looking at it, 'and I am afraid that after I have mended my barn-roof there won't be any left for you to mend the wheelbarrow with; but, of course, that is not my fault. And now, as I have given you my wheelbarrow, I am sure you would like to give me some flowers in return. Here is the basket, and mind you fill it quite full.'

" 'Quite full?' said little Hans, rather sorrowfully, for it was really a very big basket, and he knew that if he filled it he would have no flowers left for the market, and he was very anxious to get his silver buttons back.

" 'Well, really,' answered the Miller, 'as I have given you my wheelbarrow, I don't think that it is much to ask you for a few flowers. I may be wrong, but I should have thought that friendship, true friendship, was quite free from selfishness of any kind.'

" 'My dear friend, my best friend,' cried little Hans, 'you are welcome to all the flowers in my garden. I would much sooner have your good opinion than my silver buttons, any day,' and he ran and plucked all his pretty primroses, and filled the Miller's basket.

" 'Good-bye, little Hans,' said the Miller, as he went up the hill with the plank on his shoulder, and the big basket in his hand.

" 'Good-bye,' said little Hans, and he began to dig away quite merrily, he was so pleased about the wheelbarrow.

"The next day he was nailing up some honeysuckle against the porch, when he heard the Miller's voice calling to him from the road. So he jumped off the ladder, and ran down to the garden, and looked over the wall.

"There was the Miller with a large sack of flour on his back.

" 'Dear little Hans,' said the miller, 'would you mind carrying this sack of flour for me to market?'

" 'Oh, I am so sorry,' said Hans, 'but I am really very busy to-day. I have got all my creepers to nail up, and all my flowers to water, and all my grass to roll.'

" 'Well, really,' said the Miller, 'I think that, considering that I am going to give you my wheelbarrow, it is rather unfriendly of you to refuse.'

" 'Oh, don't say that,' cried little Hans, 'I wouldn't be unfriendly for the whole world'; and he ran in for his cap, and trudged off with the big sack on his shoulders.

"It was a very hot day, and the road was terribly dusty, and before Hans had reached the sixth milestone he was so tired that he had to sit down and rest. However, he went on bravely, and at last he reached the market. After he had waited there some time, he sold the sack of flour for a very good price, and then he returned home at once, for he was afraid that if he stopped too late he might meet some robbers on the way.

" 'It has certainly been a hard day,' said little Hans to himself as he was going to bed, 'but I am glad I did not refuse the Miller, for he is my best friend, and besides, he is going to give me his wheelbarrow.'

"Early the next morning the Miller came down to get the money for his sack of flour, but little Hans was so tired that he was still in bed.

" 'Upon my word,' said the Miller, 'you are very lazy. Really, considering that I am going to give you my wheelbarrow, I think you might work harder. Idleness is a great sin, and I certainly don't like any of my friends to be idle or sluggish. You must not mind my speaking quite plainly to you. Of course I should not dream of doing so if I were not your friend. But what is the good of friendship if one cannot say exactly what one means? Anybody can say charming things and try to please and to flatter, but a true friend always says unpleasant things, and does not mind giving pain. Indeed, if he is a really true friend he prefers it, for he knows then that he is doing good.'

"'I am very sorry,' said little Hans, rubbing his eyes and pulling off his nightcap, 'but I was so tired that I thought I would lie in bed for a little time, and listen to the birds singing. Do you know that I always work better after hearing the birds sing?'

"'Well, I am glad of that,' said the Miller, clapping little Hans on the back, 'for I want you to come up to the mill as soon as you are dressed, and mend my barn-roof for me.'

"Poor little Hans was very anxious to go and work in his garden, for his flowers had not been watered for two days, but he did not like to refuse the Miller, as he was such a good friend to him.

"'Do you think it would be unfriendly of me if I said I was busy?' he inquired in a shy and timid voice.

"'Well, really,' answered the Miller, 'I do not think it is much to ask of you, considering that I am going to give you my wheelbarrow; but of course if you refuse I will go and do it myself.'

"'Oh! on no account,' cried little Hans; and he jumped out of bed, and dressed himself, and went up to the barn.

"He worked there all day long, till sunset, and at sunset the Miller came to see how he was getting on.

"'Have you mended the hole in the roof yet, little Hans?' cried the Miller in a cheery voice.

"'It is quite mended,' answered little Hans, coming down the ladder.

"'Ah!' said the Miller, 'there is no work so delightful as the work one does for others.'

"'It is certainly a great privilege to hear you talk,' answered little Hans, sitting down and wiping his forehead, 'a very great privilege. But I am afraid I shall never have such beautiful ideas as you have.'

"'Oh! they will come to you,' said the Miller, 'but you must take more pains. At present you have only the practice of friendship; some day you will have the theory also.'

"'Do you really think I shall?' asked little Hans.

"'I have no doubt of it,' answered the Miller; 'but now that you have mended the roof, you had better go home and rest, for I want you to drive my sheep to the mountain to-morrow.'

"Poor little Hans was afraid to say anything to this, and early the next morning the Miller brought his sheep round to the cottage, and Hans started off with them to the mountain. It took him the whole day to get there and back; and when he returned he was so tired that he went off to sleep in his chair, and did not wake up till it was broad daylight.

"'What a delightful time I shall have in my garden,' he said, and he went to work at once.

"But somehow he was never able to look after his flowers at all, for his friend the Miller was always coming round and sending him off on long errands, or getting him to help at the mill. Little Hans was very much distressed at times, as he was afraid his flowers would think he had forgotten them, but he consoled himself by the reflection that the Miller was his best friend. 'Besides.' he used to say, 'he is going to give me his wheelbarrow, and that is an act of pure generosity.'

"So little Hans worked away for the Miller, and the Miller said all kinds of beautiful things about friendship, which Hans took down in a note-book, and used to read over at night, for he was a very good scholar.

"Now it happened that one evening little Hans was sitting by his fireside when a loud rap came at the door. It was a very wild night, and the wind was blowing and roaring round the house so terribly that at first he thought it was merely the storm. But a second rap came, and then a third, louder than either of the others.

" 'It is some poor traveller,' said little Hans to himself, and he ran to the door.

"There stood the Miller with a lantern in one hand and a big stick in the other.

" 'Dear little Hans,' cried the Miller, 'I am in great trouble. My little boy has fallen off a ladder and hurt himself, and I am going for the Doctor. But he lives so far away, and it is such a bad night, that it has just occurred to me that it would be much better if you went instead of me. You know I am going to give you my wheelbarrow, and so it is only fair that you should do something for me in return.'

" 'Certainly,' cried little Hans, 'I take it quite as a compliment your coming to me, and I will start off at once. But you must lend me your lantern, as the night is so dark that I am afraid I might fall into the ditch.'

" 'I am very sorry,' answered the Miller, 'but it is my new lantern, and it would be a great loss to me if anything happened to it.'

" 'Well, never mind, I will do without it,' cried little Hans, and he took down his great fur coat, and his warm scarlet cap, and tied a muffler round his throat, and started off.

"What a dreadful night it was! The night was so black that little Hans could hardly see, and the wind was so strong that he could scarcely stand. However, he was very courageous, and after he had been walking about three hours, he arrived at the Doctor's house, and knocked at the door.

" 'Who is there?' cried the Doctor, putting his head out of his bedroom window.

" 'Little Hans, Doctor.'

" 'What do you want, little Hans?'

" 'The Miller's son has fallen from a ladder, and has hurt himself, and the Miller wants you to come at once.'

" 'All right!' said the Doctor; and he ordered his horse, and his big boots, and his lantern, and came downstairs, and rode off in the direction of the Miller's house, little Hans trudging behind him.

"But the storm grew worse and worse, and the rain fell in torrents, and little Hans could not see where he was going, or keep up with the horse. At last he lost his way, and wandered off on the moor, which was a very dangerous place, as it was full of deep holes, and there poor little Hans was drowned. His body was found the next day by some goatherds, floating in a great pool of water, and was brought back by them to the cottage.

"Everybody went to little Hans's funeral, as he was so popular, and the Miller was the chief mourner.

" 'As I was his best friend,' said the Miller, 'it is only fair that I should have the best place'; so he walked at the head of the procession in a long black cloak, and every now and then he wiped his eyes with a big pocket-handkerchief.

" 'Little Hans is certainly a great loss to every one,' said the Blacksmith, when the funeral was over, and they were all seated comfortably in the inn, drinking spiced wine and eating sweet cakes.

" 'A great loss to me at any rate,' answered the Miller; 'why, I had as good as given him my wheelbarrow, and now I really don't know what to do with it. It is very much in my way at home, and it is in such bad repair that I could not get anything for it if I sold it. I will certainly take care not to give away anything again. One always suffers for being generous.' "

"Well?" said the Water-rat, after a long pause.

"Well, that is the end," said the Linnet.

"But what became of the Miller?" asked the Water-rat.

"Oh! I really don't know," replied the Linnet; "and I am sure that I don't care."

"It is quite evident then that you have no sympathy in your nature," said the Water-rat.

"I am afraid you don't quite see the moral of the story," remarked the Linnet.

"The what?" screamed the Water-rat.

"The moral."

"Do you mean to say that the story has a moral?"

"Certainly," said the Linnet.

"Well, really," said the Water-rat, in a very angry manner, "I think you should have told me that before you began. If you had done so, I certainly would not have listened to you; in fact, I should have said 'Pooh,' like the critic. However, I can say it now"; so he shouted out "Pooh" at the top of his voice, gave a whisk with his tail, and went back into his hole.

"And how do you like the Water-rat?" asked the Duck, who came paddling up some minutes afterwards. "He has a great many good points, but for my own part I have a mother's feelings, and I can never look at a confirmed bachelor without the tears coming into my eyes."

"I am rather afraid that I have annoyed him," said the Linnet. "The fact is, that I told him a story with a moral."

"Ah! that is always a very dangerous thing to do," said the Duck.

And I quite agree with her.

THE REMARKABLE ROCKET

THE King's son was going to be married, so there were general rejoicings. He had waited a whole year for his bride, and at last she had arrived. She was a Russian Princess, and had driven all the way from Finland in a sledge drawn by six reindeer. The sledge was shaped like a great golden swan, and between the swan's wings lay the little Princess herself. Her long ermine cloak reached right down to her feet, on her head was a tiny cap of silver tissue, and she was as pale as the Snow Palace in which she had always lived. So pale was she that as she drove through the streets all the people wondered. "She is like a white rose!" they cried, and they threw down flowers on her from the balconies.

At the gate of the Castle the Prince was waiting to receive her. He had dreamy violet eyes, and his hair was like fine gold. When he saw her he sank upon one knee, and kissed her hand.

"Your picture was beautiful," he murmured, "but you are more beautiful than your picture"; and the little Princess blushed.

"She was like a white rose before," said a young Page to his neighbour, "but she is like a red rose now"; and the whole Court was delighted.

For the next three days everybody went about saying, "White rose, Red rose, Red rose, White rose"; and the King gave orders that the Page's salary was to be doubled. As he received no salary at all this was not of much use to him, but it was considered a great honour, and was duly published in the Court Gazette.

When the three days were over the marriage was celebrated. It was a magnificent ceremony, and the bride and bridegroom walked hand in hand under a canopy of purple velvet embroidered with little pearls. Then there was a State Banquet, which lasted for five hours. The Prince and Princess sat at the top of the Great Hall and drank out of a cup of clear crystal. Only true lovers could drink out of this cup, for if false lips touched it, it grew grey and dull and cloudy.

"It is quite clear that they love each other," said the little Page, "as clear as crystal!" and the King doubled his salary a second time. "What an honour!" cried all the courtiers.

After the banquet there was to be a Ball. The bride and bridegroom were to dance the Rose-dance together, and the King had promised to play the flute. He played very badly, but no one had ever dared to tell him so, because he was the King. Indeed, he only knew two airs, and was never quite certain which one he was playing; but it made no matter, for, whatever he did, everybody cried out, "Charming! charming!"

The last item on the programme was a grand display of fireworks, to be let off exactly at midnight. The little Princess had never seen a firework in her life, so the King had given orders that the Royal Pyrotechnist should be in attendance on the day of her marriage.

"What are fireworks like?" she had asked the Prince, one morning, as she was walking on the terrace.

"They are like the Aurora Borealis," said the King, who always answered questions that were addressed to other people, "only much more natural. I prefer them to stars myself, as you always know when they are going to appear, and they are as delightful as my own flute-playing. You must certainly see them."

So at the end of the King's garden a great stand had been set up, and as soon as the Royal Pyrotechnist had put everything in its proper place, the fireworks began to talk to each other.

"The world is certainly very beautiful," cried a little Squib. "Just look at those yellow tulips. Why! if they were real crackers they could not be lovelier. I am very glad I have travelled. Travel improves the mind wonderfully, and does away with all one's prejudices."

"The King's garden is not the world, you foolish squib," said a big Roman Candle; "the world is an enormous place, and it would take you three days to see it thoroughly."

"Any place you love is the world to you," exclaimed a pensive Catharine Wheel, who had been attached to an old deal box in early life, and prided herself on her broken heart; "but love is not fashionable any more, the poets have killed it. They wrote so much about it that nobody believed them, and I am not surprised. True love suffers, and is silent. I remember myself once—— But it is no matter now. Romance is a thing of the past."

"Nonsense!" said the Roman Candle, "Romance never dies. It is like the moon, and lives for ever. The bride and bridegroom, for instance, love each other very dearly. I heard all about them this morning from a brown-paper cartridge, who happened to be staying in the same drawer with myself, and knew the latest Court news."

But the Catharine Wheel shook her head. "Romance is dead, Romance is dead, Romance is dead," she murmured. She was one of those people who think that, if you say the same thing over and over a great many times, it becomes true in the end.

Suddenly a sharp, dry cough was heard, and they all looked round.

It came from a tall, supercilious-looking Rocket, who was tied to the end of a long stick. He always coughed before he made any observation, so as to attract attention.

"Ahem! ahem!" he said, and everybody listened except the poor Catharine Wheel, who was still shaking her head, and murmuring, "Romance is dead."

"Order! order!" cried out a Cracker. He was something of a politician, and had always taken a prominent part in the local elections, so he knew the proper Parliamentary expressions to use.

"Quite dead," whispered the Catharine Wheel, and she went off to sleep.

As soon as there was perfect silence, the Rocket coughed a third time and began. He spoke with a very slow, distinct voice, as if he was dictating his memoirs, and always looked over the shoulder of the person to whom he was talking. In fact, he had a most distinguished manner.

"How fortunate it is for the King's son," he remarked, "that he is to be married on the very day on which I am to be let off. Really, if it had been arranged beforehand, it could not have turned out better for him; but Princes are always lucky."

"Dear me!" said the little Squib, "I thought it was quite the other way, and that we were to be let off in the Prince's honour."

"It may be so with you," he answered, "indeed, I have no doubt that it is, but with me it is different. I am a very remarkable Rocket, and come of remarkable parents. My mother was the most celebrated Catharine Wheel of her day, and was renowned for her graceful dancing. When she made her great public appearance she spun round nineteen times before she went out, and each time that she did so she threw into the air seven pink stars. She was three feet and a half in diameter, and made of the very best gunpowder. My father was a Rocket like myself, and of French extraction. He flew so high that the people were afraid that he would never come down again. He did, though, for he was of a kindly disposition, and he made a most brilliant descent in a shower of golden rain. The newspapers wrote about his performance in very flattering terms. Indeed, the Court Gazette called him a triumph of Pylotechnic art."

"Pyrotechnic, Pyrotechnic, you mean," said a Bengal Light; "I know it is Pyrotechnic, for I saw it written on my own canister."

"Well, I said Pylotechnic," answered the Rocket, in a severe tone of voice, and the Bengal Light felt so crushed that he began at once to bully the little squibs, in order to show that he was still a person of some importance.

"I was saying," continued the Rocket, "I was saying— What was I saying?"

"You were talking about yourself," replied the Roman Candle.

"Of course; I knew I was discussing some interesting subject when I was so rudely interrupted. I hate rudeness and bad manners of every kind, for I am extremely sensitive. No one in the whole world is so sensitive as I am, I am quite sure of that."

"What is a sensitive person?" said the Cracker to the Roman Candle.

"A person who, because he has corns himself, always treads on other people's toes," answered the Roman Candle in a low whisper; and the Cracker nearly exploded with laughter.

"Pray, what are you laughing at?" inquired the Rocket; "I am not laughing."

"I am laughing because I am happy," replied the Cracker.

"That is a very selfish reason," said the Rocket angrily. "What right have you to be happy? You should be thinking about others. In fact, you should be thinking about me. I am always thinking about myself, and I expect everybody else to do the same. That is what is called sympathy. It is a beautiful virtue, and I possess it in a high degree. Suppose, for instance, anything happened to me to-night, what a misfortune that would be for every one! The Prince and Princess would never be happy again, their whole married life would be spoiled; and as for the King, I know he would not get over it. Really, when I begin to reflect on the importance of my position, I am almost moved to tears."

"If you want to give pleasure to others," cried the Roman Candle, "you had better keep yourself dry."

"Certainly," exclaimed the Bengal Light, who was now in better spirits; "that is only common sense."

"Common sense, indeed!" said the Rocket indignantly; "you forget that I am very uncommon, and very remarkable. Why, anybody can have common sense, provided that they have no imagination. But I have imagination, for I never think of things as they really are; I always think of them as being quite different. As for keeping myself dry, there is evidently no one here who can at all appreciate an emotional nature. Fortunately for myself, I don't care. The only thing that sustains one through life is the consciousness of the immense inferiority of everybody else, and this is a feeling that I have always cultivated. But none of you have any hearts. Here you are laughing and making merry just as if the Prince and Princess had not just been married."

"Well, really," exclaimed a small Fire-balloon, "why not? It is a most joyful occasion, and when I soar up into the air I intend to tell the stars all about it. You will see them twinkle when I talk to them about the pretty bride."

"Ah! what a trivial view of life!" said the Rocket; "but it is only what I expected. There is nothing in you; you are hollow and empty. Why, perhaps the Prince and Princess may go to live in a country where there is a deep river, and perhaps they may have one only son, a little fair-haired boy with violet eyes like the Prince himself; and perhaps some day he may go out to walk with his nurse; and perhaps the nurse may go to sleep under a great elder-tree; and perhaps the little boy may fall into the deep river and be drowned. What a terrible misfortune! Poor people, to lose their only son! It is really too dreadful! I shall never get over it."

"But they have not lost their only son," said the Roman Candle; "no misfortune has happened to them at all."

"I never said that they had," replied the Rocket; "I said that they might. If they had lost their only son there would be no use in saying anything more about the matter. I hate people who cry over spilt milk. But when I think that they might lose their only son, I certainly am very much affected."

"You certainly are!" cried the Bengal Light. "In fact, you are the most affected person I ever met."

"You are the rudest person I ever met," said the Rocket, "and you cannot understand my friendship for the Prince."

"Why, you don't even know him," growled the Roman Candle.

"I never said I knew him," answered the Rocket. "I dare say if I knew him I should not be his friend at all. It is a very dangerous thing to know one's friends."

"You had really better keep yourself dry," said the Fire-balloon. "That is the important thing."

"Very important for you, I have no doubt," answered the Rocket, "but I shall weep if I choose"; and he actually burst into real tears, which flowed down his stick like rain-drops, and nearly drowned two little beetles, who were just thinking of setting up house together, and were looking for a nice dry spot to live in.

"He must have a truly romantic nature," said the Catharine Wheel, "for he weeps when there is nothing at all to weep about"; and she heaved a deep sigh, and thought about the deal box.

But the Roman Candle and the Bengal Light were quite indignant, and kept saying "Humbug! humbug!" at the top of their voices. They were extremely practical, and whenever they objected to anything they called it humbug.

Then the moon rose like a wonderful silver shield; and the stars began to shine, and a sound of music came from the palace.

The Prince and Princess were leading the dance. They danced so beautifully that the tall white lilies peeped in at the window and watched them, and the great red poppies nodded their heads and beat time.

Then ten o'clock struck, and then eleven, and then twelve, and at the last stroke of midnight every one came out on the terrace, and the King sent for the Royal Pyrotechnist.

"Let the fireworks begin," said the King; and the Royal Pyrotechnist made a low bow, and marched down to the end of the garden. He had six attendants with him, each of whom carried a lighted torch at the end of a long pole.

It was certainly a magnificent display.

Whizz! Whizz! went the Catharine Wheel, as she spun round and round. Boom! Boom! went the Roman Candle. Then the Squibs danced all over the place, and the Bengal Lights made everything look scarlet. "Good-bye," cried the Fire-balloon, as he soared away dropping tiny blue sparks. Bang! Bang! answered the Crackers, who were enjoying themselves immensely. Every one was a great success except the Remarkable Rocket. He was so damp with crying that he could not go off at all. The best thing in him was the gunpowder, and that was so wet with tears that it was of no use. All his poor relations, to whom he would never speak, except with a sneer, shot up into the sky like wonderful golden flowers with blossoms of fire. Huzza! Huzza! cried the Court, and the little Princess laughed with pleasure.

"I suppose they are reserving me for some grand occasion," said the Rocket; "no doubt that is what it means," and he looked more supercilious than ever.

The next day the workmen came to put everything tidy. "This is evidently a deputation," said the Rocket; "I will receive them with becoming dignity"; so he put his nose in the air, and began to frown severely as if he were thinking about some very important subject. But they took no notice of him at all till they were just going away. Then one of them caught sight of him. "Hallo!" he cried, "what a bad rocket!" and he threw him over the wall into the ditch.

"Bad Rocket? Bad Rocket?" he said as he whirled through the air; "impossible! Grand Rocket, that is what the man said. Bad and Grand sound very much the same, indeed they often are the same"; and he fell into the mud.

"It is not comfortable here," he remarked, "but no doubt it is some fashionable watering-place, and they have sent me away to recruit my health. My nerves are certainly very much shattered, and I require rest."

Then a little Frog, with bright jewelled eyes, and a green mottled coat, swam up to him.

"A new arrival, I see!" said the Frog. "Well, after all there is nothing like mud. Give me rainy weather and a ditch, and I am quite happy. Do you think it will be a wet afternoon? I am sure I hope so, but the sky is quite blue and cloudless. What a pity!"

"Ahem! ahem!" said the Rocket, and he began to cough.

"What a delightful voice you have!" cried the Frog. "Really it is quite like a croak, and croaking is of course the most musical sound in the world. You will hear our glee-club this evening. We sit in the old duck-pond close by the farmer's house, and as soon as the moon rises we begin. It is so entrancing that everybody lies awake to listen to us. In fact, it was only yesterday that I heard the farmer's wife say to her mother that she could not get a wink of sleep at night on account of us. It is most gratifying to find oneself so popular."

"Ahem! ahem!" said the Rocket angrily. He was very much annoyed that he could not get a word in.

"A delightful voice, certainly," continued the Frog; "I hope you will come over to the duck-pond. I am off to look for my daughters. I have six beautiful daughters, and I am so afraid the Pike may meet them. He is a perfect monster, and would have no hesitation in breakfasting off them. Well, good-bye: I have enjoyed our conversation very much, I assure you."

"Conversation, indeed!" said the Rocket. "You have talked the whole time yourself. That is not conversation."

"Somebody must listen," answered the Frog, "and I like to do all the talking myself. It saves time, and prevents arguments."

"But I like arguments," said the Rocket.

"I hope not," said the Frog complacently. "Arguments are extremely vulgar, for everybody in good society holds exactly the same opinions. Good-bye a second time; I see my daughters in the distance"; and the little Frog swam away.

"You are a very irritating person," said the Rocket, "and very ill-bred. I hate people who talk about themselves, as you do, when one wants to talk about oneself, as I do. It is what I call selfishness, and selfishness is a most detestable thing, especially to any one of my temperament, for I am well known for my sympathetic nature. In fact, you should take example by me, you could not possibly have a better model. Now that you have the chance you had better avail yourself of it, for I am going back to Court almost immediately. I am a great favourite at Court; in fact, the Prince and Princess were married yesterday in my honour. Of course you know nothing of these matters, for you are a provincial."

"There is no good talking to him," said a Dragon-fly, who was sitting on the top of a large brown bulrush; "no good at all, for he has gone away."

"Well, that is his loss, not mine," answered the Rocket. "I am not going to stop talking to him merely because he pays no attention. I like hearing myself talk. It is one of my greatest pleasures. I often have long conversations all by myself, and I am so clever that sometimes I don't understand a single word of what I am saying."

"Then you should certainly lecture on Philosophy," said the Dragon-fly; and he spread a pair of lovely gauze wings and soared away into the sky.

"How very silly of him not to stay here!" said the Rocket. "I am sure that he has not often got such a chance of improving his mind. However, I don't care a bit. Genius like mine is sure to be appreciated some day"; and he sank down a little deeper into the mud.

After some time a large White Duck swam up to him. She had yellow legs, and webbed feet, and was considered a great beauty on account of her waddle.

"Quack, quack, quack," she said. "What a curious shape you are! May I ask were you born like that, or is it the result of an accident?"

"It is quite evident that you have always lived in the country," answered the Rocket, "otherwise you would know who I am. However, I excuse your ignorance. It would be unfair to expect other people to be as remarkable as oneself. You will no doubt be surprised to hear that I can fly up into the sky, and come down in a shower of golden rain."

"I don't think much of that," said the Duck, "as I cannot see what use it is to any one. Now, if you could plough the fields like the ox, or draw a cart like the horse, or look after the sheep like the collie-dog, that would be something."

"My good creature," cried the Rocket in a very haughty tone of voice, "I see that you belong to the lower orders. A person of my position is never useful. We have certain accomplishments, and that is more than sufficient. I have no sympathy myself with industry of any kind, least of all with such industries as you seem to recommend. Indeed, I have always been of opinion that hard work is simply the refuge of people who have nothing whatever to do."

"Well, well," said the Duck, who was of a very peaceable disposition, and never quarrelled with any one, "everybody has different tastes. I hope, at any rate, that you are going to take up your residence here."

"Oh! dear no," cried the Rocket. "I am merely a visitor, a distinguished visitor. The fact is that I find this place rather tedious. There is neither society here, nor solitude. In fact, it is essentially suburban. I shall probably go back to Court, for I know that I am destined to make a sensation in the world."

"I had thoughts of entering public life once myself," remarked the Duck; "there are so many things that need reforming. Indeed, I took the chair at a meeting some time ago, and we passed resolutions condemning everything that we did not like. However, they did not seem to have much effect. Now I go in for domesticity, and look after my family."

"I am made for public life," said the Rocket, "and so are all my relations, even the humblest of them. Whenever we appear we excite great attention. I have not actually appeared myself, but when I do so it will be a magnificent sight. As for domesticity, it ages one rapidly, and distracts one's mind from higher things."

"Ah! the higher things of life, how fine they are!" said the Duck; "and that reminds me how hungry I feel": and she swam away down the stream, saying, "Quack, quack, quack."

"Come back! come back!" screamed the Rocket, "I have a great deal to say to you"; but the Duck paid no attention to him. "I am glad that she has gone," he said to himself, "she has a decidedly middle-class mind"; and he sank a little deeper still into the mud, and began to think about the loneliness of genius, when suddenly two little boys in white smocks came running down the bank, with a kettle and some faggots.

"This must be the deputation," said the Rocket, and he tried to look very dignified.

"Hallo!" cried one of the boys, "look at this old stick! I wonder how it came here"; and he picked the rocket out of the ditch.

"OLD Stick!" said the Rocket, "impossible! GOLD Stick, that is what he said,

Gold Stick is very complimentary. In fact, he mistakes me for one of the Court dignitaries!"

"Let us put it into the fire!" said the other boy, "it will help to boil the kettle."

So they piled the faggots together, and put the Rocket on top, and lit the fire.

"This is magnificent," cried the Rocket, "they are going to let me off in broad daylight, so that every one can see me."

"We will go to sleep now," they said, "and when we wake up the kettle will be boiled"; and they lay down on the grass, and shut their eyes.

The Rocket was very damp, so he took a long time to burn. At last, however, the fire caught him.

"Now I am going off!" he cried, and he made himself very stiff and straight. "I know I shall go much higher than the stars, much higher than the moon, much higher than the sun. In fact, I shall go so high that——"

Fizz! Fizz! Fizz! and he went straight up into the air.

"Delightful!" he cried, "I shall go on like this for ever. What a success I am!"

But nobody saw him.

Then he began to feel a curious tingling sensation all over him.

"Now I am going to explode," he cried. "I shall set the whole world on fire, and make such a noise, that nobody will talk about anything else for a whole year." And he certainly did explode. Bang! Bang! Bang! went the gunpowder. There was no doubt about it.

But nobody heard him, not even the two little boys, for they were sound asleep.

Then all that was left of him was the stick, and this fell down on the back of a Goose who was taking a walk by the side of the ditch.

"Good heavens!" cried the Goose. "It is going to rain sticks"; and she rushed into the water.

"I knew I should create a great sensation," gasped the Rocket, and he went out.